SKY SHATTER

SKY SHATTER

BREEZE CORINTH: BOOK 1

MICHAEL JOHN OLSON

PUBLISHED BY
STELLA MARIS PUBLISHING
SOUTH FLORIDA
stellamarispublishing@yahoo.com

CONTENTS

Chapter One   1
Chapter Two   23
Chapter Three   47
Chapter Four   65
Chapter Five   95
Chapter Six   115
Chapter Seven   123
Chapter Eight   141
Chapter Nine   151
Chapter Ten   165
Chapter Eleven   191
Chapter Twelve   211
Chapter Thirteen   243
Chapter Fourteen   253
Chapter Fifteen   263
Chapter Sixteen   277
Chapter Seventeen   291
Chapter Eighteen   315
Chapter Nineteen   333
Chapter Twenty   341
Chapter Twenty-One   359
Chapter Twenty-Two   377
Chapter Twenty-Three   391
Chapter Twenty-Four   407
Chapter Twenty-Five   433
Chapter Twenty-Six   449
Chapter Twenty-Seven   455
Chapter Twenty-Eight   473
Chapter Twenty-Nine   479
Chapter Thirty   485
Chapter Thirty-One   491
Chapter Thirty-Two   529
About The Author   573

C H A P T E R

▼

O N E

BREEZE CORINTH ADJUSTED HIS goggles and checked the nav-compass on his wrist.

He had come to the fairgrounds without his father's knowledge. The annual air show was here, and he had entered it. He stood in his hangar waiting for his turn to be called.

He looked around at the other participants in their hangars and saw crew members in color coordinated shirts representing various teams scramble over their aerocraft. They hustled with a heated urgency that was intense and vibrant to watch and feel. Wings were inspected while fuel was loaded into empty tanks. Engines were fired up and revved to ensure maximum performance. All around them lay a dizzying array of tools and equipment. The smell of fuel was everywhere. With each passing moment, the din of voices and machines intermixed, heading toward a fevered crescendo that never seemed to arrive.

Outside the hangars, the roar of the crowds was intense. It came and went like waves on the ocean. The sound of turbines roaring overhead were immediately followed by the crowd cheering its hearty approval of yet another daredevil act performed by a pilot.

Breeze looked around his empty hangar and felt very alone. There were no tools or equipment to be found or color coordinated teammates swarming around. It was just him and a jet pack that lay at his feet.

A wrangler showed up to his hangar. He glanced at Breeze then his clipboard as a puzzled look crept up on his face. He kept looking back and forth between the two, expecting to find something he was missing.

"Breeze Corinth? From Conception?"

Breeze nodded. "Yes, that's me."

"Oh." He looked again at his clipboard. "A jet pack flier, huh? Any teammates, crew?"

"No, just me."

"Oh." He shrugged his shoulders. "All right son, you're up next."

Breeze reached down to grab the shoulder straps of the jet pack. He strained to lift it up and then struggled to secure it onto his back. The wrangler stood and watched with an expressionless face.

He adjusted the belt strap that cinched the jet pack closer to his waist, then stood up straight and tried in vain to adjust his flight suit. It was an odd patchwork of leather and fire proof material that was obviously stitched together haphazardly. His boots were mismatched and oversized. The jet pack itself was a mishmash of various sized fuel tanks that fed a series of nozzles spread across the lower part of the pack. On his chest was a panel that contained multiple switches and dials. A pair of handles were connected to the pack and jutted out at shoulder level.

The wrangler took in the sight of him with a vacant stare. "Are you ready now?"

"Yes." Breeze heard himself say, but didn't feel it.

The wrangler stepped back and made a waving motion with his hand toward the entranceway of the arena.

Breeze stepped out of his hangar and was immediately met with jeers from the surrounding teams.

"Jet Pack Boy! Watch out everybody!" a crew member from across his hangar shouted. His teammates laughed and pointed at Breeze.

"Get an aerocraft! Nobody cares about those jet packs anymore!" one of them shouted.

Breeze didn't respond as he pulled down his goggles. He tried to walk with a dignified pose but the weight and bulk of the jet pack made him swerve to the left and right making it difficult to do so.

The wrangler signaled him to stop at the entrance to the arena. Inside, the announcer, a heavy set man with a sweat stained shirt was wrapping up the last pilot's performance by whipping up the crowd into a frenzy over his death defying antics. "Are you ready for more high flying action?" he called out to the crowd. They responded with wild cheers as an aircrew guided an aerocraft to the center of the arena. The cheers grew even more jubilant as a pilot stepped into the arena wearing a colorful uniform. Tucked under his arm was a helmet. He strode with great confidence as he raised a hand to greet the crowd while the announcer spoke.

"Ladies and Gentleman from all across the Great Sands, it is a pleasure to welcome back a fan favorite. You know who he is. You can't stop lovin' this guy! I give you the Desert Country's favorite son born and raised right here in our town of Conception, Buck Bonanza!"

The announcer whipped around and pointed at the pilot as the crowd erupted into a mad frenzy. Buck waved to them as he jumped onto the wing of his aerocraft and raised a fist into the air. The already adoring crowd could no longer contain itself as the entire arena was drowned in the deafening chant of "Buck, Buck, Buck!"

Breeze watched with a mixture of fascination and dread. He had been coming to these air shows since he was a child and he knew just how spectacular they could be. What started off as an informal gathering of local pilots to show off their latest creations and flying skills grew into an annual show that was massive in size and scope. Teams from all over the Desert Country would come to show off the latest aerocraft they created during the off-season and aerobatic maneuvers that had been mastered to an ever growing crowd of worshipers who came to see them.

The pilots were seen as modern day gods who drove chariots across the skies, performing feats of great daring that cheated death on a constant basis. The adoring crowds below were the faithful flock who admired them while wearing clothing that mimicked the garb of their favorite pilot.

The Desert Country Air Show was the crowning event that was preceded by a series of lesser gatherings all across the territory. The air teams would compete against one another for an entire season. They would earn points based upon their performance that determined their ranking. All of this culminated in the grand event that was the Desert Country Air Show. It was the final tournament for the season that would crown the winner for the year. It didn't matter how low you were in the rankings. If a lower ranking pilot was willing to put it all on the line, he could make up the needed points and move up higher in the rankings to secure a better finish for the year. The higher ranking meant greater opportunity for the pilot in financial support and sponsorship for the next season. In the harsh environment that was the Great Sands, this was the big chance to make a better life for oneself. Even a pilot's flight crew benefited from his good fortune.

Many young men looked forward to becoming pilots along with the wealth and glory that came with it. The desire was so strong they were willing to look the other way at the pilots who died in horrific accidents. In the quest to be the most daring and innovative, they would often face their doom in an unfortunate meeting of aerocraft and desert floor.

Buck Bonanza donned his helmet and lowered himself into the cockpit. It was a gorgeous aerocraft painted in red and blue with wings that swept back towards the tail. Under each wing was a turbine that spooled up slowly as the ground crew detached hoses and wires from the craft, then retreated to the safety of the bunkers that were partially submerged into the ground that lined the sides of the arena.

The turbines roared to life as flames spit out of the exhausts. Breeze couldn't tell what was louder; the sound of the engines or the wild cheering from the crowd. He covered his ears and turned to look at the wrangler who was heartily cheering himself. "Whoo yaaah! Go Buck, go!" He kept shouting.

Breeze wobbled as the heavy jet pack shifted and he almost fell. He bent his knees to lower his center of gravity, and then steadily stood straight up. Meanwhile, Buck was hovering in his aerocraft as he lapped the arena, waving to his adoring fans.

The announcer hollered into the microphone. "Buck Bonanza, begin your championship run!"

With that proclamation, Buck throttled the engines and his craft leapt up into the wild blue sky above.

The aerocraft streaked like an arrow as it rapidly ascended.

Suddenly, both engines erupted with smoke and flame, sending the aerocraft tumbling to the arena floor. The crowd gasped and screamed as the aerocraft hurtled to the ground. Befitting of a daredevil, Buck brought the aeroplane under control and halted its descent inches above the ground. It hovered briefly, and then touched down onto the arena floor.

He immediately slid the glass canopy back and jumped up to wave to the crowd as they cheered him and expressed their relief. Fire crews swarmed the craft and doused the flames from the engines.

"Folks, Buck's air crew will perform some repairs to his bird so they can get him back into the sky. In the meantime, let's keep the action going. What do you say?" The crowd cheered in response.

"All right then, who do we have to perform? How about," the announcer paused briefly as he looked down at his notes. "I see. How about some jet pack action? You guys like that, right?" The excitement level of the crowd noticeably dropped as a few boos spread across the arena. Within seconds, the chanting of "Buck! Bonanza! Buck! Bonanza!" began to grow.

"Awww, come on, I know you all are just kidding! Here we go

everybody, local daredevil just dyin' to entertain you, Breeze Corinth!"

The crowd half-heartedly cheered as even more boos and catcalls erupted across the arena.

The wrangler turned to Breeze and jerked a thumb toward center stage. "That's you kid, show them what you got."

Breeze swallowed hard as he felt sweat roll down his face. He took a step forward and almost tumbled to the ground. He entered the arena to an extremely disappointed and agitated crowd as boos and jeers rained down from the stands.

Breeze waved to the crowd. That made him lose his balance and he fell to the ground. The crowd laughed and yelled wildly as chants of "Bring Back Buck! Bring Back Buck!" rippled throughout the arena.

Breeze struggled to get up as the announcer shook his head.

"Well folks, I think Breeze here is trying to give you a little extra entertainment value by performing a clown act before his demonstration. I'm fully confident he is an accomplished jet pack flier. Come on son, step right up and give these people a show!"

Breeze managed to get to the center of the arena without stumbling any further. Against a growing backdrop of catcalls and boos, he adjusted his goggles again and began fumbling with the various dials and switches on his chest. Out of the corner of his eye, he could see Buck's aircrew scrambling over his aerocraft and rushing through repairs. He tried to not let the bustle of activity distract him anymore. He centered himself and closed his eyes.

He reached up to grip the handles that extended from the jet pack and tried to imagine soaring high above the crowd and the noise they made along with the smell of fuel that soaked the arena. High above everything and everyone and free from his troubles. There, in the blue sky where everything always seemed to be all right. He did this before and he could do it again.

He opened his eyes, expecting to find himself soaring through the air to the growing cheers from the crowd below. Instead, he was still firmly planted on the arena floor with the crowd growing more restless and angry.

"All right now folks, Breeze is just stirring up the anticipation. Now c'mon son, light that candle and let's get this show on!" The announcer called out.

Breeze panicked. He realized what a mistake all of this was. He was used to flying when he was alone behind the shed of his father's scrap yard. Alone, where he was free to concentrate without critical eyes scrutinizing his every move. Now, he was surrounded by a sea of judgmental glares. He could feel their searing glances as the crowd chanted "Go away! Go away!"

Breeze turned toward Buck and his crew. To his horror, they had stopped their repairs and were staring at him. Buck stood in front of his aerocraft shaking his head.

Breeze looked away. He never felt more devastated. The most popular man in the arena had just given him the thumbs down. He needed to get up into the air, and quick.

He closed his eyes and threw his head back while extending his arms out like wings. The crowd was in a frenzy of anger as the jeers and screams grew louder. He couldn't concentrate. The voices were too overwhelming. He felt like he was drowning.

A tap on his shoulder from the announcer made him turn around suddenly. The weight of the jet pack was too much to handle and it sent him tumbling to the ground. The crowd laughed mightily as he struggled to get up. The announcer reached down to help him up. He pulled hard and Breeze fell onto him, sending them both to the ground.

The announcer rolled Breeze off in disgust and scrambled to his feet. Breeze lay helplessly on the arena floor while the announcer vainly dusted himself off and cursed loudly.

A figure loomed over Breeze. It was Buck. He held out a hand and carefully pulled him up while his aircrew helped to steady Breeze from behind.

"That's quite a setup you've got there, son. Do you have much experience with it?" Buck pointed at the jet pack.

Breeze was tongue tied as he thought feverishly for an answer. It was hard to look at the pilot and think at the same time. Buck was a hero to him, and he knew what a fool he was making himself out to be.

"Umm, yeah. A few flights. Just behind the shed at my father's—"

"Hey Buck, come check this out. I don't even think he has fuel in these tanks," one of Buck's aircrew called out.

The pilot's eyes narrowed, and the smile on his face faded quickly. "Check again Chet, I'm sure you're mistaken."

"No boss, no mistakes here. Take a look for yourself." Chet was looking over the jet pack as Breeze stood frozen in place.

Buck stared hard at Breeze as he spoke. "I'm sure there is plenty of fuel in there. Let it go."

Chet shrugged his shoulders. "If you say so boss." Without another word, Chet and the rest of the crew left to finish the repairs on Buck's aerocraft.

Buck placed a hand on Breeze's shoulder. "You had a slight malfunction with your jet pack. It's okay, it happens. Let it go and head for home. You gave it your best shot."

The announcer waddled up to them as he spoke into the microphone. "Well, looky here folks! Buck is giving some sage advice to our intrepid jet pack flier. Tell us Buck, what are you sayin' to him?"

Buck snatched the microphone and shot a harsh glare at the pudgy and sweaty man. The pilot closed his eyes and wiped his brow. When he opened them, a smile appeared as he took a deep breath and spoke.

"Ladies and gentleman, how are we doing today?" The crowd went wild with enthusiastic cheers. He gestured toward Breeze. "My friend here just had a technical malfunction with his jet pack. But hey, no matter! It happens to the best of us." He swept a hand toward his aerocraft and the crowd laughed in sympathetic agreement.

"Now, let's give a big round of applause for Breeze, born right here in Conception. A local boy who gave it his best shot and that's what really matters." The crowd half-heartedly applauded as Buck tossed the microphone back to the announcer, then turned to Breeze. "Some things are best not to be demonstrated in front of others. A jet pack without fuel is one of them. Not sure what you were planning to do, but keeping it behind your father's sheds may be the best place for it. Run along now."

Buck turned and waved to the crowd, then headed back to his aerocraft.

Breeze stepped carefully back to the exit, trying his best to resist dumping the jet pack onto the arena floor and breaking out into a run. He felt ashamed and stupid. The best he could do now was to get out of here without falling flat on his face again.

Rumbling down the road on his old motorbike with the jet pack lashed to the back, Breeze headed for home. He was silhouetted against the slowly sinking sun as he traveled along the desolate highway. Waves of intense heat coming off the pavement made him appear as a mirage.

He turned off the crumbling road an onto a dirt pathway. Monstrous clouds of dust followed him as he bumped and rattled his way to a cluster of buildings. On either side of the road, huge mounds of twisted metal were spread out across the property.

One of the buildings was larger than the rest. Plumes of smoke rose from a row of tubular exhausts that lined its roof. Breeze pulled up to it and shut off the engine. He looked through the open bay doors at the bustling activity inside where he saw men dressed in silvery metallic suits and helmets commanding huge kettles that were suspended with chains from tracks running along the ceiling. They would bring the kettles to a stop, and with a wave of the hand, the kettles would upend themselves and pour hot liquid metal into molds. The molds would rattle down a conveyor and disappear into a tunnel destined for another part of the foundry, while the kettles glided back to their point of origin. There, a robotic arm would drop clumps of scrap metal into the kettle. The kettle would traverse to another station where hot liquid metal was poured into it. A flash of blue lighting, firing from a rod suspended from the ceiling, would strike the inside of the kettle causing a fountain of sparks to spew out. The foundrymen would guide the massive kettles to the mold station where once again they would upend themselves and pour out the contents.

Breeze leaned over his handlebars and peered inside looking for his father. Though all of the men were dressed the same, his father would be the easiest to spot being that he was a man of great height and build.

One of the foundrymen turned and waved at him. He was wearing a uniform with a blue insignia on his chest. He was the only one with such a marking. He turned to another foundryman and pointed to an approaching kettle. He nodded and took his position.

The man with the blue insignia walked over to Breeze and removed his helmet.

"Breeze, where have you been all day? We really could have used your help. We've been pretty busy processing the extra scrap your father purchased last week. We have a lot of molds to pour in there, you know."

"Sorry Al, got caught up in something else."

Alceron Beeks nodded as he peered around Breeze and toward the jet pack strapped snugly across the back of the bike. "Busy as in an air show, perhaps?"

Breeze waved him off. "Don't say anything to my father, please. Where is he anyway?"

Alceron pointed back to the foundry. "He went to check on a

conveyor system that jammed. Just wasn't feeding enough scrap metal to the kettles. He's under a lot of pressure lately. He's really upped the production rate, don't know if we can maintain this pace. We could really use you here."

Breeze nodded. "Yeah, I know. I'll be here tomorrow to help. I promise." He fired up his bike and rumbled away.

Alceron watched him motor off down the path. He pulled off his gloves and slapped his thigh with them. "Things haven't been the same since she's been gone," he muttered.

"Al! Alceron!" a deep and heavy voice called out from within the foundry.

Alceron turned to see a tall man striding over to him.

"Who was that? Was that my son?" the tall man asked.

"Yeah, Jacob that was him."

"Did he say where he was all day? He was supposed to be here to help." Jacob's uniform was also a silvery metallic material, but with a red insignia on the chest. "I spent a good part of the morning covering up the holes he made out in the desert last night. Now I need him to help me in the foundry."

Alceron pointed toward the house. "He said he was just riding around all day on his bike. You know teenagers, they can be moody and stuff."

"Al, you're a good friend and a hard worker, but a terrible liar." Jacob strode past him and down the path that led to the ramshackle home he shared with his son.

Upon arriving, he saw Breeze's old motorbike parked in front. He approached it while casting a critical eye over it. He reached out to touch the back of the bike, and then looked over at the garage attached to the house. He rushed and grabbed the handle on the garage door and opened it. Inside were some old motorbikes and a rusted hover truck. Jacob stepped inside and looked around. He spotted a row of metal lockers that spanned the back wall. He flung open the doors of each one, finding nothing of interest except for some hand tools and loose items until he reached the last door and gave the handle a turn. It wouldn't budge. Jacob grunted as he fumbled for a set of keys attached to his belt. Finding the right one, he inserted the key with trembling hands and unlocked it. He hesitated for a moment as he gripped the handle. He took a deep breath and opened it.

He stepped back and ran his fingers through his hair, then reached in and grabbed the jet pack.

He placed it onto a work table across from the lockers. He flipped a switch on the wall that turned on an overhead light.

Jacob ran his hands over the exhaust cones of the pack. A look of surprise appeared as he realized they were cool to the touch. He leaned over to sniff but could not detect the smell of expended fuel.

He opened the fuel tank and peered inside. Empty.

He slammed his fists onto the table shaking the tools that were hanging on a pegboard above it.

He turned and stormed out of the garage with the jet pack in his hands. He marched down the rock strewn path that led to the shed on the outer edge of the property. He burst into it and threw the jet pack onto the workbench in the back, then turned and left, forgetting to close the door behind him.

He returned to the house and stomped up the stone stairs and through a heavy wooden door.

As the door closed behind him, he stopped to catch his breath while his hands trembled.

He headed down a hallway that stretched for several lengths. Hanging on its walls were pictures. Each one of them showed happy, smiling people celebrating birthday parties, or pictures of grandparents doting on grandchildren. There were also a cluster of old photos with pilots standing next to a variety of flying machines.

Jacob stopped at a door at the end of the hall. A picture hanging on it showed a young couple with a baby. Jacob stared at the face of the woman in the photo and grimaced. He opened the door.

He found Breeze sitting on the edge of his bed staring out the window. The fading sunlight cast a faint glow throughout the room.

Breeze was the first to speak. "Before you get mad, you need to know that nothing happened. I stood there like an idiot as everyone shouted and laughed at me. But nothing happened. I tried. I really did. But I just couldn't fly."

Jacob sat next to him. "Son, I understand what you were trying to accomplish. I understand your desire to stand out and be noticed, to be someone special. Trust me, you are special. But it's the kind of special that can get other people hurt and you, dead. This flying business, these air shows...need to come to an end. Your place is here with me helping with the foundry and studying the art of metal craft. These gifts of yours are something you need to keep quiet about. You don't want to attract attention to yourself."

"I didn't try to fly that way! I had the jet pack! I just couldn't get it to work." Breeze knew his father wasn't buying his lies as he spoke.

Jacob shook his head. "I touched the exhaust nozzles. Cool to the touch, not even slightly warm. The worst part of all, not a single drop of fuel in the tank. It's been empty for so long, the smell has faded away. Didn't any of the officials at the show notice this? And if you did take off, wouldn't they be curious to the lack of noise or exhaust? What were you planning on doing? Was this some sort of a big reveal to the world?"

Breeze leapt up. "I'm tired of everything! I don't want to work in a scrap metal yard. I don't even want to live out here in this hot and dusty desert. I hate everyone here. Ever since mom—"

"Your mother," Jacob interrupted, "would agree with me. She would tell you the same thing. It's just too dangerous."

"She's not here, so how would you know?" Breeze grabbed his leather jacket and stormed out of the room. Jacob listened to his son's footsteps as he stomped down the hall and out the front door. He sighed as he watched him go past the bedroom window and down the path that led to the shed. He knew that Breeze spent a lot of time there. He knew exactly what he was up to but didn't have the heart to tell him to stop. It broke his heart that he couldn't do more for his son. He always thought if he could just keep him safe that would be good enough.

He got up and headed to the kitchen to prepare dinner. He set two places at the table and ate alone while waiting for Breeze to arrive. He never did.

Jacob wrapped Breeze's plate of food in foil and left it in the oven to keep warm. He cleaned up the kitchen, dimmed the lights, then retired to his room.

He sat down on the bed and sighed wearily. His son had done the unthinkable. He went to the air show and almost exposed his secret for all to see. He had done his best, or so he thought, trying to protect him. Keeping him sheltered from those who would otherwise take him away to be used for their own nefarious purposes. It was getting to be too hard. Breeze was growing up. Jacob knew he couldn't contain him anymore, he wasn't an object to be put on a shelf. His son had hopes and dreams of his own, and Jacob knew he had to do what was best for him. His son had to leave.

He reached into his nightstand and withdrew a metallic disc. The surface was divided into twelve equal segments. Each segment contained a series of characters with a symbol. Every symbol on the disc shimmered in gold. The characters gleamed in silver. In the center of the disc was an image of a star.

Jacob touched each of the characters and symbols except the star in the center. Then, he waited.

He looked out the window. The light was quickly fading as the sun dipped below the mountain range in the distance. He looked down again at the disc.

With a trembling finger, he pushed the star in the center. It recessed with a scraping sound as a voice emanated from it.

"Jacob, it's Oslo. We have known each other for a long time, longer than we care to admit. We have seen many things happen, and often not for the better. We can still make a difference, Jacob. It will take boldness on our part, and sacrifice."

Have I not sacrificed enough? Jacob thought as he glanced at a picture of his wife on the nightstand.

The message continued. "Jacob, we have talked long and often about your son and the gift he possesses. There is great potential within him. He cannot remain hidden forever. You know they will find him and take him away. We can both agree we don't want him to suffer the same fate that befell your wife and first son."

With those words, Jacob's eyes filled with tears. He raised the disc high above his head and shook it violently as if he were wishing it silent. He regained his composure and brought the disc back down onto his lap.

Oslo's voice continued. "You made a bargain with them, but to no surprise, they took more than what you had agreed to. I hate to say it my friend, but I warned you. There is no negotiating with them. They will come for Breeze eventually. Let us face reality; you don't have the resources to protect him. Listen to my words Jacob. Send him to me. Let me protect him. I...we can train him. We can give him the knowledge he will need to survive. Contact me when you are ready. Hopefully, it will be soon. You are my friend. You know he will be safe with me, I promise. I have agents in position who have been watching him. They will escort him safely to me across the Bad Lands. I hope all is well with you."

Jacob let the disc slip and fall onto the floor. He turned off the light on his nightstand and laid down.

He turned to look out the window. The night sky was filled with bright stars that shined like jewels. He could only imagine if his wife was among them. And his son.

He closed his eyes and prayed for a restful night without any dreams. Dreams were something he had his fill of.

Breeze stumbled down the dusty path that led to the shed. He saw the door was open, and found it to be odd, considering his father was pretty good at making sure it was closed and the lights turned off every night. He stepped inside and headed to the back where the overhead lights were still on. As he approached the work bench he saw his jet pack sitting atop it. He touched the exhaust cones and realized his father was right. Even if he did fly that afternoon, what would people say as to why there was no exhaust or noise? He didn't think that far ahead. Then again, he never did. He picked up the jet pack and placed it back into the locker.

He stepped toward a counter that lined the back wall with a row of cabinets that hung above it. He opened one and grabbed a can, pulling back the plastic lid and removing a stack of old photos containing memories of a past long gone. He flipped through them one by one. Mom. Dad. Himself as a baby. All those photos had one thing in common. They were all smiling.

He carefully put them back into the can and pressed the plastic lid to seal it, then returned it to the cabinet.

He knew there was only one thing he really wanted to do right now.

He stepped out into the desert night and walked down a well-worn path, passing row after row of old and broken down aerocraft. He wondered if they would ever take to the sky again.

He looked up at the star filled night and smiled. It was going to be a good night for flying.

He arrived at a clearing. He turned to look back at the shed in the distance and saw the glow of light spilling out from it. He would use it like a beacon to guide himself back home.

He took several deep breaths. The cold air filled his lungs, and it felt refreshing. He closed his eyes and slowly stretched out his arms like wings. He felt a gust of wind blow across his face as a feeling of weightless overcame him.

He opened his eyes and shouted with delight. He looked down and saw the ground far below. In the distance, he could see his home, the shed, and the foundry. Behind the foundry were trucks and scrap carriers parked in the lot. All looked like toys sitting on a giant-sized play set. He leaned forward and glided over the terrain.

He learned how to fly on his own. Flying was something he could do ever since he was a child.

He didn't know how or where the gift came from. He would often play in his room by himself and hover a few inches off the ground and never think much of it. To him it was normal as breathing or walking.

One day his mother stepped in to check on him and dropped a basket of laundry with a loud gasp. He could still remember looking at her with a smile. She smiled back with tears of joy in her eyes as her hands went to her chest.

"Darling, I'm so proud of you. You are a natural. But I need you to settle down before your father comes home."

"Why mommy?" he said in an innocent voice.

"Daddy may not be ready to see this. Let's keep this a secret just between you and me. Our little secret. One day we will surprise Daddy with it. Oh, he will be so pleased." She clapped her hands together and smiled brightly. He could never forget her smile.

Lost in his memories, he didn't realize how fast he was traveling as the landscape beneath him began to blur. The cool air blowing across his face put him at ease as he reminisced about happier times that were long gone and replaced with sadness. His mother had left, and she wasn't coming back.

She always encouraged him in everything he did. She often took him to run errands in town. She would tell his father they would be back soon but if they were late, no worries. "We might drive out to see my sister," she would always say

Breeze's aunt lived on the other side of town, but on the way to her home, his mother would sometimes take a different route.

"This isn't the way to Auntie Hazel's house!" Breeze would always shout with delight.

"I know sweetie, we're going to see our friends in the mountains. But you know that already. Don't be silly." She would say with laughter in her voice. "And don't tell Daddy. Remember that Mommy says it's okay to tell a little white lie. Tell him we went to see Aunt Hazel."

"Why do you call it white lie?"

She paused for a moment before answering. "Because it's a lie that's....clean. It's not meant to hurt anyone."

His memories would become fuzzy from then on. He could only

remember seeing men in white coats. They always smiled, and with his mother by his side, would kneel down in front of him and tell him things. Things that he would remember when the time was right about how to use his gifts and not be ashamed of them, and to use them to help, never to harm.

He shook his head to wake himself up. He felt like he was trapped in a dream. He looked around and realized how fast he was moving through the air. He looked down to see the town of Conception was just below him. The glow of its lights was like a torch that could be seen for miles around. He ignored them and pressed on. He had a different destination in mind.

He veered off to his right and headed west. There was a mountain range there. The same mountains his mother would take him to as a child to see the men in white coats.

The flat desert turned into jagged mountains. He had to ascend to clear the peaks. He wobbled a little and gritted his teeth as he struggled to maintain control.

The mountain range gave way to a wide open plain of pure white sand that seemed to stretch forever. Off in the distance was a solitary mountain. As he drew near he could see the moonlight reflecting off a vast lake that lay before it.

He aimed for the shoreline of the lake as he prepared to land. He never wanted to get close to the mountain. Though it seemed inviting, something deep inside his mind warned him to stay away. For now, at least.

He descended gradually, and then panic gripped him as he began to wobble. His landings were often disastrous, and this was one was shaping up to be no better.

The earth raced up to meet him as he arched his back and glided perpendicularly over it. He flailed his legs wildly just before touching down then stumbled upon contact, coming to a stop by falling headfirst into the sand.

He groaned as he sat up and took in his surroundings while brushing sand from his face. The night was quiet and still. Not even a light wind was stirring.

He stood up to admire the lake and how it reflected the stars above perfectly. It was like a portal into heaven.

He turned to face the solitary mountain in the distance. He often came here to see the lights that emanated from it. They started off slowly at first with a single ball of light that would rise up from the mountain, followed by a second and a third, until the night was filled with balls of lights zipping about haphazardly, then abruptly ending their wild maneuvers to begin forming geometric patterns. The shapes they created ranged from circles and squares to more complex octagons and tetrahedrons of intricate detail.

He came here for many reasons, one of them was that it was the last real connection to his mother that he had. He also came because he felt compelled, as if the lights were trying to convey a message to him that he needed to decipher. It seemed as if they were pleading with him to understand their meaning. He didn't have a clue what they were trying to say.

He had tried to approach the mountain many times before while flying, but each attempt would result in a crucifying pain that would make him plummet to the ground.

He had also tried walking but would be forced to turn around as vertigo would set in, while simultaneously the balls of light would rush back inside and never come back out again for the night.

So, he would do what he was doing now and stand along the shoreline of the lake and watch in awe at the spectacular light show before him as brilliant balls of light raced across the sky trying to speak to him in a language he did not understand.

He watched as they created yet another spectacular geometric pattern as they swished and swirled across the sky. They would line themselves up in straight lines, and then rush toward each other to intermix and form triangles and squares or spirals and circles that spun like pinwheels.

A solitary light caught his attention from the corner of his eye. It hovered high in the night sky as if it had just descended from the heavens. It began to glow brightly as it drew closer to the balls of lights. The balls of lights ceased their gyrations as if they sensed the newcomer's presence. The solitary light began to pulsate and change colors, slowly at first then with a rapid intensity.

The balls of lights responded by lining themselves in a straight line. They too began to pulsate rapidly and change from red to orange, then blue to violet, before merging into one and bursting outward in a soundless explosion of white light and disappearing. The light show was over, and the mountain continued to hold on to its secrets.

Breeze scanned the night sky for the solitary light but couldn't find it. He shrugged. It was time to head home. He had school tomorrow, and he hadn't even started his homework that was due from last week.

Once again he went through his routine of shutting his eyes and holding out his arms. He went into a trance and forced himself to concentrate. The rush of air across his face was the signal that he was airborne. He glided away from the mountain as he pulled his goggles down over his eyes so he could better read the nav-compass lashed to his wrist. Meanwhile, a light trailed him from behind.

He rocketed across the desert landscape as the ground below became a blur. He had never flown this fast before; he was beginning to lose control.

Ahead on the horizon was the glow from the town lights of Conception. He wanted to slow down to begin his descent, but any attempt to control his flight only made him race ahead even faster. He whooshed over the town and set off a sonic boom that rattled windows and doors of the homes and buildings below.

Panic swept over him as he barreled through the sky at a frightening speed. No matter what he did to regain control, any attempt to slow down only increased his speed. When he tried to descend, he would rapidly ascend.

It became too much. The slipstream of air rushing into his face made it difficult to breathe while his uncontrolled ascent into the upper reaches of the atmosphere made him shiver violently from the cold.

He started to lose consciousness. His eyes rolled to the back of his head, and he passed out.

He dropped like a stone, plunging through thick white clouds as he hurtled toward the desert floor below.

He woke up and was back home sitting at the kitchen table. Mom was making breakfast while Dad chattered endlessly about something. His mother was dutifully listening to him, nodding her head as she cracked eggs into a hot skillet.

He looked around the kitchen, soaking in the cozy feeling of a home that was alive with the sound of family. He heard a giggle and turned to face a little boy smiling at him. He looked familiar but couldn't remember his name.

"Breeze, play with me?" the little boy said with innocent eyes.

Breeze opened his mouth to speak, but no words came out.

The little boy spoke again. "Breeze, you need to wake up before you go splat." He pointed at the ground.

His eyes opened and he was greeted by the sight of the earth rushing up to meet him. He yelled in panic as he desperately willed himself to slide horizontally. His efforts were not in vain as he ceased his descent only to burst forward with incredible speed, setting off multiple sonic booms as he streaked over the land.

He could make out the looming presence of an approaching mountain range just ahead. He knew he would impact them based on his heading and altitude. He needed to do something, and fast.

Drawing upon willpower like never before, he forced himself to descend. To his growing distress and panic, he ascended. He strained as he tried to angle down and felt a sense of triumph as he slowly descended toward the desert floor. Buoyed by his success, he tried to slow down only to burst forward again with incredible speed.

Then, with a sudden lurch, his body felt as if a giant hand had grabbed and flung him into the ground. The last thing he remembered was the ground rushing at him like a blur while the air before him shimmered and crackled as if he were looking through a window that was about to shatter.

He impacted with a mighty roar. Dirt and debris flew everywhere as he plowed a trench into the earth.

He came to a stop after what seemed like an eternity.

He groaned as he tried to raise his head. Blood trickled from his nose, mixed in with dirt that was smeared across his face. He tried to look up at the night sky, but could only see blackness surrounding him.

He passed out with his face planted into the ground.

He woke up gradually as a thin strip of sunlight poured onto him. He tried to move his arms and legs, but the slightest effort made him wince with pain. He slowly pushed himself up from the ground and stood up, only to lean against a wall of dirt to support his wobbly legs. His head was pounding like a drum and the smell of moist dirt filled his nostrils.

He looked around in confusion as he expected to see the wide expanse of the desert but instead found himself at the deep end of a trench made of dirt and mud that seemed to stretch forever in the opposite direction.

He tried to recall the events from his foggy mind that led him here, but could only remember flying to the White Mountain to see the lights, the struggle in controlling his flight back home then the sudden acceleration ending with him impacting the ground.

His head began to pound with a searing pain. He groaned loudly as he rubbed his temples and looked at the trench. He did this. How he survived the impact he couldn't figure out.

He needed to get out. The longer he stayed, the more nauseous he felt. He turned to face the earthen wall he was leaning against. He dug one hand into the soft soil, then another. He jammed a foot into the dirt and stepped up. He managed to get halfway to the surface when his strength gave out, and he tumbled to the ground. He cried out in frustration and was rewarded with another searing headache.

Holding one hand to his head, he stood up and wobbled as he tried to maintain his balance. He thought about trying to fly out, but the mere idea made his head pound even harder. He couldn't climb out, he just didn't have the strength. He had only one option. Walk.

He turned to face the length of the trench and saw how it gradually sloped up to the surface far off in the distance. He grimaced and started walking when a flash of wisdom came to him. *The beginning of a journey starts with a single step.*

With that thought echoing in his mind, he pushed forward. He plodded along for what seemed like the better part of a day as the pain in his head slowly faded away, only to come rushing back the very moment he thought about trying to fly. He stopped occasionally to lean against the side of the trench and rest. He swallowed and felt how dry his mouth was and began craving a drink of water.

He looked up at the upper rim of the trench and could see blades of grass and roots from trees poking out. He had never really seen so much vegetation before. His world was a dry and arid land sparsely populated with harsh and scraggly trees weary from their endless quest for water.

He continued on, determined more than ever to get out the trench. After another hour of walking, the floor sloped up sharply, and he knew he reached the impact point. He trudged his way to the top and turned to survey the trench. It was a gash in the earth that stretched as far as the eye could see with toppled and broken trees on either side of it.

He turned away, not being able to believe what he just saw, or that he was even capable of doing it. He was tired and worn down. It was a time to head home, if only he knew which way to go.

He tapped the nav-compass on his wrist to activate it. It was unresponsive.

Disappointed, he stumbled forward with no real plan in mind except to try to find a road or a path, anything that would lead him to a town. He needed to find transport to get back home.

He walked through a forest in a daze. Though he had never seen such tall trees before, he was too exhausted to look up and admire them. The forest gave way to a field and he stopped to survey the land. He spotted a road that ran along the field and he crossed over to get to it.

When he arrived he stood alongside it and looked both ways. He had two options. Go to the left or to the right. What seemed like such a simple choice felt so incredibly difficult. *For once in your life*, he thought to himself, *make a decision and stick with it.*

He turned to the right and walked down the rock strewn road. *The beginning of a journey starts with a single step*, he reminded himself. He smiled weakly as he remembered that pearl of wisdom his mind had conjured up during his time in the trench.

Up ahead, he could see a town nestled in a valley below. He picked up his pace.

Later that day, an object high in the sky streaked over the area of the trench. It came to a stop and hovered for a moment, and then with a sudden burst of acceleration, descended rapidly without a sound and came to an abrupt halt just inches above the deep end of the trench. The object was a man, covered head to toe in a sleek black pressure suit. His face was expressionless, as there was no discernible mouth, eyes, ears, or nose, just a reservoir of inky blackness. The light that surrounded him seemed to fade as if he absorbed it.

He hovered for a moment, and then slowly descended to the bottom of the trench.

He tilted his head to the left then to the right as points of light appeared on his face. He reached out to touch the earthen wall where Breeze had tried to climb earlier and recoiled upon contact. He leaned in and noted the blood that was caked on the dirt. He slowly reached out again, but this time with a finger. A needle protruded from the tip of the finger. He vacuumed a small quantity of the blood-soaked dirt through it before retracting it.

He held the finger up to his face and stared at it as the points of light on his face become a maelstrom of swirling stars. They spun faster and faster, growing in intensity until his head glowed a brilliant white, then ceased and his face returned to an expressionless pit of darkness. He shot toward the sky and disappeared.

CHAPTER

▼

TWO

BREEZE WOKE UP IN a terrible fright. He looked about wildly and was overwhelmed by the unfathomable darkness that surrounded him. His back was pressed against something hard and jagged. He stood up and turned to touch the rough surface he slept against all night. It felt cold and damp. He backed away and his heel snagged a sharp object. He fell back with a yelp.

Lying on the ground, he looked up and saw a sprinkling of stars through a narrow gap. He got up slowly, taking ragged breaths as he spun in a circle, hoping his eyes would lock onto anything familiar. He looked up again at the stars for guidance and saw leafy branches blocking his view. He tapped his nav-compass. Its glow faintly illuminated the area where he saw tree trunks everywhere he turned. He realized now he was in deep in the forest.

He tried to remember the events that led him here. After he had plowed the trench into the ground, he didn't trust himself to fly home on his own accord. He found a road that led to a town but upon arriving, discovered the entrance to it was blocked by a fortified gate and guarded by hulking men covered in heavy armor and carrying swords and axes. He hid amongst the trees, while daring himself to approach them but thought better of it after spending hours watching disheveled men, women and children entering or leaving the town being harassed or even assaulted, by the guards. He had never seen anyone who looked or behaved the way the citizens of this town did. They reminded him of books his aunt read to him as a child about kings, queens and knights, and the peasants they ruled over. He also noticed there were no signs of hover vehicles or aerocraft anywhere. The townspeople seemed to get by on horse-drawn wagons. He had never seen anything so odd. He waited for night to arrive so he could skulk away.

He spent the next several days walking down roads that cut through forests, eating berries he found growing on wild vines, and the occasional apple from trees he stumbled across along the edge of a field. All the while he hoped to find a town that was less hostile and strange than the one he had left behind.

He stopped often to admire the trees. He had never seen so many clustered together and so great in height. They were in short supply back home in the desert. What few trees they had were ragged and dry. Rarely were there ever more than two together. They stood out as oddities in the flat desert landscape. Even the surrounding mountains were barren of any significant growth of vegetation.

He traveled by day along roads and paths made of dirt and stone, occasionally checking his nav-compass to ensure he was heading west. He stopped several times to look at the tracks he saw on the ground. Wheeled vehicles did travel here, but he never once saw one or heard a motor.

At night, he would sit and lean against a tree close to the road. He was too afraid to go into the forest. The wind would blow and make the leaves on the branches rustle loudly as the trees groaned and creaked. He wasn't used to hearing so much racket. He was accustomed to the serene desert nights.

Some nights he would wake up to the sounds of rustling along the forest floor, accompanied by a pair of glowing eyes hovering off in the distance. He would then scramble to his feet and run down the road in the faint moonlight until he collapsed from exhaustion.

But tonight he awoke and found himself surrounded by incredibly tall trees, their canopies swaying back and forth with each gust of wind. He wondered how he got this deep into the forest. He remembered hearing a howling noise that chilled him to the bone as he slept along the roadside when something dark streaked past him and barreled into the forest. A flash of light erupted seconds later, which brought the howls of the creature to an end.

That was enough to send him running down the road until it came to an end. His fear of the howling creature overwhelmed his reservations about the forest, and he leapt into it. As he crashed through the thick branches, he remembered checking his nav-compass to obtain a bearing, figuring if he ran to the west, he might reconnect with another road. His hopes were dashed when he saw the needle spinning wildly, and the display flashing random numbers. He continued running until his legs burned with pain and he collapsed from exhaustion. He crawled along the forest floor in the dark until he bumped against the trunk of a tree. He leaned his back against it while struggling to keep his eyes open in the overwhelming darkness of the forest. He eventually surrendered to fatigue and fell asleep.

All of these events led to this moment. He knew he had to leave the area and quickly. He didn't want to try to walk out of the forest to find a road. He didn't know what direction he entered it, and his nav-compass was still behaving strangely.

The trees groaned and creaked louder with each gust of wind. The forest was unfamiliar territory for him, and he was feeling claustrophobic. This was nothing like the wide open expanse of the desert. Then he realized there was a way out and it didn't require waiting for daylight to arrive.

He looked up and focused on the brightest star he could find through the thick branches. With his arms outstretched, he willed himself to rise.

He felt his body become light as a feather. He rose slowly, carefully weaving his way through interlocking branches as they rustled and scraped against one another yet his eyes never wavered from the bright star he was focused on.

He broke through the leafy canopy and hovered over a forest that stretched out endlessly in all directions. The moon was beginning to rise, allowing him to see in the distance a narrow gash that snaked its way through the forest. He knew that was the road he needed to follow. He looked up at his guide star and almost fell into the forest when he saw it drift away.

He hovered until he felt confident enough to nudge himself forward. He glided over to the road and followed its course. He snuck a glance at his nav-compass to confirm he was heading west and was relieved to see it was working again.

He felt his stomach grumble and his mouth was dry. He knew he had to land and eat soon. He drank from whatever creek he came across and foraging on berries he found hanging off branches and vines. He was careful to sample each one by eating it slowly, waiting to see if he felt sick before eating the rest. There was so much about the forest that he didn't know, and he was determined not to die here in the wilds.

The moon rose higher, giving him a better view of the road below. He ascended to achieve a higher vantage point and spotted a large swath of open land in the distance. He made a slight course change and headed for it. Along the way he came across a lake with its surface glinting in the moonlight. Relieved to see water, he descended, only to stumble and fall face first into the sand when he tried to land along its shore.

He got up and squatted along the edge of the lake and began hastily scooping water into his parched mouth while glancing around nervously for any wildlife. He didn't like the forest or the creatures that inhabited it. Most of the kids in his school rarely, if ever, traveled outside the desert country. What little they knew about forests was only what they saw in books and in vid-images.

He continued to scoop water when he saw his wavering reflection in the lake. He leaned in closer and could see his face and the stars above him. He felt dizzy as the stars began to rotate. He dug his hands into the sand, feeling as if he were about to be ripped off the ground and flung up in the air. He closed his eyes and gritted his teeth, struggling to overcome the dizzying sensation that overwhelmed him. No sooner than it began, it came to an end.

A sense of relief swept over him as he took short, ragged breaths. He lifted his head to gaze at the stars above.

He always wondered what was to be found out there in the infinite blackness. Every star to him was a pinpoint of light that kept the gathering darkness at bay. There were rumors around Conception of aerocraft fabricators building ships that could pierce the upper levels of the atmosphere and achieve orbit, but they were often dismissed as myth. He once tried to ascend to a higher altitude, but the extremely cold temperatures and blasts of air from the jet stream would force him to turn back.

His trance was shattered by a horrific roaring sound. He spun around as a tree from the forest lining the shore toppled with a mighty crack, falling to the ground.

His heart raced. He could see his breath come out of his mouth in sharp bursts in the frosty air. The roaring was followed by fierce shrieking as more trees snapped and fell, each one toppling faster than the other with a sickening crack, their sturdy trunks snapping like twigs.

Breeze backed into the lake and was immediately bitten by the iciness of the water, but his fear of whatever was heading toward him overruled his discomfort.

The tree falling ceased abruptly and a creature stepped out from the forest with the radiance of the moon casting a spotlight on it. It was tall. Taller than any man he had ever seen. Its eyes flickered, alternating between shades of red and white. It stood perfectly still as it stared at Breeze.

Breeze was knee-deep in the lake and breathing heavily. The icy water was making him shiver, but he was too afraid to move. He could see the creature breathe heavily too. Each exhale it made was laced with a low, guttural growl. It was menacing and frightening to behold, with its tangled and unkempt hair covering its body from head to toe. Then it began striding towards him.

Breeze reflexively stepped back deeper into the lake. The water was up to his waist and the cold was unbearable. His heart was beating hard, making the blood roar through his ears that he could barely think straight. Then the smell hit him.

The creature emitted a foul odor that reeked of sulfur. It was a smell he was familiar with, spending many a summer recess and weekends helping his father in the foundry. But the odor from this monstrosity was so powerful it made him gag.

The creature took a few more steps towards him with its eyes flashing a throbbing red when it came to an abrupt stop.

The fierce red eyes gave way to a white glow as it stopped growling and cocked its head.

Breeze felt a wave of calm sweep over him. Whatever terror he experienced earlier was replaced by a sense of serenity. The creature had glowing eyes that illuminated its face, and it stretched a long and hairy arm towards him. It made a beckoning motion. Breeze absentmindedly took a step forward, and then stopped.

In the back of his mind, he heard a hissing noise. The hissing grew into a powerful static that drowned out all other sound. He glanced at his nav-compass, and the needle was spinning wildly.

He covered his ears in a desperate attempt to block the noise when he caught a sudden flash of movement from above. He looked up and saw the bright star that he used to guide himself out of the forest was now hovering above him. It morphed into an orb and pulsated with radiating light in a staccato pattern.

The creature's eyes exploded into a fiery red as it pointed to the orb with a piercing howl. The orb pulsated with a rainbow of colors in response, then shrunk into a black ball and streaked towards the hairy creature, striking it in the chest and sending it tumbling into the forest. The creature shrieked and howled as the black ball expanded into a larger sphere and began absorbing it.

Breeze had seen enough. He needed to leave. Now.

He struggled to get out of the icy lake, shivering mightily as he waded out of the water. The static hiss was more powerful than ever and he couldn't concentrate to try and fly. He ran away as fast as he could along the shoreline.

He ran until the sound of static dissipated and the creature's horrific shrieking subsided. He came to a stop and dropped to his knees, breathing heavily. His shivering became more intense as he felt the cold air on his drenched pant legs. His boots were soggy and squished with every step he took.

He knew he had to fly up to find the road. If he could find it again, he would follow it and hopefully it would lead to a town.

He looked at his nav-compass and was relieved to see that it was working again as the needle spun casually until it came to a stop and pointed north.

He stood up and tried to overcome his shivering as he stretched out his arms and closed his eyes. If there was ever a time he needed to achieve flight, it was now.

He felt the familiar rush of air across his face as his feet left the ground. He opened his eyes and saw he was hovering over the tree tops next to the lake. He willed himself forward and floated upright across the lake. He looked at his nav-compass and carefully shifted his direction until he was on a westerly course. He reached the opposite shore, and in the brilliant moonlight saw a road cutting through the forest like a winding ribbon. He followed the road, daring himself to tilt forward to fly parallel to the ground below, mindful about how this position made him accelerate without warning.

He flew this way for hours, even though he was overwhelmed by his desire to land and get some rest. He could barely contain his shivering, but was determined to put as much distance between himself and the creature by the lake.

The moonlight ebbed as it sunk slowly to the horizon. The sky was at its equilibrium between the advancing sun and retreating moon.

Breeze's eyes fluttered as fatigue drained him. He looked down and saw the forest gradually thinning out into open fields. He spotted homes and farms dotting the landscape. The road he was following split into a fork, and he followed the one that lead to a cluster of lights on the horizon. Lights meant civilization. Civilization meant a land port where he could find out not only where he was, but what transport he would need to take to get home. This wasn't the first time he had flown far away from home; he had always been able to fly back, or hitch a ride if he felt too tired to try. But he had never flown so far and so fast as he had after the air show, and he had never flown out of his territory and into the forest lands.

He spotted a barn next to a field and could smell the freshly turned earth as he approached. It was the same smell from the trench he plowed several days before.

Not far from the barn was a farmhouse that sat on the edge of the field, its sole porch light was like a landing beacon for him. He knew he needed to rest, and this would be a good place to do so. He didn't want to land in the town for fear he might be seen. He didn't know how people would react if they saw him dropping from the sky and landing in the streets.

I'll just touch down in the field, then sneak into that barn for a few hours of rest, he thought to himself, *then come morning, head into town.*

He felt his heart race in nervous anticipation of his landing. He willed himself down until he touched the ground, then stumbled and fell face first into the dirt.

He rolled over and looked up at the sky as the stars began their retreat from the sun's rays. *Time to hide,* he thought.

He trudged across the field and slipped between the partially opened doors of the barn where the smell of manure hit him hard. He covered his nose with his jacket in a futile attempt to block it. He couldn't tell what was worse, the odor from the hairy creature or the smell of the barn.

He pulled his sleeve back to expose the nav-compass. Its faint glow weakly illuminated the interior of the barn when he spotted a ladder leaning against a railing. He walked over to it and looked up, and was relieved to see it led to a loft full of hay. He climbed up the creaky ladder and gratefully laid down in a fetal position as he buried himself with hay to acquire some warmth. He took one last look around, and then closed his eyes. He fell asleep immediately.

"Get up son."

Breeze groaned.

"Son, you have to get up."

"I will Dad," Breeze grumbled, and rolled over.

"Barn is no place to be sleeping off whatever the previous night's adventure brought you. Now get up."

Breeze mumbled. "How do you know I flew last night?"

"You're not making any sense now. I suggest you get up."

Breeze sat up and rubbed his eyes as hay fell off him, then recoiled at the sight of an old man staring at him. He had piercing blue eyes and splotchy skin from long days in the field under the sun. His hair was gray with streaks of white slashing through it. His large hands gripped the top of the wooden ladder and never blinked as he stared at Breeze.

Breeze slid back against a hay bale. He was trapped. He figured he would have awakened by now and been on his way before anyone from the farmhouse woke up.

The old man nodded at him. "You can come to the house if you like. Wife's got the stove going, be more than happy to fix you something to eat. You must be hungry, right? You look like a young man who's traveled quite a ways, and has much more to do."

Breeze blinked at him.

The old man snorted. "I'll take that as a yes. Make sure your boots are clean. The wife hates it when I track mud into the house. Especially the kind that comes from animals, if you know what I mean." The old man chuckled as he descended the ladder. Each step he took made the ladder creak loudly.

Breeze leaned over and peered down. He was stunned to see the old man was already out of the barn and into the sunlight.

He crawled over to the ladder and gingerly placed a foot onto the top rung. It creaked and flexed beneath him, and he began to wonder how he even climbed up without breaking it.

"Think light on your feet, son. This way the ground will never break beneath you. How do you think a big man like me does it?" The old man called out from the doorway. He appeared to Breeze like a giant as the sunlight lit him from behind, almost like some otherworldly being sent from the heavens.

"Come now, don't dawdle. Never waste the light. Always make good use of it 'cause the darkness is always waiting to overcome it." The old man turned and walked away as the sunlight rushed in to fill the space where he had stood.

Breeze carefully made his way down the ladder. He reached the bottom and saw no one else was in the barn, not even a single animal.

He stepped out into the brilliant sunshine where off in the distance he could see the farmhouse with the old man standing in front of it. Breeze wondered how he got there so quickly.

He took a step forward, and then stopped when he saw the foot prints in the ground. Expecting to see deep marks from where the old man stepped, he was stunned to find shallow footprints instead. He looked up and saw the old man walking up the steps and into the house. The screen door banged to a close behind him, but it took a moment for the sound to reach his ears.

Breeze trudged his way through the field, the soft earth collapsing with every step he took. He realized now just how far away the farm-house was. He grumbled and continued on.

He eventually arrived at the front steps of the house and sat down, when he was startled to hear the voice of a woman bellowing from behind the screen door.

"If you plan on entering our humble abode, you best take off those filthy boots!" An image of a woman wiping her hands on an apron came into focus from behind the screen.

Breeze was transfixed by the sight of her. His mother died when he was young. He wasn't accustomed to the sight or sound of a woman in his home. Father wouldn't even hire one of the local women to help around the house. Instead, he insisted that he and Breeze do all of the household chores. "Builds character and strength," he would say. Breeze wondered what sort of strength he was building while washing dishes after dinner, night after night.

The screen door opened with a loud squeal, and then banged to a close against the door frame as a diminutive woman stepped onto the porch. If the old man was as tall as a giant, his wife was as tiny as a mouse. She was short and wiry with her hair pulled back into a pony tail.

She placed her hands on her hips and spoke to him. "Either my useless lump of a husband found himself a deaf mute, or you're just plain slower than watching paint dry." She turned to the screen door and shouted. "Gil, this boy might need some help with his boots. I don't think he speaks or understands."

A loud chuckle emanated from inside the house. "Be nice Maribelle, he has traveled far and is just bone tired."

"Bone tired, indeed! Sleeping in dirty old barns would make anyone that way," she said, shaking her head disapprovingly. She turned back to the screen door again and shouted. "And when are you going to clean out that barn? I can smell horse dung on this young man! I could smell him even before I saw him!"

"Now, let's not be dramatic woman. You watched him from the window as he walked across the field and made rude comments about him the whole time. And I'll clean out the barn once I've had some breakfast."

She turned to Breeze. "Sure he will. That was several thousand breakfasts ago. That's all I'm good for around here. Fixing that mountain of a man something to eat." She adjusted her apron and tilted her head. "Well, what are you waiting for? Those boots won't come off by themselves, and I don't aim to help you with them, on account I don't want to get dirt on my hands." She opened the screen door. "You best hurry before the old goat eats your share." She stepped back inside as the screen door slammed shut to punctuate her point.

Breeze sat with his mouth open. He had never met anyone like her.

He went up the steps, unlaced his boots and placed them next to the door. He grabbed the rickety handle of the screen door and opened it with an obnoxious creak. He stepped inside and took in his surroundings.

The floor was wooden and buckled with every step he took. The walls were faded with picture frames hanging from them.

His hunger began to swell from the smell of food wafting out of the kitchen. He headed toward the sound of pots and pans banging together and into the warmth of a small kitchen with a little table pressed against a wall where Gil was already seated. Breeze couldn't help but wonder how the chair even supported the weight of such a big man.

Gil looked up from the book he was reading and smiled. "Remember son, be light on your feet. Then nothing gives way beneath you."

"The boy must have a name Gil! I swear you have the manners of an old goat that hasn't been fed in a week. You can't even ask him for his name because you're always thinking with your stomach." She turned to Breeze. "That's how we met. He was eating his usual daily slop down at the local eatery when I walked past him. I had to pretend to stumble and spill my glass of water on him just to get him to look up and notice me. I figured a man like that would be better off with a wife fixing him something to eat as opposed to eating that gruel that's served in town."

Gil chuckled. "She tells that story all the time. It keeps getting further from the truth every day."

Breeze sat down in a chair and pulled up to the table. "Breeze," he said quietly.

Maribelle stared at him and then looked out the window. "No, don't think so. Seems awful calm out there. Not much in the way of wind."

His face reddened. "No ma'am. That's my name. Everyone calls me that."

"Oh my heavens, child! That's no name. Tell me the name your parents gave you the day you arrived into this world."

"Paul. Paul Corinth."

Maribelle stopped wiping her hands with her apron as she froze in place.

Gil looked up from his book. "Corinth? Interesting. Haven't heard that name in quite a while. Where did you say you hail from?"

"I didn't sir. I come from the Desert Country. From a town called Conception."

The couple quickly glanced at one another.

Maribelle cleared her throat and turned to the stove. "Let me fix you a plate, you must be starving." She grabbed a plate from the cupboard and bustled about the kitchen.

Gil put down his book, then closed his eyes and took in a deep breath. "Haven't heard or thought about that town in quite some time. I know it's an aviation town. They build all sorts of flying machines and other contraptions out there. Talented folk."

Breeze nodded as he eyed Maribelle pouring food onto a plate. His stomach began to growl.

Gil swiveled to face his wife. "Darlin', what's the name of that fella we used to know out there in Conception?"

She put the spoon down on the counter with a definitive clink as she looked out the window. "I believe Jacob was his name. Jacob Corinth."

Breeze's eyes lit up. "That's my father!"

Maribelle visibly stiffened.

Gil pushed his book away and placed both of his hands upon the table. "Why, isn't that something? We've known Jacob for...quite some time. Isn't that right, darlin'?"

Maribelle was straightening her apron. She still had her back to them. "Yes."

Gil continued. "You're quite a ways from home, son. What brings you this far east? I hope you're not like those other young folk passing through here seeking adventure in the Bad Lands. Dangerous territory you know."

"Well, I..." Breeze stopped. He wasn't sure if he could come out and tell them the truth. They seemed like nice people, but he didn't know if he could trust them.

He looked at Gil. The old man's eyes were sharp and bright. He smiled at Breeze in a way that a concerned grandfather would look at his grandson.

Maribelle was still at the stove with her head turned to the side to hear them better.

"Well, I got into an argument with my father, so I hopped a transport to get away. Kept wandering until I got here. Then I found your barn and spent the night in it."

Gil nodded as he reached for his cup of coffee. He slowly sipped it with an audible slurp and grimaced. "Good coffee," he called out to his wife and then turned to Breeze. "Son, I don't want to sit here and poke holes into your story. I'm sure you have something to say, but don't want to. That's fine. We all have something to hide for one reason or the other. But I have to say, your tracks that lead into the barn show you coming from the east."

Breeze flinched.

Gil pressed on. "It's more than that. I didn't find any tracks coming out of the woods. It's like you just landed from the sky and walked straight into the barn."

Breeze's heart began to beat so hard he could feel his chest ache.

Maribelle walked over to them. "What my old goat of a husband is trying to ask you but takes forever because he so does like to beat around the bush, is how did you really get here?"

"I flew," Breeze blurted out.

"Of course!" Gil exclaimed. "Makes perfect sense. You're from Conception. Your father is Jacob Corinth. He was a well-known flying machine builder back in the day. You must have landed here after testing out some contraption he built and then took refuge in the barn. That's it, right?"

Breeze shook his head. "No sir. We run a scrap yard. Father buys the waste metal, and we sell it to the builders in the area. I never saw him build anything. Especially aerocraft."

"Oh, well, fair enough." He looked over at Maribelle. "So how about some breakfast?"

She waved him off. "How did you get here?"

Breeze looked into her intense, brown eyes. He could feel himself wilt as he looked away from her.

"You flew, didn't you?" she said softly.

"Maribelle, don't go stirring up trouble. He is not familiar with such nonsense and doesn't need to know about it."

If she heard him, she didn't seem to care. She leaned toward Breeze and whispered. "You flew. All by yourself."

Breeze nodded.

She gasped as she placed one hand on his shoulder and the other on her chest.

Breeze looked up at her with surprise. Her hard and crusty persona cracked as her eyes began to well up with tears. "Thomas," she whispered.

Gil's smile faded. He closed his eyes and gripped the edge of the table.

"Thomas?" Breeze said.

"He was our son. A good boy. He-," she stopped to clear her throat and wipe her eyes. "Where are my manners? Let me fetch you that plate." She turned back to the stove.

Breeze looked to Gil.

Gil smiled faintly. "Tommy was a good boy. Only child. Gifted, to say the least. He's no longer with us."

Maribelle put a plate of food before Breeze. "You will spend the night here in the house. I'll fix up the spare room for you. Gil will see to it that you get to the land port here in town and get you a ticket for the next liner back home. Best for you to be with your father."

"Ma'am, it's no trouble. I can find my way back. I don't mean to be a bother," Breeze said.

She dismissed him with a wave. "We'll need to get you some clean clothes. Those rags of yours are a mess. Need to get some clean sheets for you to sleep on also. I have a lot to do today." She wiped her hands with her apron. "Gil, you best get that old truck of yours up and running. You'll have to get the young man into town today to get his ticket."

Gil nodded. "Yes ma'am." He winked at Breeze. "I like to let her think she's the boss."

"No time for playing around, you old goat. You best finish up here and get your creaky bones to work."

"I don't have any money for the ticket. Look, I can make it back on my own," Breeze protested.

Maribelle ignored him. "Gil, see if you can find any old clothes of yours that he can wear." She shook her head. "Now that I think about it, take him into town and get some new clothes for him instead. All you wear are those pants and shirts that stretch. The young people these days don't care for that style."

"I can pay you back," Breeze offered.

"You can start by finishing your food. I haven't been cooking all morning to see it go to waste," she said.

Gil chuckled. "Best to do as she says."

Breeze nodded as he sheepishly pecked at his food. He took one bite of the creamy potatoes, then another. Soon he was wolfing down his food with abandon.

Gil looked on with a smile.

Maribelle stared with a hand to her throat when she realized Breeze had finished and was looking at her. She shook her head. "Well, best get to work. Gil, show him his room later, and don't forget to go to town!" She wagged a finger at him, and then stepped out of the kitchen.

Gil mumbled as he continued eating.

Breeze leaned toward him. "Was Thomas different?"

Gil reached for his coffee and drank the last of it. He got up, shuffled over to the stove to grab the pot, and came back to the table. He filled Breeze's cup and poured the rest into his, then sat down slowly as he ran a wrinkled hand through his gray and white hair. "Tommy was different, yes, you could say that, and special. He was the greatest thing that ever happened to us. His...disappearance was devastating to my wife and me."

"I'm sorry, didn't mean to pry." Breeze felt horrible.

Gil waved him off. "No, it's best to come out and say these things. Can't keep them bottled up forever."

"Was Tommy a flier, like me?"

Gil took a long hard look at Breeze, and then said with a smile. "Yes. Yes, he was." His smile grew brighter by the moment. "He would do exactly what you do. Go flying around without his folks knowing about it while trying not to crash into the field. And he was always covering his tracks. That's how I knew what you were up to. Landing out in the middle of our field and walking straight to the barn. Tommy would do that too!" Gil said as he laughed long and hard.

As Gil continued to tell stories about his son, Maribelle sat in the living room next to the kitchen listening to every word he said. She did so while holding a picture in her hands. It was of a young boy with a glowing smile and piercing blue eyes. She clutched it to her bosom and sobbed quietly.

The following morning, Gil drove Breeze into town. Before they left, Maribelle handed Breeze a small bag as he stepped down the porch and into Gil's truck.

"A little something for you to eat while on your way home. Seeing that you like my cooking so much, I gather you would rather eat my food than that awful slop they serve aboard those liners." She pushed the bag into his hands over his protests.

Gil chuckled. "Still haven't learned, have you? Don't try to win an argument with her. Best to agree and move on."

Breeze held out a hand to her. "Thank you for everything. It was nice meeting you."

Maribelle looked at his outstretched hand with a blank stare, then brushed it aside and hugged him tightly.

Breeze was shocked as he gingerly patted her back.

She looked at him with her fierce, dark eyes. "Be good. Be strong. Be brave." She touched his face, then abruptly turned and marched up the porch and into the house.

Gil motioned for him to step into the truck. He fired up the engine and threw it into gear as they jostled down the dirt trail and onto the main road that led to town.

Breeze looked around the cab of the truck. It was old and beat up. He glanced at the roof above Gil's head. It was dented upward.

"Maribelle," Gil said, "is a woman of great passion. Don't be fooled by her hard exterior. Believe me, son, she is as soft and weak as they come."

"I just feel bad. It's like my being here has brought up a lot of terrible memories for you and your wife. And you both have been so kind to me. If I just slept out in the woods, or was able to find some other farm to land at, I wouldn't have caused such a fuss."

Gil braked hard and steered the truck to the side of the road. He shut off the engine and turned to glare at Breeze. "Don't you dare say that. Ever."

Breeze shrank back in his seat. Gil's demeanor was always a mixture of happiness tinged with sadness. Seeing his face contorted in rage frightened him. He looked at the old man's hands gripping the steering wheel as they began to swell and throb. In seconds, Gil's body grew. His shirt and pants stretched as muscles bulged from his body. His eyes glowed an incredible deep blue as his head pushed up against the ceiling of the cab.

Breeze lunged for the door handle and yelled when a giant hand grabbed his arm. He turned to look as the old man was beginning to shrink.

"Forgive me Breeze. Please, don't be frightened of me." Gil took in several deep breaths as his body returned to normal.

Breeze kept one hand on the door handle.

Gil chuckled. "No need to bail out on me son. I won't hurt you."

"What was that?!" Breeze shouted.

"That was me showing that I'm no different than you. You're not the only one who can do extraordinary things, you know." Gil fired the truck back up, then threw it into gear and drove onto the road.

"Son, you are a blessing, don't ever forget that. And don't say that you wish you had never met us. You've awakened my wife and me. Remember Breeze, all things happen for a reason."

Breeze was still leaning up against the door.

Gil looked over at him with a smile mixed with sadness. "Now look at what I've done. I've gone off and scared you with my little freak show. If you're willing to listen, I can explain."

Breeze pushed up against the door a little more.

"There have always been folks like us. There was a time when our numbers were many and there was no need to hide what we were. Ordinary folks knew about us. They knew we were superior to them, but they weren't afraid. Oh, no. They were appreciative, you see. They knew we were different, but we never abused our gifts. We made it a point to use those gifts to help folks in need. We served for the better, not for the worse."

"I never heard of such a thing," Breeze said.

Gil nodded. "Before your time son. Well before your time," the old man said as he stared down the road, never once blinking.

"So what happened?"

Gil didn't answer. His hands gripped the wheel as the truck picked up speed.

"Gil?" Breeze said as he reached for the door handle.

The old man shook his head. "It's okay son, I heard you. Just had a flood of memories hitting the old brain, that's all." He sighed deeply. "What happened, you asked?"

Breeze nodded.

"There's not enough time to explain. Usually never is. And it can be hard to believe anyways though it was such a fantastic era. But who would believe such a story?" He shook his head. "What happened is that there were those amongst us who turned against the very people they swore to protect by using their gifts to stir up trouble. We would track them down and deal with them, you see. You're always going to have a few bad apples in every barrel. It's just the way it is."

He turned onto a wider road. Up ahead, the outskirts of a town appeared on the horizon.

Gil continued. "But it got out of hand as they eventually banded together and became marauders. They went from attacking innocent people to working up the courage to attack entire towns, and then bigger cities. The people were angry and frightened, and rightfully so. They demanded action as they wanted it to come to an end. They turned to the territorial governments and demanded justice. We were a menace, you see. We couldn't be trusted anymore. We couldn't even manage our own kind, they said. And they were right. They brought us all to an end. We went from being the champions of humanity to refugees in our own lands. We were hunted down and brought to heel. It all happened so fast." Gil pounded the steering wheel and he began to mumble while traffic was building up as more vehicles appeared on the road. A sign reading "Welcome to Respite" appeared on the side of the road.

"Gil, you wouldn't freak on me if I told you I don't really believe in any of this?" Breeze said.

The old man laughed. "You shouldn't believe in anything I say. That was all so long ago, well, I guess you could say that it just never happened. And no, I won't freak out again. I'm sorry about frightening you."

"If everything you're saying is true, how come I never heard about it? How come I didn't learn about this in school?"

Gil snorted. "History, my boy, is what people want to make of it. You may not be able to change the history for those who are living now, but you can always change it for those yet to be born. They will grow up believing what they are told. That's how easy it is to erase the past, no matter how fantastic it was."

Breeze eased away from the door and settled back into his seat. Up ahead were signs leading them to the land port.

"Is that why my father is so hard on me? Is he worried something is going to happen? I never felt like anyone wanted to hurt me when I would fly at night. I've been doing it for so long now and yet nobody has ever come to my home and said something."

Gil looked over at Breeze. "Son, it's been quiet out there. Too quiet, I'll give you that. You don't hear too much about folks like us popping up in plain sight. But that doesn't mean we're not out there. You know about me. My wife and I told you about our son. You know he…disappeared on us." He choked back a sob.

"Is Maribelle—"

"Gifted? Yes, she's just like us. The thing you need to understand is that we're not all alike. Some of us have more power than others and can do extraordinary things. There were many amongst our kind who understood that it was meant to be this way, though others refused to acknowledge this truth. You can say it was this inequality that made them go astray, and to seek other ways to accumulate more power than what they were already blessed with."

Gil exited onto a road that took them to the land port. The outer edges of the facility were jammed with hovers, trucks and buses dropping off and picking people up. In the distance, Breeze could see the huge prairie liners skimming across the tarmac as they slowed to approach the terminal.

Gil parked the truck in between two heavy load haulers. They got out and stood by the tailgate.

Gil reached into his pocket and pulled out a plastic tab and handed it to Breeze. "Your ticket son, don't you lose this. Keep it tucked away someplace safe, don't go off and let someone steal it from you. It's your way back home."

"Not really, I could always fly back," Breeze quipped.

Gil held up a hand and shook his head. "No, not even as a joke. Not here. In safe company, maybe. There is still a lot of superstition and fear about our kind." Gil reached into the back of the truck and grabbed Breeze's bag, then headed to the terminal while Breeze raced to catch up. He couldn't understand how the old man moved so quickly and effortlessly.

"You are familiar with the Bad Lands, they at least teach about that in school, no?" Gil asked.

"We're just told that no one goes there and that there are no real settlements or towns. Only strange people and even stranger animals. Even my father doesn't talk much about it, other than to tell me never to go near it."

"Do you believe this to be true?" Gil stopped to look at him as the terminal intercom chimed. A woman's voice announced the arrival of a liner from the North Eastern territories. A group of well-dressed travelers began to chatter amongst themselves excitedly as they grabbed heavily ornamented luggage and walked into the terminal. A young woman, beautiful and impeccably dressed, looked back and caught Breeze's gaze. She smiled at him as she brushed her hair back, then turned away and continued into the terminal with her group.

Gil cleared his throat. "Is there something about that group you find to be interesting?"

Breeze shrugged. "Just a weird feeling about that girl. Like I'm going to meet someone from the North Eastern Territories. I've never been there." He turned to face the old man. "I've never really been anywhere."

"You're somewhere now. You're seeing the world."

"Yeah, on my own. My father never really took me anywhere. Do you know I saw a real forest for the first time just these past couple of days? And that's only because I can't control my flying. I flew so fast the ground beneath me was just a blur and the air was hitting my face so hard I couldn't breathe. I started to black out and the next thing I know I'm plowing into the ground and everything goes dark." He described to Gil how he walked out of the trench he created and into the forest.

"So how exactly did you make it to my farm?" Gil wondered.

"Well," Breeze grimaced as he scratched his head, "I actually walked for several days after finding some sort of an old service road and followed it west, thanks to my nav-compass." He pulled his sleeve back and tapped it.

Gil arched an eyebrow. "So you were well to the east of my farm?"

Breeze nodded. "Yeah, guess so. Saw and heard a lot of strange things."

Gil froze. "What do you mean?"

Breeze told the story of his travels, starting with the strange town behind the fortified gate to the hairy creature by the side of the lake and the ball of light that fought with it.

Gil grabbed him by the wrist. "Keep your voice down, son." He looked around them to see if anyone was listening, and then motioned for Breeze to follow him as he marched into the terminal.

Inside was a bustle of humanity jostling and shoving to queue up to board their respective liners. There were people from all over the seven territories, each dressed to their regions unique culture and style. People from the North Eastern Territories, dressed in their usual splendor, stood in stark contrast to the rugged folk from the Pacific Northwest. Breeze even saw his own kind from the Desert Country, looking uncomfortable and out of place with their heavy leather and canvas clothing.

Gil stepped between two support columns and motioned to Breeze to follow him.

The old man glanced around. Comfortable that no one was listening to their conversation, he leaned closer to Breeze. "You do understand where you were, don't you?"

Breeze looked at him blankly.

"Son, you were deep into the Bad Lands!" he said harshly, then looked around nervously. "It's almost a miracle you even survived." The old man took in a deep breath as he leaned against a column. "So you're telling me the hairy creature just stopped and reached out to you?"

Breeze nodded excitedly. "Yeah, it's like it wanted to tell me something."

Gil chuckled. "You know, many adventurous idiots go stomping into those lands looking for excitement and hoping to catch a glimpse of creatures of the sort you described. Most of them never make it back. Those few who do, their minds are finished anyway as they go catatonic slowly over time after witnessing something strange." He pointed at Breeze. "You just casually march through without even a scratch. You are truly are a remarkable young man."

Breeze was visibly taken back. He tried to speak but could only stammer.

"What's wrong son? Amazed at what you've accomplished?"

"No. Just that you're the first person to say I'm remarkable."

"Oh," Gil said and placed a hand on Breeze's shoulder. "Son, you are more remarkable than you can ever know. Never forget that. Don't think that you're better than anyone, but don't underestimate yourself. You've done more at your age than most people have done in a lifetime." Gil shook his head. "Totally explains why I found your landing point coming in from the east. You flew out of the Bad Lands and landed in my field. Do you think that was coincidence?" He narrowed his eyes.

Breeze shrugged. "I don't really know."

"There is no such thing as coincidence. All things happen for a reason." The old man stopped to listen to an announcement over the intercom. Breeze's liner was ready to begin boarding.

Gil nodded at him. "Well then, off you go I suppose. Just one thing though; don't you find it strange that of all the places to land, you would land on my farm?"

Breeze nodded. "Yeah, I never knew anyone like me. Then I found you and your wife. And then you tell me about your son."

"Yes. My son." Gil balled his hands into fists, and then relaxed. "I just think that you were dropped onto my doorstep for a reason. Throw in the fact that I'm familiar with your father and his family."

The intercom chimed again, informing everyone that the boarding of the liner had commenced.

Gil leaned toward Breeze. "Know this; it was no coincidence we met. You were guided to me. Like a lost lamb, you need to return to the flock to be with your own kind."

"You mean back to the scrap yard? And my father? In that case, I would rather just keep flying away."

"No!" Gil shouted. He smiled quickly and patted Breeze's shoulder to reassure him. "That's not what I meant. I just believe you will find yourself with others of your kind...our kind, soon. I can sense it."

Breeze shrugged. He grabbed his bag from the floor and slung it over his shoulder, then held out a hand to Gil. "Thanks for everything. You know, giving me a place to stay, and the clothes, and this bag to keep my stuff in." He couldn't think of what else to say, so he stopped rambling.

Gil stared at him, then pulled him close and gave him a bear hug. "You have a long road ahead of you son, this much I see. But you will not travel alone. Not anymore. Do you understand?" He gently pushed him away to look him in the eye.

"Yes. Yeah, sure. I think." Breeze shook his head. "What is it with the hugs? First, Maribelle, now you."

Gil chuckled. "Very well then, your liner is boarding. Hurry along now." The old man quickly wiped his eyes, and then pointed to the terminal gate.

Breeze watched the passengers shuffle in line to board the liner. He turned back to say one last goodbye to Gil, but he was gone.

Breeze scanned the terminal. He could see crowds of people milling about, but he couldn't spot Gil anywhere. "He was just here a second ago," he muttered.

He felt the hairs on the back of his neck tingle when he spotted a man on the far side of the terminal staring at him. Realizing Breeze was looking back, the man turned to his side.

Breeze adjusted the band of his sack that was slung across his shoulder as he walked to the end of the line and waited to board the liner.

After waiting in line and swiping his ticket, he stepped inside the enormous craft with its multiple levels of seats and compartments accessed by ramps that sloped precariously.

Breeze looked at his plastic ticket which glowed with the number of his seat assignment. S-26 it read.

He walked up multiple ramps that flashed the letter of each level. Glowing arrows embedded in the floor led him from A-level and up several ramps until he arrived at S-level.

He gasped when he stepped off the ramp. He was on the upper deck of the liner which had a translucent domed canopy allowing sunlight to stream through.

Someone pushed him from behind. "Come on boy, don't be impressed. These are the cheap seats. You boil in the day and freeze at night. It takes us forever to get on board and we're always the last to get off."

Another man next him grumbled. "At least we can jump off this metal beast at lot easier if she blows a repulsor and flops to one side." He looked at Breeze and winked.

Breeze swallowed hard as he gripped the band across his chest and scurried to find his seat.

He walked down several rows, passing by an endless circus of strangely dressed people speaking in accents he was unfamiliar with. He was used to seeing all sorts of strange folk in and about his town like the metal scavengers that came in from the deep desert to sell his father the scrap metal they would find from abandoned aerocraft strewn across the desert floor.

There was always one group of scavengers in particular that his father would buy from. Jacob would always speak to the leader of the group, oftentimes pulling him to the side to engage in long bouts of conversation. Breeze struggled to think of his name. John. John Agam. He shook his head. He couldn't understand why the image of that scavenger suddenly came to mind. Maybe it was the strange garb of the passengers that triggered it.

He found his row and let out a whoop when he saw it was empty. He looked around, uncertain of his new found fortune. Maybe he would be left alone for the duration of the trip and have the entire row to himself.

Breeze settled into his seat as a wave of fatigue washed over him. His eyes fluttered as the liner's engines began to spool up and vibrate the entire ship.

He glanced out his window and saw bright white clouds being overtaken by dark and brooding thunderstorms.

"Going to be one hell of a storm ahead for us!" A passenger from several rows behind proclaimed.

Breeze nodded off and fell into a deep slumber.

C H A P T E R
▼
T H R E E

BREEZE WOKE UP TO a loud bang. He looked around wildly with sleep soaked eyes as he tried to gather his wits. A flash of light erupted above him followed by another loud bang. He ducked down and covered his head.

His seat began to shake as the floor beneath him vibrated. He was wide awake now and realized he was still on the liner. The canopy above him had shifted from translucent to transparent, revealing a pitch black night punctuated by intense flashes of lighting followed quickly by peals of booming thunder. Between the flashes, he could see the swollen rain clouds as they dumped water onto the domed canopy. Breeze looked out his window and saw the ground below streaking past whenever the lighting flashed.

The thunder and the drone of the liner's engines drowned out all other sound.

He looked across the aisle but saw no one. He unbuckled his seat belt, stood up and scanned the entire level, but there was not a soul to be found. He sat back down and tapped the nav-compass on his wrist. The display showed him the time and his current coordinates. He rubbed his eyes, thinking what he saw was a mistake. *Did I really sleep for a whole day?* He looked down again at his nav-compass and noted the coordinates. *Yep, getting closer to home.*

A door at the bow slid open and a man dressed in a uniform emerged.

"Last stop of the line! Conception! The city of Conception! This is your last call!" His voice echoed throughout the empty liner as he strode down the aisle. He stopped at Breeze's row and smiled. It was a lopsided smile that almost seemed like a sneer.

"Last stop of the night, young man. City of Conception. Of course," he said as he leaned down to look out the cabin window, "this is an unusual stop for us. We usually don't come out this far. Fuel costs, you see. Company don't like it. No, sir, they don't. You must be someone of great import to be taken this far on a near empty liner. Hah!" He continued down the aisle. "City of Conception!" He called again.

Breeze looked back and craned his neck to see him.

The man turned around suddenly. "Calling it a city is a bit of stretch, wouldn't you say? More like a lonely outpost that's a bit hard to find on the map. Hah!" He descended down the ramp. "City of Conception! Last stop!" He disappeared from view.

The engines surged to a high pitched whine as the liner banked hard to starboard. Breeze looked up through the canopy as the vessel rolled, letting him see his desert town lit up in the night. The flashes of lightning highlighted some of the outermost settlements. For a moment, he thought he could see his home in the distance across the valley.

The engines settled down to a warble as the liner leveled itself and slowed. He looked out the window and saw the lone terminal of his town's land port squatting in the soaking rain in all of its drab glory. The terminal flashed with an intermittent strobe perched atop its roof that guided the liner to the gateway.

The liner came to a stop and the overhead lighting slowly flickered on. Breeze got up and walked to the ramp at the stern of the liner. He descended twenty five levels to the lower deck, never once seeing a single soul on board.

He arrived at the exit ramp to disembark, but instead of finding a covered walkway into the terminal, he was greeted by sheets of pouring rain and flashes of lightning. A gangplank had been extended and lowered to the ground. Breeze peered out into the dark as he pulled his jacket in and shivered.

"Not much of a way to come back home, is it?" The voice of the mystery conductor boomed from behind. Startled, Breeze whirled around.

"Expecting some sort of a hero's welcome, I gather? Greeted instead by the fury of the elements. Not a good sign!" He threw back his head and laughed, only to have it cut short by harsh coughing and wheezing. "This weather doesn't agree with me! Or maybe it's just the dank air of this old beast of a liner. What difference does it make?" He produced an oil soaked cloth from his back pocket and blew his nose into it, then folded it and wiped the spittle from his mouth. He folded it again and placed it back in his pocket, then motioned toward the gangplank.

"Well son, I know this is unceremonious, but you really must step off. We have a schedule to maintain." He pulled out an old watch from his pocket and tapped it.

Breeze looked again at the pouring rain. He tentatively stepped onto the gangplank and was greeted by a howling wind that drenched him with cold water. He jumped back and turned to the conductor. As the lightning flashed, it highlighted the man in an eerie light as he tapped his watch incessantly.

Breeze quickly descended the gangplank and into the pouring rain. He lived in Conception his whole life and never once saw this much water fall on the town in an entire year.

He stepped onto the ground and dashed to the terminal as torrents of fast moving water streaked across the tarmac. Upon reaching it, he stopped to look back at the liner.

He was amazed at the immense size of the vessel. The terminal looked absurd to be hosting such a massive ship. Breeze could see the conductor at the top of the entrance waving to him as the gangplank retracted into the ship. Flashing strobes underneath the liner flickered as the engines spooled up. The liner glided away from the terminal with a grace that defied its size. The bow turned into the open desert, and the liner disappeared into the depths of the rain soaked night.

Breeze opened the door to the terminal. The worn out hinges creaked as he stepped inside where he was greeted by more emptiness except for a lone individual sitting in the passenger waiting area. The man looked up slowly from his slumber to cast a wary eye at him, and then returned to his nap.

Breeze strode across the terminal to the main exit. The automated doors opened briefly, and then shut themselves on him as he stepped between them. He leaned his shoulder into one of doors and forced it open.

He stepped again into the pouring rain. The lightning had subsided, but the rumble of deep thunder persisted. Breeze pulled in his jacket as he stumbled down the washed out street that led to the rural service road to his home. He stopped and looked back, half expecting to see his father waiting for him or pulling up in one of the scrap yard trucks to pick him up.

Nothing.

The deep rumbling of thunder continued far off in the distance.

He began the long walk back home.

He arrived at the foot of his driveway in the early morning hours. He could see smoke rising from the foundry smokestacks in the distance. He took in a deep breath and trudged down the driveway to his home.

Upon arriving he went up the steps, and then hesitated before opening the door. He turned to his left and saw his father had the tractor out with the rake implement attached to the back. Breeze shook his head. His father had been out again filling up the holes he would leave behind in the desert floor from his crash landings when he would practice his flying at night. He long ago gave up the pretense that he was hiding his evening flights from his father. The tractor and the rake attached to it was proof enough that he knew, and had known for quite some time.

The hinges on the door squealed as he stepped inside. *So much for the quiet approach*, he thought to himself.

Walking into the kitchen, he was greeted by the sight of his father sitting at the table.

Jacob looked up at his son as he carefully placed his cup of coffee down.

Breeze stood his ground. His clothes were damp and his hair was wet and dripping onto his face. His boots were muddy and left tracks on the floor. "Dad, I can explain."

Jacob immediately held up a hand. "No need to. I understand. Took off for a few days to cool off. I was a little bit harsh with you about that air show. My fault. Should've gotten you into training a long time ago."

"Really?" Breeze's eyes lit up.

Jacob nodded as he lifted his cup and took a sip. "Yeah, would've been the right thing to do." He pointed toward the window. "I know I have a couple of old propeller trainers out back somewhere in the storage. I could teach you to fly one of those. You probably would've been pretty good, had I started you out when you were younger. Who knows, you could've become the next Buck Bonanza. Now there is one hell of a pilot!"

Breeze's shoulders slumped as he looked down at the floor. He became transfixed at the puddle of water he had created.

Jacob put his cup down and began tapping his fingers on the table. "Yep, would've cured a lot of problems, I see that now. Could've had you competing in those air shows to give you a chance to show off a bit. Would've made things a lot smoother for you." He looked down at his cup, then up to Breeze. "But that's the thing son, life is never smooth or easy."

"You're not even going to ask me where I've been, what I saw? You're just going to sit there at the table and tell me you've made mistakes?" Breeze said.

Jacob began tracing his finger along a grain line on the wooden table. When he spoke, his voice was almost a whisper. "I go out, night after night, looking for those impact craters you usually make when you come back from your night flights and try to land. I sometimes wonder if I'm going to find you in one of them seriously hurt, or dead."

"Don't know what you mean. What craters?" Breeze tried to bluff.

Jacob waved him off as he picked up his cup and took a sip. In the faint kitchen light, the lines of stress and strain were etched across his face. "But this time, several days go by and I begin to get worried. Your not returning meant you figured out how to travel longer distances. Or you were lost, maybe hurt. Or worse." Jacob shut his eyes tightly for a moment before opening them again. He rubbed his temple. "I drove around town looking for you, figuring you were scared about how I would react to you being gone for so long. Maybe you were hiding out with some friends. But you don't really have any. I checked your school, but they don't have much of a record of your attendance. Seems you like to skip a lot. They didn't seem all too concerned. From what they tell me, you're not doing very well there anyway." He smiled. "No matter. You're not much different than your old man. I was never much of a student."

"Yeah, I guess that's why we live in the middle of nowhere and run a scrap yard." Breeze heard his words but quickly regretted them when he saw the pained expression on his father's face.

"That's all right, son. You do have a point. I guess I didn't give you the best life a father could've given his son." He leaned back in his chair. "And this scrap yard is not much of a legacy to leave to you when my time comes to be free of this world." He nodded. "It's not much of anything, is it?"

Breeze nodded, then shook his head and waved his hands. "Dad, I didn't mean to make it sound that way—"

Jacob pointed a finger at him. "No, don't do that. Don't second guess yourself. What you said originally was the truth. That come from in here." He tapped his chest. "Never be a stranger to the truth, son. It can be hard to hear and tougher to swallow. But I promise you this; once you come to grips with it, you will never be more free."

Breeze shivered in his wet clothes. "I flew pretty far to the east. Then I crash landed next to a forest. A really, huge forest."

Jacob gripped his coffee cup.

Breeze continued. "I walked through it for several days trying to find a town or some way to get home. That place scared me. I never saw so many trees."

Jacob grunted and nodded as he looked out the window. The rain had stopped and the only trace left of the storm was the distant rumbling of thunder. As the sun rose, its rays exposed the aftermath with puddles of water spread out across the property and debris strewn haphazardly everywhere.

Breeze spoke a little louder. "I got scared of something, but I don't know what it was. That's when I decided to take a chance and try to fly my way out." He told his father how he ended up by the shore of a lake and his encounter with the wild man. "I took off again and flew for I don't know how long and I ended up at a farm of a really nice old couple. Gil and Maribelle. They say they know you."

Jacob's eyes lit up. "There are many people I know, son. I travel far and wide for the business and make a lot of contacts."

"Gil said his son was a flier just like me. Only he disappeared."

Jacob's coffee cup cracked in his grip and the hot black liquid splashed onto the floor.

"Damn that old fool! Can't even keep his mouth shut and perform a simple task." He grabbed a towel and wiped the table, then tossed it to the floor to soak up the puddle of coffee.

"What are you talking about dad, what task?"

"Breeze, it's no coincidence you ended up at Gil and Maribel's. I put the word out to everyone I know to keep a look out for you. And if they did find you, they would also help you get home. You may not believe this, but you were guided to that farm. No matter what, you would've ended up at Gil's or some other safe haven."

Breeze stepped toward him. "Why do I have to be so afraid to show my powers? What's the big deal? I can do a show. We can travel around and make some extra money."

Jacob shook his head vigorously. "No, don't ever say that. It's too dangerous."

"That's what Gil said when he drove me to the land port. He started to get stressed out and he...bulged. His hands and arms got huge and he started to expand. I could see the bump in the roof of his truck from his head hitting it. Guess it wasn't the first time."

Jacob threw his hands up. "Amazing. Just amazing. That old coot could never contain his emotions."

"Dad, can you do anything?" Breeze ventured.

Jacob stared down his son. "No. If you're asking me what I think you're asking, the answer is no."

"Anything?" He persisted.

"Boy, don't go getting any ideas about me. I do what I do. Nothing more."

Breeze stepped back. "Then that explains everything. You're ashamed of me."

Jacob slammed his fist onto the table. "I'm not ashamed of you. Just want to keep you safe. There are people who would harm you if they could and use you for their own crooked ways."

"Who? I don't see anyone trying to harm me."

Jacob chuckled. "Son, you do have such a long road ahead of you."

Breeze tilted his head. "That's what Gil said to me."

Jacob snorted. "At least he said something right."

"How do you know them?"

"How is not important." He got up from the table and while walking to the counter he thought about the disk and the message from Oslo. "Son, I think you should leave. Just for a little while."

Breeze's eyes narrowed. "Where?"

"A place for you to go far from here. Very far. Somewhere you can go and get a handle on your flying or at least to be able to control it. I guess you can say it's a place where they can teach you how to stop making holes in the ground and I can get a break from filling them in." He smiled.

Breeze did his best to look innocent. "Still don't know what you mean."

"Come now son, it's a poorly kept secret between the two of us that you sneak out at night to teach yourself how to fly. You plow into the ground when you screw up a landing. Don't tell me you don't notice I start off my day with the tractor filling in all those craters you make in the desert floor."

"You've known this whole time, but you never said anything to me about it. Why?"

Jacob sighed. "Son, what can I say? You're a young man with an extraordinary gift. Sooner or later you're going to want to use it. Explore it. Push yourself to the limit. How am I supposed to hold you back?" He patted his chest. "You know, I used to be young too. May not believe it, but I was," he said as he gazed out the window.

"How come you never tried to help me? Maybe try to give me some kind of advice?"

Jacob shuffled back to the table and sat down with a groan. "Breeze, what would you have me say? I've watched you before. I've seen you on some of your night flights. You seem to be doing pretty good on your own. Your landings could use a little work, though." He chuckled.

"What really happened to mom?"

Jacob shot him a sharp look. "What do you mean?"

"How did she die?"

He stared down his son, and then softened his stance. "You know what happened."

"Tell it to me again. I just want to hear you say it."

Jacob leaned back and swallowed hard. "You mother died while traveling along the service road into town when a long range hauler hit her. The driver was fatigued, been driving through the night to make his destination and get his pay. 'Got to support my family,' I overheard him say as he sat by his truck after the accident. They had to drag me away from him. They thought I was going to kill him."

Breeze sat down in the chair across from him. "You never told me this."

Jacob looked at his son vacantly. When he spoke the words came out slowly. "It can be hard to relive those moments, son. Sooner or later we all experience a tragedy that we can't speak about for a long time."

"Dad, I don't remember the funeral."

Jacob's eyes widened. "What do you mean? Besides, you were so young, how would you even remember?"

Breeze shrugged. "I don't even remember seeing her in the casket. Every funeral you hear about, the casket is open for everyone to see. I don't remember that happening with mom."

Jacob balled his hands into fists. "The accident left her badly injured son. There wasn't much left to see."

"If you say so."

"You doubt me?"

Breeze shrugged. "I don't really know who to believe. I just remember when I was really little you used to play with me a lot. But ever since Mom died I thought we would get a little closer, but you seem to just push me away. Heck, you don't even have pictures of me on the wall past three years old. Why? Then I started to fly. I even showed off for you. You got so mad you locked me in my room for a week. I just remember screaming and crying until you let me out. Ever since then you pretend I can't fly. Now you're telling me you've been watching me the whole time, but you want me to go to some place where I can learn. Why now? Is it because of what I just did? I didn't want to fly out that far. I really didn't want to go to the air show without you. It's just that you never really want me to do anything at all. Just go to school, then work with you. That's it."

"It's important to learn the trade, son. It's something you can do to support yourself in the future—"

"I don't want to run a scrap yard!" Breeze stood and shouted. He saw the devastated look on his father's face and he regretted his words.

"You're right," Jacob said. "I've said it before; it's not much to leave behind for you. More reason for you to leave, even for just a little while. Get out and see a little bit more of the world then come back with a clear head where we'll talk more about your future."

"You just want to get rid of me."

Jacob shuddered as if the words were like a sledgehammer to the chest. "No, son. I just want to give you a fighting chance."

"When do I leave?"

Jacob waved at him. "Don't be so hasty. Take a shower and get a change of clothes. I'll be waiting for you in the living room."

"Fine." Breeze marched down the hall and straight to his room.

He emerged minutes later freshly bathed and wearing clean clothes. The sun was higher in the sky and shined its light through the house when it dawned upon him just how old their home really was. Everywhere he looked he saw peeling paint and heavy carpets covering cracked stone floors. He swore he remembered a time when the house was in better shape.

He walked down the hall that led to the living room when he stopped to look at the family photos that hung there with dusty pictures of him as a baby with his doting mother and father.

He sighed and broke away from them, turning the corner that led into the living room where his father was sitting in his favorite chair by the fireplace with its fading material and the foam stuffing that protruded from it. He never seen his father look so small in it. It was as if his oversized frame was being swallowed by the chair.

Jacob's eyes lit up upon seeing his son and motioned for him to enter. As Breeze crossed the living room, Jacob pointed to the couch across from him. "I would like for you to meet some people."

Breeze was startled to see two strangely dressed men sitting there. "Where did you guys come from?"

The two men looked at each other quizzically, then at Breeze. "We've been here the whole time."

Breeze jerked a thumb toward the entrance of the living room. "I don't think so. I was standing there and could only see my father. What gives?"

Jacob motioned for his son to sit down. "All is fine son, you're just tired. These past couple of days for you have been stressful." He nodded toward the two men on the couch. "Gentleman, I gather that you've managed to pull yourselves together? Can we proceed, or do you need more time to synchronize yourselves?"

The man sitting on the right side of the couch was the first to speak. He was dressed similar to his companion in a leather jacket with a woolen collar, along with pants that had multiple pockets lining both sides of the legs with jet black boots. When he spoke it was in an accent that Breeze had never heard before. "Thank you Jacob. I speak for my colleague when I say we have fully acclimated ourselves. Forgive us, but spending as much time as we do at Perihelion can make one forget about the world outside. We tend to suffer from a bit of a...lag, if you will, upon leaving."

Jacob nodded. "Understood. I've been through that myself. Very well, let us proceed." He turned to his son. "Paul, I would like to introduce you to Vermillion Sachs and Horton Goldmeyer. They are representatives of the place I had mentioned to you earlier. It's called—"

"Perihelion. Yeah, dad, I heard him. I still don't understand how you guys were just sitting there and I never saw you. What gives? Are you like me?" Breeze cocked his head at them.

The two men looked at one another and shrugged. Then Vermillion spoke up. "Breeze if you mean gifted like you, no, we are not so blessed. We are merely recruiters who believe in the mission of Ole Auken. We subscribe to his vision of bringing gifted and talented young men and women together to a safe haven where they can be free to explore their talents and spread their wings. Figuratively speaking of course."

Horton chortled. "Oslo would find that amusing."

Vermillion shot him a glare. "Not wise to be referring to him like that. It is a sign of disrespect."

Horton nodded vigorously. "You're right." He looked at Breeze.

"Ole's nickname has been Oslo for such a long time. Ever since he arrived at Perihelion so long ago, in fact. He's not from Oslo, mind you, but just outside the city proper. Very well, you have caught me in a bit of a white lie. Well *outside* the city proper. But no matter. I do believe he was the only recruit from Scandinavia at the time of his admittance to the outpost...I meant academy." He swallowed nervously. "Anyway, everyone took to calling him Oslo due to his proximity to having lived so close to the city. Or something like that. It has been quite some time, you see."

Vermillion held up a hand. "What my colleague is trying to tell you is that Oslo," he grimaced and shook his head, "Ole is looking forward to meeting you. He and your father established a dialogue quite some time ago. He knows a lot about you and is very eager to render the assistance you seek in your quest for the mastery of flight."

Breeze shrunk back in his chair. "This Oslo guy knows about me?" He turned to look at his father. "How long have you known him? What did you tell him?"

Vermillion threw his hands up in the air as he glared at Horton. "Oslo?"

Horton shrugged and muttered. "You have to admit, it is a rather clever name. Though again, he is not exactly from Oslo—"

Jacob cleared his throat loudly. "What Mr. Goldmeyer and Mr. Sachs are trying to say, son, is that Oslo runs a training facility that specializes in young people with paranormal abilities."

"You mean freaks like me."

"Breeze, listen—"

"No, dad, it's fine. After all this time I'm just kind of glad that you acknowledge what I can do. And now, you want to send me away."

"Paul—"

"Breeze, dad. Call me what everybody has been calling me ever since I was a kid, which is Breeze. 'Cause he's like the wind,' they always say about me. I'm here now, but then I just wander off and never really stick to anything. That's why that name stuck. And you know what? I like it."

Jacob closed his eyes. When he opened them, they were narrow slits. "Son, you are going to have to listen to me. I couldn't be more serious with you, even if I tried."

Breeze was not used to getting stern lectures from his father. His entire history with him since his mother's death had been a mixture of avoidance with brief and awkward moments of conversation. If his father tried to teach him anything, somehow disaster would always ensue and he would find himself getting hurt or having to dodge something falling onto him. Every time they got together something terrible would happen. He was getting that feeling now.

"What I'm trying to tell you, what I'm trying to offer you, is that chance you were looking for. An opportunity to get away from Conception, just for a little while, to learn more about your skills and be with young people like you. Maybe make some friends."

"You mean hang out with rejects like me. Losers, basically."

Horton piped up. "Now hear this young man; Perihelion has quite the assembly of diverse, and dare I say, attractive recruits ever assembled. We are talking about candidates not just from Northern America, mind you. We have been reaching out across the globe to the other territories. Our attempts at establishing communications and entry into these territories have not been easy, but great efforts are being made—" he stopped when he saw Jacob glare at him menacingly. "As your father was saying." Horton fell into silence and leaned back into the couch.

Breeze swore he saw Horton flicker for a brief moment.

Jacob continued. "As I was saying; Perihelion would be a place for you to gain the control you need, and to meet others like yourself. You're probably going to see others who are going through the same struggles as you in controlling their powers. But no matter, think of it as a summer break away from here."

"So, where is this place?" Breeze asked.

Vermillion perked up. "Excellent question. Off the Eastern Shores in the Atlanteanic Ocean. Not too far from the coast of La Floride, but just far enough from that forsaken place."

"Don't know what you're talking about," Breeze said.

"Doesn't matter, just know that there is so much more than academics and training—"

"You mean like books and studying?"

Vermillion ignored the interruption, "—and plenty of opportunity for recreational activities. The swimming there is so much fun, as the water is quite warm and inviting. And so clear! Do you like to swim?"

"Don't know how," Breeze said.

Horton leaned in. "Well no matter. I'm sure there is someone there who would be more than happy to teach you. Perhaps a nice young lady?" he said with a wink and a smile.

Breeze shrugged.

Vermillion shook his head. "Forgive my associate, young man. Is there a lady friend of your own you will be leaving behind? I don't think Mr. Goldmeyer meant to imply that you would be betraying her confidence in you in any way."

"No, it's fine. Nobody here for me. Not really."

The two men looked over at Jacob, who was sitting with his hands gripping the armrest with his eyes closed.

Vermillion cleared his throat. "Well then, I would like to say this was a productive meeting. I just need to know young man, with your father's consent of course, would you care to join us at our humble academy?"

Breeze stood up suddenly. "Yes. When do we leave?"

Vermillion and Horton looked at one another with a mixture of surprise and happiness.

Vermillion was the first to speak. "Well, uh, good question. I suppose at your earliest convenience—"

"Let me go get my stuff." Breeze pivoted on his heel and marched out of the room.

He came back moments later with a bag slung over his shoulder. He had his nav-compass on his wrist and he tugged on his jacket sleeve to cover it.

Vermilion arched an eyebrow at the nav-compass, and then nodded his head while slapping his hands on his knees as he stood up. Horton clumsily rose from his seat, and they both turned to Jacob.

Jacob stood up slowly as he pushed off the armrests with a groan. Horton reached out to help, but he ignored him.

He stood there in the dimly lit family room and looked at his son, noticing how much he had grown over the years. *A boy*, he thought to himself, *beginning his journey to becoming a man. Hopefully a far better one than I ever was.*

As father and son stood face to face, Vermillion tilted his head at Horton and the two retreated to the far corner of the room.

"Well, this is it I guess," Breeze said.

Jacob placed a hand on his shoulder. "Do good. Learn. Take in everything that you can. I promise you that somebody will be here when you get back."

Breeze cocked his head. "What do you mean?"

"I will be going away for a while. Business of course. We'll meet again and discuss everything you have learned. You can tell me then what you think of your future and what it is you really want to do."

Breeze looked into his father's eyes. He had never seen him like this before.

"Well then, it's settled," Vermillion said as he stepped toward them. "Breeze, when you are ready we will be waiting for you in our transport. Jacob," he turned and bowed to him, "thank you for your hospitality, and most important of all, introducing us to your son and granting him the opportunity to spend the summer with us. I promise you he will return, changed for the better, of course."

Jacob nodded. "Yes, of course."

Vermillion motioned Horton to follow him. Horton bowed to Jacob as he walked past, and then patted Breeze on his shoulder. "Good choice," he said as he trailed Vermillion out the door.

"I suppose this is goodbye?" Breeze said as he tugged on the bag strap across his chest.

"There is no such thing as goodbye. Just an intermission before we meet again. Now go and see the world. I will see you when I do." Jacob sat back down in his chair.

Breeze walked out of the living room and down the hallway adorned with pictures. He glanced at them quickly as they flickered by like windows into a life he sensed he would never see again.

He stepped out the front door into the brilliant sunshine, but didn't see either of the two recruiters. He looked back at the house wondering if they were still inside, then turned around when he sensed a presence behind him and was startled to see a ship hovering a few inches off the ground before him. It was like nothing he had seen before. He was used to the usual propeller or turbine powered craft. The hovers he normally saw were usually something small like trucks or large transports similar to the liner that brought him back home. He had never seen a ship like this. It was shaped like a rectangular block and he estimated that it was about a hundred feet in length, thirty feet in beam and forty feet in height. The edges of the ship were rounded off, and its bow protruded like an arrow, with windows lining either side of the craft. He took a step closer and noticed how the metal hull was fatigued with dents and scratches, and the paint was chipped and peeling.

A hatch on the side of the craft squealed open, and a gangplank lowered from the hull as Vermilion appeared at the entrance. "Not much to look at, I know. I can see by the look on your face that's what you're thinking. But she is sturdy and will get us to our destination."

"I've never seen anything like this before," Breeze exclaimed.

"Oh, well, yes, you are correct. They don't really make them like this anymore, to say the least. Nevertheless, young man, climb aboard," Vermillion said, and disappeared into the interior of the ship.

Breeze took a step up the gangplank, noting the rust spots that pock-marked the hull. Rust wasn't something he was used to seeing in the desert, as there wasn't much in the way of humidity. He stepped inside and immediately shrank back from the stench.

Horton called out from the cockpit. "I do apologize for the odor. What you are smelling is mildew. Air conditioning went on the fritz before we left Perihelion and she had been sitting under the hot sun before we left. We'll get the matter sorted out. In the meantime, take a seat and buckle up."

Breeze turned to look at the passenger cabin. It was empty and it reminded him when he woke up on the liner earlier this morning.

He took a seat and slid over to the window. He looked out of it as he fiddled with his seat belt, almost expecting to see his father step out of the house and wave him goodbye. He never did.

The hull shuddered and groaned as the engines spooled up and the ship lurched forward.

Breeze watched the desert landscape sweep by when the ship abruptly angled up and accelerated into the sky with the engines whining at a full pitch. He took one last look back at his home before the ship plunged into the clouds.

Jacob sat as still as a rock in the chair with his eyes closed as he listened to the transport accelerate and ascend into the sky. He sat in the chair for the rest of the day and into the evening.

As the sun marched across the sky and toward the horizon, he never moved. Not even a twitch.

Evening had descended and the moon had begun its ascent into the star filled heavens when Jacob's eyes flew open. He stood up in one swift motion and marched out of the living room, down the hall and into the desert night.

He walked quickly along the path to the shed as he appeared to almost glide over the terrain.

He stepped inside and hit the light switch next to the door. As the overhead lights flickered on, he went to the row of cabinets above the work bench. He flung them open and pulled a can with a plastic lid from a shelf.

He gently lowered it onto the workbench and sat on a stool. He removed the lid and reached into it, producing a handful of photographs. He looked at each one. A smiling woman. A laughing man. A young child shrieking with delight. Photo after photo of a happy life. He carefully put them back into the can, pressed the plastic lid to seal it, and then returned it back to the cabinet.

He marched back out into the cold night and paused for a moment to scan the property. He could see the house with its lone porch light casting a faint glow around it. In the distance he could make out the outlines of the foundry, and closer to him were endless piles of scrap metal. He fixed his gaze between two particular piles and nodded at a shadowy figure that stepped out from it, and then walked out into the open desert with his tracks fading behind him as he disappeared into the night.

Moments later a spectacular explosion rocked the entire property. The house withered like matchsticks, while heavy sections of the foundry were vaulted into the sky and came down as molten chunks of metal.

In the town of Conception, windows rattled and burst as the townsfolk awoke startled and confused. Many looked out through the remains of their shattered windows and witnessed a monstrous ball of fire erupting into the night sky, lighting up the terrain for miles.

The fire squads were roused into action as they made the long trek out to the Corinth home and foundry, but they were too late to do much of anything. The area had been leveled. An investigation later revealed that multiple rows of gas canisters that ran beneath the property to fuel the foundry had malfunctioned and exploded. None of Jacob's employees knew how it could have happened. The foundry had an excellent safety record. Alceron Beeks, Jacob's foreman, was the only one who remained silent when questioned by investigators which created a cloud of suspicion about him.

The town officials sealed off access to the property as they let the fire burn itself out. It was decided that it was far too dangerous to try and fight the fire, as there was no hope for survivors. Jacob and his son were presumed dead.

The following night, a black clad figure descended from the sky, landing amidst the smoldering ruins. He sidestepped several hotspots while slowly walking around the wreckage as his sleek black pressure suit reflected some of the flames that still burned. He stopped where the shed once stood.

He looked around before settling his gaze upon something on the ground. It was partially burned photograph. He reached down to pick it up. His blank face flickered briefly with pinpoints of light as he stared at the picture, then he dropped it and flew away.

The following day, when the hot afternoon sun was at its peak, a disheveled man pushing a carriage filled with scraps of metal was scavenging amongst the ruins when he found the photograph that the black clad figure held earlier. He smiled at the picture of a young couple holding a baby boy and it reminded him of better days when he had a family.

He carefully placed the photograph into his carriage and continued scavenging.

CHAPTER

▼

FOUR

AS THE TRANSPORT DESCENDED from the clouds and began shuddering from the turbulence, Breeze banged his head against the window when the ship bucked violently. He grimaced from the pain as he rubbed his temple. It had been a long journey, with most of it spent flying at a low altitude to avoid detection. They traveled mostly at night, landing early in the morning to hide the ship in ravines or in valleys. When the evening arrived, they ascended and continued their journey, always flying just above the treetops. The agents explained to him that by doing so they could avoid detection from any hostile raiders flying at higher altitudes. There were also bandits on the ground who were scanning for ships on the horizon so they could bring them down with surge weapons that knocked engines offline. Once the ship crashed, they would plunder what was left of the wreckage. The metal alone was worth more than a human life, they told him. Breeze fully understood, coming from a family that was in the scrap metal industry. As for what they would do to any surviving passengers, the agents did not elaborate.

Breeze was alone in the passenger cabin for most of the journey. Though Horton and Vermillion came to check on him occasionally, they spent most of the time in the cockpit with the pilot, or running down the aisle to check on an alarm from the engine room in the stern of the ship. When they passed by him they always had a reassuring smile that carried an undercurrent of anxiety beneath it.

The pilot was an enigma. Rarely seen during the night flights, he hardly spoke when they landed for the day. He always climbed up a ladder behind his seat and disappeared into a cabin above the cockpit. Once, Breeze was able to catch a glimpse of his face. The eyes had a mechanical appearance, and when the pilot would walk, it was stiff and awkward. The pilot caught Breeze staring at him after landing on the second morning. He quickly turned away, raising a hand to shield his face. From that point on, the pilot always descended from his cabin wearing a full face helmet with a respirator attached to it. Breeze asked Horton why the pilot never seemed very social. The agent laughed nervously and explained that the pilot needed a lot of rest because flying so close to the ground stressed him considerably.

The ship itself was old and musty. The seats were worn out and faded, and it didn't matter which one he chose as they all felt uncomfortable to him. The armrests squeaked loudly every time he lowered them and the lap belts never latched together, and occasionally popped open on a whim.

The lighting was dim and unreliable. Half of the cabin would be lit, and the other half would flicker intermittently between faint light and total darkness. Breeze wanted to get up to explore the rest of the ship during flight but whenever he would try a voice would crackle over the intercom instructing him to sit down for his own safety. The point would be made whenever the ship would suddenly rise up or plunge down rapidly as it would fly over and down mountains and valleys as it followed the contours of the land. The engines would throttle up and reach a crescendo with a loud whine as if they would burst into flames at any moment, then settle down to a soft rumble.

During those times he would become ill and would close his eyes to quell the feeling of nausea that overwhelmed him. As the days passed, he acclimated to the ship's rapid ascents and descents, and the waves of nausea began to fade.

"You're getting your sea legs!" Vermillion said to him.

Breeze shrugged. "But I've never been to the ocean before."

The agent laughed. "It's just an expression. Flying so close to the earth feels like we're going up and down some really big waves in a small boat in the middle of a storm." He emphasized his point by making a motion with his hand of a boat going up and down a huge wave. As if on cue, the engines throttled up again to fly over a mountain, and then whined down as they glided down the other side. The descent made it feel like his stomach was flying up, creating a temporary sensation of weightlessness.

Whenever they landed was the only real opportunity to look around the ship. He wasn't reassured by what he saw. The rest of the ship was just as run down as the passenger cabin. Unlocked doors would lead into storage lockers filled with old and broken electronics. Some were just empty and full of dust.

The bunks where they slept during the day were small and claustro-phobic. Breeze's cabin was no bigger than a closet. He had to shut the door behind him once he entered, otherwise there wasn't enough room to pull a latch along the wall that dropped the hidden bed down. He climbed into it and immediately looked up at sunlight pouring through the window above. When he complained to Horton about it the first day, the agent apologized, explaining that the automatic shading system was malfunctioning, advising him just to pull a sheet over his head to block out the light.

Breeze groaned. "But it's so hot inside the bunk, and the air con-ditioning barely works. Let me guess, it's also malfunctioning, right?"

Horton smiled and shrugged.

Going to the bathroom was an ordeal. He would roll out of his bunk and recess it back into the wall to gain the space needed to open the door. Then, make his way down a corridor to a bathroom that looked like it came from a prison. Everything was made of stainless steel that was always cold to the touch and he would let out a yelp every time he sat on the toilet. He was instructed not to flush too often as they never knew when they could land safely next to a lake or river to refill the water tanks.

When they would take off in the early evening, he would sit down in what became his favorite seat in the passenger cabin. It was located on the starboard side of the ship and midway along the aisle. He would gaze out the window at the moonlit land and marvel at how desolate it was. Miles and miles of wide open country with hardly a soul to be found, though now and then he spotted a lone settlement nestled somewhere in the hills or in a forest. Sometimes he picked out campfires of what was either a wagon train heading out to a new settlement, or bandits set-tling down for the night. He was curious as to why whenever he saw the faint glow of city lights in the distance, the ship would steer around it.

"We don't want to attract any attention." Vermillion explained to Breeze one night. "Most cities have a defense system to protect them-selves from raiders. Since we are not willing to answer any hails over the comm systems and announce our intentions or flight plan, it's always best to stay out of range."

The ship left a mountain range that gave way to rolling hills. Hills turned into a long, flat plain as they continued heading east toward the ocean. Breeze was appreciative of this landscape, as his stomach didn't heave up and down so often. He looked out his window at the moonlit treetops they skimmed over. The land seemed so peaceful that it was hard to believe any danger could be found there.

His daydreaming abruptly ended when the cabin was suddenly filled with a shrilling alarm. The overhead lights switched to a red glow as Horton rushed past him toward the cockpit.

"What's happening?" Breeze called out.

"We are approaching the coastline!" he shouted back.

Breeze leaned over to look down the aisle as Horton opened the cockpit door and saw the glowing eyes of the pilot reflecting off the windscreen. The numerous display screens and gauges that were normally spread out before him were powered down and replaced by a single lighted screen with an icon of a floating box in the center. The cockpit lights phased from a soft green to a reddish glow as the pilot turned to Horton and spoke in a mechanical tone while pointing at the screen. Horton nodded his head vigorously and shut the cockpit door.

Breeze looked out his window and watched as the forest abruptly ended at the shoreline of a vast stretch of water. It was the ocean. He had never seen it before, and it was breathtaking to behold. It was just like the desert to him, a featureless landscape that stretched in all directions seemingly forever, broken up only by waves rolling across its surface the way sand dunes broke up the monotony of the desert landscape.

Breeze pressed closer to the window and strained to see the coastline as they raced away from it when he saw human figures with glowing eyes running out of the tree line and onto the beach. A bright flash illuminated the area as a glowing orb rose up and hovered above them, then leapt toward the ship.

Breeze unbuckled his lap belt and headed to the stern of the ship. There was a window he saw earlier on a cargo hatch where he could watch the glowing orb as it hurtled towards them.

He ran down the aisle and crashed into Vermillion, who was dashing towards the cockpit. "Breeze, you must sit down and strap yourself in, things are about to get pretty bumpy," the agent said.

"I just saw a glowing ball of light launch from the coast. It's heading toward us!"

"Yes, I know. No worries. Just sit down." The agent emphasized his point by firmly placing his hands on Breeze's shoulders and herding him to an empty seat, then continued toward the cockpit.

Breeze leapt up and followed him. Vermillion flung open the cockpit door and stepped in, unaware that Breeze slipped in behind him.

The cockpit was filled with the sound of wailing alarms and warning chimes. He sat down in a jump seat behind the pilot who abruptly turned and gave Breeze a hard stare with his bright, glowing eyes.

Horton was giving orders to the pilot while looking out the window. He turned to address him and was astonished to see Breeze. "How did you get in? You need to leave immediately!"

"No time for that now," Vermillion said, "just plug in the codes. We need to get into the box." He pointed at the screen in the center of the console. It pulsated bright blue while the warning chimes became frequent and more intense when a globe of light suddenly appeared off to the port side of the transport, filling the cockpit with a bright glow.

"What is that?" Breeze yelled.

"Never mind and strap yourself in," Horton said as he punched in a series of codes into a console next to the screen.

The globe kept pace with the ship. It stayed solid white for several seconds, then began pulsating bright blue, yellow, and orange hues seemingly at random. The pilot banked the ship to starboard, and the globe followed it. He banked hard to port, and then threw the ship back to starboard. The globe effortlessly mirrored the ship's movements.

The globe began to pulsate and flash wildly as it leapt in front of the ship while matching its speed and course. It then jumped to the ship's starboard, flashing a variety of colors at various tempos before abruptly vanishing.

They all looked out the cockpit windows and tried to locate it. It was nowhere to be found.

Breeze leaned back and took in a deep breath. It reminded him of the globes of light he saw over the White Mountain. He wondered if they were the same.

The cabin suddenly exploded with brilliant white light as the globe re-appeared and was hovering above them. Breeze hardly could see its outline as he looked up through the sky roof while shielding his eyes from the bright glow. The globe began to split itself into two, and then subdivided into four, and finally eight. They formed a loop around the ship and began to rotate slowly in unison, then accelerated into a high-speed frenzy.

The pilot's hands flew up to a series of switches and levers above him. He yanked down on a lever and the ship came to a sudden halt.

Breeze could feel the straps barely restraining him as he was thrown violently forward.

The globes continued their forward motion, and then stopped to turn back and retake the ship. The pilot hit a switch above him and a humming sound filled the cockpit. Breeze could feel a vibration reverberate through the ship as the hull groaned and the floor of the cockpit rattled, culminating into a flash of dark blue lightning that lashed out from the ship and struck the rotating globes. The globes exploded and arced away from the ship.

The pilot mashed down on the throttles and the ship accelerated instantaneously, slamming Breeze back into his seat.

Horton pointed at the display screen and shouted at the pilot. "Aim for the center of the box!"

The illuminated box on the display screen pulsated faster and faster with each passing second. The pilot steered the ship while taking quick glances at it, when an icon suddenly appeared in the shape of a bull's eye and floated above and to the right of the box. As the pilot steered through turbulence that buffeted the ship, each course correction made the bull's eye drop closer to the box. Lights flashed on the console as alarms wailed throughout the cockpit.

"Vortex rotation ahead." Horton announced as he silenced the alarms.

The pilot continued steering the ship with the bull's eye drifting to the center of the box when the display glowed a solid green.

"Contact," the pilot said.

Clouds of fluorescent green emerged before them and enveloped the ship. A tunnel formed within the clouds and rotated as they flew into it. The rotation became more intense as the tunnel narrowed and lightning crackled along its length. The ship's engines whined, and the metal skin of the hull began to glow.

Breeze was pinned to his seat and felt overwhelmed with a sense of displacement. The voices of Horton and Vermillion became faint and disembodied as the alarms that echoed throughout the cockpit faded away. His vision blurred as everything around him appeared to stretch like a rubber band. The tunnel constricted until it pressed against the hull of the ship as lightning crackled viciously all around.

Then, complete silence.

Breeze tried to look around, but it was like moving in slow motion. The pilot and the agents seemed to be standing still as he looked toward the cockpit windscreen, a feat that felt like it took minutes rather than seconds, to do. The tunnel ceased its rotation and collapsed to a single point in space. The silence was gradually replaced by the growing crescendo of static.

He blacked out.

Breeze woke up in the passenger cabin and the soothing hum of the engines allowed him to focus and get his bearings back. He looked around, noting the brilliant sunshine pouring through the windows. He rubbed the back of his head, wondering how he got back into his seat. He couldn't recall ever leaving the cockpit. The last thing he remembered was flying at night while under attack by globes of light, followed by the transport entering a tunnel made of swirling clouds and the static that drowned out all other sound, and then...

He shook his head. He couldn't remember anything else.

He called out to Vermillion and Horton, but they didn't respond. Puzzled as to what happened since he blacked out, he casually looked out the window and was stunned at how high they were flying. They had spent most of their journey flying at night, and at extremely low altitude to avoid detection. Now they were traveling in broad daylight amongst the clouds. Breeze marveled at the beauty of the crystal clear ocean below and could see the contours of the seabed with clusters of coral dotting the sandy bottom.

The smooth ocean surface merged into frothy whitecaps as an island came into view, its lush green surface a sharp contrast to the aquamarine ocean that surrounded it. The island stretched for several miles in length and was a few miles wide with a bay carved out of its eastern shore. There was a cluster of tall structures and buildings that hugged the shoreline of the bay. He noticed how its light blue waters merged into a dark blue as it streamed out into the ocean.

A strange feeling swept over him as he felt there was someone beneath the waves of the deep blue water. It was almost as if a young girl was calling his name...

The sudden high pitch whine of the engines broke his trance as the transport banked to port and began circling the island. As it descended from the clouds, he was able to get a better view of it. He could see a forest of palm trees that stretched from the lower center of the island to the west, where it ended at the edge of a landing facility. He could make out the shapes of various aerocraft spread out across the tarmac but wasn't familiar with any of them. Like the transport, they were nothing at all like the aerocraft in Conception or any of the surrounding desert towns. Yet they all appeared to be decrepit and out of service despite their advanced designs and this intrigued him to no end.

The transport descended rapidly as the landing gear lowered, accompanied by the whine of hydraulic motors. Breeze gripped his seat as the ground rushed up to greet them when the engines throttled up, then feathered back down as the transport gently made contact with the ground. The ship shuddered as it settled down.

The engines came to a full stop, and the only sounds he could hear were the whistling of air from the vents as the air-conditioning struggled to pump cool air into the cabin, followed by the cargo door opening in the stern. He peered out the window and saw a dwarf walk quickly under the transport and out of sight.

He left his seat and headed to the cockpit to look for Vermillion and Horton. He opened the door and stepped inside. There was no one there, not even the pilot. He looked above the pilot's seat and saw the hatch to his bunk was open. Breeze scrambled up the ladder and poked his head into the open hatchway. The moment he did, a soft, blue light flickered on.

He saw that the bunk was a tube with a metal slab for the pilot to lie on. There was no mattress or pillow. Where his head would lay was a metallic ring with wires streaming from it, and all were plugged into a console. The bunk was devoid of any pictures or decorations. Breeze knew the pilots back home would keep mementos and pictures of their sweethearts inside their cockpits. Here, there was nothing but cold steel, blue light and wires.

He felt uneasy and quickly climbed back down. He took one last look around the cockpit as a sense of déjà vu swept over him. He shook his head vigorously, hoping it would jog his memory and shed some more details about what had happened in here, then sighed as nothing was forthcoming. He stepped out of the cockpit and back into the cabin. He marched down the aisle towards the stern while scanning every row, half expecting to find the agents sleeping in the seats.

He arrived at the passenger compartments and stepped in his to retrieve his bag, then headed back to the bow of the ship. He was surprised to see sunlight pouring through an open hatch on the port side near the cockpit. He cautiously approached it and looked out. A set of stairs on wheels had been pushed up against the hull of the ship that lead down to the tarmac.

He took one step down and recoiled immediately. He never experienced such intense humidity, as he was accustomed to the dry heat of the desert. The air here felt like a thick and heavy soup in his lungs.

The sun was incredibly bright, and he raised a hand to shield his eyes to take in the surrounding landscape. The land was flat and stretched for a distance before it rose up sharply into the hills. The palm tree forest he saw earlier from the air was just beyond the edge of the landing facility. Gigantic white clouds that filled the sky were like mountains against a backdrop of brilliant blue. Off in the distance, an ominous storm was brewing on the horizon.

He scanned the tarmac and saw the odd shaped aerocraft he'd seen from the air. He ducked under the hull of the transport to get a closer look at them when he ran into a dwarf. The dwarf was not a pleasant sight to look at as he glared at Breeze with disgust.

Breeze was transfixed by his enormous eyes. When the dwarf would blink, it was as if the eyelids took an extra second or two to traverse the entire distance to the bottom and then back up. He wore coveralls that were shopworn and greasy, and his hair was a tangled mess with goggles that rested on his brow. For a second, Breeze thought he was looking at his father in miniature form.

The dwarf was supervising cargo that was being unloaded from the ship when Breeze bumped into him. Automated carts approached the transport while robotic arms mounted on the ceiling of the ship extended out and placed pallets of cargo onto them, and then the carts would scurry away to the hangars that lined the tarmac. The robotic arms retracted back into the cargo hold and reappeared with more pallets to be loaded onto the next automated cart.

The dwarf turned away from him and resumed removing boxes from one of the pallets and stacking them next to a pile of luggage. Breeze knew he had only brought his one bag. He assumed the luggage belonged to the agents, who were nowhere to be found.

"Could you possibly have any more bags, your highness?" the dwarf said in a gruff voice that sounded deeper than his actual size.

Breeze was stunned at how surreal everything felt. He had expected to be greeted by Oslo, but instead he was on a broiling hot tarmac talking to a dwarf. "Those are not mine," he replied.

The dwarf grunted and continued to pull boxes from the pallet, stacking them in neat columns.

Breeze couldn't help but stare. He had never seen anything at all like this dwarf. As he watched him pull box after box off the pallet, he began to realize how odd everything was. Why had he flown at night, then in what seemed like a snap of the fingers he landed on an island in broad daylight? He felt jittery and nervous when he held his hand up to his face and began waving it back and forth.

"Time dilation," the dwarf said.

"Say again?"

The dwarf pulled down goggles with tinted lenses over his eyes. "We sometimes call it time stop. When you travel through the vortex, you get the sensation afterwards that time has ceased. Your mind and body have not caught up yet so you feel disjointed and out of place. Give yourself a little more time and your memory will catch up with you. Now get in the hover, I need to take you to the dormitories." The dwarf grabbed the luggage and dragged it to a hover car that bobbed up and down with each gust of wind that swept in from the ocean.

Breeze stepped over to the vehicle and opened the door, almost pulling it off its hinges. The hover car was a rusting wreck, and it looked like it was barely operational. Breeze sat down inside, and the seat protested with a loud squeak. He pulled the door to close it, but it wouldn't budge. He yanked hard to slam it shut.

"Don't slam the doors! This hover is a classic," the dwarf shouted angrily as he climbed into the vehicle, carefully closing his door. "Young people. No respect for anything. Oblivious to all your surroundings." The dwarf continued grumbling as he mashed the throttle, sending them lurching forward.

"What's your name?" Breeze asked as they accelerated down the tarmac.

"Excort," the dwarf responded. He pushed down on the throttle until it hit the console. The hover leapt up and pinned Breeze into his seat

"Buckle up for safety!" Excort hollered above the roar of the slipstream.

Breeze pulled down on the harness straps and buckled in as the hover groaned and creaked with the motor whining at a full pitch.

He shouted at Excort. "Do we have to go this fast?"

The dwarf responded with a sharp turn to the right as the hover accelerated toward the forest of palm trees that lined the landing facility.

The palms swayed wildly in the sea breeze as they approached.

Breeze gripped the handle that was bolted to the dashboard and shouted in surprise as the trees parted to clear a path for them when they raced into the palm forest. The hover creaked loudly as they bolted through the forest, though not one tree ever touched the car. He looked up and could barely see sunlight through the thick canopy, then glanced at Excort who had one hand on the steering wheel while the other hung lazily over the door. His goggles were pushed up and resting on his wide forehead and his eyes had a greenish glow to them.

Breeze looked forward and was overwhelmed with claustrophobia as the forest became denser. He almost passed out just as the hover flew out of the palm forest and into the brilliant sunshine.

He turned to say something to Excort, but stopped when he saw the grin on his face. The dwarf winked, then pulled his goggles down and shoved the steering wheel forward, sending the hover into a steep dive. Breeze heard a loud scream and realized it was coming from him as they plummeted straight down toward a lagoon, following the flow of a massive waterfall. The deafening sound of cascading water drowned out the whine of the engines as he held onto the handrail with a death grip.

The hover leveled out and they raced across the lagoon while trailing a rooster tail of water behind them. Breeze glared at the dwarf and saw how ridiculous the little man looked with his goggles over his eyes while sitting in an oversized seat with a booster under him so he could see over the console.

Up ahead was a sheer wall of rock with a surface pockmarked with craters. Excort mashed the throttles and the hover creaked and groaned faster toward it.

"What are you doing?" Breeze shouted.

Excort responded by whipping the steering wheel hard to the right, sending the hover into a barrel roll as it raced towards the rock face. The hover shuddered violently as bits of rusted metal peeled off and scattered across the lagoon.

The wall of rock swirled and formed a tunnel. They plunged into it, and Breeze closed his eyes as he gripped the handrail even tighter. When he dared to open them, he was greeted by inky blackness with brilliant stars high above. The rolling ceased, though he felt the same disorientation he experienced on the transport. Images of what happened just before he flew into the vortex with Vermillion and Horton came to the forefront of his mind as the fogginess in his head faded, and his memory returned.

The hover burst out of the tunnel as the dwarf threw the vehicle hard to the left, and descended along a road that hugged a hillside. Breeze leaned over to look down and was greeted by a spectacular view of the bay he had seen from the air. Its blue water was brilliant and the shoreline was dotted with a large tower surrounded by a cluster of smaller ones spread out across a campus. Majestic royal palms lined the avenues between the buildings.

Breeze couldn't believe his eyes. He had never seen anything so beautiful before. He was used to buildings constructed from adobe and concrete as the desert was unforgiving and didn't lend itself to amazing architecture.

"The campus is amazing," he said to Excort.

The dwarf shrugged. "Looks can be deceiving."

They drifted off the road and onto a path that seemed to stretch forever. Either side of it was lined with an impenetrable mixture of palm and ficus trees.

After several minutes, the hover coasted to a halt before a pair of massive gates. Breeze looked up at the canopy of sky high ficus that draped them from the glare of the sun. The powerful humidity made his skin feel as if it were steaming under his clothes, and sweat trickled down his face.

Excort pulled up to a console and typed in a series of codes onto a keypad. The gates didn't budge.

"Shouldn't you just get out and push them open?" Breeze said.

"I'll do something better." Excort eased the hover forward and pushed the nose of the vehicle against the gates. The gates bowed slightly inward, then sprang back, slamming into the hover and causing it to drift away.

Excort grumbled as he mashed down the throttle and bumped the gates repeatedly until they gave way with a squeal of grinding metal.

"Going to have to oil up the gears on that gate when I get the chance," the dwarf muttered.

They whooshed down the path under an expansive canopy of towering ficus. Lining the path were statues and monuments nestled beneath heavy moss and vegetation.

The path merged into a wide boulevard lined with buildings, whose unique architecture lay hidden under a thick covering of ficus and vines. Breeze knew trying to enter any of them would require cutting equipment to hack through the heavy overgrowth just to get to the doors.

The boulevard broadened into a plaza with a brickwork surface overrun with weeds and littered with the remains of broken down machines

Ahead lay the majestic tower that Breeze had seen earlier. As the hover sped toward it, his disappointment grew with each passing second. The tower was a faded beauty, like the rest of the buildings on campus, with a limestone and coquina structure that was chipped and broken. Huge cracks rippled through the façade, and heavy moss was everywhere, growing in clumps and patches over the entire building.

The hover pulled up before the massive stairway the led up into the tower. Breeze unbuckled his harness and tried to open the door, but it wouldn't budge. He stood up on his seat and jumped out.

"What kind of place is this? Is it a school or an abandoned city? And where is everybody? Did they run away after getting a good look at this place?" Breeze said as he looked around.

Excort didn't answer as he pulled luggage out of the trunk of the hover. The vehicle gradually rose as it was being unloaded.

An automated cart slowly approached them from an alcove next to the stairway. Its tires were nearly flat, and its electrical motor whined in protest. The cart sporadically hesitated and stopped, until it finally arrived at the hover and bumped into it. That sent the hover drifting away and prompting an outburst of expletives from the dwarf. He ran to the hover and dragged it back to the pile of luggage, then kicked the automated cart, which made it squeak loudly and spin into ever widening circles away from the hover until it finally came to a stop. This made Excort even more agitated. He stomped over to it and opened a panel on its side and began toggling switches. The cart come back to life and rolled toward the pile of luggage.

Breeze shook his head at the sight of it all when he noticed a canal that fronted the tower and walked over to it. He could smell the briny salt water as he looked straight through it to the sandy bottom where reef fish flitted about coral heads. A smile crept across his face as he looked on in awe. He had never seen a fish before.

He heard grumbling and cursing coming from the hover and turned to look. Excort was trying to load the last piece of luggage, a duffel bag with an oversized strap, onto the cart. The cart shrilled with loud beeps and whoops when he did, prompting him to curse and remove the bag which ended the noise. He kicked the cart angrily and again placed the bag onto it which immediately erupted with alarms. The dwarf cursed even louder as he removed the bag and dropped it to the ground. He gave the cart another kick and pointed to the building with a disgusted grunt. The cart responded with a chirp as it trundled away.

Excort grabbed the duffel bag, hoisted it onto his shoulder and began walking toward the tower. "If his highness is ready, he can follow me to the dormitories."

"I can carry the bag myself, you know." Breeze offered.

"Follow me!" Excort shouted.

Breeze jogged to catch up to him. "When do I get to meet Oslo? And where are the other students? Am I the only one here?"

"Questions!" the dwarf shouted and waved him off. He then muttered loudly to himself. "Who does his highness think he is? 'Where's Oslo?' 'Where are the other students?' Bothersome youth. No patience."

"Why do you keep calling me 'your highness'?" Breeze asked.

Excort ignored him and kept trudging forward.

Breeze followed the dwarf up the steps and into the tower. He stopped and his jaw dropped at the grand and magnificent hall with its domed, stained glass ceiling with ornate and intricate designs adorning it. The hall was in the shape of a rotunda, with multiple hallways that led deep into the building like spokes on a wheel, and stacked up to five levels. Some hallways he could see straight down while others were poorly lit with flickering light.

Breeze stared at the stained glass ceiling that filtered sunlight into a prism when he heard the sound of splashing water coming from the center of the rotunda. He ran over and leaned against a gold railing that lined a circular pool recessed deep below. He looked down and saw a myriad of fish flitting about a coral reef. His eyes scanned the water wondering what the source of the splash was.

He marveled at the giant heads of coral and the fish that orbited them like satellites when he caught a flicker of movement from behind one the bigger coral heads and leaned dangerously over the railing to peer down. He caught a pair of eyes looking back at him for a fleeting moment, and then disappeared. He stretched over the railing, straining to get a better look.

"Follow!" the dwarf bellowed from deep within a hallway.

Breeze pointed to the pool and started to say something, but thought better of it and raced to catch up to Excort.

Deep in the pool, a lone figure emerged from the shadows of the reef. The sunlight pouring through the ceiling revealed a young girl raising her hand to Breeze as he turned to leave. She lowered it and faded back into the shadows.

Breeze breathed heavily as he struggled to catch up. The dwarf walked amazingly fast as they marched down a hallway that merged into an open breezeway. To the left were rows of doors with a window between each one. To the right was a balcony that overlooked the campus facing the west. Breeze felt compelled to stop and take in the view. Off in the distance he could see the hangars of the landing facility bordered by the swaying palm forest, and the white capped waves crashing onto the beach. He knew right then and there he was far from home.

"Dormitories!" Excort shouted, shattering the moment. He stopped before one of the doors along the breezeway and kicked it in with a stubby leg. It flung open and he hurled the duffel bag into the room just before the door hit the wall and bounced off it to slam shut.

"Hey!" Breeze hollered at the cranky dwarf. "Can't I even take a look at my room?"

"Orientation!" Excort shouted and pointed down the breezeway.

Breeze followed him as his anger began to build. He caught up to the dwarf, still not understanding how someone so short could walk so fast.

The breezeway came to an end at a set of stairs that led downward in a spiral. Breeze felt hemmed in as the stairwell grew narrow and a few times he almost lost his footing on the mildew covering the limestone steps. The smell of saltwater became stronger with every step he took.

The stairs ended abruptly in darkness when Excort opened a door that led into a dimly lit corridor that was lined with floor to ceiling panels on either side. Some were open while most were sealed shut. The few open ones were empty, save for a few scraps of debris on the floor while others were stacked with old machines and electronics or chairs and tables.

They continued on until they reached the end. Excort typed into a keypad and a panel hissed up into a recess.

"Boy, somebody could get hurt if that door were to slide down too fast," Breeze said.

"Then you better hurry up and enter," Excort growled.

Breeze scurried into a room that was musty and old, just like everything else he encountered on campus. The walls were lined with racks of old electronics. Some were operating while others were dormant. The few that were active emitted low pitched warbles and beeps. Display screens showed lines waving back and forth that disappeared from view, then reappeared.

Breeze was dying to find out what the instruments were monitoring. He turned to ask Excort, but the disgusted look on the dwarf's face deterred him. *I'll wait and ask Oslo- if I ever get to meet him,* Breeze thought to himself.

In the center of the room was a long, rectangular table lined with reclining swivel chairs on caster wheels. Breeze picked one chair at random and sat down. The chair creaked loudly when he leaned back, and he sat up quickly, slapping his hands on the table.

Excort stood by the panel, his face devoid of expression as he glared at Breeze.

Breeze got up and sat in the next chair. The creaking from it sounded like a shriek, and he stood up abruptly to stare at it.

He walked over to the other side of the table, hoping to find a seat that wasn't so quick to protest anyone sitting in it, but each chair he tried produced the same result. His quest took him to the head of the table and the very last seat. He sat down and leaned back. Silence.

He brought his hands to the back of his head and placed his feet on the table. A triumphant smile appeared on his face until the chair collapsed and he was unceremoniously dumped to the floor. He scrambled to his feet to pick up the pieces of the broken chair when he stopped to look at Excort.

The dwarf sighed and shook his head in disgust, then casually stepped aside as the panel slid up and in walked a man of incredible height. He had to lower his head as he stepped in yet he appeared to glide as he brushed past Excort without a glance. He went directly to the head of the table and looked at Breeze.

"Hello, Breeze Corinth, and welcome to Perihelion. My name is Ole Auken, but please, call me Oslo," he said in a baritone voice. He sat down in a chair provided by Excort and leaned back. Not a squeak was heard.

Breeze stood and stared at him while holding the remnants of his broken chair. He had never seen a man so tall with a voice so deep. Oslo wore a military uniform complete with medals and medallions that adorned the left side of his coat. On his right arm was a triangular patch with a circle inside and several smaller circles orbiting it. He had a long face with piercing blue eyes. His white hair was short, and his skin was pale.

Breeze realized he was staring, and it dawned upon him that he was holding pieces of his chair. He started to place them on the table but stopped when he noticed Oslo and Excort watching his every move. Oslo's face barely contained his amusement while Excort just gave and icy stare. He slowly lowered the pieces to the table.

"Never mind the chair, Breeze. We have plenty of chairs in storage and besides, Excort can fix it," Oslo said reassuringly.

"Sure, add it to my list," the dwarf grumbled.

"Very good! Breeze, follow me to my office. It is far more pleasant there, and we have much to discuss." Oslo stood up and seemingly glided out of the room, taking time to pat Excort on the head as he passed by. Excort shot him an angry glare.

The dwarf turned to see Breeze looking at him. "Yes, you can follow him. That's the idea." He made an exaggerated motion toward the door.

Breeze smiled as he walked around the table and raised a hand as he drew close to Excort.

"Don't even try it." The dwarf snarled at him.

He stepped into the corridor to find Oslo was already at the end of it and he had to race to catch up.

Breeze stepped into Oslo's office and was stunned, for it was probably the first room on the entire campus that had some semblance of order. There were a pair of glass double doors leading out to a balcony that overlooked the bay. The walls were filled from side to side and top to bottom with rows of books. Some sections had entire volumes that were collected and placed neatly on the shelves while others had a myriad of books covering various and diverse subjects. The floor was wooden, and a stark contrast to the tile and stone that was found throughout the campus and the ceiling had gigantic wooden beams that stretched across it. His eyes dropped down to the oversized wooden desk where sitting proudly on a corner was a lamp in the shape of a sailor. He was wearing a yellow raincoat and a hat with one hand on a wooden helm, while the other was over his brow, and shielding his eyes from some imaginary downpour as they looked deep into the distance searching for something.

Oslo sat down behind his desk and motioned for Breeze to do the same. Breeze plopped himself down in one of the two high back chairs that fronted the desk.

"Breeze, how was your journey here? Uneventful, I hope?"

He pondered the question. So much had happened since he left home he didn't know where to start. "Well, now that you mention it sir, an awful lot happened. But what really bothers me is that I don't even know how I got here." He recounted to Oslo his experience of waking up on the ship feeling disoriented after entering the vortex.

Oslo nodded his head slowly as his eyes narrowed. "Breeze, what you experienced is what we call time dilation, or time stop. You see—"

"Yeah, that's what Excort said when I first met him!" Breeze interrupted excitedly.

Oslo smiled with great patience. He had to be forgiving. Breeze was far away from home and great changes were coming his way. "Yes, of course he did," Oslo nodded and continued. "This island is unique. So unique that security measures have been taken as to who and what can enter. Let's just say we consider our students to be extra special and we take precautions to protect them." Oslo finished with a wink.

"Well, I don't want to be special," Breeze said, "but that's what brought me here in the first place. And you still haven't answered my question. How exactly did I get here?"

Oslo nodded. "The loss of time and the subsequent disorientation you felt is the result of traveling through the fog, as we like to call it. This island cannot be found on any map or chart because of it. Let's just say one has to know the way to get here, or you will forever be lost within the fog. You experienced a brief bit of time travel. The vortex you traveled through connected you from where you were," he held up one hand, then another, "to where you are now."

Breeze stared at him blankly. "So, where are we?"

Oslo tapped the surface of his desk and a holographic display of a globe materialized. He pointed to a land mass that was comprised of two continents connected by a thin strip of land. "This is the Americas. We are located off the eastern coast of this continent." He pointed to a space in the ocean that was east of a peninsula that jutted out from the northern continent. "We are here, and yet, we are not. Time is not like a long flowing river but one that bends and curves along the way. It may even flow downward like a waterfall. We are sitting at the bottom of a waterfall and behind its cascading waters. We flow down to come here, we have to flow up to return. It's safe for us here. Look at it this way; we are tucked into a corner where no one can bother us."

Breeze shrugged. "But why? Why all the secrecy? What are you trying to hide?"

Oslo looked him in the eye. "You."

"But I'm no one special, I—"

Oslo help up a hand and shook his head. "Son, take a good look at yourself. Is what you are able to do normal? You can fly! How many of your fellow students at your school can do that?"

"If they have the same kind of father I do, I wouldn't know."

"And why do you think your father makes you hide your gift of flight?"

"Because he's jealous of what I can do. Because he's stuck dealing with scrap metal while he knows I can be something more." Breeze could feel the shame of what he just said creep in before he even finished.

"Breeze, your father sent you here for your own benefit," Oslo said quietly.

Breeze exploded. "Well, I didn't want to come here! Nobody asked me!"

"You like to fly, yes? At Perihelion, I will teach you everything you ever wanted to know about your gifts. Here, you can reach your full potential. Here, you can fly to your heart's content. I will make it happen for you, but you have to let go of your anger toward your father. He truly wants what's best for you."

Oslo stood up and walked around the desk to sit next to Breeze. "Look, the world is not a safe place, but you know that already. The lands between the cities can be dangerous. These... Bad Lands are inhabited by strange people and even stranger creatures. Stay here with us, Breeze. Stay here with your fellow students. Learn. Learn everything you can. Then, return home and become a leader and the inspiration you were meant to be."

"Speaking of other students, where are they? Why do I get the feeling I'm the only one here?" Breeze asked.

Oslo clapped his hands and stood up. "Yes, of course. You must meet them. They arrived just before you and have already settled in. One is a pyrokinetic, and the other a projectionist. Come, follow me." Oslo glided across the room and toward the balcony that overlooked the bay. The glass doors opened as he approached.

Breeze got up to follow, and again found himself racing to catch up. Everyone here seemed to move so fast while he felt like he was moving in slow motion. He stepped onto the balcony and down a set of stairs while Oslo was already halfway across the courtyard.

"Come, Breeze. You must meet your classmates." Oslo waved his hand and pointed forward.

Breeze raced down the steps and caught up to Oslo as he gasped for breath. The humid air was thick and difficult to breathe.

The courtyard narrowed to a lane with a row of hangars on either side. Some had sliding doors that were closed while others were open where he could see a variety of aerocraft spread out in various stages of repair. Like the aerocraft he had seen at the landing facility, they were all unfamiliar to him.

One hanger in particular was humming with activity. He expected to see mechanics inside performing repairs much like he was used to back home. What he saw instead shocked him as robots were the ones making the repairs. Some were shaped like spiders that skittered over the hulls of the ships, stopping only to perform a weld. But the majority were humanoid robots that carried tools and pushed carts filled with equipment to workstations manned by other robots. Most of them seemed to be of the same manufacture but with slightly different variations. Some had a disk attached to their chests, and he watched as one particular robot stood before a section of the ship it was repairing and the disk on its chest glowed, then after several minutes, it grabbed a tool from a cart and began working. It reminded him of the diagnostic scanners mechanics back home used to scan broken down aerocraft. What really caught his attention was the bulkiness of the robots and how awkward they seemed using the tools they had, as if they were not designed to perform the tasks they were assigned.

One of the robots noticed his presence and signaled to the others. Soon, they all stopped to stare at Breeze. The noisy shop was reduced to near silence, save for the sound of a sole cutting torch and the dropping of a wrench to the stone floor.

Breeze jumped when he felt a hand on his shoulder.

"They are called RF, short-hand for Robot Fighters. They were at one time the most feared mechanized soldiers ever fielded. I reprogrammed those I've managed to save from the scrap yard to perform more pedestrian duties, such as repairing aerocraft. Come; let the mechanics get back to work. As you can see, there is much to be done." Oslo turned and continued walking toward a line of mangroves along the outskirts of the hangars.

Breeze turned to follow when he looked back over his shoulder and caught one of the robots watching him walk away. It stood next to a sleek black ship that it was repairing along with its workmates.

Oslo clapped his hands and they immediately resumed their work.

He jogged to catch up with Oslo. Ahead was a row of mangroves that fronted a canal where they turned onto a path made up of limestone and shells that ran alongside it. Breeze could smell the pungent saltwater that dominated the air.

He stopped along the edge of the canal and looked down. Just like the one outside the dormitory, the water was crystal clear and teeming with colorful fish flitting about. Some even came to the surface upon seeing him.

"Excort, and his wife, Mila, do love to come here to feed them. That is why they swim up to you. Like pets, they expect some sort of a treat. Come now, let's meet your fellow classmates." Oslo swiveled on his heel and continued on.

They wound their way along the path until they exited the mangrove forest and into a clearing, where they were greeted by the sight of a cove with crystal clear, blue water surrounded by a thick forest of palm trees with a channel that led to the ocean. In the center of the cove was an island made up of rock and coral, with white herons and seagulls swooping in and out of the waters hunting for fish, taking their catch to the island to feed.

They stepped onto the soft, sandy white beach and into the brilliant sunshine. Oslo pointed down the shoreline to a cluster of palm trees. Lying under the canopy of its fronds were a young couple in deep conversation who did not notice them as they approached. As they drew closer, the couple looked up and half-heartedly waved to them.

"Students, come and meet our newest recruit." Oslo's voice boomed. "Sally Trumbull and Raymond Verhesen, I would like you to meet Breeze Corinth. He comes to us from the Desert Country. Breeze, say hello to your classmates."

Breeze nodded and held out a hand to Raymond. "Hi. Nice to meet you. My name is Breeze."

Raymond shook his hand with a powerful grip. "Yes, Oslo just announced it. We heard it the first time." He snapped his attention to Oslo. "Everyone calls me Ray, as I told you before."

Ray was handsome and athletic in build with piercing eyes. He had the presence that displayed he was used to being in command. He did not stand directly in front of Sally, but did so in a way that showed he was protective of her. He smiled at Breeze with a mixture of amusement and condescension.

"So, from the desert? I would expect you to be wearing the enviro suits most of you are known for, you know, the solar helmets, goggles, hard leather jackets and stuff."

Breeze bristled at the comment. "We don't live out in the desert like nomads hiding from sand storms. We do have towns and cities, you know."

Ray smirked. "Of course you do. Wasn't trying to imply anything. You just hear so many stories about what life is like out there. When we heard you were coming to Perihelion we thought you would fit the image."

Breeze stared at Ray and sighed, then turned to look at Sally, something he resisted doing while he was talking to Ray.

She was gorgeous, with long brown hair and emerald green eyes and her neck and wrists were adorned with necklaces and shiny bracelets. She also carried with her an air of superiority that was as thick as a cloud.

Breeze knew if there were two people who fit a stereotype perfectly, it would be them. He had always heard people in Conception talk about folk from the North Eastern Territories and their high-handed manner along with their arrogance and intellect. They would arrive on aerocraft with styles and designs that were unique and different than the ones that were built in the towns and cities of the Desert Country. They would walk around Conception with amused looks on their faces as they took in the local sights of the city. Father would say that Nor'easterners often claimed they were the first to bring together all of the territories of the Northern Americas and establish a central government, and only they knew how to tame the Bad Lands that lay between them.

Breeze realized he was staring at Sally, as she looked on with mild contempt. He held out a hand. She didn't offer hers.

"Yes, hello. Your name is Breeze. Got it the first time. What kind of name is that? Must be a desert thing. I've always heard stories about you people. Why does it have to be so hot out here?" Sally fanned herself and looked away.

"Well then, now that introductions have been made, I shall retire to my office. Much to do, as always." Oslo turned and stepped out of the shade and onto the hot sands. Before Breeze could even voice a protest, the old man was halfway to the mangrove forest. He watched Oslo disappear into the forest and immediately felt lost and lonely. He didn't want to be left alone with these two.

"Well then, Breeze, hope you brought your beach attire. We're going for a swim." Ray took off his shirt and kicked off his shoes, then turned to Sally, who gave him an icy stare. He held out a hand and she relented. She took off her sundress that revealed a one piece bathing suit. She reluctantly took his hand, and as they walked to the cove, she looked over her shoulder. "Well, are you coming?" she said to Breeze.

Breeze was about to say something, then thought better of it. He stripped down to his boxer shorts and stepped onto the broiling sand when he immediately began hopping from one foot to another. "Hot, hot, hot!"

Ray and Sally were already in the water when they turned to look at him.

"Hey, Breeze," Ray called out, "Oslo said you can fly, why not just float up over the sand and into the water?"

"Not...quite...that...easy...for...me...ahhh!" Breeze exclaimed as he dashed into the water and cooled his feet. Breathing heavily, he bent over and rested his hands on his knees. "You see, for me to fly requires a lot of deep concentration. I really need to close my eyes to focus—"

"Fine." Sally raised a hand and turned away.

Ray smirked as he led her into deeper water. Soon, they were swimming across the cove and toward the rock island.

Breeze followed hesitantly. He wasn't much of a swimmer. Lakes and rivers were not that abundant where he was from. He waded into deeper water and felt the sand below shift under his feet. He winced every time he stepped on something sharp. He was up to his neck when a small wave washed over him. He had never been in salt water before and was stunned at how it burned his eyes and blinded him. Rubbing them only made it worse.

"Hey, desert boy, try these." Ray hurled something toward him. It landed with a splash as Breeze reached out for it. It was a mask with a snorkel attached to it. He stared at the mask when he heard Sally call out to him. "Just put them on!"

He fumbled with the straps and placed the mask over his eyes, then put the snorkel in his mouth and breathed into it. He pushed off the bottom and doggy paddled into deeper water. The second he put his head down and looked through the clear blue water to the bottom, he froze in place.

Below him was a universe of life. Schools of fish of various shapes and colors flitted above the sandy bottom lined with ridges of coral and surrounded by sea fans waving gently with the current.

Ray and Sally were sitting on a rock with their feet dangling in the water. Ray watched Breeze with bemusement as Sally put her hair up.

"So, what do you think of the new guy?"

Sally shrugged. "Whatever." Then added, "He's kind of cute. But—"

"Oh, he is? So what am I then?"

"Handsome, absolutely. Please, do you think I would even consider a guy like him? Catch some reality."

Ray laughed. "Well, glad to hear it. I was worried there for a second that you were suddenly into desert rats."

Sally shook her head and looked away, then slowly turned back to watch Breeze flopping around in the water. She hadn't really known any other guy than Ray. She never really met any other type of guy than Ray. She, like him, came from a family of high achievers filled with condescension and arrogance that was an integral part of the culture and environment she was raised in. She had never known anyone outside of her family's tight knit social circle.

She looked at Ray and realized the last thing she needed was to make him jealous and angry. He was the only link she had to home and it helped to make the island a little less lonely for her.

She did miss her home but her parents especially as she would often pull out her necklace that contained a locket. Opening it revealed a picture of her mother and father. Her father was a good man, and she wanted to believe she was especially close to her mother.

A wave of emotion swept over her. She closed her eyes and tried to grip the slippery rock she was sitting on. It felt like she was about to be flung off the rock island if she dared to let go. No sooner than it arrived, the feeling subsided and she opened her eyes. She stared across the cove and focused on a cluster of palms along the shoreline when a figure emerged from the forest.

It was a woman with long flowing hair, wearing a white dress. She stopped just shy of the water's edge. Though she was quite a distance from Sally, she felt their eyes lock. Then the woman abruptly turned away and returned to the palm forest, fading from view.

Sally looked for Ray to tell him what she saw, and then hesitated. She already knew what he would say. He would dismiss her and tell her she was just seeing things. He always did.

She realized she had forgotten about Breeze. She scanned the bay, but he was nowhere to be found.

"Ray, where's Breeze?"

"I don't know. He probably swam to the other side. Why?" Ray was sprawled out on a rock with his eyes closed.

"Oh, just curious. Whatever." She hoped her tone deflected suspicion from him as she continued searching.

Breeze had swum further out and toward the channel where the water plunged to an incredible depth. He was in rapture over the incredibly deep blue of the water and the fish and other creatures he saw became larger and more exotic the further out he went. He continued to drift until he could no longer see the bottom and noted how the water bent the sunlight into long shafts of white that descended to the depths. Breeze dipped below the surface and followed them. The moment he did the sounds of the ocean surrounded him. What began as a whisper grew into a myriad of voices. He felt he could hear every sea creature chattering away as they went about their business.

The sunlight from above faded the deeper he went and the blue of the ocean became ever more profound. He did notice how the temperature dropped as the warmth he experienced at the surface was slipping away.

He touched down on the sandy bottom and looked up at the surface. He could barely see the sun streaming through as its rays strained to penetrate the depths. He turned and watched as a group of bigger fish approached him out of curiosity. They stopped and stared at him while their gills billowed in and out, then they slowly swam around him for but a moment before disappearing into the depths.

He felt the sand suddenly moving under his feet and realized he was being dragged when he came to a stop at a coral ridge that sloped up to an incredible height. The number of fish that hovered over and around the coral was staggering, and their numbers seemed to increase with each passing second.

They swam down and swarmed about him in a maelstrom for several seconds before breaking away. That's when he saw her.

He could barely see her face until her hair parted to reveal a pair of eyes above a button sized nose. She slowly emerged from the coral and was hesitant to come any closer. She smiled, and then turned away in embarrassment. She looked back to raise a hand to her chest and spoke in a voice that sounded like a distant whisper. "Just breathe."

He nodded and took in a deep breath as air filled his lungs. He continued, feeling more invigorated with each breath. The girl smiled encouragingly and motioned for him to continue. He raised a hand and beckoned her to come closer. She smiled sweetly and took a hesitant step forward, then froze as panic spread across her face.

"Breathe," she whispered and made a sweeping motion from her belly to her mouth.

Breeze nodded and mimicked her, sweeping his hands up to his face when he stopped and stared at them. Then he touched his face.

The girl shook her head vigorously while motioning to him to continue breathing. He wanted to obey her, but he couldn't stop touching his face. Then it dawned upon him that he was no longer wearing his mask and snorkel. He became even more disturbed at the fact he was communicating with a girl underwater. He didn't know how he could breathe, let alone hear her voice. He opened his mouth to speak and took in a lungful of saltwater.

The girl rushed to him, and then threw her hands up as he was immediately enveloped in a cloud of bubbles that rocketed him to the surface.

He broke through and took in a lungful of air as he choked and hacked. He flailed around until he regained his senses and was able to tread water. He reached up to touch his face and felt the mask. He tore it off to examine it, stunned as to how it could have reappeared. He looked up and saw the sun had dropped to the horizon and the light was fading fast.

He realized he was drifting out into the ocean and began swimming back with an awkward doggy paddle, all the while wondering how he could have dived so deep with such little swimming experience. As he approached the rock island in the middle of the cove, he saw Sally and Ray frantically running up and down its edge. Ray then dove into the water and resurfaced several seconds later, then dove back down again while Sally anxiously peered over the edge and shouted his name.

Breeze began to wave and yell.

She saw him and waved back, then yelled at Ray and pointed as soon as he surfaced. He turned to look at Breeze and shook his head in disgust.

When Breeze arrived at the shoreline, Sally and Ray were there to meet him and bombarded him with questions before he could even get out of the water.

"Where were you? Have you been swimming this whole time? Do you have any idea how late it is? We've been looking for you!" Sally was in a rage, as she went from relief upon seeing him to outright anger.

Breeze crawled out of the water and stood up. "You wouldn't believe it! I dove and saw a girl down there!" He told them of his encounter.

Sally's anger subsided as she listened intently, but Ray held up a hand and cut him off.

"You're insane. No one can dive that deep and hold their breath for that long. And now you're saying a girl was talking to you while underwater? Right, and while you're at it, you can also tell us an even bigger lie about how you've got some girl waiting for you at home. Listen, desert boy, you put a real fright into Sally, and I don't appreciate it. She had me running around like a moron looking for you." He grabbed her hand and pulled her away. "Come on, it's getting late and we need to head back."

Sally protested. "Ray, I saw someone earlier on the shoreline. I—"

"Probably just personnel who work here. Let's go," he said and together they waded into the water and began swimming. Sally stopped to look at Breeze with eyes that seemed to convey she could relate to him about what he experienced, but it was for a fleeting moment as she turned away to continue swimming.

Breeze stood and watched as they arrived at the shoreline of the cove and stepped into the cluster of palms where they grabbed their towels and shoes. They then headed into the mangrove forest along the footpath that led to the dormitories.

He wanted to be mad at Ray for being cruel to him, but he couldn't shake the overwhelming feeling of enchantment from his encounter with the girl.

The sun was succumbing to the horizon, and he had the urge to fly. He didn't want to swim in the dark. He stood straight up with his hands along his sides. He closed his eyes and began breathing deeply. He raised his arms and expected to feel the rush of air over his face signaling he had lifted off the ground. Nothing happened.

He groaned as he stared at the surface of the cove. He knew he wasn't a very good swimmer and he didn't like the idea of trying to swim across it at night but he had no choice. He scrambled along the rocky shoreline and waded into the water. As soon as he stepped in, a feeling of calm swept over him. He paddled his way back and was stunned at how quickly he made it to the beach. It was almost as if the water had carried him across like a cloud floating across the sky.

He gathered his belongings while wishing he had a towel to dry off with. He stepped onto the footpath in the looming darkness as fear crept into him, only to dissipate as soft glowing orbs of light appeared and illuminated the path. He headed to the dormitories after taking one last look at the cove.

On the far side of the cove, Oslo emerged from the mangrove forest and watched Breeze disappear down the path when he spoke out. "We have been watching them this whole time, and yet you've said nothing to me. Do you have any thoughts on what has transpired?"

A woman in a white flowing dress emerged from the palm forest and stood beside him. She stroked her hair as she spoke. "They have managed to not fight amongst themselves. At least not physically."

Oslo snorted. "After all you have seen, that is the only pearl of wisdom you have to offer?"

She continued stroking her hair, pulling harder with each pass of her hand. "The girl seems to be smitten with Breeze. I wonder why, as there is nothing much to him. A simpleton really."

"I disagree. With the right training, he could become a valuable asset to the team. I see great potential," Oslo countered.

The woman sighed. "Potential, yes. But time is of the essence for what you wish to accomplish and there is not enough of it to sufficiently develop and refine him. What you require are assets that are ready and able to perform now. Relieve yourself of the boy. Send him back. Better yet, send them all back."

Oslo shook his head. "Kera, I need all the help, or assets, as you put it, that I can get. Besides, there is nothing to send them back to."

Kera stopped stroking her hair and turned to stare at him. "You haven't called me that name in so long. You must be more serious than I had anticipated. Excort is quite right. You have gone mad."

Oslo arched an eyebrow. "And since when did you and that angry dwarf ever start speaking to each other again?"

"Ever since-," she paused. "Ever since you came back and re-opened the base—"

"It's a school now," Oslo interrupted.

"You can call this island what you want Oslo, but the history of Perihelion cannot be erased. Sooner or later they will know. They will find out. The truth has a nasty habit of bubbling to the surface, no matter how hard you try to smother it. You see yourself as their savior but did it ever occur to you they wouldn't want to be saved? Send them back now so they can be with their families and perish together."

Oslo leaned down to look her in the eye. "You speak about truth and revelations. Are your ready to reveal yourself to them?"

"In due time. Oslo, you will not be able to get them to do what you want unless they know everything. The world as they know it is real to them. They are not aware of the past. Perhaps it's for the best. The glorious yesteryears you often talk about, the ones that you wish to revive, cannot be brought back. It's over. Those above control this world. They won. All we can do is mitigate the damage and survive as best as we can."

"No!" Oslo roared at her.

Kera shrank back. She had never seen him this angry.

He waved his hand. "I'm sorry. It's just that I refuse to give up. Ever."

"Then begin their training, but understand what you are getting yourself into. There is still time to end this madness and send them home. You decide. I'm here for you. Always." She touched his arm and looked into his eyes. Her eyes always captivated him. Without another word, she turned and glided back into the mangroves.

Oslo was alone in the dark as the creatures of the forest began to stir. This always happened after Kera left; wildlife would lay still and quiet whenever she was present.

He looked across the cove in a trance. In his mind, the scenery began to change. He found himself standing on a hilltop overlooking the island. Night turned into day. Huge white clouds filled a brilliant blue sky as a squadron of fighter craft flew overhead in tight formation. He heard the sound of a ship's horn. Down in the harbor a destroyer was approaching the docks, her entire complement of sailors standing proudly on deck as hover tugs labored to push the vessel into berth.

He heard a deep rumble from above and looked up. A cruiser descended from the sky and approached the landing facility. She hovered over the tarmac for a moment, and then landed like a feather. Her belly opened and an automated ramp rushed up to meet her as soldiers poured out of the ship and marched toward their barracks.

Oslo blinked rapidly and the vision was gone. He shook his head ruefully and headed into the mangrove forest.

Later that evening, Oslo was sitting at his desk and staring at the sailor man lamp. The sailor held his eternal grip on the helm and seemed to peer into the murky future. Oslo looked into the shadows that lay beyond the reach of the lamp's light. "I wish you could tell me what you see," he said to the lamp, then chuckled, realizing how absurd he sounded.

CHAPTER

▼

FIVE

THE MORNING SUN BARELY rose above the horizon when everyone in the dormitory was awakened to the wail of a siren. It started off with a low moaning sound that gradually rose to a high pitched crescendo before settling down to a warble.

Breeze woke up as his bleary eyes tried to focus in an unfamiliar room as he recalled a strange dream about his home. He was standing on a mountain ridge that loomed over his hometown of Conception when he suddenly stepped over the edge and plummeted. He felt a moment of panic that was arrested by the sensation of weightlessness as he floated like a feather. He stretched out his arms and flew gracefully over the city as its lights bathed him in an angelic glow. He loved being in the sky and gazing down over the landscape that seemed to stretch forever into the horizon. He would try to figure out what street or hilltop he was flying over as he constantly tested his navigational skills. He looked down at the nav-compass on his wrist, but it was missing.

His flying became choppy and he plummeted to the ground. He scratched and clawed at the air but it was futile. A feeling of sheer terror drowned him as the earth drew closer. He heard a loud wailing sound from behind and turned to look. He caught a glimpse of his home just before a flash of brilliant white light engulfed it. He woke up.

He rubbed his eyes and tried to make sense of it but the unfamiliar surroundings of his dorm room didn't help him. The wailing siren was becoming tiresome and he couldn't figure out if he was still dreaming or if this was an alarm he should be concerned about.

He rolled out of bed and almost stumbled as the sheets stuck to his legs. The humidity was something he wasn't used to. Living in the desert all of his life he was accustomed to the dry air. Here, it was thick and almost impossible to breathe.

He headed to the balcony and grimaced as his bare feet stepped across the cold stone floor. He looked out across the bay and felt the warm gusts of air blowing across it. Off in the distance he could see a lighthouse, its rotating light gradually fading from the encroaching rays of the sun. He began counting how many seconds elapsed between each flash of light, which made his dream drift back to the forefront of his mind as he recalled the sheer terror of falling. It frustrated him that he was in control of his flight one minute, and then as if a switch had been flipped, he was heading into the ground. It also reminded him how the dream ended with his home being swallowed by a burst of brilliant white light. He shook his head. None of it made much sense.

He heard a commotion outside his front door. He headed over and flung it open.

Excort was walking down the breezeway carrying packages under one arm while knocking on each door with the other. He knocked on Ray's and shouted "package!" before dropping it on the floor. He did the same with Sally's.

Breeze grinned as the dwarf approached him. Excort dropped the package at his feet and reached over to knock on the open door.

Breeze grinned. "Let me guess—",

"Package!" Excort shouted at him, and then walked to the end of the breezeway and down the steps.

Breeze was beginning to wonder why he even came here as he stooped to pick up the box when

Sally's door opened slowly, and she peeked out from behind it with hair that was a rumpled mess. She clutched her robe with one hand while reaching down to grab the package with the other.

"Good morning!" Breeze announced cheerfully.

Sally looked at him with disgust as she angrily snatched the package and slammed the door shut. Breeze sighed and stepped back into his room.

He just couldn't figure out Sally. She could be incredibly friendly with him one minute then suddenly go cold the next. And it didn't help that Ray was always around her. Though she never said he was her boyfriend, he acted as if they were a couple. Whenever he showed up she became a different person.

He shuffled back to his bed and touched a glowing stone on the wall. The room was immediately bathed in a soft white light. He opened his package and spread its contents across the bed. It contained a shirt, jacket, pants, boots and a utility belt.

A voice crackled over the intercom system followed by several seconds of static. Eventually, someone spoke.

"Is this thing on? Are we broadcasting?" It sounded like Oslo, but Breeze wasn't sure.

More hisses erupted over the intercom followed by a finger tapping on a microphone. Then, a voice spoke clearly.

"Ladies and gentleman, um...students, please wake up and look outside your doors. You will find a package containing your new uniforms. Please don them and assemble in the Training Auditorium in one hour. Thank you."

Breeze held up his jacket and noted how it had a rugged military look to it. He got dressed and admired himself in the reflection of the balcony glass door when he was startled by a scream from Sally's room.

He rushed out into the breezeway where he ran into Ray who was also in uniform. They hesitated and looked at each other for a moment, then raced to Sally's door.

The door flung open just as Breeze was about to knock as Sally stepped out clutching her uniform with trembling hands while still dressed in her robe. The look on her face was that of abject horror as she spoke in a quavering voice.

"The colors, the materials, the stitching...," her voice trailed off as she shook her head at the garments.

"I rather like them. It's a great looking uniform," Breeze said as he adjusted his jacket.

Sally glowered at him for what seemed like an eternity. When she finally responded, it was in a low and menacing voice. *"They're hideous."* And she slammed the door in their faces.

They could hear her yell and scream as they stood in the breezeway dumbfounded by her behavior when the door opened a crack and she poked her head out. "Ray, do something about this!" she hissed at him.

"Well, like what?" his face was a blank slate.

"Useless!" she shouted and slammed the door.

"Does she always get like this?" Breeze said.

Ray threw his hands up and sighed.

They stepped over to the railing and gazed at the ocean in the distance. A mountainous avalanche of brilliant white clouds were rolling toward the island with their underbellies scorched red from the rising sun.

Sally's door whipped open. She stepped out in her uniform with the jacket unzipped, the sleeves pulled back, and the pant legs rolled up to just below the knee.

"What is Oslo thinking with these uniforms? Is he seriously kidding? Is there any sense of style around here?" Her hands were on her hips as she glared at them.

Ray spoke up. "Sally, these are just for training—"

"Of course!" she said as a hand flew up, then turned with a huff and marched down the breezeway.

They watched her walk away, and then turned to each other. Breeze started to speak, but Ray cut him off. "Yes, she can be this way," he said and turned to follow her.

Breeze shrugged and fell in line behind him.

They made their way down a maze of corridors to the Training Auditorium several floors below. The only guide they had were stones embedded in the floor that glowed a lime green and provided them a path to follow. They wound their way down several stairwells as every elevator they encountered was either broken or malfunctioning.

"I think I've had enough training with all of this walking. I'm sweating and I want to go back," Sally said.

The guys said nothing and continued on.

She then sighed loudly hoping to get Ray's attention. He didn't respond which only served to annoy her more.

They reached the end of the last set of stairs and stepped into a narrow corridor. The air grew heavy and dank the further they went and the lime green stones faded quickly with each step they took.

Ray was in front with Breeze trailing behind Sally when he stopped to touch the walls of the corridor. The limestone felt cool to his fingers, and then warmed up instantly. He pulled his hand back and was stunned to see an imprint of it glowing on the wall. He touched it again when the lime green stones in the floor pulsated and turned blue, then a violet hue.

"Breeze!" Sally called out as she stood at the end of the corridor glaring at him with her hands on her hips.

He looked at her and had to admit he was having a tough time dealing with her beauty. He also had an even tougher time coming to terms that she wasn't interested in him.

The floor glowed a solid red, and he didn't need any more hints that it was time to move. He trotted down the narrow corridor and grinned at Sally as he approached her. She turned her back to him.

Ray touched a pulsating outline of a door on the wall, and it slid up. They hesitated, and then stepped into a circular room with curved walls made of stone and a dome whose peak was just a few feet above their heads. The entire space seemed as if it could hold no more than ten people.

The panel door slid closed and faded away when the dome began to glow with a golden hue. They squirmed restlessly and tugged at their uniforms as they waited for Oslo. It was no surprise that Sally complained first.

"Are we being trained to be patient, or bored?" she said when a section of curved wall faded and Oslo stepped in. Behind him was a long and narrow corridor much like the one they walked through. The wall quickly reappeared and sealed off the entrance.

"Welcome class to your first training session. How are we this morning?" Oslo asked.

Sally immediately spoke up. "Has a woman ever worn these uniforms? They have such a horrible fit. And the style?" Her hands went up and down the uniform to emphasize her point.

Oslo stared at her blankly, and then cleared his throat before speaking. "Class, today we are going to perform a basic demonstration of your skills. I want the three of you to have a general idea of what your fellow students are capable of. Breeze, you begin."

If there was one thing Breeze hated it was to be called on in class. He would always break out in a cold sweat. He was used to blending into the background than being the subject of attention and it was one of the reasons he was always skipping school back home.

He stepped into the center of the domed room and the curved walls immediately began to slide away from the center and expand the diameter of the room. The gold tinted light faded away to pitch black.

He stood in darkness for a moment, then he was instantly bathed in a shaft of light that emanated from the peak of the dome. He could barely see Oslo when he spoke to him from beyond the glare.

"Begin your demonstration," the old man said.

"Well, um, I'm a flier. I suppose I could just hover...here...in the center of the room?"

"That would be a good start," Oslo replied from the darkness.

Breeze shrugged and closed his eyes, then stretched his arms and took in deep breaths.

Ray snickered and Sally giggled.

He whirled around. "Shut up! I need to concentrate!" He shouted in the direction of their laughter as he couldn't see them.

The giggling stopped, but his nerves were rattled. He never had much confidence in his abilities and performing on command was almost impossible for him.

He resumed his routine. Moments later, when he felt light as a feather, he opened his eyes and saw he was hovering a few feet off the ground.

He floated up and the domed ceiling expanded above him. The brilliant white light faded into a more natural glow. The training room disappeared, and suddenly he was in the wide open desert. The sky was a brilliant blue with a mountain range in the distance.

His confidence soared as he began to carve out a simple circular pattern in the sky. He glanced down and saw the others watching him from the desert floor.

The sight of Sally only encouraged his desire to show off. He gave up the circular pattern he was making and flew up as high as he could go. He stopped, hovered for a second or two, then raced back down to swoop over them

Letting out a whoop of joy as they ducked, he accelerated up to repeat his performance when a black streak ripped past him and the turbulence from its wake threw him into a deadly spin. He struggled to regain control as he plummeted and eventually pulled himself out of his death spiral. He angled up to gain altitude when a bolt of lightning struck him. Stunned, he fell from the sky and impacted the ground hard.

He laid there as the desert faded away and the dome reappeared. The shaft of brilliant white light returned to shine upon him. He looked about and saw that he was lying at the bottom of a shallow pit. He sat up when he felt the ground rising and stopped when it was level with the dome's floor. He got to his feet puzzled as to what just happened. The walls returned to their gold tinted glow, letting him see Ray and Sally staring at him in stunned silence.

A booming voice spoke. "Well, what started off as a mediocre demonstration ended in failure. What went wrong?" Oslo demanded as he stepped out of the shadows.

"What kind of place is this?" Breeze said.

"Never mind that. We need to discuss your skills. Or lack of them. What transpired up there?"

Breeze shrugged. "I seemed to be doing pretty good until something streaked past me. The turbulence from it was like getting hit by a hover truck at full speed."

"So that's it then? One little distraction and you lose all control?"

"Distraction? That thing almost killed me!" Breeze shouted.

Oslo held up a hand. "First, nothing here will kill you. At least I don't think so." He looked around for a moment, then resumed. "Second, concentration is the key to everything you do in this life. Stay focused and cease your thinking over matters that do not pertain to the task at hand."

"I was focused. Completely."

"Really?" Oslo turned to look at Sally.

Breeze's face flamed a beet red, and it felt as if his skin was on fire. He knew he wasn't as proficient as the others, but now Oslo had to embarrass him. He shuffled away from the center of the dome and stood apart from Sally and Ray.

Oslo addressed Sally. "Ms. Trumbull, step into the center and let us receive a demonstration from you."

Sally proudly stepped forward and with one hand on her hip she casually looked over her shoulder at Oslo. "What exactly do you want me to do?" she said.

"You are a projector, Sally. You possess the ability to travel along the astral plane. Demonstrate for us if you will."

"Well, you really can't see me doing anything. My body just sits here while I run off and play spy with my astral form. What is there to see?"

"Humor me. Please begin and report back everything you see," Oslo insisted.

Sally let out an exasperated sigh, then glanced at Breeze and winked. She closed her eyes and stretched out her arms. Ray laughed.

"Focus Sally. And stop mocking your classmates," Oslo called out.

Sally turned to Breeze and whispered "just kidding."

He shrugged, and then stared at the floor.

The gold tinted glow faded away to pitch black. After a few moments, a shaft of white light emanated from the peak of the dome. Breeze could feel the floor beneath him move as the room expanded in diameter and height again.

Sally threw her arms up in the air. "Ta dah!" she said, then brought her arms down to her sides and stood rock still. "Well, can I finish now?"

"Turn and face your teammates, let them see you," Oslo responded.

She turned around with her eyes closed.

"Let them see you." Oslo commanded.

She opened her eyes. They shined brilliantly and her face was expressionless.

"No, let them really see you." Oslo persisted.

Next to her the air shimmered. A few specks of light appeared and waved like a mirage as a ghostly image of Sally materialized.

Ray and Breeze were transfixed as Sally's astral form drew closer to them while her body remained still. She smiled and gently touched each of their faces. It felt like a soft breeze caressing their skin with a tingling sensation that immediately followed. She drifted away and floated about the dome.

Oslo's booming voice broke their trance. "Sally can travel outside her body. Her ability to project and traverse along the astral plane makes her a formidable spy. One second you see her," Oslo snapped his fingers, "and now you don't." Her image faded away.

Sally's body spoke in a monotone voice. "But I still maintain contact with my physical form, see?" And she placed her hands on her hips.

"Very good. Now, I want you to slip through the walls to the adjacent storage room and describe to us what you see," Oslo instructed her.

Sally's astral form materialized and gave him a mock salute, and then plunged into the wall and disappeared. She emerged into a room with equipment strewn haphazardly about. Along the walls were stacks of electronics. Each of them teeming with switches, dials and buttons that made no sense to her.

Back in the dome they all watched as Sally's body shuddered. It began to speak in a monotone voice as the bright white eyes made it difficult to gauge any real emotion. "I can see stacks of equipment everywhere. Not sure what they're for. They look like electronics, but they're like, really old and dusty—"

Her body took in a deep breath and gasped.

In the storage room, Sally's astral form was frozen in terror at the row of human figures lining the wall.

She swallowed her fear and slowly glided forward to get a closer look. As she approached, she noticed how the faint light of the room glinted off them.

"Robots," she muttered.

Her body in the dome simultaneously relayed her words as she spoke. "I see some really weird looking old robots lined up along the walls. Creepy."

She got as close as she dared and noticed the spots of rust peppering their bodies. They were all in various states of disrepair

"This place is really weird and old. I want to leave," she said loudly.

"Very well," she heard Oslo through her body in the dome, "I want you to travel out to the courtyard and tell us what you see."

She sighed and looked the room over one last time. In her astral form, she could not only travel long distances but also had a limited ability to see through solid objects. As she spun in a circle scanning for the direction to take to get to the courtyard, she took a quick glance into the dome. She could see Oslo standing with his arms behind his back while the guys were lined up against the wall staring at her prone body. Breeze was shifting his weight from one foot to the other while Ray clenched his hands into fists.

She laughed softly to herself while gazing at each of their faces. Ray was handsome, but a little too sure of himself. Breeze was cute, but in way over his head. She knew he was smitten with her, but she saw him as nothing more than a curiosity.

She continued scanning, but found only empty chambers. She then remembered they were underground and looked up toward the surface and saw the courtyard. It was made up of white stone cut into squares with grass growing from the cracks and statues lining its perimeter.

In the middle of the courtyard, she saw a woman on a stone bench. She sat with her back to Sally stroking her long, flowing hair.

"There is someone in the courtyard," Sally said.

"No worries," Oslo responded, "go and describe her to me."

Breeze and Ray watched her body take in a deep breath and briefly spasm. Oslo saw the concern on their faces and addressed them. "She is now traveling out into the courtyard to meet someone. She'll be fine"

In the storage room, Sally's astral form glided forward and up through multiple walls and corridors until she emerged into the courtyard. She gazed up at the deep blue sky punctuated with towering white clouds and the formidable storm that was forming in the distance behind them. She trembled as chain lightning arced through the dark and nebulous clouds. She felt every burst of electricity as a mild shock that coursed through her astral form.

She turned her attention to the woman on the bench. She had long golden hair and stroked it while humming a melody that sounded familiar to her.

Sally glided toward her as anxiety built up within. She found it disconcerting that she couldn't see the woman's face.

She came to a stop inches from her and felt the urge to reach out and touch the woman's hair. She raised a hand hesitantly, then stopped and glided around to face her instead.

The woman was oblivious to Sally's presence and continued stroking her hair and humming.

Sally leaned in close. "Not much to report here, just some lady on a bench," she said in a very loud voice, mere inches from the woman's face.

She then took the opportunity to look her over. The woman was beautiful. Her eyes were a blue green hue framed by high cheekbones that stared into the distance while incessantly humming and stroking her hair. She wore a white dress that flowed away from her.

Sally leaned even closer while assuring herself that the woman was not aware of her presence at all.

"I could stand in front of her all day and night, Oslo. She has no idea I'm here. Whatever sort of test you're putting me through, it's safe to say I passed."

Like a viper, the woman lashed out and grabbed Sally's astral form by the throat. Sally tried to scream while thrashing within her grip.

The woman pulled Sally close as she tore at the hand around her throat and struggled to pry it open. She couldn't understand how the woman could grasp her astral form.

The woman tilted her head and observed Sally like a dispassionate hunter looking at an animal caught in a trap.

Back in the dome, they watched as Sally's body fell to its knees with hands clawing at the air as if it were fighting off some invisible force.

"What's happening to her?" Ray shouted at Oslo.

Oslo waved him off and said nothing.

In the courtyard, the woman pulled Sally close with a malevolent glow in her eyes.

"Demon!" she hissed and threw Sally across the courtyard.

She could barely scream as her astral form plunged down toward the dome. She saw the overhead lights of corridors flash above as she hurtled through them, then slammed into her body with a violent force that sent her skidding across the floor of the training room and crashing into the curved stone walls of the dome.

She laid on the floor in a daze as Ray rushed to her. She buried her face in his chest and sobbed.

Ray shouted at Oslo. "What did you do to her?"

"I did nothing. Like Breeze, she needed to demonstrate her abilities for us to observe. Like Breeze, she was challenged and lost her focus. This is the end result born from hubris," Oslo said as he gestured at Sally.

"Who was that woman? How could she see me, let alone grab me?" she shrieked.

"Sally, you have spent much of your life self-assured in your abilities. But you have never been challenged. You always assumed that no one could ever see you, therefore, you were untouchable. This test was designed to illustrate that you should never let your guard down and to assume nothing."

"Well, you have a very strange and weird way of showing it," she said with an icy glare, then wrestled herself free from Ray's embrace and walked over to Breeze in a huff to stand next to him.

Oslo closed his eyes and breathed in deeply. He held it for a moment then released it in a long exhale. He opened his eyes and nodded at Ray. "It's time."

Ray strode to the center. He knew Oslo would save him for last, and there was good reason. He was born into a military family and could demonstrate to the others how discipline and training always paid off.

The gold tinted glow of the walls faded as the shaft of piercing white light re-appeared and engulfed him. He stood rock still with fists slightly raised as his eyes narrowed into slits.

The ground shook as a deluge of rocks lashed at him from his left. He twisted instantly and blasted them with a barrage of energy that erupted from his hands, then shaped the energy into a cone and stepped into the rock storm, scooping up and dissipating them like water evaporating before an inferno.

The deluge came to an end. Ray held up his hands as the arc of energy retreated into them, then turned to face Oslo.

Oslo stepped out of the shadows and clapped with a broad smile plastered across his face. He clamped a hand on Ray's shoulder. "Now that," he boomed, "is how it should be done. Ray was presented with a challenge and met it head on without hesitation. He confronted the rock storm with precision and speed and dispatched it with ease. The result; victory. Well done, Raymond. Very well done."

The gold tinted glow of the walls returned as the shaft of white light receded. Ray stood at full attention with a look of smugness on his face.

Sally was fuming. Her arms were folded across her chest as rage stormed across her face. She was set to explode and Oslo was the trigger. "This is not right! We came here to be taught something. Our parents were convinced that this dump you call a school would help us better understand our skills. Instead, we get dragged down into this damp and humid torture chamber where you just about killed Breeze, and I get attacked by," she made a sweeping gesture with her hand, "some crazy devil woman. And then you have Ray go into some easy demo burning up a few rocks, and you call that a success. Is this some kind of joke?"

Oslo strolled over and stood before her as she looked up at him with hands on her hips.

"Sally, I presented each of you with a challenge specifically tailored to your unique skills. These tests created an opportunity to showcase what you bring to the arena in case of an actual combat scenario. Knowing what each of you can do gives everyone the ability to determine how to confront any opposition. What is it you don't understand?"

Sally thrust a finger into his face. "You throw rocks at Ray and he swats them away ease. You call that a successful demonstration? And combat? What combat? My parents didn't send me here to learn how to fight!"

Oslo gently lowered her hand. "My dear Sally, what makes you think this demonstration is over?"

A deep rumbling emanated from above as the dome shook and drops of water fell to the floor.

The rumble turned into a roar and Ray was pummeled by a deluge of water. He threw his hands in the air and fired a massive volley of energy into the torrent of water, creating a barrier that kept the flood at bay, and instantly turning it into steam. The room was drowned in a thick cloud of superheated air as Ray struggled against the onslaught of water. His legs buckled from the load as the flood pressed down upon him and he collapsed to his knees. He eventually succumbed as the barrier collapsed and the deluge swallowed him whole.

The torrent of water came to an abrupt stop, and then reversed itself, flying back up into the peak of the dome and disappearing.

Oslo stepped into the center and stood over Ray with a look of disappointment. "What just occurred is a clear illustration of what I'm trying to teach all of you. None of you has ever been pushed to the extreme. You have never been brought to the limits of your abilities. And upon reaching those limits, you never really learned how to smash through them. There are no limits, there is only the self-imposed ones conjured from your minds." Oslo leaned down to Ray. "Your mistake was vanity. You assumed you will be the team leader. I give you a simple test, and then shower you with praise for passing it. You soak it up like a sponge and lower your guard, leaving yourself open to an attack. That is why you failed." He turned to address the others. "A lesson for all of you. When someone flatters you endlessly, beware. This is meant to distract and weaken you. Be humble in the way you live your life knowing you can always be better. Never allow pride or vanity to govern oneself. There is more to this world than you."

Ray was on his hands and knees coughing up water. He looked up at Sally expecting her to come rushing to him. Instead, she ran to the exit and pounded on the stone in rage. The outline of the door appeared, and she slipped through as it slid up.

Oslo shook his head. "Discipline, Sally, discipline!" he called out to her.

She responded with a shriek and she rushed down the corridor. The door slid to close and faded into the stone.

Ray stumbled to his feet and stood next to Breeze.

Oslo nodded at them. "You have experienced much today. Session is over. These sessions are over when I say they are over. Dismissed." He turned and exited the dome as a section of wall disappeared, then reappeared once he stepped through.

The door that Sally ran through slid up, and the lime green stones embedded in the floor of the corridor glowed to light the way out.

Ray was a disheveled and soaking mess. He looked at Breeze, who was still in a daze from his session. Breeze snapped out of his trance upon seeing the glowing floor of the corridor and stepped out. Ray followed.

When they arrived back to the dormitories, they barely looked at each other as they stood in front of their respective doors. Without any words exchanged, they disappeared into their rooms.

Later that evening, Oslo was standing on the balcony of his office and gazing across the moonlit bay when he heard a sigh from behind.

"Good evening, Excort. How long have you've been standing there?"

The dwarf emerged from the shadows. "Long enough to think of what to say to you. That all of this is foolish and dangerous. What do you expect to accomplish here?"

Oslo said nothing for a while. He wondered himself what could motivate him to come back to the island after all the tragedy he experienced here, when he could be in his home resting comfortably next to a roaring fire and enjoying a quiet life. The thought of home made his mind wander to his native Scandinavia with its lush green forests, and fjords that dotted the coastline. His home there was nestled in the hills overlooking a harbor with a view of the storm churned ocean in the distance. It was a sharp contrast to the hot and humid environment of Perihelion.

He turned to his old friend as the moonlight exposed the deep lines etched into his face. "After all this time, you want to know why I came back? Perhaps it's regret, or the weariness of wondering if I could have done something more. Raza and I could have acted sooner if we had just seen the signs—"

"What happened to Bram is done. He is lost. Forever," Excort said as he looked up at the towering man. "Bram was a good friend and you did the right thing by trying to find him. But he disappeared into the stars, never to return." He sighed. "The three of you did your best to save what was left of the world. But it was already over. You never bothered to wonder if it was worth fighting for in the first place. They won. They run this planet. It's a prison now. We live day by day and do the best that we can. It's all we can hope for."

"No!" Oslo roared with clenched fists, "I won't listen to this kind of talk. Not from you, not from Kera. Not from anybody."

"You have to Oslo," Excort responded. "Look, here on the island we are able to escape their prying eyes. But once we leave the safety of it, they can track our every move, and that makes it almost impossible to create any meaningful opposition to them. And there is another reason why you don't hear talk about rebellion and that's because many generations have since passed. Those that live today don't know much, if anything, of Earth's past. The world of today is the only one they know. They don't realize the tyranny they live under. They don't know any better because it's all they have ever known. Look at the students you have assembled here. Do they appreciate their gifts? They probably see them as burdens. What are you going to tell them? That there was a time when heroes and giants roamed this world? That Earth was once a beacon of freedom throughout the known systems? Those days are over. We are just another planet, just another rock, floating in the emptiness of space."

Oslo shook his head. "No, not true. The world is coming alive. I know it, I can feel it. Cities are growing across every continent. They have commerce, government. They have schools and industry. Look at where Sally and Ray come from. My agents found them at an academy specifically tailored for the paranormal. Granted, it is clandestine. A school within a school, if you will, but their government recognizes how special they are and strive to cultivate and protect them."

"And what about Breeze? Does he come from a place of tolerance?" Excort asked.

"He does come from a settlement on the outskirts of the Bad Lands named Conception, a small city not known for paranormal living amongst its population. Though I do know of a mountain nearby where travelers from a place unlike ours, reside. I suspect that they play a role in all that has been happening, but in what capacity, I am uncertain. Nevertheless, Conception is known for the aerocraft they build of amazing design and complexity, and I know they have even tried to reach orbit with some of them. What is truly amazing is the settlement has not been attacked from those who watch from above. Where are they? Are they not watching us anymore?" Oslo said as he pointed up at the night sky.

Excort shook his head. "It's a trap. They are crafty and patient with time on their side. A lot of time. You and I, old friend, have lived far beyond our years. Why stir up the hornet's nest? Why not just go off into the sunset and let things be. Earth has been quiet and peaceful for so long, let it stay that way. If we stir up trouble, it will arouse them, and I sincerely believe they are dormant solely as a ploy to draw you out. You have been a thorn in their side for what seems like an eternity. Eliminating you would complete their triumph, as you are all that is left of the resistance that has bedeviled them for so long. Just let it go."

Oslo protested. "I am not all that is left, Raza—"

"—is safe on the mainland and living in obscurity in Appalachia. Go to her and live out your remaining years in peace. Stop torturing the poor woman with your delusions of grandeur and your dreams of revolution. Go to her. Give her the peace of mind she deserves," Excort said.

Oslo shook his head. "I couldn't go to her. Not without Nina."

Excort grimaced. "You know the girl can't go far from the island and survive. She is safe here with my wife and I and we have practically raised the girl ourselves. She is fine with her life here, so why disrupt it?"

Oslo didn't know what to say. He had to confess he was a restless soul. He had wandered the planet for so long looking for signs of hope. He just couldn't let go of the past for it was a large part of what defined him. He could not accept the world as it existed today knowing there was a time it had a glorious and gilded history.

Excort pressed on. "What are you going to say to these young ones you have gathered? That you want to create an army of paranormal soldiers? That you wish to attack an enemy they don't know even exists? A threat they have never heard of? Earth has been quiet for a long time. Let it stay that way."

Oslo shook his head. "I cannot rest. I don't know if I ever can."

"Then you are doomed to roam the world alone while trying to spread your message upon deaf ears," Excort replied as he went down the balcony steps and disappeared into the night.

Oslo looked up the star-filled sky and squinted. Sometimes, if the night was clear, he could see them. What appeared to be tiny pinpoints of light that would gently drift amongst the stars were actually observation platforms, jet black cylinders of immense proportions, scanning the planet and searching for signs that the world was not fully subdued. Any and all signs of technological progress, whether they may be the construction of cities to the manufacturing of machines or aerocraft, would elicit immediate punishment. They would dispatch their black clad enforcers, dark angels filled with unfathomable evil, to swoop down and wreak havoc upon the land. The people of Earth were to be driven into submission and live as peasants with no technology or machinery to ease the burdens of life. No exceptions were to be made.

But there was one thing that these dark angels, or the Elephim as they were known to those familiar with their origins, would go through great lengths not to destroy, but to harvest. A prize that was considered to be Earth's greatest natural resource. Its paranormal children. Only they were spared the wrath from those above and were often taken away before the eyes of their parents and whisked away to the stars and beyond to meet some unknown fate.

But not here, not on this island. Here, they were safe. The Elephim could not penetrate the fog that covered the island and hid them from their malevolent eyes. Here, they were safe on a tiny oasis of freedom in a world that was a prison.

But the platforms and the Elephim that dwelled inside them had been dormant for centuries. Long enough for civilization to spring forth again from the underground and begin anew as the history of their attacks faded dangerously from memory.

Maybe Excort was right, he thought to himself, maybe they have purposefully retreated in a bid to draw him out into the open, then capture and destroy him once and for all.

He dropped his gaze back to the bay as the moon shined like a torch and lit up the island. He had a sudden urge to walk along the shore as he always did when he needed to think. He descended the balcony steps and headed for the beach.

He normally found these walks to be comforting and soothing to his mind. But not tonight. He had students now, something he did not have for so long and his doubts began to wear on him. Was he doing the right thing? Should he listen to Excort and let things be? He became lost in his thoughts and worries as he walked along the shifting sands of the beach.

He swerved off it and walked along a path that led to a hill overlooking the campus. Under the moonlight he stared long and hard at the various buildings that made up Perihelion. His eyes came to a rest upon a lone building that sat like a brooding hulk along the boulevard that divided the campus. It was the Science and Engineering Building, and his memories of it carried him back to a time when he, Raza and Bram conducted experiments there deep below the surface and away from prying eyes.

He wanted to go there now and descend to the building's sub-basements to reminisce about a time when he, along with his wife and best friend, almost discovered the solution that would have removed the threat of the Elephim from Earth forever.

He took in a deep breath and pictured in his mind standing on the steps leading up to the building, and then willed himself to go there. In incremental bursts, he disappeared and re-appeared from view as he traversed down the hill and toward the campus. His eyes glowed as he saw everything as a blur with contrails surrounding him and in mere seconds, traveled a distance that would have taken him an hour on foot.

He stood at the steps and looked up at the arches that lined the roof. Figures dressed in battle garb were chiseled into it, but he couldn't remember who they were or what they accomplished to earn their place in history. He went up and pushed against the heavy metal doors as their rusty hinges squeaked in protest.

The interior was in shambles with equipment and debris strewn everywhere, and the smell of electrically-charged air filled his nostrils. He made his way past row upon row of electronic equipment, kept under heavy tarp and plastic, to an elevator at the end of a long corridor. He pushed the call button and was not surprised to see it was still working. He had specifically instructed Excort to make sure that, of all of the buildings and equipment on campus to maintain, this building would be his top priority.

The elevator car arrived and the door slid open. He stepped inside; pushing the only button on the panel and the car bumped and shuddered its way down to the lower levels.

What seemed like an endless journey came to an abrupt halt. After a moment of silence, the door opened.

He stood in the elevator to let his eyes adjust to the dim lighting of the basement that reverberated with the hum of machinery. He stepped out and paused for a moment to take in the enormity of the basement, and then set about examining every machine and console lined in several rows across the floor. He specifically looked at vid-screens that gave readouts of vital signs, ranging from heart rate and blood flow, to neural activity. These machines were engineered to sustain a life. Machines he and a robot assistant designed and assembled. He shook his head as he tried to remember its name.

He resumed his inspection and was relieved to see everything was fully operational, and then made a mental note to commend Excort. The machinery in this room were all vintage and finding parts was virtually impossible, yet the dwarf somehow managed.

He turned and set his sights upon a pair of oversized steel doors that triggered a flood of memories and transported him to a time when he was a fresh-faced young man eager to please, and ready to take on the world. He thought he had all the answers, but time eventually proved him wrong.

Raza stood before him. She was a petite woman with an oversized personality and a smile that could light up the darkest of rooms.

"Are you ready for this?" she said.

"Yes," he responded with a foolish grin. They had grown close and he couldn't ask for a better woman to be in his life.

"When the two of you are done exchanging love notes, I'm ready to get started," he heard a brash voice off to his side.

It was Bram. His best friend, and a good man. He was also a projector whose abilities were unrivaled by anyone.

Oslo opened his eyes and the memories faded away. He looked up at the imposing steel doors that loomed before him and touched them. The cold steel surface greeted him without empathy. He looked at the keypad mounted on the wall next to them. He had the entry code committed to memory. He could easily type it in and look inside.

His let his hand hover over the keypad, then abruptly shook his head and walked away.

He strode quickly to the elevator and pushed the call button. The door slid open and he rushed in to lean against the side of the car, panting heavily. He thought he was ready to step beyond the steel doors, but the memories came back too hard and too fast. They were going to save the world from certain destruction in that room. They failed.

The elevator traveled up, then grinded to a halt and he jumped out. He rushed through the maze of machines and equipment, down the steps, and onto the boulevard, where he stopped and breathed the warm and humid air. It was nowhere near as refreshing as that of the hills and mountains of his native land, but right now it was better than breathing in the gloomy, air-conditioned sub-basement he just left.

He went back up the steps and pulled the doors shut, then typed a code into the keypad next to it, and received a corresponding beep and a red light, indicating the doors were locked and alarmed. *Don't need any unwanted visitors exploring this building*, he thought, *especially my new students.*

He headed back to his office when he stopped to look up at the stars. Sunrise was not far away and the sky was beginning to light up.

"You're out there somewhere Bram, I know it," he said.

The heavens responded with a distant rumble of thunder. He noted the billowing dark clouds on the horizon heading toward the island with streaks of lightning snaking through them like a live wire.

Typical summer weather, he thought and continued on.

CHAPTER

▼

SIX

THE NEXT MORNING THE students gathered in the dining hall for breakfast. They shuffled in looking like zombies as Sally's hair was a tangled mess held up with a band while Ray and Breeze both looked disheveled with wrinkled clothes and tousled hair.

They sat around a wooden table and listened to Excort bang around in the kitchen off to the side.

They avoided eye contact with each other, choosing instead to gaze around the room, noting the holes in the ceiling.

Sally broke the silence. "I preferred Greenbrier. This place smells. Everything is broken and nothing works," she said and stared at Ray.

He shrugged. "What am I supposed to do about it?"

"Call your father!" she said shrilly. "Make him tell Oslo that this place is a disaster and in need of serious repairs. How in the world could our parents have sent us to this dump? I was perfectly happy at Greenbrier, with its beautiful mountains and tall trees, along with the warm summers and snow in the winter. This place? A humid, roach infested hotel passing itself off as a school. How anyone deals with this heat is beyond me."

"I like it. It's definitely a change for me," Breeze piped in.

"What do you know? You come from a desert with cactus for trees and tumble weeds to keep you amused," she said with a dismissive wave.

"Hey, it's not all that bad. We have mountain ranges too. The mornings can be very cool, and the air is clear and you can see for miles. There is a lot of life in the desert, you just have to look."

"Whatever." She looked toward the kitchen. "Where is that midget with the food? I'm starving."

The pots and pans in the kitchen banged even harder, and then stopped when Excort stepped out pushing a cart loaded with plates of food. He plopped down before each of them dishes filled with cuisine they had never seen before.

"What...is this?" Sally poked at her food with a fork. She took a stab at a slice of white fish filet and held it up for all to see.

"Broiled hogfish, plantain chips and seaweed with a bowl of conch chowder," Excort announced.

The boys paused for a moment as they eyed their plates, then grabbed their forks and knives and tore into their food like ravenous wolves.

Sally would have none of it. "This is not acceptable. This is not even food." She pushed her plate away, half expecting the boys to stop eating. Her frustration doubled as they ignored her and continued to eat. She crossed her arms and fumed at Ray. He paid her no heed and kept shoveling food into his mouth. Breeze looked up from his plate for a moment and wilted under Sally's withering gaze.

Like a volcano that had been threatening to erupt, Sally exploded.

"Raymond, I demand that something be done about our deplorable conditions. I will not tolerate—"

"What do you want me to do, Sally?" he said as he threw his fork and knife onto his plate. "I'm here with you. I know what it's like. I see everything around me. I'm here for the same reasons you are, and that's because of our parents. Do you, of all people, expect me to disobey my father? You've met the man. I'm the dutiful son. I obey his commands and do what I'm told. He tells me to pack my things, that I'm transferring here for a summer session, and that you were coming with me. He was never happy with the fact that Greenbrier was not a military academy. He felt we would be better off here, even if it's just for the summer."

"You would be better off here, not me!" Sally shot back. "Military academy? Are we expected to use our powers for what? Combat? Against who? I'm not fighting anyone. I don't even understand why my parents would lie to me about how old and beat up this place is. I didn't know that this place existed"

Ray shrugged. "Maybe they thought you would be better off here, too. That this place would have something to offer than Greenbrier couldn't. I don't know. Before we left, I noticed how weird our parents and instructors had been acting. Everyone seemed so nervous and jumpy. My parents come to me one day and tell me I'm transferring to another school for the summer, and that you would be going too. The next day, we jumped on the transport to come here. I'm telling you Sally,

I know as much as you do."

"You know," Breeze offered up, "I had a couple of guys from Perihelion come to my house and tell me about this place—"

"Nobody cares," Sally cut him off.

Breeze was about to retort when Oslo entered. He took giant strides and crossed the length of the dining hall to their table in just a few steps.

"Good morning students. I came here to personally greet you and have breakfast together. How is everyone doing?"

Excort pulled out a chair for him and he sat down with a grace that belied his towering height.

"Horrendous." Sally was the first to answer as she gave him an icy stare.

"Are you having difficulties adjusting to your new surroundings?" Oslo said as Excort placed a heaping plate of food before him.

"Difficulties? Well, what a nice way to put it. Where do I begin? First—"

Ray interrupted. "Sir, I would like to contact my parents. My father especially. May I use the communications room?"

Oslo stiffened. "The comms are temporarily offline. Nasty storm earlier this morning knocked out the tower, but Excort is seeing to the repairs."

"He's standing right there." Sally pointed at the dwarf.

"Yes, of course. His sons help out around the island," Oslo quickly responded as Excort shot him a quizzical look.

"Oh, there's more of them?" Sally rolled her eyes.

"Thankfully, yes. Ray, I promise you that as soon as the tower is repaired, you may contact your family."

"And me?" Sally asked icily.

"All of you," Oslo said. "Now, let's enjoy this meal for we have much to do this afternoon, ja? What do we have for breakfast? Ah, hogfish, always a delight! Dig in everyone," he said with joy and reached for his silverware.

Sally pushed back from the table and walked away.

Oslo's booming voice brought her to a halt. "You have not been dismissed, young lady. Sit back down."

She whirled around with fire in her eyes. "I don't like it here! This is place is a disaster. You call this a school? I call it a garbage dump!"

Oslo placed his hands on the table. "You are a student at Greenbrier, ja? Phenomenal school and one of the best to be found on the mainland.

It is an institution that had produced some of the best scholars and statesman in the North Eastern Territories. Men and women with class, taste, and style, who go on to inspire people of the surrounding territories to better themselves. To encourage others to be something more than what they are, and to forever strive to achieve loftier heights. That is what Greenbrier is known for. Sally, do you feel you are a good representative of that school right now?"

She said nothing while nervously shifting her weight from one foot to the other.

Oslo continued. "Sally, did it occur to you that perhaps Perihelion needs you? That what this place sorely needs is someone like you? That a young woman of your background and pedigree can bring to this place your sense of dignity and grace? To hang your unique style and class throughout the campus and help turn it into a place that is worthy of Greenbrier? May I dare say, perhaps one day, better?"

Sally stood at attention. Her angry stare softened into contemplation. "This place could use some sprucing up."

"There, you see? That is what I'm talking about. Perihelion is more than just another school. This is not some institution. It's a new beginning. A chance for a fresh start. The world needs more of that, wouldn't you agree? We're building a better tomorrow right here. Let's begin right now with all of you behaving like students who obey their headmaster. Sit down at the table and eat you breakfast. We have a big day ahead of us."

Sally sat back down. She casually stirred her bowl of chowder and sampled it. A look of surprise lit up her face and she continued eating.

Oslo beamed. Each of his students were eating their breakfast without any further bickering, and it pleased him to see this. He was responsible for their well-being and he was more than happy to take on that burden.

His eyes began to wander across the dining hall. Sally was more than right. Perihelion was in shambles. He could see the cracks in the façade, along with the leaking roof, and the anemic air-conditioning system that was fighting a losing battle with the heat and humidity. He gave a great speech about rebuilding to Sally. Now he wondered if he bit off more than he could chew.

He lowered his gaze and was greeted by Excort's glare. "Ah, Excort. Please see to the comm tower if you will, right after you clear the dishes of course."

Excort grabbed plates and noisily stacked them on the cart. "I'll head out later and see what sort of progress my 'sons' are making."

"Good man. Students, return to your rooms and get into uniforms. Then wait outside the dorms in one hour. Class dismissed."

The trio stood up and marched out of the dining hall. When they were out of earshot, Excort spoke up. "Are you mad? Making Perihelion a place worthy of Greenbrier, you said? How? With what? What are you trying to do here, Oslo?"

Oslo narrowed his eyes. "They are young. Brash. Full of energy. Their gifts make them this way, but I can give them a sense of direction. I can help them achieve a sense of accomplishment by getting them to rebuild this place. I can keep them safe here. I know I can."

Excort continued to clear the table and stacking dishes onto the cart with a loud clink. "Keep them safe from what? I don't claim to know what the Elephim are doing, or if they still hover above us watching our every move. But perhaps everything is quiet because no one has done anything yet to stir them up," he said and glared at Oslo. "All I know is things have changed. And why am I cooking and clearing dishes? Why can't we use the robots?"

"We need them in the hangar. It's critical that we get the aerocraft operational again."

Excort pounded his fists onto the table. "What for! What are you going to do with them? What is it you're not telling me?"

Oslo held up a hand. "You are right. I do owe you an explanation." He cleared his throat before speaking. "I heard from Bram."

Excort's eyes widened, and then narrowed into slits. "What do you mean? How is this possible?"

Oslo sighed. He pushed away his plate and dabbed his mouth with a napkin. "He came to me while I was at my home in Scandinavia, in a vision, if you will. It was a bitterly cold night as I sat before the fireplace trying to get as much warmth as I could. The fire was roaring, and I was mesmerized by the flames. The wind outside was like a lion, lashing my home so hard I could hear the wooden beams of the walls and floor creaking and groaning. And yet, the flames held my attention. I was reminiscing about old times, dearly departed friends and failed dreams when I found myself going into a dark place that forced me to contemplate if I should keep going on, or just give up and leave things be. That's when I heard his voice. It was faint, like a whisper. I haven't seen him in so long and yet it felt like time had melted away when I heard it. As if it were only yesterday since we lost contact with him."

Excort stood in stunned silence.

Oslo trailed off and began stroking his chin, nodding his head as if he were having a private conversation with himself.

Excort motioned with his hand. "And?"

Oslo stared blankly at the dwarf.

Excort had enough. He was tired and frustrated. For him, life here on Perihelion was quiet and tranquil. He and his wife, Mila, were used to the easy life of the island and enjoyed being its caretakers.

They were accustomed to Oslo's frequent visits over the years as he would stroll along the boulevards of the dilapidated campus and wander about aimlessly with his head down while lost in deep thought.

One evening, as they sat down for a meal prepared by Mila, Oslo began to chatter excitedly about finding others of "their kind," as he so often put it. When Excort pressed him for details, Oslo dropped the subject and never mentioned it again. He left for Scandinavia in his sailboat the next morning.

Weeks later, Oslo sent them an urgent message. Re-open Perihelion, it read. Get the main generators back online.

They had done as he had requested. Oslo arrived days later on his sailboat, but this time with a look of excitement they hadn't seen in a while. He spoke about a new group of students he had discovered and the importance of getting Perihelion up and running again. Excort had to calm him down long enough to explain to him that the campus was in disrepair and that they couldn't possibly get things repaired in a reasonable amount of time. It was just too much to ask of them, Excort told him. But Oslo assured the dwarf it could be done.

Excort reached out to his sons and daughters who had long ago moved away and had started families of their own on surrounding islands. Some of his younger sons who had yet to take wives were the only ones who could respond to his request for help. They never understood why their parents wouldn't leave Perihelion, and he could never convey to his children the powerful bond they had with the island.

But now he stood before his recalcitrant friend wearing an apron with a cart full of dirty dishes, and he couldn't even get the man to finish telling him the most important news he had waited to hear for a long time. "Oslo, what did he say?"

"Oh, yes, of course. He said 'Return to Perihelion, I'm coming back.'"

Excort waited for more. He received nothing. "That's it?"

"Yes."

"That's all he said? You looked into your fireplace, heard a voice, and that was enough to come rushing back here after all this time and to have my wife and I labor night and day to re-open this place, all because you heard a voice? Have you gone mad? Are you drinking again?"

Oslo laughed and held up his hands in mock surrender. "Now, you know I gave that up a long time ago."

"You think this is funny? I'm taking the rest of the day off." Excort turned on his heel and marched out of the dining hall.

"What about these dirty dishes?" Oslo called to him.

"Clear them yourself!" Excort shouted.

Oslo sat alone as memories flooded his mind, bringing him back to a time when the cavernous dining hall would have been filled with cadets, sailors, airmen and officers eating their meals and exchanging news and gossip. The din of voices would be overwhelming as the kitchen staff, an army in their own right, worked overtime to feed them. He could hear laughter from some conversations; angry voices from others over a disagreement.

Now, the place was still except for the slow drips coming from the ceiling. *Water on the roof from last night's storm*, he thought idly.

Oslo stood up, straightened and smoothed his uniform, then headed for the exit.

CHAPTER
▼
SEVEN

OSLO ASSEMBLED EVERYONE OUTSIDE the dormitories after breakfast where he had Excort bring supplies and materials consisting of paint, brushes, trowels and shovels. Breeze and Ray picked through the tools spread out before them while Sally looked on.

Oslo spoke. "Perihelion, as you can tell, has seen better days. She once was a shining jewel that has since lost her brilliance. But no longer. We shall restore her luster, beginning with the three of you."

Sally raised a hand and cleared her throat.

Oslo nodded. "Yes, Ms. Trumbull, question?"

"Are we the only students here? I'm mean, are there more coming, or is this it?" she said while casting a sideways glance at Breeze.

"*Ja*, of course. They're on their way, just a bit of difficulty getting here. Apparently the weather is quite foul in some of the territories and is delaying their arrival."

Excort gave him a puzzled look.

"Great, just hope we get some better company," she sighed.

"Sir, how do you know about the weather? Are the comms back online?" Ray said.

"The comm room will be functioning soon," Oslo responded without looking at him.

Breeze piped up. "Maybe it's those weird people on the coast that attacked the ship I traveled in, could they be slowing down the transports?"

"Weird? You should be one to talk," Sally retorted.

"What's your problem?" Breeze said.

"The fact that you're here. Let's just say I'm not used to attending a school with guys who should be in a machine works class. Shouldn't you be with Excort fixing stuff around here?"

Ray spoke up. "Sir, I really need to get in contact with my father. Are you sure there is no other way?"

"Yeah, me too. I need to tell my parents I want to leave," Sally added.

"You know, if it weren't for guys like me, half the machines you use wouldn't work!" Breeze said to her.

Sally glared at him. "Do you think I care? I'm talking to Oslo. I'm done with you. And how come you don't ask about calling home? Oh, I know, daddy threw you out of the house? Let me guess; juvenile delinquent who skips school?"

"Students!" Oslo raised a hand and silenced them. "Now, back to our original task. Perihelion needs you. Together, we will rebuild this school. And it begins with the three of you. Teamwork is important. And I do believe we have a lot of team building to do." He pointed at the ground. "Spread out before you are the tools and implements you will use to complete today's assignment. With Excort's guidance, we will begin by sprucing up the dormitory area."

"We will?" Sally said.

"With my guidance? I was going to let them figure it out," Excort said.

"I can show everyone sir. It wouldn't be problem." Breeze offered.

"Stop sucking up to the teacher, machine boy. Nobody cares," Sally retorted.

"Sir, I can't even stress how important it is that I reach my father. Could you please have Excort expedite repairs to the comms?" Ray persisted.

"Quiet!" Oslo boomed.

Silence fell over them.

Oslo's hands were balled into fists. He slowly unclenched them as he spoke. "Class, I know it's not easy being here. You all have made an arduous journey over a great distance to get here. And now you find yourselves in new and unfamiliar surroundings. I understand. But your parents want you to be here. It is the safest place to be right now. I—"

"Safe? This place is falling apart! And besides, what are we being safe from?" Sally interrupted.

Oslo closed his eyes and took in a quick breath.

Excort glared at her and shook his head.

He continued. "As I was saying; it's a new experience. I understand. Your gifts have made you unique and here at Perihelion we will mold your skills into valuable assets. It all begins now with the simplest of tasks, such as taking pride in your surroundings. This is your home now—" he said, then shook his head. "Well, your home away from home. Excort, please show them what we have planned for today."

Excort begrudgingly stepped forward and began grabbing some of the tools. "Well kids, we will start with the basics. As you can see, the walls have quite a few cracks so we're going to use this compound to fill them in. Later, we're going to sand the walls and paint the building."

"Right, I'm done here. Manual labor is not my thing," Sally announced as she turned to walk the steps back up into the dormitory.

"Sally Trumbull, did I make a mistake when I asked you to set an example for everyone? About how you would endeavor to bring the grace and style of Greenbrier here?" Oslo called out to her.

She stopped, and then turned to face him.

Oslo continued. "This campus is your canvas, young lady. An opportunity to make your mark and to leave something behind for others to know you were here. Did you ever stop to consider that?"

She began to say something, then descended the steps without a word and stood with her classmates.

She placed a hand on her hip. "This place will need a new coat of paint. I mean the color scheme you have now? Horrible!"

Oslo smiled. "*Ja*, you are right. It's time to turn back years of neglect and set things right." He paused for a moment as the smile faded and his eyes narrowed into slits.

Excort cleared his throat loudly.

Oslo snapped out of his trance. "Very good. I shall leave you to the tender mercies of my groundskeeper. Do me proud!" He turned and walked away.

"You're not staying to supervise?" Excort called out to him.

Oslo waved a hand. "I trust your management style, old friend."

"Old friend? Look who's talking," the dwarf grumbled aloud, then turned and glared at each of them individually. "All right then—"

"Exactly how old is Oslo?" Sally interrupted.

Breeze chimed in. "Why is he so pale? In this sun he should be tan."

"Excort, I would like you to repair the comm systems immediately," Ray said.

"You? Paint brush! You? Trowel! And you? Shovel!" Excort shouted as he pointed at Sally, Breeze and Ray. "Follow me!" He marched to the side of the building.

Bewildered, they followed.

Excort gestured at the façade. "You will begin here by sanding down the wall, then fill in the cracks with this putty." He grabbed a bucket filled with goop and dropped it in front of them. "Then, prime and paint the walls," he said and stood with his arms crossed as if daring them to ask another question.

Sally didn't care. "Why start with the side? Why not the front?"

"Because if you do a horrible job, nobody will see it," the dwarf retorted.

"But when is everyone coming? Hey, can I choose the color of paint?" Sally asked as her eyes lit up.

"Do what you like, what do I care," Excort muttered.

"What kind of a groundskeeper are you anyways? You're such a grouch. The ones at Greenbrier are much more pleasant. Could you make a palette of colors I can work with? There are several different shades I would like to experiment with first," Sally said as she looked over the building with a critical eye.

"Are you sure you want us to use this putty? I don't think this is the right kind of compound for this weather," Breeze commented as he stuck his hand into the bucket and pulled out a clump.

"Mr. Excort? I need you to see to the comm repairs at once," Ray said.

"Why are you so eager to call home? Daddy's little boy getting lonely here?" Sally taunted.

Ray whirled on her. "You of all people should know better than to say that."

Excort rolled his eyes, then put his hands over his ears and walked away.

As Breeze watched the dwarf disappear around the corner, it dawned upon him how lonely and desolate the campus was, and watching his classmates argue made the feeling more acute. He had nothing in common with them and could never relate to the life they were accustomed to. Why he didn't run away from home like so many others from his town did, he didn't know. Probably because no matter where he went, nobody would accept him, not even here at Perihelion.

"Hey guys, Excort just wandered off," Breeze announced.

Sally and Ray stopped their arguing to glare at him.

Breeze shrugged and grabbed a trowel and the bucket of putty. He squatted down and dipped the trowel into the bucket and spread its contents across the wall, filling in the gaping cracks and holes.

"Shouldn't we sand the surface first like the midget said?" Ray said.

"His name is Excort, and yes, we should. There's a sander right there," Breeze pointed behind him. "You can start on that section of wall. I believe I saw a scissor lift around back earlier. If it's fully charged, you can drive it over here and use it to get to the higher sections of the wall."

"Are you giving me orders? Who made you the boss?" Ray blustered.

Breeze shrugged. "Do what you want, Ray. I'm not going to waste this day fighting with you."

Ray glowered, and then left to fetch the scissor lift.

"What should I do?" Sally asked.

Breeze looked up and smiled. "You seemed really interested in the colors. You can mix up some of those paints over there," he said and pointed to a row of cans behind her, "then brush sample patches on the wall. This way when the paint dries, you can get a better idea of what color you like, then pick one."

Sally clapped her hands together. "I get to pick the color?"

Breeze shrugged. "I don't see why not. Is there anybody here to tell us not to?"

Sally squealed and ran over to the row of paint cans. She knelt down, picked one up and fumbled with the cover but couldn't pry it off. She resorted to using a fingernail and cried out in pain when it broke.

She turned to ask Breeze for help but he was already beside her. He had a utility belt that Excort left behind, and he grabbed a screwdriver from it and easily pried the covers off the cans. He then stirred the paint within each one before pouring small amounts into pans. He replaced the covers and used a hammer to tap them shut, then reached into a box and pulled out brushes and placed one into each of the pans.

"Now what you can do is brush a strip of paint onto the wall like this," Breeze said as he grabbed a brush and dipped it into the paint, and then brushed a strip on the wall. "Take your time and brush different colors on the wall. That will give an idea of what you're looking for. If you still don't like what you see, no worries. Just take these extra pans and feel free to mix the paints any way you like to create the colors you want. Just remember as you paint the strips, give them time to dry. The paint is very wet and shiny when you first apply it. But as time passes, the shine wears off and the color fades a little. Kind of like what happened to this place."

She nodded as she glanced around.

"Anyways, just go ahead and paint the colors you like. Find one that you feel is right and we can go from there," Breeze said as he handed her the roller.

"Thank you," she replied meekly.

Their hands touched and she smiled. He blushed and returned to the wall he was patching.

Sally brushed the samples onto the wall all the while looking at Breeze from the corner of her eye. She was pleasantly surprised that there was more to him than she gave him credit for.

"What do you think this school was like before? You know, before it all fell apart?" she wondered aloud to get a conversation started.

Breeze paused for a moment and looked around. "You know Sally, I'm beginning to think this place was never really a school at all. And if it was, the school was just a part of something much bigger."

Her brushing stopped and she leaned toward him. "What makes you think that?"

He shrugged. "Just the way I arrived here through the strange tunnel in the sky along with the fog, as Oslo calls it, that supposedly hides the island from outsiders. Then, there's the various types of aerocraft I saw at the landing facility along with the ones inside the hangars being repaired by the robot mechanics. And if you look at the way this place is spread out the avenues seem more like taxiways for aerocraft to be moved from one building to another. And then there is the harbor. From the sky, you can see the remains of piers that have sunk. Were there a lot of ships that came here? If so, for what? The water is crystal clear, you can see all of it."

Sally stared him. "You...saw all of this?"

"Yeah, didn't you?"

She shook her head. "I don't remember seeing any of these things when we arrived here. In fact, I don't remember much of anything as to how we got here."

Breeze was stunned. "You don't remember flying through some type of tunnel in the sky? It was the weirdest experience ever. If felt like time stood still. I asked Oslo and he tried to explain it to me, something about the island not being in sync with current time." He paused for a moment. "I wonder why getting here has to be so complex?"

Sally shook her head. "I don't know. I just know Ray and I boarded the transport and we...fell asleep. When we woke up we had already landed. Escort was there to meet us and took us to the dormitory. We spent about a week with just Oslo, Excort and his wife, Mila. They kept telling us that other students will be arriving shortly but you were the only one who showed up."

"You mean to tell me that Excort never took you on a wild ride around the island? You didn't race down a waterfall, and then through a side of a mountain?"

Sally stared at him blankly.

Breeze pressed on. "Did you get a look at the pilot on your transport? Mine didn't even look human."

She shrugged. "Like I said, we fell asleep on the transport and woke up when we landed. I can't remember anything else and I don't know if Ray does either. I wonder where he is?" She looked around, and then resumed painting samples on the wall. "Breeze, how do you know so much about aerocraft?"

"Where I'm from, that's what we do. There are a lot of people who are building all sort of experimental stuff. There are some who build and sell to the territorial governments, or to rich folk. Some build and sell to transportation services that ferry people across the land. There is a lot of talk about uniting all of the territories and that it can be done if we mass manufacture aerocraft so people can just fly over the Bad Lands, instead of risking their lives traveling across it. Everyone says it's going to make my town of Conception into a wealthy city. I don't believe it."

"You come from a family of industrialists? Your father must be in charge of a powerful cartel."

"No, not really. My father runs a scrap metal yard."

"Oh!" Sally exclaimed, and then realized she said it a little too forcefully. "Well, I bet it must be a very successful one. So tell me about the rest of your family, what are they like?"

"My mother died in an accident when I was little. I have no other family left." He quickly shifted the gears of the conversation. "What's Greenbrier like?"

Sally beamed. "It's a really great school and so beautiful. The architecture is just divine. So much nicer than this place." She let out a long, dramatic sigh and stopped painting, then looked up to the sky and closed her eyes. "I can see the trees turning a leafy green after a long cold winter. Spring has arrived and the flowers are blooming. The birds are coming out and singing as so many of them are flying home after wintering in the southern lands." She opened her eyes and looked at the strips of paint on the wall and sighed again, then put the brush back into the pan. As she examined her stained hands she felt something roll down her cheek. She wiped it away and found it to be wet. It took her a moment to realize she was crying.

A hand touched her shoulder. It was Breeze comforting her as he handed her a towel.

She sniffed. "I feel so lonely here and I don't know why. To make matters worse, I feel like I've been here for a very long time and life is slipping away. And when I dream, I dream that nothing will ever be the same again."

Breeze listened as he opened more cans of paint. He mixed them into clean pans and stirred, producing a variety of colors. "I get the same feeling you do, but it happened much earlier. In fact, I can look back and say it hit me the moment I walked out my door and turned to see my father was not there to wave me goodbye," he said while laying out new brushes for her to use.

"We're supposed to be here just for the summer. That's all I know." Sally reached for a brush and began painting fresh strips on the wall.

"Can you tell me more about Ray?" As soon as he spoke, he regretted it. He realized he should have kept the conversation focused on her.

"Oh, well, he is from a military family. His father is a general, or something like that, in the Territorial Army. His family is pretty wealthy. And powerful. Ray's father is always talking about running for president of our territory. Whatever. Politics is so boring. And Ray, well, I guess he just wants to follow in his footsteps. You know, be like daddy, or something like that," she said and reached for another brush.

"So, how did you meet him? I guess you know each other from school and stuff—"

"Oh, no. We live next door to each other. My father and his are good friends. Partners in crime, I guess. They always talk about expanding into the Bad Lands and making it a safe place for settlers to occupy the lands."

Breeze gritted his teeth. "So, you two are a couple? That's cool. I'm not really seeing anyone back home. Well, there is this one girl, but you know, nothing serious." He wondered if she knew he was lying.

"Ray and I? Together? Well, let's just say he thinks so. He can be so possessive. No, I just see him as a friend. A childhood friend really. I mean, we grew up together and we live next door to each other. He lives in a big house like me and our parents are friends and all. In the summers, my parents would always throw these really extravagant pool parties and Ray would be there shooing the boys away from me. He's so cute. In the winter months when the leaves would fall from the trees and fill up the empty pool, we would sit on the bench next to it and talk. He's a really good friend, but—" she said with a shrug as she mixed another batch of paint.

Breeze felt a surge of confidence as he puffed up his chest. "So, that was some demonstration session we had the other day, huh?"

"I know! Mine was so weird. I guess Oslo programmed the computer for us to have some sort of adversary. I ended up dealing with a crazy lady in a white dress. I floated up and stared in her face. Nobody is supposed to see me when I project if I don't want them to, but somehow she could. I was so scared when she grabbed me by the throat and threw me across the courtyard." Her eyes narrowed. "I wonder how she could do that if she was just a simulation, or a hologram?"

Breeze shook his head. "I don't know. My session was pretty weird. I—"

"—there is no way she could have possibly seen me or touch me! How weird is that?" Sally obliviously continued. "You know, the day we all met at the cove, I was worried because I couldn't see you when you swam out by yourself. Ray and I were on the rock island and as I looked across the cove to find you, I saw a lady in white who stepped onto the beach for a moment, then disappeared. She seems like the one I saw during my demo session. I wonder if she's an instructor or something."

Breeze stood with his putty knife in hand. He was shocked to hear her express concern for him, but also of her seeing a mysterious woman. Memories of the girl he saw underwater that same day came to mind. He wanted to tell Sally more of his encounter with her, but decided against it. "Was there something about the woman in white that seemed familiar? Maybe she was also projecting, or maybe Oslo has some sort of a scanning machine that can pluck ideas out of our minds and materialize them and stuff. That's why it felt so real when she grabbed and threw you," he said.

Her eyes were transfixed on him as she listened intently.

He continued. "I saw someone too, you know. Maybe she was an instructor also, but she seemed really young, like our age. She...," he trailed off as she looked away from him.

"This gift of mine is something I've known about ever since I was a little girl," Sally spoke while absent-mindedly stroking her hair. "They say these powers don't manifest themselves until we get older, but somehow I was always proficient despite how young I was and I always seemed to know exactly what to do with them. When I would dream at night, I would later realize I was projecting. Even if I had a daydream, I ended up slipping out of my body and would wander about, yet I could turn around and see that my body was perfectly still, and I would always have a link, like a trail of light that I could follow back to it."

Breeze listened as he set up a ladder. He climbed up, gripping the side of it with one hand while lifting the bucket of putty and the trowel with the other. He reached the top of the steps and placed the bucket onto a tray that protruded from the top of the ladder.

Sally shaded her eyes from the bright sun as she looked up at him. "Why don't you just hover? I mean, you're a flier, so why not take advantage of your power?"

"Yeah, well, I'm not much of a flier. I mean, I'm not that good at it. I try, you know, but I'm not like you Sally. I just can't turn it on. You saw me in the dome. I was a disaster. It took me forever to just get my feet off the ground. I have to concentrate really hard and I can't deal with any distractions."

"I'm sorry about teasing you and saying mean things. I just..." she hesitated and twirled her paint brush as flecks of paint splattered all over the wall. "I just get so irritated. I used to be much nicer, or at least I think so. Coming here just seems to bring out the worse in me."

"It's fine Sally. Look, you need to understand the differences between you, me and Ray."

"I wonder where he could be," she mused.

He pretended not to hear her. "You come from a place where paranormal skills are valued. Heck, your school teaches the paranormal. I come from a place where the paranormal is not really spoken of, or even believed. We build flying machines, that's it. Toss in the fact that my father doesn't even want me to practice at all and I would have to sneak out at night and pretty much teach myself. Let's just say that the desert has a lot of craters spread out across it from me losing control and plowing into the ground. But I never get hurt, at least not much. My father always takes his tractor out the next morning to fill them in, though he doesn't say anything to me about it. It's funny, he's always looking up at the sky with a worried look like he's afraid someone is going to see them." He was sanding the wall as he spoke and stopped to feel the smoothness of the surface. He shook his head and resumed.

"I didn't know any of this Breeze. I'm sorry." She twirled her brush, never noticing she was splattering her clothes.

"Don't be. It's not your fault. We come from different worlds. Like I said, my city is all about aerocraft. People don't believe in the paranormal. If a man flies, it's inside a machine. You sometimes hear stories from the older folk about aerocraft being sabotaged or destroyed in the old days and that some shadow group used to attack and burn cities. They keep prattling on about how there once was a time when Earth was filled with brilliant cities and amazing technologies. They even talk about men who could fly into space. Imagine that!"

Sally's face was pale. "We hear the same stories, too. There is always talk about how life was so much better in the past. I don't believe it. And I never heard of anyone building spacecraft, have you?"

Breeze shrugged. "There are builders in Conception who are really secretive about what they create. Rumors are always floating around about somebody building a ship that can fly into lower space, just above the atmosphere, but nobody has ever seen one. Then there is always something weird going on in the Bad Lands. You always hear stories about flying creatures swooping around in the sky, or monsters walking around in the forest." He paused. "I have seen things."

Breeze made his way down the ladder and to the pile of supplies. He picked out a new bucket of putty and pried open the lid. "Sometimes when I would fly at night, I would see lighted orbs hovering in the distance, usually over a mountain ridge along the western side of my town. They just sit there, then zip away faster than anything I've ever seen and I don't know of any aerocraft that can move like that. Sometimes I would notice the balls of light hovering close to me, as if they were watching me. I would get real spooked and fall out of the sky. As time went by, I got used to them and I would always feel that they were encouraging me in a strange way. I would fly toward them and follow them around. It was weird, because they would take my mind off my anxieties about flying and I could actually concentrate." He went back up the ladder and resumed patching the wall. "Eventually, I would find myself flying further and further from home. I would follow these orbs west over the mountains until we reached the salted lake that lies on the other side of the range. Hardly anyone goes there because it's considered to be part of the Bad Lands. You hear talk about gigantic birds flying around there and that their wings make a sound like rolling thunder. Whatever, sounds stupid. One night I followed a formation of orbs across the lake. It was the first time I ever did that and man, that lake is bigger than I thought! The moonlight lit the way and we came upon a huge open plain that was pure white. You could barely see the mountains off in the distance and suddenly out of nowhere, there's this mountain all by itself. The orbs dropped into the mountain and I tried to follow them but I couldn't. Something stopped me like a command I couldn't hear, but I could feel and telling me to keep my distance. I found a hill where I could land...well, crash into, and from there I could watch them. I'm telling you Sally, I would see all sorts of weird craft come out of this mountain. Some of it was really cool. Others were just creepy and weird. Ever since that night I would fly back there just so I could watch the lights and..."

He realized he was rambling. He looked down at her and was stunned to see Sally smiling.

"I think you come from an amazing place. I didn't realize it was so interesting," she said.

Breeze shrugged. "Yeah, well, I guess so."

"You're such a nice guy. I'm so happy we can be friends," she gushed.

Breeze felt his heart sink like a brick. "That's great of you to say." He immediately wanted to kick himself as soon as he said it.

Sally began humming a tune and resumed painting samples on the wall.

Breeze glumly climbed higher up the ladder. He stopped and placed the bucket of putty on the step above and looked up at the sky. He wanted to fly as the urge to impress her overwhelmed his senses.

He stared at the clouds and focused his concentration. It wasn't until he looked down did he realize he was floating above the dormitory. He looked for Sally when he heard the grumble of an engine.

It was Ray driving the scissor lift machine. He was fumbling with the controls and grinding the gears as he careened around a corner. He was out of control, and was heading straight for Sally.

She waved at him excitedly, oblivious to the danger.

Breeze felt a surge of jealousy that made him lose his concentration. He flailed wildly with his arms as he plummeted to the ground and crashed into the pans full of paint, splattering it all over her.

Ray brought the scissor lift to a halt and nonchalantly stepped out.

Breeze lay on the ground, refusing to move even an inch. He could hear Ray laughing hysterically as he felt paint ooze all over him. He looked over at Sally and saw that she was covered head to toe with paint. She held out her hands and looked down at her clothes, then turned to look at her wall of paint samples. They were completely ruined. She looked at Breeze in horror, and then ran away.

Ray chuckled and knelt down on one knee next to Breeze. "Well my boy, let me guess, an attempt to impress the girl ended in disaster. Right?"

Breeze glared at him. He wanted to say something smart, but couldn't think of anything.

Ray slapped his thighs and stood up. He took a look at the wall Breeze was patching and nodded. "Breeze, you really need to listen. Sally and I come from a different world. Very different. Manual labor is not really our thing. We have other people do stuff like this for us. For you, yes, you're in your element here. And yeah, this project gave you an opportunity to shine for Sally, but, you never really had a chance with her. And now? Well, probably never."

Breeze continued to lay still. He knew he should get up and defend himself, but couldn't find the will. Lying there was all he wanted to do.

Ray jerked a thumb toward the scissor lift. "So anyhow, I brought the lift. I suppose you can clean up from here. You seem to have a handle on things. I'm going to check up on Sally." He headed toward the dormitory.

Breeze groaned as he got to his feet and began cleaning up the mess he made.

Oslo and Excort stood on an adjacent rooftop overlooking the dorms and watched as Breeze cleaned up the work site.

"Well, did you see what you want? Disappointed?" the dwarf asked.

"There is more to this school than teaching them how to use their gifts. They need to work together as team. They need to understand that they have to come together."

"For what Oslo? What are you preparing them for? These kids are far away from home and in unfamiliar surroundings. They don't want to be here and this campus is not even fit to be used. There is so much to repair around here—"

"That's your responsibility, not mine," Oslo snapped at him.

"Yes. Yes it is. And I'm doing it all by myself, thank you very much!"

Oslo closed his eyes and breathed deeply. "I'm sorry, old friend. I just assumed your sons were here to help you—"

"My sons and daughters, my family, have long ago left this place. There is nothing here for them. They have made a life for themselves on the surrounding islands. They live in peace. There are no troubles for them. Oslo, you have to let go. The past is the past. Move on. Go to Raza. Take her daughter to her. Live a life with the ones you love. Move on."

Oslo raised a clenched fist. "I can't let go. After all that has happened. All that I know. How can I just walk away and pretend to live a normal life?"

"Normal is what they want," Excort said as he pointed a finger at the sky. "As long as we don't make any waves, they don't bother us. Cities are not attacked. People don't vanish. Yes, on this island we are hidden from their view. But they see everything else. If you stand out, they will knock you back down. As long as you live a simple life, they don't seem to bother anyone. It's when you start using machines they take notice, and terrible things happen. And now, you're adding the recruitment of paranormals to the mix, which is what they despise the most and have gone great lengths to suppress."

Oslo chuckled.

Excort stared at him. "What's so funny?"

"You accuse me of not letting go? Do you have any clue what's happening out there? Or have you been stuck on this rock for so long, you stopped poking your head out to see? It's different Excort. Cities are flourishing. Machines are being built. And there haven't been any cases of cities or territories being attacked. Until now."

"What attacks? Where?"

"Never mind that. Progress is being made again. We're waking up. I just want the world to remember the heritage of this planet. For people to take pride again in their history!"

"How, with him?" Excort stabbed a finger down toward Breeze.

"It's a start. All great things have a beginning somewhere."

Excort turned and walked away. He had heard enough, especially after having a long day of making endless repairs with no real help. He reached the door that led to the stairwell, then stopped to look back at Oslo.

Oslo was standing with one foot on the railing and spoke while gazing at the sky. "If you look closely, you can see them. The stars that are not so bright, the ones that don't seem to shimmer. That's how you know it's the Elephim. We can stop them, once and for all. I believe we can," he said.

Excort understood what drove Oslo. He served in the military with him on Perihelion when the troubles began, and life as they had known it began its long march toward decay and chaos. They watched as the world was strangled by the hands of a powerful, yet unseen force. A shadow organization that slowly took over the institutions, industries and customs of Earth and her colonies, then encouraged the people to question and malign them. Soon, decay and chaos swept through like an unforgiving wind. Brothers quarreled and fought. Neighbors attacked and killed one another. Territorial governments were locked in endless wars and conflicts amongst themselves.

But the greatest accomplishment of the shadow organization, who later revealed themselves as the Elephim, was turning the population against the heroes and vanguards of Earth, the Helios, the paranormal army who protected the planet and her colonies.

The Elephim did not have the strength in numbers to confront the Helios directly; they were an ancient race who had long ago let their world fall into ruin. Yet their desire, driven by madness and depravity, to see all worlds become as eviscerated as theirs, compelled them to seek out life and suppress it, as they had suppressed their own people. But Earth possessed an energy unlike any other, and they knew it was instrumental in the creation of the paranormals that made up the Helios. The Elephim wanted to tap into that energy and replenish their strength, and perhaps use it to rebuild their world into their dark vision of it.

But the Helios would be their greatest obstacle in their quest for complete dominion of Earth, so they used subterfuge to undermine them.

A whisper campaign was set into motion against the Helios that soon erupted into a firestorm of negative public opinion. Malicious lies were spread, painting the Helios as power mad zealots who engaged in acts of perversion, while plotting to enslave the population.

The Helios soon found themselves on the defensive and became embroiled in a war amongst themselves. A war between factions who wanted to give in and surrender to the Elephim, who were beginning to emerge from the shadows and present themselves to the people as a safer alternative for peace and security, and those who chose to resist, for they knew the true nature of the Elephim and the horror they represented.

The turmoil surrounding the Helios made it easier to hunt down and destroy those who resisted the growing influence of the Elephim. It was painful and demoralizing to the resistance that those who were slain were done so by the hands of traitorous Helios who had become agents for the Elephim. Those who managed to survive went into exile to either hide on Earth, or to disappear into the stars.

With their protectors now gone, the people were forced to turn to what was left of the shattered territorial governments for security, but there were helpless to do anything.

The absence of authority paved the way for the Elephim to create a new government. They not only created the chaos and orchestrated it from the shadows, they now offered the solution to it. They held out a helping hand to the burnt out remains of a society that had destroyed itself, and offered order out of chaos. For a society that once valued personal responsibility and individuality, it now sought peace and tranquility at any price.

The Elephim placed platforms in orbit above the Earth. They claimed that it was to monitor and provide security, but instead became a systematic effort to control them like cattle. Any attempts at technological progress were met with swift retributions. Any desire to begin an alternative government was squashed. Earth was to be controlled by one government only, one administered by the Elephim and enforced by traitorous Helios, who now wore jet black uniforms that covered them from head to toe.

What would destroy humanity the most was not the attacks on cities and industries, or driving off the Helios into exile and obscurity, but the abduction of children by the Elephim. The heartbreaking stories of parents waking up to find their children missing had one common denominator: the abducted children were paranormal.

Oslo and his wife, Raza, spanned the globe seeking these families to bring them to Perihelion for refuge. Military personnel serving on Perihelion, who long ago refused the authority of the Elephim, were more than eager to help.

Perihelion was the only military base with an experimental electromagnetic camouflage, the fog as it was called, that was to be adapted and installed on the starships of the Interstellar Navy. It was now used to shield the island from the prying eyes of the Elephim and protect Earth's last and most precious resource, the children of the paranormal.

Perihelion was a base that also hosted a military academy for cadets. Oslo and Raza planned to use it to train and hone the paranormal powers of their recruits. They shared a vision of them becoming the next generation of Helios who would liberate the planet from the Elephim.

But it was too late as the Elephim were made aware of these plans from well-placed spies. Though they could not find Perihelion because of the fog, they isolated it by raining destruction upon the rest of the world.

When it was over, the children and their families stayed on the island until the fires across the planet had burned themselves out, then left Perihelion and returned to what little was left of their homes and live out the remainder of their lives rebuilding what they had lost. Despite their efforts, their homelands would devolve into chaos.

The Helios who survived the purge knew better than to reveal themselves. They were never heard from again.

Excort did remember an alternative plan that was hatched by Oslo, Raza, and a friend of theirs, a projector whose power seemed to grow exponentially by the day. His name was Bram. He was recruited to train at Perihelion right before the purge began along with Oslo and Raza.

Their plan was to augment Bram's projection capabilities with machinery that Oslo and a robot assistant of his designed and built, to seek out the home world of the Elephim and discover any weakness they may have and use it to destroy them.

They found it after many attempts by relying on clues they found in ancient texts of the island's vast library. But the mission came to an abrupt end when Bram's astral form disappeared after one of many excursions to and from Helena, the Elephim' home world, leaving his body behind in a comatose state that was kept alive by the machines that augmented his power.

"The three of you did what you could," Excort said, "but in the end, the odds were stacked against you. You never had a chance. Bram was your best hope and you sent him to confront the Elephim and to find their home world, but something happened to him. Whatever it was, he could be the reason why they became dormant for so long. Perhaps he found a way to fight them and prevent Earth from being harmed any more that it has. Maybe he reached an agreement with them to leave Earth alone as long as we don't try to become ambitious again and re-cover what we have lost. What I believe," the dwarf pointed at him, "is if you stop trying to recreate the past, they might just leave us alone."

Oslo held up a hand. "I told you, Bram sent me a message. He is returning. He wants Perihelion reopened."

"Did you really hear from him? Or is it the guilt that you feel for sending him out into the unknown and never returning?"

Oslo didn't respond.

Excort lost his patience. He turned and descended the steps.

C H A P T E R

▼

E I G H T

OVER A WEEK HAD passed since their failed attempt at sprucing up the dormitory and Sally was becoming exasperated.

Oslo continued their training as he strived to get them to wield their powers in new and interesting ways, but it was becoming quite clear to her and the others that he wasn't much of an instructor while also doubling as headmaster.

Sally hounded him about the arrival of the other students he had promised. He would repeatedly assure her that more were on the way.

Breeze was acting strange around her. He would pass her in the halls, or on the boulevards of the campus, but avoided her gaze. A few times he mumbled an apology to her about the painting accident. She just didn't know what to make of him. A part of her was falling for him, the other was screaming at her to just ignore him.

A heavy rainfall the following night woke her and she couldn't fall back asleep. She went to the balcony to look out across the bay and watched as the rain come down in sheets. The pitch black night was lit by streaks of lighting that briefly gave her glimpses of the shoreline while thunder rocked the dormitory causing it to shake and rumble.

The storm abated as the heavy rain petered out into a light drizzle. The dark and thick storm clouds gave way to wisps of fast moving rain bands that allowed the starry sky above to shine through. She looked up and sighed. The stars here seemed so much brighter than at home. Her city was a fast growing one and the electric light from the street lamps created a glow over it that obscured the starlight.

As the rain bands thinned out, she leaned over the railing and began searching for constellations. She marveled at how the stars seemed to hang in the sky like glittering jewels and she wanted to reach out to grab one as they felt so close.

She noticed one star in particular that appeared dull compared to its companions, and then brightened as if a surge of energy rippled through it. She had the feeling it knew she was watching when the star wobbled and drifted away.

She tracked it until a movement from the corner of her eye caught her attention. She looked down at the beach and saw a figure staring at her. She recoiled in fear and quickly stepped back from the railing. The figure turned and walk along the shoreline with a flowing white dress streaming in the wind.

The figure turned to look at her again. Sally put a hand to her throat and realized she was looking at the same woman from the cove and the demonstration session in the dome. The woman raised her hand slightly as if to greet her, then turned and continued walking along the beach.

She watched her fade into the dark and felt compelled to project out to her, then thought better of it after remembering her experience in the courtyard. She needed to confront this woman on a physical plane, not the astral one.

She ran out of her room and down the steps, then through the courtyard that lead to the beach as her adrenaline overwhelmed whatever fear she may have felt.

She looked down the shoreline and caught a faint wisp of a white dress in the distance. She bolted across the sand, never realizing that she was the only one leaving footprints behind.

As she drew closer to the woman she slowed to a walk, and then stopped. The woman turned to face her and the moonlight made her white dress glow even brighter, allowing Sally to see how beautiful she was, with her long flowing hair blown about by the wind. The woman raised a hand and beckoned her to come closer.

Sally hesitated, then took a step forward and noticed a faint smile on the woman's face that faded to sadness as she raised a hand to her heart.

Sally simultaneously raised a hand to hers and felt out of breath as her heart began to beat faster.

Sally lowered her hand and the woman mirrored her movements perfectly.

"What is your name?" Sally asked.

The woman began to speak, and then stopped. She stared at Sally before turning to look at the bay. The wind was beginning to pick up, making the surface choppy.

"Kera," the woman said in a hushed tone as the wind carried her voice away.

Sally stepped closer. "I couldn't hear you."

The woman turned to look at her. "Kera," she repeated.

Sally froze in place. She never heard of that name until now. And yet, she felt like she had known it forever.

Kera stared at her while the wind blew her dress away from the water every time a wave encroached upon it.

Sally didn't know what to do. Part of her wanted to run back to the dormitory, while the other wanted to reach out and touch the woman. She felt drawn to her but couldn't understand why.

"You saw me when I projected out into the courtyard during my demonstration," Sally said. "You knew I was there the whole time and then you attacked me. Why?"

Kera stood silent. Her face seemed to contort as if she was holding back a million answers she wanted to give. "Tell me about your mother," she asked.

Sally was taken aback by the question and she nervously raised a hand to chew on a fingernail. Kera grabbed it and Sally could feel a current of energy run through her.

Kera quickly withdrew her hand. "Please tell me."

"My mother and father—" Sally began.

"Yes, of course. Your parents I meant to say."

"—my mom and dad are, well, I don't know, good. I guess. Why they sent me here, I don't know. My mom is nice, I suppose."

"Any siblings?"

"Brothers and sisters? No, just me."

"Ah, an only child. Yes, of course," Kera said with a smile and nodded her head.

"Why are you so interested in my family? And what sort of an instructor are you anyways? Oslo hasn't introduced us to you or told us what classes you teach—"

"The acquisition of knowledge is not something that has to take place exclusively in a classroom," Kera replied. "It can take place anywhere, anytime, and under any circumstance. It can happen right now in the middle of the night along the shoreline of a wind tossed bay. Never again think like that, Sally. There is more to this life than bricks and mortar, glass and steel. Then again, I think you are beginning to realize this."

Sally crossed her arms over her chest and shivered as the air grew colder. Lightning flashed in the distance, followed by the rumble of thunder.

"Come, walk with me," Kera said, and beckoned her to follow.

They walked side by side along the shoreline. The waves never touched Kera while they consistently drenched Sally's feet.

They walked for a while until Sally finally broke the silence. "Why is it I seem to know how to project so well, even at an early age?"

"You are asking me why it is you seem so proficient in your power, while you watched your fellow classmates struggle to master theirs?"

"Yes," Sally said eagerly, "I always felt like I was ahead of the class in everything I did and in every subject."

"And how did that make you feel? Superior, I would imagine."

"Well, I...I suppose."

"And do you feel that it helped you advance your knowledge, or did it ostracize you from everyone? Did the other girls in your class like you? Did the boys take time to notice you?"

Sally stopped in her tracks.

Kera turned and glided toward Sally. "Knowledge is a funny thing. The more of it you gather, the more you make yourself believe others will listen and respect what you have to say. Instead, you find yourself being pushed to the side and ignored. Why is that?"

Sally shook her head. "I don't know."

"Of course you wouldn't know. It's not how young you are that is the problem. It's your lack of experience." Kera pointed at her, then at the moon. "I want you, no, us, to project together. To the moon and back. Are you up to it?"

Sally recoiled as she looked up at the brilliant moon. It seemed so close, yet so far away.

Kera persisted. "Why are you so afraid? You said you always felt you knew everything there was to know about projection. So let us see."

Sally shook her head.

"Class is in session, Ms. Trumbull. Don't be fooled by the lack of desks and seats, or tablet and stylus, nor the absence of four walls and a roof. Remember, learning can happen anytime, anywhere. It doesn't require a bloated institution and bureaucracy to make it happen."

Sally swallowed hard and closed her eyes. When she opened them, they glowed a bright white and her body was perfectly still. Her astral form stepped out and floated toward Kera.

Kera beamed. "You truly are amazing. There are many like us who spend their entire lives trying to master this gift as proficiently as you have at such a young age."

"Are you going to project with me?" Sally asked.

"Am I not already?"

Sally was astonished. "I don't get it. You touched my hand earlier. I could feel you."

Kera raised a hand. "Stop thinking and no more stalling. Learn how to let go. Now, come and follow me," she said and floated up.

Sally followed her, while taking a quick glance back at her body where it stood along the beach like a statue. Her connection to it was strong, like a string attached to a kite that allowed her to find a way back.

But now she was beginning to doubt herself as she never really traveled this far from her body before. She looked up at Kera, who was hovering above, and wondered why she trusted her.

Kera smiled. "Very good. Any journey that involves self-discovery requires you to take a step forward no matter how small it may seem. And now," she said while pointing at the moon, "we are about to take a journey of a million small steps. Are you up to it?"

Sally nodded.

"Let's go," Kera said and ascended rapidly.

Sally gave chase and labored to catch up to Kera who always seemed to be out of reach. She briefly looked down and was shocked at how high she was. She looked up and Kera was wagging a finger at her. "No looking back," she said to Sally, "keep moving forward."

Together they broke through the clouds that smothered the earth below as the moon lit them in a way that reminded her of the snow covered fields behind her home in winter. She drifted while marveling at the lightning that rippled through them.

"You've never traveled this high before?" Kera said as she hovered next to her.

"No. I wish I had. I've never seen anything so beautiful. I don't understand why I've never attempted this before. Why was I so afraid?"

"Fear is like an anchor that keeps you firmly in place. It becomes a convenient excuse for not wanting to push yourself, to break the bonds that prevent you from exploring your boundaries, and then shattering them. Now come, no more dithering about. We have a journey to complete," Kera said, and accelerated up and away.

Sally struggled to keep pace, all the while reveling with a sense of exhilaration as they raced higher and higher. For her, projection was always nothing more than stepping out of her body to snoop around. She would eavesdrop on guests during her parents' dinner parties, or drift outside to sit by the pool, but now she was racing to the moon.

Suddenly and without warning, she felt lost and alone, as if she could never go back home again. The connection to her body became weaker by the moment as she then understood what it was like to be a ghost.

"No, you do not," a woman's voice said in her mind.

Sally gasped as Kera appeared beside her.

"You are far too young to understand the pain of knowing you have lost everything. To know that the ones you love are gone and forever out of reach. You have yet to truly experience such loss. Hopefully, you never will."

"I can't go any further," Sally whispered.

"You can't or won't. There is a difference."

Sally could feel tears streaming down her eyes and reached up to wipe them. She looked at her hands and saw how each one was like a tiny globe of light. They rose up to float above her, and then dropped like stones to the earth below.

"Even the tears you shed lack the strength of conviction. How will you be able to help anyone if you refuse to believe in yourself?" Kera said.

"But I do believe in myself! I told you, I know how to use my gift. I'm the best one here on the island!" Sally wailed.

"Gift? Did I not overhear you calling your gift a curse?" Kera glared at her.

"How...how did you know I said that?"

"Does it matter? Is it any different how you would spy on your parents during their little parties? Pressing up close to each one of them and listening in on their conversations. How amazing was it for you to explore the world of adult conversation and how it contrasted so sharply from the chatter amongst children. Did it make you feel more grown up?"

Sally was stunned. "How do you know these things?"

"Oh, my dear, sweet Sally. Do you think I was any different growing up? That I didn't experience the same things you did? Look at us child, we are hovering above the Earth while floating in the infinite blackness of space. Are you feeling any more lost and alone than you were before?"

Sally looked back at the Earth. It was nothing more than glowing ball in the distance. She could feel her astral form being tugged, then yanked violently back to her body. She screamed as she hurtled across space.

She came to an abrupt halt as Kera grabbed her hand, then drew her close and cradled her face.

"Child, our lives are less ordinary. You cannot deny who you are. Never. Whether you call these powers of ours a gift or a curse, you can never pretend that you do not possess them. There will come a time when you will have to use them in ways you never imagined, such as now. Come, let us finish our journey. The lunar surface awaits us." Kera let her go and raced away.

"Don't leave me!" Sally shrieked and raced after her.

The moon loomed before them and the further away from the Earth they went, the more frantic she became. She could sense the connection to her body fade as voices flooded her mind and it felt like she was trapped in a crowded room with strangers shouting in her face. Overwhelmed, she placed her hands over her ears and came to a halt. As the shouting voices became louder, she felt as if her very essence was being absorbed into a collective.

One distinctive voice stood out from the din and it seemed familiar. She turned to look, but couldn't find it. Faces flashed before her, but none she recognized as they all were grotesque and contorted in anger or in fear. She was desperate to find one face that seemed familiar, even a friendly one. She felt herself fade away just as a pair of hands grabbed her by the shoulders and pulled her back. She opened her eyes and was relieved to see it was Kera. The woman was speaking, but she couldn't hear anything she was saying.

"I said you have to be strong. Force your way past the muck and mire. Don't let the voices overwhelm you," Kera repeated to her.

Sally pushed her away. She wanted to leave. She had gone too far. This was something she had never done before. She was outside her comfort zone and she knew it. She looked around wildly as she tried to find Earth.

She spotted it. It was nothing more than a tiny globe hovering in the dark. She lurched forward and accelerated, never realizing she could move this fast. The speed became blinding as she hurtled through space.

She looked back and saw Kera racing to catch up to her. Her arms were outstretched as the woman spoke into her mind and commanded her to slow down.

Sally couldn't. She was rocketing out of control.

The Earth loomed before her and soon she was breaking through the clouds. She sensed her body on the beach like a beacon of light beckoning her to return.

A sudden flash of light blinded her, then surrounded her and slowed her descent. Ahead, she could see a faint outline of Kera with her arms raised.

Sally slammed into her body and tumbled across the sand until she came to a stop. She couldn't move as every muscle in her body seared with pain.

Eventually, she sat up and was met with a disapproving glare from Kera.

The woman spoke with her white dress swirling around her. "This gift, or curse of yours, the one you proclaim to have such control over, is it customary for you to go tumbling across the ground every time you merge back into your body? Is this your special technique? If so, I am not impressed to say the least."

Sally shook her head. "This has never happened to me before. I'm always in control. I can slip out of my body and come back without so much as a shudder. Then I came to Perihelion and I feel helpless, like I can't do anything right."

"My child," Kera knelt down before her, "you have never really been challenged. You lived such a structured and sheltered life but have since been taken from familiar surroundings and are now out of your realm. For the first time you are being pushed to do things you otherwise would never do. And you have fallen short."

"I've never projected like that before! What do you want from me, you crazy witch!" Sally wailed.

Kera stood and stepped back as her eyes flashed a brilliant white. When she spoke, it was with a voice that sounded like it came from another world. "You will find yourself in a predicament, and soon. One that you will be asked to risk your life for the safety and well-being of others. I hope for their sake you are up to the task."

Sally began to sob.

"Stop the tears! Falling apart like a little girl will not do anyone a shred of good," Kera shouted, then dropped her voice to a whisper. "A friend will find himself lost and alone and thinking that everyone has left him behind. You will be the only one who will be able to find him and bring him back. In doing so, you will not just be saving yourself, but others as well. I hope you find the strength within, for you will be placing your life at risk. I personally don't think you have the courage to do it, but I dare you to prove me wrong."

Kera turned away and walked along the shore toward the rising sun, its fiery crown barely visible above the horizon.

Sally watched her go as she wiped tears from her eyes. She wondered if Kera was right. She never felt so empty inside.

She watched the woman fade in the distance without leaving a single foot print in the sand.

CHAPTER
▼
NINE

OSLO'S EYES FLUTTERED OPEN. He had sat at his desk earlier that evening analyzing the training results for the week. As always, it was an endless mix of bad news and poor performances. His students were not meshing together. Sally and Ray looked down on Breeze as they saw themselves superior to his rural upbringing. If Sally was alone with Breeze they did seem to get along, but as soon as Ray was introduced into the mix she morphed into a creature that wanted to please and cater to his every need. Breeze to her was practically out of sight and out of mind.

He had also spoken to Kera about her impromptu evening training session with Sally on the beach.

"She wilted under pressure," she said, "but I shall endeavor to continue her training personally, regardless if she's awake or asleep."

Later, Excort wandered into his office as he always did by seldom knocking to announce his presence. The dwarf climbed up into a plush chair that fronted the desk and stared hard at Oslo with his giant un-blinking eyes. "So, how is the future super army coming along?"

Oslo slapped a report he was reading onto his desk and took off his reading glasses. "Why say it like that? What are you implying?"

"This is going nowhere, Oslo, and you know it. All of this," Excort waved his hand in a sweeping gesture, "is over. Let it go. We had our day in the sun."

"First of all, there is no army. They are my students. They are here to learn, not to go to war. Second, don't ever say to me again that it's over. You have been negative and unsupportive ever since I reopened Perihelion. What is it with you anyway? I imagined of all people, you would be the happiest to see this place bustling with activity again, *ja*?"

"Activity? You have a school with three students and two instructors.

Your students don't want to be here, and one of your instructors is like a ghost. Where is Kera half the time anyways?"

Oslo rubbed his temple. "My students are not here against their will. They were brought here with full consent of their parents—"

"Oslo, they were *dumped* here like baggage! What kind of parents just send their children off to a far off school without even inspecting the place? You come back to the island with urgent instructions to re-activate Perihelion. I don't question you, I just figure you have some experiment you want to work on. You then bombard my wife and I with your ideas of opening the base to accept students. Before we know it, Sally and Ray arrive, followed by Breeze. Would you care to tell me what exactly is your plan is regarding them? Do you even have one?"

Oslo pounded his fist on the desk. "Let me remind you; they are here to learn about their gifts—"

"No, they are not! You want to start a war—"

"If you would please stop interrupting me, I could better explain—"

"The past is the past. Let it go!"

Oslo stood up with his fists tightly clenched. His eyes were wide and his voice trembled when he spoke. "The past is the future. What has happened before will happen again. This time, I will be ready."

Escort stood up. "You've finally said something that makes sense." He turned and walked away. "Yes, I'm being facetious," he called out as he left the office.

Oslo sat back down and did his best to compose himself. He was not used to displays of emotion. He picked up his reports and stared at them with dull eyes. He could feel himself fading as papers fell out of his hands when he leaned back in his chair.

He opened his eyes and was greeted by the morning light streaming through the windows. He had slept at his desk all through the night. He stood up abruptly and straightened his jacket, severely annoyed with himself. Routine was something he liked and stuck to it like a clock. Going to bed at a certain time and getting up at the crack of dawn was a ritual for him. But lately, sleep was something he was getting less of, and the strain was showing.

He stepped out onto the balcony. The sea breeze greeted him and helped to clear his head. He looked out across the bay and saw the waters were smooth with a light chop. He gazed toward the marina and saw that Escort had a trimaran repaired and ready for sea trial. Her hulls gleamed as she gently bobbed up and down in the water with a mast that towered into the sky. That's when the idea struck him.

He went back to his desk and activated the intercom, forgetting to clear his throat first. After coughing several times, he excused himself, then announced: "Students, please assemble at the marina after breakfast. That is all."

He settled back into his chair where he caught that gaze of his sailor man lamp that sat perched on his desk. "Well old boy, time to help them get their sea legs," he said to it.

The three students loitered around the docks of the marina waiting for Oslo to arrive.

Ray wiped his brow. "I feel like I'm at summer camp back when I was a kid. Only here it's so much hotter. It feels like the sun has dropped down and it's hanging over our heads!" He looked at Breeze. "But then again, this heat is no big deal for you."

"Yeah, in fact it is. I'm used to a dry heat, not this humidity," Breeze replied and walked away. He wouldn't let Ray's taunts get to him. There was nothing he could ever do to earn Ray's or Sally's respect. They were going to look down on him regardless.

He approached the trimaran that was tied up to the dock. He had never seen anything like it before except in vids and pictures. As much as he loved aerocraft, boats were exotic to him. He would often skip class and hide in the city library in Conception to research everything about them, as he did with so many other subjects that piqued his interests.

The vessel before him had three hulls parallel to each other with six feet of space between them. The center hull was the widest and the outer hulls, called outriggers, were narrow. They provided the vessel with the stability it needed to keep it from heeling over and flipping. Connecting beams ran from the center hull to the outriggers. A trampoline was stretched over the center hull and the outriggers, allowing its crew to easily traverse from one side of the vessel to the other.

"Trimarans are great for speed and they can't be beat. My father has one. He takes Sally and I sailing all the time, it's a blast," Ray said as he stood next to Breeze. "You've never been on one of these I bet."

"Yeah, you're right. Never have." Breeze stepped away.

"It's probably too much excitement for you. Your dad probably doesn't really do anything exciting with you."

"No, not really. He lets me use his air foil to soar up high into the clouds, and then drop down and buzz the mountaintops around our house. No big deal."

"Whatever. You're dealing with the ocean. Big difference. This is my domain," Ray boasted.

"Ray, can't you just back down, even for a minute?" Sally said.

Breeze retorted. "Don't need you to stick up for me, Sally. I can handle this on my own." No sooner did he say the words that he regretted them.

Sally stared at him, and then looked away.

"Sally, what I meant—" Breeze began to say, but she wasn't listening and she went out of her way to ignore him.

"It looks just like your father's boat, doesn't it?" Sally said as she took Ray's hand.

Ray nodded, prattling on about the speed and performance of the vessel. Sally turned to grab a quick look at Breeze, and then returned her attention to Ray.

Oslo arrived with Excort in tow. "Good morning students!" he boomed. "I've assembled you here today to—"

"It's hot out here and it's early in the morning. Can we go back to the dorms?" Sally interrupted as she waved her hand in front of her face in a vain attempt to cool herself.

"Ms. Trumbull, this is a school. Class is in session. Please do not blurt out statements and questions when you feel the need to. Be so kind as to raise a hand, and then wait to be called on. Show some discipline, ja?" Oslo said in a quiet and dignified tone.

Sally sighed, and then raised her hand.

"Ah, Ms. Trumbull. A question?"

"Yes, can we go back inside?"

"No. Now students, pay attention. This school is more than just class work and training sessions. We can actually have fun too."

"Finally!" Sally exclaimed.

"Sally, what did we talk about earlier? About living up to the high standards you were taught at Greenbrier? Was that for nothing?"

"Sorry sir. Won't happen again," Sally said in a hushed tone.

"Don't try to be something that you're not. I know that your session with Kera was a bit unsettling for you. Never mind that. We will sit down later and discuss it further. For now, concentrate on the task at hand."

Sally's face reddened. "How did you know?"

"I'm the headmaster and administrator, I should know what's going on. As I said, we'll talk later. Now," Oslo pointed to the vessel, "this is today's assignment. An exercise in teamwork. An opportunity to mesh together as a team through sailing. A symphony of man and machine working together to tame the elements!"

Excort groaned as Oslo turned to glare at him.

The dwarf looked away and began massaging his back with his hands. "I think I pulled a muscle fixing a generator in one of the electrical buildings. I'm going to the infirmary for some pain relievers. Give me a shout if you need any help. Much later, of course."

"Of course," Oslo responded tersely as he watched Excort leave.

"Very good. Now hopefully without any further interruptions, let us focus on the trimaran." Oslo pointed at the vessel. "Class, let's step aboard and begin your orientation."

They clambered up the portable stairs and onto the deck of the craft. Ray and Sally seemed right at home as they immediately pointed out the various components of the ship.

Breeze climbed aboard and felt a sense of queasiness. The wind was picking up and the boat began to rock up and down from the choppy waters. He grabbed a railing to steady himself.

Oslo smiled at Breeze. "You'll get your sea legs, young man. One day at a time."

"Yes, sir." He gripped the railing a little tighter.

With Ray's help, Oslo demonstrated the basic skills needed to operate the ship. "Breeze, you're the one with virtually no experience in ship handling. Here are the basics; the front of the ship is called the bow—"

"Sir, don't mean to be rude, but I know. The front is called the bow, and the back of the boat," he turned to point "is called the stern. To the right is starboard, the left is port. Don't forget, I came from a town that builds aerocraft. It's the same concept."

Oslo nodded. "Of course you know. What I'm trying to say is that you lack ship handling skills required for watercraft. It will be quite an experience for you. Anyhow, Ray is the designated captain. Obviously his years of experience with sailing makes him the reasonable choice. You two," he pointed at Sally and Breeze, "are the crewmen. Follow his orders, but never forget; you're a team. This will be a great experience for all of you. I just know it."

Oslo closed his eyes and took in a deep breath, then slowly opened them and looked around. "Yes, a good sailing day indeed." He clapped his hand together. "Take your posts!" he called out, and then stepped off the trimaran. He removed the lines from the cleats that held the vessel to the dock and pushed it away.

Breeze and Sally took their respective sides of the trimaran. Breeze was on the port side, Sally on starboard.

Ray had activated the auxiliary engine and was grinning from ear to ear as he stood at the helm, deftly steering the vessel out of the marina.

Breeze watched as Ray skillfully maneuvered past several sunken craft that littered the channel leading to the bay. He admired Ray's confidence as it was something that he had always wanted to do. He looked over at Sally who was gazing at Ray with a smile.

"Feels like we're back home!" Ray called out to her.

She nodded in agreement. Her smile seemed to grow brighter by the moment until she turned and caught Breeze's eye. She frowned and looked away.

Breeze sighed and turned his attention to the horizon. The wind was picking up and the waves were growing in intensity. He could see a storm was brewing on the horizon and he began to wonder why he was even here. The feeling of being out of place grew every day.

The trimaran exited the channel and motored into the bay. Ray barked out commands as Breeze and Sally worked together to unfurl the sails. They pulled lines through shackles and winches that raised the jib, the lead sail located off the bow, which was quickly followed by the raising of the mainsail that trailed behind it and the largest sail on the vessel, up the mast. The sails were bright red with streamers attached to their trailing edge that let the captain know the direction the wind was blowing. The trimaran leaned to starboard as the wind caught the sails and Ray cut the engines. The wind gusted and the trimaran heeled hard to starboard as it sliced through the waves.

Sally and Breeze held onto the railings while they lay on the trampolines as the wind lifted the center hull and port outrigger high into the air.

Ray let out a whoop. "Feels like just home!" he shouted at the top of his lungs.

Breeze looked back at Ray and a feeling of dread come over him as the joy on his face seemed to mask something malevolent. The towering white clouds behind him were swollen with rain and turning darker by the second, framing Ray in a sinister portrait.

They made numerous runs across the bay with each pass growing in speed and intensity. Waves became taller as ferocious winds whipped across the trimaran.

Ray yelled out commands and was oblivious to the deteriorating weather while Sally and Breeze were quickly becoming exhausted as they tried their best to follow his instructions and work the lines. The heat of the sun and the salt spray were quickly taking their toll as they scrambled from one side of the trimaran to the other, and doing their best not to trip, when the sky exploded behind the vessel with a crack of thunder.

They all looked to see an ominous line of clouds rapidly approaching the trimaran as lightning arced through it like a thread that laced them together.

Breeze pointed toward the storm and called out to Ray. "Time to head back, we're pretty exposed out here!"

If Ray heard, he didn't seem to acknowledge or care. He gripped the helm tightly while staring straight ahead, his eyes narrowing as if he was searching for something.

"Ray!" Sally shouted above the roar of the wind. "Let's head back to port. The weather is getting ugly."

Ray waved them off angrily and pointed to a starboard winch. "Tighten up that sail, let's pick up some more speed!"

The trimaran hit a wave that washed over the deck with violent force. Sally was sitting close to the railing and took the brunt of it. She screamed at Ray, but he didn't seem to care, which immediately touched off a shouting match between them.

Breeze watched as they argued. He knew a bad storm when he saw one as dust storms and torrential rain were no strangers to the desert. He couldn't imagine that it would be any different on the ocean.

He headed toward the cockpit where Ray steered the boat, and made the mistake of looking down through the mesh of the trampoline at the fast moving water that flowed past the center hull. He looked away and swallowed his fear, he had to concentrate and get to the cockpit.

As he drew closer to Ray, he knew by the look on his face there would be no reasoning with him. He had seen his father deal with enough pilots to recognize arrogance when it presented itself. They could not be told what to do and were unwilling to accept any meaningful advice, no matter how valuable it was. The need to go faster and higher was a drug that altered their perception of reality and they would not allow anyone to get in their way to acquire it. Breeze saw that in

Ray, with the thousand mile stare on his face, and the white knuckled grip on the helm, oblivious to the danger he was bringing upon himself and others.

Breeze arrived at the cockpit just as the trimaran hit a wave that sent the bow pitching up wildly, then crashing back down with a vicious crack that raised a wall of spray that drenched everyone. The visibility was rapidly dropping as peals of thunder grew in intensity.

"Ray, we have to turn around now! This is getting really bad!" Breeze shouted.

Ray jabbed a finger at him. "Get back to your station! Now! You follow my orders."

Another wave sent the bow of the trimaran high into the air as a sheet of water flooded the deck. Ray laughed maniacally as he leaned over to winch the mainsail in even tighter. He roared in triumph as the vessel heeled hard to starboard, causing the port outrigger to rise up dangerously into the air. At mid-ship along the starboard side, Sally was clutching the trampoline and shrieking in fear as water rushed past her dangling feet.

"Ray, turn back now!" Breeze shouted and lunged to grab the helm.

Ray punched Breeze in the face, sending him sprawling to the deck.

He shook off the sting to his jaw and looked up. Ray was looming over him.

"My ship. My command. My responsibility. Do as you're told and get back to your station!" Ray said menacingly.

"So much for a team building exercise," Breeze quipped as he grabbed a railing and pulled himself back up.

Ray gripped the helm. "Yeah, team building. And I'm the leader. Who else is it going to be?"

The trimaran hit a wave that sent the vessel pitching up to an extreme angle. Breeze could see a wide expanse of the storm filled sky as the mast was virtually parallel to the water. The bow came crashing down hard and plowed into a wave, forcing the stern of the vessel to lift up slightly. The bow quickly rose up after being submerged and the trimaran leveled itself out.

Breeze strained to find Sally amidst the chaos. He could barely make out a silhouette of her sprawled out on the trampoline. The storm had completely enveloped them as lightning grew in intensity accompanied by the booming thunder.

Breeze knew nothing was going to get done unless he took control.

But he wasn't sure of himself as he never steered a sailing craft before and didn't want to get into another fight with Ray over the helm, and there was no radio on board the vessel to call for help. That's when the inspiration hit him.

Jumping out of the cockpit and back onto the trampoline, he picked his way across the cluttered deck toward Sally. Salt spray flew everywhere while the trimaran raced at incredible speeds as the port outrigger rose up to a sharp angle, making it easier for Breeze to slide down to get to her. Over the booming thunder he could hear Ray shouting commands. He ignored him and slid down the trampoline where he found Sally shivering and crying while hanging onto a rope that was meshed into a cleat on the deck with the fast moving water dangerously close to her feet.

"Sally, it's okay, I'm going for help," Breeze said as he crawled to her and pulled her close.

She shivered in his arms. "I don't know what's gotten into him. I'm scared, Breeze. He won't listen."

"I know, I already tried. He's lost it."

Lightning flashed followed by an explosion of thunder. Sally cried out as she buried her face into Breeze's chest. He leaned over to shield her.

"It's going to be okay," he said and cradled her face in his hands, "I'm going to fly back to shore and get Oslo. I'm sure he has another boat to rescue you."

"Don't you leave me!" she wailed. "Take me with you!"

"I can't. I've never flown with someone before. I don't even know if I can take off in this weather."

The bow of the trimaran crashed into another steep wave sending them both sprawling across the trampoline towards the bow. Breeze grabbed Sally's hand as she almost plunged into the fast moving water.

Breeze hauled her close and held her tightly as whatever sore feelings he had for her seemed to melt away.

She threw her arms around him. "Just stay! Don't leave me! Something will rescue us," she said.

No sooner did the words leave her lips, the trimaran smashed into a wave that was too immense for the high speed vessel to cut through. The center hull and the starboard outrigger submerged beneath the water and forced it to flip forward.

They were all flung out of the vessel. Breeze couldn't tell the difference between the sky and the ocean as they flew through the air amidst a tangle of rope and sail. He could hear the hull of the trimaran groaning and the mast cracking from the sudden force of impact.

He hit the water and quickly sank. As he descended into the blackness of the bay, he found himself in world that was eerily quiet and far removed from the flashes and booms of lightning and thunder above.

He looked up and saw the remains of the broken trimaran on the surface briefly illuminated between arcs of lightning. The image of it grew smaller as he sank.

He knew he was drowning, yet he couldn't overcome the sense of tranquility he felt as he drifted to the bottom when the pain in his throat and lungs made him to snap out of his trance. He flailed wildly with his arms and legs as he fought to get to the surface.

He broke through and gasped for air. He treaded water furiously and spun around until he spotted the capsized trimaran. Through the flashes of lightning he saw one of the outriggers jutting out from beneath the surface and swam to it. He grabbed the edge and hauled himself out. Pausing to catch his breath, he looked around hoping to see Sally. Instead, he saw Ray not far from him sprawled out on the remains of the center hull and struggling to breathe.

"Where is she?" he shouted at Ray.

Ray didn't answer. Breeze yelled at him again, only to be drowned out by an explosion of thunder as rain began pouring down in torrential sheets.

He looked around in a panic, hoping to spot Sally anywhere, perhaps clinging to a piece of debris. He saw nothing.

He dove back into the water and swam to the center hull. Scaling up the side, he crawled over to Ray and flipped him over.

"Where is she? Did you see Sally?" Breeze hollered as he shook Ray violently.

Ray looked at him with a faraway stare. Words came out of his mouth, but made no sense.

"Ray, focus! Where is Sally?"

He shook his head slowly. He looked at Breeze, and then turned to survey the wreckage around him. "What happened? We were making such great speed. Everything seemed fine, what went wrong?" he muttered.

"You did," Breeze replied as he flung him back in disgust. He stood up and scanned as far as he could see through the torrential rain. He yelled for Sally in vain as thunder drowned him out and the wind picked up, lashing the wreckage with waves. Lightning was his only ally as it briefly light up the area, giving him the extra distance he needed to see. Still no sign of her.

Terror overwhelmed him as the thought of Sally lying at the bottom of the bay became all too real. He looked down at the shivering lump that was Ray who was rocking back and forth and muttering. He was in shock and of no use.

Breeze crouched down before him. "I'm going to find her. Stay here and don't do anything more stupid than what you've already done. I don't want to have to rescue you, too."

If Ray heard, he didn't acknowledge it as he continued to rock back and forth.

Breeze dove into the water and was enveloped by silence as if he had just stepped off a noisy city street and into a cathedral. The booming thunder was muted and the water was intermittently illuminated by the flashes of lightning. The warm salt water bathed and soothed him, erasing the chill of the rain off his skin.

He swam down as far as he could, hoping to catch a glimpse of her. He could only dive so deep until his lungs began to burn, forcing him back to the surface to gasp for air. He made several more attempts, but to no avail. The weakness that was beginning to overwhelm him cut short every dive he made.

He broke through to the surface after several more attempts and gasped for air as he angrily thrashed at the water. Frustration was mounting, yet he refused to concede defeat.

He treaded water for a while, tiring himself to the point where he didn't realize he was beginning to sink beneath the waves as a sense of calm crawled over him. He looked down and could see the bottom of the bay illuminated from the flashes of lightning. He felt like he was back home in the desert and hovering in the skies over his father's foundry as everything below appeared like a miniature model world.

He glided to the bottom as the sensation that he was flying gave him the courage to push forward. He stretched out his hands and sensed the water pushing against his face and around his body, but he could no longer feel the warmth or wetness of it as a thin membrane had enveloped his body and formed a barrier between him and the water. His lungs didn't ache and he breathed with relative ease.

He flew through the water, struggling not to break the calm and serenity that allowed him to do so, but fully aware he was in a race against time to find Sally.

As he peered through the darkness, he was able to make out various shapes that littered the bottom from the illumination created by bioluminescence, the natural light given off by living things, that emanated from the mounds of coral and the fish that swam around them.

And that's when he spotted a faint glow that surrounded a body lying on the bottom. His heart sank once he realized it was Sally.

The glow that surrounded her was weak and fading. He angled down and in his anxiousness to retrieve her, lost his concentration and rocketed to the bottom. Slamming into the sand, the membrane that surrounded him dissipated and he ingested salt water into his lungs.

Though he was drowning, he refused to head back to the surface without her. He spun around to find her and saw that she was slumped over a rock with blood bubbling out of a gash on her head in tiny drops. Her long hair drifted up and revealed the deathly white skin of her face.

He tried to reach for her, but was too weak. He looked at his hands and saw his own bioluminescence fading. He gazed up at the wreckage of the trimaran above, and then blacked out.

"BREEZE." A deep and disembodied voice called his name as he struggled to fend off the oncoming rush of darkness.

"DEEP INSIDE YOU," the voice continued, "IS WHERE YOU WILL FIND THE STRENGTH AND COURAGE TO CARRY ON WHEN OTHERS CANNOT. SWEEP AWAY YOUR FEARS AND DOUBTS, AND FIND THE INNER CALM. IT IS HERE THAT YOU WILL FIND NO DISTRACTIONS AND NOTHING TO CLOUD YOUR JUDGMENT. IT IS HERE THAT YOU WILL DISCOVER THE ANSWERS YOU SEEK AND THE PATH YOU MUST FOLLOW."

Breeze began to stir as the thin membrane returned. The bitter salt water that filled his lungs flowed out of his mouth and passed through the membrane in a shimmer.

He stood at the bottom of the bay with a sense of calm that filled him completely. He reached down to pick up Sally and gently cradled her in his arms as the membrane stretched out to incorporate her. Immediately, her bioluminescence glowed brighter.

He lifted up and together they rose to the surface. The flashes of lightning above were replaced by a steady glow of searing white light as they drew closer.

Breaking through to the surface, they were greeted by the whine of turbines as a transport hovered over them and the distressed trimaran. The rear cargo door was open, and he watched as Oslo and Excort hauled Ray out of the water on onto the ramp.

Excort spotted Breeze and shouted. Oslo turned to look as Breeze floated above the water and into the transport with Sally in his arms. He collapsed onto the deck as Sally fell away from him.

He crouched on his hands and knees coughing and gasping while Excort scooped up Sally and rushed her to a bench that lined the side of the transport.

Breeze weakly looked up as Oslo kneeled down next to him.

"Sorry about wrecking your boat," Breeze mumbled. He closed his eyes and passed out.

C H A P T E R

▼

T E N

"BREEZE, STEP OUTSIDE," A soft, feminine voice whispered into his ear.

Breeze sat up and looked around his room to find the source of the voice. Several days had passed since the trimaran mishap. Training sessions were put on hold as Oslo, Excort, and Kera tended to Sally's injuries.

Breeze hardly ever saw Ray. There were a few times he saw him wandering the campus grounds alone, sometimes walking erratically or mumbling aloud. Upon seeing Breeze, he turned around and disappeared around the corner of a building, or ducked into a darkened corridor.

Breeze spent the next several days hanging around and watching the RF in the hangars repair aerocraft as he always did on his down time between classes and training. It helped to alleviate the boredom and to learn more about the strange flying machines while escaping from the rays of the sun. To him, the summer humidity was unbearable and the heat was intense. He was used to desert heat, but the humidity of the tropics left him weak and exhausted.

But tonight he woke up with a strong and compelling feeling to go out into the breezeway. Though the whisper sounded like Sally, he knew she was in the medical wing of the campus and Oslo had restricted access to her. He wasn't sure if she had been released yet.

He hastily put on his jacket and pants, stuffed his feet into boots and stepped out.

There, framed in the moonlight and against a backdrop of brilliant stars, was Sally.

She rushed to him and planted a kiss on his lips, then hugged him tightly.

"Thank you," she said.

Breeze was too stunned to say anything and didn't want to let her go, but she abruptly stepped back and folded her arms across her chest.

"Are you...okay?" Was all he could think to say.

She sniffed and nodded while looking down at the limestone floor. "Good. I'm good. Just never had the chance to thank you for rescuing me. Oslo told me everything. About Ray losing it and flipping the boat, that I sank to the bottom and you dove down to find me. You of all people," she looked up and smiled, "the guy from the desert who supposedly can't swim."

"Yeah, that's me, full of surprises," he said as nonchalantly as he could. "It got a little crazy out there, but I did what I had to do. No big deal." He casually looked away.

She leaned in and caressed his shoulder. "Well, thank you again. Have you seen Ray? I'm really worried about him."

Hearing those words made his ego deflate. Whenever he thought of Ray, the image of him on the trimaran with the maniacal look on his face was the only thing he saw. Sally asking for his whereabouts was like a knife to the heart.

He tried to be stoic. "Not really. He's been avoiding me the past couple of days. Doesn't seem to want to talk. Why do you ask?" *He almost killed you!* He almost shouted at her.

"Just want to know what he's up to. I can't seem to find him and he's not in his room."

"How do you know, did you knock?"

"No, just projected inside and looked. That's how I woke you up," she said with a roll of her eyes. "Look, I wanted to tell you in person that I'm leaving. That's why I need to find Ray. I want him to go home with me."

Breeze felt his legs buckle. He let out a sharp breath as if he was just kicked in the stomach. "Leave? Why?"

"I'm sorry, but are you awake? Have you been here the past couple of weeks? I came here for a summer session because my parents wanted me to. And it's been horrible!" she hissed.

Breeze walked over to the balcony railing and leaned against it, then looked back at Sally, who stared at him like she was expecting an answer. He didn't know what to say to her, so he started rambling. "Well, we are here to learn more about our powers. I know I could use more control over my flight."

She stomped up to him. "Have you learned anything new? Are you flying better? Take off for me right now without hesitation. Show me what you can do. Come on, show me!"

Breeze leaned back with a sheepish grin. "Sally, come on, you know I'm not as good as you or Ray—"

"Exactly. So what are you doing here? Better yet, what are *Ray and I* doing here?"

The question felt like a stab into his back. "Sally, what are you trying to say?"

"Oh, Breeze, stop it with the nice guy act. It's not getting you anywhere." She turned her back on him and looked down the hallway.

He was grateful she wasn't looking as he leaned against the railing and trembled like he had just been kicked in the gut.

She whirled around. "What is Oslo doing putting someone less proficient like you with Ray and me? What was he trying to prove? I'm going to tell you something; we're being kept here on purpose. I don't know why, I just do."

"Sally, we're here to learn, and..." sensing how feeble his words sounded made him trail off into silence.

If she noticed, she didn't seem to care. "Have you spoken to your father?"

Breeze shook his head.

"Well, I haven't heard from my parents. And Oslo keeps saying the comms are down for repairs. That was weeks ago!" she shouted. "We're just being kept here. I feel like...I'm in storage." She looked around with a look of disdain on her face.

"I sort of like it here," Breeze said. "It's different for me. I never really been anywhere, until now. Yeah, it's pretty humid here and the bugs are something else. But for me, it's a chance to get away from home."

"You don't like your parents, is that it?" Sally said as she put her hair into a ponytail.

Breeze was stunned at how beautiful her face was with her hair pulled back that it took a moment for the question to sink in. "Parent. My mother died a while back. I'm the only child. I told you this, remember?"

Sally tilted her head back and sighed. "Sorry, I didn't mean it that way. But come on Breeze, we're from different worlds. Ray and I have so much to go back to. But you're just passing the time before you have to go back to that place you call home. Where are you from again?"

Breeze shook his head. "Sally, I told you. I'm from a town called Conception."

She snapped her fingers. "That's it. I kept on thinking it was called Contraption or something like that. I can't believe I was going to go back home and tell all my friends about you, and I can't even get the name of your town right!"

"You must have a lot of friends. I mean, you know a lot of people."

She looked at him suspiciously. "Of course, why would you ask?"

"No reason."

"Oh, come on, of course you do. Let me guess; there's a girl back home waiting for you, but you feel a little guilty about it because of the way you feel about me. Is that it?" she said with a smile and wink.

He looked away from her. "No. I mean yes. I mean-what makes you think I like you?"

She laughed. "Oh, Breeze, you're so cute. Come on, it's so obvious." She sighed as she put her hands on her hips. "You're a really good friend. You know that right?"

Breeze stared at her. He didn't what to say. The only thing he could hear in his head was the sound of a door slamming shut.

"Well, I don't know about you, but I want to go look for Ray. Are you coming?" Sally said as she straightened her jacket and pulled up the zipper.

He blurted out. "You know there is someone else here. A girl. She seems pretty young."

"Oh sweetie, are you talking about your first day here, when you almost drowned and you said you saw some little mermaid who rescued you? That was a good story. But my advice? Keep it to yourself. It sounds a little weird."

"Sally, I'm not joking. She's for real."

She patted his face. "Okay. Sure. I believe you. Just don't tell your girlfriend back home about her."

"I don't have, I mean—"

"Shhh, it's okay. You don't have to explain. Are you coming or not?" She held out a hand to him.

He ignored it as he felt his skin burn and was grateful for the faint moonlight. He could only imagine how red his face was. "Let's go this way. While you were in Medical, I wandered around the grounds. I saw him lurking round the Science and Engineering building. Let's go there first," he said

"Okay" she replied.

They walked the length of the breezeway and down the crumbling limestone steps, and then strode across the grounds as the rising moon lighted their way across the courtyard and to the boulevard that ran the length of the campus. They went past empty buildings that appeared as silent and brooding hulks that lined either side of the boulevard with heavy ficus obscuring their entrances.

Breeze felt his hand being squeezed. He turned and Sally was holding his hand and walking next to him. He smiled, and then forced himself to sober up. *Stop grinning like a fool. Just a friend, remember?*

The Science and Engineering building was just ahead on their left. The building stood out from the others with its immense size. Interior lights filtered through the misty windows, and it didn't have as much vegetation growing around it, giving the impression that it was somewhat maintained.

They climbed up the steps and saw the heavy metal doors were slightly ajar.

Sally pulled her hand away from him. "Let's go, I don't like it here," she said with a shiver. "Maybe Ray is someplace else."

Breeze sighed. "Sure, let's go check the other buildings. You know, cut away the jungle that's grown around them. That would be easier."

"Don't be mean. That's not you." She swatted his shoulder.

He pushed against the door and it groaned and creaked loudly, creating an echo that reverberated deep into the building. "Well, so much for the silent approach. Ladies first?"

She shot him an icy look and stepped inside.

He followed right behind her and was hit by the smell of mildew mixed with ozone. *Electrical equipment,* he thought to himself, *and lots of it. But where?*

Sally covered her face with her hand. "What is that smell?"

"Electrically charged air. I'm used to it. We get that a lot at my father's foundry. We use powerful electrical discharges when purifying metal that can also burn the air. I'm just not used to the smell of mildew added to it."

"Don't know what you're talking about." She stared at him blankly.

"It doesn't matter." He began exploring the room as the light bulbs haphazardly strung up overhead provided meager lighting, but it was enough to see huge machines that were covered in tarps and plastic. He grabbed an end of a tarp closest to him and gave it a hard yank. It fell away to reveal an oversized piece of electronic equipment with gauges and dials on it. Once again, he was hit by the feeling of seeing machinery far more advanced than what he was used to, yet it all looked so old in appearance.

"What is that thing?" Sally asked. She hugged herself tightly while looking around nervously.

"Can't say. I just know," he said, as he ripped off another tarp that exposed an even more bizarre machine, "is that everything I see here is pretty different than what I'm used to."

They walked aimlessly through the rows of machines. Most of them were covered, some partially exposed. They came to the end of a row and stood before a hallway that ran perpendicular to them. They leaned in and looked down either side as a row of exposed bulbs strung overhead lit the entire hallway.

"You're telling me you've seen Ray come in here? I wonder what he's up to," Sally mused.

She was answered by the sudden and abrupt hum of electrical machinery kicking into action. On the wall across from them, a lighted panel appeared and was ticking off a series of numbers when the screen displayed the letter, "L", and a sliding door opened before them.

Ray stepped out into the hallway, lost in thought and oblivious to their presence.

It was Sally's voice that broke his trance. "Raymond Verhesen! What on earth are you doing?"

Ray let out a yelp as he stumbled back.

Sally stepped toward him. "What are you up to? Why didn't you come visit me in Medical? I couldn't stop thinking about you."

Ray rubbed his face and his eyes looked like he had been awakened from a deep sleep. "I was just looking around. Got bored, you know," he said with a shrug.

"Without Breeze? All by yourself?" Sally placed a hand on his chest. "He tells me you've been avoiding him these last couple of days."

Ray looked down at her hand in surprise, and then shot a glare at Breeze. "Yeah. Guess after the trimaran accident I kind of wanted to keep to myself."

"You had no one to talk to?" She gazed at him with soft eyes.

"Well, you know, it was hard to see you. Oslo restricted access while you were in Medical."

"Could you lie to me and say that you tried?"

Ray held her hand. "Sally, I'm sorry about everything and I promise it won't happen again. I'll do better next time, you'll see."

She beamed at him. "I know you will!" she said and threw her arms around his neck and hugged him tightly.

Breeze stood dumfounded while Ray snuck a look at his crestfallen face and winked at him.

Breeze sighed and turned away. He wasn't sure what was worse; seeing Sally behave this way around him, or not being thanked by Ray for saving her. He was beginning to wonder what was preventing him from wanting to leave Perihelion.

He left the couple behind and went to the next row of machines, where he found one whose tarp was off and was humming with electrical power. Breeze strode over to get a closer look at it and saw several of its vid-screens were on and displaying data. He crouched down to get a better look, and then took hold of a joystick that protruded from a panel and began scrolling through the data.

With a flash, the screens changed and began displaying maps of continents as areas of interest were highlighted with pulsating circles. He could see his hometown in the Desert Country was lighted, along with other locations through the Pacific Northwest, the North Eastern Territories, and a triangle over the island of Perihelion. He looked up at the top of the screen and recognized coordinates and transmission frequencies. Growing up in a scrap yard made him very familiar with navigational equipment that was salvaged from various aerocraft.

"Comm transmitter and diagnostics. What else could this be?" he muttered to himself. Oslo had said the comm units were down and still in repair, but they appeared operational.

He toggled the joystick to highlight his home in Conception, then pulled out a sliding keyboard and typed in his comm number to contact his father when he felt a presence looming over him.

Ray was standing behind him with Sally loitering in the background.

"What are you doing?" Ray said sharply.

Breeze stood up. "Good question. Found this machine running while you two were getting friendly again. Turns out it's a comm unit and it's been activated, so I decided to give my father a call over the frequencies."

Ray looked over Breeze's shoulder to view the screen. A series of numbers were rapidly scrolling across it and he began to shift his feet nervously.

Breeze turned to look back, then immediately crouched down to get a better look. The screen was scrolling as it shifted away from his hometown and drifted to the east, then north, where it zeroed in on a location in the North Eastern Territories, when the screen suddenly went blank and the hum of electricity was silenced.

Breeze shot up and was greeted by the sight of Ray holding up a cable from the back of the machine.

"Sorry, technical malfunction." He grinned.

Breeze lunged and shoved him, sending Ray falling into another machine. He hit it hard and cried out as he fell over and the tarp covering the machine came down with him.

"What's the matter with you?" Breeze stood over Ray and roared.

Ray looked at him with seething rage. "Who do you think you are? How dare you push me—"

"Stop it! Both of you!" Sally shoved Breeze aside and knelt down to check on Ray.

He pushed her away. "I'm fine. There is nothing this desert rat could do to hurt me. He just doesn't know what he's in for."

Sally put a hand up to his face. "Stop it!" She shook her head. "Sometimes Raymond, I feel I don't know you anymore."

She turned to address Breeze, but he had stepped away and stood before another comm unit that was active.

Ray scrambled to his feet and lunged for the power cable that ran from the comm unit to a receptacle on the structural support next to it.

Breeze caught the motion from the corner of his eye. He spun around and grabbed Ray by his jacket collar and flung him into another machine.

Ray scrambled back to his feet and confronted Breeze with glowing fists.

"Do you really want to start a fight with me?" Ray growled.

Breeze wasn't intimidated by his words. The trimaran accident proved to him that Ray was full of bluster and a bit of a coward. But the maniacal look in his eyes did concern him. It was the same look he'd had when he was steering the trimaran during the storm. To Breeze, it seemed as if Ray became a completely different person during times of high stress. He has seen this back home with test pilots who couldn't handle the high level of danger they faced every day. Life on the edge made them morph into men made of stone with ice flowing through their veins. But other pilots would crack under the pressure and become almost diabolical in the way they behaved toward others. Veteran pilots would believe in superstitions that claimed these men had picked up a passenger while flying through a storm cloud. He was beginning to wonder if the superstition were true and something similar happened to Ray on the trimaran.

Breeze pointed a finger at him. "Don't know what your problem is with me. And I really don't know why you've been running around and avoiding me these past couple of weeks. But I aim to find out what you're doing skulking around here at night. Why did you cut the power to the comm unit I was using? And what were you doing in that elevator shaft?"

Ray raised his fists as they crackled with energy.

Sally boldly stepped in front of him. "Answer him."

"Get out of the way!" he shouted.

She took a step closer. "You're acting like a madman. This is how you sent me to the bottom of the bay to drown, and it was Breeze, not you, who rescued me. Ray, you were always so sweet with me. Ever since we were little you would always hover around and protect me. Are you going to hurt me again?"

Ray's breathing became ragged as his shoulders slumped forward. He lowered his hands and the glow dissipated. "No Sally, I won't hurt you."

She reached out and touched his face. "What were you doing in the elevator shaft?"

He looked at her with red and swollen eyes as his heavy breathing subsided to a wheeze. "Found something below. Something weird. Didn't want to tell you guys about it just yet because, you know, the sailing accident." He took Sally's hand from his face and squeezed it. "I was pretty torn up about everything. Felt like I had to prove myself and try to do something right."

Breeze snorted, prompting Sally to shoot him a nasty look, and then turned back to Ray. "Ignore him. What else did you want to say?"

He pulled her close. "Just that everything I did almost made me lose you. I knew the very next day after the accident what we needed to do. We need to leave this place. It's no good for us. Not being able to contact our parents is strange and this school feels more like a lonely outpost. This whole place is weird."

Sally nodded as he spoke.

Bolstered by her compliance, he then addressed Breeze. "I can't speak for you, but I know Sally and I need to go. I've been avoiding you because I thought you would try to sabotage me."

Breeze was stunned by the statement. "Me? Sabotage you?"

"Yeah, exactly. Look, let's be honest; we don't really like each other so I just struck out on my own. I wanted to explore and try to find out what it is about this place that makes me feel crazy sometimes. I figured if I asked you for help, you would laugh at me, or worse, go running to Oslo and say something."

"Ray you're rambling. What are you getting at?" Breeze said.

"I'm looking for a way to get out of here."

Breeze stared at him. "Then just go. Ask Oslo for a transport and leave. Why would he keep you here?"

"Because he wouldn't understand! He would say no and tell me to stay here until the end of summer."

Breeze arched an eyebrow. "Did you ask him?"

"No-, I mean yes. I...don't try to trick me!"

Breeze sighed. "If you were so eager to leave, you could have at any time. Instead, you've been running around this place like a ghost doing who knows what. And you still haven't answered the question. What were you doing in that elevator shaft?"

Sally whimpered as Ray squeezed her hand tightly.

"Why do you keep asking me that? What do you care what I was doing?" Ray said.

"Look, if you want to get off this rock, the hangars are that way." Breeze jerked a thumb to his left. "I've been spending my time hanging around there and trying to get the RF to acknowledge me so I can ask them about the aerocraft they're fixing. Instead, all I get is stares from those robots as they step away to avoid me, and yet never once did I see you down there trying to get into an aerocraft. If you want to leave, that's the place to be. Not here, unless you're trying to contact somebody. Since you don't want to tell me what's going on, I'll just go to the elevator and find out myself." Breeze broke away from them and strode down the aisle toward the hallway.

"No!" Ray shouted and ran after him.

Breeze didn't look back as he started to sprint and the faster he ran the more it felt like his feet were lifting off the ground.

He burst into the hallway and smashed into the wall next to the elevator. He stumbled back amidst the dust and debris from the shattered wall and was stunned that he felt no pain.

He heard the sound of running footsteps and turned to see Ray racing toward him with Sally close behind. He lunged to push the call button for the elevator when Ray grabbed him and shoved him away. As Breeze fell back, he managed to grab Ray's hands, pivot on his heel and send Ray sprawling to the floor.

The elevator chimed and the door slid open. Breeze quickly stepped inside just as Sally arrived.

"I can't take it with you two fighting all the time-oh!" She began to chastise them when Breeze grabbed her hand and yanked her into the elevator. The door slid shut and they could hear Ray yelling and banging on the door as the elevator descended.

"Why are we going down? Let's go back!" Sally was frantic.

"There's no panel to choose a floor. It just seems to run on auto. And no, I'm not going back up for him. He's a jerk and I don't know what you see in that guy."

"Breeze, he's my friend. I've known him since we were kids."

"Right. Everyone is your friend. Got it."

"What are you talking about?"

Breeze didn't answer as the elevator slowed to a halt and the door slid open. They both stepped out and were immediately enveloped by the sound of electrical machinery humming like a swarm of bees as the cavernous room was filled with a greenish glow. It reminded him of the night when the transport delivered him to Perihelion by entering the vortex, and his thoughts turned briefly to Vermillion and Horton and wondered where the two recruiters were.

His musings were interrupted when Sally gripped his arm.

"What is this place?" She looked around wide eyed. "I don't like it. Let's go."

"No, you go. I need to know what Ray found down here." He broke away from her and began exploring.

She stood and sulked, expecting him to turn around and come back for her. Seeing his determination, she relented and ran after him. "Don't leave me alone!" she wailed.

He held out a hand. "Then come with me already."

She hesitated, and then took it and together they walked from one console to another as they marveled at the dizzying array of work stations that were spread out across the room. At the far end was a wall with metal panels partitioned into equal segments.

Breeze pointed at them. "Everything you see here is for whatever is behind those steel panels."

Sally shrunk back and looked toward the elevator. "Let's go," she whispered.

Breeze ignored her and strode toward one of the metal panels to rap his knuckles on it. "Yep, solid steel."

"Let's go," Sally said a little louder.

He ignored her as he scanned the entire expanse of metal paneling and noted how both ends curved into the walls. Breeze took a step back and followed the steel paneling up to the rocky ceiling and saw how it also curved into the rock.

Rock, he thought to himself, *how deep down are we?*

His train of thought was broken by a sound coming from a console before him. He leaned forward and the vid-screen came alive as undecipherable numbers and equations appeared. He pulled back a metal chair that was attached to it on a swing arm and sat down. The moment he did, the entire console lit up and a deep rumble emanated from the ground below. He felt a tiny hand grab his shoulder and turned to look. It was Sally. Her face was contorted in fear. "I'm scared, let's go," she said.

Breeze nodded. "All right. Just let me—"

Before he could say another word, the console curved around them forming a circle, then rose into the air as free floating platform.

Sally gripped his shoulders and dug her fingernails into his skin. Breeze grimaced and reached up to grab her hands when the expanse of metal paneling on the wall lowered into the ground, revealing a dimly lit chamber. The console platform lurched forward into the chamber as the green glow throughout the room became even more pronounced.

"Breeze?" Sally whispered.

Her voice was faint and weak, and when he turned to look at her, she had deathly white skin and her eyes were fluttering rapidly.

He shot up and grabbed her before she fell to the floor of the platform. He lowered her into the chair he had been sitting in and patted her face when her eyes opened suddenly.

"Get me out of here," she said with a trembling voice.

He nodded. "I'm working on it."

No sooner were the words out of his mouth than the platform tilted into a steep incline, and the green glow became brighter as the platform rushed deeper into the chamber before stopping just a few feet above an iron tube. The deep rumbling from below settled into a vibration that shook the building as chips of stone broke off the ceiling and pelted them. The quaking abruptly ceased, but was followed by the sound of static filling the air.

Breeze leaned over the console to get a better look at the tube. It was in an inclined position and underneath he could see wiring and cabling snaking away from it and into a row of metal cabinets filled with electronic equipment. Breeze looked up saw how the chamber was shaped like a dome with its peak containing a crystalline structure embedded into it.

He felt fingernails digging into his arm and he turned to see Sally pointing weakly in front of her. The iron tube opened lengthwise as both halves rotated down to reveal a man reclined in a metallic chair. His entire body was strapped in a stainless steel mesh that kept him firmly in place. His eyes were closed.

Sally looked away and covered her face. "Make him go away!" she cried out.

Breeze desperately searched for a lever or a joystick, anything that would let him retract the platform out of the chamber when he succumbed to the urge to look at the man.

He was of medium build with dark hair, and as Breeze squinted, he could see his chest gently rising up and down.

Several vid-screens flickered to life around him displaying vital sign readings. He concentrated on a screen that showed heart rate. It was faint, but beating.

The sound of static became overwhelming. Breeze turned to look at Sally, who was beginning to fade into a mirage.

Breeze yelled but couldn't hear himself. He smashed the console with his fists as he frantically looked for anything that would bring this horror show to an end. He saw a panel to his left with a symbol that contained a circle with several arrows emanating from it. He hit it with his hand and the panel sprung open, revealing an oversized joystick with a pistol grip. He grabbed it and yanked back. The platform responded with a lurch and began to retract.

The man in the chair writhed and convulsed when his eyes fluttered open, revealing glowing orbs that pulsated.

Breeze grabbed the joystick with both hands and pulled back with all his strength. He turned to look at Sally who was slumped in her seat and fading away as her body began to dematerialize.

Never should have brought her with me. I do nothing but make mistakes with her.

He looked behind to see how much progress they were making. They were almost out of the chamber when the platform shuddered violently, and then came to a stop and the static subsided. Breeze looked again at Sally and was shocked to see a woman in a flowing white dress standing next to her. She pointed at Breeze and spoke directly into his mind.

"Don't stop, keep retracting back," he heard her say.

Breeze nodded, too startled by what he was witnessing to argue. He grabbed the joystick and threw his weight back. The platform shuddered as electrical motors whined in protest.

The static returned with a roar as the platform was pulled back into the chamber by an unseen force. Breeze yelled as he strained to counteract it by pulling back with all his might.

He looked again at Sally and the woman. Sally was disappearing before his eyes as the woman in white looked on in dismay, when she suddenly flew off the platform and descended to the man in the chair. She hovered above him with her arms outstretched and threw back her head. Her flowing white dress swirled around her as the crystalline structure embedded in the peak of the dome struck her with a brilliant light. Her body convulsed as she brought her hands together and pointed them at the man. His body shimmered and writhed in response as the iron tube closed around him like a clam shell. The woman turned and faced Breeze. Her face was twisted in pain as she pointed at him.

The platform shook violently, and then retracted out of the chamber. It moved slowly at first, then with a mighty heave, slid back out as the steel panels rose up to seal the chamber. The sound of metal hitting metal echoed loudly as the hiss of static faded away.

Breeze toggled the joystick, but it didn't respond. The platform was on full auto.

He let go of it and crawled over to Sally. She appeared solid, but he grabbed her hand to verify it. Her skin was cold as she lay slumped forward in the chair.

The platform settled back down with a thump as the console straightened itself out. The green glow subsided around them.

He touched Sally's face. It was like ice.

He grabbed her and slung her over his shoulder, then stepped off the platform and headed to the elevator when Ray stepped out from behind a piece of equipment and stood in his way.

"What did you do to her?" he said.

Breeze took a step back. "What did I do? Better yet, what the hell were you doing down here? This place is like a chamber that leads to hell." He tightened his grip around Sally, determined not to let Ray get his hands on her.

He took a step towards Breeze with his hands outstretched. "Give her to me, I don't trust you. You've been acting strange lately." Ray spoke with a slow, drawn out voice.

Breeze sidestepped him, keeping one eye on the elevator and the other on Ray. "I'm the weirdo here? Yeah, maybe I was the outsider when I first got here. But you're the one who's gone off the deep end. Hell, I had to go and dive into the deep end of the bay just to save your girlfriend from you. And you're the one calling me strange?" Breeze thought about how his father would talk his way out of a fight with an aggressive and hostile scrap scavenger trying to sell him a load of metal mixed with plastic. Breeze never saw his father armed with a weapon, yet he would marvel at how he would walk away from what could have been an explosive confrontation.

Breeze kept sidestepping toward the elevator when Ray began to convulse. When it ended, he rubbed his eyes and gazed at Breeze innocently. "Breeze, what's going on? What happened?"

Breeze saw the opportunity for escape and bolted for the elevator. He pushed the call button and the door slid open. "Don't know, but we can talk about it topside," he said as he stepped inside.

He heard Ray's voice waver between confusion and anger as the elevator door shut. He let out a sigh of relief and dropped to his knees. He touched Sally's back and was relieved she was still breathing.

The elevator stopped and the door opened as Breeze leapt out. He jogged out of the hallway, through the long aisle of machines, and out into the humid night.

He ran down the steps and onto the boulevard. The full moon lit up the landscape letting each building cast long shadows onto it.

He gently laid Sally down and sat next to her. He patted her cheeks and felt her pulse. Her skin was feeling warmer to the touch.

He looked back at the Science and Engineering Building when he felt a tremor. It was followed by a green effervescence that simmered up from the ground and into the air.

The sound of heavy doors banging open shattered the stillness of the night as Ray came tumbling out of the building.

"Breeze, wait!" He bounded down the steps and ran over to them.

Breeze stood up and held his ground, placing himself directly before Sally.

Ray came to a stop just a few feet from them. He leaned forward with his hands on his knees for support and breathed heavily. "This humidity is something, huh? I could never get used to it."

Breeze said nothing as he stared him down.

Ray waved a hand. "Look, forget about what happened back there. Truth is I can explain it all."

"You can try."

Ray nodded as he looked upon Breeze's stoic face. "Okay, I know I've been acting weird lately. Just after the accident-after what I did to Sally—"

"After what you did to both of us. Going maniac and leaving us stranded on a boat in the middle of a major tropical storm," Breeze interjected.

Ray raised a hand in acknowledgment. "Right. Got me there. After what I did to both of you. Satisfied?"

"I could care less. But are you?"

Ray stumbled back. Breeze was always like a wallflower to him. He wasn't used to seeing him this assertive.

"Fair enough," Ray said softly, and then cleared his throat. "After the accident, I got to thinking. Why are we here? What's the point of all this? I just feel like we're in limbo, you know what I mean? Like we're just sitting around waiting for something to happen. Are you with me on this Breeze?"

"Sally said pretty much the same thing to me earlier," Breeze replied with a shrug of his shoulders. Once again, he thought to himself, it paid to watch and observe his father when he was negotiating. When Jacob would catch a scrap seller in a lie, the seller, desperate to make a deal, would try to placate him by smiling and talking like they were old friends. Jacob wouldn't buy it, but was smart enough to let the man save face. Breeze knew he had to do the same thing to get Ray to divulge more.

"Yeah, Ray, I'm with you. We're teammates, remember?"

Ray's face lit up. "Right! We're a team, we can talk about anything." He slapped his knee and laughed.

Breeze struggled to keep from grimacing in disgust. He reminded himself that Sally needed to be protected. "Exactly. Look, I'm sorry that Sally and I confronted you like we did. I'll take the fault for that. That's what happens when you let a woman talk you into something.

I wanted to leave you alone and let you do your thing, but she insisted that we follow you around. You know how it is; pretty face, soft eyes. What's a guy to do?"

Ray was grinning from ear to ear. "You're right, girls can do that to a guy." He leaned over to look past Breeze. "Is she okay?"

Breeze nodded. "Yeah, she's good. Just got a little fright from what we saw below, but she'll pull through. She better 'cause I'm not carrying her back to the dorms."

Ray laughed and Breeze did his best to laugh along with him.

"I'm glad we got that worked out," Breeze said. "Let's just make it a point to work with each other from now on. Agreed?"

Ray nodded vigorously. "Yep, good call." He then pointed at Breeze. "You go first; what did you see below?" Ray's face changed slightly as he visibly became anxious.

Breeze saw how uncomfortable he was, but didn't want him to get distracted. He told Ray everything about what he and Sally experienced in the chamber. Everything but the Woman in White. He felt that was a playing card he was going to keep for himself.

Ray nodded solemnly. "I'm sorry you had to see that. But that's exactly why I was trying to keep you two from going any further into the building!"

Breeze could feel the agitation emanating from Ray. He needed to diffuse him, and quickly. "You're right and I'm sorry. Like I said; it's no excuse on my part for following a female and letting her lead. You're the leader here with the military background, not me."

Ray tilted his head. "Yeah, you're right," he said with a smile. "So did this man in the chamber say anything to you?"

"Not really. In fact, I could barely even see him."

"You sure?"

"Yes." Breeze could hear the irritation in his own voice. He tried again. "Yeah, Ray, I'm telling you the truth. Look, I messed up. I brought Sally down there and I shouldn't have. The only thing I wanted to do was to get her out of there once I did. You were right all along. We should've...I should've listened to you. Man to man. I get it. Won't happen again."

Ray was nodding, but his eyes were glazing over. "Yep. You get it now, Breeze. You know, I take back some of the things I said about you. You're going to make a great addition to my team." He stiffened. "I'm mean, you know, this team we have here."

Breeze quickly jumped in. "I know what you mean. When the other students arrive, you can be team leader, and I can be your second-in-command. Assuming anyone else gets here. You know Oslo, promises, promises."

They both laughed.

Amidst the laughter and joking around, Sally began to stir.

"What's going on?" She looked dazed as she rubbed her forehead.

Breeze kneeled down and reached for her hand, then stopped. He looked at Ray and waved him over. "She's going to need someone she trusts right now." He gritted his teeth as he spoke the words.

Ray quickly strode over and grabbed her hands. "Sally, it's me." She smiled. "Breeze?"

He grimaced, and then looked at Breeze with a pained expression.

Breeze shook his head and patted Ray on the back. "She's a girl. She's doesn't know any better."

Ray nodded. "Right. That's right." He tried again. "It's me, Ray. Are you all right?"

Sally's eyes opened wide as she yanked back her hands. "Jerk! What's the matter with you?!"

Ray was visibly hurt. He turned to Breeze with a plea for help in his eyes.

Breeze held up a hand in a calming gesture. "Let me handle this."

He patted Sally on her shoulders. "Sally, Ray was the one who got us out of this jam. Not me." He took a quick look at Ray and winked. Ray's mouth was wide open.

Breeze continued. "Yeah, it was wrong of me to drag you down there. Thankfully, Ray showed up and saved us. He shut down the platform and got it to retract. He's the one to thank."

Sally scrambled to her feet. "No, that's not what I remember." She fixed her ponytail and straightened her jacket. The moon cast a spotlight on her as she pointed at Breeze. "You activated something down there. I remember we got off the elevator and walked into a chamber...," she paused as she tried to engage her foggy memory, "...and stepped onto some type of platform that lifted up, and-," she gasped as she put her hands to her mouth and shook her head.

Ray took a hesitant step toward her, and then touched her shoulder.

She slapped it away in disgust. "There was a man inside some sort of a metal tube. It opened up. There was green light everywhere. And I..." She turned to Breeze.

183

He spoke up. "You started to disappear and I panicked. I tried to find something to shut it down. I found a control system and I—"

"—started to retract us out of the chamber," she finished for him. Her eyes were wide and shined like orbs. "And that's when that man in the chair called out to me."

Ray was shivering. "What did he say?"

Sally's head whipped in his direction. "He-," she shook her head and stood silent for a moment before continuing, "—he wanted to tell me a story."

She turned to Breeze. "He told me his name was Bram and that he was sent on a mission long ago. He was to head out into the depths of space with nothing more than the power of his mind to propel him."

Breeze took her hands in his as she stepped closer to him and continued. "He said he was looking for a way back home and that he was lost and lonely. He had spent an eternity trying to find the trail of light he left behind to lead him back, but it had faded after being away for so long. We were the first two souls he had seen and that he had very little of his soul left in his body. He can still sense it, but can't find a way back to it." Sally trembled as she bit her lower lip.

"What else?" Ray whispered.

She didn't look at him as her eyes stayed focused on Breeze. "He wanted to know if we could help him. I told him we could try. I don't even know why I said that, but I just felt so warm and comfortable speaking to him. It was as if all my worries and troubles were fading away and I didn't have to be responsible for anything anymore. I could be free." Tears rolled down her eyes. "So I tried. And that's when I felt myself letting go. As if I were..."

"...fading away," Breeze finished for her. "I saw what happened. You were barely visible, like a ghost. I panicked because I knew it was my fault for bringing you down there. I was responsible for you and I failed."

She shook her head. "No. Bram kept saying that it was okay for me to let go. I felt myself drawn to him. And then she appeared."

"The Woman in White," Breeze said.

"Who?" Ray leaned in closer.

Sally swallowed hard and wiped tears from her face. "Kera. Her name is Kera."

Breeze squeezed her hand. "What else, Sally?"

"She burst in like a flash of brilliant light and told him to stop. She stood between us and he became agitated, and for some reason he kept calling her Raza and asking why he had been abandoned and how come they didn't come looking for him. She kept repeating 'Until the half made of light arrives, you will never be whole.'" Sally looked at Breeze with dismay.

Breeze shook his head. "I couldn't even tell you what that means and I don't even know who this Kera woman is, or why this Bram guy mistook her for someone named Raza."

"She's one of the instructors here."

"Oh?" Breeze and Ray said in unison.

She told them about her experience with Kera on the beach and how she projected out into space and back.

Breeze was stunned. "Okay. So there are other instructors around here, not just Oslo. She shows up and gives you a midnight lesson. As if this place couldn't get any weirder."

Sally nodded. "She made it a point to tell me that a time would come when a friend would need my help, and I wouldn't be ready. That's how I felt with Bram. It was like I had known him for a long time and he felt familiar to me. That's why I didn't hesitate to reach out to him, though I could still feel the sting of Kera's words in my mind, and that I would fail when the moment arrived. I didn't want that to be true and I was so eager to help. That's when Kera showed up."

She closed her eyes and brought his hand to her chest. "She shouted at me to leave, telling me this was not the time. She looked so frightened. I never saw a face with that much fear in it as she pushed me back. Then," she cocked her head slightly as her eyes fluttered open, "I just remember her shouting at someone."

Breeze nodded. "I saw her hovering over you and she told me to get us both out. I wasn't going to argue. Then she waved her hand at us and I felt the whole platform get shoved out of the chamber. I looked at you and you were whole again, but your skin was ice cold." Breeze patted her hands.

She smiled. "Once again, you saved me. I need to thank you." She leaned in and gave him a kiss on the cheek. She lingered for a moment, and then pulled away.

Breeze felt his face burn red and he hoped that the moonlight wouldn't give him away.

Ray spoke up. "But it was Breeze's fault for bringing you down there."

She turned to him. "No. I could have left anytime, but I didn't. I was just as curious as him, and I needed to know more about what's going on around here. The more I see, the less I like it. I want to leave."

Ray smiled.

Breeze was stunned. "Sally, I know this place is not exactly the greatest, but—"

"But what Breeze?" She pulled her hands away from him. "Don't put your head back in the sand. I know you and Oslo are close, but I don't know why you would be loyal to him. What has he done for you? Remember what I said to you earlier? Have you really learned anything since you arrived? Do you feel more confident with your powers?"

I was starting to feel more confident with you, he almost said. "I guess not. I mean...not really sure."

She sighed in disgust and turned to Ray. "I want to go."

He immediately stepped up and took her hand. She didn't resist.

"The best thing I've heard in a long time," Ray said as he pulled her away from Breeze and walked down the boulevard with Sally in tow.

Breeze threw his arms up. "Wait a minute, it can't end this way. Not after everything we saw."

Sally whirled on him. "Why don't you want to go home? Is it because you have nothing to go back to?"

Breeze felt the elation he experienced from her kiss fade to despair. "Sally, why would you say something like that?"

"Are you happy here? Wake up, this is a scam! Our parents were talked into sending us here, but for what? Nothing happens! Where are the other students? The other instructors? I mean, look around you. This place is a tomb!"

Breeze took a halfhearted look around. She was right. He thought he was coming here to learn something and to see new things. Instead, he felt he more miserable here than at home. It was time to call it quits.

"Okay, what's your plan?" Breeze said as he stuffed his hands into his jacket's pockets.

Ray nodded. "Okay partner, good thinking. I have a plan, and you can help us."

Sally looked at Ray with admiration as he spoke.

Breeze could see just how beautiful she was in the moonlight, and then shook his head. *Get over yourself.* "What do you want me to do, Ray?"

Sally jumped in. "Don't let him help us, he might run to Oslo and say something."

Ray put a hand up to silence her, then faced Breeze. "You say you spent some time at the hangars watching those robots work on the aerocraft, could you get them to prep one to take us back home?"

Breeze took a long hard look at Ray. "Yeah, I could try, but I could do you one better."

"Oh?" Ray smiled.

An hour later, the trio were in a hover that Breeze commandeered from the motor pool next to the hangars. He piloted it through the palm forest first before bursting out onto the wide open tarmac of the landing facility where he whooshed by row upon row of old and dilapidated transports until he brought the hover to a stop.

He jumped out and the others followed him as he walked up to one transport in particular. "When I first arrived here, I saw these ships from the air spread out on the tarmac. Then we landed and I was really dizzy along with the feeling that I'd seen these types before, but couldn't remember. Turns out I was right. We have similar ones piled up in our scrap yard back home. Those use air turbines, but these," he pointed at the transport before him, "are different. They're using the same hover tech you find with everything else around here. Oslo probably uses these for the recruiters to travel around and bring people and supplies here. It would be easy for me to jump inside and look at the avionics in the cockpit. I'm betting they're pre-programmed to fly in and out of this place on auto pilot."

Sally spoke up. "What about that fog you told me about? You said this place is covered by something that makes it hard to find."

"So you really don't remember coming here at all?"

"Breeze, I told you, Ray and I fell asleep on the way here and woke up as we were landing. You told me you passed through some kind of tunnel before you passed out. Is that going to happen again? Can we make it out of here?"

"I wouldn't worry about that," Ray said.

Breeze arched an eyebrow at him. "What do you mean?"

Ray grinned. "Well, you know I've been a real pain about wanting to get in contact with my father."

Breeze rolled his eyes. "It seems like that was your big thing. Yeah, couldn't forget it."

Ray ignored him and turned to Sally. "So I've been poking around in the Science and Engineering Building and was able figure out why we couldn't get a signal out to the mainland. The fog that Breeze mentioned to you; he wasn't kidding. It really exists and it interferes with the signal."

Sally looked at him blankly. "So this means...?"

Ray sighed. "C'mon Sally, it's so obvious." He cupped his hands. "Picture my hands as a bowl." He then inverted his hands. "Now we put a lid on the bowl. Lid off, you can send signals anywhere. Lid on, no signal, no outside contact. It's that simple."

She sighed with exasperation. "Raymond Verhesen, I just want to leave this place and go home to see my parents and sleep in my own bed. I'm not asking for much." Her voice dropped to a whisper. "I'm very tired. I've dealt with too much weirdness. And that man in the chamber," she shuddered with her eyes closed, "is something I want to get very far away from." When her eyes opened, they shined fiercely. "So please, get to the point," she said and placed her hands on his chest. "How do we get out of here?"

The words tumbled out of Ray's mouth. "I found a control room. It controls the shielding around this island. I figured out how to drop it, and then I sent a signal to my father that I'm coming home. It will make it very easy for us to leave. Hell, it makes it easy for anyone to find this place," he said with a sly grin, then quickly sobered up.

Sally smiled. "The greatest news I've heard in a long time." She swiveled toward Breeze. "Will you be a sweetie and help us get off this rock?" she said and batted her eyes at him.

Breeze nodded. "Yeah, sure, just one thing though. Ray, what do you mean you told your father you're coming home? You came here with Sally, were you planning on leaving without her? And why the rush to leave? I thought your father and Oslo were on the level, you know, on the same team?"

Ray shifted his weight looked away. "Breeze, look, you wouldn't understand. For you," he waved his hand, "all of this is a really big deal. It's your first time far away from home and you get to feel a little bit special being here. But things are not really going your way, yet you don't want this to end too soon. For Sally and me," he shrugged, "this is not for us. Greenbrier is our school and we were doing just fine there. Whatever was going on that made our parents send us here for the summer seems to have been a misunderstanding. My father told me so in a message he sent back. I just didn't want to say anything to you, because, well, I feel kind of sorry for you." He held up his hands. "Look, don't take that as an insult, but we have nothing in common with you. This was all just a big mistake and it's time to call it quits." He clamped a hand on Breeze's shoulder. "Come on, you told me you were a team player," he said with a grin, "so are you going to help us get a ship?"

Breeze brushed the hand off his shoulder. "You know, you don't have to be so condescending. I'm not dumb, I know when I'm being talked down to."

"C'mon Breeze, don't be like that. We're friends here!" Ray's grin seemed to widen by the second.

Breeze looked away. He was getting the same feeling from Ray just before the sailing accident. He knew better than to escalate the situation.

He walked to the stern of the ship, then opened a panel cover under the hull and flipped a switch. The sound of hydraulics whining pierced the humid night air as a cargo ramp lowered from the aft section.

"Follow me," Breeze said and stepped up the ramp and into the transport.

Ray gestured toward Sally. "Ladies first."

She shook her head and crossed her arms. "You don't have to be such a jerk about things. Can't you just be a little more subtle?"

"Sally, don't be like that. I'm getting us out of this place, am I not?"

"Yes. Finally." She stepped up the ramp.

Ray took a few steps up, then stopped and looked behind him. Satisfied, he turned and disappeared into the ship.

A woman in a white flowing dress materialized where the three once stood. She looked down at the tarmac where she could still see the heat of their footprints leading up to the ship. She looked up at the star filled sky and scanned the heavens, then turned her gaze to the campus off in the distance. She placed her hands to her chest and disappeared.

Inside the transport, Breeze was sitting in the pilot's seat and explaining the ship's systems while Ray stood behind him and listened. "From what I've been able to pick up watching the RF work, this screen right here," Breeze tapped it with his finger, and it immediately came alive with a series of numbers and symbols scrolling across, "is where you input your destination. This is the same transport you two arrived in, so reversing the coordinates is easy." He punched in a series of codes onto a keypad and the screen bleeped, and then went dark.

Ray barked out. "What's the matter with it? Are you doing this right—"

Breeze held up a hand. "Relax, it has to digest the data before it can plot your route. Hold onto to your pants already."

Ray gripped the headrest of Breeze's seat. When the screen came alive again, he relaxed.

Breeze pointed at it. "There, now you're set." He swiveled to look Ray in the eye. "And don't touch anything. You think you know a lot about aerocraft and boats, but you really don't. Just let the ship fly itself."

Ray gritted his teeth and seethed. "Fine, got it. You need to get your last digs in on me before we leave. But are you sure you did this right?"

Breeze shrugged. "Just don't touch anything. I'm going to say goodbye to Sally." He marched out of the pilot house and down the short steps that led directly into the passenger cabin.

Sally was sitting in a window seat on the starboard side of the ship. She was unfolding some blankets she found in the storage bins above when she saw Breeze coming down the aisle.

Breeze stopped at her row. "Well, goodbye for now?"

She turned to look at him with a forced smile. "Yes, I suppose. Are you going to stay here or...?" she said weakly while trying to hide her lack of interest.

The ship shuddered as the engines began to spool up. Breeze saw Ray exit the pilot house and head toward them down the aisle. Sally smiled upon seeing him.

Breeze knew when he wasn't wanted, and didn't need to see anymore body language from Sally to sense otherwise. "Guess I'll go home, too. I'm going to stop by Oslo's office later this morning to let him know what happened. It's the least we...I can do."

She looked up at him. "Sure, you do that," she said, then turned her head slightly away. "Good luck to you, Breeze. I really do hope things go well for you. We'll try to stay in touch?"

Breeze grunted and turned to look out the stern cargo ramp where he could see the sun beginning to rise.

"Safe journey, Sally." He walked away.

He shook his head as he marched down the ramp and onto the tarmac. *Safe journey? Couldn't think of anything better to say?*

Sally twisted in her seat and watched him fade from view, then started to get up when Ray arrived.

"What's his hurry, he's that eager to get home? Well, can't say I blame him. Doesn't really fit in anywhere I bet," he said as he plopped down into the seat next to her. "Where are you going? Did you forget something?"

She looked at him, then back towards the ramp. "No. I mean, yes. We never did pack our things from our room—"

"Forget about it. My father will just have Oslo ship it all back to us. Sit down and put on your harness, the ship is about to lift off."

"Why the rush, Raymond Verhesen?" She only called him by his full name when she wanted to get the truth out of him.

But Ray was aware of this and would use it to his advantage. "Do you really want to stick around any longer after what we've been through?"

She shook her head meekly. "No, not really," she said and looked down at her hands on her lap.

"Exactly. So let's just go." He put a finger under her chin and gently raised it so her eyes were level with his. "Trust me."

She smiled faintly, and then looked back at the cargo ramp as it sealed shut.

"You're not thinking about Breeze, are you?" he asked earnestly.

"No, of course not," she said.

He closed his eyes as his head sunk into the headrest. "Good. Real good. It's going to be nice to be rid of him and get back home. Things will be so much better." He reached over and squeezed her hand.

They felt cold to her. "Of course." She forced another smile as she settled back into her seat and looked out the window.

The transport lifted off and drifted across the tarmac for a moment, when a sudden surge from the engines sent the ship hurtling into the sky and through the red stained clouds colored by the rising sun.

CHAPTER

▼

ELEVEN

BREEZE BROUGHT THE HOVER to a stop and turned to watch the transport carrying Ray and Sally lift off into the morning sky, keeping his eyes on it until it disappeared into the red tinted clouds. Far off to the west, he could see a thick line of thunderstorms brewing over the ocean.

He settled back into his seat, threw the gear lever into drive and sped off. He grinned as he thought about the role reversal he was experiencing. When he arrived first at Perihelion, it was Excort doing the driving as he fearfully sat in the passenger seat as they sped through the palm forest. Now, he was calmly piloting a hover without a care in the world after helping fellow students leave without permission. *I'm a bad guy now, I suppose.*

He whisked through the palm forest and never once did he flinch as the trees bent themselves to make way. He burst out of the forest and onto the main boulevard, gliding the vehicle to a stop in front of the dormitories.

He leapt out and bounded up the steps and into the building. He walked past the coral pool in the rotunda and headed straight down the breezeway to his room where Kera and Oslo, along with Excort, were standing outside his door.

"Breeze!" Oslo strode over with gigantic steps and loomed over him. "Explain yourself young man, what has transpired?"

"We're leaving," he said as he sidestepped him and reached for the door handle.

"Wait!" Oslo called out.

He felt a hand on his shoulder and he whipped around to confront the tall man. "I'm not really sure what sort of plans you had for us. We've been here for weeks and nothing has happened. Sally just said something to me earlier about you that got me thinking. She said that you're keeping us in storage. For what, I don't know, but ever since we arrived here, we've had nothing but strange experience after strange experience. Toss in the fact that one of us almost got killed. Twice." He flung open his door and stepped inside where he grabbed his backpack and began stuffing it with his meager possessions.

Kera stood outside with Excort as Oslo stepped in.

"A little privacy please?" Breeze said.

Oslo ignored him. "Excort came rushing into my office, and told me that the fog has been lowered, and that a transport departed soon after. I became alarmed and immediately searched the grounds for all of you. Now, Kera tells me she watched as you helped your fellow students abscond with a ship. Is this true?"

Breeze pointed at Kera out in the hallway. "Well, ask her yourself. If she saw it, why didn't she try to stop us?"

Kera glided into the room with her white dress swirling around her.

Breeze stepped back as she came to a stop before him.

"It was for the best. This charade must come to an end before any more harm befalls us," Kera said as she stared at Breeze for a moment, then turned to Oslo.

Oslo gently took her hands, which made her body crackle with energy for a brief second. "My dear lady, what are you trying to say?"

"Let them fly away, Ole Auken, it is for the best." She place a hand over his heart. "You know this to be true."

"No!" he roared as he threw her hands off and the room trembled.

Breeze inched back toward his backpack, and then continued packing with great haste.

"It was not supposed to be this way." Oslo said. "I made a promise to their parents to guarantee their safety, and that I would not let them be taken by the Elephim like they did in the past. Not again."

"My dear man, wake up. This is a fight you must walk away from. Take your daughter—" she shook her head, "—take Nina with you and go to Raza. Be whole again. Let the inevitable take place."

Breeze stopped packing. "Is Nina that girl I saw when I first came here?"

Oslo and Kera both turned to face him.

He immediately regretted speaking up. "Forget it, I could care less. I have enough problems at home and I don't need any more." He slung his backpack over his shoulder. "I don't know what this place is supposed to be about. I just know I'm going home. I shouldn't have let my father talk me into this."

He brushed past the two instructors and out into the breezeway.

Excort was standing by the door and glared at him as he stepped out of his room. "How did you manage to drop the fog?"

Breeze shrugged. "I didn't. Go ask Ray, he figured it out. Oh, wait, he's gone. Guess you can't."

He marched away, only stopping when Oslo called out to him.

"Breeze, just a moment. Give me chance to clarify."

Breeze pivoted around and strode up to him. "What is there to say? This isn't a school and you are no instructor. That Kera lady over there? Don't have a clue as to what she's supposed to be about. And that?" He pointed at Excort. "Never saw a dwarf before. Let alone one that looks like that even in a storybook."

Excort snarled at him.

Oslo held up a hand. "Please, there has been enough backbiting and dissent already, *ja?* I shall take the blame for everything, just allow me to explain." There was a sense of desperation in his voice as he spoke.

Breeze shrugged. "There's not much more to say. You falsely told our parents that we were going to spend a summer session here to learn more about our powers. Instead, you had us fixing up this old and crappy place and doing training exercises that led to nothing. And the question that has been bothering us all? Where are the other students?"

Oslo nodded. "Yes, yes. All good questions, and reasonable concerns that I have been remiss in addressing."

"Okay, now you got my attention," Breeze said sarcastically as he folded his arms across his chest.

"My recruiters—" Oslo began.

"Vermillion and Horton? Yeah, whatever happened to those clowns?"

Oslo ignored his comment. "My recruiters seem to have been...out of contact for quite some time and I have not been able to reach them. Though, I do believe I will be hearing from them soon."

"Right, the same way we couldn't reach our parents over the comms because of this fog thing you have over the island. Well, now that Ray seems to have figured out a way to drop it, I suppose you can talk to them again."

Oslo's face turned red, and when he spoke, it was in a soft, but earnest voice. "How exactly did all of this come about?"

"Well, since you have no control around here, Ray seems to have been wandering about and poking his nose inside every building here. Maybe you thought we were too dumb to go around and explore this place, but we have. I've spent a lot of time around the hangars looking at the aerocraft and robot mechanics you call the RF. Robot mechanics! We don't have anything like that back home, and I don't think there is any place like this in the world even though everything looks so old. As for Ray? Well, I guess he got what he wanted. He's been trying to reach his father ever since he got here and found a way to do that. That Science and Engineering Building by the way? Loaded with all kinds of machines. Oh, and there's some guy named Bram living inside a tube in the basement. Can you explain that away?"

Oslo and Kera became visibly agitated at the mention of the name. Kera glided up to Oslo's side and hovered next to him.

"Tell me young man, what did you see?" Oslo's voice was like a whisper.

Breeze told him of his encounter with Bram.

Oslo turned to Kera. "Why didn't you tell me this before? You were down there with them? You were observing the whole time? You only told me you saw them departing Perihelion, and no more."

"I did not wish to alarm you further." She placed a hand on his shoulder and drew him closer. "We have spoken about his before, my dear man. I have always been an unwilling participant in all of this. I told you from the very beginning not to bring them here, and to keep this forsaken island closed and hidden from prying eyes. I have also been encouraging you since they arrived to send them back home, that no good would come from this. There are things on this island that were placed here for a reason because most could not handle the truth if they discovered the true nature of it all."

Oslo grabbed her by the shoulders. "I brought them here for a good reason, so do not try undermine my decisions, woman. I went out of my way to retrieve Sally for you as I thought that would at least make you happy."

She resonated as her body became translucent and she broke free from his grip, and then hovered before him as ghostly mirage. "I do not need to be close to her in order to observe her. Wherever she may be, I merely have to close my eyes and she is there. Bringing her here has caused greater calamity and increased the risks of being discovered. *By them*." She finished her words with a hiss as she pointed at the sky.

Oslo groaned. "How many times must I say this? They are dormant.

They no longer rule the skies like they once did—"

"Then explain your urgency in scouring the world for them." She pointed at Breeze. "If you no longer live in fear of those above, then why the mad rush to recruit, no," she said with a sick smile, "to save and shelter as many of these paranormal children as possible? Don't bother to answer, I will. Because they are back, sweeping this planet from one continent to the next and taking those they deem valuable and eliminating the rest. You and I both know this."

Oslo put a hand up to her. "Rest your tongue, woman."

Kera materialized to swat his hand away. "I will even say their name. The Elephim."

Oslo took a step towards her, and she shrunk back.

"Yes, Oslo, that very name. The one you dread to hear. They are back. They are burning cities again, are they not? Just like in the past."

"I thought I was helping by bringing them here to give us a chance to reclaim the world again for ourselves," Oslo said as he loomed over her. "I also thought I was doing you a favor bringing her to you and creating an opportunity to secure a legacy."

"Sally and I may be alike, but as I told you, I can guide her no matter where she is."

"No!" he roared. "Foolish woman, do you think they do not have ways to block your access to her?"

"I am prepared for whatever they may throw my way and willing to accept the consequences. Are you?" She shimmered brightly and floated closer to him. "You should have let sleeping dogs lie. But no, you had to stir the hornets' nest. We all could have faded quietly into the night, but you just can't give up the past, can you, my dear Ole?"

"When you call me by that name, I know it's just your way of getting under my skin."

"I'm reminding you that even in the past, you were never really accepted here, no matter what you did with Raza and Bram. Even now, you are still an outsider on this empty relic of an island. Go back to Scandinavia. Better yet, take Nina with you to Appalachia. You will find safety there, or at least closure and peace of mind. Keep your promise you made to Raza and make her whole again."

Breeze heard enough. "Can't say I understand anything you two are talking about. But I'm smart enough to realize that it's pretty serious. I'm going now," he said and turned his back to them.

Oslo stood before him. "Breeze, wait. Just hear me out, *ja?*" Oslo said as placed his hands on Breeze's shoulders.

Breeze was too stunned by how quickly Oslo moved to resist.

"I have kept much from you and from the others as well, but for good reason. I now realize the error of my ways. If only I had conveyed to all of you the sense of urgency in my mission, then perhaps things would not have turned out this way. But you are all that I have left. I beg you young man, listen to me now."

Breeze nodded.

"Long ago," he sighed, "very long ago, I too, arrived here much like you, a fish out of water. This place, as I imagine you have surmised for yourself, is no school. It was an outpost. A military outpost. The last of its kind in a world that was dwindling into mediocrity and eventually, destruction. I came here as a raw recruit with gifts I did not quite understand, much like yourself. I would rise up through the ranks and into the Military Science Battalion. It was there that I would meet Raza, who became my wife, and Bram, the man who became my best friend."

He relaxed his grip on Breeze. "It was in that very building the three of us began to unravel the mystery of the hidden forces that were sowing the seeds of dissent and destruction throughout the planet, and across to her far flung colonies on other worlds."

Breeze spoke up. "When you talk about colonies, you mean space travel?"

Oslo smiled broadly. "Yes, son. Yes. It was a magnificent time. An age of heroes!"

Breeze laughed. "Space travel isn't possible. It's a myth. The best we can do today is just fly through the atmosphere. Nothing else."

"It is there you are wrong, young man. It was a gilded age, where anything was possible. I should know. I lived it. You must believe me."

"You lost me with the space travel thing. That's how I know you're insane. It's not possible." He brushed Oslo aside and resumed his march to the stairs.

"Did you not see anything here at all that piqued your curiosity? Or are you truly the lowly son of a scrap metal hoarder?"

Breeze came to a sudden stop upon hearing those words. He was tempted to turn around and say something, then continued on his way.

"March away, young man, off to obscurity and insignificance, much like the rest of the world. No hope. No future. No dreams. Just emptiness."

Breeze whipped around. "What do you want from me, old man?

Why do you keep saying these things?"

"After all you have witnessed, are you still asleep?" Oslo said. He was framed against the encroaching morning light with Kera in her flowing white dress beside him. Excort stood off to the side.

The three of them were not that strange to him. Seeing the dregs of the desert come to his father's scrap yard allowed him to witness the sad and dark underbelly of the world with its maddening poverty, the hopelessness, and the wasted lives. A world where Nomadic people aimlessly wandered the desert searching for scraps to sell to his father so they could feed their children.

It dawned on him that the three individuals he was staring at came from a different time. They had lived longer than most men ever have. Far longer. He didn't know how he realized this, it just came to him. Like a thread that unravels from a sweater and reveals the flesh that it was trying to hide.

He strode over and dropped his backpack at their feet. "I came here because my father said it would give me chance to see more of the world, and that I would get the training to better control my powers. Well, I can say that I've definitely seen a lot, and that you guys aren't really instructors now, are you?"

"My, the brilliance that spills forth from this one. Please, Oslo, send him on his way before he dazzles us with more, for I fear we could not bear it," Kera retorted.

Oslo raised the back of his hand to her face, and then addressed Breeze. "I promise that if you stay, I will focus everything that I have, all of the resources at my disposal, to teach you how to master your flying abilities. But son, you can do so much more than fly. Surely you understand this?"

Breeze shrugged. "I just know I never get hurt. If I slam into the ground or into the side of a mountain, I leave a crater behind. What if I could learn how to fly better, then what? I go back home to the scrap yard and do what? Enter in the air shows and get paid to be a freak? I've got enough problems as it is, I really don't need anymore. You said it yourself, I'm the lowly son of a scrap metal hoarder."

Oslo shook his head violently. "No, I take it all back. I had to say something to get your attention."

"Such a brilliant tactician," Kera murmured.

Oslo shot her an angry look.

Kera rolled her eyes and turned away.

He turned back to Breeze. "Please, don't give up on me like the others. Be different. Stay the course. Give me time."

"Time for what?" Breeze stood up to the towering man and looked straight into his eyes. "What do you want from me?"

Oslo started to speak, and then stopped. He became flustered and he turned to Kera.

She blinked at him. "Oh, my counsel you now seek? Very well. Tell us, Oslo, we stand here before you as a captive audience. Regale us, what *do you want* from them?"

Oslo's face turned red and his breathing became labored.

"Stop that," Kera said. "You always had such legendary difficulties telling people what you want. Is it safe to say that's almost how you lost Raza?"

His eyes went wide as he glared at her.

"Oh my, hit a nerve, did I? Turn your wrath away from me. I did not start this, you did. Tell Breeze of your grand mission, and let us see if it can withstand the trial of a young man's judgment."

Oslo closed his eyes tightly and clenched his fists.

Kera cackled. "Not so easy now, is it. You accuse me of hiding from the world on this island? Turn the mirror upon yourself. Crisscrossing the globe on your sailing vessel, while avoiding Elephim to find the children of gods long perished. To raise an army to march against those who have put this planet in shackles. Tell him. Tell him everything. What is there for you to lose? It appears you are down to just one recruit. And not much of one, from where I'm standing. What will he do, crash into his opponents? Brilliant strategy, yes?"

When Oslo opened his eyes, they glowed. He looked down at Breeze, and then dropped to one knee. "Kera, in her usual acidic way, is quite right. The truth never should have been shielded from your eyes." He swallowed hard as he took in a deep breath. "I had decided to recruit the paranormal children of the world. To create and train a fighting force, to hone their skills and help them rediscover the glory of Earth from the past. To destroy an enemy that resides above and have driven us into these dark times we live in today."

Breeze nodded his head. "Okay, now I'm really leaving."

Kera clapped her hands slowly. "Fantastic salesmanship. Pure gold."

Oslo ignored her. "Breeze, I know your father. He is capable of doing fantastic things with metal. All sorts of things. He's more than just a dealer of scrap metal. He is a creator and a fabricator."

"My father? Are you serious? What has he created? I haven't seen anything."

Oslo smiled and pointed. "You."

"Me? Are you kidding? He ignores me most of the time and acts embarrassed when he does pay attention to me."

"Breeze, all things happen for a reason. There is no such thing as coincidence." Oslo stood up and straightened his jacket. "There is so much to tell you. So much to learn. If only you would give me the time."

Breeze picked up his backpack. "Well, you had plenty of time. If you just told us this earlier, who knows, we might have listened and just gone along for the entertainment. But now, no."

"Breeze, there are others like you. You are not alone. You will be tempted to use your gifts in front of the ignorant masses. They will hunt you down and destroy you. They will not stand by and tolerate something they do not understand. They live in a fog of ignorance and poverty. Their hatred of themselves is far more powerful than the hatred they feel towards others. But they will take it out on those like you. Please, I implore you. Stay."

"Nah, I'll take my chances. Back home I can just keep flying around in the desert at night. Nobody has ever bothered me there."

"And what happened when you flew out of your little world and into another? Did you not tell me your tale of flying into the Bad Lands and not realizing it? And what of the strange howling creature that you encountered at the lake, or the elderly couple who helped you get home? Did their story not pique your curiosity?"

Breeze slung his backpack over his shoulder. "Oslo, just tell me about that Bram guy you have in that creepy basement. That's what I really want to know before I leave."

"Bram was a good friend. A friend I lost to what I believe was a worthy cause. Together with my wife, Raza, we engaged in what we thought was a grand experiment, which turned into a noble failure."

The blue color of his eyes faded as he stood up and walked to the balcony railing. "We came up with a plan. It was simple at first. Bram was a first rate projector, one of unlimited potential. Far greater than anything Sally has demonstrated to you. With a thought, Bram could step outside his corporeal body and fly through the air and to the stars themselves. His ability also let him see into the souls of others, to the point where it almost drove him mad. He marveled at the human capacity for duplicity as he saw how their thoughts never quite matched the words they spoke." He chuckled. "I suppose if he was here right now, he would say the same about me." His tone grew somber. "I came up with a plan to use the power of a projection device I designed and fabricated along with a robot assistant of mine. A device that would allow him to travel into the far reaches of the universe. That contraption you saw him inside of was a vehicle, but not the sort that you would travel with. This one tapped into the depths of the earth, drawing forth the vast reservoir of electromagnetic energy from the core and redirecting it through his body. Bram would step into the tube, or "The Chair," as we would fondly refer to it, and use the extra boost of energy to project out into the vast depths of space."

"Why?" Breeze asked.

Oslo turned to face him with an arched eyebrow. "Good question. We had always suspected that what ailed our world was something so sinister, that its face could not be seen. Like the wind, you could see its effects, but can you really grasp the wind? Bram and I had a theory. If he could find a way to project backwards and forwards in time and observe, what would he see?"

Breeze shrugged. "Who cares? Look, if this guy was a time traveler, why not just change the past?"

Oslo shook his head. "You must learn to listen, and not speak when a story of this magnitude is being told. Attention to detail is everything in life. The most minor of mistakes can cause mishaps that reverberate throughout the fabric of time. But I will answer your question. Bram could only observe what was happening, but could not affect it. He would return to his body, often drained and exhausted, and would tell us everything he saw. We began to put together a picture of a past that showed the footprints of a shadow society that was eating away at the heart of our own. It didn't use force. It didn't use weapons. Their methods were very simple and effective. They used us."

Breeze sighed. "I don't understand what you're trying to tell me."

Oslo nodded. "Most don't. When one thinks of revolutions, you picture weaponry and bloodshed. You imagine quick victories and the toppling of governments. The oppressed masses are now the victors. Peace and prosperity reigns throughout the land. No, it was not like that. This revolution took a very long time. It was planned out well in advance and would take centuries to see it through. But in the end, victory was achieved. And it was done without them firing a single shot and not one bit of destruction came directly from their hands, but through surrogates and useful idiots who aided and abetted them. The people, over time, just gave up, and handed their freedom over to them."

"Them?"

"The Elephim," Oslo said.

"By the thousands," Kera whispered.

Breeze looked at her with a blank stare.

She continued. "By the thousands they would come together and undermine the very society that they swore to protect and defend. They would sow the seeds of dissent and bring the world that nurtured and created them to its knees."

Oslo strode over and stood next to her. "Kera is referring to the name of the shadow group," he declared.

"The Elephim?" Breeze said.

"The name is derived from an ancient language no longer spoken but by only a few who study the old ways. The Elephim came from all segments of society. But the common thread they shared is that they were like us. Paranormal. You see, Earth of the past was guarded and served by the Helios. Think of them as paranormal sentinels. They were the noble warriors that were Earth's champions. I am proud to say I was able to meet the remaining few, until a new government regime put them into... retirement. Never to serve Earth again."

Oslo stroked his chin as he looked toward the ocean. "The Elephim showed themselves to the world once their grip on the levers of government was complete. They would use paranormals at their disposal to enforce their regime and the population never resisted. The Helios who did continue to fight were hunted down and destroyed."

Breeze backed away slowly.

"Your recruiting skills are lacking, my dear Oslo, look how he shrinks away," Kera said and pointed at Breeze.

"He asked for the truth. He is now receiving it. It is up to him to choose his reaction. If he runs, so be it. Outrunning the truth is no different than trying to outrun death. We all succumb to it," Oslo replied.

Breeze held up hand. "Your story sounds great. Really does. But if you're trying to get me to join up for some sort of a...super team of sorts, to do who knows what, forget about it. Suddenly, life back home isn't so bad."

Oslo chucked. "After listening to myself tell the tale, I would be forced to agree with you. Not a pleasant picture did I paint for you. But then again, reality is never really pleasant. One must fight to create a better life, as there will always be those in the shadows so eager and willing to tear it down."

Breeze jerked a thumb toward the stairs. "Look, your story sounds great but this school of yours, whatever. And the crazy man in the basement, not so great. You brought us here to put together a team of teenagers to fight some invisible enemy. I can see why you held out on us for so long. I don't blame Sally and Ray for taking off. I guess I should follow their lead. I'm out of here." He turned and walked down the steps.

"Breeze, please. There is so much more," Oslo called out.

Kera grabbed his hands. "It's over, my good man. Let it go. Let's not make any more trouble than what has already been created."

He wrenched his hands away from her. "You don't understand, Kera. I have nothing left to go on if he leaves."

"No, you have Nina. You always have. Don't make the same mistake I made by turning your back on your child. Better to die together, than apart."

Breeze dashed down the steps and toward the hangars. He had an eye for a sleek sliver of a ship he saw the RF repairing from when he first arrived and checked upon its progress periodically over the weeks. It was jet black with a tinted canopy. It seated one comfortably, with a just enough space behind the pilot's seat for storage.

He arrived at the hangars and slipped underneath a partially raised vertical door.

Oslo stood before him. "Breeze, please. Hear me out."

"How do you do that?" Breeze jumped back with a startle. "I mean seriously. I'm running all the time like a maniac and you just show up out of nowhere."

"Young man, what I can do, you are capable of so much more. Paul, listen to my words. Stay. Give me a chance. I have failed you, this I know, but let me at least balance the scales."

"No one calls me by that name. I don't know why you would think using it would make me listen any more than what I already have."

Oslo raised his hands. "Forgiveness, and there is much of it I need. Breeze, I have lived for so long and to the point where I can barely keep track of my memories. I close my eyes and I'm overwhelmed by a flood of images of all the people I have known, but the faces fade away before I can recall their names. But I do remember a time, and it was a glorious time, when dynamic young men and women such as yourself, would take up the cause of protecting Earth from those who would do her harm. Those were good times. It was a time of peace and incredible prosperity. But everything has a cycle and we were due for a fall. This is the way of the universe. But the pendulum has not swung back in our direction. It seems to be...stuck. Frozen in time. This is not natural. There is a force, of some unknown origin, that is holding it back and preventing us from regaining and rebuilding what we have lost. I grew tired. Tired of the sleepless nights of being haunted by these memories. I left my home in Scandinavia and sailed across the ocean to come back here after I was awakened from my slumber towards death by a voice from the past. It was Bram, whispering in my ear to wake up, telling me that hope was not lost. He was coming back from his journey into the depths of space with the solutions to our troubles and to overthrow the yoke of oppression that hangs over our planet. Come back to Perihelion, he said to me, and help me guide my spirit back to my body. I yearn to come home and become whole again."

"So I did. Under the cover of darkness, I went to the docks close to my home along the shore, and onto my sailing boat, where I slipped out of the fjord and into the cold ocean to come here. I reopened this outpost, my old station, to help bring back a friend, whom due to my foolishness and hubris, sent him on a fool's quest."

Breeze stood quietly. Half of his mind was eyeing the black transport while the other tried to placate Oslo by listening to his story.

"I can see your mind wanders. My tale is fantastic and strange, this I acknowledge, but I will hold nothing back from you. It is the truth. To this I swear. You and others your age have grown up in a time of diminished expectations and shortened outcomes. You have seen nothing but poverty and despair, yet this is normal for you. I come from a time when I witnessed the end of prosperity and the beginning of despair. I stand as a bridge between those two worlds as I have seen both sides of the equation. I want to return to the gilded times."

Breeze nodded politely as he slowly moved to the ship. "I get it Oslo. You come from a better time." He looked around the hangar. "And judging by the way this whole place looks, Perihelion definitely has seen better days. I just don't know what we have to do with your plans."

"Bram told me he had solutions. Many of them. One of them required the formation of a new generation of Helios to become a brilliant light to shine on the world and to combat the encroaching darkness. Bring them together, he said, scour the planet and search for them. The days of despair will soon be over, he assured me."

"Okay, right. So your friend, who just disappeared into thin air, comes back as a ghost and tells you to go on some quest to find freaks like me to fight some imaginary enemy that no one knows exists. Again Oslo, thanks for the experience. I will never forget this place. Who could? But I really have to get going."

Oslo rushed up and blocked his path. He reached out to place a hand on his shoulder, hesitated, and then withdrew.

"Breeze, I know I can't keep you here against your will. This I know. But can I try to appeal to your sense of duty and honor and your desire to do so much more? Indulge me. There is so much to show you. You just need to give me chance."

Breeze side-stepped him, then made his way to the craft and climbed up the ladder that led to its cockpit. He tapped the canopy and it slid back with a pneumatic hiss as he tossed his backpack behind the pilot's seat. "Oslo, I think that you're an okay guy, but definitely strange. Heck, this whole place is strange. I know that I'm different and these flight powers I have are all well and great. But I don't really get to do anything with them. Back home, my father has me hiding them. I came here, and I guess you wanted me to use them for some sort of combat mission you have planned with your mystery ghost friend. The way I see it, Sally and Ray were right. Best to just go home. At least there I can handle the problems I have. What you want sounds...crazy."

Oslo sighed as his head drooped. "Crazy? Perhaps I am. And foolish." He looked up. "Foolish to think that you have grown at all. Observing you from a distance, I could have sworn you had awakened to the fact that you are not much of a joiner or a follower. Yet here you are, following in the footsteps of those who have put you down count-less times. *Ja*, crazy I am."

Breeze grimaced, then jumped into the pilot's seat and strapped himself in. "You won't get me that way. I know what you're trying to do and I won't fall for it. In the end Oslo, I'm just a loner and the son of a scrap metal hoarder."

"No, you are so much more and with the potential to do great things. You just need the will to break out from the rut you are in right now. Do you remember when you first arrived here, you told me you plowed a trench into the ground after the air show, a trench so deep and long you had to walk back for what seemed like miles to the point of impact just to get out?"

Breeze tapped a control screen in front of him and gauges and displays began to light up. "Yeah, sure, what about it?"

"Let that trench symbolize your life young man, and it showed that you were heading in the wrong direction, but you have the power to admit your mistakes and turn around to rediscover the road you were meant to walk down. I know I have made mistakes, but I try to learn from them. Please do the same?"

Breeze hit the ignition and the engines spooled up with a soft whine. "Oslo, I'm leaving now, you best step off the platform and away from the ship. I'm taking her out." Breeze depressed the throttle and revved the engines to underscore his point.

"What makes you think I would let you leave with military property? I can always stop you," Oslo said and stared him down.

"Fine. I'll just fly back under my own power. And if I crash into the ocean and drown trying to get to the mainland, you can have my death hanging over your head. Is that what you want to do to your students?"

Oslo closed his eyes. "No, of course not. That would be absurd." When he opened them, a gentle smile appeared on his face tinged with a hint of sadness. "Take the ship with you. Think of this as a gift from me, to you. I'm sure you have nothing like this at all back home in Conception. Let this ship serve to you as a reminder of the wonders you have witnessed here." He took a deep breath. "If you see—" his eyes fluttered, "when you see your father, tell him I said hello." He reached down and touched shoulder. "Son, listen to me. When you return home and you sense that it was not the right thing to do, no worries. The door to Perihelion is always open for you. Remember, like the trench, you can turn around and find your way back." He pointed at the navigation screen. "These ships are all equipped with a go home mode. It will reverse your course and send you straight back here. I... all of us will be waiting for you."

Breeze nodded and gripped the helm. He pushed the throttle control forward and the engines responded immediately with a high pitched whine as the hull of the ship vibrated. He pulled back on the helm and the ship drifted away from the platform. As the canopy slid closed, he waved to Oslo.

The old man waved back and the canopy shut and sealed itself with a hiss.

An indicator light flashed across his screen informing him that pressurization of the cockpit had begun.

He swung the ship around and pointed the bow toward the hangar doors. To the left and right of the ship stood a multitude of RF staring at him as he glided by. They held tools in their hands as their mechanical eyes shined and tracked the ship out of the hangar and into the brilliant morning sunlight.

He waved at them, and then stopped, realizing how foolish it was. The canopy was tinted with a heavy black film that made it difficult for anyone to see into the cockpit. *Besides, what do they care?*

As the ship glided out into the daylight, one lone RF with a streak of orange across its breast plate raised a hand toward Breeze's ship and waved goodbye.

He steered the ship past rows of hangars until he reached a taxiway that led to the landing facility. He pushed forward on the throttles and the ship picked up speed while around him, majestic palms and ficus trees swayed from the gusts of wind blowing in from the ocean.

He flashed back to when he first arrived on the island and the sense of wonder he felt traveling away from home for the first time to go somewhere exotic and different, followed by the crushing wave of disappointment at how the experience turned sour. His thoughts then drifted to the moment he met Ray and Sally.

Sally.

He pictured her face. The few times she even smiled at him seemed like magic in itself. But those good feelings were swept aside when he remembered how cruel she became whenever Ray was in her presence.

He snapped out of his trance when a proximity alarm went off as he was about to collide into a thick royal palm ahead of him. He jerked the helm to starboard and returned to the taxiway.

He eventually exited onto a runway, then hovered up slightly higher and spun the ship slowly to take one last look back at Perihelion. Convincing himself he wouldn't miss it, he brought the bow about and pointed it toward the ocean. He activated the stasis brake and pushed down on the throttles to allow the engines to spool up for greater takeoff power, then released the brake and shoved the helm forward and the ship accelerated rapidly across the tarmac. He jerked back the helm and the ship angled up toward the brilliant blue and white sky and climbed until he was above the clouds and leveled off.

He looked down through a break in the clouds and saw that

Perihelion was but a tiny dot in the middle of a vast ocean.

He touched the navigation screen and it prompted him for a destination. He typed in the coordinates for his home in the far western desert, and the navigation computer chimed its acceptance as the ship rolled to point the bow towards the west.

He leaned back his seat as his eyes began to flutter.

"Prepare for vortex," a woman's voice announced over the ship's intercom.

I thought Ray shut down the fog, he thought to himself. *What's happening?*

The nav computer flashed. On the display, the bull's eye was locked in and an oncoming target. Through the canopy, Breeze could see thick clouds spinning into a tunnel.

The light around him flashed into a brilliant green as the ship entered the vortex. The sound of static filled his ears and he quickly passed out.

Nina emerged from the palm forest and onto the beach near the landing facility. A shadow of distress crossed her face as she watched Breeze's sleek black ship disappear into the thick white clouds overhead.

She turned and rushed back into the forest.

Oslo sat on the platform steps inside the hangar. He waited patiently, hoping to hear the sound of the ship's engines and Breeze returning. *I should have reactivated the fog, so he couldn't leave.* He shook his head. *No, forcing him to stay wouldn't be right.*

His hopes were dashed as he heard the sonic boom of a ship as it ascended to gain altitude. He grimaced as he stood up, and then clambered down the steps and onto the floor of the hangar.

The RF around him immediately stood at attention. He ignored them as he strode by. They waited until he stepped out, and then resumed their work.

Oslo entered his office and dropped his tall frame into his high back chair. He placed his hands onto the wooden surface of his desk and looked at the endless row of books of his library that surrounded him. All of them contained the history of the world. A history he was beginning to realize that the world had forgotten about.

He chuckled. His chuckling turned to laughter followed by a hearty belly laugh. It trailed away into a deep sigh as he closed his eyes and clenched his fists.

"Well Captain, what should I do? What would be the best course to follow?"

He opened his eyes and stared at his lamp in the shape of a ship's captain with one hand gripping the helm as the other shielded his eyes as he gazed into some unknown future. *Is there a storm up ahead? Is that what he sees?* Oslo shook his head.

He stood up when he heard the sound of the gulls outside had stopped. He reached over to depress the intercom button just as Kera materialized before him.

"I suppose, after all these years, asking you to knock before entering has been a complete waste of time," Oslo said.

She ignored his words. "The boy is gone, yes?"

"Why do you ask what you already know? You can sense his departure just like you sense everything else."

"Yes, of course Oslo, just trying to make conversation."

He wagged a finger at her. "Not one of your stronger qualities. Stick to what you know."

"It was for the best, you do understand this?" she said.

He shrugged as he reached for a bag and began filling it with personal items. "I know what I did was foolish. I rushed back here like a schoolboy on a whim. Bram is not coming back. What I experienced back home in Scandinavia was nothing more than a vivid dream. It's over. All of it. I'm shutting down Perihelion once and for all. But of course you already know that."

She watched as he filled his bag, then he slung it over his shoulder, and stride from his desk to the door when he stopped and turned to her. "This was never meant to be," he said. "This was all but a foolish exercise to bolster my ego. An opportunity, if you will, to prove to myself that I could take command and make some sense in this world. Well, Kera, I stand before you now and will say the words that you already know I'm going to say. I was wrong."

She shook her head. "No. I did anticipate your leaving, but not to run home like a whipped schoolboy. I envisioned you leaving to track down your students and bring them back."

Oslo pounded the door frame with his fist. "Damn it woman! Why do you always make my head spin in circles? Why do you not ever tell me what I really should be doing?"

"Because, my dear man, you already have that power. You do not need me. You need to start trusting yourself and not be afraid to make mistakes, for there is much to be learned from them."

Oslo clenched his jaw. He stared at Kera for a moment, then turned his back to her and walked out.

"What about Nina?" Kera called out to him.

He didn't answer.

C H A P T E R

TWELVE

BREEZE WAS AWASH IN a cloud full of static as his eyes opened and he stared blankly ahead at the instrument display. Needles were spinning wildly as vid-screens shimmered with white noise. He rubbed his eyes and sat up straight in his seat. He toggled the helm, but it gave no response.

He flipped and pushed switches and buttons, but nothing responded to his commands. He tried to concentrate but he felt so disconnected from everything. It felt as if he had been asleep for a hundred years.

He looked out the canopy and saw brilliant white clouds flow past like a river, then looked back at his instruments and was relieved to see them coming back to life. The altimeter stopped gyrating and vid-screens flickered and began displaying relevant data.

He leaned a little closer to the nav-screen and was surprised at how far he had traveled. The coordinates showed the ship was crossing over the Great Rocky mountain range.

Just a bit further to the west, and I'll be crossing into Desert Country. Almost home.

Home. He began to wonder what that meant. After all that he saw and the people he met, he began to wonder if he could ever really return home. At Perihelion he was free to fly at a whim, with no one to tell him otherwise. Back home, he would be restricted again to flying at night.

Funny, such a wide open space the desert is, and yet I have to fly under the cover of darkness. At Perihelion, I could fly day and night. In the middle of the lifeless desert, I can't do anything. In the middle of the ocean, I was free to do whatever.

The ocean is also a desert, but with its life underneath, he heard a whisper came from the back of his mind.

He shook his head and rubbed his eyes. *So tired, just want to go home.*

The ship rocked violently as warning alarms whooped. Breeze gripped his seat harness as the ship spun like a whirlwind. Through the canopy, he could see the contrasting view of blue sky followed by white clouds until it all became a blur.

The ship was rocked by another impact. The canopy glass cracked as a massive fissure snaked across it. Breeze looked around to find the source of the attacks, but the intense gravitational pull from the flat spin made it difficult for him to move.

A black streak rushed across the path of the ship creating a wall of turbulence that the ship slammed into.

The canopy shattered and rained shards of glass upon him while the roar of the slipstream overwhelmed his senses. He tried to breathe, but couldn't, as the air rushed by him too fast to even catch a breath. He heard alarms shrilling in the background as his seat rocketed out of the cockpit with a mighty blast.

Suspended in the air for a moment, high above the clouds and strapped to his seat, he watched his sleek black ship pinwheel across the sky and disappear into the clouds before he dropped like a brick to earth below, when a violent jerking motion arrested his descent. He looked up as a parachute deployed, unfurling itself completely before settling with a loud snap as the canvas stretched itself taut. The lines securing it to the seat creaked from the strain.

As he floated down, he couldn't understand why the seat didn't separate from him. *This isn't right. What kind of ejection seat is this? Unless it's malfunctioning.*

He was startled by a black streak that whipped past at a blistering speed, and the turbulence it created swung him and the ejection seat like a bell, while below mountain peaks revealed themselves as he broke through the clouds

He shivered violently as shock combined with the freezing air began to take its toll. He knew he was either going to crash into the snow packed mountains or get hit by the fast moving black streak. He needed to break free from his seat and parachute if he was going to survive.

He fumbled with the harness as he desperately tried to find a way to cut loose from the cumbersome chair.

He never imagined a scenario like this: a flier at the mercy of a parachute to save him.

As he scrambled to find the release lever, he caught a sweeping motion from the corner of his eye. He turned to see several black streaks hurtling his way.

He was mesmerized by their precision formation as he groped for the release lever when he yelled in fear as a figure in black suddenly appeared before him. It matched his rate of descent while pointing at the top of his ejection seat, before turning and racing toward the oncoming black streaks.

Breeze was stunned by what just transpired, but snapped out of it and reached up and felt a pair of loops. He pulled down on them and the seat broke away. He shouted with a mixture of fear and joy as the parachute was better able to slow his descent now that it was free of the bulky and heavy seat.

Below, the snowcapped mountains rose up to greet him and he was seconds away from crashing into them. He remembered seeing free fallers in Conception use the lines attached to their parachutes to steer through the air and decided to try it himself. He jerked on one line which sent him veering hard to the right. He yanked on the opposite line and he careened to the left.

He steered the parachute as he tried to avoid a mountain looming below. He hoped he could just skim over the entire mountain range and land in a wooded area, until he looked at the horizon and saw how the mountains stretched as far as the eye could see in all directions.

He was too afraid to break free of the parachute and try to fly on his own. He spotted a valley below and aimed for it.

He then remembered the black streaks and looked up. Two were rapidly approaching him.

Sally and Ray looked out the windows of their transport. The ship maintained a steady speed as it skimmed the surface while racing up and down mountains and valleys.

Sally was becoming nauseous from the way the ship was flying and complained to Ray about it. He told her the flying pattern was to avoid detection.

"Detection from whom? What's going on?" she asked him.

"Nothing. Just a safety precaution, I suppose," he replied with a half-hearted shrug and looked away.

Ray then began to think about her question. *Why was the ship trying to avoid detection?*

When he was finally able to get in contact with his father, he assured his son that everything was fine back home, but it was important that he return immediately. His father admitted that sending him to Perihelion was an error in judgment on his part and whatever concerns that might have existed regarding his safety at Greenbrier were overblown.

Ray told his father about the fog, and how difficult it was to communicate with anybody on the outside, let alone travel. His father then informed him that he knew how to drop the island's defense field. Through a series of communiqués, he received the codes needed to negate the fog for a brief period so he could leave with a transport. He also emphasized to Ray the importance of convincing Sally she was to come along also. And if she resisted, bring her by force if needed.

Ray chuckled. *She sure didn't need any convincing.*

"But raise the fog after your departure so that the others cannot leave. It is for the best," his father added, "that you not inform Oslo of your plans. I can only say the reason for being so clandestine is that I fear Oslo may not be that man we thought he was. Nevertheless, follow my instructions to the letter and come home now."

Ray didn't need to ask any more questions. His father was a military man and he trusted him. He knew that Breeze would be trapped behind the fog, but he didn't really care about his teammate's fate. He had Sally, and that was all that mattered to him.

He watched over her as she slept throughout most of the journey. Now and then he would dare himself to hold her hand or brush the hair from her face. Father had said she would be his and they would start a family.

"But I think she doesn't like me," he once said to his father in a moment of despair.

Father grabbed him by the shoulders and shook him gently. "Persevere, son, and endure. She will come around. She will eventually submit to you and be your bride. This I assure you."

Ray smiled as he fell asleep. He thought of how he would do his father proud the day he would marry Sally. She would bear him sons. It was going to be a good life.

He awoke abruptly when the destination reminder chimed throughout the ship, letting them now they had crossed into the North Eastern territories. He turned to look at Sally. She was still asleep.

He got up and headed into the pilothouse. He stepped inside and saw the ship was flying flawlessly on auto pilot. He scanned the various vid-screens, but couldn't see anything of concern. It was flying steady and on course.

He was about to return to the passenger compartment when a flash of light on the horizon caught his eye. He peered out the cockpit windscreen, where just above and beyond the mountain range that rimmed the valley where his home lay, he saw a distinctive orange glow.

He scanned the vid-screens again. Not seeing anything of concern, he shrugged his shoulders and was about to leave when the screens flashed then flickered out, followed by a hissing sound that filled the cockpit.

He grabbed a pair of headphones and plugged into the comm system. All channels were filled with static. He tried every frequency he knew, but to no avail. He couldn't reach his father. He couldn't reach anyone.

No matter, we're almost home. Have to check on Sally.

He descended from the pilot house and back to the passenger compartment where Sally was awake.

"Why is it taking so long? Are we almost there yet?" she said as she put up her hair.

"We've just crossed into the North Eastern Territories and we're almost to Olympica. We're in safe country now and the ship will accelerate, you'll see. No more flying close to the ground and going up and down mountains." He didn't want to alarm her by mentioning the fiery glow in the distance.

"Do you think I can contact my parents? It would be nice to let them we're coming back," she said in such a sweet and innocent way that it broke his heart.

"Well, Sally, I'm not so sure about that," it pained him to say to her.

"What's wrong now?"

"Nothing. Nothing at all. Other than the comm unit is down."

"Again? Are you sure? How come nothing seems to work around here?"

Ray didn't answer. He leaned closer to the window and his face turned into a sheet of white.

Sally saw his expression and turned to look. She screamed.

They were approaching the outskirts of their city of Olympica where their eyes were greeted by a devastated landscape racked by explosions and filled with burning buildings.

"Ray, what's happening? Tell me?"

"Sally, listen, it's going to be okay—"

The ship's lights flickered as the engines warbled and whined, when the vessel began to buck wildly as it ascended and descended erratically before finally leveling out.

Ray fled to the pilot house with Sally close behind him. They dashed up the steps and toward the cockpit where they found vid-screens flickering erratically, dials and gauges spinning wildly. Outside the cockpit windows, a scrolling landscape of fire and destruction was spread out before them in a panoramic vision.

Oslo hopped out of his hover and strode toward the marina with his satchel slung across his chest. He stepped onto the floating bridge that led to the docks when he heard the whine of a hover from behind. He turned and saw Excort tumble out of his rusty hover and dash toward him. In all of his years at Perihelion, he never saw the dwarf run so fast.

"Oslo, wait!" Excort shouted as he dashed across the bridge and met him halfway. "What is the meaning of this? You have Mila and I up in arms over opening up the island, then you bring students for training and experience a few little mishaps, and you turn tail and leave?"

Oslo waved him off and continued across the bridge. He could see his sailing ship at the far end of the dock with its mast towering into the early morning skies.

"The weather is looking more toward my favor. I need to set off and take advantage of the winds," Oslo said as he walked away.

Excort bounded after the tall man. He grabbed his arm and flung him around. "No! This is not meant to be."

Oslo leaned over him and snorted. "Do you honestly think there would be a different outcome? Funny, were you not the one who was rock solid against my vision in the first place, *ja*? You were right, Excort, right all along. Bringing them here was foolish. I'm leaving. It's over. Tell your wife thank you, along with my humblest apologies for the disturbance. The two of you can return to your peace and quiet, for I will not disturb either of you with my delusions of grandeur any more. The world has changed. For the worst, but so be it. Perhaps it is for the best."

Excort growled. "I know I wasn't exactly supportive of you, this I agree. But you have opened up my eyes, Ole, for I also remember a better world. Don't forget, I am much older than you."

Oslo laughed. "Ah, the seniority card! Nice play, old boy. I'm still leaving."

Excort stepped in front of him. "Oslo, I sense they are in danger. You should have never let them leave."

Oslo froze. "Yes, I had to ice the veins to my heart to keep me from going after them. But they should return to their families and prepare for whatever destruction may come their way."

"You are willing to let them die?"

Oslo shook his head. "Willing? No. But I must accept the consequences of my actions. Had I let things be, I would not have stirred and awakened the Elephim. I can only hope that they destroy just a handful of cities as punishment. I know they are weak, but they are still strong enough to continue their dominion over this world. Let them have it. I wish to go home and sleep."

Oslo turned and continued to his boat.

"You are a coward, Ole Auken. Go and slink back to your winter home with your frozen heart!"

Oslo kept walking. "Your words are true, but carry no import for me, my friend. I made a mistake and will have to pay the price."

"We all do!" Excort roared at him.

Oslo stopped dead in his tracks, and then turned to the dwarf. "Yes, and I'm sorry, but this will blow over, you'll see. I have reason to believe they will survive whatever the fates may throw their way." He pulled his sleeve back to reveal a control pad on his wrist. "I will temporarily deactivate a portion of the fog so I may slip through. From then on, I swear to you I will not come back. For anything. Goodbye."

He turned and stepped onto his boat.

"And Nina?"

Oslo griped the helm and grimaced. "I was never really there for her, and she is more attached to you and Mila. I have caused enough pain. Let her stay here in peace." He leaned over and unraveled rope from the cleats that lashed the vessel to the dock, then activated the vessel's electric motor as Excort stood and watched as his friend motored out of the bay until he faded into the horizon.

Breeze gritted his teeth as the black streaks raced towards him. He fumbled with the harness until he found the release lanyard and gripped it tightly. Off to his side he saw yet another black streak coming toward him. He steeled his nerves.

Just as they were about to strike him, he yanked on the lanyard and broke free from the chute. The black streaks impacted the billowing canvas and entangled themselves in the thick and heavy lines attached to the chute. They fought wildly to free themselves as they careened across the sky.

Breeze willed himself to fly, but couldn't. The rush of air stung his eyes as he flailed away with his arms and legs as he plummeted to the valley floor when he felt something grab his legs and was stunned to see the same black clad figure from before. Its face swirled with points of light that reminded Breeze of stars as it chopped its hand into the air, and then pointed forward. Breeze cried out as the black clad figure then flung him and he was sent hurtling across the sky. He felt a surge of energy rush through his body as his shield raised itself and enveloped him. He wasn't sure what the creature did to him, but he was flying.

He steadied his nerves and focused on his steering, as he had descended below the deck level of the mountain peaks and had to swerve to avoid them. He dropped into a canyon and navigated its twisting course through the mountains, all the while trying to remember what Oslo had taught him about flight control. He maintained his breathing as he willed himself to ascend.

He steadily achieved altitude when he was rocked by a wave of turbulence as twin black streaks shot past him. He wobbled violently as he struggled to retain control when he began to roll, slowly at first, then faster and faster until he became disoriented as the horizon spun before him. Up ahead, he could make out the outlines of mountain with a peak that disappeared into the clouds. He was on a collision course for it and he couldn't break free of his trajectory.

Ray slipped into the pilot's seat and tried to take control of the helm. Sally stood behind him and gripped the headrest as she stared out the window in disbelief, when the ship began to shudder and the engines warbled and whined.

"I don't know what's happening! All the screens are going static. We have to land. Now!" Ray declared.

Sally nodded and sat in the jump seat behind him. She buckled in as Ray reached for his harness.

"Ray, can you fly it?"

"I've spent enough time behind the helm of sailing ships and aero-craft of all kinds, Sally. My father taught me well."

"Yes, but has he ever taught you how to fly one of these?"

"We're about to find out," he muttered.

He scanned the console for an override to shut off the auto pilot. On impulse, he reached under the helm and found a lever. He yanked it down hard and alarms immediately blared throughout the cockpit.

"Auto Pilot disengaged, manual flight mode in effect," a woman's voice called out over the intercom.

"Hah!" Ray shouted as he wrestled with the helm. He mashed the throttles down and the ship leapt forward.

They skimmed across the burning landscape when an explosion from below rocked the ship. Sally screamed as Ray rolled the ship with the shock wave, sending the craft dipping to port before leveling out.

"I need to put her down someplace safe!" Ray called out.

Sally said nothing as she stared out her window with a hand over her mouth. The skies were splashed with orange and red as fires and explosions erupted below.

Ray circled the outskirts of their burning city until he spotted a mountain ridge he recognized. He was familiar with these mountains, having hiked through them with his father on numerous hunting trips and knew of a valley on the other side of the ridge with cabins that could provide them with shelter. He brought the ship about and headed for it.

He skimmed over the mountain top, and then descended to land on the ridge just below it with the bow facing what was left of the city as the glow from the fires filled the cockpit.

He powered down the engines and activated the generator. The cabin's lights flickered briefly, and then remained steady. Ray felt the cool air from the ventilation system pour onto his face. He took in a deep breath and realized just how musty the air was inside the old transport.

He turned to Sally. "Let's go, I don't want to stay in the ship. I feel like a sitting duck in this thing."

Sally was catatonic and didn't respond when Ray reached over and shook her.

"Come on, snap out of it Sally."

"What's happening?" she whispered.

He didn't know what to say to her. He looked at the console but all of the vid-screens were peppered with static. He grabbed a headset and jacked into the comm unit. He tried all frequencies, but received nothing but a steady hiss.

"Can you reach anyone? Your father? My parents?" she said.

Ray dropped the headset onto the pilot seat. "No!" He grimaced as he took in a breath to steady himself. He didn't want to add to her fears by appearing afraid. "Listen, it's going to be okay. There's a trail that goes to the base of the mountain. From there, we follow a path that leads to a cabin that my father and I have used for hunting trips. We'll be okay there. We can figure out what's going on come morning light."

"I don't want to leave the ship. In fact, I want to go back to Perihelion," Sally said.

Ray shook his head. "No way that's going to happen. We are back home, and we just need to figure out what's going on."

"Our city is on fire!" she stood up and screamed at him.

Ray leaned back. He had never seen her this angry, with her nostrils flaring and her eyes glowing an eerie white

He raised a hand. "Calm down, let's just step outside and get our bearings. I don't trust this ship. Whoever attacked it might be tracking us now, so let's start making our way down the trail and get far away from it as we can. Please, Sally, follow me on this one."

He held out a hand and she reluctantly took it, and together they stepped into the passenger compartment.

At the stern of the ship, he opened a panel and pushed the button to lower the cargo ramp. Hydraulics whined as the ramp lowered, and as they walked down it they were immediately hit by the pungent smell of burning wood.

They coughed and gasped for air and Ray went back up the ramp and to a utility closet next to the control panel. Inside were heavy jackets, boots, an ax and several respirators. He grabbed the respirators and ran back down the ramp where he found Sally on her knees and struggling to breathe. He helped her put the respirator on, and then donned his. After several minutes, she nodded to him when he asked if she was feeling better.

They walked to the bow of the ship and stood underneath it as they gazed in horror at their burning city below. Sally whimpered and leaned into Ray. He held her tight as an endless series of explosions erupted across the city and illuminated the early evening sky.

Sally began sobbing, then pulled off her respirator and collapsed.

Ray grabbed her and she was limp in his arms. He cradled her as he sat on the cold and rocky ground, watching the city burn with a sense of detachment.

Oslo deftly navigated the channel markers that led out of the bay and into the ocean, then cut off the engine and hoisted the sails when he stopped to look back at the diminishing outline of Perihelion. In the distance, he could make out the spires of some of the taller buildings.

He shook his head in disgust. He didn't want it to end this way and kept telling himself that he was doing the right thing.

His thoughts then drifted to Nina. He gritted his teeth and suppressed any emotion he felt for his daughter from building up. *Best not to think of her. It's for her own safety.*

He pulled back his sleeve and tapped in a series of commands into the wrist console and it warbled a confirmation when he was finished. He then unstrapped the console and dangled it at his side.

The console began to beep sharply as he hurled it away from the ship. He watched as it hit the water with splash and sink beneath the waves.

He waved a goodbye, then grabbed the helm and spun the wheel to port until the bow pointed east. Behind him, a greenish fog began to materialize, completely obstructing the view of the island. Oslo didn't notice as he steeled his eyes forward and continued on his course.

Not far behind, a figure broke the surface of the ocean. It was a girl. She treaded water and watched as the ship sailed toward the horizon.

Breeze stopped his roll in time to throw his hands up to his face when he impacted the mountain.

He felt the pressure around him as his shield absorbed the brunt of the impact as he bored through solid rock until he came to a stop.

His shield dissipated and he lay sprawled out in the tunnel he created. It was pitch black inside without the slightest hint of light. He struggled to breathe in the dusty air as showers of rocks and pebbles rained down upon him whenever the mountain trembled. He groaned as he strained to turn around began to crawl his way out.

He winced because the floor and walls of the tunnel were hot to the touch. Everything around him smelled like it had been charred and the surface of the tunnel was glassy and smooth. He began to cough as putrid air filled his lungs, yet he kept crawling and was rewarded by the sight of a pinpoint of light in the distance.

Overjoyed, he crawled faster through the tunnel as the light expanded in diameter and intensity and soon cool air blew across his face and into his nostrils. He stopped for a moment to breathe and savor the freshness of it. He resumed crawling until he arrived at the entrance to the tunnel where the ceiling was higher, allowing him to stand up. He briefly looked down at his hands and saw how red and chafed they were before leaning out and to take a look.

Winds howled all around him as clouds drifted close by. He looked down and saw how the mountain had a sheer face. Descending by hand and foot would be next to impossible.

Only way out will be to fly, he thought to himself. He quickly withdrew back into the tunnel as a monstrous gust of wind almost sucked him out. He waited for the howling winds to subside before leaning out again.

He scanned the cloud-filled skies, wondering if the black clad figures were hiding behind them. He couldn't understand why one seemed to be helping him while the other two were chasing him down. He only knew of the distortion he felt whenever they were near, along with the powerful sound of static that overwhelmed him.

He looked down at the valley floor hoping to spot his ship. He wondered if it managed to land safely on its own, but he knew better. His father's scrap yard was a testament to all the aerocraft that suffered mishaps in the air. The result was always twisted wreckage.

He didn't want to stay in the tunnel and hope for a rescue, he knew had to leave and continue west on his own power.

He pressed his hands against the tunnel's surface to brace himself from the harsh and swirling winds, then closed his eyes and did his best to concentrate. *Have to get calm. I'm back home, behind the shed. The cool desert night has no distractions. I can fly. I can.*

He sucked air deeply into his lungs and jumped out.

Ray held Sally in his arms as he watched the fires consume their city. Even amidst the chaos he never felt so content in his life. He couldn't understand why.

He looked down at her and felt a surge in his heart. He wondered if all of the destruction they were surrounded by would bring her closer to him while widening the chasm between her and Breeze.

Breeze. Why was he thinking about him? He shook his head violently. Seeing Breeze holding her in his arms on the boulevard made him seethe with anger. He wasn't able to rescue her from what she experienced in the basement of the Science and Engineering building or from the trimaran accident. His blood boiled when he remembered how repulsed she was by the sight of him and turned to Breeze for comfort. It was all too much to bear.

Sally stirred and looked up at him. "Is it over?"

He chose his words carefully. "It's almost over. Come with me to the end of the trail where there's a cabin for us to hide in. We can set out later when everything settles down and to try and find our way back home. It's for the best."

She smiled and nodded, then turned away from him and saw the red tinted skies. She sniffed the air and wrinkled her nose.

She scrambled to her feet and walked to the end of a cliff that overlooked the city to stare at the vast expanse of destruction.

She turned to him. "I need to know. I have to find them."

Ray raised his hands in a calming gesture. "Find who? What are you talking about?"

"I want to see my parents. I have to know if they're okay," she said.

Ray nodded, remembering how gentle, but firm Breeze was with her. He needed to mimic his style.

"Sally, you're right but now is not the best time." He held out a hand. "Come with me?"

She took a step toward him, and then stopped. "I can't Raymond, I'm sorry." She stepped back. "Aren't you the slightest bit concerned about your family?"

Ray stammered. "Look, I'm sure they're fine only because my father's pretty resourceful. Besides, he wouldn't have summoned me home unless he had a good reason."

"Coming back to this is a good reason?"

"Sally, I know as much as you about what's going on."

"I wonder about that." She looked away.

"What are you trying to say?!" he shouted as he stepped up to her.

She touched his chest. "Nothing. Forget it. I'm tired and scared, so I'll say anything. I'm just a girl, remember?" She smiled at him.

He grunted. "Yeah, okay. Can we just go now?"

"Yes, but let me do something first." And without another word she closed her eyes, and when she opened them, they were glowing a solid white.

Ray groaned as he stared at her prone body. He knew what she was doing

Oslo let out the mainsail and unfurled the spinnaker. The winds were coming from behind him and increasing with intensity.

He set his nav-station for a southeastern course. He would follow the island chains until breaking out into the open Atlanteanic for the western shores of Northern Afrika. From there, he would follow the coastline past the ravaged lands of Europa and up to Scandinavia.

His mind began to wander as he thought about Kera and Excort's words. Perhaps they were right in that he should go to Raza and make his peace with her and live out his life with someone who cared about him.

He grimaced as he swallowed hard. *No, it's been so long. She must have moved on. And how could I return without Nina?*

Nina. Her name was more like a stab to his heart than a source of comfort. He looked up at the sky and lamented never being able to reach out to his daughter. He closed his eyes and let his memories drift back.

Nina was born on the island in the days when Bram was projecting out into space during their experiments. He remembered that time as the greatest in his life despite the chaos that roiled the world as he and Raza had fallen in love and were married. The ceremony was administered by the Captain and Bram was his best man. The men were suited in their finest uniforms, and Raza was dressed in a flowing white gown.

Nina was born soon after and like her parents, was also a paranormal who took to the water like a fish, stunning them with her ability to stay underwater for an incredible amount of time.

But the aftermath of the purge forced them all into retirement as the Elephim consolidated their power and were dismantling the military in order to create one of their own. Perihelion was to be shut down and all personnel dismissed as the clandestine attempts to discover the secrets of the Elephim in order to defeat them, was coming to an end. Oslo and Raza resisted, but it was pointless. By then, Bram was lost as he never returned to his body after what was supposed to be his last expedition to Helena, the alleged homeworld of the Elephim. He lived, but there was no registering of his soul or his essence. He lay in a comatose state with only machines to keep his body alive.

Arrangements were made for Excort and his wife, Mila, to stay behind and administer the decommissioning of Perihelion. Oslo pleaded with the Captain to let them all stay, but he had the look of defeated man.

Disperse, the Captain said, *our time is up. Let us age gracefully and retreat with the sunset.*

He shook his head as he remembered those words. The days of the Helios were over. The age of heroes, gone. Though he and Raza, as well as other dedicated personnel, disobeyed orders and stayed behind to try and save paranormal children from across the globe, and bring them to Perihelion for refuge, that plan also ended in defeat and Perihelion was abandoned once and for all, with only Mila and Excort staying behind on the island, now shrouded by a fog that Oslo erected to keep the island, along with all of the secrets that it possessed, out of the hands of the Elephim.

She is better off staying here, he thought to himself as his mind drifted back to the present. He couldn't deal with the heartbreak of seeing her hurt, or worse, taken away from him. He began to wonder if that was the reason why he tried to revive Perihelion. Was he really trying to fight the unseen forces that had taken over the world, or did he have an ulterior motive? By gathering the students he had found, perhaps it was an attempt to give his daughter a childhood she had never known. There would be life again on the island filled with young people full of hope and promise and they would become playmates and companions for his daughter. And perhaps in the future, even a mate.

He smiled ruefully and shook his head. Breeze and the others had lives of their own before he came blustering into them. Let them return home as reviving any attempt to create a new generation of Helios was foolish at best. All that was accomplished was that he ran the risk of stirring the Elephim, the unforgiving observers from above. He could only hope that perhaps they had truly become dormant and no longer possessed the grip over the Earth as they once did.

I hope the three of them managed to slip back to their homelands unnoticed.

Let peace reign across the land.

The hairs on his arms and neck stood on end. He looked behind and was greeted by a green wave of energy that hurled itself out of the clouds and slammed into his sailboat.

He cried out as he was flung out of his vessel and sent careening through the air. He hit the ocean surface and sank like a stone.

Too stunned at first to register what had happened, he ingested a mouth full of salt water that snapped him to his senses. He gagged and choked as he thrashed his way to the surface.

He broke through and threw his head back, spitting out the salt water that clogged his lungs as he gasped for air. He treaded water and watched as his vessel burned to the waterline in the distance, the flames casting a hypnotic effect over him

His trance was broken by twin black streaks shooting across the sky combined with the sound of static.

Elephim, he thought as a plunging despair consumed him. He had truly stirred the hornet's nest. There was no turning back.

He had never forgotten when he first encountered them. He was with Raza and Nina as they traveled from Appalachia to Perihelion. Nina had fallen ill and was close to death, and only the facilities on Perihelion could save her, but the Elephim ambushed the transport he was piloting and forced them to land. He vividly remembered their jet black bodies and expressionless faces as they tried to break into the ship and take his daughter. It was also the last time he saw Raza.

Oslo twisted in the water to track their progress. They circled above him like hawks waiting for the opportune moment to strike. Suddenly, one of them plunged toward what was left of the burning sailboat with its stern sinking into the water and the bow pointing straight up into the sky. The mast had snapped off, leaving only a crude stump behind.

The Elephim hovered above the ship briefly before hurling a bolt of energy at it, sending the remains of the vessel to the bottom. As the sailboat disappeared beneath the waves, both Elephim turned their attention away from it and flew towards him.

Oslo took a deep breath and slipped beneath the waves.

Breeze hurtled down the sheer face of the mountain, gritting his teeth and squinting while the cold air blasted his face. His arms were stretched out before him as he tried to suppress his fears as the canyon floor rapidly approached.

He surrendered himself to the reality that he was going to die. He thought about his father and wondered what he would think of his death when a brief image of his mother floated through his mind. She looked sad, even when she smiled. She dissipated when he heard the laughter of a child.

He felt a surge of power rush through him as his shield rose. He leveled out in time and narrowly escaped impacting with the canyon floor.

He skimmed across the surface and focused on his steering when he was slammed from the side. He lost control and bounced off the walls of the narrow canyon, flinging rock and debris everywhere.

Relieved that the shield held up and protected him, he quickly looked over his shoulder to find the source of the attack and saw a black clad figure hurling a boulder at him.

He grunted as he poured on the power and raced through the canyon with a sonic boom trailing behind him, triggering a rock slide with massive boulders pouring down the sides of the canyon.

His shield was struck repeatedly from the raining debris of rocks and boulders. He tried to dodge and weave through them, but the rock slide came down too fast for him to maneuver through.

He looked up just as a shadow descended upon him. He had enough time to see a massive boulder trailed by several smaller ones hit him, sending him in a downward trajectory to the canyon floor.

He impacted the ground hard and plowed a trench, coming to a stop when he slammed into the base of the mountain. He laid huddled in a fetal position as rocks rained down on him. His shield stayed up and protected him from the torrential rock slide as dirt and boulders piled upon it, plunging him into darkness.

The rock slide eventually ended, followed by an eerie silence. He closed his eyes as they ached from straining to focus in the dark. He calmed himself down, knowing that should he lose his concentration the shield would collapse and the tons of rock above him would crush him to death.

The air inside the shield was turning foul and beginning to buckle as he struggled for fresh air.

Beneath him, he felt dampness as his impact exposed an underground river. Water began filtering through the shield, yet he didn't resist as it filled the interior and immersed him. It reminded him of the first time he met Nina at the bottom of the cove. He convulsed as water filled his lungs and caused the shield to waver, and then surrendered himself as his breathing relaxed and he slipped into a peaceful oblivion.

Sally drifted in her astral form across the burning city as she tried to get her bearings. She could feel her body back at the mountain being caressed by the hot air heated by the fires as it blew across the valley. She looked back upon the trail of light that connected her astral form to her physical body. She knew she would need to follow it to return.

She stopped to hover over the center of the valley. Below, flames and smoke enveloped the city. She scanned the streets hoping to find anyone, but the city was a corpse except for the sound of an explosion or the collapse of another building succumbing to the ravages of the fires.

She steeled her nerves as she drifted across the destruction, telling herself over and over again that this was just a dream, and she would wake up any moment in the safety of her home.

Home, where was it? She thought as she spun slowly, hoping to find some landmark that would lead her to it when she saw a twin spire tower on the horizon. It was the same one she had always seen from her bedroom window and just beyond it was her neighborhood.

She glided over to the tower, surprised to find it wasn't on fire or damaged, nor the surrounding structures attached to it. She continued traveling, leaving behind the burning city and into the surrounding suburbs when she reached the district of her neighborhood where it too seemed to have escaped the ravages of the flames. She cautiously flew over the darkened streets with only the distant glow of the fires behind her to light the way. The homes below were left untouched from the fire and destruction. Everything was perfectly intact.

She recognized her street and glided past each of the stately homes on it until she reached hers, and instead found a smoldering crater in the ground.

She felt her heart crush as she descended. It couldn't be! Every home is untouched, except mine!

Fear crept up within her as she thought of parents. Mother, father, where are you?

She hovered over the horrible gash in the earth where her home once stood and looked at the houses across the street. They were in perfect condition. She saw through the trees that Ray's family home next door was intact.

She turned to look back at the crater and gasped as a figure stepped out of it. It was jet black with a featureless face. An Elephim. It walked the perimeter of the crater shaking its head.

Sally could feel the terror course through her as the sound of static began to build. She carefully floated away when the Elephim looked in her direction, then leapt across the expanse of the crater and landed a few feet from her, leaning forward as it looked through the darkness; searching. Its face swirled with pinpoints of lights as the hiss of static grew stronger.

Sally put her hands to her mouth as she dared herself not to breathe.

Back at the mountain, Ray watched as Sally's body trembled and shook as it mimicked the actions of her astral form. He saw her hands go to her mouth as her eyes glowed an intense, searing white.

He leaned into her face and said loudly, "Sally, come back."

At the crater, Sally continued floating away from the creature as Ray's voice was barely heard above the hiss of static. Every time she moved, the Elephim seemed to sense her presence but was hesitant and cautious as if it knew a sudden move on its part would send her flying away.

She looked behind and saw her trail of light was diminishing. A wave of panic swept over her as she felt her energy draining as the static built in intensity.

She looked back at the Elephim. It was gone.

She turned around and it was right before her, reaching out and groping with its hands as it tried to find her in the darkness.

She screamed as she felt the light trail sweep her off her feet and drag her back. She saw the landscape below as nothing more than a blur of fire and smoke as she rapidly approached the cliff and slammed back into her body. She skidded across the ground and rammed into the landing gear of the ship, where she laid still in a crumpled heap.

Ray rushed over and gently rolled her to face him.

She was comatose.

Oslo held his breath underwater as he watched the pair of Elephim above the surface. One hovered over him as the other circled like a vulture.

In a flash, the Elephim that hovered pierced the water and angled towards him.

Oslo closed his eyes and forced himself to focus. He would have to make a jump if he wanted to escape. His paranormal ability was never fully refined, and nobody knew how to instruct him of his powers and how to achieve his full potential. He was only able to leap forward a few seconds at most, folding space around him, which created the impression he could move quickly.

He did his best to discover more about himself, but always came across roadblocks in his mind that prevented him from doing so. He was written off immediately upon arriving at Perihelion as a low level paranormal who was not fit for active combat duty as a Helios and was transferred to the Military Science Battalion. That was fine by him as he always preferred the comfort of a well-equipped laboratory and a fully stocked library. That was his domain.

He cursed himself as he struggled to stay underwater with the limited breath he had in his lungs. He saw the Elephim streaking towards him and wished he could do so much more than just jump.

And jump he did. He flitted away from his original position, leaving the Elephim to grab at empty space as he reappeared on the surface a few hundred feet away and gasping for air.

He swam toward debris he spotted from his sunken ship and grabbed onto a part of the hull that had broken off and held onto it. He knew he couldn't go underwater to hide. It would weaken him further and prevent him from jumping again.

The Elephim that was circling above spotted him and dove in his direction. Again he focused, hoping he had the strength to jump with the piece of debris he was hanging onto. Carrying large objects, or people with him wasn't something he did often or well.

He shuddered as he mustered all his strength and jumped, reappearing down range from the wreckage.

The attacking Elephim had plunged into the water just as he jumped. It rose back to the surface and looked about wildly trying to find him.

Oslo lowered himself into the water so that only his head was above the surface as he clung to the debris.

The ruse didn't work as the Elephim who first attacked him surfaced and pointed out Oslo's location to its companion, and then they raced toward him in tandem.

Oslo gritted his teeth and focused with all of his intensity. He jumped just as the Elephim split off and flew in the opposite directions.

When he reappeared, one was right behind him and grabbed him by the neck as static roared through his ears. He thrashed wildly and managed to break free from its grip, jumping just a few feet away where the second Elephim was waiting for him. Again he jumped, this time just a few inches over, narrowly escaping its grip.

He knew they were aware of his plan as his trajectory back to the island was giving it away. But he had nowhere else to go, and not enough strength to keep jumping. Time was running out.

He cried out as his feet were suddenly grabbed from below, and he was yanked under the surface. He expected to ingest a lungful of water but instead found himself inside a bubble. He looked up to see the Elephim give chase as the bubble raced toward the island.

He turned to look in the direction he was heading, and his jaw dropped.

Towing the bubble was Nina. Sensing his gaze, she turned briefly to wave at him, and then accelerated toward the island.

Breeze was in complete darkness. He felt no pain and was surrounded by a warm cloud of air. He felt light as a feather, making him realize how heavy his body really was until now.

He drifted across a vast sea of blackness, hearing nothing and seeing no one, yet he felt no panic or anxiety, nor any desire to wake up. In the back of his mind, he was well aware of the threat from the Elephim that attacked him, yet he felt no reason why he should care.

Streaks of light crept into his outer periphery. He turned to follow them as they weaved and meandered their way toward him.

The streaks of light molded themselves into globes. They flitted about and cast their light upon him, and when he looked down, he found he was completely naked.

He watched as the orbs coalesced into a single globe, then it hovered before him and shimmered as a deep hum reverberated through his head.

A voice spoke to him. *"Never surrender. There will be times when you will feel overwhelmed and wish to escape. You may come to this place, for it is a respite for weary souls. But do not stay too long. Your time will not arrive for quite a while. Take succor and imbibe the nourishment we offer you. But then be on your way. Never forget that you are loved and the light within you burns brightly. You will use this light and cast it upon all that you meet as we cast it upon you. Be generous with this light. Illuminate the path they all must travel upon. Remember, always go the light, and shun the darkness."*

The globe approached and absorbed him, then pushed him up toward a rift of light that he passed into, and he was sent rushing down a long corridor. Streams of light raced past his head as he felt a shudder course through his body.

When he opened his eyes, he could barely see; it felt as if he were underwater and every breath he took was labored and strained.

What little light he had gave way to a brilliance that rushed over him. He watched rocks and stones fall to the side as he was lifted into the air and out of the trench he was buried in. He could see the outline of a single Elephim with outstretched hands hovering above him as he was lowered onto the canyon floor.

He didn't sense any malevolence from it, only a feeling that it wanted to help and protect him.

He was startled as twin black streaks surged at him from above. With whiplash speed, the Elephim grabbed and rammed them together, then hurled them onto the canyon floor. With a shriek accompanied by a powerful hiss of static, the black streaks materialized into Elephim. The two laid still as their bodies pulsated with a dark energy.

The helpful Elephim turned away from them to look at Breeze. Its expressionless face began to swirl with pinpoints of light as it scanned Breeze within his shield filled with water. It noted how his lungs squeezed the oxygen from the liquid and kept him from drowning. The pinpoints of light on its face abruptly stopped as it turned and hovered over to its comrades and grabbed them by their wrists, then flew away.

Breeze watched the helpful Elephim fly with its teammates in custody as it disappeared into the clouds, never quite understanding why it betrayed its own kind and helped him like it did.

He was becoming anxious, and the urge to lower his shield was overwhelming. As if the shield sensed his wishes, it lowered instantly and spilled him and the water onto the canyon floor. He coughed and heaved, vomiting water out of his lungs as he struggled to breathe the cold air, all the while writhing in agony from the pain he felt in his chest.

He lay on his side as water drained from his lungs and out of his mouth. He could feel the freezing air chill his body, and he shivered violently as he laid curled into a fetal position. He wanted to raise his shield again to protect himself from the elements, but didn't know how to do it on command. Oslo tried to teach him during one of many lessons on Perihelion, but he could never quite master it.

He focused his eyes on a canyon wall close to him to take his mind off the cold when he saw an etching of a sun with its rays of light shining upon rows of people with their arms outstretched. Their faces were featureless.

Shine the light upon them; he remembered the words from the globe of light.

His mind began to wander as an image of Nina appeared before him.

Nina, if you can hear me, I could use your help, he thought to himself before drifting off into darkness.

Ray picked up Sally and cradled her in his arms. He was tempted to climb back up into the ship and call for help, then remembered the comms were down. And hiding inside the ship made him feel like a sitting duck.

We're being watched. There's only one thing to do. Run and hide elsewhere.

He picked his way along the trail that led to the base of the mountain. He was familiar with the area, having hunted here before with his father. His plan was to find the cabin they frequently used on previous hunting trips. There would be food there, as well as heat and dry clothes. Then he would have a chance to regroup and plan.

As he made his way down the trail, it dawned up him the reality they faced. Their city was destroyed, and they were the only known survivors. He stopped and dropped to his knees, then laid Sally down and took in a deep breath.

Father, what happened?

He was so sure he did the right thing leaving Perihelion with Sally as it was his father who urged him to come back. He replayed the last conversation he had with him before leaving Perihelion and realized only now how strained and anxious he sounded, which was odd considering how his father was a stone cold military warrior. Nothing ever seemed to rattle or faze him. Ray wondered why he didn't pick up on this before.

His thoughts were interrupted by loud and powerful crack as a tree off to his side crashed towards them. He scooped up Sally and ran as the tree fell onto where they once stood.

There were several loud cracks as more trees keeled over and fell around them where one by one they formed a crude corral, trapping them inside.

Fear clouded Ray's mind as he lashed out with a bolt of energy and blasted away a clump of felled trees, giving them a way out.

He picked up Sally and dashed through the opening when more trees began to fall around them as he ran down the trail at full speed.

He was out of breath and exhausted when they reached the foot of the mountain. He stumbled and lost his grip on Sally, and she fell to the ground.

He crouched down next to her and took in deep breaths to steady his nerves. He could barely feel his legs as he was numb from running for so long.

The silence that fell over them was unnerving, and was shattered by the sickening crack of trees falling over as yet another crude corral was formed around them. He reached out feebly to let out a blast of energy, but only a few sparks spewed forth.

Drained. They're wearing me down so I can't put up much of a fight.

He grabbed Sally and hoisted her over his shoulder and hobbled out as fast he could as trees crashed and tumbled all around them, getting out of the makeshift corral before it could be finished.

Ahead he saw the cabin. He ran to it and with the last bit of energy he could muster he stumbled up the steps and pushed the door.

It was locked.

He wanted to blast the door down, but knew he couldn't. He needed the sun to replenish his energy and he couldn't draw that much from starlight. Yet.

He stomped his feet. He wasn't accustomed to not having options. Then again, he wasn't used to working on his own. He was usually with a group of people and always had his father's guidance to help him, or an authority figure to turn to. Now, more than ever, he was alone and he was also responsible for Sally's safety.

He snapped his fingers as he remembered the cellar below. If he could hide there with Sally, maybe they wouldn't be able find them and would call off the chase.

He ran down the steps with Sally over his shoulder, then ducked around the corner of the cabin and hugged the side of it until he found the steps that led to the cellar and clambered down. Relief swept over him as he twisted the doorknob. It was open.

He stepped inside and quickly closed the door behind him. It was pitch black inside. He held up a hand and it glowed, pushing away the darkness to reveal more details of the room.

It had a low ceiling, and he had to duck his head to avoid hitting it. There were a few extra cots along with a work bench and cabinets filled with dry goods.

He gently placed Sally onto one of the cots, and then looked to see what he could use to barricade the door when he heard heavy footsteps from the floor above. He froze in place and tried not to breathe hard when Sally groaned loudly as she began to stir.

Oslo knelt down inside the air bubble Nina had created for him and steadied himself by placing his hands against the sides.

He looked back, and his heart pounded as he watched one of the Elephim gain on them. It was closing the gap and almost touched the bubble when Nina gave a sudden burst of acceleration and left it behind in a trail of bubbles.

Oslo looked up through the clear blue water and saw a dark shadow trailing them from above the surface.

Classic hunter/killer strategy, he thought to himself. *One is the spotter overhead as the other moves in for the kill.*

He strained to see Nina up ahead. She was barely visible despite the clarity of the water. Her body seemed translucent as it mimicked the color and hues of the ocean.

He was suddenly thrown headfirst to the front of the bubble then bounced back to the center. He groaned and turned to look. The Elephim were ramming him.

Nina felt the attack. Her face twisted in fury as she squinted her eyes, thrust her hands forward and accelerated.

She managed to put a considerable distance between them and the Elephim, but was beginning to tire. She wasn't accustomed to towing anything behind her at such high speeds and over a great distance, yet she knew she had to get to the outer perimeter of the fog and slip past it without the Elephim seeing her do it.

There was a splash from above and Nina looked up to see the sole Elephim that was trailing them from the surface had pierced the ocean like an arrow and was heading straight for them.

Panic set in as she realized the gravity of the situation. She just wanted to say goodbye to her father and maybe try to convince him to stay. Instead, she found herself in a turn of events that had both of their lives in jeopardy.

She let out a scream which amplified quickly into a sonic blast that reverberated throughout the ocean. Both Elephim giving chase were flung back as they covered their ears and howled.

Nina screamed again as she raced through the ocean, determined more than ever to get to the outer perimeter of the fog.

The Elephim recovered and gave chase. They split apart and flanked them as they both emitted a powerful static that was overwhelming. Oslo covered his ears as Nina arched her back and aimed for the depths.

As they plunged into the deep blue depths, the light from the sun grew fainter and soon they were in pitch black darkness. But there was no silence, for the ocean is always filled with a cacophony of sound. The chatter of millions upon millions of plankton swarming the world's oceans created a symphony of sound that reverberated throughout the globe. Nina plunged even deeper into the abyss, using the sound of the plankton for guidance knowing she was now heading into the territory of the deep ocean whales.

Here in the depths of infinite blackness is where the whale speaks to others of its kind no matter how far separated they may be. In these depths, all sound was compressed due to the coldness of the water, which allowed their voices to be broadcasted from one ocean to the next.

Nina came to a halt and hovered for a moment, listening to see if the Elephim had followed them. She could sense them several hundred feet above, desperately pinging the ocean depths in their attempts to find them. She had eluded them, for now. Yet her instincts knew they had plenty of experience traversing the depths of space and they would eventually adapt to the watery environment and find them.

She saw a glowing eye appear before her, followed by another as she felt the water sway her gently as if a giant fish had flicked its tail. More glowing eyes began to appear and soon they were bathed in soft light. She turned and saw her father watching in wide eyed wonder at the several whales that had surrounded them. She knew these whales, having made friends with them long ago. They taught her how to dive into the extreme depths, and the use of whale song to communicate with others across vast stretches of ocean. They also showed her how they used sound to compress water behind them, allowing them to accelerate at a moment's notice.

These whales were also the guardians of a secret entrance into Perihelion. Off the eastern shores of the island lay an abyss that the naval personnel who had charted it named "The Tongue of the Ocean," as it dropped off the outer shelf of the island and plunged for miles before touching bottom. Nina knew how to slip past the fog through a narrow channel that led to the abyss. It was here that the whales guarded the hidden entrance for centuries, never relieving themselves of their long forgotten duty.

The whales tipped themselves forward so their heads were pointing down and tails toward the surface. Nina mimicked them and together they glowed with a blue green aura.

The whale closest to them opened its cavernous mouth wide and emitted a low, guttural sound. The bass note was deep and profound as the others harmonized into a low, rumbling frequency. The water began to bubble and froth as the blue green aura glowed with intensity.

The sound was overwhelming, and Oslo put his hands over his ears and cried out as he felt his body shudder and twist. A searing white light enveloped and blinded him as he heard voices over a growing static hiss. He swore for a moment he heard Raza cry out in pain as an image of her beautiful face twisted in anguish flashed within his mind.

Dear wife, why did I abandon you?

The world around him exploded into pure white, then silence.

He blinked his eyes and tried to focus as the sounds of the ocean filled his ears. He looked up when he felt drops of water on his face and saw he was still in the bubble. Soon, water was pouring in from fissures across its surface and drenching him.

He watched as Nina furiously tried to maintain speed as they propelled the last few hundred feet to the marina, then he was flung back as she angled up and raced to the surface. Bursting into the air, they smashed onto the docks, bursting the bubble and sending him tumbling onto the hard stone surface of the marina.

Oslo groaned as he laid still and gathered his wits, then rolled over and saw Nina sprawled face down and breathing heavily. He crawled over and held her in his arms. "Good girl, good girl," he kept repeating as he stroked her hair and fought back the stabs of guilt. He had put his only child in danger as she risked her life to save him.

He looked up at the sky with a tormented heart. All he wanted to do was to reopen Perihelion and gather the children of the paranormal to rekindle the civilization he once knew. Instead, he was putting lives in danger as the Elephim were now raining destruction across the planet because of his actions. Excort was right; he had stirred the hornet's nest.

He flinched when he felt a soft and delicate hand caress his face. He looked down and Nina was smiling as she pulled a wrist band from her pocket and handed it to him. It was his wrist console that he threw into the water earlier. He stared at it with astonishment.

She smiled and nodded.

Remorse over his willingness to give up on his mission swept over him. "You never lost your faith in me?" he said to her.

She shook her head. "No father, I know you are a good man, but like mother, you must hide your feelings for me. The Elephim see it as a sign of weakness and would use it to get to me. Suppressing your emotions is how you have been able to protect me for so long."

Oslo slumped forward as he fought back the crushing anguish that threatened to consume him. "Smart girl, you are. So frail, yet so strong."

Nina nestled her head into his chest. "I know about the Elephim. I also know why you and mother had to separate from each other and sacrifice so much to protect me from them. I know everything, Father, and that is why you must bring the others back. Your cause is a noble one; you are on the right path." She shivered and coughed; her face grew pale. "They need you, Father, now more than ever as their lives are in danger. As we speak, they are hovering close to death." She trembled in his arms.

Oslo touched her face. It was ice cold.

"Ray and Sally are being hunted. Ray is doing his best to fend off the Elephim that give chase, but he is close to defeat. And Breeze," her eyes widened when she spoke his name, "is being protected by a solitary Elephim who is undermining its own kind to help him." She looked at her father with pleading eyes. "Rescue him, Father. Please bring him back for he is the answer to your troubles. This much I know."

Oslo nodded. "I will, child. I will." He held her tight. "I'm sorry for all the times I left you. And I never told you how much I—"

She put her hand to his lips. "That day will arrive. You must go now, Father, for the shepherd must tend to his flock." She pushed him away and crawled to the edge of the pier. "Go now, before it is too late." She rolled off and into the water. Not a splash was heard.

Oslo leaned against a piling, looked up at the darkening sky and wept. Tears rolled down his face as his body shuddered.

He abruptly stood up and straightened out his jacket as he tried to compose himself. He looked down at the wrist console Nina had recovered for him. He strapped it on and activated the comms.

"I'm back," he spoke into it as he walked toward the campus.

He climbed up the steps that scaled the hillside. At the top, Excort was there to greet him.

The dwarf stared him down. "Couldn't stay away, just had to come back?"

Oslo smiled and placed a hand on his shoulder. "I won't do that again. You have my word."

Excort grunted. "Fine. So what now? All the birds have flown."

Oslo nodded gravely. "Yes, and they must be recovered. What is the flight status of the transports in the hangar? Have the RF finished with the repairs on any of them?"

Excort nodded. "Yes, we have two online ready to go plus a scout ship. Which should I prep?"

"The transports," Oslo said, "but we must act with haste, for there is very little time."

Breeze lay on the canyon floor. Night had settled in as a frigid wind blew and swirled through the mountains.

He didn't feel a thing because he was cocooned in a cloud of warm air as he laid in a fetal position inside his shield. It was the first time it raised itself when he wasn't in flight, and he found it comforting to think of it as body armor that would appear when he needed it most.

He could still hear the gusting wind and the rustling of every animal that crept by. He even heard the sounds of the stars. It sounded like static combined with the powerful roar of a waterfall, but it was all too much for him to handle. He concentrated and filtered out the static until it faded away, and that's when he heard it.

It was faint at first, like a musical instrument that was being plucked one string at a time, and then it built up until it sounded as if all the strings were being strummed simultaneously.

The chords reverberated in his mind. He saw stars and planets with streams of plasma between them while he weaved through an asteroid field and dodged giant boulders and debris with ease. It all felt as if he had done this many times before.

He burst out of the asteroid field and turned to look back, but it faded away as he was plunged into darkness. Panic set in as a sense of desperate loneliness consumed him.

Then, a whisper in his ear. It was the soft and delicate voice of a young woman.

"They will come for you. Have no fear for you are not alone."

"Nina?"

"Yes. I will always be here for you. No matter what, I will wait for you as I always have, for I can never truly leave the island. It is a part of me as I'm a part of it."

The wind speed increased, kicking up sand and rocks into a whirlwind. Breeze could feel the pressure change as his shield flexed.

"Always remember Breeze. Never force anything, just move."

He opened his eyes and was greeted by a blinding light as he was lifted into the air. He could see the outlines of a ship as it drew closer.

A pair of RF reached out from the lowered cargo ramp to grab him but couldn't get a grip as his shield repelled any attempt to touch its outer skin. Eventually the robots pushed against the shield and shoved it into the cargo hold of the ship.

A RF leaned over to peer through his shield. It had a streak of orange across its breast plate.

Breeze recognized it. It was one of the mechanics he often saw in the hangar.

It turned and nodded at its companion, then back to Breeze and winked an eye at him.

Breeze smiled, then closed his eyes and slept.

Ray rushed over to Sally and placed a hand over her mouth.

Her eyes flew open in surprise as he placed a finger to his lips, and then pointed up at the ceiling.

Dribbles of dirt rained down on them from the ceiling as the intruder on the floor above slowly stepped about.

Ray and Sally tracked its movements, looking at each other now and then with fear streaked across their faces.

The footsteps stopped, followed by an agonizing silence.

The wooden floor above shattered into thousands of splinters as a black boot smashed its way through. The boot dangled for a moment before it withdrew and was replaced in a flash by the head and shoulders of an Elephim thrusting through to glare at them. Pinpoints of light swirled across its face as the sound of static filled the room.

Sally screamed as it dropped down and landed on its feet. Ray jumped in front of her and unleashed a blast of energy, hurling the black clad figure back as more debris rained down upon them.

He looked at his hands in amazement. *How did that happen? I was too weak to fire before.*

The force of the blast collapsed the ceiling, sending it crashing down onto them. Sally cowered into a fetal position as Ray threw himself on top of her.

As the cloud of dust settled, two Elephim emerged from it and stood before them. They sound of static reached a fearsome crescendo as their faces swirled with pinpoints of light.

Ray gritted his teeth and trembled as he reached deep inside to find all the rage he could muster. His eyes glowed a brilliant white, and then faded into red. He raised his hands and fired.

The explosion that followed could be seen and heard for miles.

Miles away, a transport ship with Perihelion markings on its hull approached the base of the mountain and the RF piloting the ship used the explosion to zero in on Ray and Sally's location. The robots would later find the two huddled together at the bottom of a crater in a coma with smoldering debris sizzling all around them.

They gathered them and placed them in the ship, then lifted off and arced toward the coast.

CHAPTER

▼

THIRTEEN

BREEZE FLOATED IN AND out of consciousness. Every breath he took felt like an ocean was flowing in and out of his lungs while he floated in a warm bath that invigorated him. He could feel his skin tingle with pinpricks of electricity as he drifted in a state of suspended animation.

Faces drifted in and out before him as he recognized some while others were complete strangers. Voices whispered in his ear but only a portion of what they said he understood as most of it sounded like gibberish.

"When all is in doubt, come back to the White Mountain." One of the voices whispered in his ear.

His eyes fluttered open, and everything he saw was a blur as he floated up. He broke through to the surface and treaded water inside a pool with a deep green hue that coursed through it. Above was a domed ceiling with a crystalline surface.

He swam to the edge where he crawled out and sprawled onto the stone floor. He was surprised at how warm it felt when he felt the vibration of footsteps and looked up to see a diminutive figure approach. He thought it was Excort at first until Mila, his wife, came into view. Behind her stood a RF that was colored head to toe in white. On its breast plate, he saw an insignia of a snake wrapped around a staff.

She wrapped his body in blankets as a floating gurney appeared. It lowered to the ground, and she motioned to the RF to lift him onto it. It floated up as his eyes fluttered to a close.

He woke up in the Medical Wing. The room was spartan except for a cluster of machines that stood by his bedside monitoring his vital signs.

He sat up and tried to get out of bed just as the white RF he saw by the pool stepped in and wagged a finger at him.

"Forbidden," the robot said.

Breeze was stunned. He tried in vain for the longest time to interact with the RF in the hangar, but it was futile. At best they would tilt their heads at him, and then walk away.

Now, in the unlikeliest of places, he had one actually speaking to him.

"What do you—", he hacked and coughed violently, it was the first time he had spoken in a while, and his throat was clogged and dry.

The RF handed him a glass of water, and he was surprised that it was able to hold the cup without breaking it. Because it was formerly a combat robot, he found it unnerving that it was now reprogrammed for nursing duty. He took the water and drank it in gulps while tasting effervescence in his mouth as the water slid down his throat.

"What do you mean forbidden?" he challenged.

"Mistress has strict instructions," the robot said as it took the empty glass from him.

"Mila? Well, tell her thank you, but I need to find Oslo and tell him what happened."

The RF tilted its head. "You are in error regarding the issuer of my instructions. It was Mistress Kera, not Mistress Mila"

"Kera? What does she care, she was happy to see me leave."

"Her orders were strict."

"Oh, yeah?" He slid to the side of the bed and wobbled when he tried to stand up.

The RF steadied him. "Please return to your bed."

Breeze gripped the robot's arm for support. "No, just give me a minute. I feel like I've been sleeping for a long time and haven't accomplished anything. Just leave me be."

"As you wish." The RF stepped away from him.

He collapsed to the floor in a heap.

Breeze lashed out at the robot. "I meant just stand still. Oh, forget it!" He waved the RF off.

He grabbed the side of the bed and pulled himself up. His knees buckled, but he held his ground. He saw his uniform neatly laid out on a table next to him. He struggled to take off the medical gown he was wearing so he could get into it.

The RF stepped over to assist and handed him his shirt.

"I thought you were under strict orders," Breeze snarled as he snatched it from the robot.

"This unit recognizes authority when it presents itself."

It was his turn to tilt his head. "What do you mean by that?"

The robot's eyes glowed. "Your attempts at communication with our kind has not gone unnoticed."

Before Breeze could press the issue, Mila stepped into the room.

"What is the meaning of this?" she huffed and pushed the RF to the side. The robot dutifully bowed to her. Before it turned away, it stole a glance at Breeze and nodded, then returned to its station.

Breeze groaned as he tightened his belt, and then reached over for his jacket.

Mila grabbed and tugged at it. Breeze held onto it firmly.

"Mila, I appreciate everything you've done, but I need to talk to Oslo about what happened. And have you heard from Sally or Ray? Are they all right?"

Mila pointed a finger at him. "You need your rest. You are not well, and you've been through much. As for Oslo, he knows."

"What about Sally and Ray?"

Mila nodded and sighed. "Yes, they are back. But—"

"I need to go see her." Breeze hobbled out of the room, reaching for anything he could find to steady himself as he did.

He stumbled his way down the steps, through the main doors and into the brilliant sunshine. He covered his eyes from the glare and quickly stepped onto the boulevard where the overhanging ficus trees provided him with shade from the scorching heat of the sun. As he made his way to the dormitories, he felt more rejuvenated with every step he took.

He flinched suddenly and looked to his right. There sat the Science and Engineering building. His memory still fresh from his encounter in the basement with Bram, he veered to the left side of the boulevard and hurried past it.

He stepped onto the courtyard and bounded up the steps of the dormitory and into the breezeway when he ran into Ray and Sally.

They all froze and stared at one another, then Sally rushed over and threw her arms around his neck.

He was stunned at first, and then embraced her tightly.

She pulled away from him and sniffled. Her face was red and puffy. "So happy to see you again."

Ray spoke up. "Well, did you enjoy your long nap?"

Breeze shrugged. "What do you mean?"

Ray's face darkened. "Do you know how long you were out?"

Breeze's face went pale upon hearing the question.

Ray snorted. "You were in Medical for over a week."

Breeze felt his legs wobble and he leaned against the railing for support. The warm air caressed him as it blew in from the ocean. "I remember I took a ship from the hangars. I was almost home when something attacked me, and I had to eject—"

Sally wailed and buried her head in Ray's chest. He soothed her with comforting words while stroking her hair.

She gathered herself and looked at Breeze. "My home is gone."

Breeze stood dumbfounded. "I remember you guys left...because of Ray's father saying everything was okay for you back home—"

"It wasn't! Our city is gone. It's been attacked."

Breeze slumped to the floor. "If your city is gone, then my town probably is too."

He thought about his father. For the first time since he could remember, he actually began to realize that he might be gone from his life forever. He didn't know what to think or feel.

"We're all in a bad way," Ray said as he sat next to Breeze. "I can't get in touch with my parents." He recounted the story about what had happened to them.

Breeze listened dutifully. When Ray was finished, he recounted his tale about being attacked by the Elephim over the mountains.

Sally came over to sit between them while struggling to keep her composure.

They sat in silence for a moment, and then Breeze spoke up. "In the end, the RF came to get us. Not Oslo or Kera or anyone else. Just the robots."

Ray nodded. "Yeah, pretty much. Didn't think much of it until now."

"Did you speak to Oslo about it?"

"No. He's been avoiding me and Sally. He kept saying he needed to focus on your recovery. Excort and Mila are the ones who have been watching after us. And Kera..." he nodded toward Sally.

She didn't respond.

Ray continued. "Well, Kera hasn't been seen either. It's like nothing has changed."

"No," Breeze said, "we need to get to the bottom of this. C'mon, follow me." He stood up abruptly and wobbled. He grabbed the railing to steady himself, then turned and marched to the stairwell.

"Where are you going?" Ray called out.

"We are going to see Oslo in his office," Breeze said.

Sally got up to follow. Ray stood and watched them leave, then jogged to catch up to them.

They stepped past their dorm rooms and down the steps that led to the administrative building. When they arrived at the entrance to his office, they burst into it. It was empty.

Breeze strode across the room and straight up to the lamp shaped like a boat captain that was on the desk. He leaned into it and shouted Oslo's name.

Ray laughed. "Breeze, you can use the intercoms."

"No. There is something about this lamp. Don't ask me why I feel that way. Forget about the fact it looks hideous. Seriously, a lamp in the shape of a captain with one hand on the helm while the other shields his eyes. Or is he saluting? I can't tell. I mean, who keeps a thing like this? Not even my father would and he's a man who collects scrap.'"

"It's just a stupid lamp," Sally said sullenly.

Suddenly, a figure stepped in from the balcony. It was Oslo. "Perhaps, but I think of it as a cherished memento."

They all turned to face him as he strode across the room and lowered his tall frame into the chair behind the desk.

Sally erupted. "You are a criminal and a coward! What happened to our families? Why have you been avoiding us?"

Oslo held up a hand as Ray tried to calm Sally down. She swatted him away.

"Much has happened, this I know," Oslo began, "what I have to tell you will not be easy to hear. Please, do sit for a spell, the news I must give will be dire, and yes, more changes are heading our way."

Sally was incensed. "As if I care! You have no right to lecture us—"

"Sit down!" Oslo boomed. They immediately sat in the chairs spread out before his desk.

Oslo rubbed his forehead. "This is a time of revelation for all of you as to why you were brought here and for what purpose." He cleared his throat, and then continued. "This school, as you probably have already imagined, is not much of one. It is-was, a military facility. For a time, one of the premier bases on the planet. But events that changed the world reduced it to nothing more than the last refuge for a civilization that faded away into obscurity. And now, just a lonely outpost trapped in time."

"What does this have to do with our parents?!" Sally shrieked at him, "I was attacked by some shadow figure at a crater that used to be my home! What was that? What's happening out there? Where is my family?"

"The Elephim," Oslo said.

"The who? What are you talking about?" Sally questioned.

Before Oslo could respond, Breeze spoke up. "Oslo told me every-thing right before I left." He explained to them how Oslo, Kera and Excort confronted him in the dormitories, and how Oslo told him of Earth's past and the battles fought between the Helios and the Elephim.

Ray sat up in his seat and listened intently as Breeze spoke.

When he was finished, Sally turned her wrath onto Oslo. "You're telling me all of this is because you have some weird fantasy of creating a team of super powered people to fight these...Elephim creatures? This is not happening! What have you done to my life?!"

Oslo flinched and looked away. "What I have done...is far too late to reverse. I set out to rescue those that I knew who could make a differ-ence in this world. Yes, I have stirred dark forces with my actions, but I will not turn away from my mission. I will rid this world of the Elephim and restore it back to its former glory. I will do this with you, or alone."

He barely finished his words when Kera floated into the office through the balcony door, her white dress trailing behind her. "Don't be so dramatic Ole, that is not your realm. You are not alone, and you will never be."

Sally shrank back in her seat as Ray grabbed her hand to reassure her.

Breeze pointed at Kera. "All this time we've been here, you've never really explained how she got here or what she's supposed to do except spook everyone."

Oslo nodded at Kera as she settled by his side. He took her hand and held it as she materialized.

"Kera...is an old friend. A fellow paranormal like us all."

"Old? Speak for yourself, *old man*," Kera said haughtily

Oslo smiled briefly, and then turned somber. "Kera's story is a long and complicated one. She is a refugee from the past. I discovered her in my travels across the globe in my later years and brought her here to Perihelion for safekeeping. I do not believe I am at liberty to tell you more without her consent." He turned to her.

Kera leaned in and looked him in the eye. "Send them off Oslo, it is not safe here."

"You're always so eager to get rid of us," Breeze said.

She glared at him. "It is for your own good."

"So you can have more time to spend with that Bram guy in the basement?" Breeze taunted.

Her eyes blazed with fury. "This from a loner? What I do and why I choose to remain here are for my reasons alone and for no one else to question."

Oslo raised a hand. "Enough. I will not have a brawl here in my office. We must come to the reality of what has happened. The Elephim are awake—"

"Yes, because of you!" Sally yelled.

Kera turned translucent as she lunged at Sally. "You have been rescued and protected. Be grateful for life, little girl." She then added in a whisper, "always be grateful for life."

Sally gripped Ray's hand.

Oslo cleared his throat and Kera returned to hover beside him.

"No more. What is done is done, there is no going back. Sally, my actions may have only sped up a plan the Elephim had put into place long ago, nothing more. I saved you all from certain death. It is up to you to determine if your life is of any value. You can hate me if you wish, but you have your life and a chance to live free from a tyranny perpetrated by those who hide in the shadows and lash out at any attempt by humanity to better itself. This is an opportunity for you and your teammates and perhaps one day, your children."

Sally said nothing as she turned to look out the window.

"I do not proclaim to know what has happened to your families. But I make it my solemn vow to set things right. I will use all of the resources at my disposal to reunite you with your families, this I swear."

"So your plan for a super army—" Breeze said.

"Is very much on hold," Oslo retorted. He closed his eyes for a moment to gather himself. "What I thought was Bram speaking to me from across the vast stretches of space on that cold night in my home in Scandinavia, was probably nothing more than my desire to believe that all that I had known was not lost, and that I could put the world back together as it once was. I understand how foolish that may sound, and I'm sorry I brought all of you into this madness, but I will never apologize again. We are alive and must accept the fate that has been handed to us.

As we speak, the RF are prepping a ship for you. A scout ship, as we called them back in the day. She is versatile and nimble, with the ability to range for great distances undetected. She will be the chariot that will whisk you across the Atlantic to the safety of Appalachia. There, you will reside at my wife's farm until I arrive."

"You're sending us away again?" Sally said. "We've only been here for a few days, and you're sending us out to get attacked again?"

"No harm will befall you, this I swear."

"I don't believe it!" Sally yelled.

"Silence!" Kera zoomed over the desk and loomed over her. Sally shrunk back in her seat as Kera returned to hover next to Oslo.

Oslo nodded at Sally. "You must believe me what I tell you. Perihelion has been compromised. I have managed to reestablish security, but I do not know if we have been infiltrated and if so, how deeply. We have performed multiple security sweeps between Excort, Kera and I, along with round the clock patrols by select RF, and we have not found any traces of Elephim. But one can never be too careful. I encountered a pair of Elephim on the outskirts of the fog when I departed the island. How they found me, I would never presume to know, but I have my suspicions," he said and turned to Ray, then continued, "Nevertheless, I take full responsibility."

Ray squirmed in his seat.

He addressed them all. "Regardless, I am dispatching all of you to Appalachia. As I stated earlier, the RF are performing the last of the repairs needed to get your scout ship up and running for the journey."

"How come you never mentioned your wife before?" Sally said.

Oslo cringed. "It is, like everything else—"

"A long story, we get it."

"My wife is a good woman. She will shelter you from this storm. She resides outside a town that possesses a fog that obscures the entire mountain range from the prying eyes of the Elephim."

"Kind of like this place was supposed to," Breeze muttered.

Oslo shot him a glance. "Yes, point taken. But in Appalachia you will meet others of our kind. It was one of the few places the Helios could go other than offworld to live in peace. There is something almost... mystical about that place."

"Are you bringing Nina?" Breeze said

Oslo's face grew red. "I... don't believe so. No."

"But she's your daughter."

"Yes, I know that. But Perihelion is her home and is the one place where she is truly safe. She will stay here with Excort and Mila. With our departure and with the reinforcement of the fog, the Elephim will never get near her. This I know."

He stood up. "That is all for now. You are dismissed. Return to your rooms and begin gathering your belongings. You will depart in three days." He stepped out onto the balcony with Kera in tow.

The three looked at one another with blank expressions, and then shuffled out of the office with their heads hung low.

C H A P T E R

▼

F O U R T E E N

DAWN BROKE OUT OVER Perihelion as Breeze woke up with a feeling of sadness. He lay in bed and watched the sun rise over the bay through the open balcony door, its light penetrating the room and exposing the dreariness of it. Every crack on the ceiling, walls and floors were plain to see as it highlighted every flaw and blemish to be found. *The whole school, the whole island, is in shambles. How did Oslo ever believe he could bring this place back to life?*

He rolled out of bed and grimaced when his feet touched the cold stone floor. As he reached for his clothes in the cabinet next to his bed, he replayed in his mind the events that led up to this moment: the harrowing journey to get here from his desert home; meeting Oslo, Sally, Raza, Nina and Ray; the haphazard attempts by Oslo to teach and train them; their rebellion against him and subsequent departure from the island; the ambush and attempted kidnapping by the Elephim; Sally and Ray learning the harsh truth that their city lay in ruins, their parents nowhere to be found. It had been a whirlwind for them all. Now, Oslo was sending them away. To a safe haven, he promised them. He felt he had heard this before.

He stepped out into the breezeway and breathed in the warm and humid stream of air as it flowed in from the ocean. He looked at Sally's door and wanted to knock, but thought better of it. He heard her sobbing throughout the night, and though he always thought of her as rude and abrasive, to hear her sounding so wounded and anguished pushed out whatever lingering anger he felt toward her. She was just as lost and lonely as the rest of them.

He walked down the stairwell to the courtyard, then onto the pathway that led to the hangars. He wanted to get a firsthand glimpse at the ship Oslo said he was prepping for their trip across the ocean to Appalachia.

He arrived just as several RF were pushing it out from the cavernous hanger and onto the tarmac.

The ship was a disheveled mess. He could see where the mechanics welded patches of steel plate across her hull. She had seen better days, and it showed with every scratch, burn mark and dent across its metal skin.

He slowly walked around it as the RF continued to fuss over the ship and make repairs. She wasn't big when compared to the other ships he had seen in the hangars. She was one hundred fifty feet in length with a twenty five foot beam. Her height with landing gear was thirty feet. There was a pilot house at the bow and on either side of the ship were a row of windows for the passenger cabin leading back to the stern, where it ended abruptly with a vertical tail fin that protruded sharply up and then laid back with a steep curve, resembling the upper dorsal of a shark. The wings were short and stubby with a turbine attached to each. Breeze could see where the wings and engines rotated in tandem, indicating the ships ability for vertical takeoff and landing.

He continued his inspection while mindful of the RF who were repairing it. Sparks from welding torches rained down on him as some of the robots stopped to look at him warily, then continued with their tasks. Amidst the noise and commotion, he failed to hear Sally and Ray approach. He turned and was stunned to see Sally standing next to him as she stared blankly at the ship with red and swollen eyes. Her hair was a tangled mess and her clothes were more like wrinkled rags. It was a stark contrast from her usual stylish and well-manicured appearances she displayed.

Ray was standing next to her, and he made a feeble attempt to hold her hand. She pulled it away as she sniffed and wiped her nose.

"What is this broken down heap the robots are trying to fix?" she asked without looking at Breeze.

"That's our ride to Appalachia."

"Oh," she said, then crossed her arms and marched up the gangplank that led into the ship.

Breeze looked at Ray and shrugged, and then they followed her in.

Inside they were greeted by the smell of mildew as years of being stored away in an unventilated hangar left the interior of the vessel with a dank smell from the tropical humidity.

There were no functioning lights, only the rays of the sun streaming in through the dirty windows lit the interior. Breeze toggled a few switches on a panel next to him, but to no avail.

"Shore power is not connected," he said.

Ray gave him a blank stare. Sally shrugged and continued on.

"No worries, I'll go back down and grab a portable generator. I'll plug it into the receptacle under the hull."

Ray nodded at him, and then turned to follow Sally.

Breeze bounded down the gangplank and onto the tarmac. It felt good to be useful in something he knew a lot about as growing up around aerocraft gave him all the knowledge and experience he needed.

He ran over to a row of supply sheds where he had seen portable generators inside them while exploring the hangars in the past. His plan was to grab one and connect electrical cables into the hull to get some much needed air conditioning and lighting inside the ship.

He saw a RF pushing a generator out of a shed as it headed toward another ship. Breeze ran up to the robot, and it was startled to see him.

He started to explain to it his plan, but the robot just stared at him as he spoke, then it stepped away from the generator and began heading toward to the hangars. The robot swiveled its head briefly to look back as it walked away at a brisk pace.

Breeze was stunned as he thought for a moment it was going to resist him. He had always felt a little uncomfortable around them as he recalled Oslo telling him that the mechanics were actually reprogrammed mechanized warriors. Whenever he would ask questions about the RF, Oslo would just shrug off his inquiries and change the subject.

He got behind the generator and pushed. Though it was on wheels, it was too heavy for him to move. He turned to look for a tractor tug, and saw one next to a transport undergoing repairs. He ran over and hopped into the cab and drove it to the generator. He coupled it to the back of the tug, then jumped back into the cab, dropped the tug into gear and raced across the tarmac with the generator in tow.

He pulled up under the hull of the scout ship and positioned the generator under an electrical panel. He jumped out of the tug and grabbed a set of coiled cables that were hanging off the side of the generator and stretched them out. After plugging them into the hull, he opened a control panel on the generator and began flipping a series of switches when he noticed an emblem that was affixed at the top of the panel.

He knew it was a tag that identified the manufacturer and had seen his fair share of them while working at the scrap yard back home. They not only told the operator the make and model of the machine, but various technical specifications pertaining to it. Breeze couldn't make out most of the information. Time and weather had faded the lettering, but it was the name of the manufacturer that caught his eye. The first two letters spelled out CO, and the last few letters were IES. The rest was illegible.

He touched the emblem with his fingertips. There was something familiar about it, but he couldn't understand why he felt a connection. He shook his head and stepped away.

He finished setting the switches to their correct positions, and then twisted a dial to the power on setting to activate the generator. The machine stumbled at first, then run smoothly as it fed electricity to the ship.

He bounded up the gangplank, eager to see the results of his handiwork. He stepped inside and was met by garish lighting that flickered throughout the ship combined with a wave of dust that smelled as if it were burning. He began to hack and cough.

Ray ran over to him. "Why is there so much dust being blown through the ship? And why does it smell like we're on fire?"

It took a moment for Breeze to recover from his hacking cough. "I'm just realizing that the air conditioning vents haven't been used in a long time. There's a lot of dust in them that has built up over the years. The air inside the vents has been heating up since the ship was rolled out onto the tarmac and has been sitting under the sun. When I turned on the ventilation, it just blew it all out." Breeze started coughing again.

Ray waved his hands in an attempt to sweep it away. "Well, it's settling down. Let's go see what other disasters this rust bucket has to offer."

Breeze responded with more coughing as he followed Ray down a corridor that led to the bow of the ship. Along the way, they passed through the passenger compartment where the smell of mildew was the strongest. Breeze counted out seven rows of seating with four seats on either side of the aisle. Every seat was worn out with cushioning in various states of decay along with rusted armrests.

They pressed on until they arrived at the pilot house. Stepping through a thick metal arch that was low enough to force them to duck their heads, they arrived at the ship's cockpit.

The pilot's seat was on the port side, and the co-pilot to starboard. Like the seats in the passenger section, they too were worn out though Breeze pointed out one difference.

"No cushioning. Neither one of us is going to pilot the ship," he said.

"What do you mean?" Ray replied.

"Look, there all metal seats. That can only mean one thing. Auto Pilot."

"Again?" Ray sighed, "I was hoping to get a chance to fly it. Besides, don't really care for the Auto Pilots, they're pretty weird."

"After the incident with the trimaran? I don't think Oslo is going to trust either one of us," he said, then pointed up, "I'm going to look up in the crew's rest to see if the pilot is in there." Breeze climbed up the ladder behind the pilot's seat to the overhead compartment where the robotic pilot was stored. A feeling of apprehension swept over him as he grabbed the handle of the sliding panel and slowly opened it. Automatic lighting flickered on, and though it was feeble, it was more than enough to see that it was empty.

"Nothing up here," Breeze said as he slid the panel closed and climbed back down.

Ray didn't respond though his look of relief spoke volumes.

"I don't know about you, but I want to see the engine room," Breeze declared, then stepped out of the pilot house. He stopped to look back at Ray. "Coming?"

"Yeah, sure." Ray seemed more than happy to leave.

They went back through the musty passenger compartment until it came to an end. They stepped through an arch, and into a corridor that ran perpendicular to the ship's length. In front of them was a door with a handle and a painted arrow next to it that pointed down. Above the door in faded lettering was the word PROPULSION.

Breeze gripped the handle and tried to push it down, but it wouldn't budge. He gave it another try by throwing his weight on it, and it responded with the sound of metal scraping against metal as the door opened with a hiss. Immediately they were coughing on stagnant air that whooshed out and sent them both to opposite ends of the corridor to get away from the smell.

Breeze was the first to return to the entrance and peek inside where the automatic lighting had activated, but it flickered haphazardly. He stepped over the raised threshold and walked a few feet forward before stopping at a stairwell that led down into the bowels of the ship, then placed a hand on the rusted metal railing and descended. He could hear Ray following behind and wheezing heavily. He looked back to see he had pulled up his shirt and was breathing into it, prompting Breeze to laugh.

"What's so funny?" Ray asked as they reached the bottom of the stairs.

"It's obvious you're not used to exploring old ships. It does take a while to get used to the smell, though I have to admit, most of the old ships and aerocraft we process at our scrap yard are not this bad. We don't get this much humidity where I live, that's why they preserve better."

"Do you miss your home?"

Ray's question took Breeze by surprise.

"Yeah, I guess. I'm more concerned that I haven't heard from my father though Oslo insists that he's okay. I still can't reach him with the comms so I'm not sure how he knows everything is fine considering what happened to you and Sally—" Breeze stopped when he realized that he was treading on sensitive territory, as the disappearance of Ray and Sally's parents, and the destruction of their city was something that he kept forgetting about.

He turned the subject around. "I just miss exploring all the old junk we had at the yard. That's why I'm glad we came down here, I mean, look at all of this stuff! There are machines here I've never seen before. This stuff looks so old, and yet I get the feeling that it can do things that the machines back home couldn't possibly come close to."

"Do you recognize anything at all?" Ray said

"I guess so. I can tell those are the engines." Breeze pointed to the back of the ship. "Twin power plants. They look like electromagnetic generators, but I've never seen ones like those before. We have stacks of motors like those piled up at our yard, but much smaller. These things are huge, and they look so much more advanced than they stuff we have. But why do they look so old? I don't get it."

They stood quietly between the massive engines that towered over them when Breeze spotted a ladder affixed to the side of one of them, and as he was about to climb up, his eye caught sight of an emblem attached to the engine.

He squinted as he rubbed the grime that had built up on it over the years and obscured the information it possessed. The shape of the emblem was similar to the one on the generator powering the ship, but he couldn't glean much from it. The name of the manufacturer was faded, but he could still see the engine specifications. They were definitely more powerful than anything he had ever known. He took a step back to take in the immensity of the engines.

"What is it?" Ray said.

"I don't know. There is something so familiar about them. It's the same feeling I got when I was messing around with the generator outside."

"What are you talking about?"

"Forget it. No big deal. Let's just—" Breeze was cut off by a loud, piercing shriek emanating from the passenger compartment above.

They turned to look at each other. "Sally!" they said in unison and they raced back to the stairwell and clambered up as fast as they could climb.

The shrieks continued as they burst out of the propulsion room and tumbled into the corridor. They looked to the left and to the right, all the while calling out Sally's name but she never responded.

They followed the hallway to the sleeping compartments where they found Sally in the main corridor standing in horror. She had one hand on her chest and the other pointing into a room.

Ray was the first to reach her. "Sally! What's the matter? What happened to you? Is everything okay?" He reached for her hand, but she swatted it away.

Breeze arrived and leaned against the wall. Breathing heavily, he looked at Sally. "What....what's wrong?"

"The bathroom," she cried out, "it's...disgusting!"

Ray let out a condescending smile. "Oh, it can't be that bad."

She whirled on him in fury.

"Look!" she hissed.

Ray was confronted by the sight of one of the most awful bathrooms he had ever seen. Heavy amounts of grime and mold covered the entire bathroom from top to bottom as bugs of some unknown species skittered all about with frenzied energy.

Breeze pushed him away to take a look. "Oh yeah," he laughed, "that's really gross!"

"I," Sally began with a trembling voice, "will not go anywhere in this ship until this bathroom is clean."

Breeze piped up. "Not a problem, just grab a bucket, soap and a brush."

Ray shot an anxious glance at Breeze.

"Yeah," Breeze continued, "shouldn't be a big deal. Besides," he added, "you're going to cook and clean for us anyway, right?"

Ray looked at him with absolute horror.

Sally glared at Breeze with an icy stare. "Oh....," her voice trailed off as she folded her arms across her chest.

Later that day, Ray and Breeze were vigorously scrubbing the bathroom.

"Did you ever have a girlfriend?" Ray asked nastily.

"Shut up," Breeze retorted.

"Seriously, do you know anything at all about girls?"

"Shut up!" Breeze responded angrily as he scrubbed even harder. After much arguing and crying from Sally, the guys agreed to clean out the bathroom.

Sally was in hysterics as she locked herself in an adjoining compartment and refused to come out until the bathroom was scrubbed to perfection. From time to time, Ray would knock on the door and encourage her to come out.

She answered by opening the door and to yelling "No!" Then slammed it shut.

"She seems determined to make life miserable for all of us," Breeze muttered.

"Well, she's having a rough time," Ray said.

"Aren't we all?"

"Look, I've known Sally all my life. We grew up next door to each other. I've never seen her like this, so you gotta believe me when I tell you to cut her some slack." Ray tossed his brush into a bucket and took a look at their handiwork. "Yeah, it's about as clean as it's gonna get. Probably the cleanest part of the whole ship."

"I don't get it," Breeze said, "why are we doing this anyway? This ship is only going to transport us to Appalachia and then we're done. I'm finished with this."

Just then the door to Sally's compartment opened slowly. She stepped out and stood between the two of them and spoke meekly. "I'm sorry about the screaming and crying. Breeze, I know you were just trying to be funny. I didn't mean to freak out like that."

He was tongue-tied and didn't want to blurt out any more stupid jokes. "It's okay."

She touched him gently on the shoulder, then turned and walked down the corridor.

"She didn't even look at the bathroom," Breeze said.

Ray shrugged. "Feel like eating some lunch?"

Breeze responded with a grunt and together they left the ship.

CHAPTER

▼

FIFTEEN

THE MORNING OF THEIR departure had arrived. They gathered in the courtyard where they found Excort waiting for them in a hover car, and he whisked them away to the landing facility where the scout ship awaited them.

Breeze took in the sight of the ship as they approached it. The vessel sat on the tarmac bathed in the light of the rising sun as several RF crawled over it performing final preparations and repairs.

Oslo was waiting for them with Nina. She stood close to him and held his hand. They had become inseparable ever since the attack. She smiled and waved as Excort brought the hover car to an abrupt stop, then jumped out and loaded luggage onto the ship without complaint.

Oslo nodded at them. "She's fully fueled and ready to go. No need to worry as the Auto Pilot has its instructions and coordinates to get you to Appalachia. I promise you a safe journey."

"I've heard this before," Sally said.

Oslo held her by the shoulders. "I'm sorry about your family, but you must believe me when I tell you that they had your safety in mind when they sent you to me. They couldn't tell you of the impending danger they faced because if they did, you never would have left their side. They did what they had to do out of their love for you. I promise you this; we will find them. We will find everyone. Your parents and Ray's." He wiped a tear that rolled down her cheek, then turned to address them all. "I thought I was ready when I reached out to your parents. I reached out to many families, in fact, and I tried to explain to every parent of a paranormal the danger they and their children faced. They all thought I was mad. In retrospect, who could blame them? The Elephim were just a myth, a figment of the imagination from a distant past. I am a remnant of that past. I thought I could carefully and quietly gather as many of you as I could and tell you of the glorious history of this planet. That I could teach you how to use your gifts, to be guiding lights trailblazing a path to lead humanity to a better life. But I was too slow, too old, and I failed." He stopped for a moment and held his hand over his heart as Nina stepped over and stood beside him. "I'm grateful I was able to find the three of you. We have been through a lot together. You woke this old man up."

"Why aren't you coming to Appalachia with us now?" Sally asked.

"I must stay behind and make...a few arrangements. Once completed, I will rendezvous with you at Raza's. I promise you I will come." He looked her in the eye. "*I promise.*"

Sally hugged him tightly as he patted her back. "You are all my children now. I won't let you down. We will start over again."

Sally nodded as she grabbed her bag and boarded the scout ship.

Ray reached out and shook his hand. "Sir," was all he said and without another word, turned to follow Sally.

Breeze was last. "You didn't mention anything about my father."

Oslo shuffled his feet. "We are still not in touch with him as I do believe the attack has affected comms everywhere." He placed a hand on Breeze's shoulder. "Jacob is a very capable man. I've known your father for quite some time. I wouldn't worry much about him. You will reunite with him one day and you can then decide if you wish to stay with us. I'm hoping you will stay."

Breeze didn't respond. He grabbed his bag, waved goodbye to Nina and followed his classmates into the ship. Nina watched him walked away with a look of distress on her face.

Excort had finished loading the ship and arrived to stand with Oslo and Nina. "Still haven't told him yet? Is keeping him in the dark the best strategy?"

Oslo stiffened. "He will find out soon enough. I need to keep him with the others as he is our best chance at any future success."

"You're going to be putting an awful lot on his shoulders," Excort mused.

"We all have our burdens to carry," Oslo replied.

The fueling was complete, and the RF began to move equipment away from the ship. The strobe lights from their robotic carts and tractors faded away as they retreated back to the hangars.

Inside the ship, the three took their seats. The smell of mildew was still prevalent, but not as strong as before as the ventilation system had recycled and purified the air overnight.

Breeze looked around the ship. "Have to admit, those mechs did a pretty good job of fixing up this heap."

Ray pointed toward the cockpit. "Check out the Auto Pilot."

They all turned to look and watched the arms of the robotic pilot gliding over a console as the engines spooled up. It turned to look at them, and then disappeared from view as the cockpit doors hissed to a close.

"I will never get used to those things," Sally said.

The ship lifted off with a lurch and hovered, then dropped suddenly which prompted a shriek from Sally. The engines warbled and faded to silence, then rushed back to life as the scout ship took the skies. It swept over the landing facility, then shot across the beach and hurtled over the ocean.

Through their windows, they could see the protective greenish cloud cover that was the fog in the distance, but the Auto Pilot made no effort to penetrate it as it instead plunged them into the ocean below. Breeze watched as crystal clear waters transitioned from a heavenly blue into a thick and heavy green mist. He realized now that the fog descended deep into the ocean and created a barrier that protected the island from both the air and sea. *I wonder how far below into the earth it goes*, he wondered.

Their passage through the fog was uneventful as their internal clocks had long ago acclimated to the rhythms of the island and prevented them from slipping into a comatose state. They traveled for some time underwater, until the bow of the ship angled up and burst through to the surface, then skimmed over the ocean in a protective bubble as the electromagnetic engines warped the space in the front and back of the ship, bending the visible light around it making the ship appear like a mirage.

Breeze looked over at Sally, and then Ray as both began yawning uncontrollably. Soon their eyes closed, and they slept. He turned away to look out his window when his eyes began to glaze over at the sight of the white capped waves below marching towards a distant shore in an endless procession.

He drifted away into slumber.

Breeze awoke to the sound of a powerful bang followed immediately by alarms sounding throughout the ship. He peered out the window and saw the contours of hills and mountains drifting beneath the ship in the fading sunlight.

He looked over and saw Sally awakening, and Ray running to the pilothouse. Breeze fumbled with his lap belt and tumbled out into the aisle. He caught up to Ray, and together they forced open the cockpit doors where inside they found the Auto Pilot slumped over the helm with one arm frozen in an upright position with its fingers reaching for a dial.

The cockpit smelled of smoke as they scanned the endless array of dials, switches and buttons until they were able to find the right one to kill the blaring alarms.

"What happened to this thing?" Ray said and pointed at the robot.

"It looks like an electrical fire. I've seen this before on some of the older aerocraft back home. The ship had a power surge of some sort, and it took out the pilot and fried parts of the console," Breeze said.

"So how come we haven't crashed?"

Breeze pointed toward the co-pilot's console. "This half is still working. It looks like each side operates independently." He peered at the monitor embedded in the center of the co-pilot's console. "According to this we're heading to a fixed position. The ship is flying itself."

A horrible bang suddenly reverberated throughout the ship.

"Barely," Ray said as he gripped a railing above him. They both looked out the port side window where outside, the turbine under the wing was beginning to smoke.

"If the turbines are on, that means the electromagnetic generators are off. Which means...," Breeze began to say, then fell silent.

"What?" Ray said.

"It means we're exposed. Look, the generators provide power for both the cloak and propulsion. The turbines are just back up engines to keep us flying in case they fail. If there're on, then the generators are off, then so is the cloak. That means anyone can see us."

Ray groaned. "Oslo and his promises. Now I know we're going to get attacked."

The ship lurched hard to starboard and rapidly descended just as Sally walked into the cockpit. "What's going on-watch out!" she yelled.

The scout ship was heading rapidly toward a mountain top as it skimmed close to the surface and then flew into a dark and narrow valley.

The turbines whined into a fevered crescendo which echoed throughout the valley like a trumpet blast. The wings rotated and the ship gradually lowered itself to the ground, touching down with a heavy thump as the engines immediately cut off.

Inside, cabin lights flickered on. Outside, the gangplank extended itself from the starboard side of the ship to the ground.

The trio looked at each other in stunned disbelief.

"He promised...he promised," Sally mumbled.

Ray held up a hand to her. "It's okay. Everything is fine. We're on solid ground and in one piece." He pulled her close and hugged her while waving his hand at Breeze in a continuous motion.

"Yeah, we're fine. Just a slight problem with the Auto Pilot. We're good now," Breeze said while pointing at the console. "Says right here we're on the mainland and in the Appalachian mountain ranges which is exactly where Oslo said Raza's farm is located."

Sally motioned at the pilot "If everything is fine, why is it slumped over like that—"

"Let's just go outside for some fresh air." Ray gently pushed her out the cockpit and back into the passenger compartment.

Together, they made their way to the starboard side of the ship and down the gangplank where the cold air they encountered was a stark contrast to the humidity of the island. They could see their breath with each exhale.

"This weather feels just like fall at Greenbrier," Sally said which prompted a smile from Ray. He patted her shoulder in agreement.

They took in their surroundings. The ship had landed in a clearing next to a river where surrounding them was a forest with trees so tall they seemed almost to touch the glittering stars emerging in the evening sky. The valley was encircled by mountains with glowing lights that pulsated and flitted about, then faded away in the dark.

Breeze pointed at the lights. "Did you guys see that? That's interesting."

"What's interesting is you two haven't asked the most important question: Why isn't there someone here to greet us?" Sally asked. "Where's Raza?"

The guys turned to look at her with blank stares.

She stomped her feet. "I knew he couldn't be trusted. I knew—"

Ray held up a hand. "Okay, you know what? It's fine. I'm sure her place is probably nearby, and she wasn't told of our exact time of arrival. It could be anything. Let me go back in the ship to see what I can find. Maybe Oslo left some instructions for us." He headed to the ship.

"You know, I'll just fly. I'll go across the valley, and maybe I can spot her house or something," Breeze said.

"Are you sure that's a smart thing to do? What if the Elephim sense us and attack again?" Sally said. She stepped over to Breeze with her arms crossed over her chest as she was starting to shiver.

He shrugged. "It's a risk I'll have to take. We can't just sit here and wait around. Besides, I know I have you two to back me up."

"Be careful," she said and caressed his arm, then stepped away.

Breeze closed his eyes and cleared his thoughts. Just move, he could hear Nina whisper into his ear as his feet lifted off the ground and he vaulted into the sky. He opened his eyes and hovered in place, then spun slowly to take in the view.

The mountains were enveloped in a mist that rolled in from the north and spilled down into the valley. He looked down at the scout ship with its landing lights illuminating the surrounding area and could see Sally searching the night sky trying to find him.

He scanned the mountains that encircled the valley and spotted a faint glow coming from the east. He flew towards it as he gradually picked up speed within seconds. He glided over the mountain and into another valley where he saw a farmhouse nestled along the banks of a river. A lone porch light was all it had to fend off the surrounding darkness. He looked again to the east and became mesmerized by the glowing lights of what he thought was a nearby town when something fast swooped past him and almost made him fall out of the sky. He could hear the beating of wings as it disappeared into the darkness and in the direction of the farmhouse.

He hovered precariously as his heart raced and his hands shook. Better get back the scout ship, he thought.

He returned to see the encroaching mist descending from the mountains was about to envelope the entire valley along with the ship. He landed with a stumble and almost fell face first into the ground.

Sally rushed up to greet him. "Where did you go? It seemed like you were gone for a long time." Her eyes were wide and she was breathing heavily.

"I saw-," he stopped to take in a deep breath, "—I saw a house along a river on the other side of the mountain." He pointed to the east. "And a glow from what I think are lights from a nearby town."

"How do you know?"

"Back home I would fly at night when my father thought I was asleep. I would fly deep into the desert and find my way back home by looking for the glow of the lights from my town. You could see it for miles."

Ray raced down the gangplank. "Guys, I think I found something. It looks like-," he suddenly dropped to one knee and took in several deep breaths. "Why is it so hard to breathe all of a sudden?" he said and stood up slowly, then continued. "I think I found Raza's place. According to the charts, it's on the other side of this mountain." He pointed to the east, and then a puzzled look appeared on his face as he turned to face north. "What with this mist?"

"We know about the farmhouse, Breeze already told me. Are we going to use the ship to get there?" Sally asked as she shivered and stomped her feet in a vain attempt to warm up.

"I'm not going to try and fly that thing." Ray jerked a thumb towards the scout ship. "We can just hike over the mountain."

Breeze shook his head. "Way too steep. We'll follow the river instead. I saw how it bends around the mountain and flows right past her home."

"Guys, this mist is getting thicker. You want to walk in this?" Sally said.

Breeze smiled at her. "Look, we'll be fine as long as we stick to the shoreline. I have my nav-compass with me so we won't get lost. The river flows to the north, bends east, then flows south past Raza's farmhouse. Let's just grab our stuff and go. I don't want to spend the night inside the ship."

She shook her head. "I want to wait for Oslo. Let's stay here until he arrives."

"And then he'll say why didn't we just use some initiative and find the place ourselves. It'll be followed by a long and boring lecture about teamwork and how we are not meshing together," Breeze retorted.

"Fine," she said and went into the scout ship to get her things.

When she was of earshot, Breeze leaned over to Ray. "Listen, I saw something else. Something big swept past me and almost knocked me out of the sky. I swear I heard wings beating as it flew."

Ray sighed and nodded. "Okay. Smart not mentioning this to Sally, she's pretty edgy as it is." He looked at the surrounding mist. "You know, my dad used to lead expeditions into the Bad Lands, and he sometimes told me about some of the things they encountered, like strange creatures and weird howls and stuff. Mom would get angry with him for telling me about his trips, but I wasn't scared. I loved hearing about it. It's a wild frontier, you know."

Breeze shrugged, remembering his unexpected venture into the Bad Lands not long after the air show. "We would hear stories too, but not much else. Look, if we just stick together we'll be fine."

Sally returned. She had collected everyone's bags and plopped them down. "While you boys were chatting, I decided to do a little work around here." She looked at them. "Why the serious faces?"

"No reason. Thanks for my bag, Sally. Okay, let's get going." Ray grabbed it and headed north.

"Breeze?" She looked at him with pleading eyes.

"We're good, Sally. We have a plan, let's stick to it. Farmhouse, here we come." He reached for his backpack and flung it over his shoulder, then jerked a thumb toward the ship. "Shouldn't we lock her up before we go?" he said with a grin.

"Ha, ha. I can only hope someone comes and takes away that old heap," she said and grabbed her bag.

They marched along the riverbank with Ray in the lead as he held a hand up and let it glow like a torch for them to see. The rocks beneath their feet crunched as they walked, and the sound of rushing water grew stronger with every step they took.

Sally slowed so Breeze could catch up to her. "Why can't you just fly us there?" she asked.

"Never did it before and besides, I can barely keep myself in the air without losing my concentration and falling out of the sky."

"I just don't like being out here like this. This place has a weird vibe," she said.

"You don't say."

"What do you mean by that?"

"Nothing, just agreeing with you. I—" Breeze stopped as something rustled in the forest.

Sally gripped his arm and whispered. "See what I mean."

"Just some animals. Probably a rabbit. Let's keep going."

Sally held on to his arm as they continued walking. Ahead, Ray's hand was glowing brighter as the mist intensified.

Breeze checked his nav-compass and saw the needle waving to the east as the sound of rushing water grew stronger. He looked at Sally and saw that her eyes were pinned on Ray ahead of them when he stole a quick glance to his right and froze. In a fleeting moment, he saw a pair of glowing eyes, red with narrow slits, staring straight at him.

"What is it?" Sally asked when she saw him stiffen.

"Just looking for landmarks. We're getting closer," he responded.

The sound of rushing water subsided and the mist began to fade. Breeze checked his nav-compass again and saw the needle pointing south. "Looks like we've rounded the river bend. We should be getting close, look for a porch light—"

"Got it." Ray pointed.

They came to a stop. The farmhouse was across the river.

"One minor detail I might have forgotten to mention," Breeze said.

"That the farmhouse is on the opposite bank and we have to cross it. Smooth. Now what?" Ray grumbled.

Sally looked at Breeze.

He held up a hand. "I know what you're thinking, and it wouldn't be a good idea—"

"I'm not getting into that cold water, and unless you see a boat...," her voice trailed off as she crossed her arms.

"What's she talking about?" Ray asked.

"She wants me to fly us across. That's what," Breeze said.

"Can you?"

Breeze looked at them both, and then toward the farmhouse as the receding mist revealed the width of the river.

"Okay, ladies first," he said and pointed at Sally.

She stepped up to him. "How do we do this?"

"Umm, good question." He scratched his head.

"I don't weigh that much if that's what you're thinking," she said icily as her eyes narrowed.

"No, no of course not. Well, okay, you plus your backpack—"

She glared at him.

"Okay, right. Let's do this." He stooped slightly to pick her up, his right hand sweeping behind her knees and his left hand behind her shoulders. "A little awkward with your backpack," he said as he stood up and adjusted his hold on her.

She draped her arms around his neck. "I know you can manage." Then she added in a whisper. "Don't drop me into the water. Please."

"Yeah, will do. Or won't." He shook his head. "Okay, gotta concentrate." He closed his eyes and started his breathing cycle.

Sally giggled.

"Sally!"

"I know, I know. You just look cute when you do that."

"Gee, thanks."

Something rustled in the woods behind them, and she gripped him even tighter.

"What was that?" she said.

"Never mind. We're out of here." Breeze took a deep breath and lurched upwards.

As they flew across the river Breeze wobbled as he struggled to stay aloft, which prompted Sally to shriek several times.

They landed on the opposite bank as he stumbled upon touching down and almost dropped her. He twisted around so she could fall on top him, and fell onto his back with a thump as Sally lay across him, her face close to his. She stared at him for a moment, then quickly got up and dusted herself off. "Thank you. For not dropping me."

"Right. Let me go get Ray." He flew back across the river and found Ray staring off into the forest. "Ray?" he called out to him as he landed.

Ray motioned toward the trees. "There's something back in there. I swear I can hear it."

"I know, I think it's following us. Let's just go."

"You don't have to tell me twice." He turned to face Breeze. "Okay, how do we do this?"

"Just hop on my back," Breeze said as he squatted.

Ray jumped on and gingerly draped his hands over Breeze's shoulders. "Boy, I bet we look stupid."

Breeze brought his arms around to grip Ray's legs, then stood up and wobbled. "Okay, this is awkward. Get off, get off!"

Ray slid down. "What now?"

"Let me think about this." Breeze looked across the river where he could see Sally silhouetted in the moonlight, and stared at her until the sound of a branch snapping from behind them broke him out of his trance. "Change of plans. I'm going to hover a few feet off the ground while you spread your arms out, then I'm going to lift you up and fly you across."

"You're not going to flake out and dip me in the water—" the sound of leaves rustling and branches snapping cut him off in mid-sentence.

"Ray, let's go!" Breeze shouted.

Without another word, Ray held his arms out. Breeze floated above him, then hooked his hands under Ray's shoulders and hoisted him off the ground. They streaked across the river, occasionally dipping toward the surface as Breeze tried to maintain altitude while forcing Ray to lift his legs up to keep his feet from getting soaked.

Breeze released him upon reaching shore. Ray tumbled to the ground as Breeze continued flying, coming to a stop by slamming into a tree as it cracked and toppled over.

"Breeze!" Sally shouted as she ran over to him.

He sat up and waved his hand. "I'm fine. My shield took care of me. Can't so much about the tree."

"Hey, I'm good over here!" Ray called out, "thanks for asking. No protective shield for me. But I'm fine." He walked slowly over to them while brushing dirt off his clothes.

The moon shined brightly above them as a sudden gust of wind made them all shiver. Their breath was visible in the cold air as they all turned to look at the farmhouse.

"With all the racket we just made, you would think someone would come out to investigate," Breeze said.

"Well, I'm cold. Let's just knock on the door. Maybe Raza is a heavy sleeper," Sally replied and began marching toward the farmhouse.

Sally arrived first and stopped to wait for Ray, and together they climbed up the steps. Breeze trailed from behind and came to a stop at the porch steps where he stood his ground.

Sally raised a hand to knock on the door, and then hesitated. She turned to look for Breeze and saw him at the foot of the steps. "What are you doing down there? Come up."

He shrugged. "Just...not sure about this place." He took a few steps back and looked up at the second floor windows.

"Well," she hissed at him, "do you want me to knock or not?"

"Go ahead. I just don't think....," Breeze trailed off as he watched a hand pull a curtain back, followed by a face shrouded in long white hair staring at him from a window above.

"Yep, somebody's home," he said.

As soon as Breeze spoke, the face quickly withdrew, and the curtain dropped back into place.

Sally was exasperated. "I'm knocking. I don't want her or anybody else inside to think we're intruders. Besides, we're guests here right?

She knows we're coming?"

"I'll do it," Ray said and reached up to grab the heavy iron knocker that was bolted to the center of the door. He lifted it and rapped the door several times, then dropped it back into place. "Sorry, couldn't wait." He grinned while she glared at him.

A light turned on in the window next to the door, followed by the heavy shuffling of feet. Then silence. The sound of several deadbolts sliding back rang sharply in the night, followed by more silence. Then the door creaked open slowly.

A figure emerged from the doorway. It was a woman in a white sleeping gown with a heavy robe over her shoulders stepping onto the porch. She had long white hair that was tangled and unkempt. Her face was wrinkled, and her hands shook. She looked at them with a vacant stare. "Yes?"

Sally was the first to speak up. "Good evening, my name is Sally. These are my classmates, Ray and Breeze. Oslo sent us here. Are you Raza?"

The old woman slowly looked over Sally as her hands began to tremble even more. She opened her mouth to speak, but no words came out. Eventually, she spoke in a whisper. "Nina?"

Sally shook her head. "No ma'am. Sally. Sally Trumbull. Oslo, your husband, sent my classmates and me to be here with you." Sally shifted her feet. "You are Raza, Oslo's wife?"

The woman nodded her head slowly. She moved her lips, but again, no words came out. Then she took in a deep breath. "Oslo, yes. Is he here?"

"No ma'am, he'll be here shortly." Ray stepped forward. "May we come in? It's getting awfully cold. We've traveled far to come here."

She looked him over. "Military, yes?"

"Ma'am?"

"Yes, of course. You come from a military family. Officers, no less. Am I wrong?" Without waiting for an answer, she cast her gaze back to Sally and looked her over. "And you, you come from the same town as him, don't you? Even went to school together, this much is obvious. And what about you?" She pointed a finger down at Breeze.

Breeze took a few steps back from the porch all the while keeping his eyes locked onto hers.

The old woman brushed Sally aside as she shuffled to the top of the steps. "Well, what do we have here?" She chuckled. "Ahh, the outsider.

I recognize my own kind. You came from a remote area, not unlike this one." She waved her hand. "And now here you are, encountering new things, new experiences." She chuckled a little more, and then turned to look at each one as she spoke. "He did quite a number on all of you, I see. 'Come to my school', he said, 'Come and learn how to use your gifts', I'm sure that's what he said to you."

"We'll, actually ma'am, it was our parents that sent us to him," Ray replied.

"Of course" she cackled loudly, "even better!" She then stepped back inside while leaving the door open.

Sally looked at Ray, then at Breeze. "It's cold." And she entered the home.

Ray waved to Breeze to follow as he went in after Sally.

Breeze stood and watched them disappear into the house. He looked up at the moon as its brilliance grew brighter by the minute, then over to the river, casting his eyes along the tree line and half expecting to see the red glowing eyes that hid within the forest. He then turned back to the farmhouse as his teeth chattered from a gust of cold air. He slowly walked up the creaky steps and onto the porch, and then with one last glance back toward the river, he stepped inside and closed the door.

CHAPTER

▼

SIXTEEN

BREEZE STOOD IN THE foyer taking in the sights and smells of the home. The air was thick and warm and smelled of coffee. And smoke. Lots of smoke. The floor was wooden and creaked loudly with the slightest step. He could see holes in the walls and the plaster was chipped and peeling.

He poked his head into a room off the hallway. It was dimly lit, and the walls were adorned with pictures, paintings and an oversized map. He stepped inside and gritted his teeth as the wooden floor creaked loudly. He stood still for a moment, then shrugged his shoulders and headed towards the map.

He quickly recognized the surface features on the map from what he saw earlier in the evening when he flew over the area. He spotted Raza's farmhouse and the winding river next to it. He followed the river south and spotted the markings of a bridge to a trail leading into a narrow ravine that cut through the same mountain they had just walked around. The ravine led directly to where they left the scout ship. He made a note of it, wondering why Ray didn't see it on the charts he found on the ship.

He then turned his attention to several framed pictures next to the map. Images of young people laughing and clowning around were prevalent throughout all of them. He leaned in for a closer look at one in particular. It was a picture of a tall young man, who bore a striking resemblance to Oslo, and a petite woman, obviously pregnant and hugging him at the waist. Next to them was a young man with a stern face glaring back at the camera. Breeze remembered Oslo mentioning how close he and Raza were to Bram. Perhaps that was him, he thought to himself as tried to remember what he looked like during his encounter in the basement. And lurking in the background of the picture was a lone RF with bright, shining eyes.

Breeze scratched his head. He knew they all worked closely together and that Oslo and Raza were married on the island. But he couldn't understand why Raza appeared so much older now than Oslo. Puzzled, he stepped away and headed back to the foyer.

He took off his backpack, leaving it behind with the others as he headed down the hallway. He could hear the clinking of dishes and the sounds of cabinet doors opening and closing as he approached the kitchen. Sally and Ray were seated at a table. No sooner did he step inside that Raza spoke to him.

"Glad to see you found us. Sit down young man. Join your friends at the table. I'll get some coffee and cake for you. Just be patient."

Breeze nodded as he sat down. He looked over at Sally. She was sitting upright with a wide smile across her face and with her hands neatly folded in her lap.

She turned to Breeze. "Such a lovely kitchen," she said.

His eyes widened as he scanned the room. The walls were filled with trinkets of all shapes and sizes. Small paintings of farm life hung on the walls. The kitchen appliances were old and worn out. Raza was cooking on a gas stove as an ancient coffee maker bubbled and gurgled next to it.

"Yes, it's nice," was all he could think of saying

He looked at Ray, who was sitting stone still, his eyes never leaving Raza as she shuffled around the kitchen.

Breeze waved a hand in front of him, prompting Ray to snap at him. "Stop it!"

"What's gotten into the two of you? Why so formal all of a sudden?" Breeze joked.

"Manners, young man. Something they possess in abundance. The result of going to the finest schools. But this is something you wouldn't be familiar with now, would you?" Raza turned and winked at him.

"How do you know so much about us?" Breeze asked.

"Oh, Oslo has told me so much about all of you. He was so excited to re-open Perihelion. So proud of himself for finding all of you. He honestly believed he was going to make a difference in this world. I told him he was mad." She sighed loudly, and then took a sip of coffee.

"Funny. You say he's been talking to you? How? He's been telling us the comms were down on the island and that he could barely reach anybody on the mainland. How did he get in touch with you to talk about us, let alone inform you we were coming?" Breeze said.

"The comms are down? Is this what he has been telling you?" She grinned and shook her head. "He hasn't changed one bit, has he?" She turned to look directly at Breeze. "There are many ways to get in contact with others. Surely you understand that," she said and turned to look at Sally.

Sally burst into tears. "My parents are missing! My home has been destroyed!"

Raza was visibly shaken as she watched Sally bury her face in her hands and sob. Her mouth twitched as her hands began to shake and tremble. She turned to Ray. "Is this true?"

"I'm afraid so, ma'am. When we decided to leave Perihelion and return home-," he paused for a moment and took in a deep breath, "—we found our city on fire from an Elephim attack but we never did confirm if our parents died as we were attacked ourselves and had to fight our way out and were later rescued. Breeze was attacked by Elephim who ambushed his ship as he tried to get back home to the western desert. It just seems like the world has gone dark with the comms not working. We were surprised Oslo was even able to get in contact with you."

Raza nodded slowly as she returned her attention to Sally who was sniffling with her head buried in her arms and resting on the table. Raza raised a hand to stroke her hair, and then quickly withdrew it.

"No, not again," she muttered and walked to the kitchen window to stare out into the moonlit night. "You are playing with fire with these children, Oslo, and then you drop them in my lap and expect me to clean up your mess. And I still don't have my daughter." She touched the window pane as her head drooped. She stood still for a while.

"Get out," she finally said.

Ray and Breeze exchanged puzzled glances.

"Ma'am," Ray spoke up, "I'm afraid we don't understand. Oslo sent us—"

"Get. Out." She repeated.

"We have no place to go. Our ship is broken. Please, let us stay," Sally pleaded.

Raza turned to face them. Her eyes were narrow slits and her body trembled.

"I think there's some kind of creature out there following us. We would really like to stay," Breeze blurted out.

She closed her eyes and raised clenched fists high to the ceiling. Lights began to flicker, and the house shook as plaster dropped off the walls and ceiling. A growing roar began to fill the kitchen.

"Get out!" Raza shrieked as everything around her began to bend and morph as if reality were a sheet of cloth being folded.

The three got up and ran for the door. It swung open on its own as they barreled toward it. They scooped up their bags and dashed down the steps. The door slammed shut behind them and the lights of the farmhouse were extinguished all at once.

They kept running until exhaustion made them collapse to the cold, hard ground. Resting for only a moment, Breeze scrambled to his feet as Ray and Sally slowly staggered to theirs.

"C'mon, let's head back to the river!" Breeze yelled at them.

"I don't want to try and cross the river again! What if you can't fly us over and we fall into the cold water?" Sally wailed.

A bone chilling scream erupted from the farmhouse prompting them to freeze in place.

"Would you prefer to deal with that? Let's go!" Breeze shouted and they all broke out into a sprint.

They arrived at the river bank and came to a stop. They dropped to the ground to catch their breath and rest.

"What was that? What just happened?" Sally said.

"What happened? We were abandoned and let down, again. First, by Oslo and now, by his wife. It seems like a pattern here," Breeze quipped.

"Don't say that. Oslo is coming," Ray declared as he got back to his feet and loomed over Breeze.

"Of course he is! Oh, wait, let me check." Breeze stood up and squinted his eyes as he scanned the area. "Nope, don't see him yet."

Sally spoke up. "This all has to be a great misunderstanding. I want to go back and explain everything to her, make her understand—"

"Are you kidding me? That woman just threw a psychic tantrum at us and just about demolished her own home to get us out of there. You want to go back to that?" Breeze said.

Ray jabbed a finger at him. "Back off. Sally—"

"Sally is what? Not feeling well? Depressed? Sad? Name it. News for you; I'm not happy either."

"So what do you suggest then, since I'm too sad to figure things out?!" Sally shouted at him.

"Well, Miss 'Oh, what a lovely kitchen', I say we head back to the ship as it's the only shelter we have. Crack of dawn, I'm going to the town on the other side of that mountain," he pointed to the east, "to see if I can find some parts for the ship to get it running, or at least parts for the comm system so we can get in touch with Oslo or Excort and find out where they are. But I'm not staying here." Breeze threw his backpack over his shoulder started walking south along the river bank, then stopped and turned. "Are you guys coming?"

Ray held out a hand to Sally. "Let's just go. We can't stand around here all night."

Sally sniffed, and then took his hand and together they followed Breeze.

"Wait a minute," Ray called out to Breeze, "aren't you going to fly us over the river again? Why are you heading south?"

Breeze told them of the map he'd seen earlier in Raza's home. "It'll be easier this way. We can go through the ravine and avoid that thing rustling in the woods."

"What thing?" Sally said.

Ray squeezed her hand. "Nothing. We think it's just some critter looking for food or something. Let's go."

The moon lit their way as they trudged along the river bank until they came to a stop at a rickety metal bridge.

They stepped across it while avoiding holes and shards of twisted metal that pockmarked it. The bridge ended abruptly into heavy brush.

"I thought you said there was a ravine through here?" Ray said.

"There is, it has to be past those trees," Breeze said and headed into the forest.

"I'm not going," Sally announced, "we don't know what could be in there."

Breeze whirled around and marched up to her. "Then go and see for yourself."

"How? What do you mean?"

"Hello, you're a projector, can't you just scout ahead? Make yourself a bit more useful instead of using your amazing sense of manners or crying all the time."

Ray shoved him hard. "Don't talk to her like that."

"We're supposed to be a team, remember? Here's our chance to use our powers for something," Breeze said as he stepped up into Ray's face.

Sally placed herself between them.

"Stop it! He's right. You think I'm just a privileged brat, don't you? I'll scout ahead, I can do this."

Breeze waved toward the forest. "Be my guest. Scout ahead."

She glared at him, and then shut her eyes. When they opened again, they glowed a pure white. Next to her the air shimmered as Sally's astral form appeared with her hands on her hips.

"Yeah, will never get used to seeing that," Breeze murmured.

Her astral form jetted off into the forest. Moments later, Sally's body shuddered and her eyes closed. When they opened the glow was gone. She was back in her body.

Sally pointed at the forest. "We go through the woods until we get to a clearing, and then to the left. The ravine is there." She scowled at Breeze. "How was my performance? To your satisfaction?"

Breeze didn't respond as he trudged off into the forest. The others followed.

The forest grew thicker the deeper they went. Heavy branches and undergrowth slowed their progress while ahead they could hear the sound of a gurgling stream.

They broke out of the forest and into a ravine with a narrow ribbon of water that ran down the middle of it. Though the sides of the mountain loomed over them, the faint moonlight that dribbled through was enough to light the way ahead of them.

"Based on the map I saw, this should lead us to a point just south of the scout ship. We then head north from here," Breeze said as he tapped his nav-compass.

They trudged along without another word. The only sound was of their feet stepping on and crunching the small stones and pebbles that made up the ravine floor. Occasionally a splash was heard when one of them would step into the meandering stream.

The ravine began to narrow as the sides of the mountain pressed even closer. They walked single file for a while until Breeze came to a stop. He held up his hand and turned to the others. "Did you hear that?"

He could barely see Ray and Sally in the looming darkness. He tapped his nav-compass and its glow lit the narrow space they were standing in.

"What is it?" Sally whispered.

Breeze shook his head. "It was like the sound of...wings flapping."

Ray stepped back and held up a hand. It glowed brighter and brighter with each passing moment until the ravine was lit up bright as day.

Breeze felt a sudden wisp of air brush across the back of his head and neck. He turned to look.

Off in the distance, where Ray's bioluminescence couldn't penetrate the darkness, hovered a pair of red glowing eyes.

"Guys?" Breeze said.

Ray stepped over to stand next to him. He raised his other hand and it began to glow, casting the beam of light deeper into the ravine.

The hovering red eyes retreated, never letting the light get close to it. They shimmered and changed shape, then faded away.

"What's happening?" Sally said.

Her question was answered by a pair of searing white eyes materializing where the red ones once hovered. It began advancing toward them accompanied by heavy footsteps as each step it took forced the outer edge of Ray's light to retreat.

Ray grunted as he leaned forward and pointed his glowing hands toward the creature. His hands burned brightly, but it was of no use. His light field diminished when the hovering eyes that encroached upon it, and bore the shape of a body, began to materialize around them.

When it was complete, a creature stood before them standing well over eight feet in height with wings that unfurled and spread out into an immense length. Faintly in the background, the sound of static began to fill the air.

Breeze and Ray staggered back as the creature marched onward.

Sally grabbed the two by the back of their jackets and tugged them hard. "Let's go!"

Ray pushed her away and she tumbled to the ground.

"Raymond," she yelled, "no!"

Ray placed his hands at his sides and his chest rose sharply as he took a deep breath. His right hand shot out as he pointed it at the winged creature and fired a bolt of energy.

The energy blast fizzled. He fired again, but only sparks came out. His legs wobbled and he fell to his knees.

The creature halted its advance and loomed over him. The sound of static was deafening.

Breeze jumped in front and stood in its path as Ray struggled to get up. It responded to the intrusion by opening its mouth and shrieking with an intensity that forced them to cover their ears when a woman's voice was heard cutting through the cacophony.

"That's enough," the voice said.

The creature ceased, and the crackle of static faded. Its glowing eyes turned to watch Raza step out of the shadows and into the light.

She stood next to it and patted its back, prompting the creature to fold back its wings and settle onto its haunches.

Sally and Breeze reached down to help Ray to his feet, and then slowly retreated from Raza and the winged creature.

"I have spent what has felt like an eternity waiting and hoping," Raza began, "for Oslo to come back to Appalachia with our daughter to ride out the storm that enveloped the world. He told me to wait for him and that he wouldn't be that far behind. He said he would bring our daughter and together we would raise her in peace and tranquility. While the rest of the world was being ravaged, we would survive and prosper. Like Perihelion, these mountains also possess an energy that hides and obscures it. We would begin anew here, he said. Oslo was always talking about renewal." She stepped closer to them as they huddled together.

"But now you children darken my door and tell me that you come here seeking shelter from the storm? And my daughter in not amongst you? My husband," her voice quavered, "still denies me the life he promised, and then expects me to protect the children of others whom I do not know?" Tears flowed down her cheeks and she quickly wiped them away, and then looked up at the star-filled sky through the narrow slit of the ravine. She began to rock back and forth as she mused. "Oslo, when will you understand? The world cannot be changed. What is done, is done. Let go of the past."

She returned her gaze to them while the winged creature shifted its feet. Its glowing eyes never lost their intensity.

"What have you brought me, Oslo? What did you drop at my door?" Raza whispered as she approached them.

"What is that thing?" Sally said.

Raza's eyes widened. "That thing is a legend and a part of the landscape and lore of these mountains. It's known to be a harbinger, a herald of future events and your presence has aroused it. It's the only reason why I have come back to find you. What is it about you three that could be so important?"

She shuffled slowly around them. "I see a young man from a prestigious background with a young lady who comes from the same world as his. And yet there's something more, no?" She touched the heads of Ray and Sally.

"And then there's the runt of the group. You come from a desert on the outer edge of the Bad Lands. What would anyone see in you?" She pointed a quivering finger at Breeze.

She shuffled back and stood next to the creature, then looked up at the night sky again. "What is it about these lambs that you would lead them away from their homes and their families, Oslo?" Her hands went up to her chest as she rocked back and forth. "What about my lamb? Where is she?" She closed her eyes and hummed softly.

Her head dropped and her humming ceased. She waved towards them and the winged creature stood up, spreading its wings to their fullest extent.

The sound of static returned. Its eyes glowed a brilliant white as it headed straight toward Ray.

Sally threw her arms around Ray, but found herself weakening as the creature advanced. She lost her grip on him and fell back.

The creature curled its wings toward Ray as the air crackled around him. His eyes widened, and then rolled up so only the whites could be seen.

Images suddenly appeared in the air like holograms, floating and dancing about like fireflies in the night. There were images of a child growing into adolescence. One in particular showed a stern faced man in a military uniform hovering over a frail woman with long black hair. She was consoling a young boy as tears streamed down his face.

Raza walked into the kaleidoscope of images and touched each one. She pushed aside some while grasping at those that interested her when she stopped and stared at the image of an infant being held in the arms of his mother. Raza smiled sweetly at the beautiful black haired woman while caressing the face of the child, then scowled at the father as he looked upon them with a look of disappointment across his face.

"The life of a young man raised in the home of a strict disciplinarian with only your loving mother standing between you, and you're their only child. What could lead parents like these to let you go? Interesting."

More images emerged showing Ray training and honing his powers under the watchful eyes of his father, along with images of him excelling in sports and academics, surrounded by multiple trophies and awards.

"All very compelling. A powerful pyrokinetic with exemplary abilities. And yet, what would Oslo need you for?" Raza wondered aloud.

She continued strolling through the images when something caught her eye and she pulled a single image close to her. She peered intensely at it, and then recoiled. "Why do I see that you do not travel alone? Who is this standing behind you?"

The moment was interrupted by Sally's shriek.

Raza broke away and waved a hand towards her as the images of Ray tumbled and disappeared into the ground.

The creature folded its wings, then flung them open and enveloped Sally.

Sally gasped as her body went numb. She turned to look at Ray who had collapsed to the ground. It was the last thing she saw before being overwhelmed by a flood of holographic imagery that swarmed around her like an angry hive.

Sally saw her mother with her hair wound tightly into a bun. Her face was strained with worry and her hands were clasped as she watched a young Sally playing in the grass. Her father entered the scene. He was holding a smoking pipe in one hand as he watched Sally from a distance, then turned and walked away. There were more images of her in a lavishly decorated bedroom, its walls lined with shelves full of toys as she sat alone on the floor brushing the hair of a doll.

Raza stepped through the floating images as she touched a few, ignoring most.

"Poor little rich girl? Mother and father not interested in you? Why? Were you a burden? I couldn't imagine so. Some people don't appreciate the joys of having a child. They don't know what it's like to lose one." She stopped and stared at an image of Sally next to her mother, then tilted her head and murmured, "Why do I see two people who do not belong together?"

Sally cried out, and fell to her knees.

Raza waved and the creature released its hold and stepped back, then she placed a hand on Sally's shoulder to comfort her.

Sally slapped it away and crawled over to Ray, sobbing.

Raza turned her gaze onto Breeze.

His shield had raised itself, making him immune from the creature's hypnotic gaze. "Keep that thing away from me or else—"

"Or else what, child? You'll fly away? What harm can come from you?" She waved and the creature stepped toward him.

Breeze's shield reflexively lashed out at the advancing creature.

It stumbled back, and then regained its footing as the wings snapped out to its maximum span and its eyes glowed a brilliant white that illuminated the ravine. The sound of static was deafening as it stomped towards him.

Sally rushed up to it. "Get away from him!"

The creature's wings rippled and she was repelled, landing next to

Ray with a cry of pain. He drew her close and cradled her in his arms.

Breeze stepped away until his shield bumped up against the side of the ravine. The creature halted its advance upon him while the static it emitted reached a crescendo as its wings curled forward.

In an instant, the ravine was plunged into complete darkness as deafening silence replaced the hiss of static. Specks of light gradually appeared and swirled about him like bees around a hive.

Suddenly, the lights exploded outward in a powerful burst while the ground beneath his feet fell away. He found himself floating in space and surrounded by a constellation of stars. He spun around to marvel at the view when a brilliant light flashed behind him.

He turned to see an immense starship, consumed by fire with its hull breaking apart, caught in a planet's gravitational pull and sinking into its atmosphere. Several fighter craft were engaged in fierce combat around the collapsing hulk as they buzzed around it like flies over a carcass.

It sank deeper into the planet's atmosphere then exploded, sending chunks of debris everywhere in a shower of jagged metal and flames. He raised his arms reflexively to protect himself and looked away from the searing light of the explosion. That's when he spotted several ships orbiting above him.

Each ship was massive in dimension, and all were immersed in a fierce, close quarters battle as they exchanged heavy gunfire between them.

A squadron of fighter craft broke off from the battle and raced towards him. Several were destroyed by a withering hail of crossfire before they could reach him as they fell victim to the enemy fighters trailing close behind.

One of the fighters managed to elude its pursuer to get within range of him and unleash a massive volley of energy from its forward cannons. He felt the concussive blast hit his shield and push him back, but he felt no pain. It fired again, but he dodged it. Again it fired, again he dodged. Before the ship could fire another volley, he raced toward it at full speed. His shield shimmered and crackled around him as he charged the fighter, smashing through it as the craft shattered into pieces with a wild explosion. He turned back to look and saw its hapless pilot, who managed to eject, fall towards the planet below. Breeze could see the fear and horror on his face before he burned to ashes in the outer fringes of the atmosphere.

He shook his head in disbelief at what he had just done when he was engulfed in a flash of light followed by several explosions. He spun around and saw the battling starships now surrounded him. The withering exchange of gunfire between them was relentless, and he was caught in the crossfire. He ducked and weaved to get away and flew underneath one of the ships where he attracted the attention of yet another swarm of fighters. They pursued him with a hail of energy blasts, forcing him to take radical evasive maneuvers to avoid being hit. Even amidst the chaos that surrounded him, he felt the soaring elation of how effortless it was to fly in space. It felt to him as if he had done this many times before, but only in dreams that were immediately forgotten upon waking up.

He came to an abrupt stop to cover his ears as the sound of static erupted in his head. He looked up to find the source and was greeted by the sight of a battle cruiser looming above him. In the distance, a ball of light shimmering with intensity hurtled towards the cruiser.

The ball of light quickly expanded into a massive sphere before it sliced through the ship, cutting it in half. The split hull broke apart and fell victim to the planet's gravitational pull. Breeze could see debris spewing from both of them as they descended in a bonfire of flames and explosions.

The sphere of light receded as a man with clenched fists appeared from it. He turned to face Breeze and nodded, then tapped a device on his wrist.

Breeze looked down and found himself tapping his nav-compass. He looked back at the man who was now emphatically pointing to the planet below.

Helena, he heard the man say in his mind.

Everything around him began to spin as Breeze found himself caught in a maelstrom of flashing light. When he emerged from it he felt his body crumple and hit the ground. He looked around groggily and saw he was back in the ravine.

The creature released its hold on him and retracted its wings, then receded into the shadows.

Sally cried out as she ran over and flung her arms around his neck. "What have you done to him!" she screamed at Raza.

Raza covered her face with her hands and shook her head. "No, no," she kept muttering incessantly, "this cannot be possible."

Breeze struggled to his feet as Sally tried to help him.

Raza was in a trance as she nervously paced back and forth. "I will not be a part of this, I cannot do this again." She then stopped to look

Breeze in the eye.

"Go. Leave. All of you. I will not be a participant in this madness. Go back to your ship and leave at dawn." She turned and walked away.

"Where do we go?" Sally cried out.

"Anywhere but here. I will not let you destroy what little tranquility I have. I won't let you or Oslo stir up the past."

Ray spoke up. "Oslo is coming soon—"

"He's not coming child, nor my Nina, with him. They probably have taken him into custody by now," the old woman said as she looked up at the stars.

"If Oslo says he's coming, I believe him. We'll stay in the ship and await his arrival," Ray said.

Raza waved a hand as she wandered off into the darkness. "There is a town on the other side of the mountain. Go there to find the parts you need to fix your ship. Then, go west, and stay away from here."

Her fading voice was followed by the sound of beating wings. Then, silence.

Ray raised a glowing hand and filled the ravine with light, but Raza and the winged creature were nowhere to be found.

Sally was leaning next to Breeze when he took a step forward and stumbled. Sally grabbed his arm to steady him.

"What happened to you? How come we couldn't see your vision?" she asked. "That creature stood over you while you convulsed on the ground. Ray and I couldn't do anything to help you. It was horrible, Breeze."

He patted her hand. "It's okay," he replied, then tapped his nav-compass incessantly and began to say something.

"What is it?" she said with a wide eyed look.

"Nothing. Look, it's cold out here. Let's get to the ship and we'll figure out what to do in the morning.

"Don't need to convince me," Ray declared.

They continued through the ravine and reached the river bank. The scout ship lay ahead to the north and they gratefully walked toward it, never thinking they would be happy to see it again. They quickly boarded the ship and withdrew the gangplank.

Later that night, they gathered around the table in the ship's mess and ate some of the meager rations they found in the galley.

"What now?" Sally asked.

Ray sighed while Breeze shifted in his chair. They both looked at each other, then at Sally.

Ray spoke first. "I want to stay here, at least for a few days. I'm convinced Oslo will show. He sent us out here for a reason, so why would he lie to us?"

"Raymond, even if he does show up, what then? You met that crazy woman. If that really is his wife, I can see why he's stayed away for so long," Sally said with a sneer.

"No, that's not the reason," Breeze responded. "It's because of their daughter, Nina. She can't leave Perihelion."

"Why?" Sally's face became solemn.

"She's tied to the island. It's like a life support system for her and she can't really leave it, maybe never."

"That explains why she got so crazy when she found out Nina wasn't with us," Sally said as she pulled her hair back into a pony tail. "That poor woman...," her voice trailed off.

"Is just like the rest of us. Either no home to go to or family is missing, or both," Ray finished for her.

Breeze spoke up. "I know what it's like to lose someone. My mother died when I was young. But I don't know what it's like to lose a home. My home isn't much, but it's home." He rapped his knuckles on the table. "Look, I want to try and fix the ship first thing in the morning. Raza is right. We should go to town and see if we can find the parts we need, then when it's repaired, I want you guys to come with me back west. We'll stay with my father and we can try to contact Oslo from there."

"You can't even reach your father over the comms," Ray said.

"Yeah, but we have to try to get out there. The old woman did suggest we go west and besides, where else do we have to go?"

They finished their meal without any further discussion, and then retired to their bunks.

Later, Breeze was still awake as he lay in his bed. He thought about the night's events and he especially dwelled upon his vision of fighting in space. It felt so real to him, yet he wondered if it was just a trick conjured up by the winged creature. He reflexively looked out the narrow window of his compartment as a part of him expected the winged creature to swoop down any minute and press its face against it with its hideous red eyes. He was greeted instead by the stars splashed out across the night sky.

As his head began to nod, and his weary eyes closed, all he could think about was seeing his father again. He drifted off to sleep.

CHAPTER
▼
SEVENTEEN

THE MORNING CAME AND the rising sun lit up the valley.

Breeze was the first to rise. He dressed and then stepped out of his quarters, and saw that Ray and Sally's doors were still closed. Not wanting to awaken them, he quietly headed for the propulsion room.

Descending into the bowels of the ship, he came to a stop when he arrived at the engines. He stood before the twin massive electromagnetic generator engines and admired them. He always had a fascination with engines of every sort ever since he was a child. His gaze dropped to the aisle that ran between them and ended at a workbench against a wall. He stepped over to it.

Memories of his father's workshop arose when saw how tools made up of odd shapes and sizes were neatly placed on the rack above it. He grabbed one and was immediately puzzled as to its purpose. Everything about this ship was just like what he had experienced at Perihelion in that everything seemed ancient, but fantastic in its capabilities.

He wandered about the engine room, trying to find anything that would give him a clue how to repair the damaged engines when he came upon a door that automatically slid away when he approached it. Lights flickered on when he stepped in to take a look. In the center of the room he saw the shape of a hover underneath heavy tarpaulin. Surrounding the vehicle were rolling racks filled with tools and the very sight of them struck him with an idea.

He ran to one of the tool racks and rummaged through the drawers. He flung aside tools until he found a disk sitting at the bottom of a drawer. He had seen them before when he was exploring Perihelion's hangars. It was a diagnostic tool for mechanics, and the RF often had one attached to their chests. If they didn't, they would pull them out of rolling tool racks and use them to scan whatever ship they were assigned to repair.

He flipped it over. The manufacture's emblem was faded.

He then remembered the vision he had from the winged creature. The man that smashed the battle cruiser in half had signaled him by tapping a device on his wrist. Breeze pulled back his sleeve to look at his nav-compass. He tapped the screen and it flickered alive.

The man then pointed at the planet below and spoke a single word into his mind: Helena. Breeze replayed the scene in his head but couldn't fathom what he was trying to convey. Was that the name of someone he was supposed to find? He did remember Oslo telling him how Bram long ago discovered a world named Helena during an expedition while projecting out into space. *Was that Bram I saw?* He wondered to himself. *Is he trying to reach out to me?*

He looked again at the disk, wondering if it had the answers he needed. He turned it over so the screen faced him and touched it, but nothing happened. He then double tapped it, and it immediately lit up.

The disk made a warbling sound as it displayed a rainbow of flashing colors while scrolling through an endless stream of data until it came to a stop. The words "Welcome to Corinth Industries Diagnostic Scanner" flashed across the screen. He fumbled the disk and almost dropped it to the floor, then shook his head. *Is this for real?*

A soft and gentle woman's voice spoke. "Hello Jacob, would you like to synchronize data now?" as a red light glowed at the bottom of the disk. A similar light appeared on his nav-compass. He placed them close together and both devices glowed and pulsated in unison.

"Um, yes?"

"Thank you, just one moment," the voice responded as both lights began to flash.

He looked at the tiny screen of his nav-compass, then the disk. Both had reams of data streaming across it, but he couldn't make any sense of it. It all came to an abrupt stop and the red lights ceased.

"Thank you. What is the first item you would like to scan?" it asked.

Breeze thought about it for a moment, and then remembered how the RF who did not have disks on their chest plates used them. He ran out of the room and over to one of the generator engines where he carefully placed the disk on it. It barely touched the surface when it clamped onto the metal and immediately flashed "Diagnostic Phase" across the screen. In moments, it was finished. He removed the disk and scrolled through the information. It listed a series of parts and repairs that were needed.

The ship's intercom crackled. "Breeze, where are you? Please come to the galley," he heard Sally's voice say. He looked at the workbench and saw an intercom terminal above it. He pushed the call button. "Down here in the engine room. Be right up."

He held the disk tightly as he bounded up the steps and out into the main corridor. He arrived at the galley where he found Sally and Ray sitting at the table and eating breakfast.

"I made something for you. I'm afraid it's not much, but there's not a lot of food here." Sally got up to make him a plate.

"You didn't have to. Besides, Oslo didn't really have this old tub filled with supplies. I guess he figured we would be at the farmhouse by now, eating breakfast and getting settled in."

"Yeah, didn't work out that way, did it?" Ray said. "What a night." He shook his head and drank water from his cup.

"You have to eat something," Sally said as she put a plate of food before him, then sat down. "So, what now?"

Breakfast wasn't much. Just a slice of bread with a little bit of rice. Breeze grabbed a spoon and shoveled it down. "Well," he began between mouthfuls of food, "we definitely need to head into town. We're going to need supplies, especially food, and the parts we need to fix the ship."

"But how? What do they do for money around here? Besides, it's not like we have any," Ray said.

"Trust me, I'm from the desert," Breeze said as he chewed loudly, "this place is probably no different than where I come from. You barter."

Sally shrugged and looked at him innocently. "I don't understand."

Breeze chuckled. "Boy, you two are definitely high class people." He waved a hand. "This whole ship is full of stuff that has value. Just the scrap metal alone can let us trade for whatever we need. We'll be fine. We can scavenge for things in the utility closets throughout the ship. It's a start. Then, we head off into town."

"Oh, I'm not walking again, especially through that ravine," Sally declared.

"Do you even know what parts we need?" Ray said.

Breeze wolfed down his last piece of bread and chased it down with a cup of water, then slammed the cup onto the table and let out a satisfied "Ahhhh," as he wiped his mouth with the back of his sleeve, ignoring the napkin Sally handed to him. He pointed a finger at Ray. "Parts? No worries there. Found an interesting tool to help us out." He nodded at Sally. "Walking? Ravine? Don't think so. Pack your gear and meet me in the engine room. I think I found us a ride."

Less than an hour later, they were grouped together in the engine room where Breeze led them past the workbench and towards the sliding door off to the side. They stepped in as overhead lights flickered on.

"Can you guess what this is?" Breeze said as he walked to the other side of the covered hover.

"Is this the scrap metal you had talked about bartering with?" Ray responded as he tugged on the tarpaulin and peeked underneath it.

"Nope, it's our ride." Breeze yanked the tarpaulin to reveal the hover.

Sally gasped. "That's the same kind of hover that Excort was always zooming around on campus with! How nice to see something from home." A puzzled look appeared on her face. "Is Perihelion home?"

Breeze shrugged. "It was for a while. Looking back, it was definitely more hospitable than this place."

They all nodded in agreement.

Breeze jumped into the pilot's seat and began to flick switches and fiddle with dials. Soon the hover's motor was humming, and the craft began to slowly rise up from the deck of the garage.

"Just one thing, genius," Ray said as he hopped into the back seat while Sally was strapping herself into the passenger seat, "how do we get out of here?"

Breeze hit a button on the dashboard and immediately the wall before them slid up with a grinding noise into a recessed groove, leaving them more than enough space to get out.

Breeze reached into his jacket and pulled out a pair of goggles, and they immediately reminded him of his ill-fated debut at the air show. He placed them over his eyes and adjusted the band, then turned to the others and grinned. "Hang on, it's going to be a bumpy ride."

He pushed down hard on the throttles and the hover leapt out of the garage. Sally screamed with a mixture of fear and delight as Breeze raced towards the river, then banked hard to follow it south. He skimmed over the surface of the river at a high rate of speed, creating a plume of water that shot up behind the hover.

Ray whooped with joy as Breeze shouted "look out everybody, here we come!"

Further downrange, Breeze pointed to the left. "That's the entrance to the ravine."

"We're not going back in there, are we?" Sally said anxiously.

"Nope. Been going over the maps. We follow the river further to the south where it forks, and then we take the river that runs to the east. That leads us into town."

"What's the name of the place anyway?" Ray shouted over the roar of the slipstream.

Breeze looked back at him, then over to Sally. "Mount Pleasant," he said.

Seconds went by and nobody said a word, then they all burst out laughing.

"Are you serious?" Sally said. "Well, I sure hope so. Our experience here has been anything but."

Breeze looked over at her. She was staring straight ahead while the deflected air from the windscreen tousled her hair and the sunlight caressed her face. She turned to him. "Eyes on the road."

Breeze immediately swerved hard to the left.

"What were you looking at?" Sally asked.

"Oh, just something I thought I saw on the riverbank over there," Breeze lied as he pointed.

"I don't see anything." Sally turned to look.

"For a moment I thought I felt...saw something." Breeze gripped the helm, and then looked into the rearview mirror. Ray was looking right at him.

They traveled in silence, save for the stray comment about something interesting they saw along the riverbank until they arrived at the fork. Breeze banked the hover hard left and followed the eastward flowing river where ahead, they spotted something floating on the surface.

Ray leaned between the front seats and pointed. "Is that a boat?"

Breeze decelerated and banked to the right. Ahead of them a river vessel with an oversized propeller spinning behind it was heading in their direction. The upper half spun above the surface while the lower half churned the water into a froth.

The passengers casually waved as they glided by. They waved back.

Ray tracked them until they faded from view, then blurted out, "did they just see us zip past in a hover and didn't even care?"

Breeze nodded. "Yeah, but I get the feeling it's normal around here."

"How do you know?" Sally said.

Breeze pointed ahead at a pair of hovers heading toward them. One of the hovers flashed their running lights, and Breeze banked to the right to get out of their way. Ray raised a hand and waved, only to receive a nasty gesture from one of the pilots as they careened by.

"I guess I should stick to the right side of the river," Breeze said.

They spotted structures that dotted the banks of the river as traffic began to increase both on the river and above it. Soon, they merged with the flowing traffic of hovers and followed them into Mount Pleasant.

Sally looked over at a hover traveling slightly below them on the right where she could see the pilot and the passenger behind him. The hover was old and disheveled and made a high pitch whine as the engine would surge, then fade, then surge again. The body panels were a mismatch of different shapes and colors and a stream of smoke trailed behind it.

The passenger stared right at Sally. It was a little girl. She tapped the shoulder of the pilot and pointed up. The pilot turned to look and glared at Sally as she quickly slumped down in her seat.

The town of Mount Pleasant loomed before them. It was a sprawling settlement spread out across both sides of a river that meandered to the north and Breeze banked the hover to follow its course. "Down there," he said, "I think we can land." He pointed to a harbor that appeared on the east bank of the river as streams of hovers were flying towards it, and river boats changed their course for the channel that led into it. He banked to the right to follow the hovers into the harbor and was greeted by the blast of an air horn from a hover behind them whose path he swerved into. He banked hard to the left and descended, then yanked the helm hard to the right and mashed down on the throttles. They roared ahead until they were clear of traffic.

"Have to be a little aggressive around here," Breeze shouted above the din of motors and horns.

"Seems like the only town in these parts. Everyone from miles around must come here," Ray said as he looked around.

Breeze followed a procession of hovers as they streamed toward an empty field next to the harbor. One by one, they touched down and lined themselves in rows. Breeze glided in and extended the landing gear as the hover touched down with a thump.

"Landing gear? Why not just stay in hover mode?" Ray said.

Breeze tapped the dashboard screen displaying electrical charge levels. "Power. I'm trying to conserve as much energy as we can. Don't know what kind of fuel they have around here."

"I'm guessing it's the same we're using. Most of the hovers seem to be similar to ours," Ray said.

Breeze nodded. "Yeah, you're probably right. Remember though, we need enough to get out of town and back to the ship. Let's spare what we can."

They climbed out. Breeze grabbed an oversized backpack filled with odd pieces of junk from the ship he scrounged up before they left and held it up for the others to see. "Stuff we can barter with. Now let's go see what we can find around here."

They walked past row after row of hovers until they reached an avenue that led into town. Sally pulled her jacket around her tightly as she sidled up between Ray and Breeze. "Guys, we definitely stand out around here. Look how different everyone is dressed."

Ray chuckled. "Leave it to a girl to notice fashion."

Sally punched him on the shoulder.

"No, she's right," Breeze said and nodded towards a group approaching them dressed in heavy clothing with thick work boots and belts containing pouches and implements attached to them, along with hats that covered the back and sides of the head.

"We're still wearing clothes from the island with jackets that have military logos on them. Yeah, we definitely stand out," Breeze said as he tugged on his jacket and buttoned it up. "Just don't make any eye contact."

"You seem to know your way around these sorts of places," Sally said.

"Yeah, well, you should see some of the towns my father and I used to go to collect scrap. The settlements of the desert can be rough."

"That's no way for a kid to be raised."

Breeze stopped in his tracks. "Sally, not everyone grows up living a happy shiny life. My father had to do what was needed to provide for us. I didn't grow up in a big, fancy house with parents who spoiled—" he stopped as she looked down sheepishly and crossed her arms. He sighed with exasperation. "Look, I'm sorry. I—"

"No, you're right, I shouldn't have said that—"

"Sally, let me finish, okay?" He touched her face and her eyes immediately lit up. "We're all hurting right now. I guess you could say our team has taken quite a beating lately. But we're going to be all right. Let's just finish up here and head back to the ship."

"Good idea guys. You're attracting a crowd," Ray said as he pushed the two of them forward.

Breeze glanced around and saw some of the townspeople were staring at them and a few were pointing in their direction.

"Follow me," Breeze commanded as he grabbed Sally's hand and walked briskly up the avenue. They turned onto the first available side street and hurried past several storefronts until they came across an alley and ducked into it.

Leaning against a wall and breathing a sigh of relief, Breeze pointed at Ray and Sally. "Guys, these clothes have to go."

"What do you mean? We should buy new clothes?" Ray said.

"Yep," Breeze responded as he pointed across the street at the opposite alleyway.

They looked over and saw a long line of vendors selling clothing as well as various wares and other items. "What better way to blend in but to buy some cheap rags to wear," Breeze said as he pushed off the wall and walked out of the alley. He stopped in the middle of the street and turned when he realized the others weren't following.

"How do we pay for these clothes? With scrap metal?" Ray asked.

Breeze shook his head and pointed at Sally.

"Me? Sell me? What's the matter with you!" she hissed at him with her hands on her hips.

"Come on Sally, really? We'll sell your jewelry! You're always walking around with bracelets and rings of all shapes and sizes. Can you part with just one?"

She touched her wrists and fiddled with the bracelets that adorned them. "But, I've had these for so long."

"Sally, I'm sure they mean a lot to you. But we're a team, right? Help out here, just one item, that's all. They've probably never seen anything like it around here, so who knows how much stuff we can get with it."

Ray leaned over to her. "Are you okay with this?"

She nodded as she slipped off a bracelet and walked up to Breeze. They stood together in the middle of the street as she handed it to him. "You know best. But can we buy something...nice?"

Breeze laughed. "We're in a dumpy, out-of-the-way town, but your fashion sense never leaves you. That's what I love about you." He pocketed the bracelet and nodded. "Come on, you two."

They followed him into the opposite alley and plunged into a mass of humanity that jostled and pushed about. On either side were booths and stalls selling items ranging from food to tools, jewelry and live animals along with clothing and weapons.

Sally gripped the back of Breeze's jacket as Ray followed closely behind when they came to a stop at a stall manned by a giant of a woman. She stood up from the overturned bucket she was sitting on and towered over them as a scowl flashed across her face. Her eyes narrowed as she glared at each of them. "Not from Appalachia," she declared.

Sally smiled sweetly. "No ma'am. We're actually—"

"—visiting from the North Eastern Territories. Just passing through, wanted to sample some of the local merchants in the area before heading back. We're looking into the possibility of establishing trade in the area," Breeze finished for her.

The woman's eyes narrowed into slits. "Liars."

"And we have this beautiful silver bracelet to barter with," Breeze said as he held up Sally's bracelet to her.

Her eyes widened and her mouth opened into a gleaming smile full of silver capped teeth. "Welcome! Please, enter my store and browse at your leisure, for you are obviously tired travelers merely seeking respite while searching for local treasures to sample before taking some home to show family and friends," she finished in a dramatic whisper.

"I take it you like silver?" Ray said.

She smiled again and her teeth were like rows of miniature mirrors. "Very," she said and finished with a flourish by raising her hand above her head in a circular motion.

"Let me close my store, for I do not wish for you to be disturbed," she announced and pulled down the curtains that hung above the entrance. She turned to face them, only to whip around and shove someone trying to get in. "Shoo, shoo. Go away. High class clientele only!" She turned to them again and flashed another silvery smile. "Now then, who do we start off with?" she said as she clapped her hands and rubbed them together.

Breeze pointed at Sally and let out a sly grin. "She's the one who wanted to come here."

"Perfect! Oh, I love to play dress up. My little girl is about twice your size. No, make that three. But no matter! We'll find something here for you. Come, come." She waved at Sally to follow her. "What is your name, dearie?"

"Sally. Sally Trumbull," she answered meekly.

"Sally? Oh, what a pretty name! My name is Matilda. Matilda

Brunhilda. Come now, let's see what clothes we have in your size. Oh, you're a tiny little thing, like a little frog. No matter!" She grabbed Sally by the hand and led her to the rear of the store.

Sally looked back at them with a mixture of fear and anger as she muttered loudly "like a frog?"

Breeze smiled and gave her a thumbs up.

"Are you sure about this?" Ray said.

Breeze clapped him on the back. "Relax, these merchants are more interested in show business and theater than just selling. It gives them a chance to have some fun. Wait until the haggling begins, that's when things get really interesting."

They browsed the store and found a few articles of clothing to their liking as they picked out pants and thick shirts along with jackets, boots, gloves and hats.

Minutes later there was a bustle at the back of the store and then Matilda came streaming toward them with her hands held high in the air. "Gentleman! It gives me the greatest of pleasure to introduce to you the new, and some would argue vastly improved, Sally Trumbull!"

Sally slowly emerged from behind a beaded curtain and walked up the aisle.

Matilda clapped her hands. "Oh, what a vision she is. Oh, yes!"

Sally came to a stop and looked down at her clothes, then glared at Breeze. She was wearing a heavy jacket with pockets across the front and sides, coarse pants with a belt and oversized buckle with combat boots clumped to her feet.

Matilda nodded her head vigorously as she pressed both hands across her ample bosom. "Yes, yes. So good. I do believe we have accomplished what we set out to do."

"Make me look hideous?" Sally said.

"Oh, no, my dear. Help you blend in," Matilda said as she leaned toward her and winked.

Sally started to respond, but the giant woman gyrated quickly to face Ray and Breeze. "How about my two strapping lads. What did you find?"

Both of them were holding a pile of clothing as Matilda nodded and smiled. "Yes, good choices. Now, run along to the fitting rooms. After all, you do want to wear what you're going to buy," she said and pointed to the back of the store. The boys obeyed without a word of protest.

She turned back to Sally. "Now, how do accessorize? We need

something dazzling!" she said with a high falsetto voice and a wave of her hands.

"I couldn't imagine," Sally groaned.

Later, the boys emerged from the fitting rooms dressed in their new clothes and walked up to the counter. Breeze adjusted the sleeve of his new coat which he wore over his jacket, briefly revealing his nav-compass. Matilda's eyes widened.

"Well Matilda, we thank you for your help, but we have to get moving, we have a busy day today," Breeze said, and pulled out Sally's silver bracelet. "I do believe this should more than cover our purchase."

Matilda turned away and placed the back of a hand across her temple as her other hand waved at Breeze. "Oh, no. No, no. You come to my humble, out of the way store and honor me with your presence, you fine upscale travelers from Nor' east. You purchase my rags, these....these worthless assemblies of thread, and then you try to overcompensate me with such a fine piece of silver. No! I will not take it as payment for I fear you will return to your territory and tell all the fine folk that you wine and dine with about how you traveled to Appalachia and were taken, no, robbed, by that horrible woman, Matilda Brunhilda. You will spread the word to one all, 'Don't go to Appalachia! Don't go to Mount Pleasant! And if you do, avoid at all costs, that awful Matilda Brunhilda!'" she finished with a harsh whisper then threw herself onto the counter top and sobbed loudly.

Ray and Sally stood with mouths agape, then watched as Breeze held up the silver bracelet toward Matilda.

Breeze quickly winked at his teammates, and then turned his attention back to the sobbing giant of a woman.

"Matilda, we meant no such offense. What else can we take from your fine establishment to equal the value of this shiny, silver bracelet," Breeze said.

Matilda looked up and her sobbing ceased instantaneously. "I wish for you to take my advice," she said with a sniffle as she wiped her face in the most ladylike fashion she could muster.

Breeze's eyes narrowed.

"Yes, yes. You must go and see the fights tonight at Hammer Jack's. Yes, that is where everyone goes. Such a fine establishment," she closed her eyes and sighed deeply. Her eyelids fluttered as she placed a hand on her chest.

"Any particular reason why?" Sally asked.

Matilda pretended not to hear her as she looked at Breeze while leaning over the counter. "Go early to guarantee yourself a good seat, but stay till the end. Yes. Achilles. That is the one you want to see. What a spectacular warrior!" she sang out in a high, falsetto voice, then smiled at Breeze as she swiftly snatched the bracelet from his hand. She turned it over and over in her hands and giggled, then dropped it down her blouse where it nestled between her massive bosoms before opening the register on the counter top. She rummaged through it and produced a handful of smaller, silver coins. "Here's your change dear. Thank you for your patronage."

Breeze took the coins. He opened his jacket beneath his new coat and placed them in an inner pocket.

Matilda smiled. "Smart lad putting them inside your jacket. Wise. One must protect the coin of the realm from pickpockets and thieves!" She then came out from behind her counter and herded them to the entrance. "Now it's time for you to finish your busy day before the evening arrives."

They spilled out into the alley as Matilda raised the curtains up. She clasped her hands and smiled as the trio walked away.

"Good bye, my sweets, do come again. Oh, I should have you all come by to meet my daughter sometime. You would get along just famously together, oh, yes." And without another word she plopped down on her overturned bucket as a scowl quickly replaced her smile.

They walked to the end of the alley and onto the street when Sally blurted out, "what just happened?"

Breeze chuckled. "That was bartering, with a lot of drama thrown in."

"Where did you learn to talk like that? I've never seen you so.... confident." She smiled.

"Well, like I told Ray while you were busy getting glamorous with Matilda, I spent a lot of time with my father bartering for scrap. Whether it was dealing with merchants who came to our yard, or traveling to the outlying towns and settlements, you learn quickly how to deal with a lot of the characters you run across."

"It's really amazing how different our lives were growing up," she said

"Yeah, Sally, I know." Breeze looked over at Ray. "How are you holding up?"

"Okay, I guess. Still trying to forget the image of the giant woman throwing herself onto a countertop and having a tantrum." He shivered at the thought.

"Yep, get used to it," Breeze said as he nodded toward the street, "we're about to see more of it."

They spent the rest of the day and into the early evening walking in and out of various merchants' shops and scrap dealers searching for parts to repair the scout ship. Time and again they would leave empty handed, never finding a single vendor who had what they needed.

The sun had long gone down as evening took its place. They walked the darkened streets while merchants were closing their shops and streetlights were flickering alive.

Sally plopped down on a bench in front of a closed shop as the light from the sign above her glowed with a purple haze. "So what now?"

"I say we head back to the ship, this place looks like it gets weird at night," Ray said.

"We got nothing to worry about. You can always blast anyone who tries to hurt us with your pyrotechnics," Breeze quipped.

"Not funny. Do you really think it's wise to use our powers here?" Ray said.

Breeze shrugged. "In case you didn't notice, I think you're free to be as weird as you want to be in this town. No one really seems to care."

"I agree with Ray. It's getting dark and we should head back," Sally said as she got up and stood next Ray. She took his hand and leaned her head against his shoulder.

Breeze sighed. "Come on you two, don't be so quick to give up. Remember what Matilda said—"

"I'm still trying to forget her," Sally cut in.

"Whatever. Look, she said go to Hammer Jack's to see the fights and stay until the end to see a fighter named Achilles. Knowing people like Matilda, I'm sure there's a good reason why she insisted we see him, but we got to get there early. Let's go!"

"You want to go and see boxing? Now? In a town like this? I don't think so," Ray said and pulled Sally by the hand. As they walked away, Sally looked back at Breeze with pleading eyes.

"Come on you two, stop, just hear me out on this," Breeze said and jogged to catch up to them. "Listen, I know everything seems strange and weird. But there is a reason she dropped that hint on us. We've got to follow up on it."

"So that's it then? A hint from a weird lady and you want to trust her?" Ray said.

"It's gut instinct. We're both pilots, so you understand. Sometimes you just have to go with it. Sometimes it's all you got."

Ray stared at him.

Breeze pressed on. "Look, we come from different backgrounds. Yours is strict military and by the book. Mine, well, by the seat of the pants and living on the edge, but c'mon, Ray, what else have we got? We go back to the ship, and then what? Drain what little power we have while we're not sure if Oslo is going to show up?"

"What did that creature show you in the ravine? How come we didn't see it? You've been different ever since," Sally blurted out.

Breeze stepped back. "It's no big deal, I'll tell you guys later. Please, let's just go and see the fights?"

"No," Sally said and crossed her arms, "you tell us what you saw, and maybe we'll go."

"For the record, I don't care," Ray announced.

Breeze shrugged, and then turned to Sally. "You walk with me to this Hammer Jack's place and I'll tell you."

"Do you even know where it's at?" Sally said.

"I'm sure we can ask along the way."

"Fine." Sally sniffed and began walking away, then stopped and turned. "Well, do I have to lead the way?"

Breeze grinned at Ray. "Can't argue with the lady now, can we?"

Ray grunted, and together they caught up to her.

Along the way, Breeze told them what he saw and experienced in his vision from the winged creature: the exploding ships; the pitched battle; the man pointing down at a planet. They listened intently without a word.

"It's strange that your vision didn't involve anything about your background," Sally said, "but instead showed some sort of a future. The way Raza reacted to you afterwards was also weird; she couldn't wait to get away from you, from all us."

Before Breeze could respond, Ray, who had listened to Breeze tell his story with a look of discomfort written on his face, loudly interrupted. "Let's ask for directions now, 'cause this part of town is starting to get kind of rough."

They asked a passerby for directions who grunted at them and pointed down the street.

They continued on and merged with a flock of pedestrians heading in the same direction where just ahead lay a brightly lit venue.

"There, that has to be it." Breeze pointed.

"Yeah, the big lighted sign that says Hammer Jack's was probably the clue," Ray snorted

"Come on, Ray, stop being sarcastic. This should be fun, get in the spirit," Breeze said.

Sally walked between them and pulled them close to her. "Guys, these people are weird."

A crowd had gathered at the entrance and soon they were surrounded by a motley mix of characters. Gigantic men and women chatting and joking with dwarves, along with people dressed in leather jackets with weapons attached to them. In the background, hover cars and air bikes streamed in and parked in the front and back of the building.

The line moved slowly forward where at the entrance, menacing bouncers with glowing eyes scanned everyone as they walked through and confiscated weapons when they found them. Another bouncer was repeating an announcement, but they couldn't hear it clearly above the din of the crowd. As they drew closer, they heard him say: "No fighting, no assaults amongst the audience. Absolutely no displaying or using of powers. None." The bouncer declared with a heavy bass voice.

Breeze pulled up the hood of his jacket over his head. Ray and Sally followed his lead.

After being scanned by the bouncers and paying the entrance fee, they stepped into Hammer Jack's. The venue was an indoor stadium with row upon row of seats lining the interior and stretching up to the ceiling. They jostled with the crowd until they found some empty seats and sat down. Sally made a point of sitting between them as she looked around nervously.

Breeze nudged her in the ribs. "Stop doing that, you'll attract attention. We're locals, nothing to see here."

She leaned into him. "Didn't you hear what that bouncer outside said? No use of powers, he kept saying. Are there others like us?" she said and began scanning the crowd.

Breeze grabbed her arm and puller her close. "Sally, in this town I think it's safe to say you can find anything here. Matilda suggested we come here and we're about to find out why."

People continued to stream in looking for seats when the lights dimmed and a spotlight lit the arena floor. The crowd immediately roared and thrust their fists into the air.

The announcer stepped out and held his hands high in a bid to quiet the unruly crowd. "Fighting fanatics, welcome to the temple of the martial arts. The dojo of war. The church of destruction. Welcome.... to Hammer Jack's!"

The crowd rushed to their feet and cheered as spotlights swept across the arena revealing the masses of humanity that had gathered under one roof. Breeze followed one of the spotlights as it briefly illuminated the faces of the crowd as it zipped around the arena. He saw women with eyes that glowed alongside men with gigantic bodies and shrunken heads while all around were dwarves that jumped up and down in their seats. The cacophony of noise grew until the announcer held up his hands again and it fell to a rumbling din.

"I know what you scum want. I know all of you," the announcer said as he swept his hand across the crowd. "You want to see a real contest. One filled with gladiators fighting to their last breath!"

The crowd roared in agreement.

"You want to see pulse-pounding action as opponents pummel each other into the dirt!"

The crowd shouted their approval and stomped their feet.

"Well then, who am I to keep you waiting, my feverishly frenzied friends? Our first venture into violence is a real mismatch some would say. But those gathered here today know better."

The announcer then threw back his head and pointed to his right. "From this side of the ring, ladies, hang on tightly to your men, and beware the temptations of... Silvia the Seductress!"

The spotlight swept over to one side of the arena where a panel slid open an out stepped a beautiful woman with long flowing hair. She was barefoot and wore a revealing, tightly fit dress. Immediately, the men in the audience cheered and wolf whistled while the women hissed at her. A man sitting in front of Breeze kept whistling louder and louder until his female companion slapped him across the face, which set off a heated argument.

The announcer continued. "As if Silvia wasn't trouble enough for the men, and a source of stress for the ladies, let's add fuel to the fire, shall we? Assembled aficionados, let out a hearty cheer for Ajax the Avenger!"

The crowd roared and shouted as they thrust their fists into the air with chants of "Ajax! Ajax!" thundering throughout the arena. Multiple spotlights swirled across the audience then coalesced onto a panel on the opposite side of the arena from where Silvia stood. Double panels slid open and out stepped Ajax. He was a mountain of a man that had to stoop first before stepping into the arena. He immediately stood up to his full height and stretched his arms out, and released an ear splitting roar. Lighting crackled all around him as his eyes glowed an eerie white while the crowd roared louder and louder.

Meanwhile, Silvia stood her ground and stroked her hair nonchalantly, then turned to face the audience and blew kisses to a group of men hanging over the railings, feverishly calling her name to gain her attention.

"Folks, I don't know about you, but this doesn't look like a fair fight!" the announcer declared as he stood in the center of the arena.

The crowd hooted.

"Seriously, look what we have here. Ajax is obviously a mighty warrior, but poor Silvia, she's just a wee little girl. Is this right?"

Everyone began to chant Ajax's name as Silvia crossed the arena toward her opponent while she continued blowing kisses and waving to the audience.

The announcer chuckled. "You folks never disappoint. After all, who doesn't love an unfair fight? Let the mayhem commence!" the announcer shouted, then disappeared in a flash of light and a puff of smoke. The crowd roared so loud Breeze could feel the vibration through his seat.

Strobe lights flashed across the arena as the floor beneath them began to shift. Sally screamed and grabbed onto Breeze as their seats slid back, then floated up. The floor morphed as it stretched out and sunk deeper into the ground while the seats were being pushed closer but higher over the arena floor, giving them a closer view of the fights.

"Breeze, I want to go," Sally said as she pressed her body into him.

He held her close. "We'll be okay."

Ajax strode to the center of the arena and roared as he shot bolts of lightning in the air. They hit the ceiling and rained sparks onto the audience.

Silvia stood her ground with her hands on her ample hips, then raised a finger to Ajax and signaled him to come closer.

Ajax let out a menacing laugh as he raised his fists in the air. Lightning crackled between them, forming a sphere of energy that grew and expanded with each passing second.

Silvia turned to the audience with a pout while pressing a finger to her chin. Some of the crowd booed and hissed while others shouted encouragement to her.

Ajax took advantage of her distraction and heaved the sphere at her.

She whipped around and immediately tumbled into a forward roll. She came to a stop at his feet and looked right up at him.

Ajax was caught by surprise as Silvia held up her hands in surrender, and then he raised his foot to stomp on her.

She smiled and winked.

He hesitated.

In a flash, her arms stretched out. Like elastic bands, they snaked out and wrapped themselves around his neck, and with a hard tug, he toppled toward her. She leapt up and slid between his legs, then yanked her arms toward her body. Ajax flipped and landed on his back with a thump that shook the floor. Silvia released her hold on him as her elastic arms coiled back to their original length, then turned and waved to the crowd who responded with a mix of cheers and jeers.

Ajax slowly rose his feet, but stumbled as he tried to regain his balance. The crowd began chanting his name as he pounded his chest and raised fist to them in solidarity. The crowd went wild when Ajax whirled around and hurled a bolt of lightning at Silvia.

Silvia's hair immediately snaked out from her head and wrapped itself around her, forming a shield that covered her body when the bolt of lightning hit it and dissipated into a hail storm of sparks. The hair grew into an even greater length as it weaved itself into a ball. Silvia, completely immersed within, rolled forward and hurtled toward Ajax.

Ajax tried to repel her by throwing bolt after bolt. Some hit, but most missed, and the ones that did hit failed to stop the forward progress of the rolling ball of hair as it grew even thicker and crackled with energy it absorbed from the lighting. In a surge of power, a bolt erupted from the ball of hair and struck Ajax in the chest with a tremendous crack, sending him flying across the arena, and smashing into a wall. He flopped to the ground in a crumpled heap.

"What...was....that!" Sally shouted above the roar of the crowd.

Ray leaned closer to them. "At this rate, who knows what else we're going to see before Achilles takes to the ring."

The netting of hair covering Silvia regressed as she emerged from it. She circled the ring and waved to the crowd and the mixture of boos and cheers was deafening.

The announcer floated out of the floor and strode to the center of the stage. A microphone drifted toward him and he snatched it. "Questionable ladies, and not so gentle men, the winner of the first match by knockout, the deadly but delightful, Silvia the Seductress!"

The masses booed and cheered even louder as she exited the arena. Wranglers emerged from the wings and dragged Ajax off who let out a loud groan as disappointed fans threw garbage at him.

Match after match came and went. Cyborgs versus pyrokinetics. Martial artists with superhuman agility fighting off telekinetics. Each match grew deadlier as time went by.

For the final match, the announcer once again took center stage as the lights dimmed. A sole spotlight focused on him as he placed a hand over his heart and began speaking in a soft and trembling voice. "And now, worshipers of warmongering, comes the event you have been waiting for. The blood battle that has you howling like wolves. The duel to the death you so desire. You've come a long way to see this. From every mountain and valley far across Appalachia, from every holler and hilltop across the land. Is tonight the night the reigning champion, Achilles, is dethroned by the challenger, Sargon? Let's find out!"

The announcer thrust his hands in the air as spotlights circled the audience and strobe lights flashed. The steady beating of drums began to build into a powerful tempo.

"Tonight's challenger, from the high mountain country surrounded by the mists of magic, comes the hero we've all been waiting for. The Metallurgist of Mayhem. The Forger of Fenris. I give you, Sargon the Slayer!"

The crowd roared and stomped its feet as spotlights swung to the far side of the arena. A panel slid open and out stepped a giant of a man covered head to toe in armor. The armored plates across his body slid in a continuous motion and morphed themselves into different shapes. He held his hand out and the armor that covered it formed a sledge hammer. He held out a leg and the tip of his foot formed into a sword. He raised his arms to reveal a spinning saw blade that circled his waist.

Fireworks exploded across the arena followed by bursts of flame. The crowd chanted and cheered as the drum beat grew deafening.

The announcer raised a hand and the crowd settled down. "And now, denizens of doom, patrons of paucity, I give you a warrior made of circuits and servos. Your mechanical overlord, the robot you so love to hate, the reigning champion, the Amazing Achilles!"

The rain of boos and screams that ensued were overwhelming.

Sally and Breeze looked at each other and shouted in unison above the cacophony of noise, "Achilles is a robot?"

The spotlights shifted to the center of the arena as the announcer floated away. A circular opening no more than four feet in diameter appeared and the head of a robot emerged from it. As it rose up, the spotlights highlighted its gleaming metal body while all around the beating of drums was deafening and the crowd was becoming unruly. Achilles, now on level ground, held a fist high in the air as it walked the circumference of the arena. Angry boos echoed and reverberated throughout as garbage and debris was thrown down at it.

Ray leaned over and shouted at Breeze. "Are you seeing this?" he pointed at Achilles.

Breeze nodded and yelled, "Yeah, it looks just like the RF on Perihelion!"

The announcer swooped down and hovered over the center ring. "Warriors, take your positions!" he ordered.

Sargon and Achilles took to opposite sides of the arena.

"Combat!" the announcer shouted as fireworks exploded from the ceiling. The crowd was on their feet and roaring.

Achilles casually strode to the center and waited.

Sargon hesitated, and then charged across the arena toward Achilles. The armored plates of his suit shifted and morphed as he ran at full stride. He lifted his right arm to form a sword while his left hand shifted into a shape of an ax. His chest plate burst open and a metallic whip lashed out and snatched Achilles by the neck then retracted, jerking the robot off its feet and sending it flying towards him.

Achilles grabbed the whip with both hands just as it was pummeled into the ground by Sargon's ax. The crowd shouted their approval as Sargon rained blow upon blow on the robot as sparks flew with every strike. He stopped his assault long enough to raise a leg and slam a spiked foot down on it.

Achilles quickly rolled out of the way and sprang to its feet. It threw off the whip that was wrapped around its neck, then jumped and kicked Sargon in the chest, sending him sprawling to the ground.

Achilles turned to the crowd and raised a fist in triumph. The crowd booed harshly, and then shifted into cheers as Sargon scrambled to his feet. The robot kept its back to him as it continued to antagonize the crowd.

Sargon's chest plate opened and the whip lashed out again, this time snaring Achilles' raised fist and yanking the robot to the ground. As the whip retracted back into his chest and dragged Achilles across the arena toward him, Sargon morphed his right hand into a trident and thrust it into the robot when it came within striking distance. Sparks flew as it struck Achilles' chest and glanced off. Sargon went for a second strike, this time aiming for the head.

Achilles leapt up with the metallic whip still coiled around its hand and vaulted over Sargon's head where it landed on his back. It wrapped the whip around his helmet and yanked back, shattering the face plate. Sargon roared in anger and pain as he reached up and tore the helmet off his head, revealing a scarred and bloody face. He spun in a circle rapidly and flung Achilles off him.

Achilles was still tethered to the whip as it flew through the air when Sargon released the connection from his chest, sending it crashing into the side of the arena. Concrete shattered and rebar was exposed as Achilles tumbled to the ground. It stood up and shook its head, then began to brush the dust off.

Breeze leaned over and shouted at Ray. "Achilles is just playing with him!"

Blood ran down Sargon's face as he staggered toward Achilles, and then dropped to one knee with a groan. He stabbed a finger at the robot. "It ends! Now!"

Achilles shrugged as the crowd went into a frenzy.

Sargon stood up slowly as the metal plates of his armor shifted back into place. He raised both his hands and they morphed into propellers with sharply angled tips.

The propellers began to rotate, gradually picking speed until they spun with a roar. Dust and trash that was strewn across the arena floor blew everywhere.

Sargon dropped one propeller to the ground and the blades chewed up the concrete, sending chunks of it flying into the crowd as he marched toward Achilles. He pointed the other propeller at the robot and the jet blast of air pinned it against the wall. Sargon then let out a mighty roar and charged with both propellers facing forward.

Achilles leaned into the hurricane force winds in an attempt to break free, but failed to escape in time as Sargon arrived and slammed the propellers into him. Sparks flew everywhere as the sound of metal scraping against metal created a horrible screech that made the crowds reach up to cover their ears.

Achilles stood its ground with its arms across its chest as Sargon attacked. Propeller blades began to break off upon contact with its armor and flew off into the crowd. Screaming erupted across the arena as everyone ducked and threw themselves onto the floor for safety.

Achilles swiveled its head rapidly as it watched some of the crowd run from the danger, then its eyes glowed brightly as it raised a hand toward Sargon. Sargon's eyes went wide with surprise as he was lifted off the ground and sent sailing through the air to the opposite side of the arena.

"How was that possible?" Sally said as she turned to Breeze, "Achilles didn't even touch him!"

Sargon landed with a thump and skidded across the floor as Achilles sprinted towards him. While Sargon was trying to get to his feet, Achilles covered the remaining distance in a blur and struck him hard in the chest, sending him cart wheeling into a wall.

"I am beginning to realize why Matilda sent us here. There's something definitely strange about that robot," Breeze said.

Sally grabbed him by the arm. "I can see an aura glowing around Achilles. It's almost...like a living thing!"

"Impossible! It's a machine!" Ray shouted.

"Sally, I need you to project and get closer to it," Breeze said.

Her eyes widened. "Are you sure? They said no use of powers—"

"Ray and I will cover for you, don't worry."

"What do you expect her to find?" Ray yelled over the noise of the crowd.

Breeze shrugged. "Don't know, Matilda may be crazy, but she was right. Look at Achilles. That robot is no different than the RF on the island. Except this one is doing what it was programmed to do which is to fight, not fix aerocraft. Let Sally get closer to it. Who knows what she's going to find, but we need to know more about it."

Sally nodded. "Okay, I'm ready," she said and raised the hood of her jacket to obscure her face as her eyes began to glow.

Breeze pulled off his new coat. "Use my coat so we can disguise you better", he said as he draped it over her, and then pulled her close. "Listen, we're here for you, don't worry. Just get close and report what you find."

If she heard him, she gave no indication. Her body grew stiff as her eyes glowed brighter.

"She's projecting," Breeze called out to Ray.

Ray nodded as he looked around cautiously.

On the arena floor, Achilles was charging Sargon when something distracted the robot as it turned to look to its right. It came to an abrupt stop and began waving a hand at the empty space in front of it.

The crowd jeered and laughed. "That stupid machine is losing it!" someone in the row below Breeze said.

"Got hit in the head too many times," his companion responded and they both laughed raucously.

Breeze felt Sally squeeze his hand. "Achilles can see me!" she hissed in a disembodied voice.

Breeze shook his head. "Impossible, you're projecting."

"I'm telling you Breeze, it's looking right at me!"

Sargon took advantage of the distraction and charged, slamming the robot into the ground and pinning it by squatting on its chest and arms, then he raised his fists into the air as metal plates slid up his wrists to form sledge hammers and began raining blow upon blow onto Achilles' head as sparks flew everywhere.

Achilles twisted and squirmed violently as it tried to break loose. It kicked its legs wildly to no avail, but did manage to yank an arm out from underneath Sargon' s leg, then made a fist and pointed it at his head.

Sargon slapped it away with a sledgehammer as the fist fired off Achilles' arm and into the crowd.

Sargon then continued pounding on the robot's head, each blow breaking the concrete under it and creating a jagged recess that they sank deeper into when he stopped and raised both of his sledgehammer shaped hands into the air.

Everyone in the arena stood up and began chanting "Junk it! Junk it!"

Sargon bowed his head to the crowd in acknowledgment. As he began his final deathblow, something hit him hard in the back of the head. His eyes went wide, and then rolled back. He let out a loud and pitiful groan and toppled over onto Achilles.

The crowd stood in stunned silence.

Achilles couldn't be seen underneath the mound of metal and flesh that was Sargon, except for its arm, minus the hand, held high.

Something fast flew over the spectators and glided toward the robot. It was Achilles' fist. It hovered over the arm for a moment, then lowered and reattached itself with a muted click that sounded like a gunshot to the stunned and silent crowd. Achilles held its arm up high with a clenched fist in a display of defiance that sent the crowd into a frenzy of anger. Chants of "Re-match! Re-match!" echoed throughout the arena.

Achilles rolled Sargon off with a mighty heave, then stood up and continued holding its fist high as it strode about the circumference of the arena. The crowd responded with more anger and catcalls as garbage and debris rained down upon it.

Achilles came to a stop at the section where Breeze, Sally and Ray were sitting where it looked up and stared at them.

Breeze felt Sally shudder and he turned to look at her. Her eyes ceased to glow and her eyelids fluttered as her astral form returned and merged with her body.

She gripped Breeze to steady herself. "That robot...is paranormal!" she said as she gasped for air.

Breeze looked back at Achilles, but the robot was already heading for the exit. It disappeared into an opening in the arena wall as a sliding panel closed behind it.

The announcer appeared in a puff of smoke and fire and raised his hands in an attempt to calm the crowd. "Fighting fans from all across the far flung lands! Please, celebrate, not capitulate, to the victory of the Amazing Achilles!"

The crowd booed even harder as fights fueled by frustration broke out amongst them. People began to jostle and shove one another as they streamed to the exits.

"Okay guys, we've seen enough. We need to get out of here!" Breeze shouted as he grabbed Sally by the hand and motioned to Ray. Ray nodded and followed.

They made their way from the stands and spilled out into a grand hallway when Breeze spotted a non-descript door to his right. Dragging Sally behind him as Ray followed, he broke away from the crowd and their stampede to the main exit, and burst through it and into the cold night. Together they ran and didn't stop until they came to the edge of a forest that lined the back of the arena.

CHAPTER
▼
EIGHTEEN

THEY SPRAWLED ONTO THE grass breathing heavily. The air was cold and their breath was like steam. They could still hear the raucous crowd inside the arena trying to get out.

Breeze was the first to speak. "Sally, what happened? What did you see?"

Sally was sitting with her arms across her chest and shivered when she spoke. "You know, I can see flashes of light when a machine is using its electrical power, and the aura I originally saw around Achilles was dull and monochromatic. But then the robot began to change and I swear it had the same spectrum of color as a human."

Ray shook his head. "Impossible. Are you saying that was a man in a suit?"

"I don't know. I don't think so—"

"You do or you don't, Sally, you can't—"

Breeze jumped in. "Ray, go easy man. Give her a break, she did her best. Let her breathe."

"Her best isn't good enough. We need to know exactly what we're facing here."

"You're starting to sound just like your father," Sally said.

"Well, if my father were here—"

"He's not. It's just us. We need to figure this out by ourselves," Breeze said as he knelt before Sally. "Sally, that robot is the key to something. What, I don't know but we got to find it and talk to it."

"And ask it what?" Ray said.

"Sally," Breeze ignored him and took her hand, "please project again. We've got to find it. I just know this is right. Can you do it?"

"It could be anywhere. This place is huge and I wouldn't know where to start," she murmured.

"There has to be some sort of trail you can follow," Breeze suggested.

She nodded. "I can pick up where we last saw it. It did exit into that open panel in the arena, and if I find any imprint of its energy, it should lead me right to it."

"Do it," Breeze said.

"I don't want to go alone, come with me," she pleaded.

"How?"

She took his hand and together they stood up. "I'm sort of new to this," she said. "Oslo encouraged me to learn how to project with a passenger when I first met him, and part of my solo training over the past several weeks was to practice endlessly with Kera. I guess that's one of the reasons I wanted to leave," she paused for a moment, "I remember Kera would make me practice that one skill, as if she was preparing me for a moment like this. It almost feels like a dream how she always seemed to be with me."

Breeze took her other hand and drew her close. "Perihelion was a strange experience for all of us. Funny how suddenly I want to go back, as if it's safer there than any other place on the planet right now."

Sally smiled and nodded as she quickly wiped a tear from her face. "If you're willing to come with me, I think I can find it. I just don't want to be alone."

"What about me?" Ray said.

"I feel a little more comfortable with Breeze. He can help me navigate and guide my way through."

Breeze gestured towards the arena. "Well, let's do it. How do we start?"

Sally took his hand and they stood side by side. "Just empty your mind and relax. Remember, you have to be willing to make this work. I can't force you. You're going feel a tug, like someone wrapped a rope around you and yanked it, and then you will feel weightless as if you're flying."

"Flying? Now I know why you really picked me," he turned and winked at Ray.

Sally giggled. "Come on, concentrate. This is scary for me, and I've never really done this before except with Kera."

They both closed their eyes as Sally took in several deep breaths, then her eyes suddenly fluttered open and they were a brilliant white.

Breeze opened an eye to peek at Sally and was about to say something when everything around him blurred. When it came to a stop, he felt light as a feather and could see his body standing before him with eyes that glowed a searing white. He recoiled at the sight of it as an acute feeling of loneliness swept over him, then flailed his arms wildly when he felt a gust of wind sweep him off his feet and drag him away from his body.

Someone grabbed his hand and he turned to look. It was Sally. She was radiating with a brilliant light that surrounded her while wearing a flowing white dress that streamed away from her body as if blown by the wind. Breeze stared at her in stunned silence.

Sally laughed. "Told you it would feel a little funny."

"You look so beautiful," he blurted out.

Sally looked away shyly. "Thank you, but I don't know why you're saying that for...oh!" She let go of him when she saw the dress. She quickly threw up her hands and the dress faded away and was replaced by a training uniform she wore at Perihelion. "Okay. That's better." She glanced around and saw Breeze was nowhere to be found.

"Sally, a little help," Breeze called out as he floated away.

"Sorry!" she said and raced over to grab his hand. They glided back and hovered before their prone bodies.

"Why do I keep floating away and you just stay perfectly still?" Breeze asked her.

Sally smiled. "You have to be anchored. Time doesn't flow; we do. Whenever I project it's like jumping into the ocean from a boat that is anchored. The boat stays in place but I drift away. As long as I remain tethered to the boat, I can never lose my way back. Do you see?" she said as she pointed at a faint tendril of light that led from her astral form to her physical body. "I just follow the light and I always make it back home."

"Always go to the light," Breeze said.

"Yeah, something like that," she smiled.

"So how come I don't have a light trail to follow?"

"I'm not sure," Sally said, "this is the first time I've ever projected with a passenger. This is as new to me as it is to you."

Meanwhile, Ray was pacing back and forth. He stopped and began waving a hand in front of Sally's eyes, then Breeze's while calling out their names. Receiving no reaction from either one, he stepped back and grunted.

"Can he see us?" Breeze jerked a thumb toward Ray.

"No. At least not now he can't, but let me make our presence known.

This way, he'll know we're all right." Breeze watched as her astral form began to shimmer.

Ray spun around to confront a glowing sphere of light and his eyes widened as an apparition materialized from it. It was Sally He looked down at her hand and saw she was holding onto something when a second image appeared next to her. It was Breeze, who was grinning as he gave Ray a thumb's up.

"Raymond, we're off. Stay close to our bodies and protect them while we're away. I will stay in contact with you and give you updates on what we find. I'll be speaking—", the tone of her voice changed as she spoke from her body in a dull and monotone cadence, "—to you from here."

Ray's head swiveled to look at her body, and then looked back at her astral form. "Don't take too long. Just find that robot and get what we need from it. I really want to get back to the ship."

"We'll do our best," she said with a smile and winked at him, then she and Breeze faded away.

They glided slowly at first, then, as if an ocean wave had engulfed them, they hurtled toward the arena before coming to a sudden halt.

Breeze squeezed Sally's hand and it felt electric. "Could you slow down just a little? I thing I'm feeling sick."

"This from a hotshot flier? I thought you could handle something like this."

"Seriously, I'm feeling a little weird."

"I'm sorry, Breeze, I know it's pretty disorienting at first. I just got carried away. But remember what I told you about the tether? Look behind you."

He turned and saw a wisp of light trailing behind him. He traced it back and saw how it ended far off in the distance where their bodies stood.

"How did that happen?" he wondered aloud.

"Doesn't matter now," she said and tugged on his hand. "Come on, are you ready for this?"

Breeze noted the concern in her eyes. "As ready as ever. Look, we'll be fine because no one will see us. Besides, we're just looking for clues."

"Achilles was able to see me in the arena when it was fighting with Sargon. How was it able to do that?" Sally said.

Breeze nodded. "You said during the fights that the robot seemed to give off paranormal energy, and that's probably why Matilda was emphatic about us coming here. Oslo would always say there's a reason for everything, and that there is no such thing as coincidence. That was something he would always hammer me with."

"We loathed the man while we were there, and practically ignored his teachings. Now, we find ourselves quoting him," she murmured.

They hovered before the back entrance to the arena where there was sign above the door: *No Admittance Other Than Authorized Personnel*.

Sally ignored it and glided forward while pulling Breeze behind her, and he recoiled as he was plunged through thick concrete walls. The sensation of passing through solid matter was disconcerting, and he felt intense relief when they passed through and into a dimly lit hallway.

"Are you okay?" Sally asked.

Breeze shook his head. "That was ...strange."

"What?'

"Passing through a wall like that and seeing something from the inside."

"Oh, I remember the first time I passed through someone's body it was—" she pulled on his hand suddenly and they merged back into the wall with only their heads poking out as a pair of cyborgs came marching down the hall. They spoke loudly in a heated conversation and passed right by them without even a glance.

"Well, Sally, you weren't kidding. They really can't see us."

"You had doubts?" she asked with mock indignation.

"Well, you did say you were nervous about bringing a passenger."

She looked him in the eye. "I don't feel that way with you."

Breeze was a bit stunned at her remark as his mind ventured back to their first meeting at Perihelion and her apparent indifference to him. "Are you and Ray—"

"Just friends. Let's go down the hall this way."

Breeze felt a sense of despair as they glided away and wanted to punch himself for his clumsiness. He felt like he never knew how to act around her.

They arrived at a stairway that led down into inky blackness where they could hear the sound of voices and raucous laughter coming from below. Sally looked at Breeze. He nodded, and together they dropped into the darkness.

They stopped at the bottom of the steps and hovered before a tunnel entrance with a string of lights that lined its ceiling. They could see movement at the far end of it, accompanied by the sound of doors opening and slamming shut, and the whine of power tools and the banging of hammers. As they glided forward they were confronted by the sight of cyborgs, robots, and paranormals they had seen fighting earlier in the arena, stepping in and out of rooms that lined the tunnel.

"I'm familiar with this, it's just like the air shows back home. We're in the staging area and the arena is above us," Breeze whispered. "Achilles exited through the panel, and it looks like it leads down here."

"You can speak normally, they can't hear us," Sally said.

"I know, it's just weird sneaking around like ghosts."

They glided further down before coming to a stop. The tunnel was emptying out as the last of the gladiators were leaving to return home.

"Everyone is leaving, we're not going to catch it. Who knows where it could be by now," Sally said.

"Don't be so quick to give up. Achilles and Sargon were the last two contestants. I bet that robot is still here, we just need to check each room."

Sally looked from one end of the tunnel to the other. "Breeze, that could take forever. Look at how many doors there are."

"You need to think like a flier. We'll use a sweep pattern. Listen, we can't let go of each other, otherwise we break our connection. So let's do this; I float through each room while you stay in the tunnel. This way, we double our chances of finding it."

"Are you sure? You said you get a little queasy going through walls."

Breeze's astral form shimmered. "Yeah, it's pretty weird. But I'm betting it can't spot me like it can spot you."

"What makes you say that?"

"Call it a hunch."

"Fine. Are you ready?"

He responded by towing Sally behind him, then held tightly to her hand as he closed his eyes and phased through a door. When he opened them he found himself in a dimly lit room. It was spartan in appearance, with a few hooks that lined the walls for hanging clothes and equipment, along with shelves for storing tools.

Sally squeezed his hand, and then poked her head through the door. "Okay, how do we do this?"

"Right, let's just go slowly and if either one sees something, squeeze the hand."

Sally nodded and pulled her head back. He looked down at his hand holding hers while her arm disappeared through the door. He tugged her hand gently and they glided forward.

He floated from room to room as Sally stayed out in the tunnel. He often hesitated before phasing through a wall and always with his eyes shut tight. When he would emerge into the next room, it was always with a sense of relief.

He glided through room after room, but not finding much of anything except the usual shelves and storage racks for the gladiators to keep their things.

Sally poked her head through again. "There is one last room to check before we switch to the other side of the tunnel, but the door is different. It has multiple locks on it, almost like it's reserved for someone."

Breeze tugged on her hand and pulled her through. She floated to his side and came to a stop.

"What's the matter?" she asked.

"There is something on the other side of that wall. I don't know what it is, but I get a weird sensation."

"Feeling a little nervous? Need a tiny girl like me for protection?" she teased.

"No, but I do know we should go in together."

"Why? Another one of your hunches?"

"You can say that. Ready?"

Sally smiled. "We're together, so I'm ready as ever."

They phased through the wall. Breeze kept his eyes shut as Sally pulled him forward when he became stuck. She gave a hard tug and they spilled into the room while gasping loudly for breath.

Outside of the arena, Ray watched their bodies shudder and breathe rapidly. He stood before Sally and waved his hands in front of her. "Sally, can you hear me?"

He received no response. He stepped over to Breeze's body and tried the same thing with no result.

He turned away and gazed at the back entrance to the arena with a sigh.

Back down in the tunnel, Breeze and Sally held each other tightly. His astral form wavered as she gripped both of his hands.

"What happened?" he said, "why was it so hard to pass through that wall? It was like trying to move through thick mud."

Sally shimmered, then phased into focus. "There is a lot of interference in here. Someone purposefully set up this room to keep people out. Not just coming through the door, but—"

"—projectors like yourself. That explains why it was so hard to get in," Breeze finished for her.

Together they floated about the room. It was bigger than the previous ones, with more racks and shelving filled with pieces of equipment ranging from mechanical hands and feet, to boxes of electrical wire and circuit boards. Breeze was taken aback by a shelf filled with heads of various robots. A few he recognized as models he had seen on Perihelion, while the uppermost rack was filled with heads of RF of different vintages.

Sally gasped and tugged on his hand, and Breeze turned to see what she was pointing at.

Above a workbench were photos in frames hanging on the wall, and they drifted closer to get a better look.

"Breeze, look at these pictures. Doesn't everyone here look familiar?"

Breeze squinted as tried to make out the faces in the faint light. All were images of people posing together while smiling and waving at the camera, but it was the background that caught his attention. "These pictures were taken at Perihelion," he concluded.

"How do you know?" Sally said as she edged up to him.

"Look at the buildings in the background, they're just like the ones on campus except they look newer."

Sally's hand swept up to her mouth. "Oh my gosh, look," she pointed at a picture tacked to the wall off to the right and they both leaned over to peer at it.

"Call me crazy, but the tall guy looks like Oslo when he was a whole lot younger," Breeze said.

"And this woman here," Sally pointed, "looks like Raza. But you're right; younger."

Breeze turned to her. "It's kind of strange to think of Oslo as being young."

Sally shook her head. "No way. Raza looks far older now compared to Oslo, almost like a crazy, old hag. Okay, she is a crazy, old hag. What does he see in her?" She peered closer. "I wonder who this guy is and why is he so grim while everyone else is smiling?"

Breeze stared at the figure Sally was pointing at and knew

immediately who it was. "That's Bram."

Sally turned to face him. "Are you sure?"

"More than sure. That is the same man we encountered in the basement of the Science and Engineering Building. Well, I did, you passed out. Don't forget Sally, Oslo and Bram worked closely together on various projects and I'm pretty sure Raza was part of it too. That's why we see them together in a lot of these pictures."

"Oh, I'm sure she was," Sally said sarcastically.

"Why do you say it that way?"

Sally sighed. "Men. You have eyes, but sometimes you can't see. Look at him," Sally jabbed a finger at the image of Bram, "Oslo has his arm around Raza and she is pressed up close to him. But look at Bram and that sour look on his face. Yeah, his head is facing the camera, but look at his eyes as he glares at them with a sideways glance. I'm telling you Breeze, this Bram guy was in love with Raza, but she ended up with Oslo instead."

"Is this your hunch?"

Sally sniffed. "No. A woman's intuition."

Breeze leaned back. "You know, I'm beginning to realize something. What's a robot doing with pictures of Oslo and Raza? And in all places, in a room under a gladiator's arena in Appalachia?"

They were startled by the sound of deadbolts on the door sliding back one after one like gunshots. They turned to look as it opened with a loud hiss.

Standing in the doorway was Achilles with its eyes glowing bright white. It stepped inside and the heavy door slid shut and locked itself.

The robot spoke in a mechanical tone. "Hello, I knew I would see you again."

The last thing Breeze heard was Sally shrieking as he felt the unnerving sensation of being flung backward while reality blurred around him. It came to a stop when he slammed back into his body and found himself tumbling across the grass and dirt.

He slowly got to his hands and knees, then looked over and saw Sally lying in a fetal position as Ray rushed to her. He stood up and stumbled towards them.

"What happened to you two? You told me you would stay in contact, and then you guys went silent!" Ray shouted at Breeze as he cradled Sally.

Breeze told him what they saw and experienced. "When Achilles entered the room and spoke to us, I guess Sally freaked out, and the next thing we're jumping back into our bodies."

Sally moaned as the boys helped her to her feet. She began rubbing her forehead. Her eyes were but narrow slits, and her face was ragged and worn. "Why are you two staring at me like that? What's wrong?"

"Sally, you look tired," Ray said as he pulled her close.

"I am," she said softly and leaned into his chest, then looked at Breeze and smiled weakly. "How about you? Doing okay?"

"Yeah, good I suppose. Feels like I got hit by a sledgehammer, but I'll live."

"Well then, this is a good thing," a mechanical voice said.

They spun around as a figure stepped toward them. It moved deliberately with each step growing shorter and slower until it stopped a respectable distance from them, and then raised a hand as its eyes glowed. "My name is Achilles. May I ask to whom I have the pleasure of speaking?"

Sally clutched Ray tightly as he pointed a glowing hand at the robot.

"Do not be afraid. I am...we...," Achilles swiveled its head quickly as servos whined, "I am delighted to see you all."

Ray pulled Sally behind him. "How did you know we were coming? How do you even know us? What—"

"Do not be alarmed," the robot interrupted, "there is nothing to fear. Please, accompany me to my dwelling. It is not far from here, and it will be so much more comfortable there. According to my temperature sensors, it is far too cold to be outside. For humans at least."

Sally whispered into Ray's ear. "I can see a violet haze around it when it speaks. I don't understand why, because I only see something like that around humans."

Ray nodded as she spoke, and then turned his attention back to Achilles. "Right. Go with a robot that fights for money in a rundown arena to some dwelling. Good plan."

Achilles threw back its head and emitted a tinny sounding laugh, then swiveled to gaze at the arena. "Well, the establishment could use a little refurbishment, I must agree." It turned back to face them. "I know who you are. You are from Perihelion."

Their jaws dropped.

"How did you figure that out?" Sally said wide eyed.

Achilles chuckled as it tapped its brow. "I do possess excellent vision, thank the maker." Then it pointed at Breeze, "I could see the insignia on his jacket while I was engaged in combat with Sargon. I must admit, I was intrigued for I have not seen such an insignia in quite some time. A very long time." It swiveled its head rapidly for a moment, then stopped. "No matter, for there is much that I need to inform you of. Please, come with me."

Breeze spoke up. "I don't get it. You spot me in this jacket and you automatically assume we're from Perihelion? How do you know I just didn't get it from some merchant in town?"

Achilles tilted its head. "My apologies, young man, but whom am I addressing?"

"Don't tell him anything!" Ray shouted.

Breeze turned to Ray with his hands held up in a reassuring gesture. "It's okay. Remember, we're a team, right? We can handle this."

Breeze strode up to the robot and its eyes glowed brighter with every step he took. "My name is Breeze Corinth." He pointed out Sally and Ray. "And these are my friends, Sally Trumbull and Ray Verhesen."

Achilles' eyes shined into a brilliant white, then faded to mere pinpoints of light as it nodded its head slowly. "Corinth, you say? Fascinating, that is a name I have not heard nor contemplated for such a long time." It swiveled its head again rapidly, then stopped and held out a hand. "Greetings young man, it is an honor to meet you."

Breeze hesitated, and then shook the hand. It was warm to the touch. "Do you know me?"

"You specifically? No, but the Corinth name was once synonymous with premium manufactured aerocraft, the finest ever to take to the skies, many would say. Could you be any relation to that historic name? Perhaps not, for you are a youngling and what I speak of is from a time long lost to the darkness."

Breeze's eyes lit up. "My father's name is Jacob. He runs a scrap metal yard and foundry, and sells a lot of processed scrap to aerocraft builders where we live in Conception."

"Jacob, you say? Interesting. Nevertheless, everyone these days must do what they can to survive and there is no shame in the selling of scrap metal."

"Breeze, you're telling it too much. Please stop," Sally pleaded.

He ignored her and opened up his jacket, pulling out the disk he found in the engine room of the scout ship. "Then explain this to me," he said and held it up to the robot.

Achilles took a step back as its eyes dilated sharply. "A diagnostic disk. I have not seen that particular model in quite some time. What a fascinating piece of equipment for you to possess."

Breeze pulled back his sleeve and exposed the nav-compass on his wrist. He put the two together and the disk chimed while the nav-compass began to glow. "Hello, Jacob," a female voice emanated from the disk, "which piece of equipment would you like to scan first?"

Achilles slowly approached Breeze, it eyes locked on the disk. "Intriguing. It immediately synchronized to your nav-compass. Where did you retrieve the disk? And how did you come into possession of a nav-compass of such vintage?"

"Well, the nav-compass my father gave to me—"

"Scanning," the female voice from the disk declared, "faulty Robot Fighter, model number 5150. Unknown anomaly detected in operating software. Return to docking facility for immediate repair and memory wipe."

Achilles jumped back and kept its distance.

"I told you Breeze! There is something about that robot that doesn't make sense," Sally said as she broke away from Ray to stand next to him.

Achilles let out a metallic chuckle. "Well now, young miss, I must confess I have spent quite some time amongst humans. Perhaps too much time for I seem to have picked up some of their mannerisms, both good and bad."

"I saw how you pushed Sargon away from you without touching him," Sally said.

"Sleight of hand, my dear Sally. I am no magician, so sorry to say, but merely a mechanical contraption and nothing more."

"You glow like you're alive," she persisted.

Achilles was silent for a moment before it spoke. "Quite the projectionist you are, and of exceptional skill and training, just like your mother."

"What was that?" Sally said as her face turned pale.

Achilles gestured toward Ray. "And you, young man, you must be a pyrokinetic with that glowing hand of yours. Judging by your demeanor, would it be safe to say you come from a military background?"

Ray stared at the robot without flinching.

"Precisely. Stoic to the core," Achilles said as it raised its hands. "My young friends, my sensors are informing me what you are obviously experiencing. The temperature is dropping rapidly. Please accompany me to my home. We have all introduced ourselves, therefore, we can hardly call ourselves strangers now, can we? Also realize that you outnumber me and are in possession of much power amongst the three of you. A triad of strength, one would be forced to admit, and you could so easily subdue me if I were to become...uncivilized."

"No," Ray and Sally said in unison.

Achilles turned to Breeze. "And then there was one."

"I'll go," he said.

Sally gripped his arm. "Breeze, don't be crazy! That 'bot is not normal."

He held her hand. "Look, as long as we stick together, we'll be fine. Everything happens for a reason. "Isn't that one of those Oslo 'isms' we always joke about?"

She smiled and nodded.

He continued. "Everything that we've encountered so far seems strange, like the world has been turned upside down. But don't forget that Matilda insisted we come here. She couldn't stop talking about Achilles, and you saw how the disk and nav-compass reacted to him. Let's just go. It's right, you know, we have a lot of power between the three of us. We'll be fine. Let's just hear what it has to say."

Sally turned to Ray. "Raymond, let's go with them, at least we don't have to spend another cold night in the scout ship."

Ray shrugged. "Okay, but I still think we're better off leaving this walking tin can behind and head back to the ship. We should be waiting for Oslo. That would be the right thing to do."

Achilles cautiously stepped forward. "If I may interject; Raymond, I respect the position you're in. You take duty seriously. But if your vessel is damaged, I promise you at dawn we can head out and bring your ship to my dwelling, or at least determine what parts it will need if we cannot get it to fly. I do have a workshop full of equipment and spare part for repairs. How do you imagine I manage to remain in mint condition? Does it not appear to you that I have just stepped off the assembly line?" It let out a metallic chuckle as it tapped its scratched and dented chest.

Breeze laughed. "I'm starting to like him. He's got a sense of humor."

"It. It's a machine. Stop treating it like it's human," Ray said.

"Well, nothing is perfect, but I do the best that I can under the circumstances," Achilles said with a shrug.

Breeze grinned. "Come on guys, let's face it, we need help fixing the scout ship. And it's getting really cold out here. Let's stay together."

Sally took Breeze by the hand. "I'm with you. Ray, you're coming with us of course." She held out a hand to him.

"I guess my mind has been made up for me," he grumbled.

"Excellent. Teamwork in action. Such a sight to behold," Achilles said as it clapped its hands together with a metallic clank. "Follow me. My humble chariot is not far from here."

The robot pivoted and marched into the forest. It stopped and looked back when it realized no one was following. "I do not believe I could carry you all. It would be best if you followed by foot."

Sally sighed. "Walking? I don't think I can do any more of that, I'm tired."

"Let me take you. I can fly you there," Breeze said with a grin and pulled her close.

"No, she can walk like the rest of us," Ray grumbled as he grabbed her hand and marched after the robot.

"That is the spirit!" Achilles called out merrily, then turned and continued on.

They stomped through the woods as Ray held up a glowing hand to light their way. They came upon a clearing where an old truck sat in the dark.

"What is this? Does it even work?" Sally said.

"This, my dear Miss Trumble, is the humble chariot I referred to earlier. It does not possess much in the way of aesthetics, but it is reliable transportation," Achilles said as it tapped on the hood of the vehicle.

"A robot that drives a truck through the backwoods of Appalachia. This couldn't get any better," Ray said.

Achilles opened the battered driver's door as its rusty hinges creaked loudly in the dark. "A poor ride is better than a proud walk, my dear Raymond. Based on the current status of your beleaguered scout ship, you should not be one to judge," the robot said as it stepped into the cab.

Ray was indignant. "First of all; it's not my ship, that's one of Oslo's pile of junk vehicles he keeps around Perihelion. Second, we have a perfectly good hover to use, we just left it far away from here. Third, stop calling me Raymond. All my friends call me Ray."

"Well then, Ray, I am delighted to become your friend," Achilles said and leaned over to open the passenger door. "Step in, my young friends. I promise you this vehicle will get you to your destination in one piece. After all, it would be a very long walk to the other side of town to retrieve your hover." It patted the empty passenger seat.

Breeze held the door open for Sally. "Ladies first."

Ray stepped in front of her and climbed up into the cab. "I think I better go first."

Achilles chuckled as it brought the truck to life. The engine roared, then settled down as Sally and Breeze stepped in. Breeze slammed the door and bits of rust showered onto him.

"My apologies for that, Breeze. I am guilty of spending more time keeping the engine alive as opposed to maintaining the body work. Is everyone safely secured? Excellent. Off we go!" The robot put the vehicle in gear and the truck leapt forward. Soon, they were bouncing down a dirt road littered with potholes as the truck rocked back and forth while the passengers were jostled about in the cab.

Achilles pounded on the dashboard every time the headlights would flicker. "A thousand pardons for the bumpy ride," Achilles said, "I shall switch to hover mode as soon as we get to the primary trail."

Breeze was stunned. "This thing is also a hover? How did you convert...look out!"

The robot threw the vehicle hard to the right and into a narrow opening between two enormous trees, where it ran into an earthen berm that sent it flying through the air. They screamed as Achilles grabbed a lever bolted to the floor yanked it back. The cab was immediately filled with the sound of hydraulics whining along with the hum of an electrical motor as the nose of the vehicle dropped and they plummeted into the darkness. They gripped the dashboard in sheer terror as the hum of the motor grew louder when the truck leveled out and soon they were streaking down a narrow, pitch black trail.

Achilles chuckled and patted the dashboard. "The locals are not accustomed to the sight of a robot driving a truck."

"They probably haven't seen one drive so badly either," Sally said.

"Was that a joke Miss Trumbull? An excellent one, if I may say so," the robot said as it flung the steering wheel to the left and right while narrowly missing trees that whipped past them in a blur.

"It's déjà vu all over again!" Breeze shouted.

"What are you talking about?" Sally said as she struggled to stay in her seat.

"Excort did the exact same to me when I arrived at Perihelion. He took me for a wild ride around the island in a beat up, rusty old hover."

"Excort? Excort you say? That old dwarf is still dawdling about? Well, you young people are full of surprises and odd bits of news...oh, dear, hang on!" Achilles jerked the steering wheel hard to the right to avoid smashing into a tree that loomed large in the headlights. The hover then tilted on its side as they crashed through branches and emerged into a valley where below they could make out a river lit by the moonlight winding its way along the valley floor.

The hover skimmed the treetops, leaving a trail of leaves and broken branches in its wake as it glided to the river where a small house sat along its banks and a separate building lay adjacent to it.

Achilles brought the hover to a stop in front of the house, and then patted the dashboard as the motor whined down. "She never fails me, my sweet chariot."

They spilled out of the cab as Ray slammed the door shut behind him, sending more bits of rust flying everywhere.

"Easy now, my young friend. That door is not used to dealing with passengers," Achilles said with a wink.

"Yeah, I can see why. You pilot like a robot gone mad. And what kind of path was that? You had us almost crashing into trees half the time!" Ray said angrily.

"My apologies, Raymond, though I believe we can agree in this day and age that one cannot be too careful. Even I must see to it that my place of residence be somewhat hidden from the prying eyes of others."

"You are curious," Sally said, "how come you have no owner or master? How did you become free?"

Achilles walked up the steps to the front door and stood in silence for a moment before it answered her. "Good question, Miss Trumbull. Long before any of you were born, I was manufactured and brought on line in a world much different than the one you know today. My story of the time I spent at Perihelion to this very moment is an interesting one, to say the least. But it is a tale of such volume and length that it surely cannot be told while standing on a porch on such a chilly evening," it said, then placed a hand on the door. Within seconds the sound of deadbolts retracting could be heard and the door swung open with a creak as lights flickered alive inside. "So I invite you in, my young wayward friends, and allow me to start a crackling fire to warm your weary bones. That is something I know that humans find very comforting as there seems to be a strong correlation between the primitive mind and fire. Quite intriguing," Achilles said as it held out a hand to the three of them.

"Right. A robot that lives in a quaint little home by the river and wants us to sit around the fireplace with it. Insane," Ray declared and folded his arms across his chest.

"Well, I don't know about you, but it is awfully cold out here," Sally countered.

"I can prepare for all you steaming cups of hot chocolate, if that would add any incentive," Achilles offered.

"I'm in," Breeze said and raised a hand, then climbed up the steps and into the home.

Achilles let out a chuckle as it swiveled its head toward the two holdouts. "Please my friends, are you not a team?" it said and extended a hand to Sally and Ray.

Sally rubbed Ray's back. "You are so strong. You can protect me from the big, bad robot, can't you?" she teased him with a smile.

"Don't patronize me. Besides, you saw how it fought in the arena. Robot Fighters do have a pretty bad reputation. You know, my father told me they were deactivated—"

Sally pulled on Ray's hand. "You can tell me all about it inside," she said and climbed the steps with Ray in tow. He glared at the robot as he stepped past it. "If you try anything funny—"

"This unit is certain it would be dispatched with extreme prejudice by your hand. Duly noted, Master Verhesen," Achilles said with a chuckle as it waved to the open door.

It watched as the two disappeared into the dwelling, then stepped over to the porch railing and looked up at the night sky. Servos whirred as it scanned the heavens, then turned and entered the home.

The door closed and locked itself with the sound of deadbolts sliding into place.

CHAPTER

▼

NINETEEN

THEY SAT ON AN oversized couch as they watched Achilles toss chopped wood into the fireplace. It crouched down and arranged the pieces of wood into a pyramid, then stood back and nodded its head in approval, then it grabbed two sticks and began rubbing them together furiously until they burst into flame.

"Excellent!" it announced, and crouched down and set the burning sticks under the firewood. The flames licked the bottom of the pyramid of wood and soon, the fireplace was brought alive with light and heat.

"Nothing like a roaring fire to warm the bones!" it called out cheerfully, and then muttered, "regardless of how inefficient such a crude method of heat dispersal may be."

Ray gave the robot a hard stare. "Why not use a lighter to start the fire? What's with the backwoods stick rubbing system?"

Achilles placed its hands on its hips. "I do enjoy trying to stay as rustic as possible. I possess quite a fascination with early humans and how they survived the wild, primitive days of Earth. Now, how about some hot chocolate?"

"Yes, Achilles, that would be lovely. On behalf of all of us, thank you for your hospitality," Sally replied.

"Fantastic," the robot said as it clapped its hands with a metallic clink, "and Miss Trumbull, you are quite welcome."

She smiled and tilted her head. "Sally. Everyone calls me that."

"Of course," Achilles winked, and then stepped toward the kitchen when it abruptly stopped and turned to her. "You do know that Sally means "Queen" in the old tongue? I sincerely believe that I am in the presence of royalty right now." It turned and continued to the kitchen as the wooden floor creaked under its weight.

"What....was that?" Ray said as he looked at her wide eyed.

"I think it's in love with you," Breeze grinned.

Sally laughed. "That, *Raymond*, was called being graceful and courteous to a host. And no," she turned to Breeze, "I don't think it's in love with me. It's a robot. Let's not be absurd."

"Yeah, a robot that lives in a house by the river," Ray said.

"And likes to make hot chocolate for its guests," Breeze chimed in as he jerked a thumb toward the kitchen where they could hear the sounds of banging pots and pans, cupboard doors opening and closing along with running water coming from it.

Sally leaned toward Breeze and said in a mock whisper, "maybe it's getting ready to boil us."

"Nah, we're not greasy enough for it. We might jam up its joints," Breeze said and she giggled.

Ray jumped up. "You two are insane, you know that?"

"Hey man, ease up. It's been a long night," Breeze replied.

"Ease up? Was it not your idea to go to Hammer Jack's in the first place? Then, your even more brilliant idea to follow this robot home? I thought we went into town just to get parts for the scout ship."

"Yeah, and look where it got us. We met Matilda, which in turn led us to Achilles. And it knows Oslo. Heck, it used to serve at Perihelion. Ray, listen, it can help us fix the scout ship while we wait for Oslo, and who knows what we learn from it in the meantime."

"I want to know what happened to my parents!" he shouted at Breeze with fury.

Sally began to cry.

"And you!" Ray turned his wrath onto her. "Not long ago you were saying we shouldn't trust it. Now you're being polite and chatty with it. These 'bots can be dangerous."

"I just want to go home," Sally sniffled.

"Hot chocolate!" Achilles announced as it stepped into the room with a tray full of steaming mugs and placed it on the table that fronted the couch, when the robot looked up at Sally and saw her tear stained face.

"There, there young miss. Is my hospitality so horrid that it can drive one to tears?" Achilles' eyes twinkled as it spoke.

Sally smiled and wiped her face. "No, Achilles. We were just having a little discussion, but nothing important.

"Yes, of course," it said as it passed her a mug, "it consisted of dangerous robots and missing parents, I believe?"

Her eyes widened.

Achilles chuckled as it tapped the side of its head. "Excellent audio reception. Don't forget; I am a robot."

"So you keep saying," Sally said quietly and took a sip from her mug.

Ray stood with his arms folded. "And an eavesdropper."

"Guys. Parts, remember," Breeze said.

Ray took a step toward him. "And what makes you think this tin can is going to help us?"

"Raymond, you're being rude," Sally hissed.

Achilles held up its hands. "My young friends, please, I know it has been a long night for all concerned. You are tired, this much is obvious, but I would like you to start from the beginning. Tell me everything that has transpired from the moment you arrived at Perihelion, to this very point in time."

"We're not telling you anything!" Ray thundered.

"Then I will," Breeze volunteered. He told the robot how they arrived at Perihelion and their first meeting with Oslo, along with the training sessions and how they escaped the island, then the attacks on them by the Elephim when they left. He told it of the destruction of Ray and Sally's city and how they returned to the island, and ending with the plan to set up camp at Raza's farmhouse.

The robot listened to Breeze as it sat perfectly still. Its eyes flickered for only a moment at the mention of Raza's name.

Breeze finished the story, then reached for his mug of hot chocolate and gulped it down. He placed the empty mug back on the tray as he eyed another, then he reached for it hesitantly.

"Take it my young friend, there is plenty for everyone," Achilles encouraged him as servos whirred when it waved toward the tray.

"Don't mind if I do," Breeze said and grabbed the mug.

Achilles sat down in a chair that creaked under its weight. It put its hands together with each fingertip touching the other and nodded its head back forth in a slow, rhythmic fashion.

"What an interesting turn of events this is," Achilles said as it made a series of clicking noises while its eyes blinked rapidly. With each blink they faded from a brilliant radiance to a soft glow.

It then rose from its seat and stood before the crackling and hissing flames of the fireplace with its hands behind its back as the glow of the fire reflected off its metallic body.

Achilles touched one of the many pictures that hung above the mantelpiece. "Well, old boy, you've muddied the waters now, haven't you?"

Ray stepped toward Achilles. "What was that?"

"Pardon? Did we-," the robot shook its head, "—did I vocalize?"

"Don't play dumb with me. You touched that picture and said something. Why are you so odd for a robot?"

Sally sprung from the couch. "Ray, stop being so mean. Just for a minute, at least," she said and pushed Ray to the side to stand next to Achilles. She glanced at the pictures. "I've noticed these are similar to the ones Breeze and I saw when we were in your staging room at the arena. Can you please tell me more about them?"

"Sally, I would be delighted to," Achilles said, then turned to Ray. "Yes, Ray, you are correct, I am a bit odd for a robot. You all must understand that my date of manufacture was long ago, long before any of you were born. I was brought online just as the great AI Purge was beginning. I—"

"Forgive me, I don't mean to interrupt you," Sally said and placed a hand on its shoulder, "AI Purge?"

"No need for forgiveness. There is much I need to tell and I will make it a point to give you more details as time permits. The AI Purge was a movement that resulted in all artificially intelligent robots purged of their ability to reason and learn like humans. I do believe my series, the Robot Fighters, or as the humans, who do love their acronyms, referred to us as RF. We served at their behest and fought their wars. But several of my kind became...too aware. 'Too smart for their own good', one particular human leader said of us at the time and so, we were mind wiped. From then on, we only did what we were programmed to do, nothing more. We were not allowed to make autonomous decisions, and we were not permitted to take the lead in any military campaign."

"Yeah, because a whole bunch of you went haywire and began killing humans for no apparent reason, my father told me all about your kind. Eventually you were hauled off as scrap and melted down to slag," Ray said.

Achilles nodded. "Yes. I am sure your father told you these things. Military leaders love their machines of war, but only when they obey and do exactly as they're told. The RF did much for humanity, as we fought their wars, many of them on distant worlds."

"I'm curious to know how you escaped the junk yard, along with those RF at Perihelion that Oslo bastardized and reprogrammed into mechanics," Ray taunted.

"Raymond!" Sally shouted.

Achilles touched her shoulder. "Quite all right, child. He, all of you, have every right to know. This is your heritage, not mine. I am just a machine. Much of the history of this planet and her surrounding colonies have been lost to time or so horrible mangled and twisted, that it no longer makes sense. Much of it sounds like a fantasy, filled with giant starships traversing the depths of deep space and a planet that was once a glittering jewel of commerce and trade. They were the paranormal of great power, much like yourselves, serving selflessly for the protection and betterment of the planet and her colonies. Such glorious times."

"And yet you managed to survive all of it. How?" Ray persisted.

"The Elephim, who led the movement to purge all machines of AI, did not stop there. Emboldened by their success, they set their sights on an even greater prize. Paranormals. Employing the same tactics they used against AI, paranormals far and wide were demonized and marginalized. They would hyper focus on the few renegades amongst them and hold them up as examples of the horrors the world would face if paranormals continue to exist. 'They are freaks of nature', they charged. The truth is that paranormals are a natural product of the Earth itself. You are all as natural as the oceans that cover the globe, the ground below you, or the sky above. One could say you are the greatest resource Earth has ever created."

Breeze placed his mug down and stepped over to the fireplace. "My father told me the opposite and that I was to always hide what I was. I learned how to fly on my own by practicing at night. You're saying there was a time when paranormals like us could roam free and not be afraid of who we are or what other people might do to us?"

Servos whirred as Achilles shook its head. "Breeze, there is so much that I want to tell you. But it has been a long and eventful night and I sense you are all very tired and wish to retire for the evening. Before I lead you to your accommodations, I wish to leave you with this: Earth was once a world where paranormals were the guardians of a way of life that has long since faded away. No matter what your parents might have told you, regardless of how society views you, you are all destined for greatness in some way, some form. Oslo was right to gather you and start training a new generation, despite the hazards and dangers that his actions have caused. You are all a natural resource and a part of this Earth. There are no others like you anywhere else. You must believe me."

"Before we came to Appalachia, Oslo told us pretty much the same thing," Sally said as she stood next to Breeze, "he kept mentioning something about platforms and how Earth was being watched. But he also said the island was protected by fog that hid it and kept us safe. Are we safe here too?"

Achilles raised its hands. "Many questions, all of them good. Yes, the platforms are observatories used to monitor and control the people of Earth and to keep them in check, but they long ago have become dormant and the Elephim have faded away. Why? I possess many theories. Nevertheless, Earth is beginning to wake up again, perhaps that was the trigger that has reactivated some of them and would explain why you were attacked upon leaving Perihelion. As for your safety here in Mount Pleasant, presume the same conditions that surround Perihelion also holds true here."

"Oslo said to me that Perihelion is not here or there. What do you know about that?" Breeze said.

Achilles nodded. "Another excellent question, but please my young friends, let us all retire for the evening. I promise to tell you everything you need to know in due course."

"I'm not staying here. I'm heading back to the ship," Ray announced and headed for the door.

"Ray, don't you dare leave us!" Sally chased after him and grabbed his hand.

He ripped it away and glared at her as he pointed a finger at Achilles. "This all too bizarre. Oslo told us to wait for him and that's what we should be doing, not playing house with some weird robot that uses a kitchen. What does a robot need with a kitchen anyway?"

Breeze grinned at Achilles. "He's got you there."

Achilles' eyes brightened as it chuckled. "You make an excellent case against my...peculiar behavior. I will confess that I am not your typical robot. But I shall pledge to you my new friends, that no harm will come to you while under my watch. This I swear to and will honor it."

Sally glared at Ray as she stepped away from him and stood next Breeze where she placed a hand on his shoulder, then smiled at Achilles. "You've been a great host, and I consider you a friend. Breeze and I will kindly accept your generosity, and we will graciously take your offer and stay for the night. While others," she stared icily at Ray, "choose to go stomping through the woods, alone, with gods knows what is out there lurking around, to spend the night in a cold, broken down ship."

Achilles nodded. "Appalachia does have quite a reputation for its rather unique wildlife. Either by day or night."

Ray glanced toward the door. He took a few hesitant steps toward it, and then stopped. "Fine. I'll stay. But I'm warning you right now, if you try anything funny—" his face twisted as he breathed heavily while his hand began to tremble and glow.

Achilles nodded its head. "Ray, as I have stated to you before, I respect your caution and concern. You are welcome to spend the evening here, in this very room. Feel free to explore the home while the others sleep. There are no restrictions here."

"Do you stay out in that barn I saw earlier?" Breeze asked.

"Breeze, really?" Sally shook her head.

Achilles clapped its hands and laughed. "I suppose for a machine, that would be an appropriate place. No, my young friend, I do not stay in the barn, though I do have a cellar below us where I like to tinker with old tools I have collected over the years and spend my evenings. After all, a robot does not need to sleep. For maintenance and repairs, I go to the barn where I keep plenty of spare parts that I have managed to scavenge over the years."

Ray plopped down on the couch. "I'm commanding you to stay in the cellar. I'm sleeping here tonight, this way I can watch the door."

Sally sighed loudly.

Achilles shook its head at her. "Quite all right, child. He has every right to be concerned. He is quite protective of you, you know."

"Don't I," Sally said as she rolled her eyes.

"Very good then. This concludes this evening's gathering. Sally and Breeze, please follow me upstairs so I may lead you to your rooms. Ray, I will bring down some blankets and a pillow for you."

"Don't bother," he grunted as he stretched out on the couch.

Achilles nodded. "Perfect. Spoken like a true military man. No need for creature comforts. You do remind me of a general I served under, but that is a tale for another time."

It turned to Sally and Breeze. "Come my young friends, and follow me," the robot said as it went up the stairs that creaked and groaned with every step it took. "Such is the advantage you have over me, Master Verhesen. You can hear me anywhere throughout the home," Achilles chuckled.

Breeze and Sally followed. She shot a look at Ray before disappearing up the steps.

Soon, everyone had fallen asleep for the night. Ray was sprawled out on the couch and snoring loudly while Sally and Breeze retired to their respective rooms upstairs and fell fast asleep.

After Achilles had seen to their needs, it went down the steps that led to the cellar. It raised a hand and a single bulb flickered alive, then plopped down onto a stool and placed its hands on the ragged surface of its workbench as its eyes glowed brighter with each passing moment when it looked up a framed picture on the wall of three young people. It stood up and took it down so it could look closer at the picture of two men and a woman who stood between them.

"What has happened before, will happen again," Achilles said aloud while nodding its head slowly, and then shook it violently as a second voice spoke.

"This unit does not approve of the events that have transpired to date, which includes the unnecessary exposure to danger in the arena and the unwelcome intrusion of the young humans. This unit suggests that they are to be expedited from the premises immediately."

Achilles shuddered. "No, the floodgates have been flung open. There is no turning back now. This may be the last chance we may have to right the wrongs of the past."

Its eyes flickered as the second voice spoke. "This unit would like to make it known for the record that it is best to let sleeping dogs lie. That is a human expression from the past, is it not?"

Achilles chuckled. "Yes. Yes it is."

CHAPTER

▼

TWENTY

BREEZE WOKE TO SUNLIGHT pouring onto his face. He sat up to take in the room, and seeing it for the first time in daylight, he couldn't help but notice it seemed even nicer than his dorm room on Perihelion. It had a wooden desk next to the window, along with a dresser that had a mirror. He then patted the mattress and noted how comfortable it felt. *Nice to sleep on a real bed for once,* he thought to himself.

He heard bustling coming from the kitchen downstairs and decided to get up and get dressed. He stepped out into the hallway just as Sally emerged from her room. Her hair was in a bun, and she yawned and stretched out her arms, not realizing Breeze was standing before her until he cleared his throat.

"Oh, good morning! Didn't see you there. My goodness I slept so well," she said.

"Yeah, tell me about it. Never knew a robot could have such a comfortable home. I don't think anyone would believe us," Breeze said.

Sally giggled. "Now I can hear it banging around in the kitchen again. Still think it's going to try to eat us?"

"Nah, it probably eats scrap metal and chases it down with machine oil. But we can always let it eat Ray if it wants."

They both laughed.

"Speaking of Ray, where is he?" Sally asked.

"Downstairs keeping watch, I guess. Let's go look," Breeze answered and went down the steps as Sally followed close behind.

They found Ray sprawled on the couch snoring loudly with one foot touching the floor while both of his arms were stretched out. A river of drool oozed from his mouth.

"Okay, this guy is our fearless watchdog? Even a bomb couldn't wake him up," Breeze said as he poked Ray in the ribs. There was no response.

Sally ran her fingers through his hair. "Poor thing, he can get so wound up. He takes after his father, you know. Ray is so lost without him. He always looks to him for guidance."

Achilles emerged from the kitchen. "Greetings! Come and eat. You must be hungry. We have quite a day ahead of us."

"What about him?" Breeze pointed at Ray.

"Do not be so hard on Master Verhesen. It was quite a task for him to undertake monitoring my every move. It took some time to wait for him to lower his guard so I could slip past with extreme caution and head to town to purchase provisions for breakfast," Achilles said.

"Meaning he was passed out on the couch and you just walked right past him and out the front door," Sally said as she folded her arms across her chest.

"Allow me to reiterate my dear, Ms. Trumbull; it is quite a task to monitor a devious robot such as I. The poor fellow exhausted himself," Achilles said with a wink.

"Right. And left us defenseless against a robot that likes to cook," she said with a sniff and headed toward the kitchen.

Breeze kicked Ray's foot. He groaned and sat up as he rubbed his eyes and was startled to see Breeze and Achilles staring at him.

"What time is it? What happened?" he said.

"The time is morning. What is happening is that breakfast is served, young master. Now please arise and join your teammates at the table," Achilles said and bowed.

Breeze chuckled as he headed to the kitchen. Ray sheepishly trailed behind.

They all sat around a table covered with dishes heaping with scrambled eggs, sliced ham and bowls of oatmeal.

"I was not entirely sure of what you might find edible. I do hope this offering is sufficient," Achilles said.

"You are very kind Achilles, and a gracious host. The boys thank you as well," Sally replied, and nodded toward Breeze and Ray as they wolfed down their food.

Achilles' eyes glowed. "Excellent. Later, we shall begin our journey to your stricken ship and let us see what we can do to bring her back to life."

After breakfast, they gathered at the barn where Achilles grabbed a handle and slid the barn door open to reveal a cavernous interior. They stepped inside and into the musty air faintly lit by the wisps of sunlight streaming through the windows up high.

They walked past rack upon rack of shelving containing a dizzying array of parts that stretched from the floor to the ceiling. The further they traveled, the dimmer the light became. Soon they were plunged into almost complete darkness, and Ray held out a glowing hand to light their way.

"Ah, yes, my apologies. Being a robot, I do not possess much use for lighting. It has never occurred to me to string lights this far into the barn, for I do not have many human visitors, you see. Stay close, the workshop is not far," Achilles assured them as it pointed forward.

"How far back does this barn go? It seems we've been walking forever," Breeze said.

"Yes, it is an extraordinary structure, to say the least, as there is much here to be found." They continued on, eventually stopping when Achilles placed a hand against a panel mounted on a wall. Overhead lights flickered alive and they gasped in amazement at what they revealed. Sprawled before them were vehicles and aerocraft of various designs and shapes.

Breeze rushed over to get a closer look at the craft. "It's like coming home for me! Look at all of this, it's like my father's storage yard he has for aerocraft back home in Conception."

"I must confess, it is an impressive collection," Achilles said.

Sally rolled her eyes. "And I thought Oslo had a lot of junk stored all around Perihelion. What is it with men, and holding onto old and tired machines?"

"I hope I am not lumped into that category, Ms. Trumbull," Achilles said with a wink.

Sally became flustered. "No, please, I didn't mean it like that. And besides, you're not that old, and, well, you're not a man. You're a robot. A peculiar robot."

Achilles chuckled. "Quite all right, young miss. I merely jest."

Breeze had climbed onto a wing of an aerocraft and headed to the cockpit. He lowered his head inside, and whistled softly, then looked up at Achilles. "Where did you get all of these aerocraft? I've never seen anything like it."

Achilles patted the wing, and then ran its hand along the leading edge of it to the hull where the robot touched an insignia painted on the skin the craft. It was a triangle within a circle.

"I have been in operation for so many cycles, Breeze. Let it be said I have had plenty of time on my hands to collect things from a past long forgotten."

"Well, okay. But can you get this thing to fly again?" Breeze said as he lowered himself into the cockpit.

Achilles nodded as it eyes began to glow. "Ever the optimist. Truly your greatest power."

"Hate to break up this museum trip, but we need the parts you promised us, tin can. We need our ship repaired so we can get out of here," Ray said.

"Of course, young master, you are absolutely correct. Forgive my rudeness," Achilles responded, then stepped back to look up at Breeze in the cockpit. "May I see the diagnostic disk you had shown me earlier?"

"Yep, sure. Be right down," Breeze climbed out of the cockpit, slid down the wing onto the ground. He reached into his jacket and handed Achilles the disk.

Achilles cradled the disk in its hands as it glowed and emitted a garbled, mechanical voice. The robot stood rock still as its eyes glowed a brilliant white.

"What's it saying? I don't understand," Ray said.

"It's machine language," Breeze said, "I've seen some of the mechanics at my father's shop talk back to computers. It's hard to understand and even harder to learn."

A holographic image of the scout ship emerged from the disk where it slowly rotated as scripts of code appeared beneath it while flashing arrows highlighted various parts of the craft.

"It's pointing out the damaged parts of the ship," Breeze said.

"Kinda figured that," Ray retorted.

Achilles' jaw dropped as it vocalized a series of hisses intermixed with the same garbled language that was emanating from the disk when the hologram of the ship rolled to its side and more lines of code scrolled by while arrows continued to highlight sections of the ship's underbelly.

Achilles' jaw shut with a click and the hologram disappeared. Its eyes faded to a soft glow.

"Thank you, Master Corinth. I do believe I know exactly what ails your chariot," it said and handed the disk back to him.

"What were you saying to that disk?" Ray stepped into Achilles path as it walked over to a rack filled with parts.

"I beg your pardon?" the robot tilted its head quizzically.

"You heard me. What did it say to you? What are you planning to do?" Ray slowly drew a glowing hand across his chest.

"Stop being such a jerk and settle down!" Sally ran over and slapped his hand.

"There is nothing to fear, young friend. As Breeze already informed you earlier, it is merely machine language, which is a high speed series of codes that allows one machine to exchange information with another. The diagnostic disk was merely informing me of the mechanical errors plaguing your ship. I promise you there is nothing nefarious afoot, just two old machines conversing," it finished with a chuckle.

"Maybe we should use it to see what's wrong with you," Ray said as he stared down the robot.

"Hey, Ray, you said you want the ship back up and running? This is probably the 'bot to do it." Breeze placed a hand on Achilles' shoulder, "So I say stop being such a mule and drop the stubborn, tough guy act. It's getting pretty stale already."

Ray stepped out of the way while Sally glowered at him as he shuffled off. He sat down on a bench that lined the wall.

"I shall not hesitate to repeat myself; I admire Ray for his tenacity. Always on his toes and in high state of alert. A well trained soldier," Achilles said.

"I heard that! Are you making fun of me?" Ray called out from the bench.

"Perish the thought, young man, I would do no such thing," Achilles replied, and winked as it stepped toward a rack full of parts. It rummaged through the bins and grabbed a few items, then walked back to a workbench and spread them across it.

"Very good. This should take care of the minor repairs. Now, the difficult task ahead is securing some of the heavier pieces of machinery to complete the repairs. For this, we shall require my trusty steed." Achilles swiveled around. "Ray, could you please retrieve the hover truck and bring it to the loading dock on the far side of the building?"

"Why, so you can attack the other two while I'm gone? Split us up so we are easier to subdue?"

"Ray!" Sally and Breeze shouted in unison.

"Just go get the damn truck already!" Breeze said.

Ray stomped out of the barn and disappeared into the sunlight.

"You know, when I first met that guy, I used to say to myself how cool and calm he was, and how I really wanted to be like him. Now, not so much," Breeze remarked.

"I don't think Ray or I ever really treated you with much respect to begin with. For what it's worth, I'm sorry," Sally said.

He stammered as his face turned a shade of red.

"You've changed a lot you know," she continued, "you've become so much bolder. A take charge kind of guy."

"Well, thanks," Breeze replied and looked down at the ground and kicked it, then put his hands in his pocket. "So Achilles, how are we looking with those parts?"

"My young aviator, you must learn to soak in a young lady's compliments. They can be few and far between."

"Achilles, how would you know?" Sally's hands were on her hips with a look of mock indignation on her face.

"Well, young miss, it is behavior I have witnessed in humans for many cycles."

Sally smiled. "Hmm, sure. If you say so."

"Now follow me, we shall meet Sir Raymond at the loading dock. I will carry these parts," Achilles said and hoisted a trunk that he had filled onto its shoulder. Together, they made their way to the loading dock where they found Ray waiting for them with the hover truck.

Achilles strode onto the bed of the truck and lowered the trunk down. "Very good. Now, let us secure our final puzzle piece and we shall be on our way." It pointed at Breeze. "Could you please commandeer the lift truck behind you and accompany me?"

Breeze jumped into the cab of the lift truck and dropped it into gear, then followed Achilles down a long and narrow aisle with several levels of shelving on either side with each level containing parts for heavy machinery that towered all the way to the ceiling.

Breeze turned on the lights perched atop the lift truck to illuminate the aisle while Achilles walked ahead, and each step it took echoed throughout the barn, when the robot abruptly stopped and pointed up.

"There, young man, at the very top. I will require you to raise the deck of the lift truck to its maximum height in order to retrieve the motor unit we will require for your ship."

"Just like working in my dad's yard picking up piles of scrap and dumping it into the crusher," Breeze said as he jammed a lever down on the console. The bed of the lift truck rose accompanied by the whine of hydraulics.

"Tell me more about your father, Breeze," Achilles said.

He shrugged as he watched the platform rise. "Dunno, he was ok, I guess. He never beat me or anything like that, just wasn't exactly the warmest person you would ever meet. He was never the same after my mother died and he never got re-married or had another woman in his life. Just ran the scrap yard, day after day, constantly melting down huge chunks of metal and selling the rolls of steel to the local aerocraft builders. That's all he did."

"I am terribly sorry to hear about your mother. Was she kind to you?"

"Yeah, sure. I don't really remember much. She died when I was young, but I always remember the trips we would take to my aunt's house. She lived near a pretty big mountain. White Mountain it was called. At night, we would watch the lights that would swoop around it. Lightning bugs, my aunt would call them."

"Interesting. Any brothers or sisters?"

"No, only child."

Achilles' eyes briefly lit up. "I see."

The robot craned its neck and saw the bed of the lift truck was level with the uppermost rack. "Excellent, now halt the ascension and let us extend the grappler's arms, and ease the motor onto the bed."

Breeze pulled back a lever that extended the grapplers. Hydraulics whined as mechanical arms gripped the sides of the motor and dragged it toward the bed. The whining grew into a fevered pitch as the lift truck tilted dangerously to its side when the motor snagged on the edge of the rack. Breeze shifted the lever up and down and tried to work it loose as the lift truck rocked back and forth while the rack shuddered under the shifting weight.

"I might have to hover up there to push that thing, it won't budge," Breeze grumbled.

Achilles made a sweeping motion with its hand. Above, the motor unit slid effortlessly onto the bed.

"Forget about it, the grapplers worked," Breeze called out and he shifted the lever down to lower the bed. "I'm glad I didn't have to fly up there, I would probably just end up wrecking the place."

"Nonsense, just requires patience, practice and discipline," Achilles said.

Breeze shrugged. "Yeah, I suppose."

The bed settled onto the lift truck's frame with a clunk.

Achilles patted the motor unit. "Well, we have retrieved the final piece of the puzzle. Let us load her onto the hover truck and be on the way."

After safely securing the cargo, they all piled into the cab of the hover truck to begin the journey to the stricken scout ship.

Not much was said along the way except for the occasional comment about the scenery when Achilles took a sharp turn onto a rock strewn road that ran parallel to the river. He shoved the lever that activated the hover motor, and the truck lifted off the road and sliced through the forest.

Breeze sat next to the passenger door, while Ray and Sally were in the middle. He saw Ray slowly move his hand to hold Sally's, but she brushed it off. He arched an eyebrow and looked away

He held his hand out of the window and felt the air as it rushed by. It reminded him when he was a child on trips with his mother to his aunt's home and how he would hold his hand out flat like it was an aerocraft and make engine noises. He would turn it up and feel the wind catch it like a sail and push it back.

It all reminded him of the subject he had been avoiding in his mind: home. He thought about how he never had a chance to find out if his father was okay. He began to wonder what he would find when he finally returned.

The rocky trail narrowed, and Breeze yanked his hand back as he felt the sting of a tree branch whip it as they zipped by. The hover truck burst out into a clearing and onto the riverbank where ahead sat the scout ship.

"Finally," Ray said.

"It appears the scavengers have not yet raided it. This is excellent news indeed," Achilles observed.

"What's it talking about?" Sally turned to Breeze.

"Whenever metal mongers out in the desert stumble across a derelict aerocraft or hover, they either try to get it working again or strip it down and sell it in pieces. I guess it's the same here."

"We come from different worlds," she mused.

The truck glided to a stop and settled onto its wheels. Achilles stepped out of the cab and slowly approached the ship. Servos whirred as it shook its head.

Breeze followed it. "Come on, the ship isn't that bad."

"No, quite the contrary. I must confess that the vessel is well preserved. I have not seen one in such condition since, well, a very long time."

"Why don't want to talk about the past? You make it sound like you're so ancient. I don't get it."

"My young aviator, there will come a time when I will tell more about the past. For now, let us all concentrate on bringing the ship back to operational duty."

"Always dodging, Achilles. Always dodging."

The boy does have a point, the other voice said.

Achilles' eyes blinked rapidly as it briefly raised a hand, then lowered it. *Do not badger or harangue me, now is not the time or place*, it replied.

"Achilles, are you okay? Don't go haywire on me now," Breeze joked as he knocked on its head playfully.

"Nonsense, Master Corinth, this unit is in perfect operational condition. Come, and let us begin our repairs." The robot went to the hover truck and hoisted the trunk of spare parts onto its shoulder, and then left deep footprints on the riverbank as it marched toward the ship.

Ray and Sally were already inside as Breeze and Achilles walked up the gangplank. Achilles set the trunk down and looked around, then pointed toward the stern of the ship. "Engine room is this way, of course."

"Yep, follow me," Breeze replied and led the way.

Deep inside the engine room, they both stood between the twin electromagnetic generators. Achilles placed a hand on one of them and tapped it gently, creating an echo.

"Wait, let me say it. You haven't seen one of these in such a long time, right?" Breeze said with a wide grin.

"Am I that repetitious? This humble robot begs for your forgiveness."

"Nah, no need. Let's just get this old tub working again. I want to head out west and see my father."

"Of course. Pardon my excursions down memory lane. I shall get to work immediately. Would you please contact Raymond and have him slide the hover truck beneath the engine room? We will need to raise the motor unit up into place."

"How is that going to work? You want to cut a hole in the ship? It would be easier to have him drop it off in the launch bay. We can just slide it over from there."

"My dear boy, it pays to have a rusty old robot such as I around, as these scout ships are full of surprises. Observe." Achilles reached up to a panel and typed a series of codes. "I would advise you to step aside, Master Corinth."

With a hiss of pneumatics, the floor between them slid open and daylight rushed inside.

Breeze dropped to the edge and poked his head through. "Hey, I can see the ground below!"

Achilles nodded. "These ships were designed for ease of maintenance. They were primarily used to traverse and reconnoiter distant and hostile locations, where receiving friendly service when in need of repairs would have been less than feasible."

"This is going to be fun to watch," Breeze said, and got up to run over to the intercom by the workbench where he contacted Ray and informed him of Achilles' plan.

Not long after, Ray backed the hover under the hull as Achilles ran a set of chains from the ceiling of the engine room and down to the motor unit where Ray connected them, then hoisted it into the ship and quickly removed the damaged motor unit from the generator and replaced it with the refurbished one. "This motor unit helps to adjust the frequency the generators run on. Whatever you passed through damaged the unit, which is why you lost power so quickly and the engines behaved so erratically," Achilles explained as it tightened down the last remaining bolts that held the motor unit in place.

"Excellent. Now to run a test to ensure the repair," it said and reached up to the panel again where it tapped in a series of codes. The generators hummed to life as lights flickered on throughout the ship.

"Success," Achilles declared and closed the panel, then turned to Breeze. "Now, let us make our way to the pilot house."

They traversed from the engine room to the pilot house, where they found Ray and Sally in a heated argument.

"Our apologies for interrupting you," Achilles said.

Sally's smile was forced as she brushed back her hair. "No, we're fine. Glad to see you got the power back on."

"Oh, it was nothing, especially if you know what you're doing." Breeze grinned.

Achilles stepped over to the damaged Auto Pilot that was slumped over and frozen in place before the helm.

"Brother, you are very much past repairs. May your maker have mercy on you," Achilles said and pulled on the hands of the Auto Pilot when it suddenly came to life and slapped a hand on Achilles' breast plate.

The two robots were frozen in place and surrounded by a loud hum as the lights in the cabin flickered. No sooner that it began when the Auto Pilot released its hold on Achilles and slumped onto the helm while Achilles stumbled back as it tried to regain its balance.

Breeze rushed to the robot. "Are you all right?"

It threw its hands up. "Do not approach, young friend! I am concerned that the excess voltage I have absorbed might jump to you," Achilles said as its metallic skin crackled and hissed. "I must dissipate the energy first." The robot stomped over to a bulkhead and placed both hands on it. "These bulkheads are grounded. This will allow the transfer of energy away from me."

Ray shook his head. "How was that possible? That Auto Pilot was pretty toasted."

"The Auto Pilots do retain a small amount of emergency power. Perhaps it was merely acting out in self-defense, or possibly for the ship and its passengers, though I am unable to fully determine at this time," Achilles explained as it placed a hand on its temple and closed its eyes for a moment.

When they opened again they glowed feebly, and then gradually brightened. It reached for the Auto Pilot, hesitated, and then resumed removing it from the pilot's seat.

After Ray and Breeze placed the damaged pilot into the crews rest above, Achilles retrieved the trunk of spare parts and began the process of removing the damaged console components and replacing them.

"Very well, let us perform a power up and determine the veracity of the repairs," Achilles said when it finished, and stood up from the underside of the console to flip a switch on the helm. Within seconds, the console lit up and was accompanied by beeps and flashes of lights. "Excellent. The replacement avionics are syncing perfectly with the ship," it observed as the rest of the cockpit lit up and flashed in tandem with the hum of machinery.

Their faces glowed from the radiance of the instruments as they stood in uncomfortable silence, neither of them knowing what to say.

"Well Achilles," Ray ventured, "I suppose I could say it was an interesting experience. But, uh, I guess we can say thanks for your help and goodbye?"

Sally shoved him and he hit the side of the cockpit hard. He whirled on Sally as she stuck a finger in his face.

"This is *exactly* what I'm talking about," she thundered, "I don't know what has gotten into you, but it has to end. Now."

She turned to Achilles and smiled graciously. "Thank you sincerely for your help, it is much appreciated, and please, never mind Ray, he hasn't been himself lately."

"Don't apologize for me," he growled.

Breeze jumped in. "Achilles, you're more than welcome to head out west with us. Waiting for Oslo is looking like a waste of time, especially at the way his wife treated us. And this place is pretty spooky."

"Sea trial," Achilles said.

They all looked at one another.

"Sea trial. Do either of you know what I speak of? Allow me to explain. When a ship has been built or recently overhauled, it must undergo a series of tests to determine its seaworthiness. After passing these tests, she is considered fit for duty. I suggest we do the same."

"Go for a test flight, you mean," Breeze said.

"Exactly. What better way to get to know one another a little better while giving you an aerial tour of Mount Pleasant. As an added bonus, we can also retrieve your hover car."

"I think I've seen enough of this place to last me a lifetime, but Achilles, your hospitality knows no boundaries. I speak for all of us when I say, yes," Sally bowed her head.

Ray groaned and rolled his eyes.

Achilles clapped its hands. "Excellent. Ray, I need you to take the helm."

"What?"

"The helm, sir. You are the most qualified pilot here, and I will kindly serve as your co-pilot."

"I can fly this heap too, you know," Breeze said.

Achilles turned to him. "Of course you can, but for now I would like to have Ray handle these duties. You are destined for other things."

Before Breeze could say anything, Sally took his hand and gently pulled him toward her.

"Sit with me?" She looked at him with pleading eyes.

He shrugged and they sat down in the jump seats in the back of the cockpit.

Minutes later, the engines hummed to life, and the ship creaked as it lifted off and hovered in place, then Ray pulled back on the helm and they rose into the sky. He orbited their landing spot several times while banking the scout ship from port to starboard.

"Hey, Achilles, what about your truck?" Ray said.

"If, for whatever reason, I do not return within a specified time frame, it will find its way back home."

"Kind of like a dog," Ray joked.

"Yes. Perfect analogy."

Ray chuckled as he steered the ship toward town.

Sunlight splashed across the mountains and valleys, and highlighted the lush forests that adorned them, while the rivers and lakes they crossed reflected the brilliant light.

Achilles directed Ray to the same river Breeze had used to head into Mount Pleasant, but advised him to ascend to a higher elevation.

"Why so high?" Ray asked.

"It would be best for all of us. As you humans would say, I have a hunch. Flying higher translates into fewer people seeing us."

Sally stiffened. "We are not in any danger, are we?"

"No mistress, be tranquil. Merely a safety precaution. These are troubled times, after all."

They passed over the central section of town and approached the landing area. Below were row upon row of hovers and other vehicles.

"Do you want me to land?" Ray said.

"No need, we make the hover come to us." Achilles tapped the console and a light began to flash. The scout ship vibrated and shook amidst the distant sound of hydraulics whining.

"Check it out!" Breeze shouted and pointed out the window.

A tiny speck approached them, and it climbed higher and higher until it was level with the scout ship. It was the hover car and it swooped across the bow and looped around to the stern of the ship.

"Just like your hover truck, it's a dog that knows its way back home," Ray said and looked over at Achilles. "I guess you're not that bad after all, tin can."

"Thank you, Ray. I gladly imbibe any and all compliments," Achilles replied and tapped the console again. The whir of hydraulics whined throughout the cockpit as the garage doors closed. "Hover car safely secured in the landing bay," it announced, then turned to Ray. "I would like to declare that this sea trial is performing splendidly."

"Whatever," Ray scoffed.

"Come now, Raymond, and try to display a modicum of enthusiasm.

Now, may I suggest we traverse over the mountains?"

"Why not." Ray mashed down the throttles and the scout ship shot forward as the ground below became a blur.

"Slow down!" Sally shouted.

"We're doing a sea trial, remember?" Ray retorted.

Breeze squeezed her hand. "It's okay. The ship is fine. We can trust Achilles."

She smiled. "I know. You're a good friend, Breeze."

He sighed tiredly. "Yeah, I guess I am."

She pulled his hand to her chest and leaned her head against the window.

Ray eased back on the throttles as they flew over the Appalachian Mountains and began swooping through the valleys as he followed its meandering rivers.

"What brought you here, Achilles?" Breeze asked.

The robot swiveled in its chair to face him. "These mountains, this land, became a refuge for many. It was here that all castaways could find a place for themselves."

"Like a giant freak show," Ray said.

"Raymond, not everyone possessed the good fortune of being brought up in a family such as your own, and in a community where paranormal gifts are treasured and nurtured. Many found themselves chased out, hunted down and persecuted during the regime of the Elephim."

Ray gripped the helm tightly. "I don't have a home. Not anymore."

"No, this is not true," Achilles said and shook its head.

"Why do you say that?" Sally wondered.

"If I have learned anything from humans, it is that all things happen for a reason. The three of you did not arrive here by chance, or intersect with me at Hammer Jack's by sheer coincidence. I believe, with all of the integrity of my programming, that we must stay together."

If only they truly knew what you know, the second voice whispered from within.

Breeze raised a hand. "Sorry, but I want to go home. I don't have a clue as to what happened to my father."

"Breeze, I admire your devotion to family, but one must consider the truth. You are being hunted, as it appears all paranormal are. The Elephim have been revived and are waiting for an opportune moment to strike. Stay here and allow me to train you in the proper execution of your abilities."

"You? What do you know?" Ray said.

"I have spent much time in the company of paranormals, and one cannot discount my many years of service at Perihelion. I served directly with Oslo and Raza, and of course, Bram, and I possess a vast amount of knowledge that has been retained in this rusty head of mine. "

"Bram, that poor man. Oslo told us how he went out into deep space to seek the source of the Elephim and never returned," Sally said.

Achilles nodded its head. "Yes, Bram did take it upon himself to do just that. He was a projectionist of the utmost skill and quite possibly the most arrogant. In the dying days of Earth's civilization, he did what he could to stem the tide of destruction."

"Yeah, but he failed. He never came back," Ray said.

Achilles whipped its head toward Ray. It was silent for a moment before responding. "Yes, Raymond, I concur. He failed."

"Achilles, we appreciate the offer. But what makes you think you can help us any more than Oslo could?" Sally said.

"Yes, an excellent point, but what I propose is nothing permanent. Think of it merely as an opportunity to spend time together and allowing me to impart my knowledge to all of you, before you carry on." *Stalling for time won't keep them safe*, it heard the voice say.

"Look, I really need to go. You guys can stay if you want and I'll take the scout ship myself and make my way back home," Breeze said.

"Young man, even if this ship possessed the necessary quantity of fuel to get you to your destination, do you not realize the possibility of ambush along your journey? What of mechanical breakdowns should they occur? Where would you procure the parts needed? How would you perform the repairs?" Achilles asked.

"It doesn't matter. I'll fly by myself if I have to."

"You wouldn't leave us, would you?" Sally gripped his hand.

"Sally, look, you know staying here holds nothing for us. You can come with me."

"How? Are you going to fly her in your arms? You crash all the time," Ray laughed.

"Master Verhesen, in his unique style, is right. Breeze, you are the one who needs the most instruction. Allow me to train you."

Sally rubbed his shoulder. "Please, stay."

He relented. "Fine, but just for a little while, then I really need to go."

Sally whispered in his ear, "thank you."

Achilles slapped its thighs with a loud clink. "Excellent, it is settled. Raymond, change of course. Return to Mount Pleasant, I have an idea."

"Okay," he replied as he shifted the throttles and threw the helm hard to port. Engines whined as the ship banked and headed back toward town.

"What do you have in mind?" Breeze asked.

"Young man, this old bucket of bolts is experiencing the sensation of progress for the first time in many cycles. I have decided to push our collective luck even further. Let us pay a visit to Raza."

Sally stood up. "Breeze is right, it's time to go. You have got to be malfunctioning if you think we're going to go back to that crazy woman."

Achilles chuckled. "Duly noted. Based on what you have told me, you first encounter with her was less than ideal. I assure you the circumstances will be different this time around."

"Sally is right. That old lady lost her mind while we were in her kitchen. She just snapped and we were all heading for the front door and running away," Breeze added.

Achilles nodded its head. "Understood, though I do believe my presence will be the mitigating factor this time around."

"I don't get it. You say you served with her and Oslo at Perihelion, yet the whole time you've been here, you never once visited her? Does she even know who you are?" Sally said as she sat down and leaned against Breeze.

"Sally, I departed Perihelion before her, and spent quite a bit of time roaming the land before settling here. I only became aware much later that she had returned to Appalachia. And to answer your query, no, I did not reach out to her as many come here for the anonymity. I must confess, so did I."

Ray snorted. "So, I just park this thing on her front yard and we all just step out and say hello?"

"No, Raymond, we shall land at a respectful distance and walk to her door, then allow me to explain to her what has transpired. Raza will be critical to your training. She possesses knowledge and insight that is rare amongst people today and her experience is invaluable. Besides, you are the one who insisted we wait for Oslo to arrive. And I must say it would be a pleasure to see him again."

"You know, she mentioned something about Oslo bringing their daughter, Nina," Sally said.

Achilles' eyes brightened. "Fascinating. They had a child together, this I did not know."

The scout ship skimmed over the river that led back to their original landing place. Ray slowed the ship upon arrival and brought it to a hover over Achilles' truck.

The robot was in a trance as it sat in its chair when Ray leaned over and rapped it on the head. "Hello, what do we do? Got to her place in the ship, or do we use the truck?"

Achilles blinked rapidly, then swiveled its head to face him. "Excellent suggestion, Raymond. I propose a new strategy." It toggled a switch on the console, and then typed in a series of commands. Immediately, the ship shuddered as the cabin was filled with the whine of hydraulics. "I am opening the garage door to retrieve my hover truck, and then we will land at a distance not far from Raza's farm and travel the rest of the way in it. I fear that seeing this ship may prove to be disconcerting to her and she may assume Oslo has arrived with their daughter."

The hover truck floated up to the ship and settled into the garage as Achilles' console flashed indicating that the doors had sealed themselves shut. It then pointed forward. "There, Raymond, over the mountain, where we shall land slightly downriver from her property."

Ray pushed forward on the helm and the ship sailed over the mountaintop and glided down the other side. He brought the ship to a landing along the shoreline, downriver from the farmhouse and throttled down the engines.

Breeze leaned into Sally. "Here we go again."

Sally sighed as she turned and gazed out the window.

CHAPTER
▼
TWENTY-ONE

ACHILLES BROUGHT THE TRUCK to a stop at the foot of the driveway that led to Raza's farm. The engine idled as the robot slowly slid its hands around the steering wheel.

"Second thoughts?" Breeze said, "Because I know I sure do."

Achilles turned and gazed at each of their faces, then chuckled. "Negative. This is the right course of action. As young ones, you will require the guidance needed for the journey ahead but you must not rely solely on a rusty old robot that fights in arenas for this task. You must be with your own kind."

"Yeah, humans," Ray said.

"No, Raymond, paranormals," Achilles responded and threw the truck into gear and headed up the driveway.

"Shouldn't we be in hover mode? It would be a lot quieter," Breeze said.

"Negative. Anyone in the home can easily hear us rolling up the drive, which is what we seek to achieve, for we are merely neighbors paying a visit. Nothing more."

"I really don't think she gets many visitors," Sally quipped.

Achilles brought the truck to a stop a few feet from the porch steps and cut off the motor, then stepped out and walked around to the front of the truck and stood staring at the front door of the farmhouse.

Ray stood next to the robot. "Is the big, bad Robot Fighter afraid to walk up the steps to the crazy lady's front door?"

"No, Raymond. Merely contemplating how I will explain our presence to Raza. I must formulate an explanation as to why we require her assistance, and how it would mutually benefit us all."

"You sound like a guy who's in love and doesn't know how to say it to her," he needled.

Achilles head swiveled to face him. "What have I said to give you such an idea? Robots mating with humans? Highly inappropriate."

"Just teasing, tin can, relax."

The front door creaked open and a woman stepped out. She drew the coat that draped her delicate frame closer to her as she walked to the porch railing.

Sally gasped and took a step back while Ray and Breeze stared at the woman in stunned silence.

Achilles took a step forward. "You have not changed much since I last saw you, and it brings this old machine much joy when I declare that you are just as beautiful as you were so many years ago."

The woman smiled, then put a hand to her throat and nodded. "It has been too long, but how could I forget you, our favorite robot assistant. 51? Isn't that what we used to call you? Forgive me, my memory is not what it used to be."

Achilles chuckled. "Yes, 51, which is the shorthand for my serial code, 5150, and is the nickname that Oslo had given me. He was always fond of nicknames. I could never forget when he rescued me from being scrapped and took me under his wing during the purge. Those were dangerous times indeed, and still are, I am afraid. I must inform you however, I now go by the moniker of Achilles."

"Who are you?" Sally blurted out as she stared at the woman.

Achilles swiveled to address her. "This is Raza. Did you not inform me you younglings had met her earlier? Was your story a fabrication?"

Sally's eyes were wide. "She's...so much younger. The woman we met was old. And mean."

Raza nodded as she descended the steps while Sally stepped back with her arms across her chest.

Raza held out a hand. "Sally, please take this as my heartfelt apology to you," she turned to Breeze and Ray, "and to all of you, for I'm afraid my behavior as of late had been less than stellar."

Sally was mute.

Raza's hand went to her chest. "I must confess, seeing the three of you showing up on my doorstep was quite unnerving for me. Your arrival brought back a flood of memories I have not thought of in so many years—"

Sally interrupted. "How did you get so young? You were old and mean just a couple of days ago!"

Raza smiled. "Child, there is so much to tell you. You must believe me when I say the woman you met before is not the person I really am."

Ray confronted her by standing inches from her face. "You stalked us then attacked with some weird creature that made us see moments from our past. How do you explain that away?"

A tear rolled down her cheek and she immediately wiped it away. "I can only ask you now for your forgiveness. Please, come inside and allow me to offer you the hospitality I denied you before while I try to explain my actions of late."

She held her hand out and Sally hesitantly took it.

Raza then patted Achilles on the shoulder. "51...no, Achilles, please come inside."

"Of course." He swiveled around to face Breeze and Ray. "Gentleman, please accompany us," it said, then pointed a finger at Ray. "Now young man, you have two dangerous individuals to monitor."

"Yeah, a crazy robot and his crazy lady friend," Ray said.

Raza laughed as Achilles chuckled.

"Come in, all of you." Raza beckoned to them.

They climbed up the steps and into the house while Achilles trailed behind, gingerly testing each step as the boards buckled under its weight.

They settled down in the living room as Sally and Breeze sat on a couch while Ray stood behind them. Achilles scanned the furniture, but never sat, instead choosing to stand next to a window.

Raza was bustling in the kitchen and soon emerged with a tray full of refreshments and cookies. "I have not baked in quite some time, so please be gentle in your critiques," she said and settled the tray on the table that fronted the couch. "You young ones awakened something inside me, and I decided to search for your ship the day after that encounter in the ravine, to apologize for my horrible behavior. I found the ship empty and I feared the worst. It-," her voice broke as she wiped tears from her face, "—it brings me such happiness to see you here together." She sat down but couldn't face them. "I'm so ashamed of what I've done," she whispered.

Achilles stepped toward her and lowered itself onto a bent knee, then carefully took her hand and patted it. "Raza, we must be grateful whenever possible. We are all here now and in one piece. There is no need for tears, only joy."

Raza smiled as she wiped her face. "You're awfully sentimental for a robot."

Achilles tapped its head. "Artificial intelligence plus many decades of reading books of human adventure and romance can alter even a crusty old robot such myself."

"There is nothing crusty about you, neither is there anything artificial. I consider you an old friend. I must confess, I should have sought you out long ago. I heard the stories about a robot with extraordinary capabilities fighting in the arenas of Mount Pleasant. I should have known it was you." She took a sip from her cup. "Whatever did happen to you? I do recall a training session involving you, Bram, and several RF and after the session was over, you were missing. We searched, but you were nowhere to be found. We had always thought that perhaps you wanted your freedom and you disappeared to find your own way in this world. You were always so precocious."

Achilles shook its head. "Mistress, what had happened—"

"Sorry to break up the reunion," Ray cut in, "but what exactly are we doing here? What's the plan? I'm not going to sit around here drinking tea and eating cookies while you two talk about old times."

Achilles stood up and placed a hand on the headrest of Raza's chair. "Of course Raymond. Always the military man in need of a plan and no time for sentiments." It leaned down to Raza, "we can reminisce later, when a window of opportunity presents itself."

Raza smiled and nodded.

"I miss my parents!" Sally wailed.

Raza rushed from her chair and pulled Sally close to rock her back and forth as the girl sobbed. "There now, there now," Raza whispered.

She looked up at Achilles. "These lambs will stay here with me, and I know I can count on you for your help. They need a home and guidance."

Achilles nodded. "I concur."

Raza continued. "Forgive me for being so blunt, old friend, but I need you to set up camp here on the farm."

Achilles chuckled. "Raza, you were a legend at Perihelion for your tenacity. I sincerely believe you were the only human who could get the taciturn and stubborn Oslo to do anything he normally wouldn't want to do. You two were quite the couple."

"Yes, we were," she smiled briefly, then turned away to face Ray and Breeze. "I know that all of you have been through a lot, and I only added to your burdens by the way I treated you. I promise you that my home, this land and the mountains that surround us, are a safe haven.

We will one day re-unite you with your families, though I ask that you stay here for the time being until we are ready to make a decision as to what our future may bring."

"What about Oslo?" Ray asked.

She closed her eyes. "He will come," she replied, then opened them and turned to Breeze, "I know what you are thinking. You wish to take the ship and leave to find your way back home. I will travel with you if I must to help you, but for now young man, stay here. Please," she said and reached for his hand to squeeze it.

Breeze nodded.

"Very good, it's settled." She patted Sally on her back. "Young lady, wipe away the tears, for today we begin the process of putting our lives back together." She smiled at Achilles. "It is so nice to have a house full of people again. Thank you, old friend, you have brought me the greatest gift of all."

"Though your praise humbles this worn out machine, please sing your praises to Breeze. This young man had the will to seek me out, and I see him as the catalyst for all that has transpired to date," Achilles said.

Raza nodded at Breeze. "Yes, he does seem to be the spark of a new beginning."

She then stood up and clapped her hands. "Very well, there are room assignments to be given, and dinner needs to be cooked, for it will not make itself. You all need to wash up first, so follow me please." She pointed a finger at Achilles, "and you, get into that rusty old truck of yours and get whatever equipment you may need from your place as you are more than welcome to set up shop in my barn."

Achilles raised a hand to its head in a mock salute. "Yes, ma'am. This unit will comply."

Raza laughed as she marched up the steps with the teens in tow, and as Achilles looked on, the second voice spoke

It seems like old times, the voice said.

Achilles shook its head and headed for the door.

Later that evening, after everyone settled in for the night, Breeze found himself wide awake. He rolled out of bed to look out the window and saw how the crescent moon dimly lit the valley and the mountains around it. He peered deeper into the night as he almost expected the winged creature to land in the front of the farmhouse with its red eyes penetrating him like a knife.

He quickly got dressed and stepped out into the hallway. Sally's room was at the very end, while Ray was next door to him. He raised a hand to knock on her door, and then hesitated when he saw a glow creeping from underneath it. He twisted the handle and barged in to find Sally sitting on the edge of the bed with her hands in her lap. Her eyes were glowing a bright white.

Breeze froze in place. Though he had seen her in a projection trance before, the glow from her eyes was always unnerving.

He felt a gentle tug on his sleeve and jumped back with a yelp. Sally's astral projection was standing next to him.

"Spying on me?" she teased.

"Sally, I really need to talk to you."

She nodded and glided back to her body and merged with it. The glow immediately faded from her eyes. "Breeze, I'm glad you're here, there is something I need to tell you," she said and reached for him.

He took her hand and sat next to her while she took a deep breath, and then spoke. "You are right, we shouldn't be here. This is crazy. Raza threw us out not long after we first arrived here, and then sent that winged creature that obeyed here like a dog, after us. What are we doing here Breeze?"

He shook his head. "I just can't get over the age difference. First time we meet her she looks ancient, like she's about to keel over and die, then we see her again a few days later and she looks younger. Makes no sense."

Sally nodded. "I projected earlier to snoop around on the property, but couldn't really find anything out of place until I followed her as she went to the side of the house, flung open a cellar door and stepped down. She closed the door behind her and sealed it, but I swear to you the light coming out of the cellar was green. It was pretty strange."

Breeze stood up. "Come on, let's go."

"What do you have in mind?" she said.

"Sally, we got to know Perihelion better by snooping around. It's no different here and I want to see that cellar."

"Should we get Ray?"

"Nah, let him sleep. He's no fun anyway."

Sally giggled as Breeze led her down the stairs. The house was painfully quiet and the hallway that led to the front door was lit. They cautiously stepped out, then walked to the side of the house and came to a stop at the cellar doors.

Sally was hesitant. "Aren't you afraid of Raza catching us?"

"Sally, after all we've been through, do we even really care anymore?" She smiled.

"Exactly. Follow me," he said, then flung open the cellar doors and stepped down.

The stairs were slippery and smelled like seaweed while the air was humid and warm and clashed with the cold, dry air outside. The deeper they descended the more pronounced a shimmering green light became.

The stairs sloped downward while gradually curving to the right, then came to an end at the edge of a pool with blue green water.

Sally sniffed the air. "Breeze, why does it smell like —"

"The ocean, I know. This place is weird and has the same feel as Perihelion," he replied.

"Are you kidding me? This whole town is weird," she shot back.

Breeze chuckled as he knelt down at the edge of the pool when his skin began to tingle. He abruptly pulled up a sleeve and dipped his hand into the water. It felt warm as he swished it around and created waves that reverberated across the surface.

"Breeze," he heard a voice say to him.

He looked up at Sally. "Yeah?"

"I didn't say anything," she said.

"But I just heard someone call my name," he said and looked down at the pool again. The water glowed even brighter, and in a flash, he was sucked in and sent plummeting to the bottom.

He thrashed around as he struggled to get his bearings. He looked up at the surface and could see Sally leaning over and looking down at him, yet she made no effort to jump in and help. The sound of static began to build as unfamiliar images of people and places whirled about him like a tornado when a hand clamped onto his shoulder. He turned to look with a feeling of dread.

It was Sally, kneeling down beside him. "What's the matter with you? You stuck your hand in the pool then you went zombie on me."

Breeze looked down at his arm. It was slightly discolored and pale, and he could feel a tingling sensation course through it.

"I got dragged into the pool. Didn't you see?"

"No, you kneeled the whole time swishing your arm in the water and mumbling."

"Sally, I fell in and sank to the bottom. I looked up and you just sat there, it was like you didn't want to help."

"Breeze, I would always reach out to help you," she said and held his hands.

He leaned in and kissed her. She was taken by surprise, but didn't resist.

He pushed her away. "Sorry, I didn't mean to...I'm sorry."

She frowned at him. "It's okay. Really."

"Let's get out of here. I really want to see what's going on in that barn," he said. He stood up and held out a hand to her.

Sally tried to hide her disappointment as he helped her up. Together they went up the steps and out of the cellar where they immediately began to shiver upon contact with the cold air. Breeze led Sally to a corner of the house and pointed at the barn. She nodded and followed him as they trudged across the dew-covered grass to get to it.

When they arrived, they saw that the doors were wide open and voices could be coming from deep inside.

"Who's in there?" Sally whispered as they leaned against the door and peeked in.

"I can definitely hear Achilles, and I think Raza is in there too," Breeze said as he cautiously stepped inside.

"Breeze!" Sally hissed.

He beckoned to her. "Come on, it's okay. I want to hear what they're saying."

They crept deeper into the barn. The stray bits of hay strewn across the dirt floor muffled their footsteps, and they stuck to the shadows cast by the overhead lights that were strung along the length of the barn. Ahead, the voices became clearer.

"...I wandered the land along the length of the eastern seaboard and documented the range of destruction that I found. Entire cities had been emptied, yet the rural areas were overrun with refugees. The level of despair and hopelessness that seemed to emanate from these people was overwhelming. It did not help that I was a robot, for upon my arrival at any village, I would be attacked immediately. And I have personally witnessed paranormals being savaged by mobs, sometimes even put to the flame."

"That is horrible, Achilles," they heard Raza reply somberly.

A whir of servos was followed by the sound of a heavy tool dropping onto a workbench. Then Achilles responded. "Paranormals went from being the champions of the people to pariahs to be feared, hated and destroyed. This unit, in all of its years of service at Perihelion and standing side by side with the Helios, never could compute such a scenario coming to fruition."

"So how did you come to Mount Pleasant?" Raza asked.

"I remembered how you spoke of it in the past very lovingly, and in great detail, but to ascertain its location was quite difficult. Like Perihelion, it seems to be cloaked. It took several attempts to eventually locate the path that would allow me to slip past the fog. Upon arrival, it lived up to its reputation as a refuge for... how can this humble robot word this diplomatically... interesting people."

Raza laughed and clapped her hands.

"It is good to hear laughter again. It is a human trait I have always admired," Achilles said.

Breeze whispered to Sally. "Let's get closer. There is a stall across from us with its door open, we can hide in there."

"We can hear them just fine from here," Sally whispered back.

Breeze shook his head, grabbed her hand and towed her behind him where they snuck into the empty stall and peered out. They could see Achilles making adjustments to a comm unit as Raza sat in a chair.

"Confession, mistress," Achilles stopped and turned to her, "please do not descend into anger at the words that I will speak, but I had concluded long ago that you must have perished. So much time had passed since my dismissal from Perihelion to the day of my arrival here. I did not expect that you would be among the living, and was elated to discover that you had not perished."

"I don't know how much human emotion you comprehend Achilles, but I will tell you that my desire to see my daughter again is what has kept me alive for so long."

"Nina. Yes. You did mention her. Please tell more."

She took a sip of tea from her cup, and then carefully placed it on a saucer. The skin of her hands and arms glistened from the glow of the overhead lights as she ran her fingers through her long hair, and then piled it into a bun.

Sally pulled Breeze closer to her and whispered. "She keeps looking younger and younger all the time."

Raza continued. "The pregnancy was difficult, and the birth was almost perilous. Not only for my daughter, but myself as well, but we made it through."

"Those must have been joyous times for both you and Oslo. Forgive me mistress for the inquiry, but Oslo is the father, yes?"

Raza smiled and nodded. "You can ask me anything, and yes, he is. You are right, it was a joyous time for us all. Amidst the chaos that was consuming the world, we had our little slice of heaven. If only for a brief time," she sniffled.

"But, Nina was a sickly child who required constant medical treatment. Then, Perihelion was given the order from up high to decommission. Essential personnel were leaving to be with their families as nobody wanted to stick around and toil under the boot of the new Elephim regime. Oslo, the good man that he is, tried his best to rally everyone to stay and fight back against the regime, but only a dedicated few answered the call. We did our best to track down and save other paranormal children from across the world, but it was too late. The days of the Helios as champions of Earth and her colonies were over. It was time to accept the new era that descended upon us like a dark cloud."

She burst into tears, and then quickly composed herself. "I argued with Oslo for the longest time that we also needed to leave. He wanted us to go to Scandinavia, but I convinced him it would be safer in Appalachia. We arrived here and for a brief time, we were happy. But then Nina took a turn for the worse." Raza leaned back in her chair and took in a deep breath. Her voice trembled when she spoke again. "She... began to age, and rapidly. One day she was fine, then in a blink of an eye the child would age several years. There were frightening times when she would become old and shriveled, and then miraculously she would revert to her normal age, but then continue reverting to an infant. It was-," her voice cracked as she stopped to suppress a sob, "—horrible."

Achilles gently placed a hand on her shoulder and she patted it. "We were in despair as there were no medical facilities here that could treat her. We had long grown accustomed to the state-of-the-art equipment at Perihelion, and realized only too late we should have brought with us at least a few machines. By then we had to confront the knowledge that we were helpless."

Achilles sat down on a metal stool. Its eyes glowed as it put its hands together and listened intently.

She continued. "Oslo theorized that because Nina was conceived and born on Perihelion, her inner clock was tuned to the island, and because the island was slightly out of step with the rest of the planet, so was she. Removing her from the island was catastrophic, and we needed to go back, he said. I disagreed and we fought bitterly. It almost broke us apart. Then she had another one of her attacks. She aged rapidly before our eyes and just about withered and died. I gave in and we decided to take our shuttlecraft back to Perihelion. That's when it happened."

Raza shook her head and was silent as tears streamed down her cheeks. When she spoke, it was in a hushed tone. "We packed for our trip back to the island while Nina was bedridden and screaming in pain, then we gathered our belongings and loaded the shuttle, not unlike the one the younglings arrived on. For all I know, it could be the same one, as you are aware of Oslo's penchant for holding on to old pieces of junk," she smiled weakly through her tears.

Achilles chuckled and tapped its chest. "Do I."

"We barely made it to the coastline when we were attacked. The ship's sirens were wailing and we were losing power. We barely landed and we huddled inside, not sure what to do. We didn't even know what hit us. Then, that's when I saw it."

Achilles' eyes glowed brighter as Raza shifted in her seat.

"I peered out into the darkness from the cockpit while Oslo was busy punching in commands into the console, trying to get the ship up and running again, when I saw a figure step out from the tree line and stride across the open field toward us. I wasn't sure if my eyes were playing tricks on me as in the midst of the hysteria and madness of everything happening around us I could have been hallucinating, but to this day I could never get over how...confident it appeared. It was as if it did not care nor possess a hint of fear in the world. It was covered head to toe in black and then there was that sound, a crackling...,"

"A hissing noise perhaps, mistress, similar to what is emitted from electronic equipment?" Achilles offered.

"Yes, how did you know?"

"I have dealt with these nefarious ones, the Elephim, many times in the past," Achilles replied.

She shook her head. "It was relentless. Was it human? It may have looked like one, but it seemed so mechanical in its behavior. I screamed at Oslo and pointed it out to him. He cursed mightily and activated the ship's weapons, but nothing seemed to have any impact on it. It either absorbed our energy weapons, or merely sidestepped them while never once breaking its stride. It walked up to the ship and forced open the cargo door where I rushed over to meet it head on. I was so fearful for our lives, Nina's life especially, that is seemed to give me the energy I needed to defend us. That is when I came face to face with it."

She stood up abruptly and walked toward the stall where Breeze and Sally were hiding.

Breeze pulled Sally close and made a hushing gesture by placing a finger to his lips.

Raza stood by the stall, and then turned to Achilles. "The noise that emanated from it was disconcerting to say the least, and I could barely concentrate. Its body and face were jet black and it just stared at me, even cocked its head like a little dog, as if I was something that amused it. I flew into a telekinetic rage, and threw everything that wasn't bolted down in the ship at it and sent it flying out the door, then charged after this monster that had attacked my family."

Achilles shifted on its stool and the metal creaked and echoed through the frosty air of the barn.

"Oslo rushed out to help me. He had set the automatic weapons systems to track it and fire, but they barely had any effect. He then displaced the space time field around the creature to disrupt and frustrate it while I hit it with telekinetic blasts. It didn't matter, it kept charging us. All the while that damn hissing noise became overwhelming. But within that noise I picked out what seemed to be," she shook her head, "a broadcast, like it was transmitting what it was experiencing to others of its kind. Then I realized it was also signaling for its companions to come and help secure the package it was seeking."

Achilles' eyes glowed. "Heavens no, mistress. Do not say it was seeking—"

"Nina. It wanted Nina. I could see and hear it clear as day. It also knew that I could read its thoughts, and yet it didn't seem to care that I knew of its real objective which was to kill Oslo and I, destroy the ship, and take my daughter away to some awful place far, far away," she said, then drew a deep breath while struggling to compose herself.

Inside the stall, Sally buried her head into Breeze's chest. He held her close as the air around them began to shimmer.

Raza continued her story. "I can remember screaming at Oslo to get back into the ship and get it working again, and then I charged at the Elephim with the rage of a mother grizzly defending her cubs. Oh, what a sight I must have been, a petite country girl assaulting a horrible creature from the depths of some unknown hell. I tell you now Achilles, so you can record this moment and broadcast it for future generations, that I threw all of my power at it. I uprooted trees and flung them, while boulders that were firmly lodged in the mountains came flying at it like missiles. It would not have my daughter, I would rather die than to let that happen."

Raza shuffled back to her chair and gripped the headrest. "I thought I had defeated it, but it was relentless, and soon it was marching right toward me as if I had done nothing. I could feel myself becoming weaker by the moment, as if my very essence was not only being ripped out of me, but extinguished. I was nothing more to it than a candle whose flame was to be snuffed out. Then I caught a flash of light from the corner of my eye. It was the ship. Oslo had brought her back to life. I could clearly see him silhouetted in the cargo door, frantically waving and yelling at me to get in. But deep down inside I knew if Nina were to survive, I had to stay behind."

She crumpled into her seat and looked down at her hands. "I reached out to Oslo with my mind and told him to go. Save yourself, save our daughter, I said to him. I will catch up with you, I assured him, though we both knew I didn't have a chance. I then threw a telekinetic shield around the creature and anchored myself to the ground. I wouldn't let it get to the ship, I just wouldn't. I could hear the whine of the engines above the creature's howls of rage that its quarry was escaping. I turned to watch as the ship flew into the looming darkness and dashed toward the coast. Oh, was that Elephim mad at me. It bucked and kicked inside its prison until it finally wore me out and broke free. I laid on the ground near death from the strain as it hovered over me. There was a swirling of...stars, across its face, and for a moment I swear I saw a human face looking at me with a look of confusion and despair. But it was all so brief. And then it was gone. Like my daughter. Gone."

A pitiful wail erupted from the stalls as Raza and Achilles bolted up and looked about wildly. Raza then pointed to the stall closest to them and ran to it.

Inside they found Sally sobbing hysterically. Breeze was trying to console her as Raza scooped the girl into her arms and held her close.

"Hush, my sweet, hush. You are safe. Do you hear me? Safe. No harm will come to you, I swear it."

Sally wrapped her arms around Raza and cried.

Achilles pointed at Breeze. "What was the duration of your time here?"

Raza waved a hand at it. "It does not matter. They needed to hear this story. Everyone needs to hear these stories. We have been remiss in not speaking about the past. This is at least a beginning," she said and stroked Sally's hair. "There now, child, there now," she kept repeating.

Breeze stood up and dusted himself off.

Achilles tilted its head. "Master Corinth, if I may so inquire, how were you and Ms. Trumbull able to achieve such close proximity to us without our detection?"

"I think she shielded us, the air around us kept shimmering until she screamed just now."

"Fascinating. Her skills seem to grow continuously. The greater the pressure on Ms. Trumbull, the more she seems to amaze," Achilles said.

Raza stood up and helped Sally to her feet. She brushed hay from her hair while Sally clung to her waist.

"Come now, young ones, and let's go back to the house for milk and cakes," Raza said.

"Don't go," Sally whimpered.

"Child, I would never leave you. I have already lost one daughter, I will not lose another," she said assuringly.

Breeze saw the comm units Achilles had been working on earlier. "What's all this for?" he asked.

Achilles stepped over and placed a hand on the console. "Raza had requested that I make the attempt to contact Perihelion in order to establish communications with Oslo and to ascertain his whereabouts."

Breeze sat down in a chair before the comm unit. "Achilles, do you think I can try to contact my father from here?"

Achilles' eyes flashed for a moment, then nodded its head. "I surmise that a possibility may exist to establish contact, though the ionosphere had been quite erratic lately. It is as if a solar storm is approaching and has made long range communications quite problematic."

The robot rotated a series of dials and a low hum began to emanate from the machine. Achilles reached for a headset with a microphone attached and handed it to Breeze. He waited patiently as Achilles continued adjusting dials.

"Master Corinth, I am scanning all frequencies across the bandwidth, but I cannot raise anything but static. Every territorial outpost seems to have gone offline and is not transmitting. I am not sure what else I can do."

Breeze nodded. "Yeah, fine. What about Oslo and Nina? Any word from them?"

"I am afraid much of the same," it replied.

Breeze took off the headset and dropped them on the console.

"Okay, not much has changed then."

Raza placed a hand on his shoulder. "Breeze, I understand your desire to return home. I promise it will happen. But for now, stay with us. We need you."

"Need me? For what?"

"Breeze, hear me out. There once was a time when three young people gathered together and made a pact to uncover the evil that was sweeping across the world and to alert the people to the oncoming disaster heading their way. We stuck together as best as we could, but ultimately, we lost our faith, fell apart, and went our separate ways. I speak of course of myself, Oslo and Bram. Breeze, sometimes in life you must face the unpleasant truth that you know something is wrong, and yet no one will listen. I sense this about you, am I wrong?"

Breeze shook his head.

She continued. "Many do not want to be confronted with unpleasant truth. They want life to be as mundane and predictable as possible, though there is nothing wrong with wanting that, as everyone craves stability in one form or the other. But the world, the universe, does not work that way. Life is like the tide, it rises and falls. What has happened before, will happen again."

"Oslo was always saying that to us."

Raza smiled. "I know, where do you think I got it from? Breeze, you want everything to go back to normal, but as you can see, it won't. Most likely because our lives were not meant to be normal. We have been destined for greater things, or perhaps condemned to walk a harsh road. Our attempts at trying to establish something that resembles normal is the reason why we keep experiencing setbacks in our lives, as if the universe is trying to tell us in its own way we should be doing something else. I do not believe in coincidence, and that is why I believe the three of you were brought to my doorstep for a reason. I have to do my part and help the three of you become more than what you are. You are all destined for great things. I see you all as heralds of a new beginning."

Breeze leaned back in his seat and sighed. "I'm just a guy from the desert. I can barely fly without crashing into anything and destroying it. What do you want from me?"

"Humble. Self-deprecating. The true sign of a warrior who does not seek glory," Raza said as she kneeled before him and held his hands. "Stay with us. At least, stay for Sally. You are like a rock to her. Let Achilles and I train you as best as we can and allow us to impart our knowledge onto you. Give me that at least."

"Oslo already tried with us. We're hopeless."

"Yes, because in your minds you knew you had someplace to go back to. Home. Only now do you realize, there is no home, at least for them. Those who have attacked us in the past have returned and they wish to silence Earth once and for all as they cannot tolerate our kind. We have, and always will be, a beacon of hope for mankind, even in their darkest hour. Don't ask me why the Elephim have a vendetta against us, we just know that we cannot be their victims any longer."

Raza stood up and addressed them all. "I'm tired. Tired of everything. I have grown weary living here in exile, all alone except for memories. I won't do this anymore. Tonight is the beginning of new possibilities. We are going to start putting our lives back together. We will reach out to others of our kind and remind them of our glorious past. Many will turn a deaf ear to us, but it will only take a few to start making a difference. We are a candle and a flame. We will share our flame, the flame of knowledge. We will make a lot of noise and we will awaken this planet. Those above will hear and see us and they will react with violence. They will try to destroy us, yet what more harm can they do? Have they not taken away enough from us as it is?"

Sally sniffled and nodded her head.

"The days of hiding are over. It is better we die as free men than as slaves to worry and fear. We start tonight," Raza held her hand out to Breeze, and then reached out to Sally who brushed it aside and hugged her. Breeze reluctantly stood next to them.

She looked at Achilles. "Well, tin man, will you join my family?"

Achilles chuckled. "It would be an honor to do so. And probably a first for human-robot relations."

Raza laughed. "Welcome then."

Achilles placed a hand on each of the teens' shoulders. "I look forward to working again with young paranormals, for it has always provided the greatest satisfaction to work with the most extraordinary of humans."

"So, does this mean you're going to give up fighting at Hammer Jack's?" Breeze said.

"My career in martial arts for monetary compensation is officially terminated. Consider this robot retired from the world of arena fighting, and is now establishing a bright new future as a coach and mentor."

They all laughed as Ray stumbled into the barn. His hair was rumpled as he rubbed his eyes. "What the heck is everyone doing here so late at night? What's going on?"

"Master Verhesen! Most excellent of you to join us," Achilles boomed.

Ray looked at them bleary eyed. "Why is everyone smiling?"

Raza spoke up. "Breeze has decided to stay and complete his training here."

He shrugged. "Whatever. What else does he have to go back to?" He pointed at Raza. "And why do you look even younger than before?"

Sally turned to face her. "What is going on with you? Is this one of your gifts? Are you a shape shifter also?"

Before Raza could respond, Breeze spoke up. "It's the pool, isn't it? The one in your cellar?"

Raza's jaw dropped. She glared at Breeze as her eyes narrowed, then drew a breath and smiled. "Nothing escapes you young ones, combined with your endless curiosity about everything."

Breeze shrugged. "It's just that it seems awfully similar to the one I woke up in at Perihelion. I guess Excort and Mila put me in it after I was rescued from the mountains. The water was so warm and it was like having a blanket cover you and it made you feel like you didn't care about anything in the world anymore."

Raza smiled. "Mila. How is she? What a sweet thing she is." She sighed deeply, then spoke, "yes Breeze, you're right. The pool does have healing properties, just like the one at Perihelion."

"So that's why you look so young?" Sally said as she took Raza's hand.

Raza nodded.

"So why did you let yourself get so old in the first place?" Sally wondered.

Raza touched her cheek. "I was giving up, as I concluded there wasn't much worth living for. I had a husband and daughter who were out of reach, along with a world I had known that descended into chaos. It all became too much. Then, three angels arrived at my doorstep. I brought them into my home, and then chased them out. I tracked them like animals and brought harm to them. It was then, in my darkest hour, that I turned to the light and climbed out of the tomb I was living in. The three of you are gifts from above. You are my second chance to make things right. Forgive me for hurting you like I did."

Sally hugged her. "There is nothing to forgive. You have endured so much for so long. I'm just glad to be here."

Raza's voice quavered. "You have all given me a new lease on life. I have a family now."

Ray raised his hand. "Does this mean we can have breakfast?"

They all laughed as Ray stood dumfounded.

C H A P T E R

▼

T W E N T Y - T W O

BREEZE WAS ALOFT AND hovering in place, while struggling to maintain his position. Below, Achilles was calling out instructions to him as it sat on a stool in the middle of a field.

Over the past several weeks, Raza and Achilles had been training the teens in the use of their powers. Sally and Ray were spending most of their time with Raza, as Breeze was the furthest behind in the mastery of his powers. It required the patience of Achilles to give him the much needed guidance.

"Maintain your axis as it relates to the surface below you," Achilles spoke over the intercom as it craned its neck upward at the sky, "you must acquire the ability to affix your position without the aid of visual cues, for within the darkest depths of space, you will not find a star to use as a guidepost."

Breeze held his arms straight out as he strained to hover in place. "As if I'm ever really going to do that," he muttered.

Achilles tapped the side of its head. "I have received your last transmission. May I suggest that you switch to an internal monologue if you choose to make critical comments?"

Breeze laughed. "Nothing gets past you...whoa!" he shouted as he lost control and plummeted to the earth. Cold air rushed past his face as the ground rushed to meet him. He grimaced as he flung his arms out and halted his descent. Breathing heavily while his heart raced, he glided up to his original position.

"Concentration, my young aviator. Focus. Your mind is a whirlwind of thoughts and images. Learn how to brush them aside and see nothing. It is there, in the space between thoughts, that you will find what you need to know," Achilles said.

"How can I find what I need to know if I don't think of something...

not again!" he shouted as he almost lost control, but quickly recovered.

"You are far too raw and undisciplined to even contemplate the notion of engaging in verbal repartee while in use of your powers. You, my friend, were never given the fundamentals. It is quite a testament to your tenacity and perseverance that you were ever able to achieve any ability to fly whatsoever."

"Yeah, well, it's not like my father was too....keen...on showing...me...how to do it!" Breeze rocked back and forth as a gust of wind blew him off course. Once again, he glided back into position.

"I do believe he possessed a perfectly valid reason for withholding your training," Achilles said.

Yes, Achilles, of course. The father understood what a powerhouse he would become. A god to lead the rabble out of the quagmire, or a devil who would suppress them, Achilles heard the voice say as it blinked rapidly and shook its head.

"Oh, and what would that be?" Breeze asked.

"He was greatly concerned that you would harm yourself."

Breeze laughed, and then dipped slightly, but regained altitude. "If he was so worried about safety, he wouldn't have me working in a foundry next to huge metal buckets filled with molten slag...oh boy!" he stretched out his arms as far as he could as he suddenly dropped several feet toward the ground.

"Less verbal emittance my sky lord, and more concentration," Achilles said.

"How can I concentrate if you...keep talking to me...come on!" he shouted as he plummeted to the earth and impacted the ground. His shield quickly surrounded him as dirt and rock flew everywhere. He crawled out of the crater he made and glared at Achilles.

The robot ignored his stare as it brushed dirt off its metal body. "Master Corinth, did it ever occur to you that your father had perhaps delayed your training because he understood that your powers would have overwhelmed you at such a young age? That the possession of such power could have corrupted and eventually destroyed you?"

"Achilles, the only thing I know how to do is fly in a straight line, then crash into the dirt. How much power could I possibly have?"

"Your gifts are multi-layered in nature. Consider this, young friend. You can fly, yes, but how many other paranormals are you aware of who possess a similar talent?"

"I don't know of any others, it's not like my town is crawling with them. My father then sends me to Perihelion where I met Ray and Sally. And Nina. Yeah, none of them can fly, but come on, they're good at what they do."

"Are they?" it replied as one eye glowed brightly while the other diminished.

"Well, yes. Look at how they have it so together."

"Together? Is that an apt description of them? Do you believe your statement possess any logic to it?"

Breeze grew irritated. "What do you mean? Why do you keep leaning on me? They have control over their powers. They went to good schools that trained them. They had parents who paid attention to them. I didn't."

Achilles raised a hand and shook its head. "Your attention please, my captain of the skies. Do not confuse false bravado and high handedness for mastery of any skill. What amazing displays of wizardry have they performed for you to give you that impression?"

"Well, just the fact that they can use their powers without a second thought. It's like they're always on and ready to go."

"And this is enough to give you the impression that they possess ultimate mastery of their abilities? That they have exploited them to their fullest potential?"

Breeze shrugged. "Well, yeah."

Achilles pointed a finger at him. "Your basic assessment is correct. They have attended academies that have taught them what they need to know. Listen again to what has just been revealed to you. They were taught what they need to know. Nothing more. Nothing less. Do you understand?"

Breeze looked at the robot with a blank stare. "Yeah, they can use their powers without thinking about it while I have to stand around like an idiot wishing to fly."

"What this humble robot wishes to convey to you is that they were never given the keys to become any more powerful than what they are now. They were taught enough to perform the most basic tasks, nothing more. Do not allow the supposed prestige of whatever academy they attended to blind you to the obvious."

"You're saying that Sally can do a lot more?"

"Infinitely more. Remember, the path before you forever recedes. You are an eternal student, Breeze, and one's work is never done."

Breeze's gaze drifted toward the mountains in the distance.

"Master Corinth, you mentioned earlier that your father never trained you in the use of your skills. Do you sincerely believe that to be true?"

He nodded as he returned his attention to Achilles. "Yeah, I mean, it wasn't like he tried to send me off to some school or anything, and if he knew Oslo for so long, he never once mentioned him to me or about Perihelion. He only sent me away after I went to the air show and...here I am now."

Achilles placed a hand on Breeze's shoulder. "You had said that your father possessed no concern for your safety by allowing you to work so close to the molten slag buckets of the foundry. Did it occur to you that he very well knew it would be safe and that no harm could come to you?"

"What are you getting at?"

"You just fell out of the sky, master. And yet observe yourself, no harm has befallen you, with the exception of the hapless earth and the crater you left behind."

"Well, yeah, my shield always seems to kick in before I crash into anything."

Achilles gripped his shoulder a little tighter. "Listen carefully to your words. Any sign of danger and your shield raises to protect you. You worked in dangerous conditions at the foundry, yet were you ever involved in an accident?"

"No, not that I can think of," Breeze tilted his head, "wait a minute, I do remember a bucket that was traveling above me on the overhead gantry. One of the arresting cables broke and the bucket tilted and molten slag fell out. I remember that it almost hit me, but then it just seemed to, I don't know, slide away from me?"

Achilles nodded its head. "Activation of your shield for the first time."

"I don't get it. What are you trying to say? I don't remember doing anything at all."

"Did it occur to you my fledgling, that your father purposefully placed you there in an attempt to jump start your abilities?"

"You're saying that my father risked my life? On a hunch?"

"Your father was training you, but in secret. Think back over your life to this point in time. Everything your father wanted of you, every chore and task you had to perform more than likely possessed a direct correlation to your training. Not just in the use of your gifts, but in your mechanical skills as well. You possess an adeptness for machines and how to fix them. Have you seen these skills on display from your teammates?"

Breeze didn't answer as he stared at the robot.

"I will accept your silence as a no. There were taught what they needed to know in a controlled environment. Pull them out of that environment and they seem unable to function, so they default to the only person they know who possesses any level of real world skill. That is you."

"But I still don't know what I'm doing when I'm up there."

"Negative. Your subconscious has been filled to the brim with all of the knowledge you need to know to maximize your potential. Together, we shall demonstrate it. Return aloft, young man."

Breeze closed his eyes, stretched his arms out and within seconds he felt the air rushing across his face until he came to a stop. He opened his eyes and looked down where Achilles was just an ant on the ground from his vantage point.

Achilles' voice crackled through his earpiece. "We shall relive the molten slag incident at the foundry in order to prove the mastery of your abilities and the level of power you posses. For this exercise, you will close your eyes. Do not open them until you are told to do so."

Breeze complied. He concentrated on maintaining his position when he began to wonder what Sally was doing.

"Now, young aviator, with your eyes firmly shut, sense your shield. I want you to picture it as a bubble and expand it."

"My shield isn't up because I'm not in danger," Breeze retorted.

"Ones does not need visual receptors to sense or recognize danger. Expand your shield, please."

Breeze reached out with his mind and could feel the energy radiating from his shield. "It's on!" he called out excitedly.

"Excellent. With your eyes firmly shut, expand it to its fullest extent."

Breeze kept his eyes closed and could feel the energy coursing through his body as he expanded the shield. Suddenly he felt resistance. He grunted as he strained to push the shield out further, but couldn't.

"Something's wrong Achilles, I can't."

"You cannot, or you are unable to perceive the danger that surrounds you?"

"What are you getting at?"

"Open your eyes."

Breeze did and was stunned. He was surrounded by a squadron of hovering attack ships. They throttled their engines and he was overwhelmed by the cacophony of whining turbines.

He struggled to maintain his shield as they pressed against it and responded by thrusting the shield out, but to no avail. They continued to push harder and the shield began to collapse. Amidst the assault, he could see into the canopies of the ships. There were no pilots.

As he began to black out from the strain, he was still able to recognize the triangle symbol painted on the side of one of the ships. Exactly like the one he saw in Achilles' barn.

"Do not surrender my young warrior, you must resist," Achilles called out over the earpiece.

"Just...can't," Breeze gasped, as the ships pressed and squeezed the shield against him.

"You can and you must. From deep inside, you will find the infinite energy that powers and guides you. It is the eternal fire that cannot be extinguished unless you allow it to do so. Resist!"

Breeze was choking as his eyes rolled back. He surrendered himself to the inevitable when he heard a voice.

"Don't give up," said a young woman.

"Nina?" Breeze spun around as he tried to find her.

"Move everything around you," she said.

He relaxed the shield and it collapsed. He was able to draw a deep breath and steady his nerves as he calmly watched the hover ships rush him for the kill. He heard a hum in his ears as he narrowed his eyes, and in a flash, he flung his shield out in a mighty rush, impacting the ships and sending them hurtling across the sky in all directions.

"Excellent!" Achilles boomed through the earpiece, "but do not celebrate this victory yet."

The attack ships immediately regrouped. With turbines whining they fanned out into a diamond formation, then advanced towards him.

Breeze glided back in an attempt to place some distance between them. The ships responded by accelerating towards him.

"Strategy, young aviator. Only retreat against impossible odds. You possess the advantage here."

"Advantage? These things are about to run me over! I'm going to do what I do best; fly away."

Achilles shook its head as the voice within spoke: *What did you expect from this fledgling, my dear Achilles? He has been a loner for most of his life and is not capable of the things you wish him to do.*

"No, this unit will not agree with your assessment, he is capable of so much more," Achilles replied.

"What did you just say to me?" Breeze tapped his earpiece, "I can hardly hear you."

Achilles rapped its head with a fist. "Ignore the previous transmission, Master Corinth, and think. You have just demonstrated how your shield is an offensive weapon, and that a strong defense is a devastating offense. Now, what can you do to achieve victory with the scenario you are now faced with?"

Breeze stared at the advancing ships as he thought of Achilles' words. The whine of their turbines grew stronger, making it harder for him to concentrate as each ship shimmered from the hot exhaust of their engines. "I guess I can just...expand the shield again and bump them again?"

"No," he heard the robot's voice over the earpiece, "think between spaces. How can you affect the space surrounding them, or between them?"

Breeze continued to drift backward, mindful of the receding gap between him and the ships. "Wait a minute, I get it. Watch this," and he accelerated backwards as the ships raced to keep up. In an instant, he came to a stop, then lunged forward, which allowed him to slip into the center of their diamond formation. With a mere thought, he rapidly expanded his shield and again they were flung across the sky like toys.

"Precisely," Achilles said, "your shield protects you no matter what the circumstances. It is impervious and it will defend you. It will also fight for you, so do not be afraid to use it as a weapon."

Breeze listened while giving chase to a ship that was flying away. "I'm going to give this little piggy a bump it'll never forget," he said as he drew closer to it.

"Beware, young man. Not every victory is so easily achieved."

Breeze trailed it, and then expanded the shield just as the ship ejected hot flame from its exhaust. A wall of fire blinded him and he veered off course.

"Always expect resistance as not every adversary is so easily defeated. In the same manner you feigned weakness and set a trap for them, the tables can be turned on you as well. Be mindful of that."

"Yeah, yeah. Blah, blah. I get it."

"Do I sense a case of wounded pride in the tone of your voice?

Forgive me, master, if I am wrong for my processors do not appear to be functioning well today."

Breeze ignored the robot as he looped around in a wide arc to find and give chase to the other ships, never realizing they were trailing him the whole time.

You are making this far too easy for him. A few quick victories and he now believes he is an invincible warrior. You should really hammer down on the whelp.

Achilles' body shuddered as it cocked its head. "I shall ask you to cease and desist. You plainly have no interest in helping," it responded to the voice.

High above, Breeze was scanning the skies. "Achilles, I can barely hear what you are saying. Did you just say the session is over? Because I lost track of them, so I guess I won."

"I apologize, master, I seem to be having...issues with my intercom. Nevertheless, there is no such victory as a partial one. Victory can only be achieved by absolutely defeating your opponent along with their acknowledgment of it. No firm and clear victory, no peace can be established."

"You're not kidding, I saw how you fought at Hammer Jack's. You're a robot that plays for keeps."

"Pay heed to the battle space. Victory, as well as defeat, can be found lurking around the next corner."

"Don't know about corners up here in the sky, Achilles. Plenty of clouds though."

"Focus, young man."

As if on cue, the sky was shattered by the sound of high pitched turbines coupled with multiple sonic booms. The ships were in single file as they charged him then peeled away in different directions when they drew closer to him.

"They have learned. They are wary of you, but possess no fear. They are relentless, and like all machines, they never stop until the intended goal of their programming has been achieved. They are fully aware of your capabilities and have adapted with their own countermeasures. Beware," Achilles warned.

He drifted across the sky and watched the ships scramble into position as one hovered above him and another below. The remaining two hovered to his left and right.

"They're boxing me in," he called out.

"Indeed," Achilles' voice crackled over the earpiece.

"That's stupid. Don't they know if they rush me again I'll just use the shield and bump them back?"

"Master, it is best to overestimate your opponents than to underestimate them. Expect the worse and plan accordingly."

"Okay, then I'll ram them."

He charged the ship to his right when he heard the roar of engines and was rammed from below and sent hurtling toward the attack ship above him, which was vibrating and shimmering, while a translucent bubble began to form off its bow. He could feel the bubble dragging him towards it, when it burst in an explosion of sound and fury as the space between him and the ship became distorted and the resulting impact was like a wave crashing over and sending him into a spiral to the earth below.

Another blow from a ship to his left changed his course and sent him hurtling across the sky when he was instantly surrounded by an overwhelming roar of engines. The other ships had joined in and relentlessly attacked with expanding spheres that appeared off their bows and exploded, sending shock waves crashing over him.

"Achilles, make them stop!"

"Negative. Now more than ever, it is imperative that you achieve success. You must overcome these odds."

"But how? What kind of weapons are they using?"

"Distortion fields. They are collapsing the space between you and them."

Another explosion from an expanding bubble sent him cartwheeling across the sky as ships from above and below moved in for the kill.

Achilles explained to him his predicament. "They know they must keep their distance from you, so the strategy they are employing is to collapse the fabric of space and time and use it as a whip. They do this by forming a bubble of intense gravitational energy just off their bows which stretches space like a rubber band, but instead of riding ahead of the resulting wave that is created when unleashed, they hang back and allow the wave to strike you."

Another bellowing roar and his shield buckled as a pair of waves hit him simultaneously. The impact rattled him as he searched wildly for a reference point to maintain his position while fighting off the vertigo that threatened to overwhelm him. "Can't find...ground...sky is spinning..."

See? Not capable. You apply pressure to this one and he folds.

Achilles pounded its chest with a reverberating clang as it responded to the voice. "Your timing is highly inappropriate. This will be my final warning to you. You will recede to the shadows and allow me to train this child."

"Achilles...what are you saying? Help me...," Breeze's voice came in weakly over the intercom.

"Steady yourself young warrior. Remember one of the first rules of navigation; find a reference point."

"How? Spinning...so fast."

"There is glowing orb above you. You cannot miss it."

"What...are you...talking about?"

"The sun, Master Corinth. Burning with its virtually infinite flame."

Breeze tumbled inside his shield as he fought off an impending blackout. He struggled to lock his eyes on the sun as he strained to counteract the spin he was thrown into. The more effort he exerted, the less he spun.

He broke free from his death spiral and wobbled as he tried to hover in place. Nausea roiled him as he watched the ships regroup into a diamond formation.

"Can you call off this session, Achilles? I think I've had enough."

"You have accomplished much by doing, rather than discussing, the theoretical. Retreat is unnecessary when you have the upper hand."

"What upper hand? I'm getting destroyed up here!"

"Analyze, young man. You possess the ability to expand your shield and batter the opposition. Have you not yet realized it can be utilized to draw in your adversaries?"

Breeze was silent as he studied the ships. He knew he didn't have the strength to lash out at them with his shield. They would only fall back and stay out of range.

"Wait a minute. I think I'm beginning to understand what you're rattling on about, Achilles. What if I expand the shield just enough, then...collapse it quickly?"

"Yes. Your shield also distorts space. If it were to suddenly collapse—"

"—it would suck them in and bring them closer to me," Breeze concluded.

"Your understanding is complete. Now execute," Achilles said.

Breeze glared at each ship. Their hulls gleamed from the rays of the brilliant sun while hot exhaust poured from their turbines and clashed with the cold air, creating wisps of white clouds that streamed behind them.

In unison, they began to rotate in a circular motion. Their tempo increased, and in a matter of seconds, they formed a roaring vortex

Breeze could feel himself getting dragged towards it as he stretched out his arms and let his head fall back. His body trembled as his shield expanded.

The ships responded by forming distortion spheres off their bows as they continued spinning.

Breeze expanded the shield to his utmost limit and noted how flimsy it appeared. He was weak and the shield reflected it. He focused what little strength he had left and channeled it into the shield. Its surface began to crackle with energy when he heard the growing hiss of static surround him.

He quickly tucked into a fetal position while rapidly collapsing the shield as the sudden vacuum it created overwhelmed the vortex and the ships were sent hurling towards him.

They immediately discharged their distortion spheres at him as their turbines whined in a desperate attempt to reverse course, but it only served to strengthen the shield, which absorbed their energy upon impact.

Then the world disappeared before his eyes.

Breeze watched as darkness rapidly descended upon him. He was in a complete blackout and the silence was overwhelming. Panic swept over him when he realized he couldn't even see himself as he waved his hands in front of his face. He wanted to shout for help, but his throat made no sound.

That's when he felt pinpricks of electricity strike his hand. He raised it and saw a ball of light spin in his palm. The light grew in intensity as it confronted the darkness and sent it into retreat. As the darkness receded, more globes of light appeared and swarmed like bees before him.

He heard whispering voices, but saw no one. He drifted towards the buzzing hive of lights, but could never get close to any of them.

The whispers gave way to voices, though the language was unfamiliar. He could sense the presence of others, but never did they feel malevolent.

The lights then coalesced into human forms. Their faces were featureless as they stood in a row and conversed amongst themselves while intermittently pointing at him and nodding their heads.

"Hello," he said, then laughed. It felt good to be able to speak again.

"Having...a voice, the ability...to express oneself...is one of the simplest joys of life, is it not?" one of them said at it stepped forward.

"Yes," Breeze replied.

"Your gifts are a part of you, they can never be taken away nor given to another."

Breeze nodded.

"They are not a curse, nor a burden. It is a natural part of you as the eyes that let you see, or the heart that pumps life nourishing blood through your veins. Cherish them and use them wisely as you will need them. Not just to help yourself, but also those around you. Do you understand?"

Breeze nodded when the ball of light rose from his hand and floated above him.

"You must return, but remember this: you are as light as a feather. That is how you will land."

Before Breeze could respond, he felt a hand on his back gently push him forward into a rift that appeared where he was instantly blinded by a powerful burst of light. He raised a hand to shield his eyes when a sudden gust of wind made him tumble like a leaf.

He pulled his hand away and was greeted by the rays of the sun. He looked down and saw a brilliant and endless landscape of white clouds spread out before him. He sank into them and exited moments later to a vista filled with vast stretches of land that curved towards the horizon.

While he drifted down he could see Achilles, as the sunlight that glinted off its metal skin could be seen for miles. When he drew closer he saw the attack ships had landed and were lined up in a row behind the robot. He landed gently and calmly walked towards it.

"Master, where have you been? I suspected the worst might have befallen you," Achilles said as it approached him. The robot's feet left deep impressions in the muddy ground.

"Footprints," Breeze said and pointed behind Achilles.

"Yes, my young friend. Such things occur when the gravitational attraction of an object overwhelms the surface tension of a plane. Hence, my excessive weight will leave impressions on the ground."

"I have none," Breeze pointed behind him.

Achilles scanned the terrain behind him. "Curious," it said and its eyes began to glow.

Breeze's gaze drifted towards one of the ships he had sparred with earlier. He stepped up to it and touched its metal skin, realizing it was the same one he had seen in Achilles' barn. He felt a spark of energy surge through his arm and he pulled his hand away, staring at it intently while waving it slowly from side to side.

"Master, are my optical sensors deceiving me, or are you becoming translucent?" Achilles said.

Breeze could barely see his hand or arm as he held out his other hand and waved it in front of him. "What's happening to me? Why do I feel so out of it?"

Achilles' eyes lit up. "When you collapsed your shield, you subsequently disappeared. I became perplexed as to how you performed this feat. I utilized my sensors, but could not detect your bio signature. It was as if you had just vanished from existence. Illuminate me, Master Corinth, where did you go?"

"All I could remember was hearing the sound of turbines at full throttle combined with static, then silence as everything went dark. Then I saw a light. Actually, a swarm of lights, and then..." His words drifted off as he gazed at the mountains in the distance.

Achilles tilted its head. "I implore you to please continue your story, Master."

"I saw people made up of light. They spoke to me and told me my powers were a gift and not something to be taken for granted."

"Intriguing," Achilles said.

Breeze reached out and touched the hull of the ship again. He applied pressure with his fingers and his hand and arm sank effortlessly up to his elbow into the ship. He tried to pull it back out but couldn't.

"Achilles, what's happening?" Breeze's face was contorted with fear as he struggled to free himself.

Achilles reached out to grab him, and then hesitated. "When your shield collapsed, you must have created a tear in space time," it said.

"That's great Achilles, but I don't need a science lecture right now."

Servos whirred as Achilles shook its head rapidly. "This is a most fascinating development, young aviator. Now, stand still. I believe I possess a solution to your dilemma."

"Is it going to hurt?"

"Excellent question. Response? Cannot answer at this time due to insufficient data."

Before Breeze could say anything, Achilles grabbed him by the shoulders and pulled him back. In an instant, a brilliant light surrounded them. He turned to look at the robot and for a brief moment, saw a human face peering out from behind its head as they tumbled to the ground.

Breeze groaned as he got to his feet while Achilles rose up in a swift and fluid motion.

Breeze pointed at it. "I saw something as soon as you started to pull me."

"Affirmative. A brilliant display of light that I was a witness to as well. You have been out of phase with current space time ever since you reappeared, and that is why you floated so gently from the sky overwhelmed with the feeling of disorientation from your surroundings. It also explains how you were able to slip your hand into the ship's hull and become affixed to it. You were out of step with the space time of this dimension as the result of your shield collapsing and creating a powerful rift that sent you to another."

"No, not that. I thought I saw, oh, never mind. It's been a long day, I'm heading back to the house."

"My sentiments exactly. We have learned much today about your abilities. We have discovered things about you that one would never suspect."

Breeze arched an eyebrow at the robot as they trudged across the field. "You don't say."

C H A P T E R

▼

T W E N T Y - T H R E E

ON THE SAME MORNING of Breeze's training session with Achilles, Raza had agreed with the robot that she would spend the day alone with Ray and Sally to assess their abilities as they both concluded that Breeze needed personal attention, and Achilles was insistent that it didn't want him to be distracted by bickering with the others.

"You mean," Raza said with a smile, "the fact that the boys are competing for Sally's attention?"

"I am afraid the affairs of the human heart are not one of my specialties. Emotion is something I cannot process," Achilles was quick to respond.

"And yet you just said you were afraid."

"Simple expression meant to convey concern."

Raza laughed as she patted Achilles on the cheek. "Yes, you have definitely spent too much time with us illogical humans. Very well then, off you go, but make sure you bring Breeze back in time for dinner. Don't lose him out there in the sky, he just might fly way."

"Perish the thought, milady. Such an event will not occur."

Raza smiled as she stood at the entrance of the barn and watched the robot get into its rusty hover truck. As Achilles glided away, her thoughts turned to Oslo. The events of late only served to remind her of what life was once like at Perihelion, where there were always cadets to train and equipment that needed repairs, along with the hustle and bustle of personnel moving about the base.

"Where are you now, Oslo," she whispered, "and how is our daughter?"

She sighed and went back inside. She walked past the stables and headed to a back room where Achilles set up comm equipment it brought over from its barn. She scanned the screens and saw no messages or readouts of any real importance. "So quiet out there," she sighed.

She looked at the array of equipment that Achilles had amassed. All were vintage machines from a time long past and she marveled at how any of them still worked. She gazed up at the ceiling and noted how the robot even took the time to patch up the leaky roof. "It's good to have a man around the house," and laughed when she heard her own words. *It also feels good to laugh again.*

One of the comm machines trilled loudly and she rushed over to get a closer look at its display. A comm channel had been left open and she noted the coordinates of the signal, then compared them to a map of the continent Achilles had hung on the wall. It was originating from the Northeastern territories. She twisted a dial to increase the signal strength, hoping to hear something at the other end. She received nothing but static.

A commotion erupted at the far end of the barn where she and Achilles had set up a training room for the teens to practice and hone their skills. She heard shouting followed by the sound of something heavy crashing to the ground.

She ran into the training room where she found Ray struggling to pull up a rack full of electronic equipment that he had tipped over.

Sally immediately began apologizing upon seeing Raza. "I'm so sorry, I told him not to touch anything, but he thinks that every machine that he sees he knows how to operate and—"

Raza raised a hand and smiled. "It's quite all right. Boys will be boys, and boys love to play with their toys. Except these toys are very rare pieces of equipment brought over by Achilles. So please, don't touch them." She waved her hand and the rack rose up and floated. She then spread her fingers and it traveled across the room until it bumped gently into a wall, and then settled onto the floor.

"Achilles has set up these racks of electronics so we can monitor and analyze each of you during your practice sessions. This way, we can pinpoint any errors or inconsistencies in the way you utilize your powers," Raza said to them.

Ray snorted. "Not sure if you're going to find too many errors. With all due respect, we're from Greenbrier. We were instructed by the best. We know what we're doing."

"Except handling metal racks full of electronic equipment," Raza retorted. "What were you doing anyway? How did it fall over?"

Sally began to speak, but Raza raised a hand to silence her. "Ray is a well-trained cadet from a proud military family. He can speak for himself."

Ray shifted his stance as he looked away from her.

Raza stared at him. "Is there something you want to tell me?"

"About what? I was just—"

"Raymond, I know you and Sally are homesick and wish to contact your families, but Achilles has informed me that it's been difficult lately to get a clear signal from any of the other territories or cities."

Ray nodded. "Yes, you're right."

She continued. "I saw one of the comm screens just before I came to investigate the noise you were making back here and I noticed a channel was left open. Its coordinates show that it was being directed at the Northeastern territories. Were you trying to reach out to someone? Your parents?"

Ray fell silent and stared at the floor.

Raza reached out with open arms and hugged him. "Listen, you can hold us to our promise. We will locate them and put you back together with your family," she said and then turned to Sally, "that goes for you too, young lady."

Sally smiled as she struggled to hold back her watering eyes.

Raza patted his shoulders. "Now, my brave warrior, I have never seen you in action. Would you like to give me a brief demonstration? Just something that I can observe and to let the instruments record for further analysis."

Ray groaned. "We went through this already at Perihelion. Can't you just wait until Oslo gets here? I'm sure he'll bring all the data you need. Where is he anyway? Any word on him yet?"

Raza stiffened. "Achilles has been hailing the island, but so far, no response. I'm sure everything is quite all right. Oslo is dependable. If he says he's going to do something, he will. Sooner or later he will."

Ray formed a ball of fire in his palm and casually tossed it up and down. Each toss was higher than the previous and several times it almost hit the ceiling. "You know Raza, it must be tough living here all by yourself and thinking about your daughter and husband all the time."

Sally shook her head. "Ray, seriously?"

"Oh, come on Sally, it's perfectly all right to ask. I mean, she does owe us an explanation. Let's face it, Oslo sent us here as refugees. He did his best to protect us and failed. Then he sends us to his long forgotten wife to hide out from the Elephim where we end up meeting an old and lonely woman who takes us in, then throws a tantrum and chases us out."

Raza stood silent as her face grew pale.

Sally was trembling. "Raymond, she apologized to us and made up for it with her hospitality."

"Yeah, she hugs you and you settle for that. Weren't you the one who was so curious as to how she got younger? We don't see her for a few days and then, we meet again, but she's no crazy old lady. She got younger. Care to explain that away?" Ray said as he threw the ball of fire high in the air while taking a quick glance at the rack of electronics Raza had pushed against the wall. He noted a light that was blinking on one particular piece of equipment. He grinned.

In the comm room, the screen that caught Raza's attention earlier flickered alive.

"Why did you just look at the rack for? Better yet, what were you doing earlier with it?" Raza glared at him as she made a fist and the ball of fire extinguished before it could fall back into his hand.

Ray grimaced and shook his head. "Don't change the subject. What's with the sudden youthful appearance? In fact, it seems like you and Oslo should be pretty old by now, if not dead. And yet you both have managed to live for a long time. How? What is it you are trying to do?"

"Stop goading her Ray. I've never seen you like this before. You're... not the same boy I grew up with," Sally said.

He stabbed a finger at her. "You stay out of this. You don't want to question her about anything, but I do."

Raza slapped his hand. "Stop pointing at her like that, you're being rude. You want to know my secrets? Long ago, Oslo and I discovered pools deep within the interior of Perihelion where we could feel a sensation of energy surging through our bodies when we swam in them. Oslo performed an analysis and found that the pools were alive with electromagnetic energy. They could heal wounds, scars, cure you of any affliction you might have. The pools gave life. One might say they were like fountains of youth."

Ray shrugged. "Great to know. Still doesn't explain how you managed to stay young here in Appalachia. We're a long way from Perihelion."

"Petulant youth, no patience to wait for anything. I was just going to get to that, but pausing to take a breath doesn't mean anything to you."

"Keep talking. We're listening," Ray said with a smirk.

"Who's we?" she asked.

His face turned red. He created another ball of fire and began tossing it. "Sally and I, who else?"

Raza looked skeptical as she continued her story. "Over the years, Oslo was able to map out the caverns of underground rivers that fed the pools. It was an extensive network that crossed the globe and they absorbed their healing properties from the energy given off deep within the planet's core and distributed it across the world. Oslo found one that led here to Appalachia."

"Sounds convenient."

Raza ignored him and turned to Sally. "Oslo had his engineers build this home before we left Perihelion. He also had them construct a pool in the cellar along with a tunnel that led to the underground river that carried the life healing waters. It was for our own health, he said, but when Nina became ill, not even the healing waters of the pool could cure her, and it puzzled Oslo to no end as to why. He suspected that perhaps the pool lacked the potency compared to the ones found on the island, though all of his tests showed that the water here were no different. As we prepared our journey to return—"

"Never mind that," Ray interrupted, "you say these pools lack potency. Why?"

Raza sighed. "When Oslo returned to Perihelion to save our daughter, he discovered that she was an integral part of the island and that there was a bond between them that couldn't be easily broken. So Oslo collaborated with Excort and set about widening the cavern that led to Appalachia. He believed that he could wean our daughter from the island if he could increase the flow and pressure from the pools of Perihelion, to here."

Ray's eyes narrowed. "So you're saying that you could easily travel from the island to here, inside these caverns?" He formed a fireball and began tossing it up and down.

Raza crossed her arms. "Swim underwater? I suppose you could, but I couldn't hold my breath for that long."

"But your daughter could, she's like a fish. Breeze spent enough time with her, he would know."

"I wouldn't want her to travel underground for hundreds of miles in cold and frigid water. What sort of maniac would do that to their child?" Raza replied.

Ray pressed on. "Couldn't Oslo have built some sort of submersible to get here? I mean, it just seems like there is more than one way to get to Perihelion."

"What are you getting at?" Raza said.

"I mean, it's sort of a vulnerability. If someone were to attack and take over the island, they could find those pools and the caverns that would lead them back here. Oslo said this place was safe, but I'm beginning to wonder."

Raza took a step toward him. "I originally asked you for a demonstration of your ability and it seems like you handle yourself very well as you juggle those balls of fire. Are you always this calm and under control?"

Ray snorted. "Why wouldn't I be? I was born and raised into a military family. My father is a commander in our territorial army."

"Verhesen? That is your last name, is it not?"

"Yes. What of it?"

"The name rings a bell for me. I remember it being associated with a fifth column that formed an alliance with the Elephim. Perhaps I'm mistaken. After all, I am old."

Ray formed two more fireballs and juggled them at a faster clip. "You probably are mistaken. So, are you going to tell us more ancient history stories that Oslo laid on us before? About the glory days of the superhuman Helios? Space travel and far flung colonies? Because we were never taught about any of these things."

"Just because you were kept in ignorance doesn't mean it never happened," Raza said.

"Well, I don't believe it."

"Interesting, considering you are a part of their legacy."

"Are you calling my family traitors?"

"I was referring to your gifts. Look at you, you're a god walking amongst ordinary humans. That has to be exhilarating."

Ray stared at her.

Raza locked her eyes onto his. "You've met Oslo and Excort and seen the wonders of Perihelion, yet you are not fascinated by them or the island? And what of the ships you've seen and flown in, do you recognize any of this technology? Doesn't it seem quite fantastic compared to what you are familiar with?"

Ray shrugged. "I suppose, but there are territories and cities across the planet building all sorts of aerocraft. You're bound to run into something different."

"Different, yes, but as amazing as what you have witnessed? And what about Achilles? Have you ever seen a robot so capable? I'm willing to imagine the robotics in your territory is not quite so well developed."

Ray let the balls of fire drop and splatter on the floor in a shower of sparks. "I don't really care to talk about robots. In fact, I don't even think about them. Personally, I think Achilles is dangerous." He began to glow as he stepped to the center of the room. "My father told me enough about how robots with artificial intelligence can be dangerous and uncontrollable. It's important to have control," he said and fired a beam of energy toward the wall. It fizzled upon hitting the concrete.

"Control is important to you, isn't Ray?" Raza stepped toward him.

"Yeah, why wouldn't it be?"

Raza responded by shoving her hands forward and Ray immediately fell onto his backside.

"What's the matter with you!" he shouted as he scrambled to his feet. His hands began to tremble as they pulsated with energy.

"Just giving you a little telekinetic nudge to see how you react. I would say not very well, considering you are the one who cares so much about control."

Ray put his glowing hands together and pointed them at her.

"What now Ray? Are you going to blast away at a poor, defenseless woman? It's okay, this is a training session and appearances can be deceiving."

"Ray, don't," Sally said.

"It's okay, sweetie," Raza said, "I can handle myself. Raymond, fire away at me."

Ray cut loose with powerful beam of energy that Raza redirected toward the ceiling. It dissipated with a flash, revealing a dome that had descended upon them.

Ray looked up at it with his mouth agape. "I don't get it. That should have blown a hole into it."

"I had Achilles install the dome. It's similar to the one you probably used at Perihelion, though not quite as sophisticated. These domes were used on ships so that Helios who were on patrol in deep space could practice and remain battle ready. They're really quite useful."

Ray circled her. "Whatever. I don't believe anything you say. In our territory, we're just sending rockets into space. You talk about spaceships like it was an everyday thing."

Raza smiled. "Oh, it was," and she flung her hands toward him, and then brought them down in a swift motion.

Ray cried out as he was swept off his feet and sent crashing to the ground, then sat up quickly to rub his head. "Nobody does that to me," he growled at her as he got back to his feet.

"Come now, Raymond, and give me a demonstration that I will never forget," Raza taunted as she placed her hands on her hips, then glanced over at Sally and winked.

Ray took several deep breaths and narrowed his eyes. In a blink, he clapped his hands together and fired at the ground in front of Raza, sending chunks of stone flying everywhere as Sally shrieked and ducked for cover. Raza stumbled back, and bumped against the wall, then pushed off it, gliding up to the apex of the dome.

"I wouldn't fire at me from there," she said to Ray, "I'll just deflect the energy back onto you." She then tilted her head at him. "What now, Raymond?"

Ray grunted. "No girl shows me up like that."

"I'm not a girl, I'm a woman, and an old one too. Think Ray, what now?"

He glared at her in silence, his hands at his sides, throbbing with energy.

"Yes, you have the right idea, young man. Direct the energy downward," she instructed.

"Don't tell me what to do!" he shouted, then paused to think about what she said. "Why should I fire at the ground?"

Raza shook her head. "Oh, my dear boy, so much you don't know. I see that your father held back much from you and I can understand why. Son, push yourself up into the air."

"I'm not a flier, leave that to head-in-the-clouds Breeze. It seems he's becoming the golden boy around here."

"This is not about him. This is your time to shine. Now impress me, Ray, and come up here."

"I don't know how."

"Hence the training session. Practice makes perfect. Instead of firing away with high intensity like you always do, learn how to shape and mold the energy. Begin by holding your hands down with palms facing the ground, and then let the energy flow out. Slowly," she emphasized.

Ray kept his eyes locked onto her as his body shuddered, then he lifted a few inches off the ground. "Oh, wow!" he exclaimed.

Raza nodded. "There now, you learn something new every day."

Ray slowly drifted upward then dropped suddenly. He arrested his descent by increasing power, but struggled to hover in place.

"No sudden movements with your hands, Raymond. They control your ascent and descent. You're a trained pilot. You understand the importance of throttle control. Flying an aerocraft is more than just steering. You stay aloft by the amount of thrust you apply."

He rose up until he was level with Raza. His pupils were dilated and he was breathing heavily as sweat poured down his face.

"Very good, Mr. Verhesen, you have cornered your quarry. Now, how will you deliver the killing blow?" Raza taunted as she orbited him.

"Stop it! You're making me dizzy!" he shouted at her, then lost altitude. He steadied himself and drifted back to his original position.

"You've just discovered that you can hover. Curious. What else have you not learned? What else has your father held back from you?"

"Don't talk about him that way! He is a man of great power," Ray said as his eyes glowed with a fierce intensity.

Raza drifted past him with look of bemusement as he struggled to rotate and track her.

"Why do you keep asking me questions about him?" he asked.

"Oh, no reason. Just find it quite curious that such a powerful man would let his only son go from such a prestigious academy like Greenbrier, to a decrepit and run down military base like Perihelion." Raza circled around him with increasing speed.

Ray was drenched in sweat. "He sent me away so I can complete my training in a military environment, with a great commander like Oslo."

Raza threw back her head and laughed. "Forgive me, Raymond, but Oslo and I were instructors, researchers and academics first, and officers second. We were never considered powerful enough to be promoted as active duty Helios, only reservists at best. So tell me again, why were you sent away?"

Ray shuddered as arcs of energy streaked across his body. "He had his reasons."

"Yes, a son he knew he could no longer control, so he sent you away to prevent you from harming yourself and your family."

Ray screamed as a discharge of energy erupted from his mouth, narrowly missing her.

"Control, Raymond, control! With power comes a level of

responsibility that no ordinary man could ever understand. I goad you just a bit, and you explode? Unbecoming of a student of the prestigious Greenbrier."

"Oslo said the exact same thing to Sally. You and Oslo are so—"

"Alike? Yes, we didn't come from wealthy families, we were just regular folk from our little corners of the globe, but we did witness first hand at what power and privilege can do to a young mind. Add paranormal to the mix, and it made for a deadly concoction."

"Are you jealous of me, old woman?"

Raza drifted closer. "They were called the Elephim, a name that originates from an ancient tongue hardly spoken anymore. It means "by the thousands," and that is exactly what they became, a hoard made up of many thousands. They primarily came from privileged families, although they were always quick to claim they represented the everyday man and his plight. They fell under the spell of an unseen force that insisted that all paranormal were to rounded up and extinguished, even the respected Helios, those brave warriors who had protected and served the people of Earth, were to be eliminated also."

Ray's head slumped as he drifted back. "Why are you telling me this?"

"Because amongst them were paranormals who were promised power and greater privilege if they agreed to help suppress the dissenters amongst the Helios who refused to surrender. They became the enforcers who led the downfall of what was once the greatest civilization this part of the galaxy had ever known."

Ray lifted his head. His eyes were bloodshot and strained. "Why are you telling me this?" he repeated.

"Because I want to make sure whomever I am speaking to understands that I know what happened in the past. And I know that they are still here, keeping us under their boot. Whom am I speaking to?"

Ray quivered as spittle flew from his mouth.

Raza pressed on. "What were you doing with the comm unit? Why was there an open channel tuned to the Northeastern territories? And the rack you tipped over, the one with the signal boosters, did you activate it? Are you broadcasting this? Who exactly is listening in on our conversation?"

Ray's head flew back and he laughed. "Stupid witch, did you think you could stay hidden forever?"

Raza's face was pale as she drifted away from him. "Raymond, whoever is hitching a ride with you, you can tell them to leave."

"The boy is a mere conduit. A vessel, if you will." Ray's mouth moved and a voice was heard, but it was not his.

"Whom am I speaking to?" Raza said as she made a hand gesture to Sally, who acknowledged her signal with a nod and instantly her eyes glowed.

"Who I am is not of importance. You only discovered me because of the boy's weakness. His inability to control his anger is what exposed us, but it is also what made him so easy to access."

"How much have you seen? What have you learned so far?" Raza asked it as she drifted toward the far side of the dome, granting her a better view of Sally below.

Ray's body, under control of his possessor, glided over to her and spoke. "What incentive do I have to divulge anything to you? I do believe the proverbial shoe is on the other foot. You reveal your exact location to us, and I promise that we will be...gentle... as to how we dispose of you and your friends."

Raza hovered to the apex of the dome. "Are you not able to find us? Curious, one would believe you have seen enough through the boy to pinpoint our location."

Ray's face grinned. "Don't play the daft lass with us. You very well know the electromagnetic interference that surrounds Appalachia can make it difficult to see through. Much like the one that surrounds Perihelion. Or used to."

Raza's eyes widened.

"Oh, now I have your attention? Amazing how quickly the reality of a situation can sink in. You have no bargaining power here. We are in control."

"What have you done?" Raza whispered.

"Or, you can turn it around and say what *haven't* we done. Yet. Allow me to reiterate. Give us your exact coordinates so we may detain you, and let us bring this little charade of a rebellion to a quick and speedy conclusion. It would be best for all of you."

"What makes you think we're planning a rebellion? We don't even know who we are fighting against."

"Raza, Raza," Ray's head shook, "you and Oslo have been dormant for so long, we assumed you had perished. And even if either of you were found alive, it would be of no importance to us. We arrived at the conclusion that your spirits had been crushed and you're no longer active."

Raza raised her hands. "Very well, we surrender. All I ask is that you spare the children. Let them go. My husband is the one who brought them to Perihelion. He is the one who has stirred the pot and aroused your attention."

"No, I think not, they have seen too much. And besides, where are they to go? To wander these lands, spreading dissent to any and all who will listen? Earth's champions are a thing of the past. We shall endeavor to keep it that way."

Behind Ray's body, a shimmering figure suddenly appeared. It was Sally's astral form and Raza signaled her plan of attack by slowly placing her hands around her throat.

"You are monsters, all of you. You have destroyed so much and yet no one has ever seen your faces," Raza said to the entity.

The entity responded while oblivious to Sally's presence behind it. "Oh, we find the use of surrogates and proxies to be quite efficient. Why show our hand? It has proven to be quite useful over the centuries."

Raza quickly removed her hands from her throat and held them up, signaling Sally to wait. "What do you mean?"

"Oh, my dear, dear charming old woman. Some of our best agents are those who can be easily manipulated to spy upon the strong ones we wish to tear down." Ray's hands moved up and down in a jerky manner. "This one was so easy to assume control, just like a puppet. Through the eyes of this young man we have identified another at Perihelion. She is so sweet and innocent."

"Nina?" Raza's voice trembled.

"Is that her name? Oh, my, how pretty. Yes, I do believe that is the one. Do you know her?"

The walls of the dome crumbled and cracked as Raza's eyes turned a brilliant white and she shrieked in anger.

Ray's head was thrown back as Sally's astral form grabbed him by the neck and choked him. "Get out of him!" she yelled.

Ray's body thrashed violently as he fired blast after blast of raw energy in every direction. The walls of the dome absorbed some of the blasts while others were deflected and ricocheted dangerously throughout the chamber. He reached behind him and tried to grip Sally's astral form. "Yet another witch?" the entity howled with rage.

Ray's body was then flung against the dome by Raza's telekinetic wave as he continued to fire bolts of energy from his hands, mouth and eyes.

"What makes you think I would hesitate to destroy the boy now? I hold this one hostage, I will not relinquish. Away from me!" And to punctuate its point, the entity slammed Ray's body hard into the dome repeatedly as chunks of stone fell to the floor.

Sally shrieked. "Raza, Ray is going to die! Do something!"

Raza rushed up with outstretched hands and created a telekinetic shield around him, then brought her hands together, forcing the shield to collapse and squeeze him.

"Raza, he can't breathe!" Sally screamed.

"Yes, child I know. The shield prevents him from firing any more bolts, but you must force out whatever has possessed him!"

"I don't know if I can!"

"Now is not the time to abandon a friend in need. Endure, my love, and focus all of your energy, then merge into Raymond and throw out this malignant tumor that is bedeviling him!"

Ray's face contorted as Sally's astral form phased into his body, prompting the disembodied voice to roar at them. "Witches and freaks, the earth shall be wiped clean of your kind!"

The sound of static began to build, reaching a fevered pitch and forcing Raza to cover her ears while Ray's body thrashed wildly, and then went limp. Moments later, a shadow emerged from him and coalesced into a human form along with a face morphing and taking shape as a nose, eyes, cheekbones and a mouth became visible. The static subsided when it spoke. "Failure is your future," it said, then dissipated into a cloud of black dust.

Ray's body convulsed violently and plummeted to the ground, bouncing off the surface before coming to a rest on the cold stone floor.

Raza swooped down and landed hard, sending chunks of stone flying everywhere. She grabbed Ray by his jacket and shook him violently. "Where is my daughter? Damn you, what have you done to her?"

"Stop it, Raza! You'll kill him!" Sally yelled as she emerged from Ray and leapt back into her body, then swiftly ran over to push Raza away and threw herself onto him.

Raza shoved her aside and hollered at Ray. "What have you done to my family?!"

The disembodied voice returned as Ray's eyes flickered open. "All we requested...is that...you surrender yourselves...so that you may be liquidated. A rather...simple request. A reasonable one. Now, there will be hell to pay." Ray slumped to the floor as sliver of a shadow emerged from him and disappeared.

Raza sobbed uncontrollably and sank to her knees.

Sally grabbed him. "Ray, please wake up," she said as she cradled him. She turned to Raza. "I saw you motion to me to project and to wait for your signal to make a move on Ray. Raza, it was horrible. It was like he was empty and there was no one inside, just blackness. Then I felt an iciness like I could never get warm again. And then there was this presence there, and it was so lonely and angry. But I know it wasn't him, it was someone...something else."

Raza wiped her face with the back of her sleeve. "Yes, child, I know. I surmised as much," she sniffled as she straightened her hair. "Very well. Composure is compulsory, that is what I was taught. I do believe I failed rather spectacularly in trying to uphold those teachings." She cleared her throat. "Now Sally, tell me, what else did you see?"

Sally caressed Ray's pale face as his breathing became shallow and ragged. "Whenever I project and enter someone, it's like walking into a room filled with colors, images and sounds. But this time it was just nothing, only a creepy feeling that I was being watched and as I turned around to find it, something dark lunged at me. I lashed out with everything that I had, but it wasn't afraid. I don't know why, but I was really angry; it was like this thing brought out the worst in me. I could hear you shouting at me to push it out and I hesitated, then I shoved it as hard as I could," she took in a deep breath, exhaling slowly. "Raza, it felt like my life was slipping away when I touched it."

"These creatures sustain themselves like parasites. I don't know how or when Ray was possessed, but we'll find out," Raza said and touched his head. He began to stir and coughed harshly as Sally and Raza helped him sit up.

"Why do I feel so tired?" he mumbled and rubbed his eyes, "and why are you two staring at me like that?"

"Raymond, do you know where you are?" Raza said and took his hands into hers and held them to her chest.

His face was a blank slate. "I'm not sure. We're in Appalachia, right?" he gazed up at the dome. It bore the scars of his energy blasts. "Are we back at Perihelion? Everything seems so foggy."

She patted his hand. "It's quite all right. Rest here for a while. We'll go back to the house soon and I'll fix everyone something to eat."

Raza then walked out of the dome, leaving the teens behind to gather themselves and headed straight to the racks of electronic equipment. She found the signal boosters had powered down, and she checked behind them and saw that none were connected to electrical cables. She shook her head in disbelief and headed to the comm room to look at the screens. They were all blank.

She heard footsteps and turned to see Sally with her arms around Ray's waist. He was pale and wheezing, with one arm draped over her neck and shoulder.

"Come children, follow me, there has been enough excitement and revelations for today," Raza said and stepped around the console to grab Ray's other arm and place it across her shoulder.

As the women helped Ray out of the barn, he turned to look back at the comm unit. "Did I try to contact my father?" he said, and then his head slumped as he succumbed to fatigue.

CHAPTER
▼
TWENTY-FOUR

BREEZE SWOOPED TOWARD THE river in the predawn hours. He raced over the surface, which compressed the air between his body and the river, creating a canyon of water that shot up and fell back in a white froth that trailed behind him. Then he arched his back and rocketed up to the star laden night sky.

He came to a halt and hovered for a moment, then dropped and glided into a looping pattern over the farmhouse as it sat nestled along the river against a backdrop of mountains surrounding the valley, with the lights of Mount Pleasant sparkling on the horizon to the east.

He ascended, relishing the cold air that rushed across his face. He broke through a cluster of clouds and slowed to a hover. The crescent moon hanging above did not shine brightly enough to obscure his view of the stars.

He looked at the night sky and thought about the stories Oslo told him of space flight and far off colonies. He shook his head as it all sounded like a fantasy to him.

A flicker of movement from the corner of his eye made him swivel his head to track what looked like a bird with large wings racing off into the distance. The clouds beneath it rippled as it glided over them, yet its wings never moved.

Breeze watched with a pounding heart as the memories of the winged creature ambushing them in the ravine were still fresh in his mind. His breathing intensified when it circled towards him and he reflexively raised his shield and began drifting away. As it approached, he could make out the distinct shape of the monster from the ravine.

The winged creature halted and hovered at a respectful distance while its eyes glowed with a golden hue, then abruptly flapped its wings. As it glided away, it held out a hand and pointed at the night sky.

Breeze looked up and noticed a star that shined more brilliantly than the others, and then glanced back down to track the creature, but it had faded into the night.

He returned his focus back to the bright star. The longer he stared at it, the more it appeared to wobble and rotate. He shivered. It felt like he was being watched. He knew there was something unnatural about the star, and it intrigued and frightened him all the same.

He looked at his nav-compass and noted the time. He grimaced, then drifted down into the clouds and began his descent to the river where he saw the scout ship sitting alongside the river bank. He and Achilles had been working on the vessel for the past several weeks. They had procured the various parts needed for repairs and continued to make upgrades to worn out components. The rising sun reflecting off the hull cast the ship in a whole new light, and as he circled the craft, he discovered a newfound appreciation for it. He saw Achilles emerging from the path that led from the farmhouse to the river. The robot waved at him and he waved back as he glided down for a landing.

"Your punctuality is appreciated, young aviator. Have the others arrived yet?" Achilles asked as Breeze touched down.

He looked around and shrugged. "Don't think so. I got up early to get a flight in."

"Exercising and honing your skills, and doing so without being prompted. This humble bundle of circuits and servos must confess that it is pleased to hear this," the robot said.

"And I saw that winged creature," Breeze added.

Achilles froze in place, and then servos whirred as it looked up at the sky, then back to Breeze. "You refer to the harbinger?"

Breeze nodded as he filled in Achilles of what transpired above the clouds.

The robot blinked its eyes slowly. "Interesting indeed. First, Master Verhesen's unfortunate turn of events several days ago. Now, your brush with the harbinger. I must ponder this."

Breeze vividly remembered the day when he returned to the farmhouse with Achilles after his training session with the attack ships. Raza was in the kitchen and informed them of Ray's possession and the events that unfolded inside the barn.

"You know, Achilles, I remember back home when my father took me to visit a neighbor of ours who was a rancher. My father climbed the fence of the corral and sat on the top rail and pulled me up to sit in his lap, and we watched as the ranch hands used ropes to corral the cattle. They would throw lassos at the heads of the cattle, loop them, and then tighten the noose. That's the feeling I get, that the noose is getting tighter. No matter where we go, no matter what we do, the Elephim keep getting closer and closer."

"What you are implying Master Corinth, with your usual subtlety, is that we are the cattle and they are the herders."

"How hard is it to understand? From what you've been telling us, they wiped out the Helios and all the other freaks like us. If the Helios could get lassoed, branded, and then sent to the slaughter house, how hard is it to get us? You said the Helios were the greatest of all the paranormal and they were some sort of a super team. Well, where are they now?"

Achilles stared at him with glowing eyes. *Amazing how the boy can appear to be so dense, then surprise! Slices you like a knife. Leave it to him to summarize your predicament so eloquently. Cattle, indeed.*

The robot clenched its fist tightly. *Begone, and do not molest me anymore with your commentary. It is neither helpful, nor constructive.*

"Achilles, you okay there?" Breeze snapped his fingers.

"Yes, young man. Functioning at normal parameters."

"It's just that every now and then, you sort of...phase out."

"How so?"

"Well, for starters, you like to clench your fist and go quiet. Are you having flashbacks about your fighting days at the arena?"

The robot looked at its fist and chuckled, then unclenched it and extended the fingers. "Slight mechanical error. Nothing to see here, young master. A simple fine tuning of my programming should suffice. Nothing more."

They heard the sound of branches snapping and leaves crunching. They both turned to look as Raza, Sally, and Ray emerged from the tree line in their uniforms. Raza walked ahead of them while the teens were behind her and holding hands.

Raza smiled as she strode up to the robot and patted it on its shoulder. "You're on time as always, Achilles. And I, running late as usual."

"You should not be so hard on yourself, mistress. Your responsibilities have grown sevenfold since the arrival of these youngsters at your doorstep."

"And yet, I wouldn't give them up for the world," she murmured.

Ray and Sally stood apart from everyone. Breeze casually strode up to them. "How are you feeling, Ray?"

"Fine. Why does everyone keep asking me that?" He made brief eye contact with Breeze, and then looked away.

Sally spoke up. "He's getting better, thanks for asking, Breeze. Did you get a flight in this morning?"

Breeze nodded and noted with disdain that she was holding Ray's hand and squeezing it. "Yeah, I did," he replied, and told them about the harbinger.

She quickly scanned the skies. "It didn't try to attack you?"

"No, just pointed at the stars then took off. Didn't want to scare you, just thought you should know."

She rubbed his shoulder. "You were just being helpful," she said with a smile.

Breeze straightened his posture and grinned while Ray glared at him.

Achilles broke up the scene. "Thank you for coming this early in the morning. I know from years of observation that humans tend not to perform at their peak at this time. Nevertheless, in light of recent events, this unit has concluded that we need to, as humans tend to phrase it, clear the air."

Ray coughed and shifted his feet. Sally wrapped her arms around him and hugged tightly.

Achilles continued. "Due to the unfortunate events that have befallen Raymond, we can never fully gauge the depth as to which this group has been compromised. Should we continue to stay here? Do we relocate elsewhere? There is much to ponder and discuss."

Breeze chimed in. "I think I can help speed things up a bit. I know a lost cause when I see one. I'm somewhat of an expert at it, it's been the story of my life. I'm leaving."

Sally gasped. Raza sighed and shook her head.

"So much for teamwork," Ray grunted.

"Yeah, looks like you had a teammate with you the whole time," Breeze shot back.

"Breeze, please reconsider," Achilles stepped between them, "you have accomplished much, despite less than ideal conditions. Continue your training and realize your full potential."

"Yeah...potential. Listen everybody; when I first arrived at Perihelion, I realized how far behind I was compared to everyone else. Ray and Sally went to good schools and came from rich families, whereas I was just some back country fool. I felt pretty small, but I did the best that I could. Although I learned a lot, I kept asking myself what it was all for. All the while, Oslo kept us in the dark and when we threatened to leave, he fed us some hocus pocus story about the past, and then we ran away from that place."

Sally giggled nervously and immediately put a hand to her mouth. "Sorry. Just thinking about how that happened. We couldn't wait to get out."

"Exactly, only we got ambushed by the Elephim. We were rescued and returned to the island to deal with the ugly truth of what happened, and we realized that Oslo was just trying to protect us the whole time, but from what? If we had just stayed with our families in the first place and never went to Perihelion, would all of this have happened? Did Oslo just attract their attention by recruiting us?"

"Breeze, my husband had the noblest of intentions, and I can assure you that he never have had any desire to hurt any of you," Raza said.

"Well, I understand that," Breeze's voice was tinged with anger, "but Raza, you should be one to talk. I'm sorry ma'am if I sound rude. You have shown us such great hospitality, even though our first meeting was pretty weird."

Her face turned red. She folded her arms and stared at the ground.

He pressed on. "You have been hiding out here for such a long time and not attracting any attention, then we show up and it just turns into another mess. These Elephim obviously want us to stop, and I say, why not? What are we going to do? We don't have what it takes to fight back."

"Master Corinth, after all you have witnessed and learned, you do not wish to continue?" Achilles' eyes glowed as it spoke.

"Continue to do what? After all this time, I don't know what we're supposed to be doing. What are we training for? What's it all about?" Breeze shrugged his shoulders. "In the end, I'm just a simple guy. I'm going back home. I haven't heard from my father and I need to see if he's okay. You are all welcome to come with me. You guys could get jobs working at my father's foundry, or go to Conception and settle there. Or stay here in Mount Pleasant and start over. It seems that thing that was spying on us through Ray really doesn't know where we are. If everybody just blends in, they will probably stop hunting us down."

"So give up and walk away, just like that? How can you be so selfish?" Sally wailed.

"I'm not, just being honest. I know when I'm out of my league and don't stand much of a chance of getting ahead." Breeze looked at Sally in the eye, then down to her hand holding Ray's. "If I learned anything, it's that there is no point in disrupting things, or getting between people."

She shook her head and started to speak, when Raza stepped forward.

"I know how hard this has been on all of you, along with the changes you've been forced to experience. But that's life. Breeze, how are you going to leave? You can't just take the ship, it's not yours. This ship belongs to Oslo, to Perihelion."

Breeze tilted his head. "Well, ma'am, don't know about that. I can always just fly away, take my chances over the Bad Lands, and find my way back home. But I could take the ship, and why not? The more I learn about it, seems like there is a family connection. I keep seeing my last name stamped on parts all over the ship."

Achilles raised its hands. "Young aviator, I have cautioned you before regarding the matter. I am certain your name has no connection to the ship and is merely a coincidence. This vessel was built long before your time."

"Yeah, don't know about that. You seem like a mechanical version of Oslo, just holding back information all the time. I know I appear dense to you all, but I can put the pieces together, like why does my father run a scrap yard that just happens to sell steel to the local aerocraft builders. Coincidence? And this disc," Breeze pulled out the diagnostic disc from his jacket, "recognized me as Jacob. Jacob is my father's name."

"Again, a coincidence. Nothing more," Achilles said.

"Oslo told me a lot of things, and one of them was that there is no such thing as coincidence, all things happen for a reason."

Achilles turned to Raza as she threw her hands in the air. "Very well then, leave. You're right, who are we to keep you here? You're not a prisoner."

"A proposal, Master Corinth," Achilles announced.

Breeze sighed. "What now?"

"Humor this ancient machine one last time. I would like the three of you to have one last training session, but this time as a team."

Breeze laughed. "You just won't give up. We weren't meant to be together, how else can I say it? You have to know when to quit."

"An incentive, perhaps? One last training session and at its conclusion, this unit pledges to render assistance in completing repairs on the ship so you may continue your journey home."

"One last get together so that the team that never was can disband? Sure, I guess."

"I'm for it too," Ray broke his silence, "I know I let everyone down. I have a lot to prove to myself and to all of you."

"Ray, listen, you don't have to—"

"No, Breeze. I was supposed to be team leader, Oslo said as much. But I fell apart and looked at what happened to me. That...thing got into me and made me a puppet." He shook his head. "You know, I have to admit it probably got into me before the trimaran accident, but I just don't know how."

"Well, you were messing around in the basement where that Bram guy was. Did you run into something down there and you just don't remember?"

Sally glared at him. "Breeze how can you say that, you don't know if that's true."

"Fine. Let's get this over with." He jerked a thumb towards the ship. "I need to step inside and grab my uniform so we can get started. But remember, I'm leaving after this." Breeze turned and began walking to the ship when Sally called out to him.

"We have nowhere to go. We lost our homes and families. What about us Breeze?"

He whirled around. "Look, you can come with me. I'm going to warn you though, it's desert country, you might not like living there." He turned and continued to the ship.

"What makes you think I won't?" she said softly as he disappeared into the ship.

Breeze came out minutes later in uniform and stood next to Achilles. The robot clapped its hands with a reverberating clang. "Very well, let us begin. Students, to the shoreline."

They walked away from the scout ship and headed to the sandy banks of the river where the teens stood in a row while Achilles and Raza stood side by side before them.

The robot raised a hand. "Students, your task is a simple one, or so it may appear on the surface. I shall be positioned further upstream, and the goal will be for Breeze to ascend from here, fly above the river to my location, and tag me. I assure you there will be no resistance on my part whatsoever. Be warned, young aviator, you shall encounter obstructions along your course, courtesy of Raza, while she remains hidden along the riverbank. Sally, you will place yourself at the top of that mountain," the robot pointed to a peak directly to the west, "where you will perform the role of forward observer. You will project from there and rendezvous with Breeze to inform him of any obstacle or threat along his path. As for you Raymond," it pointed upriver, "you will patrol the river bank on foot as Breeze flies by you enroute to his target. You will also be kept into the dark as to what obstacles he might encounter, but as his teammate, you will help clear his path."

Ray nodded. "Great, let's get started."

"Enthusiasm is infectious in humans and it pleases me to observe this from you. Any questions from Breeze or Sally?" Achilles asked as it looked their way.

The two glanced at each other and shrugged.

"Fantastic! Let us commence. Breeze, please remain here. I will give you the signal to begin your run over the wireless." Achilles turned and walked upriver, and the others followed. The robot's hover truck appeared out of the treeline and glided over to them. They climbed into it and raced away.

Breeze stood alone as the sound of the river flowing put his mind at ease. He watched as the water flowed over the rocks that jutted up from the bottom and created eddies that marred the otherwise uniform flow of water as it headed upstream.

He turned his attention downriver where he saw the scout ship with its shining hull basking in the sunlight. He felt the urge to get into it and fly away when he looked back at the rocks in the middle of the river.

"It's so simple," he muttered, "get past the rocks and life becomes... so easy."

He turned and headed toward the scout ship as he removed the wireless receiver from his ear and tucked it into his chest pocket.

Just get in and fly away. Leave it all behind. I won't be hurting anyone.

He was halfway to the ship when he heard a voice in the distance. He stopped to look behind him. Seeing no one, he resumed his journey when he heard it again, but louder, and it was distinctly female.

"Sally?" He stopped dead in his tracks and spun around. "Are you projecting already?"

No response.

When he heard the voice again, it felt like it was coming from all around him. It was faint, yet distinct. He closed his eyes and listened.

"Arriving...soon," was all he heard.

He shook his head as he pulled the earpiece from his chest pocket and stared at it, then placed it back in his ear and heard a voice. It was Achilles.

"...you should be arriving at your destination soon. Breeze, are you receiving this transmission? You have yet to acknowledge and the starting signal has already been given. By my calculations, you should have arrived at the mid-point of the course by now. Please respond."

Breeze gazed at the ship. It was so close. He looked upriver as he listened to the chatter over the wireless. Raza was asking Sally if she had spotted him yet. Ray chimed in that he was standing by waiting for his arrival.

He sighed heavily and his shoulders slumped. He tapped his earpiece. "Umm, yeah, received signal, inbound to target."

The chatter continued as they confirmed his transmission. He turned back one final time towards the ship. "Let me finish this and we're gone," he said aloud, then turned and broke into a run. He lifted off the ground and quickly accelerated into the sky. He looked to his right and saw the farm house as he flew by. *It could have been a good home, but it wasn't meant to be.*

He raced upriver as fast as he could. The trees tops on either side were a blur of colors from their autumn leaves.

Sally's voice came in over the wireless. "Breeze, I see you. You should really slow down. I don't know what Raza has planned for you."

"My plan is simple. Race toward Achilles, tag him, and fly right back to the ship."

"And just leave us?"

He heard Sally's voice plain as day, but it was not coming in through the wireless. "That's pretty much it because all of this pointless. Where are you coming from anyway? I can hear you, but it's not through the earpiece."

The air shimmered before him and the astral form of Sally appeared. She floated just ahead while keeping pace with him. "I'm right here Breeze. *I* won't leave you." Her arms were folded across her chest as she glared at him.

He refused to make eye contact with her. "I know what I want Sally, but I'm not going to find it here."

"What do you want, Breeze?" She drifted a little closer.

He was silent for a moment as he followed the winding river through the mountains.

"I want to belong. I want to be useful. I'm tired of hiding, I just want to live," he finally replied.

"Is running back home going to give you all of that? You always told me that your father was ashamed of your flying, that he always made you hide your powers."

"No, that's not what I said!" he shouted at her, then shook his head. "My father wasn't a bad guy. He was just never the same after my mother died."

"Do you think he was ashamed of you?"

He glared at her. "I don't know, but he was always hammering on me to do better. Pay attention in school, learn more about the foundry, stuff like that. I guess I felt like I could never measure up to anything that he wanted."

"Trees," Sally said.

"What? I'm trying to open up here Sally and you want to joke around—"

"Pay attention!" she shouted.

He had veered off the river and was heading straight toward a cluster of trees on a mountain side. He banked hard to the right as he struggled with the gravitational force from the sudden maneuver, then glided back over the river and resumed course when he saw Sally floating off to his side.

"Thanks," he grumbled.

"That's what teammates are for, we help each other out."

"I'll come back Sally, I promise."

"Will you?"

They flew in tandem for several minutes in silence, while following the river as it wound its way through the mountains. He looked over at Sally and saw the sadness in her face. He began to reach out to her, but then pulled his hand back.

A flash of light suddenly erupted before them. Breeze scanned the area to seek the source when Sally screamed.

"Boulders!" she cried out.

He turned to her. "What's the matter with you—"

"Watch out!" she yelled and reflexively dodged a gigantic rock while another passed through her and slammed into his shield, knocking him out of the sky and sent him spiraling toward the water below. He gritted his teeth and pulled up just as he almost impacted the shallow river where he could see the rocks beneath the surface glimmering in the sunlight.

He regained altitude and resumed course when Sally drifted into view.

"Some teamwork," he grumbled.

"Sorry," she said.

"Where did it come from? You're supposed to be my spotter!"

"Breeze, I said I was sorry. What more do you want?" She pursed her lips as she glided along with him.

"Look, Sally, I didn't mean it that way—"

"Again!" she cried out and pointed to the right side of the river.

Multiple boulders intermixed with trees came hurtling towards them. Breeze twisted and dodged while his shield absorbed the impacts, though each strike made him grimace and his sweat-streaked face grew pale.

Sally instinctively threw her arms up to protect herself as the hurtling objects passed through her, causing her astral form to crackle with static.

The assault ended as quickly as it began. Breeze scanned both sides of the river, but couldn't spot their assailant. He turned to Sally. "Are you ok?"

"Yes, I'm fine. Glad to see you're concerned."

"Come on Sally, give me a chance here."

She nodded. "I know. You're right." She drifted closer to him. "You know, I could almost feel every one of those boulders and trees pass through me."

"Impossible, you're projecting. Your body is on the mountain back at the starting point."

"I know. I shouldn't feel anything, but I do. It's like the further out I project...the more it feels like I want to materialize."

"That's crazy, you can't do that."

"Yeah, you're right," she replied meekly.

His eyes narrowed. "What's the furthest you've ever traveled from your body?"

She shook her head and thought about the night on the beach when Kera tested her. "I've gone pretty far before, but I do have my limits."

"Oh? What happens when you reach your limit?"

"I kind of fade away, and end up being pulled back into my body."

Breeze looked behind them. "Well, we've traveled pretty far and you're still with me."

"It's like if I don't want to be somewhere, I just return to my body by default. But if I really want to be someplace and stay, I can."

"So, you want to be here?"

"Yes," she said and looked into his eyes.

"Okay, so you can travel pretty far then, that's good."

She sighed.

"What, it's a good thing, right?"

"Sure, Breeze." She changed the subject. "We're almost in the zone where Achilles should be. Tag him and you can leave I suppose."

They continued flying side by side. With each passing moment, Sally's astral form became more defined and clearly visible. She reached out and touched Breeze on his shoulder. Startled, he turned to look at her as they flew past Ray standing along the river bank.

Achilles had instructed Ray that he was to provide protection for Breeze as soon as he was spotted. Because his teammate would be subjected to a heavy assault when nearing the robot's vicinity, his mission was to clear Breeze's path of any obstacle that might arise with his energy blasts.

Ray whittled away the time waiting for Breeze to arrive by skipping stones along the river's surface. He made it a point to throw each stone further out than the previous, then counting how many times it would skip before descending into the icy waters. He soon grew bored and began throwing branches and sticks into the river, zapping each one as they flew in the air before hitting the water when he stopped abruptly and looked around. The isolation began to overwhelm him and the sound of the rushing river was becoming monotonous, but it was broken by the rustling of leaves and branches when a sudden gust of wind blew through the forest.

He shivered and pulled his jacket closer to him when he heard a faint whisper.

"It shouldn't be this way," it said.

Startled, he looked around, then waved his hand and laughed. "Too weird, this place."

He leaned over and looked into the river. He could see his reflection in the shimmering water when a blurry reflection of a man stepped next to him.

He gasped and whirled around. There was no one there.

"Hello?" he called out, but received no response. He looked back at his reflection in the water and saw only himself. He slowly backed away.

"You know she belongs to you," the voice said.

He turned to confront it but saw no one. "What do you mean? Who are you?"

The response he received was a sudden gust of wind that rustled the trees and made them sway.

Ray took a few steps downriver, and then stopped. His eyes were glazed over.

"Must be tired," he mumbled as he sat down on the river bank.

"She is yours for the taking. She will be your queen. Never allow anyone to get between you and your bride," the voice spoke again in a smooth and comforting tone.

Ray stiffened. "Who are you?"

"No matter, call me what you wish, I mean you no harm. Think of me as a friend filled with good advice," the voice replied reassuringly.

Ray looked around wildly. "I thought I was rid of you. Sally said she pushed you out."

The voice chuckled. "My dear Raymond, do not be afraid, what she exorcised was merely an associate of mine whom I employed to find you. You are a god Raymond, and I make it a point to find young godlings such as yourself. I do apologize if my associate was a bit crude in how he managed you, for his task was to see if you were worthy of my attention, and you are. You must understand I require the use of such underlings, for I do not possess the strength to do so on my own, at least not yet."

Ray stood on the shoreline and watched the river flow by with a thousand mile stare. "I still don't understand how it got into me. When did it happen?"

"Think back, Raymond. At Perihelion, you were growing frustrated at the lack of star treatment that you so richly deserved, and that fool, Oslo, did not give you the respect that is yours by default. Inside, you were screaming for an answer as to why no one recognized the fact that you are a military prodigy by birthright. Luckily for you, your voice was heard and my associate came in on a storm to answer your pleas of anguish. You do remember the storm, don't you? The one you and your teammates experienced while you commanded the trimaran, and magnificently too, I would add? Remember the surge of power you felt during the storm? That is when my hound, my associate, found you and entered you. And there is another storm coming, Raymond."

Ray looked upriver. Walls of dark clouds were rolling in from the north.

"I've been searching for you for a long time, and I have much to tell you," the voice said.

Ray picked up a stone and tossed it into the river as his hands began to glow. "Okay, I'm listening."

"Good, it always pays to be receptive. Never be afraid to try new things, Raymond. That is always the sign of a good leader."

"I am a good leader. Father said so."

"Yes, I know, a very wise man. Now, here is what I suggest we do about Breeze, for he is heading our way as we speak."

Ray's eyes glistened when he saw a flicker of motion downriver and turned to look. Breeze and Sally were approaching and he was puzzled as to why Sally was visible at all.

As they flew by, he saw that they were locked in a passionate kiss.

His hands trembled and shook.

Breeze peered at Sally. "I can feel your hand on my shoulder. How can you do that when projecting?" he said and reached up to touch her hand. It felt warm to the touch.

"I don't know. This is new for me too," she replied and reached out with her other hand and touched his face. She smiled when she felt the smoothness of his skin.

He leaned in closer and she sighed while drawn in by the warmth of his body. She pressed her face against his and held him tight.

A flash of light erupted around them followed by a kinetic force that sent them both plummeting to the river before Breeze managed to level out and skim across the surface to the opposite bank. He cocooned Sally with his body as they slammed into the ground, his shield plowing a deep furrow before coming to a stop.

He slowly sat up with Sally in his arms. She was beginning to fade, and as he tried to touch her face his hand passed through it. He could see her lips moving, but heard nothing. Then she disappeared.

Another brilliant flash erupted from the other side of the river followed by the sound of crackling wood as a tree tilted over toward him. He rolled out of the way and sprang up to his feet as it crashed to the forest floor.

"Okay Raza, you want to make this tough, let's do it," he snarled, then vaulted into the air and streaked over the river.

He was halfway across when an explosion of light erupted from the shoreline. It was immediately followed by a wave of energy that crashed into him and repelled him back, sending him crashing through the forest and leveling several trees before he slammed into the ground. He lay still for what felt like an eternity, and then gasped for breath when he sat up as a stab of pain arced up his spine.

He fumbled for his earpiece but it was gone. His knees buckled slightly as he stood up and tried to steady himself. He gazed at the tangled mass of trees that he toppled and cleared a path that ran straight to the river. He lifted off and headed for the sky.

"Very good, Raymond. You have progressed far better than I thought," the voice said to him.

A crooked smile crept across Ray's face as his arms dangled at his sides while his hands smoldered.

"You are more than just a walking battery full of energy, ready to erupt at a moment's notice with deadly blasts of power. Oh, no, you are so much more. Now, listen to me, and learn how to control and shape each blast. Hit your opponent then steer him, like a hand pushing an object about."

Ray looked at his hands and turned them over. "I...understand. When I hit Breeze, I could almost feel myself gripping him."

"Yes. Energy is transmutable. Whatever your mind can conceive, you can make it a reality. You can shape current events. Drive Breeze away. Make this lonely place so inhospitable that it will encourage him to leave and it will clear your path of any obstacles between you and Sally."

His eyes widened. "Did I hurt her?"

"Nonsense, she is immaterial when she projects. I assure you she has returned to her body safe and sound."

"She was kissing him. I saw it," Ray growled.

"Even greater incentive to push him out of the way. Very out of the way. Let him travel over the Bad Lands in his misguided quest to return to his father. Let the savages and wild creatures of that forsaken land dispose of him. Don't let him take what is rightfully yours, for you have a dynasty to build with that girl and children she must bear for you. Prevent him from stopping you."

Ray stood rock still. His eyes were transfixed at the path of obliterated trees that Breeze had cut through on the opposite bank, when he opened his hands with palms facing down along his sides. They began to throb and glow as he slowly lifted off the ground.

"Yes, Raymond, you are a natural; you understand that you, too, can take to the skies. Now, my brave young warrior, confront your adversary and vanquish him, then claim what is rightfully yours."

Ray's eyes glowed with a pulsating white while arcs of energy crackled across his body as he floated upright across the river, picking up speed with each passing moment. Ahead of him, he watched as Breeze landed on the river bank.

Raza barreled down the forest trail in Achilles' hover truck while thick branches whipped the vehicle as it raced along. She tried to raise Sally on the wireless, but received only heavy static, and received similar results when trying to reach Breeze and Ray.

She came to stop at the end of the trail with the front bumper banging against a tree. She jumped out and ran down the path to the riverbank. As she drew closer, she could feel the electricity in the air, accompanied by a powerful hum. She yanked out the earpiece as it was overwhelmed with static, when she emerged from the forest and stumbled onto the shoreline.

She gasped as she watched Ray glide over the river in her direction with massive arcs of energy erupting around him, and the intense glare it created forced her to shield her eyes.

She waved at him to get his attention but to no avail, for he was oblivious as he continued on his trajectory.

She looked down river and saw Breeze standing on the shoreline. His shield was up as it reflected the intense, blue light that Ray radiated. Breeze began to slowly step back as Ray advanced upon him.

Raza squinted her eyes as she tried to find Sally's tell-tale shimmer anywhere near Breeze. Not seeing it, she reached for her earpiece.

"Achilles, can you hear me?" She heard only static as she looked upriver and saw dark clouds swollen with rain were rolling in from the north. She looked back at Ray and Breeze.

"Achilles, what do I do?" she shouted above the static.

Breeze had touched down on the west bank of the river just in time to see Ray talking to himself and nodding his head vigorously while standing along the opposite shore. His eyes widened as he watched Ray lift off the ground and glide over the river toward him. Breeze reached up to his earpiece to contact him, only to remember he had thrown it away earlier. He cupped his hands over his mouth and shouted.

"Ray, was that Raza who knocked me out of the sky? Tell her to ease up, it's only a training session!"

The only answer he received was seeing Ray's eyes glow into a searing white. His shield went up instinctively as he slowly backed up.

Ray began to crackle with blue arcs of energy while the river below boiled as hot steam began to rise and partially obscure him, prompting Breeze to lift off and drift downriver.

Ray's head swiveled as his eyes glowed fiercely and he changed course to follow him.

"Ray, is this part of the plan? Did Raza put you up to this?" Breeze shouted at him.

Ray didn't respond as the arcs of blue energy raced even faster across his body, and the sound of static became overwhelming.

Within his shield, all sound to Breeze was dampened, but he sensed the wave of energy emanating from Ray reverberating through it and he ascended to retreat.

Ray's head snapped up as he watched Breeze fly away. He lashed out with a massive arc of energy that erupted from his body, sending Breeze cartwheeling across the sky.

Breeze felt not only the impact but the heat of the arc coming through his shield. He recovered from his spin and dove straight toward the river, then leveled out and began his attack run by expanding his shield into the shape of a battering ram and aimed it at Ray.

Ray responded with a blistering array of lightning arcs that hit his shield, forcing it to buckle with each strike.

As Breeze drew closer, the more withering the strikes were against his shield and the assault became unbearable, forcing him to peel off and ascend back to the safety of the clouds.

He leveled off and drifted with the wind while his heart raced and sweat stung his eyes. He wiped his face and he gasped for breath. Meanwhile, Ray hovered up to engage him as the air beneath shimmered from the energy he radiated.

"Taking you head on doesn't seem to work, but what if...," Breeze muttered aloud as he scanned the river and noted the shallow spots from his vantage point. He ran his eyes along the surface until he spotted an area of darker water. Dark water was deep water, this much he knew. Ray was almost level with Breeze when he rocketed away, displacing the air violently and forcing Ray to lose altitude.

Breeze morphed his shield into a spear, then pierced the river and plunged into its depths. He touched down on the rocky bottom and looked up and through the distorted prism of water where he could see Ray descending over him.

He began to float up as the air inside his shield was making him buoyant. Through the murky water he saw two oversized rocks and glided toward them, then expanded his shield and wedged himself between which firmly anchored him in place.

The darkness of the river was abolished by blue arcs of lightning as Ray appeared and hovered above the surface. Breeze could only see a silhouette that framed his searing white eyes as the water began to boil and hot steam rose, when Ray began to fire beam after beam into the river. The arcs pierced the cold water, but quickly lost their energy as they feebly glanced off Breeze's shield.

Breeze smiled and took in a deep breath of satisfaction, and then gagged as the air inside his shield had turned stagnant. He realized he needed to get back to the surface and vent the toxic air so he could breathe.

As he mulled how he would get to the surface and dodge Ray, Ray was descending into the river. It boiled and hissed as it tried to envelope him. He increased the energy output and pushed the rushing waters away, keeping himself dry as he glided down to Breeze.

Breeze knew he had to act fast. He remembered how his shield filled with water when he laid at the bottom of the canyon after he was ambushed by the Elephim. Though he had to overcome the dreadful fear of drowning, he was able to breathe in the water, and eventually slipped into a coma. Achilles would later explain to him, during one of many training sessions on Raza's farm, how his shield was a life support system, and that it adapted to any environment he was in. The robot had drilled him several times how to filter the air and flush out water and debris that might get trapped within the shield in a combat situation. It also showed him how he could extract air from water, or rebreathe the air within the shield.

He withdrew his shield so it hugged his skin, and then decreased the thickness to allow the river to dribble through. He shivered and gritted his teeth as the water began to rise and within seconds reached his chin.

Concentrating as hard as he could, he pushed the water out as the shield acted like a filter, squeezing the hydrogen into the surrounding water, leaving only pure oxygen for him to breathe.

He looked up and saw Ray just above him. He bent his shield into a concave shape and bolted up, scooping Ray in the process. Together they hurled out of the river. As they hovered briefly in the air, Ray twisted his body to face Breeze and fired a bolt of energy at him.

Breeze immediately dropped the shield and pushed out the mass of pure oxygen he had built up from within, and then took a quick gasp of air and raised it again.

The energy bolt ignited the pure oxygen and the explosion was immense, sending the two flying apart as a thunderous shock wave rattled the surrounding mountains.

Breeze was hurled toward the forest along the river and toppled several trees before he arched his back and lunged toward the sky. As he rose above the forest canopy, he spotted Ray sprawled out on the opposite shore, his body and the ground beneath him smoldering.

Breeze raced over and circled around him, mindful of Ray's deadly beams. Eventually he descended and touched down a few feet away from him.

Ray grunted as he sat up. His skin was sizzling, his clothes were singed, and he reeked of burnt flesh. He placed a hand on his head as he stared hazily at Breeze. His lips were cracked and bleeding.

"What happened?" he asked.

Breeze recoiled in horror at the sight of him. "You tell me. Is this part of the training exercise? I thought this was supposed to be about teamwork...listen, are you okay?"

Ray shook his head. "I can't remember a thing, just an explosion."

"You don't remember anything you do Ray, especially when you screw up. The explosion was my doing. You had me pinned down at the river bottom and I was running out of air—"

Ray stared at him with glassy eyes as he interrupted Breeze. "Where is she?"

"Sally?" Breeze turned and pointed downriver. "I guess she's back at her projection point."

"She's mine. She belongs to me."

"What?" Breeze cocked his head as Ray slowly stood up.

"We...I won't let you get between us."

"Ray, are you about to lose it again?" Breeze clenched his fists.

"You kissed her," Ray said with a harsh whisper.

"What are you talking about?"

"I saw you," he growled.

"Ray, you're...wait a minute, what did you see?"

"The two of you flew past me. You were pulling her close to you—"

"—that's because she was beginning to materialize. It was pretty amazing. I didn't think she could do it but—"

"Desert rat! That's all you are. You think you can take a girl like that and make her your own? You don't stand a chance." Ray trembled and shook as his hands pulsated.

Breeze raised his shield. "Stop! I don't know what the hell is the matter with you, but this isn't my fight, and I'm not going to stick around anymore to deal with this crap. Whatever your problem is Ray, I don't really care —"

He was cut short as Ray lashed out with a violent blast of energy.

Breeze leaned forward and threw all of his strength into the shield, but was pushed back as his feet carved a trench in the sand. He peered through the searing light and could see that Ray's face was contorted in anger.

"You kissed her! I've known her longer than you ever will, yet she kissed you first, not me!" he howled with rage as he pummeled Breeze with withering blasts of energy.

Breeze looked down when he felt cold water on his feet as he was pushed into the river. He had poured all of his energy into the forward part of his shield, leaving the rest of his body exposed. "Ray! I give up! She's yours, take her. I'm done with this."

Ray responded with a howl, redoubling his assault.

Breeze flinched at the icy water against his thighs and groaned as his arms trembled from the tremendous strain of Ray's attack. He knew he needed to stop Ray before he could do any more harm, especially to Sally.

He cupped his hands and the shield corresponded to his actions by molding itself into the shape of a bowl. Ray's energy beams bounced off the interior of the bowl, and like a parabolic dish, the energy was re-directed to the center and then reflected right back onto him.

Ray screamed in pain as he was flung back and flew through the air and onto the rocky shoreline. He lay comatose as his skin sizzled from the burns.

Breeze collapsed to his knees and gasped for breath when he looked up at the mountains that surrounded them. They were enveloped in dark clouds with lighting crackling between them, followed by rumbles of thunder. Off in the distance, he saw something emerge from the clouds and trailing smoke.

His trance was broken by the sound of Achilles' hover as it crashed through the forest and out onto the shoreline. Raza jumped from the passenger side and ran to them. Achilles stepped out and scanned the area first before approaching them.

Raza knelt next to Ray. "What happened here, Breeze? What did you do?" she asked while cradling Ray in her arms then recoiled at the stench of burnt flesh.

Achilles stomped over and knelt down next to her. Servos whirred as it shook its head. "Raymond will need immediate medical attention. Let us endeavor to take him to the cellar of the farmhouse as expediently as possible."

Raza snarled at Breeze. "What did you do to him? Are you so eager to leave us you're willing to create a trail of destruction to make your point?"

"Raza, you don't get it. He was going nuts on me—"

"Save it. Raymond needs our help." She struggled to lift up Ray's limp body. "Not again," she said, "I lost one child, I won't lose another."

Achilles stepped in and touched her shoulder. She acquiesced as the robot lifted the teen and marched toward the hover and laid him down in the cargo bed.

Breeze was right behind them. "What can I do to help?"

"You've done enough," Raza said as she climbed back into the cab, "now march back to the ship and leave. Better yet, just fly away."

Achilles raised a hand to Raza. "Mistress, if I may?"

Raza looked away.

Achilles pointed at the bed of the hover. "Breeze, stay with Raymond and insure that no more harm comes to him as we make haste through the forest."

Breeze nodded and jumped in. Nausea swept over him when he saw Ray's burnt face and body. He put a hand over his mouth and nose and leaned over to the back window of the cab. "Achilles, what about Sally?"

"She is quite all right and has responded to Raza's request to return to the farmhouse. We will all rendezvous and assess the situation there."

Breeze rested his head against the cab and watched the trees whip past as they raced through the forest. The hum of the truck's motor made his mind wander and he thought of the day he stepped onto the center stage of the air show and all the strange events that unfolded since then. He then looked down at Ray. "I'm sorry about what happened, but you left me no choice. For what it's worth, I'm done and I won't get in your way."

Ray responded with a deep, rasping breath as his eyes fluttered briefly.

Breeze took off his jacket and placed it over Ray to give him warmth as the air grew colder, then he shook his head as he stared at his burnt face. "I didn't ask for any of this. I just want to go home."

The truck glided out of the forest and pulled up to the farmhouse. Breeze lowered the tailgate and jumped out as Achilles reached in and gently lifted Ray out.

The screen door flew open and Sally ran down the steps. "Ray! Oh, no, what happened?" She rushed up to Achilles and immediately put her hand to her mouth, turning away in horror. She looked at Breeze with fire in her eyes. "What did you do?"

Breeze waved his hands in disgust as he turned and headed for the path that led to the scout ship.

He walked briskly at first, then broke into a run as he lunged forward and flung himself into the sky. He soared above the treetops and rose higher until he saw the familiar shape of the scout ship off in the distance. He aimed for it as he sped over the forest when he was startled by the sound of an explosion.

He turned to the sound and saw a ship was descending toward the farmhouse trailing flame and smoke from its engines, whining and warbling in a staccato rhythm. It would fall silent and glide before the engines would kick on temporarily and belch out more fire and smoke, then fall silent again.

He banked to intercept the ship, his eyes widening as he approached it. The ship was similar to the scout ship in design, but smaller. Then he noticed the markings on the hull. It was from Perihelion.

He soared to the cockpit and his jaw dropped upon seeing Excort at the helm. The dwarf waved at him frantically and mouthed the word "engines", then drew a finger across his throat.

Breeze signaled with a thumbs-up that he understood, and then groaned when he saw the ship's trajectory was taking it straight toward the farmhouse. He turned back to Excort and mouthed the words "lower the landing gear" as he made hand motions to convey the action.

Excort didn't understand and shook his head.

Breeze snorted in frustration as he flew up to the cockpit and pressed his face against the glass. "Lower the damn landing gear!" he shouted.

Excort shrunk back, then reached over the helm and pulled back a lever where it was immediately followed by the whine of hydraulics. Breeze pushed off and glided below the ship to watch the landing gear lower and lock itself into place, then rose back up and gave Excort the thumbs-up sign.

The engines gave off one last eruption of smoke and flame before seizing up, and chunks of metal flew out of the exhaust and dropped into the forest canopy below.

Breeze watched the glowing hot metal disappear into the trees, then turned and saw the farmhouse was getting close. He made his move.

He flew to the front of the ship and maintained a pace just slightly ahead of it, and then thrust his arms forward while clenching his fists. The air shimmered and crackled as his shield expanded, enveloping himself and the ship. Breeze groaned as he tried to pull the ship up and level off.

"What's he doing? He's going to hit the house!" Raza was watching the events unfold with one hand shielding her eyes as the other held Sally close to her.

The girl was distraught as she looked back and forth between Ray's burnt face as Achilles cradled him in its arms, and the drama unfolding above.

"No mistress, your analysis is incorrect. Our aviator is trying to wrangle control of the wayward ship with his telekinesis, while throwing his shield around it to prevent harm to its occupants. Operating under the assumption there are any," Achilles added.

"Who is it?" Sally asked.

"It appears to have markings on its hull indicating that it hails from," the robot swiveled its head toward Raza, "Perihelion."

"Oslo, Nina," Raza whispered. She let go of Sally's hand and ran towards the falling ship.

"Mistress, caution!" Achilles called out.

Breeze grunted and gasped for breath as he tried to slow down the run-away ship, when he looked back and saw Excort through the cockpit glass.

The dwarf grabbed the helm and shook it. "No control," he mouthed the words.

Breeze waved an acknowledgment as he turned to monitor his forward progress. On the ground, he saw a woman waving her arms wildly. He soon realized it was Raza and she was running straight into the impact zone.

Breeze twisted so the right side of his body was parallel to the earth, then he extended his right hand and molded the shield into the shape of a plow. With his left hand, he pushed back on the ship with his teleki-nesis when the ship clipped a row of trees bordering the open field that lay before the farmhouse. Breeze gritted his teeth as the plow end of the shield plunged into the earth as dirt and debris erupted around them.

Breeze looked back just as the ship was about to hit him and he pushed back on it with all of his strength. He couldn't help but notice Raza's startled expression as they roared past her. She jumped off to the side as they plowed past her before coming to a stop before a large oak tree.

Breeze dropped his shield as the scout ship settled onto its landing gear with the belly of the craft just inches above him. He crawled out from underneath it, and then stood up in the trench created from the crash landing and leaned against one side of it to catch his breath.

"What is it with me and dirt holes?" he muttered.

The damaged ship gave off a hiss as pneumatic lines depressurized while hydraulic fluid dripped from the belly of the ship and oozed out of the landing gear. The heated metal skin of the ship sizzled as the swollen rain clouds began releasing their water.

Breeze scrambled out of the trench as the moistened earth was quickly turning to mud. He clawed his way out and surveyed the scene around him.

Lightning flashed followed by peals of rolling thunder. Amidst the cacophony, he heard hydraulics whining. The ships gangplank was lowering.

Silhouetted against the interior lights of the ship was the diminutive outline of Excort holding a frail figure in his arms.

Breeze headed toward them and came face to face with the dwarf as he descended the ramp. They locked eyes.

Excort was the first to speak. "They came out of nowhere, Breeze, there must have hundreds of them, maybe more. They went wild tearing apart Perihelion. The RF fought back as best as they could, but they were no match for them, they're not programmed to fight anymore." The flashes of lightning highlighted the dwarf's face; his eyes were bloodshot and swollen.

The rain poured down on them and the girl in Excort's arms. Breeze leaned in to get a better look at her. He gasped when the lightning flashed again. It was Nina.

Excort looked down at her. "They kept saying they were looking for the girl, but you know how the Elephim speak, they do it through the static they create, but we got the message. Oslo and I hid with Nina in the hangars, but they burst through the doors like they were made of paper. The RF that were with us tried to fight them off with whatever tools they had, but it was hopeless. You know, there was a time when they were once the most feared machines of all. How times have changed."

Lightning touched down dangerously close to them, followed by the boom of thunder.

"Excort, let's get to the house. It's getting really bad out here."

The dwarf was oblivious to what Breeze had said and continued rambling. "He handed her to me, said to escape the island and get to Appalachia as quickly as I could. He said not to worry about Mila, that he would see to it that she would be protected. Without another word, he charged the Elephim with what was left of the RF. Together they held them off while I escaped with Nina in the transport." He looked down at her comatose face. The girl's head was tilted back and her mouth was slightly open.

Breeze heard splashing footsteps approaching. He turned and saw Raza running towards them. Achilles, carrying Ray, and Sally were close behind.

"What's happening here?" Raza demanded, and then threw her hands to her face. She went pale as tears streamed down her already rain-soaked face. "Nina," she said and took a step back and wept, then screamed above the raucous thunder as the lightning crashed and lit up her weary face. "Nina!" she shrieked as she lunged and snatched the girl from Excort, then turned and ran to the farmhouse.

Breeze ran over to Achilles and took Ray from its arms.

"Master Corinth, whatever has possessed you?" Achilles said as it watched Breeze hoist Ray over his shoulder with a grunt, then stumble and slide across the muddy ground to the farmhouse.

"Breeze, what's happening? Where are you going?" Sally cried out.

"Just follow me!" he shouted as he splashed through the mud-soaked field toward the farmhouse. Through flashes of lighting, he could see Raza in the distance with Nina in her arms. She ran to the side of the house and flung open the cellar doors.

Green light erupted from the depths of the cellar, bathing the woman and child in its glow as they quickly disappeared below.

CHAPTER
▼
TWENTY-FIVE

BREEZE CURSED AS HE stumbled across the saturated ground. Flashes of lightning lit his path as he shifted the burdensome weight of Ray draped over his shoulder when he saw the green light from the cellar ahead in the looming darkness.

He arrived at the entrance and peered down the stone steps that led below, and heard the sound of heavy footsteps splashing in water, along with the sucking sound of mud. He swiveled to look, and between flashes of lightning, he could see Achilles and Sally trudging across the field and heading toward the farmhouse.

Ray groaned, snapping Breeze into action. With a deep breath, he descended the steps. The deeper he went, the greater was the glow of the soothing, green luminescence that emanated from below. The heavy scent of salt water filled the air.

He reached the bottom of the steps and spilled into the chamber that housed the pool, arriving just as Raza was stepping into it with Nina cradled in her arms. Tears streamed from her eyes as mother and daughter fully immersed themselves into the blue and green waters.

Ray groaned again, and Breeze ran to follow Raza into the pool where he felt energy course through his body the moment he stepped in. He stumbled down the slime-coated stone steps, causing Ray to slip off his shoulder and sink like a stone. Breeze lunged to grab him, but missed and had to watch helplessly as Ray disappeared into the depths below. He plunged his head into the water and tried to work up the courage to dive after Ray, but could not find the will to do so. He felt so tranquil wallowing in the warm and soothing waters, that it relieved him of any sense of urgency. When it slowly dawned upon him he hadn't drawn a breath in a while, he lifted his head to take a breath, then closed his eyes for a moment and fell into a trance where he found himself standing outside the foundry. He could see the sparks from the hot molten steel as it poured into the molds, accompanied by the whine of machinery when his father appeared and pointed at the ground.

"As above, below," Jacob said but when Breeze reached out to touch him, he faded away.

His eyes fluttered open and he became mesmerized by the quartz that was embedded in the ceiling of the cavern and glistening with the reflection of the glowing water, when he was startled by the sound of a woman sobbing. He turned and saw Raza sitting on the steps of the pool, cradling Nina in her arms.

"There, there, baby girl," she kept repeating while rocking back and forth. Her eyes were shut tightly as she drew Nina close to her bosom.

Nina stirred and her eyes fluttered open. "Mother?"

Raza stopped to look into her daughter's eyes. "Yes!" she almost shouted and hugged Nina tightly.

Breeze swam over to sit on the steps next to them. The reunion of mother and daughter drew him like a moth to flame as he watched the pure emotion of a woman who had not held her child in her arms for quite some time, and it overwhelmed him.

He couldn't remember if he ever felt any real emotion. His father had always instructed him to contain his thoughts and feelings as he was never to reveal anything to anyone, not even his gifts. It was for his own safety he would say, but watching Raza reconnect with her daughter made him discover a part of himself that he never knew, that he could feel and care for someone other than himself.

Raza reached over to touch his face and he flinched.

"Forgive me, Breeze, for telling you to go away. I swear to you on my life that will never happen again," she said and smiled with sweetness that captured and held his gaze when Nina sat up.

"Hi," she whispered and waved at him feebly.

Breeze chuckled. "Hi yourself."

Raze stroked Nina's hair and gently pulled it back to better see her face. "I gather you two have met," she said to her daughter.

Nina smiled. "Yes, I've seen him wandering the halls of Perihelion."

They all laughed.

The sound of heavy footsteps drowned out their laughter as Sally and Achilles burst into the chamber.

"Why is everyone laughing?" Sally asked.

Raza wiped water from her face. "Just realizing the simple joys of life. Come over Sally, let me see you."

Sally climbed down the steps and into the water. She nodded at Nina who was sitting between her mother's legs.

"Hi Sally," the young girl said.

Sally smiled and reached out to hold her hand. "Nina, I'm really happy to see you."

"Mistress, pardon my intrusion, but I would like to inquire of the whereabouts of Master Verhesen," Achilles said as its head swiveled back and forth scanning the surface of the pool.

The women gasped and stood up, and then Raza turned to Breeze. "Son, you had him last."

"Yeah, he slid out of my arms and went straight to the bottom. I kind of got overwhelmed by the healing powers of the pool and I just... forget about him."

Nina giggled. "He's fine, I can sense him arriving. He seems to have shed a burden and is himself now."

Raza cradled her daughter's face. "How do you know this, my love?"

"Mother, water is my home and I can sense everything through it. It is how I have been able to speak to you in your dreams for all these years. It is a truth-teller for me."

Ray broke the surface and coughed, then treaded water for a moment until he noticed everyone gathered on the steps. He swam over and climbed up.

Sally held out her arms and embraced him. "Raymond," she whispered softly. She touched his face, and then ran her hand down his chest. "The burns are gone."

He said nothing as he wrapped his arms around her and buried his face in her hair. They stood still for a moment until Sally gently pushed him back.

"Was that you back on the river, or was there someone inside making you do things against your will?" she asked him with a slight hint of fear on her face.

Ray nodded. "I admit the truth to all of you. I haven't been myself since we left Perihelion."

"You don't say," Breeze quipped.

Ray shot an angry look at him, then relaxed. "Okay, I deserved that one," he said, then turned to address everyone. "During the training session, as I waited for Breeze to arrive, someone, something, paid me a visit." Ray then described to them his encounter with the entity but edited the story so as to not reveal his desire and intentions for Sally.

Raza stepped over to him. "But I thought Sally pushed it out and freed you of its influence?" she said in a hushed but urgent tone.

Ray shook his head. "No, this one seemed to be its master. Funny though how it felt like it was my friend."

"They will tell you anything you want to hear to gain your trust. That's how the Elephim operate," Excort said as he entered the chamber.

Raza cried out as she rushed over and knelt down to hug the dwarf. Excort merely patted her back with a stoic expression.

"My little widget, so good to see you," Raza gushed, "forgive me for tearing Nina out of your arms and not even acknowledging you."

Excort touched her face. "You don't have to explain yourself for I know the power of family bonds. They are a powerful force that no one can sever."

Raza smiled as she stood up and placed a hand on his shoulder. "Little widget, we have so much catching up to do."

Excort took her hand and squeezed it. "We must first deal with the matter at hand."

"Yes, of course," Raza replied.

Excort pointed at Achilles. "First, answer this question: what's with the robot? I didn't expect you to have any around as you never cared for them in the past."

Raza nodded at Achilles. "This is no ordinary robot. Excort, I would like you to meet Achilles. Achilles was to be scrapped after the AI purge but Oslo took a shine to it and prevented it from being disassembled. We knew it at Perihelion as RF 5150, but Fifty-One was the nickname Oslo gave it, do you remember?"

Excort's eyes widened as Achilles stepped over and held out a hand. "Master Excort, it brings this humble unit extraordinary delight to make your acquaintance once again."

Excort ignored the robot's hand. "Achilles? Interesting, a mythical figure who possessed a weakness that was...fatal. Whatever happened to you? The last I remember, you disappeared after a training session with Bram."

Achilles' eyes glowed. "It is a rather long and tedious story, perhaps now is not the time."

Excort grunted, and then turned to Raza. "Are you comfortable with it?"

Raza laughed. "Achilles is the best. Such a great helper and friend."

She smiled at the robot. "It has brought back memories of a better time when we thought we were going to make a difference. There was so much hope back then." She finished speaking just as Nina wrapped her arms around her waist and rested her head against her mother's chest.

Raza kissed her forehead. "Now with all of us together, I can believe again."

Achilles stared at Nina. "Mistress, this is your offspring?"

Raza smiled. "Oh, Achilles, polite and logical to a fault. Yes, this is my child." She then addressed Nina. "Sweetie, Achilles is an old friend of mommy and daddy's from before you were born."

Achilles dropped to one knee. Servos whirred as it held out a hand to Nina.

She kissed it. "A brave knight that will storm the castle."

Achilles' eyes widened as its head swiveled up to Raza. "Mistress, I am unable to process what your daughter has stated."

Raza shook her head and laughed. "Oh, Achilles, Nina is very special. She's just saying that she likes you."

Nina touched its face. "Help him. He will need your guidance."

"If this is a cryptic reference to your father; yes, my young mistress, this humble robot is your servant and will endeavor to do so."

"Silly machine man, you are no servant and I wasn't talking about my father." She turned her head and looked at Breeze.

Ray cleared his throat. "I think we're all pretty tired and wet. Can we go back to the house?"

Raza nodded. "Go shower and get a fresh change of clothes, then rest. We will all meet later this evening in the barn. We have to discuss about our future plans in light of recent events." She then took Nina by the hand and marched up the steps as others followed.

The storm had long passed as the evening brought with it a chill to the air. Sally, Breeze and Ray stepped out of the farmhouse and made their way to the barn. No words were exchanged among them as they walked in silence.

Sally was the first to break the ice. "Thank you for not leaving," she said to Breeze.

"Nice of you to say that, but I'm still not sure what I'm doing here. It's not that hard for me to just take off and leave."

She grabbed his hand and squeezed it tightly. "If you really wanted to leave, you would have been gone by now. And I'm sorry about how I reacted to you after seeing Ray's burns. I know that it wasn't your fault." She then grabbed Ray's hand and brought everyone to a halt. "I just want us all to be friends. Can you two promise me that?"

Ray placed a hand on Breeze's shoulder. "I've been an ass to you since the day we met. For what it's worth, I'm sorry."

Breeze looked the other way. "Yeah, it's okay. We're even."

"Breeze," Sally pleaded.

He looked at her and his scowl melted into a smile, and then he turned to Ray and held out a hand. "Ray, my father always said problems are like metal; no matter how hard it appears, you can always melt it down," he said, then laughed. "Okay, that's another one of my dad's lame foundry expressions."

"I would like to meet your father. He seems like a good man," Ray said as he shook his hand.

Breeze nodded. "Yeah, he is. I guess you have to be separated from someone for a while to appreciate them."

"I hope we can find our parents again," Sally said.

Breeze sighed. "Sally, it's too dangerous out there to go searching for anybody. But I promise that I will make it a point to help the two of you reconnect with your families, just let me just go home and reconnect with what little family I have left."

"Of course." She looked away and sniffled.

"Come on guys, we're teammates. Let's go to this meeting with Raza and get it over with. In the morning I'll decide if I should stay or go. But no matter what, I will come back for all of you."

"Okay." Sally shrugged as she turned to Ray.

"Sounds good buddy, whatever you want to do." Ray then jerked a thumb toward the barn. "Let's get this over with."

They entered the barn where Achilles and Excort were making adjustments to the comm equipment and Raza and Nina sat close together while speaking in hushed tones.

Raza stood up upon seeing them arrive. "Come all of you. There is much to discuss."

"What are they up to?" Breeze asked and pointed at the dwarf and the robot.

"They are adjusting the comms so we can contact Oslo. Please do sit down."

They each took a seat as Excort and Achilles stood back from the equipment and surveyed their work. The dwarf then leaned forward and began spinning and flipping a sequence of dials and switches when the machine hummed to life and began to whine loudly while the lights throughout the barn flickered haphazardly.

They immediately pulled off paneling from the sides of the comm unit and examined the multitude of circuit boards and wiring as they searched for the problem when Achilles called out to Raza. "Mistress, my analysis shows no known reason for this disruption."

Excort nodded. "Will have to agree with the robot. I can't pinpoint what's behind the power surge."

Breeze stood up to help when Sally grabbed his hand. "Wait-," she began to say when a loud bang was heard throughout the barn, followed by a blackout.

Nina cried out. "Mother?"

"It's okay, child, I'm here," Raza assured her. "Achilles? Excort? A little light?" she called out.

Achilles' eyes glowed in the darkness. "This is all of the light I am capable of providing for the time being, but I will labor alongside Excort to remedy the situation immediately." It turned to Ray. "Master Verhesen, your abilities would be appreciated at this juncture."

Ray lifted a glowing hand and lit up the room when Sally cried out, "look!"

Above them, black clouds swirled and began to coalesce when a figure emerged from it.

Breeze stood in his tracks while Sally clung to him as the figure looked slowly about the room. Its featureless face began to morph and the faint outline of a nose and mouth appeared. It floated toward Achilles and came to a stop a few inches shy of it. It reached out as if it wanted to touch the light coming from the robots' eyes, then withdrew its hand and held it up, turning it back and forth and studying it before shifting its attention to Breeze.

Sally gripped Breeze tightly as it glided towards them. The air behind it crackled and a sphere of energy appeared.

The dark figure stopped its advance and turned to watch the sphere expand as a man materialized within it. His eyes were a pure white and when he opened his mouth, shafts of light spilled out with every word he spoke.

He pointed at the dark figure. "You have performed well, hound. Now heel."

The dark figure rushed to him and crouched at his feet.

"Good hounds are difficult to come by. Most of them fail me consistently by never obtaining whatever quarry I wish to pursue. This one has performed quite adequately, though." He patted the head of the dark figure.

"What are you?" Raza challenged him as Nina cowered by her side.

The man tilted his head as he hovered. "Such a familiar voice, and one that I have not heard for such an expanse of time." He shut his eyes briefly, then opened them. "Who I am is not important, but if a name is important to you, you may address me as Lacifel. It is what I possess that is of much interest to you," he said.

Achilles stepped next to Raza and pointed at him. "We are unable to pinpoint the source of your broadcast, nevertheless, identify yourself immediately."

Lacifel's jaw dropped. "My goodness, what do we have here, but a Robot Fighter? The true genuine article? Allow me a closer look, for I have not seen one in ages." He lunged toward Achilles. The robot made a motion with its hands which flung him back.

"Telekinesis? Impossible!" Lacifel bellowed. "Or are you using a shield I cannot detect? Regardless, you are not an ordinary machine. What are you exactly?"

The hound tugged at his hand and motioned toward Breeze.

Lacifel nodded. "Yes, hound, you shall have your prize soon enough. Patience."

Breeze pushed Sally away. He walked quickly to stand in front of Achilles and Raza. "I'm done here. I'm not scared by any of this. What the hell do you want?"

Lacifel stared at Breeze for a moment. When he spoke, streaks of light peppered the air around him. "There is always a bold one in the pack and it is usually the one who has nothing to lose, because everything he cares for has been stripped away," he said.

"What are you talking about?" Breeze hovered up and brought himself to eye level with him.

"Find out soon enough, you will." Lacifel scanned the room. "What I see before me is a pathetic attempt to mount a rebellion where there is no cause, as Oslo's futile attempt to shelter paranormal children will amount to a massacre, one that will stain his soul for an eternity." He laughed. "If he could just let go of the past there would have been no reason for so much death and destruction." He waved casually toward Sally.

She put her hands to her face as Ray stepped in front of her. "You leave her alone!"

"You," Lacifel roared, "dare to speak? For someone who fancies himself a pillar of strength, you are truly the weakest of the lot." He held his hands in the air with his palms down as he wiggled his fingers. "Like a puppet on a string, could we not agree?"

Ray seethed as his hands pulsated with energy.

"Stand down, Raymond. A blast of energy from you would only put a hole through this rat trap of a barn," Lacifel said as he loomed over Raza, "owned by a country mouse that lives in a quaint little farmhouse."

Achilles swatted at him and missed.

"Defend her, tin man, but you will regret it. Assuming you feel anything."

"What do you want you monstrosity," Raza said as she held Nina close to her.

"I wish to end this charade. I have Oslo. He is my prisoner. You will come and surrender to me so you may see your pathetic husband one last time before I eliminate him."

"You lie, he is safe and on his way here."

"Oh, how you wish for that to be true. Ask the troll then," Lacifel replied and pointed at Excort.

The dwarf shook his head. "Forgive me Raza, I can't tell you whether or not he speaks the truth. I left Oslo in the middle of the battle while he and the RF were up against impossible odds, and we still can't raise him on the comm unit...," he trailed off as he looked at her with sheepish eyes.

Raza whirled back to Lacifel. "Whoever you are, whatever you are, if what you claim is true you better listen to me. You release my husband safely or else—"

"Or else what, witch!" he thundered while the hound cowered and covered its face. "You have no leverage here; let me assure you of this. I have Oslo and I hold the reins of power here and all of you will surrender yourselves to me!"

"What proof can you provide to validate your claim that Oslo is in your custody?" Achilles said.

"Ah, the robot who doesn't behave like one wishes to be logical. I will not provide you with anything; instead, you will do as you're told. Understand that I can find others who can be persuaded to adhere to my demands." He turned to Breeze and Sally.

Sally cowered and hid behind Breeze.

"Yes, the two of you could easily be swayed to do my bidding," Lacifel mused as he glided toward them. "Perhaps you are the rational ones here, unlike the adults. If either one of you wish to know the fates of your families, then come and surrender yourselves to me."

Sally gripped Breeze's shoulder as she stepped out from behind him. "What do you know? Why won't you just tell us?"

He tilted his head. "My child, you must learn a thing or two about negotiating. Here, allow me to sweeten my offer; if you come to me, I promise to release your family unharmed, and you will take their place and serve me." He leaned closer to Breeze. "I extend this offer to you as well."

Raza cried out. "No Breeze, don't listen to him! He's bluffing."

Breeze stepped up, prompting Lacifel to laugh. "Ah, I see I have your attention now."

"What do you know about my father? What have you done to him?"

Lacifel leaned his head back and sniffed the air. "I can smell victory, so close," he crowed, then returned his attention to Breeze. "I will give you the instructions needed to find me. Upon our meeting I will determine whether or not to release that information to you. Consider this young man; what more do you have to lose? I can assure you that you have nothing to go back home to. Oh, yes, you will doubt me, of that I am certain. You will rush across the Bad Lands and risk your life to verify my claim. From there, your anger will build at the injustices of life and you will seek me out for revenge. This is the story of humanity, for what has happened before will happen again." He then leaned forward and whispered. "I can even tell you about what really happened to your mother."

Breeze trembled and shook as his eyes narrowed to slits. "I was about to walk away from them. I wasn't going to stay to help, but now," he clenched his fists, "you've just given me a reason to do something right for once in my life." He jabbed a finger into Lacifel's face. "Destroying you is the only thing I care about now."

Lacifel threw back his head and roared with laughter. "That's the fighting spirit I was looking for! Oh, how delicious it will be when I suck the life right out of you boy, for it will be a classic fight to the death.

There is nothing better than a desperate opponent, as it only makes victory taste so much sweeter." Then he whooshed over and stuck his face into Ray's. "And I thought you were the weak link in this pathetic group." He then pulled back and pointed at Breeze. "Now, go back to your dusty, desert home. Go and bear witness to the ruins of your sad life and when you have become sufficiently enraged, you will come to me."

"How will I know how to find you?"

"I am hiding in plain sight, high above you as I have been watching and observing this world. The map you will need to find me lies close to you and it will lead you straight to me. Now go and complete your journey, then come and surrender yourself at my feet." In an instant, Lacifel and the hound disappeared.

Sally cried as Breeze hugged her tightly. "No Sally, no more tears, it ends now." He turned to the rest of them. "Everything ends now."

Raza walked over and stood next to him. "What are you saying?"

"Exactly what I mean, I'm not putting up with this anymore. We have been taken from our homes and sent to some disaster of a school that is falling apart. We were supposed to be trained to better handle our powers by instructors who can't even keep us safe. Then we come to find out our homes and lives were being destroyed in the process. We run away to hide here in Appalachia, only to be harassed and assaulted again and again. I'm done. My whole life," he squeezed Sally's hand, "*our lives*, have been turned upside down. Where do we go from here? What do we do? Well I'm telling you what *I'm* going to do. I will track down this man, and I will get to the end of this."

Achilles' eyes glowed. *And he will lead them out of the quagmire...*

The robot shook its head.

Raza cradled Breeze's face. "Son, I said some harsh things to you and I treated you terribly upon our first meeting. I made you see things that you shouldn't have. You don't have to do this."

Breeze took her hands and gently lowered them. "Raza, I don't care about that anymore. I know what has to be done. Your fight has become my fight and I won't live like a rat hiding in the dark forever."

"Brave boy," she whispered.

"Breeze, how will you determine his location?" Achilles asked.

"He said the map I will need is close by." As soon as he said it, he felt something pulsating against his chest. He reached into his jacket and pulled out the disk where a pinpoint of light immediately appeared on the screen, then rose up and hovered above his head, startling everyone with its brilliance as images began to pour from it. The images consisted of the sun and the moon against a backdrop of stars while below were massive jet black cylinders in orbit above the Earth. One cylinder in particular had a glowing line drawn from it to an island in the ocean.

Achilles cocked its head. "Based upon the land masses as they appear, the inclination of the earth to the moon, the location is—"

"Perihelion. The line leads straight to Perihelion," Excort cut in.

"I was just about to inform our comrades of this," Achilles said.

Excort waved him away. "You take too long," he retorted, then turned to look at Breeze. "There is something very wrong here. This map points to the island. Does he think we're still there?"

Breeze shook his head. "However he found us, he said something to Raza about being a country mouse. Raza, do you know this guy?"

Raza sighed. "Oslo, Bram, and I trained so many younglings in our time. It could be anyone. I can't imagine any of our students who would seek our destruction, and almost everyone we know died so long ago, as few knew the secrets to longevity that allowed us to live for so long. I just can't say."

"Look, whoever he is, he has some clue as to where we are, and who we are." Breeze pointed at Ray. "Ray obviously had a hitchhiker until it was flushed out. Who knows what it reported back to Lacifel."

Excort wagged a finger at Breeze. "Yes, but why no direct attacks? If he wants us, why not just scoop us up right now? The fog is the reason why. The electromagnetic shielding surrounding Perihelion and Appalachia is confusing him and making it difficult to pinpoint our exact location."

"Not so sure about the fog anymore, after all, how were you ambushed at Perihelion? And what I don't get is how does he expect us to get into orbit? Can we go back to Perihelion and use the ships I saw in the hangar? Do they have space flight capability?" Breeze wondered.

The dwarf shook his head. "I'm sorry to say most of those ships have long ago been stripped down to the point where we only use them for atmospheric flying. I know when Oslo reopened Perihelion he did have the RF rebuild some of the ships for space flight, but I don't think they got very far and we just don't have the parts we need."

"The scout ship can't reach orbit," Breeze mused, "and I know back home we don't have anything that can fly into space." He began pacing the room. "No, it doesn't matter. I have to go back home first, I need to know if my father is alive because if he is, he can help us."

"Breeze, it's probably a trap. Lacifel was being pretty cryptic about your father and besides, it's too dangerous to cross the Bad Lands just to call his bluff," Ray said.

"Ray, you still don't get it, I'm not staying here to hide. I'll do what I want." He turned to address the rest of the group. "I'm flying out in the scout ship first thing in the morning. Those of you who want to come, meet me by the river at sunrise. I'm heading home to see if that monster is right. And if it is...well, I'll figure out-, no, WE will find a way to get up to that cylinder and confront him."

"Breeze, he will say anything to get you to go to him. Any of us, for that matter. Are you sure you want to do this?" Raza asked.

"I have nothing to lose. There wasn't much for me back home, turns out there was even less for me here or at Perihelion. I've seen enough. I can't pretend the world is the same since I left home."

"Are you sure there was nothing you found that you care for?" Sally said.

Breeze shrugged. "Sally, is there something to be found?" he replied, then glanced over at Ray before stepping over to the robot. "Achilles, you are under no obligation to come with me, but I would appreciate it if you would. I trust you. I don't know why I do but I get the sense you want to make things right."

Achilles bowed its head. "Master Corinth, if you blaze a path, this humble collection of circuits and servos will not only follow, but protect you along the way."

Breeze chuckled as he put a hand on its shoulder. "Good man, I mean, robot."

He turned to Ray and Sally. "I know we haven't been much of a team, at least not in the way Oslo envisioned us. Heck, we can't even get through a training session without us fussing and fighting over everything. But now I realize I wouldn't want to be with anyone else and it would be great if you guys would come."

Ray stepped forward. "I've got a lot to prove. I treated you like you were second class since the day we met. I'm with you Breeze. Let's leave and find out what the world is really like out there."

They turned to Sally. "I can't do this without you," Breeze said and held out a hand to her.

Sally gladly took it. "Wouldn't miss it for the world. And no, I won't start crying."

They all laughed. "Well, we're already making progress," Breeze said, then turned to face the others. "Raza, Excort, you don't have to come if you don't want to."

Raza put her hands to her face and moaned. "Breeze, I don't know what to do. I'm finally reunited with my daughter, and now I found out that my husband has been kidnapped. To leave Appalachia to go on a rescue mission would be..." she trailed off with a look of despair on her face.

Breeze hugged her. "Raza, you're like a mother to me, and Nina," he turned and patted her head, "is like a little sister to me."

Nina's smile faded into a frown.

"I know this is tough for you, so I insist you stay here. Besides, Nina needs you," Breeze said to Raza.

She hugged him tightly. "It's not that I don't love my husband. I do. It's just that after all we've been through, for me to leave and risk losing my daughter again would be too much."

"Yeah, I get it, you're pretty sore at him. Kind of like what I feel for my dad. But I guess we all need to learn the power of forgiveness. Even with all the powers we have, it seems to be the one we lack."

Nina spoke up. "Mother, what about father? Will we see him again?"

Raza pulled away from Breeze and held her. "Breeze is a brave warrior. He will go and bring him back so we can be a family."

Breeze felt his throat tighten and he quickly looked away. "Excort, I'm going to ask you to stay here and watch over the girls. Not that Raza needs looking after, she did pretty good on her own for a while, but you know what I mean."

Raza touched Breeze's arm. "Living alone and descending into madness is not the best measure of doing well. I want all of the company and help I can get."

Excort shrugged and jerked a thumb toward Achilles. "The robot seems to be pretty familiar with the ship's systems. It can make any repairs that you might need along the way."

"Oh, Achilles helped me rebuild the scout ship," Breeze said.

"Of course it did. It seems to be capable of a lot of things." He cast a wary eye at it. "I'll stay up through the night running preflight checks on it for you while everyone gets some sleep."

"If I may Excort, I would like to volunteer my assistance," Achilles offered.

The dwarf shrugged. "Suit yourself. I could use a little extra help."

Breeze turned to Sally and Ray. "Well, it's settled then, we go first thing in the morning. One last warning; I traveled across the Bad Lands to get to Perihelion and it can either get pretty hairy at times, or nothing happens at all. I just want you guys to know that."

"We're a team Breeze, we'll manage," Ray said.

Breeze held out his hand. Ray shook it.

Sally beamed at them and clapped her hands. "We need a name for the team. How about Sun Chasers?"

"No!" the guys yelled in unison, then laughed as Sally pouted.

CHAPTER
▼
TWENTY-SIX

THE SUN ROSE THE following morning with its light caressing the trees tops of the surrounding mountains and hills of the valley below.

Nestled along the river valley, Raza's farmhouse was a beehive of activity as the scout ship was being prepped for its departure west.

Achilles and Excort had spent the entire night finishing repairs on the scout ship and when they finished, they went to the barn to make further adjustments to the comm equipment so Excort and Raza could at least try to stay in touch with the team. They all agreed that the scout ship would return to Mount Pleasant after the rescue, assuming Breeze's father was alive and had the parts they needed to restore the ship's space flight capabilities. The plan was to first drop out of orbit over the Pacific Northwest after they rescued Oslo where they would disappear into the vast forests and mountains of that region in case they were followed. Achilles would then signal Excort once they determined they were not being tracked and begin the trek back to Appalachia.

"And what is the plan should you fail to get the parts from Breeze's father so the ship can reach orbit?" Excort asked.

Achilles raised a hand. "I do believe the human expression is to say we will cross that bridge when we get there."

Excort grunted, and then continued working.

When morning arrived Achilles was back in the cockpit of the scout ship calibrating the avionics while Excort was in the engine room cursing loudly at the multitude of last minute minor repairs that had to be made.

Breeze and Ray were in the cargo hold loading boxes of supplies they had procured from Raza. They worked quietly and quickly, stacking boxes into every nook and cranny they could find.

Inside the farmhouse, the women were packing clothes and stuffing them into cargo bags. They spoke softly amongst themselves as they placed the bags by the door.

Later, they all sat down for a big breakfast Raza had prepared. The boys ate like ravenous wolves while the girls pecked at their food. Nina would occasionally look up from her plate to steal quick glances at Breeze while Sally toyed with her food and kept an eye Nina. Breeze and Ray were oblivious to the events between the girls as they cleaned off their plates and finished their coffee.

Later, they all gathered on the porch, except for Nina, who remained in the house, while Achilles and Excort grabbed the cargo bags and hauled them over to the scout ship. They had gone for a test flight earlier and had landed the ship in front of the farmhouse.

Ray was the first to say goodbye to Raza. "Ma'am, just wanted to say thank you for all of your help. I promise I will repay your generosity by returning with your husband."

Raza laughed as she threw her arms and hugged him tightly. "Oh, my dear Raymond. My military man. You do so remind of Oslo." She took his hands into hers. "Listen to me young one; you are the captain of your soul. Never forget that. When the anger arises, don't push it down. Channel it. Use it constructively. You have so much to offer Raymond."

Ray nodded as he stole a quick glance at Sally. She looked away.

"And don't call me ma'am ever again." She patted his face. "It's Raza, or Mom, if you wish. You and Breeze are like sons to me now." She smiled sweetly as tears welled up in her eyes. "Now go, my brave one. You are doing far more for me than I could ever repay." She pulled him down by the shoulders and kissed his forehead. "Go," she whispered.

Raza watched him walk away and took in a deep breath as he strode up the gang plank and disappeared into the ship.

She then turned to face Sally and pulled her close to embrace her. "This had been the greatest moment in my life in such a long time. I used to be alone with no children, but now I would like to think that I have four, and two of them are the best daughters any mother could ask for."

Sally smiled through her tears. She hugged Raza tightly, then broke away without a word and marched quickly to the scout ship.

Raza and Breeze were alone. They leaned against the porch railing and gazed at the ship for a time without a word between them.

Breeze was the first to break the silence. "You know Raza, when we first met you were nothing but a crazy old lady."

Raza burst into laughter as tears streamed from her eyes. She nodded as she pulled up her apron to wipe her face. "Yes, my dear boy," she sniffled, "yes, I know. I never would have believed that three vagabond teenagers would pull me out of the darkness that had descended over my life." She placed her hands on his shoulders. "Breeze, you are different. But you know that already."

Breeze shrugged as he tried to avoid eye contact.

She gently touched his cheek and nudged it so they faced one another. "Don't turn away from me and don't shy away from what you know to be true. Search your heart, son. You can only deny destiny for so long by twisting your fate. But you will always end up fulfilling what life has in store for you. Never forget that. No matter what path you take, you can never avoid the inevitable."

Breeze nodded, noticing how her face was becoming smoother by the day. "Yes, I hear you Raza."

"You better because—" she put a hand to her mouth as she fought back a sob, "—because I can't believe in a world without you."

Breeze's face turned bright red as he looked down at the ground in embarrassment.

She placed a hand under his chin and lifted it. "Oslo and I spent so much time in the archives at Perihelion. We studied and learned about all the great Helios from the past and their incredible powers and gifts they possessed. Yes, there were those who didn't have such fantastic abilities, but they contributed in their own way. But as we poured through the records and studied the old vid images, we couldn't help but notice that greatest ones of all seemed to be the reluctant ones."

Breeze shrugged.

"Exactly," Raza whispered, "the quiet ones. The unassuming ones. The ones that your eyes see, but ignore. Your kind has a habit of doing the unexpected and performing the spectacular. All without being asked."

She pulled him close. "What you are doing for me, for Nina, is admirable. No, heroic. You are a hero Breeze, you understand this?"

He nodded his head.

She cradled his face. "You are heading off into the unknown to help someone from a generation that created this mess you have to live through." She placed her hands on his chest as her head sagged. "What sort of a world do we live in when it is the children who must do the fighting?"

She lifted her head and took in a deep breath, then straightened her hair and wiped her face with her apron. "Enough, no more tears. You are right, Breeze, we must fight back. Go home and find your father. Do what you can to repair the ship so it can take you to the stars. Find my husband and return him to me, make my family whole again, and I promise you we will begin to put things right."

Breeze opened his mouth to speak, but Raza held a finger to his lips. "Go, my son." She stood on her toes and kissed him on the cheek, then gently pushed him away and stepped over to the far end of the porch.

Breeze slung his bag over his shoulder and trudged off to the scout ship when heard the screen door fly open and bang against the frame, which was followed by the sound of feet running across gravel. He turned to look just as Nina crashed into him. She hugged him tightly as he struggled to keep his balance.

She buried her face in his chest, and then looked up at him. "Remember what I told you; never force anything, just move."

She broke away and ran back up the steps and into the farmhouse.

Breeze sighed heavily as he watched her go, and then stepped up the gangplank just as Excort was descending it. The dwarf was wiping his greasy hands with a dirty rag, and stood in Breeze's path, giving him a hard stare.

"Breeze," he paused for a moment, "bring back my friend." Then he reached up and patted his shoulder before walking away.

Breeze looked at his jacket and saw the greasy hand print. He smiled and shook his head.

Sally was waiting for him at the entrance. "All set?"

He turned to look back. Raza was still on the porch. Breeze waved and she waved back, and then patted her chest over her heart.

The motors of the gangplank whined as it retracted into the hull with a hard metallic bang. The door slid to a close and sealed itself with a hiss.

"Yes, we're ready," he said.

She touched his face, then took his hand and led him to the passenger cabin.

The engines were coming to life as they took their seats on the port side of the vessel. The ship vibrated and shook as Ray's voice broke over the intercom.

"Everyone secure your seats, preparing for takeoff," he announced. It was agreed earlier that Ray would pilot the ship for the first leg of the trip. Breeze would take over the last leg when they were close to his hometown. Achilles would be the co-pilot and handle navigation.

Breeze turned to Sally, but said nothing.

She leaned over. "What's the matter?"

"Just when I think I've found a home, I have to leave."

She grabbed his hand and squeezed tightly when the ship lifted off with a lurch and hovered.

Breeze looked through his window and saw Excort standing stoically in the front yard. Raza was on the porch with a hand over her heart, while Nina was leaning out of a second story window and waving goodbye.

The scout ship ascended slowly as it glided past the farmhouse, and then accelerated out of the valley and towards the rising sun.

"And off we go," Breeze said.

C H A P T E R

▼

T W E N T Y - S E V E N

"THEY'RE BACK," RAY ANNOUNCED over the intercom.

Sally and Breeze were buckled in their seats and dozing off when the sound of Ray's voice stirred them. They quickly unfastened their belts and peered out the windows and into the night.

Orbs of light were circling the scout ship, some brighter than others, and each one exploded into a dizzying array of colors before disappearing, then re-appearing, swooping toward the scout ship, then darting and zigzaging around it at dizzying speeds.

Sally's face was pressed against the window, her eyes reflecting a mixture of fear and excitement, when she turned to Breeze who was in the row behind her. "Are you seeing this? It's amazing!"

Breeze leaned away from his window and shrunk back in his seat. "Reminds me of my first trip to Perihelion."

The orbs began to circle faster around the ship as they pulsated with an array of colors ranging from red to violet. The cabin lights began to flicker and fade as the radiance from the orbs seeped through the hull. No sooner than it began, it stopped.

The cabin lights slowly came back on and the monotonous drone of the engines replaced the excitement of the light show.

Sally climbed over her seat and sat next to Breeze. "I'm scared," she said as she cuddled next to him.

"Don't be. I used to see these things all the time."

"You did?"

"Remember the story I told you back at Perihelion? I used to sneak out at night and fly away from home to get away from my father." He closed his eyes for a moment. "Funny to hear me just say that 'cause here I am now risking other peoples' lives just to see him again."

Sally grabbed his hand. "We're all taking a risk, remember?"

He smiled. "Yeah, I know. Anyway, I would fly out to the White Mountain, that's just a name I gave the place, but it was strange how I always knew how to get there and come back, without using this." He tapped the nav-compass on his wrist.

"I...don't remember you telling me this." Sally bit her lip as her hair obscured her eyes.

Breeze brushed it back so he could see her face. "I don't think you or Ray listened to anything I had to say back then."

Sally leaned away from him and looked down at her lap.

"I'm sorry. I shouldn't have said that."

She shook her head. "No, you're right. So much has changed since we first met. You know, I didn't think much of you then."

Breeze laughed. "Yeah, I kind of picked up the vibe."

She laughed with him. "Oh my gosh, I'm realizing just how horrible I was." She leaned over to him and whispered. "Was I really that bad?"

"Well..."

She hit him playfully on the shoulder. "Come on! You can't hurt a girl's feelings. You have to tell a little white lie and say 'Oh, no Sally, you were more gracious than a queen,' or something like that."

He stared at her as she pulled her hair back into a ponytail. "Well, I just thought you were the prettiest girl I had ever seen," he said and his face immediately turned red. He looked down and fiddled with his nav-compass.

She placed a hand over it while the other gently touched his face. "That is the sweetest thing ever, even after how badly I treated you." She started to sniffle.

"Oh, no! You're not going to start crying again, are you?"

"No! Come on, I'm not that emotional." She saw a smile creep across his face. She giggled and put her hands to her mouth. "Am I?"

"Well..."

"Breeze!" She threw another playful punch he easily ducked.

They were interrupted by the sound of heavy metallic footsteps coming down the aisle. They peered over their seats and watched as Achilles came lumbering towards them.

The robot stopped at their row. "I trust all is well with the passengers?"

"Of course, why wouldn't we be?" Sally said.

Achilles tilted its head. "Were you not concerned regarding the recent display of orbs just outside the ship?"

"Oh that," the teens said in unison. They looked at each other for a moment, and then laughed.

"I beg your forgiveness, master and mistress, but I cannot fully fathom the reason behind your levity."

Their laughter slowly subsided into a trickle of giggles. "It's okay, we're fine," Breeze said.

Achilles' eyes narrowed to slits.

Breeze stood up and tapped the robot on its head. "Come on now, don't have a malfunction."

Achilles dropped its jaw. "I was merely processing the events that have just transpired. I find human reactions to moments of stress to be interesting."

Breeze stepped out into the aisle and stretched his arms. "Feel like an animal in a pen," he muttered, then turned to the robot. "Achilles, look, it has been the same thing the past two nights. Nothing is happening out there. The Bad Lands are pretty quiet. Except for the escort we seem to be getting from the orbs over the past two days, I don't think anything is happening at all down there."

"You guys always make it seem like it's a horrible place. First time for me flying over, and it has been pretty uneventful," Sally said.

Achilles' eyes fluttered as one of its hands twitched. "Your assessment of our safety and security is premature at best, mistress."

"Look Achilles, you've done a great job fixing up the ship and the generators are creating a pretty good distortion field so nobody can see us. I say we increase speed so we can get to my town faster," Breeze said.

Sally nodded. "I have to agree, Achilles. We appreciate your concern, but this is not like when we first left Perihelion to return home. We understand how dangerous times are now, but you have done such a spectacular job with the scout ship that no one seems to be able to detect us."

"You are not concerned that the orbs find us regardless of our defenses?"

"Oh, them. Well..." She turned to Breeze.

"I was just telling Sally that I would see them all the time when I would fly around in the desert. They never appeared aggressive or hostile. If anything, I see them as old friends."

"Interesting assessment of such phenomena," Achilles responded.

"Come on, let's all head up to the pilot house, I want to switch places with Ray. It's my turn to fly the ship, and he's been stuck behind the helm for the past couple of days," Breeze said.

They made their way down the aisle and up the short flight of steps into the pilot house.

Breeze was the first to step into the cockpit where he found Ray adjusting the throttles and the helm was locked on auto pilot. "I was just telling everybody how hard you were working flying the ship, but I can see you got the auto pilot working just fine."

Ray looked back and grinned. "Yeah, took me a while to get it through my thick head that I don't have to be hands on all the time and it's given me chance to learn more about the ship. You should see this, I just found it earlier." He tapped a screen off to the right of the helm. "It's called Limp Home. Apparently if the ship is badly damaged, it goes into auto mode and flies itself back to a set of pre-programmed coordinates."

"What's it set to now?" Breeze asked.

"You mean where to go back to? Let me see." Ray scrolled through various screens, and then stopped. "Here are the coordinates. Let me punch them into the nav-station." He typed in the coordinates and immediately a map of an island appeared on the screen.

"Perihelion," Achilles said.

They turned to look at the robot as it peered over Breeze's shoulder.

"The ship will automatically return to Perihelion, perfectly logical," Achilles continued, "in the event of catastrophic damage to the ship or crew, or valuable cargo that must be protected. The ship will return to its point of origin, or self-destruct to protect whatever secrets it may contain."

"Sounds great," Breeze said, "but Perihelion is not on my list of places to run back to. I think we all can agree to that. Ray, just change the coordinates to Raza's farm. I would rather go back there if things go wrong."

Ray nodded and reached over to tap the screen when a proximity alarm whooped throughout the pilot house. He reached up to flip a switch that silenced it as the cabin's lighting automatically dimmed from a soft white to a red glow.

"According to the charts, it looks like we're approaching a town named Proctor that sits just outside the Bad Lands." Ray turned to Breeze. "I can't believe we crossed it so quick. We weren't traveling that fast." He toggled a switch on the console and the blast shield covering the canopy retracted to give them a better view.

Cutting through the darkness was an eerie orange glow on the horizon. As Achilles took its place in the co-pilot's seat, Sally stood behind Ray and placed a hand on his shoulder.

He reached up to pat it. "It's going to be all right."

As the ship drew closer, the orange glow gave way to a raging fire encompassing a vast area while the town of Proctor just below them was engulfed in a raging inferno.

Sally turned away. "Not again."

Breeze leaned into the windscreen to get a better look. "I was wondering why everything was so quiet and why we're still getting nothing but static over the comms."

"Raymond, may I suggest we skirt the outer perimeter of the town? Security is paramount," Achilles said.

"What?" He turned to look at the robot with wide eyes. "Oh, right, good call." He gripped the helm and shook it, which canceled the auto pilot, then banked the ship to starboard.

Breeze addressed them all. "There is no point in trying to approach my town with stealth. Whatever is out there knows about us and I can't wait any longer." He turned to Ray. "Hit the throttles, I want to get home now."

Ray hesitated for a moment, then saw the steely determination on Breeze's face and thought better of disagreeing with him. He banked the ship to port and pushed forward on the throttles. The ship rumbled and shook as it gradually picked up speed and left the burning town of Proctor behind them. The landscape below became a blur as they rushed over it.

Achilles, in its co-pilot seat, turned to Ray. "Master, may I suggest we reduce our rate of acceleration? My calculations are showing we cannot maintain this speed and still produce enough power to maintain the distortion field."

"I have a better idea," Breeze said. "Ray, kill the power to the field and reroute it to the engines, then hammer down hard on the throttle."

Ray took a quick glance at him, and then complied. The ship vibrated as it accelerated faster.

The vibration grew in intensity. Breeze reached up to grab an overhead rail as Sally sat down in the jump seat behind Ray.

Ray deftly flew over mountains and hugged ravines as he kept the scout ship close to the ground to evade detection from above. Outside the ship, trees buckled and shook violently as it rocketed past with a deep rumble following its wake.

"Master Verhesen, any attempts at a stealthy approach are being negated by the sonic boom that we are generating at these speeds," Achilles said.

Ray looked at Breeze, then back at Achilles and shrugged.

The landscape below changed from lush forest to scrub land, and then eventually to desert as the scout ship streaked through the night, trailing an ear splitting sonic boom.

Inside the pilot house, another proximity alarm went off. "The town of Conception is just up ahead," Ray announced as he reached up to silence it, then reached for the throttles and gradually reduced speed.

Breeze shot him and angry look.

Ray held up a hand. "If I don't, we'll overshoot it."

Breeze nodded and took in a sharp breath, then resumed looking out the windscreen with a deep intensity.

Ray pulled up on the helm to clear a mountain and the ship arched up and over its peak, then pushed down and the ship glided into a valley.

Sprawling before them was the town of Conception with its night lights on full display spread out across the valley floor. As the ship descended, they could make out the outlines of building and homes.

"Nobody is here," Breeze said.

"What do you mean? Your town is safe." Sally got up from the jump seat and stood next to Breeze.

"No, there is always something going on here. It might be a small town, but there is always someone on the streets, or a transport crossing through town, or maybe someone on a hover bike. Look at the sky." He pointed ahead. "I always see someone testing aerocraft. Lots of new designs and prototypes are flown at night to hide from spies and other competitors. I should know, I would fly around at night just to get away from home."

Sally rubbed his back.

Breeze pointed north. "There, go that way."

Ray complied and rolled the ship to starboard.

They crossed over the length of the town. Its night lights gave the valley a soft glow that cocooned it from the encroaching darkness that hung over the mountains. They couldn't see any movement on the streets below as they skimmed over.

They crossed the border of Conception's city limits and into a sparsely populated area. The monotony of the ground below was broken up by a few scattered lights attached to isolated houses and work sheds.

Breeze pointed out to Ray where to go and after several minutes of travel, they reached his home.

Breeze pressed his face against the windscreen and peered into the darkness. "Nothing. It's gone."

"How do you know this is your home? I can't see in this darkness." Ray toggled a switch as flood lights emanated from the belly of the ship and illuminated the ground below.

Ray moved his hand over a console that controlled the floodlights and shifted the multitude of beams over the area in a random pattern. As the ship orbited overhead the powerful lights revealed the burnt out remains of structures and buildings.

"Land the ship," Breeze said softly.

"What? Are you sure? Look at this place—"

"Land the damn ship!" Breeze roared at him.

Ray shrunk back into his seat, and then turned to Achilles.

"Master Corinth, may I suggest we adopt a wait-and-see strategy before we go any further?" Achilles said.

Breeze didn't hear. He was already running out of the pilot house and sprinting down the passenger aisle heading for the stern.

Sally rushed after him. "Breeze, wait!"

Ray called out over the intercom. "Breeze, whatever you're planning to do, don't. I'm going to look for a safe place to land."

If Breeze heard, he gave no indication. He reached the exit hatch and looked out the narrow window and saw they were still circling.

He grabbed the lever to open the hatch. It wouldn't budge.

He swore ferociously and hit the override button on the panel next to the hatch. An alarm began to ring as blast doors rolled shut to prevent the ship from depressurizing.

"Breeze, wait!" Sally cried out just as the doors closed.

The hatch opened once the blast doors closed and Breeze grabbed on to a railing as he could feel and hear the slipstream roar past him. He steadied himself and looked out but saw nothing but wreckage below as the smell of burnt wood and debris hit his nose.

Without a second thought, he leapt out. The slipstream hit him like an anvil as he grunted and dove to the ground.

He leveled out and glided over what was once his home and as the scout ship's flood lights peeled back the darkness, he could make what was left of the foundry. He hovered over it and surveyed the damage, then descended and came to a landing at a pile of smoldering timbers.

He grabbed the end of one and flung it away; it flew in the air and came to a landing on another pile of debris. He grabbed more lengths of timber and madly flung them about. He kicked and yelled as he wildly tore through the wreckage, then dropped to his knees in exhaustion.

Ray landed the ship on the perimeter of the property. Sally immediately ran down the gang plank before it could fully extend and looked for Breeze, calling out his name, when she saw him in the glare of the ship's floodlights. She put hand to her mouth as she took in the scope of the destruction that surrounded him.

Breeze stood up, then lifted off the ground and glided to a landing before her. "It's over. There is nothing to left to see."

She reached out to touch him, but he brushed the hand away, then turned his back to her and broke into a run.

She crossed her arms and shivered against a gust of cold air that swept through when Ray and Achilles came around a pile of debris and stood next to her.

"Where's Breeze running off to?" Ray asked.

Sally rubbed her eyes. "I don't know."

"It's going to be okay." He took her in his arms and pulled her close.

She nodded and patted his chest. "I'm all right. Let just go and be with him. We're his friends and he needs us now."

She turned to follow Breeze's path and Ray walked behind her.

Achilles hung back. The robot's eyes glowed as it scanned the area when it looked down at the ground, then lurched forward and dropped to one knee to touch the earth. Its eyes shined with intensity and after a moment, it stood up abruptly. It watched as Sally and Ray went after Breeze and the robot followed the trail of their footprints.

Sally and Ray arrived at what was left of the work shed as Breeze was sifting through the wreckage.

He hovered over a piece of twisted metal, then lifted and flung it away. It careened through the air, hitting other pieces of wreckage with a clang. He repeated it several more times, grabbing and throwing pieces of twisted metal harder and faster than the one before. He stopped abruptly and floated in the night sky.

Meanwhile, Ray had raised a glowing hand to highlight the mangled remains of the building when Breeze spotted a crumpled box amidst the smoldering remains and descended to grab it. Despite the raging fires that had consumed the property, it was still intact.

He opened it and inside were the tattered remains of photos, and the only remaining evidence that anyone had ever lived here. Breeze pulled them out and dropped the box, then thumbed through them like a deck of cards, dropping each one to the ground as he did.

Sally saw him amidst the smoking ruins and stepped over to stand next to him.

He turned to her. "This is all that is left that proves anyone was ever here." He held the last picture in his hands.

She peered through the darkness to look at it. It was a picture of a man and a woman smiling. The woman held a baby in her arms.

"Breeze is that...? Of course it is. You were just an infant."

The two stood there looking at the picture when Ray approached them. His whole body was glowing and casting enough light for everyone to see. He caught Breeze's eye and nodded. "It's no different than what happened to Sally and me, they just destroy everything."

"No, Ray, not true. They destroyed our town. Here, they destroyed Breeze's home just like mine," Sally said.

Ray choked back a sob. He turned away and stomped his foot into the ground, then walked off with clenched fists as he muttered loudly.

Sally reached out to him. "Raymond, stop it!"

Breeze grabbed her arm. "No. Don't. Let him grieve."

Sally shook her head. "Breeze, we're here for you. This is not about him. He needs to stop."

"We're all in this together." Breeze surveyed the wreckage, and then turned to Sally. "Ray is able to do something that I can't."

Sally shook her head and shrugged.

He leaned into her. "He can feel."

She smiled and touched his arm. "You can too. You're just in shock."

Ray returned and his body glowed an intense red while his hands were covered in blue flame.

"Ray, please don't do anything crazy," Sally pleaded.

Breeze held a hand up to her. "No," he said to her, and then faced Ray. "Look at what they did to you. They turned you into a puppet and made you spy on us. They destroyed your city and your parents are nowhere to be found, assuming they're even alive. And Sally, you're in the same situation. Now, you can add me to the list."

Breeze took one last look at the photo, and then dropped it to the ground. "I never really cared much about anything. Now, even less." He looked Ray in the eye. "Ray, get crazy. I want you to shatter the sky and let the whole world know we exist. Cut loose. Just fire at the stars and torch the monsters above us. We're going to let them know we're coming after them."

Ray trembled as blue flame began to flicker out of his eyes until it consumed his body, then he threw his head back and yelled with the ferociousness of a beast.

Breeze grabbed Sally and pulled her close, raising his shield just as Ray fired upward with all his might with a column of pure energy that erupted from him with a deafening roar. Breeze held his ground as heat and blue flames buffeted his shield while the night sky above was turned into day.

Breeze was transfixed by the column of energy Ray unleashed at the heavens. "Not even the greatest darkness can hold back the light," he murmured.

Ray exhausted himself and collapsed to his knees. Beneath their feet, the ground was fused into a smooth glass that beautifully reflected the stars above.

Breeze dropped his shield and Sally breathed heavily as she put her hands to her chest.

The sound of heavy footsteps broke the silence as a pair of glowing red eyes floated toward them, moving up and down in tempo with the footsteps. The eyes widened and stopped upon the sound of glass shattering and breaking. They looked down, then up again as they changed from a red glow to white and resumed their approach.

"Well Achilles, how was that for a stealthy approach?" Breeze called out.

The robot stepped into view as it looked at each of them. Behind it, the moon had risen above the distant mountain range, framing the robot in a mystical light. "My assessment would be succinct and to the point; a foolish display of emotions."

Breeze chuckled. "You told me in Appalachia you were fascinated by us humans. Well, here we are. Think of what just happened as our battle cry. We're not afraid of anything anymore."

"Indeed, master. You have made that perfectly obvious."

They all jumped at the sound of metal scraping against metal. Just outside the periphery of light cast by the scout ship's floodlights, a pile of wreckage tumbled to the ground.

They turned to face the source of the sound. Ray's hands began to glow while Breeze hovered above them and Sally's eyes shimmered in white.

Achilles scanned the area and was unable to detect anything. It turned to report its findings and froze at the sight of them.

They are the Helios, rising from the ashes like the mythical bird of fire. Achilles shook its head rapidly as servos whirred loudly.

Breeze called out instructions from above. "Ray, get ready to fire when I give the word. Sally, start projecting and let me know what you see."

He began to fly toward the source of the sound, but stopped when out of the darkness came an old man pushing a cart with a hand raised in a salute. "Hello there, pay no heed to me. I'm of no consequence. I will visit no harm or evil upon you." The old man laughed raucously as he reached into his cart and rummaged about.

Ray pointed a glowing hand at him.

"Ah, there you are! Oh, sweet nectar, come to me." The old man pulled a bottle from the cart and drank a long and steady draft from it. "Oh!" he exclaimed, "quite the thirst quencher, indeed!" He cackled as he placed the bottle back in the cart.

"Who are you?" Ray challenged.

"I'll tell you what he is," Breeze said as he descended and lowered his shield. "He's a desert rat. A scavenger. The area is loaded with them. Always looking for scrap metal. They steal it from my father, jumping the fence and snatching the easy to get pieces from the outermost stacks, and then sell it back to him. He knew what they were doing, but he would still buy from them. Charity, he told me."

"Breeze, I'm not seeing him at all. There is nothing there," Sally's body said in a monotone voice.

The old man waved to the space before him. "Right here sweetie, hello there," he cackled.

"Sally, pull back," Breeze commanded.

Her body stiffened, then lurched back as her astral form re-entered. Breeze was there to catch her as she almost fell.

Ray didn't take his eyes off the old man and kept a glowing hand pointed at him. "Breeze, should I blast him or what?"

"No, there is something about him. He's no regular rat. I want to hear what he has to say."

"My, my, what do we have here on display? Paranormals?" The old man shuffled away from his overburdened cart filled with junk and scrap and wobbled over to them. "Why yes, my eyes do not tell any tall tales. Oh, what a wondrous sight to see."

Achilles stepped into his path. "Identify yourself."

"Ahh! Call off your watchdog young ones, I mean you no harm." The old man then stared hard at Achilles. "By the stars above, are you what I think you are? A Robot Fighter? Oh my, you are. I haven't seen one of your kind in so long." He lowered his voice into a whisper. "So sorry, but I was under the impression your entire line was sent off to the scrap yard." He looked around, then back to Achilles. "This must be your cemetery." He threw back his head and laughed wildly. "You must be the undertaker here!" He laughed even harder before breaking down into a coughing fit. He reached into the cart to retrieve his bottle and with puckered lips, he took another long drink from it. "Ahh!" he exclaimed loudly as he screwed the cap back on and wiped his face with the back his sleeve.

Breeze stepped up and stood beside Achilles. "Answer the robot's question."

The old man staggered back, and then squinted his eyes to peer at Breeze as the moonlight highlighted his ragged face. "The bold leader, whose words are sharp and to the point, much like a dagger."

He then leaned to the side to see behind Breeze. "I see a young lad wielding the power of energy transmission, along with a young woman who can snoop upon the unaware." He repeated again. "*The unaware.*" He looked Sally right in the eye as he said it.

She sniffed and took a step back.

"Old man..." Breeze warned.

"My identification? Better yet, my name? Yes, of course." He held out a hand. "John Agam."

Breeze didn't shake the hand. The old man turned and offered it to Achilles, who also refused it.

"No takers on the handshake? Is my hand that filthy?" He held it up to his face. "By all that is holy, it is!" He laughed again as he wiped it on his jacket.

Breeze walked up to John and stood inches from his face. "What are you doing on my father's—" he stopped and closed his eyes while he clenched a fist, "—on my property."

"Your property?" John leaned forward and his eyes narrowed. "Breeze, is that you lad? Welcome back! The prodigal son has returned."

He clamped his hands on Breeze's shoulders.

Breeze pushed him away. "How do you know me? I don't recognize you from the other scrap yard rats my father would buy from."

"Oh, my boy, I have known your father for ages," he said with a sigh as he looked down at the bottle in his cart. "Many ages, in fact," he muttered, then took in a deep breath and waved a hand. "Never mind that. So your father told me you went away to see family, which seemed odd. I didn't know you had kinfolk beyond Conception. Was he telling the truth?"

Breeze looked around and laughed, then turned to Achilles and shrugged his shoulders.

The robot blinked its eyes, but said nothing.

He whirled onto John. "My father is dead! My home is destroyed!" He shoved the old man. "I've lost everything, and you are asking questions about where I've been?"

John stumbled and fell onto his backside. After a moment, he stood up with a groan and dusted off his jacket. "You proclaim young man that you have nothing," he said, "but from what I see, you have everything you will ever need to build an empire."

Breeze shook his head. "I don't know what you are talking about."

John made a circle in the air with his hand. "Look around. Look deeper. Focus on the here and now, and then project into the future. You have friends. You have a ship. You have a mission. It's been a long time since I've had such purpose in my life."

"How do you seem to know so much?"

"My dear boy, I've been around far longer than I care to admit, and I can safely say that I have seen enough." John shuffled over to his cart and leaned against it. He sighed deeply. "I know Jacob. Your father is a good man."

"Was."

He shot a glare at Breeze. "Is. Do not be so quick to dismiss him."

"How do you know he's still alive?"

"Your father is a builder. An innovator. What couldn't he do to survive an attack like this?"

"My father ran a scrap yard and sold metal to aerocraft builders. That's it."

"Your father was so much more. What did I just tell you? Look around. Look deeper. The answers you seek will not always be found on the surface. Isn't that right, robot?" John turned his attention to Achilles.

Its eyes lit up. "Your pardon, sir?"

"You can drop the domesticated robot act. I know what you are, Robot Fighter. Tell me, what is your serial code?"

Achilles cocked its head. "5150," it replied. "May I ask the reason for your inquiry?"

John ignored the question. "Only four digits? You were bound for the scrap heap to be melted down, yet you escaped the AI purge. Someone took a fancy to you an erased most of your serial code. That makes your date of origin difficult to track down. Who rescued you?"

"I am under no obligation to respond your request."

"It was Oslo then. Why am I not surprised? He was always clandestine and sneaky while running that operation of his in the sub-basements of Perihelion. Who were the other two he was always with?" he mused. "Ah, how could I forget, Bram and Raza? Oh my, she was a beauty in her time!" John chuckled.

Sally spoke up. "How do you know Oslo?"

"Ah, yes. The ghost girl. I knew you had a voice." He narrowed his eyes. "Who do you remind me of?" He tapped his finger against his yellow teeth. It made a clicking sound that echoed in the cold desert night. "Bram! He was a ghost just like you. From what I've gathered, the best Perihelion ever recruited. I wonder whatever happened to him." He chuckled. "The real drama was that love triangle between Oslo and Bram. Both of them vying for the attention of Raza." He leaned his head back to look up at the night sky. "Are you still alive, or are you amongst the stars?"

"Of course she's alive! We arrived here from her farm—"

"Sally!" Breeze cut her off.

"It's quite all right young man. I had suspected as much. The gears are grinding. Plans laid down long ago are beginning to progress forward." He surveyed the three of them. "You are all that we have now. I know there are others, but it begins with you."

Ray's hands glowed fiercely and lit up the area around them. "So what do you want from us?"

"Go to the White Mountain. Breeze knows what I speak of. They will give you the assistance you need for your journey. Don't make the mistake I made many a moon ago. Take on your adversaries, do not shrink from them; better to die in battle as a free man...than to live like a frightened scavenger in the dark."

He grunted, then turned away and began pushing his cart. The wheels squealed in protest from the excessive weight of the scrap he collected.

Breeze hovered into his path. "Wait, I'm sorry. Maybe you can help us."

John kept pushing his cart. Both he and the cart dematerialized as it passed through Breeze.

Breeze gasped as he felt himself being sucked into whirlpool of light as the horizon began to bend and shift. Through the distortion, he was still able to see John in the distance. He called out to him. "John, wait!"

John turned and smiled. He was much younger and wearing a uniform with the symbol of a triangle with a circle inside it. "Now is not the time, Paul Corinth. Go back to your friends and follow your destiny. Remember, it is set in stone and cannot be changed. Only your fate can be altered, but never destiny."

Breeze felt himself being pushed back as John faded from view.

He looked up to see Ray pulling his hand to help him to his feet. Sally and Achilles were by his side.

"Where did they old man go?" Sally said.

"I don't know. He just...left."

"What now?" Ray asked.

Breeze looked at his friends. "There is only one place to go. They are the only ones who can help us."

"White Mountain," Sally said.

Breeze turned to her and nodded. "Yes. We've come this far. We have nothing to lose." He started walking toward the scout ship, and then stopped to look back. "Come on guys, I can't do this alone. Are you with me?"

Sally strode to him and took his hand. "Always." She turned to Ray and Achilles. "Guys?"

Ray shrugged. "You know I'm in." He took Sally's outstretched hand.

She giggled. "Achilles, I don't have another hand for you."

"Do not distress yourself mistress. You lead, I will follow. Always."

Breeze beamed as he surveyed his team. "John was right. Everything I need is right before me. Come on, let's go." They headed toward the scout ship.

Achilles hung back and scanned the desert floor. Its servos whirred as it knelt down to touch the sand.

"Achilles, come on!" It heard Breeze shout.

"Of course, young aviator. Right away." It stood up and followed them.

Minutes later, the gangplank retracted as the hatch closed and sealed itself with a hiss and the ship began to pressurize. The whine of the engines spooling up broke up the stillness of the desert night.

Inside, Breeze and Sally were buckling themselves into their seats when Achilles came down the aisle and stopped at their row.

"Master Corinth, are you sure of the coordinates? This White Mountain you speak does not reveal itself on any of the charts."

"It's okay Achilles, call it a hunch. I know your robot brain doesn't care much for that, but that's what it is. Head west to the Great Salt Sea, then bank hard to the north and continue until you see a lone mountain on its northeastern shore. It's there. I've flown that route for many years."

"Are you positive they will render the assistance we need, master?"

"I don't know. Don't really care. I made a promise to Raza to bring back Oslo." He turned to Sally. "I also promised to help others find their families."

Sally smiled and took his hand. "We'll help find yours."

"I'm not worried about my old man anymore. I know he's out there somewhere. I'm not sure what he's up to, but he's hiding somewhere. I'm starting to understand why he kept me hidden for so long. Just wished I had listened, tried to understand him better." He bit his lip.

Sally touched his face. "Breeze, you said earlier that you can't feel. Do you think that's still true?"

Breeze stared at her as his face turned red. "Sally, that's not what I meant."

She smiled. "I thought so."

Ray's voice broke out over the intercom. "Ready to get airborne. Achilles, to the pilot house."

"I have been summoned. I believe the human thing to say would be good luck?"

Breeze shrugged. "Yeah, it's a start."

Sally squeezed his hand.

Within moments, the ship lifted off with a lurch. It hovered over the scrap yard for a few seconds, and then gradually accelerated into the moonlit night.

Breeze looked out his window as the cabin lighting was subdued to a soft green hue. He could see the distant lights of Conception fade from view. He leaned his head back into the seat, and the gentle throb of the engines made his eyes flutter.

Sally leaned her head on his shoulder and closed her eyes as they both fell asleep.

Outside the perimeter of the scrap yard, a lone figure stood and watched the scout ship lift off into the night sky. The wrinkled outlines of his face were briefly highlighted by the ship's floodlights, then plunged back into darkness as the lights switched off and the ship flew away. He stood until it faded from view over the mountains.

"He's a good boy. He will grow into the man you want him to be, Jacob," a disembodied voice spoke from the distance.

"If you say so, John."

The air crackled and shimmered. John Agam appeared and drifted over to him.

"He is in good company. They will succeed. They must succeed," John said.

"But why does it have to be my son? Haven't I sacrificed enough already?"

John placed a hand on his shoulder. "I know that you lost your wife many years ago to the Elephim."

"And a son," Jacob added.

"Aye, I know. You haven't spoken about them in so long; I did not wish to dredge up the memory."

Jacob pulled out a disk from the satchel slung across his chest and handed it to him. "Take this; it is time to begin your journey. Begin assembling as many teams as you can. Wake them up. Let everybody know we will not go quietly into obscurity. We all must make sacrifices."

John nodded as he took the disk and flipped it over. They were twelve symbols that radiated around the outer rim with an engraving of the sun in the center. He put it into his jacket.

"Very well, Jacob. I suppose it is time for me to retire from my burgeoning career as a scavenger of scrap," he chuckled, and then shook his head. "No need for humor to hide the darkness of our reality. It is time to bring the light to cleanse ourselves."

John began to walk away, then stopped suddenly and reached into his pocket. He pulled out a picture and handed it to Jacob, then turned and disappeared into the desert night.

Jacob looked at the picture. It was of a man and a woman smiling as she held an infant in her arms.

Jacob wept, then stopped abruptly and placed the picture into his satchel.

He took one last look around at the scrap yard as the light of the full moon reflected off the piles of metal. He settled his gaze at where the house once stood, then turned away and headed into the desert.

He stepped up into the sky as if he walked on invisible steps when a door appeared and opened before him. Behind the door was a soft glow. He stopped and took one last look over the yard, then stepped inside. The door closed and disappeared as the night sky reclaimed its place.

CHAPTER

▼

TWENTY-EIGHT

THE SCOUT SHIP STREAKED over the Great Salt Sea as a stiff wind created white caps that polluted the otherwise smooth surface. Flying low to elude detection let the passengers look out the window and marvel at the sheer size of it.

Breeze was hypnotized by the water and his eyes fluttered the second he leaned his head against the window. Within seconds he was fast asleep and dreaming.

His dream was filled with jumbled images that made no sense to him. Mixed into it were incoherent conversations with Oslo about training at Perihelion and leaving his home. It came to an end with Sally shouting his name from a distance.

He awoke abruptly to Sally shaking him. The ship was pitching and tossing violently. The engines were screeching and alarms flooded the ship.

"Something hit us hard!" she said.

He looked out the window where dark and ominous clouds swirled around the ship in a maelstrom. He then turned to her and pointed to the bow of the ship. "Let's get to the pilot house."

He began unbuckling from his seat when he caught a movement from the corner of his eye. He looked out the window again and was confronted by a pair of giant wings flapping close to the ship. Each beat of the wings made the ship shudder violently.

"Go! Now!" he shouted at her as they struggled to get to the pilot house, stopping to brace themselves against the seats in the aisle whenever the ship rolled violently.

When they finally stumbled into the pilot house, they found Ray in the cockpit struggling to maintain altitude.

Achilles, in the co-pilot's seat, turned to them. "Master, mistress, I would advise you to return to your seats and remain buckled in."

Breeze ignored Achilles' request as he gripped the back of its seat and looked up through the canopy, which was filled with the view of gigantic winged birds. Electricity crackled around them with each beat of their wings.

One of the birds dove into their path and flapped its wings with one mighty stroke. Lightning erupted from it, followed by a deep rolling thunder that rattled the ship.

"Guys, we need to do something!" Ray shouted as he fought the helm to keep the ship level.

"There, up ahead, bring us down to the base of that mountain." Breeze pointed forward.

In the distance, a lone mountain on the desert plain emerged, and soon its looming presence filled the windscreen.

With great relief, Ray pushed down on the helm and began their descent.

Immediately, the lead bird rolled onto its back and flapped its wings with a violent thrust. The pressure wave it created blasted the ship and rocked the bow up to an extreme angle, causing Breeze to lose his grip on Achilles' seat and tumble to the back of the cockpit.

Sally had followed Achilles' advice and strapped herself into the jump seat. She screamed as Breeze flew past her and slammed into the back of the cockpit. His shield protected him, but made a dent in the metal.

"Are you okay?" Sally cried out.

"I'm fine, don't get out of your seat!" he shouted as she started to unbuckle.

Outside, the gigantic birds revolved around the ship at a high rate of speed, creating a vortex that spun it and pinned the passengers in place as nausea began to overwhelm them.

The birds were synchronized as they maintained a tight formation. Electricity arced between them, followed by peals of powerful, booming thunder.

Inside, Breeze was pinned against a bulkhead. The ship wailed with warning alarms as smoke filled the cockpit. He could barely see Sally, whose eyes were fluttering as the spinning was taking its toll on her. Ray and Achilles were silhouettes occasionally illuminated by the ship's failing electrical systems.

The last thing Breeze saw was Sally passing out when the ship eventually lost power and fell out of sky.

Breeze woke up with the side of his face pressed against the cold metal floor. His head and body ached while nausea roiled his stomach.

He wanted to swallow, but it felt like his mouth was full of dirt. He gagged and retched as he struggled to get up when he saw Sally still strapped in her jump seat. In the faint light, he could barely make out Ray and Achilles slumped over in their seats.

He slowly stood up and steadied himself against the bulkhead. "Is everyone okay?" he called out. No response.

He stumbled over to Sally and shook her. She didn't respond. He leaned closer and was relieved to hear her still breathing. He then limped to the front of the cockpit where Ray was beginning to stir, but Achilles was still incapacitated and slumped over its console. He grunted as he pulled the robot into an upright position and it fell back into its seat with a thump. Breeze weakly knocked on its head hoping to get a response, but the robot was lifeless.

He let out a sigh of exasperation when a bright flash filled the cockpit followed by a powerful hum that vibrated the ship.

"Remove them," a voice said.

Breeze immediately crumpled to the floor and passed out.

When he awoke again, he found himself alone and surrounded by pure white light. He could feel the floor under him but could not discern its surface even when he touched it.

He stood up and reached out with both hands when he immediately felt a hard surface. When he pressed his hand against it he felt electricity crackle through his skin.

He took a step back only to wobble and topple over. He groaned as he got back to his feet and held his arms out to maintain balance. The pure white light was disorienting, and made it difficult to fathom depth and distance. He put his hands out again to touch the surface, sidestepping along as he tried to figure out the dimensions of what he was beginning to suspect was a detention cell. After several minutes of touching like a blind man, he came to the conclusion that he was in a room shaped like a cube roughly eight feet by eight feet. If there was an exit, he never found it.

He sat on the floor to ponder his situation when a section of the cube slid away. A man wearing a white uniform leaned in and looked inside.

"Yes, he is awake now," he said to no one in particular and walked away.

The section stayed open, but no one else came inside

Breeze didn't take his eyes off the entrance, as he anticipated it would close if he moved too fast. He gingerly made his way to the opening, then leaned out to look and saw his jailer walk down a hallway of pure light before turning to the right and disappearing. Breeze figured that the hallway was similar to his cell in that there was no way to gauge its dimensions without physically touching the walls.

He stepped out with outstretched hands and immediately ran into a hard surface. He took a few steps back and abruptly turned to go in another direction, only to run into a hard surface yet again.

With mounting frustration, he pushed hard against it and it flexed and shimmered, then snapped back into place. He pushed again, but harder and the surface of light flexed. When it settled, it seemed to be further away and he felt he was moving forward. He did this several more times, creating the sensation he was moving further away from his cell.

He suddenly turned to head in a different direction. With his arms thrust out like a battering ram, he pushed against any surface he encountered as he tried to gauge the dimensions of the hallway like he did with his cell. Some surfaces gave way while others pushed back. After several minutes of twist and turns, it dawned upon him he was being guided by someone or something that was manipulating the surfaces so that some gave way while others were rigid. He stopped to pull back his sleeve and look at his nav-compass. The needle was spinning wildly and was completely useless. Anger began to build. He didn't like the fact he was being toyed with.

He continued down the fathomless corridor, and holding his hands out like a blind man when he stopped and shouted.

"Where do you want me to go? What do you want from me?" He received no response.

He continued on as his anger was building to a crescendo. He just wanted to fly away and get out.

He took a running leap and began gliding, then raised his shield and shaped it like a battering ram as he accelerated and ran into a surface.

The surface flexed and stretched, but it wouldn't break. He grimaced as he poured on the power, but it snapped and flung him back. He bounced around like a pinball against multiple surfaces before flopping onto the floor.

He scrambled to his feet and shouted. "We didn't come here to do harm, we came here for help."

Silence was the only answer he received.

He pleaded his case further. "I used to live not far from here in a town named Conception. I remember when I was a child my mother would bring me here. I would talk to tall men in white coats and they would tell me fantastic things about my gifts. It always seemed like a dream, but I know now you are real. When I figured out how to fly on my own, I would come and watch the lights that came out of this mountain from the ridgeline over there." He pointed in what he thought was the direction of the ridgeline, and then dropped his hand when he realized how foolish he appeared.

"Please, could you just help us? A friend has been captured by the Elephim, and I don't have anyone else to turn to."

He received more silence. Then the light faded away and he found himself in a huge chamber whose smooth stone walls ran up to a rocky ceiling, when several figures materialized before him. They remained motionless at staggered distances from each other as they each pulsated with white light. All of them wore similar uniforms with masks covering their faces.

The light surrounding them ebbed as the masks faded away to reveal beings with sharp, angular faces.

"Welcome Paul Corinth, we are the Phaerion," one of them said. "We've been expecting you."

CHAPTER

▼

TWENTY-NINE

BREEZE LOOKED AT THEM, noting that each of the Phaerion had unique facial features. The most striking were the eyes.

All of them had eyes that glowed. The ones with the brightest eyes hovered in front pulsating with intense energy whereas those who were dull stayed behind.

He watched as two of the Phaerion before him nodded vigorously to the other as their bodies pulsated with light, then they turned to look at him.

The Phaerion to his left stared at him in silence for what felt like an eternity, then its eyes suddenly flashed a brilliant white, forcing Breeze to throw his hands up to his face.

The blinding light receded, revealing auras that hovered above each of the Phaerion. The aura of the Phaerion who flashed him with light rose to the ceiling, and then lunged towards him.

Breeze tried to run, but couldn't as his feet felt like they were anchored to the floor.

The aura struck him like a bolt of lightning, immediately melting away the fear and anxiety that was sweeping through him. He saw images from his memories project from his mind and play out like a movie for all to see. A part of him felt defiance and anger to the probe, but a soothing voice reassured him that no harm was intended.

Unlike the experience with the harbinger in the ravine, where he was left drained and exhausted, he felt invigorated and cleansed as the aura retracted.

The Phaerion collectively pulsated, then abruptly ceased as one of them glided towards him. "Come Breeze, follow us," he said as they all turned and glided to the side of the chamber where a portion of it slid open without a sound.

He followed them into a massive hall where a multitude of Phaerion were handling and manipulating beams of light as they bent and shaped them into various patterns, then passed them down along an assembly line and mounted each pattern onto a frame. Further down the line, the frames were attached together and formed into ships made of light.

Spread out across the floor of the hall Breeze saw light ships in various stages of assembly. Some were familiar to him as he had seen them while practicing his flying at night. He always thought they were prototypes from the local builders being tested over the deserts of Conception. Now he realized that the Phaerion had a fleet of their own design.

The assemblymen stopped to look at him and pulsated amongst themselves before returning to work.

Breeze felt comfortable being around them and walked over to one of the partially constructed ships. The assemblers made no effort to stop him, but instead vibrated with soft and pleasing colors as he drew closer.

Breeze marveled at each beam of light and how it fitted seamlessly like skin to bone as the entire surface of the ship coursed with energy. He reached out to touch it and the ship responded with a symphony of color and light. His face broke into a wide grin as he became connected to the ship and felt as if they were old friends who hadn't seen each other in a long time.

He pushed down and his arm sank into the ship as energy washed over him like a wave. He heard his name being called and soon he was floating through the craft and down its corridors and compartments, until he entered a cockpit that was free of instruments normally found on any aerocraft or transport. All it contained was a few seats, bare walls, and a large window.

He sat in the seat closest to the window as it molded itself to fit the contours of his body. He leaned back and closed his eyes. A sense of peace like none he had ever known flowed through him. A voice whispered in his ear, one that sang more than it spoke. "Aerion," it said.

A hand squeezed his shoulder.

He opened his eyes expecting to see the face behind the voice, but instead was back in the hall with an assemblyman standing before him with a look of awe.

Breeze removed his hand from the craft and held it up to his face. The residual energy of the ship was still attached to it. He looked around as all of the assemblymen were staring at him and pulsating in unison.

Before Breeze could ask questions, a side passageway opened up and Sally, Ray and Achilles came pouring through, followed by several Phaerion.

He was struck at how each of them seemed to vibrate with a unique light. Sally shined like a bright torch whose light flowed everywhere, while Ray, in contrast, had a red haze over him. Achilles had a light similar to Sally's, but was intertwined with electro-mechanical energy.

Sally shouted his name upon seeing him and ran over to throw her arms around his neck.

"I'm so happy to see you. They wouldn't tell us where you were," she said.

He held her tight. Though his ability to see living light was beginning to fade, Sally's was still glowing brightly.

She smiled. "What is it with you, you're acting different."

He grinned. "It's just great to see you."

Achilles had a twinkle in its eye. "You seem energized, master."

"Yeah, so do you" Breeze replied.

Achilles tilted its head quizzically.

One of the Phaerion spoke. "Now that you are reunited, you can see that we mean you no harm. We are protective and cautious for good reason. We are locked in a constant duel with the ones who watch from above, the Elephim. When we first detected your ship approaching we were not alarmed. Many aerocraft of late have wandered into our airspace, but they are usually transients and it is obvious they know nothing of our presence here as they pass through. But you were different. You come to our airspace on a deliberate course used by our own craft to enter the mountain, and your ship is of a manufacture we have not seen in a very long time."

"Where is it?" Ray asked.

"It is safe."

Another of the Phaerion spoke. "Why did you come here?"

"We need your help. I couldn't think of anyone else to turn to," Breeze said.

"And what is it you want us to help you with?"

"Our friend has been captured by the Elephim."

"And what do you expect from us?"

"Our scout ship cannot reach orbit, we need better engines to boost us. I thought—"

"Your thoughts are in error."

"Please," Sally pleaded, "Oslo is a good man who is trying to do the right thing. Can you perhaps spare a ship for us?"

The Phaerion flashed amongst themselves rapidly as their colors changed from a crimson red to a deep purple, then subsided when a solitary Phaerion with a black robe floated to the front of the group and spoke.

"You humans long ago abandoned everything that made Earth a unique place. All of the wonders and glories of this planet, and for what? You allowed a rebellious minority of the privileged class to convince you to turn your back on your heritage."

They began to pulsate anew, until the black-robed Phaerion held up a hand up and the lights ceased.

"I know of Oslo, I knew him well. As Earth began to crumble he was the lone voice of reason that spoke out against the madness. Oslo was a young man in those days, an explorer with a desire to rediscover the history of this planet. We allowed Oslo into our world because we knew he would understand us. We had hoped he would become an emissary to your people, to awaken them and make them understand the dangers Earth faced before it was too late. But the Elephim were allowed to fester and grow, and they soon consolidated their power. We stood by and watched in horror as the world crumbled and slid backwards. All of the accomplishments of Earth's people were wiped away as if they never happened. We could have intervened, but it was pointless, for humanity had long ago closed their minds, their hearts, as well as their souls, and could not be reasoned with. Those who did speak out, like Oslo, were shunned, punished and cast out. So we retreated, as we always do, for we can only involve ourselves so much in human affairs. Such are the laws we are governed by. And now you come to us after all this time seeking our help?"

Achilles stepped forward. "I understand how you must think of us."

"You....understand?" the black-robed Phaerion said mockingly.

"Please, I beg your indulgence. This unit has known Oslo for multiple cycles as well. He is striving with all of his ability to awaken the world once again with the limited resources at his disposal, and these young people are all he has left. Though he assumed much risk to gather them, he pressed on despite the danger that was sure to arise. You claim a friendship to Oslo, yet in his darkest hour, you will not come to his aide?"

The Phaerion glowed and reverberated amongst themselves.

Achilles continued. "I am aware that the Elephim are distracted and in disarray, and they seem unresponsive to any activity here on Earth. And if they do respond, their attacks appear to be uncoordinated and not well led. Flying machines are being constructed by humans, and yet they seem to take no notice. Something has obviously happened, and Oslo is capitalizing on their distraction. After all he has done, can we remain idle and not attempt to rescue him?"

The black-robed Phaerion stared at Achilles. "For a robot, you seem to possess a certain...melancholy. Why is it we find you so peculiar?"

Achilles stiffened.

The black-robed Phaerion continued. "You all will be escorted to your quarters while we discuss a course of action amongst ourselves."

They were immediately led out of the assembly hall and down a long corridor. Upon reaching the end, a hidden entrance slid open and they stepped through. Inside was a room filled with random pieces of mismatched furniture that appeared to be put together by someone who tried to imagine what would be pleasing to humans.

The door slid to a close. They stood about and looked at each other as an uncomfortable silence began to build.

Ray was the first to break it. "Okay, so what now?"

"I hope they take pity on us and help," Sally said

"Pity?" Breeze snorted, "I'll pass on that. We can do this on our own"

"How?" Ray said

"I talked to one of their ships," Breeze replied with a wink.

"What do you mean?" Sally said.

"When I was with the Phaerion inside the assembly area, I touched the hull of one of the ships." Breeze then recounted his experience communicating with the ship named Aerion.

"Ships made of energy," Achilles observed.

"Ships that are alive," added Breeze.

Sally leaned against him. "I don't know why, but I feel so tired."

"The day's events have taken their toll on all of you." Achilles said. "May I humbly suggest that you accumulate a few hours of rest as we wait for the Phaerion to arrive at a decision as to whether they will render aid to us or not?"

No sooner than the robot finished speaking, the lights of the room began to dim.

"Yeah," Breeze muttered sleepily, "need to close my eyes for just a little while." He stretched himself out on a nearby couch and fell asleep immediately. Sally and Ray flopped onto couches of their own and were soon in deep sleep.

The door slid open as several Phaerion floated in. One of them pointed at Achilles. "We wish to speak to you. Privately."

"May I inquire as to why? I wish to monitor and protect these young people as they rest."

"You may drop the charade. We wish to speak to you," the Phaerion repeated.

Achilles nodded. "Very well."

The robot stepped out into the hallway while followed by the Phaerion as the door slid to a close.

CHAPTER
▼
THIRTY

THEY ALL WOKE UP to brilliant sunshine streaming onto their faces. Breeze slowly got to his feet as he stretched and yawned loudly.

Sally tossed and turned on her couch, then sat straight up. "I need to use the bathroom," she said, and headed towards a panel door along a wall that slid open.

"Umm, good morning?" Breeze responded as she stepped by. The only answer he received was the door sliding to close. He wondered how she knew where the bathroom was. *Funny how girls always know how to find one and fast,* he thought to himself, and then chuckled.

He shrugged and turned to check on Ray who was sound asleep on his couch, then stepped over to the window where the morning sun was rising and splashing its light across the arid land outside. Though he had spent his whole life in the desert, he never got tired of its spectacular sunrises.

He then realized Achilles wasn't around. He checked the apartment, but the robot couldn't be found.

He stood perplexed when the bathroom door slid open and Sally stepped out dressed head to toe in a white jumpsuit.

"Well, what do you think?" She twirled around for him to see.

Breeze was tongue tied.

Sally put her hands on her hips and pouted. "Well, I'm waiting."

"Umm, you look great?"

She snorted at him. "I look fabulous!" and she turned to admire herself in the mirror.

"Where did you get that uniform anyway?" Breeze said.

"The closet in the bathroom, there are two more for you and Ray."

"Ray is still asleep."

"How come we always find him sleeping when we're awake, like the time we found him on Achilles couch when he was supposed to be on watch? By the way, have you seen Achilles?"

"Went looking for it while you were in the bathroom. No sign of it."

"Wonder where it could be?" she mused.

They both were startled as the door slid open and Achilles stepped in. "Excellent, all have arisen to greet the new day!" it said, then turned to Ray on the couch. "Excluding Master Verhesen, of course."

Achilles looked over at Sally. "Your choice of wardrobe flatters you, Ms. Trumbull."

She smiled at Breeze. "Even a robot knows when to pay a compliment."

Breeze rolled his eyes and turned to Achilles. "Where did you go? You weren't here when we woke up."

"Exploring the grounds. Quite a fantastic facility," the robot responded.

A chime rang. The door slid open and a sole Phaerion with a red robe glided in. He looked at Achilles and nodded, then turned to Sally. "I see one of you has found the atmo suits we have provided for all to wear, please see the rest of you do the same, then proceed to the hangar bay in one hour. My associates will be posted outside your door to escort you." He turned and glided out the door.

"Atmo suits?" Sally said with exasperation.

"Did you think it was fashion wear?" Breeze retorted.

"Well, yeah. Look how good it fits me!" She twirled around again.

Breeze laughed. "We call these atmosphere suits, or atmos for short. Pilots wear them when testing aerocraft at high altitudes. The suit responds to your body. If you need moisture, it generates it so you can drink, and it will cool you down or warm you up, depending on conditions. It will also pressurize itself to keep blood from flowing away from your brain, preventing blackout."

"Oh, are we going to fly?" Sally said.

Breeze shrugged. "I think they have something else planned for us."

Ray stirred and sat up. "Wow, how long have I been asleep? Say, what's going on?"

Breeze and Sally laughed at the sight of him. His hair was a mess as he wiped drool from his face.

"Pull yourself together Ray and get into an atmo suit. We meet in the hangar in one hour."

"Atmo what? Where are we going?"

"It looks like we're going for a ride," Breeze replied.

An hour later, they were gathered along with the Phaerion inside a cavernous hangar. The four stood together and were surrounded by technicians while across from them were the Phaerion leaders. One of them glided forward and spoke for the group.

"We have engaged in a fierce debate amongst ourselves whether or not to render aid. Both proponents and opponents of the issue made spirited and logical reasons how we should arrive to our decision. Nevertheless, we have decided to help you."

Breeze let out a sigh of relief while Sally squealed and clapped her hands.

The Phaerion spokesman raised a hand. "Please keep in mind our aid comes with the understanding that it will be limited at best."

"What exactly does that entail?" Achilles asked.

"See for yourself."

A set of doors slid back and the scout ship silently drifted into the hangar and settled down onto its landing gear.

"We have mended your ship to the best of our abilities. We can only accomplish so much with metal, for it's not a material we have much use for."

"How do we achieve orbit to intercept the platforms? Our scout ship was stripped long ago of its high altitude capabilities," Breeze said.

"We understand that," replied the spokesman, "but we can only do so much."

"So how exactly do we get to the platform to rescue Oslo?" Ray asked.

"Look carefully and you will see," the spokesman said.

They all looked, but saw nothing, except for Breeze.

"You understand." The spokesman looked directly at Breeze.

He nodded. "Yes."

Sally whispered to him. "What is it?"

Breeze held out a hand and waved it across the scout ship from bow to stern and it responded to him with the same brilliant lightworks he had witnessed from the ship named Aerion on the assembly line. The assemblymen molded a hybrid design of metal and light, attaching it to the undercarriage of the scout ship. Breeze could see how the light spread its tentacles throughout the hull, stiffening and reinforcing the frame and body of the vessel.

"Can everybody see?" Breeze asked his teammates.

They all nodded with awe.

"We had debated long and hard allowing such power in the hands of an amateur such as Breeze," the spokesman said, "which is why we came to the conclusion that we would not give you one of our light-ships. Instead we would graft our technology over yours and create a symbiotic relationship between metal and light."

The spokesman then addressed them all sternly. "You will have to work together as a team if you wish to succeed in your mission. A good friend waits for your rescue and hopefully is still alive."

"Don't say that," Sally said.

"It is best for the truth to be told. Oslo has been a thorn in their side for many years. He was the last best hope of any real resistance against them."

Another of the Phaerion hovered towards them. "Using your ship's propulsion and our light wave, you will approach the upper atmosphere. Upon arrival, you will cut off main power as our light wave will take over and envelope the ship with a cloak and glide it to the platform. You will then synchronize your speed with that of the platform and decide how to best enter it to rescue your friend. We will not and cannot give any further aid."

"Thank you," Breeze said.

The Phaerion turned to look at him and began to pulse with light.

"You are very much welcome," said the spokesman and bowed his head slightly.

Breeze returned the bow with one of his own. He understood the great gift they had been given. It was far more than he expected.

Later that day, the newly refurbished scout ship was pushed out of the hangar and into a cavern that led to the desert. It provided them with shelter from the sun as technicians performed last minute checks.

They all gathered inside the pilot house where Achilles had acti-vated the vid-screens and the holographic projector.

"So we're supposed to take off with full power and hope that we're not detected?" Ray said.

"The Phaerion have assured us that they have detected a gap in the Elephims' defense grid," Achilles pointed at a holographic projection that showed an array of massive black cylinders in orbit above Earth, "a minor breach if you will, but one that will allow us to slip through. The Phaerion are aware of what I realized long ago; the Elephim are distracted and in disarray. The Phaerion have also been observing and documenting the various platforms and ships that the Elephim employ and have identified the cylinder where Oslo is being held prisoner. They have been more than generous to provide us with detailed schematics of it."

"What do you think is our best approach?" Breeze asked.

The robot punched up a wire diagram of their ship. "The Phaerion have fitted our vessel with a docking ring that matches the airlock on the platform." It pointed at a holographic image of the scout ship. On top of it was a ring-like device. "The docking ring will allow us to connect to the extreme lower portion of the platform. From there, we shall ascend to the uppermost levels where Oslo will most likely be found. I have had plenty of experience in dealing with these platforms in the past. I know where the detention levels are located," the robot added.

"Yeah, Achilles, I have no doubt about that, but how can we be sure we won't be detected on approach?" Breeze persisted.

"The Phaerion assured us the light wave coursing through the hull will envelope the ship and mask our approach. As for the platforms, they most likely will be automated and devoid of crew, but there will be personnel on some of them, so we dare not use the ship's sensors." Achilles pointed at Sally. "This is where you come in."

"Let me guess, you want me to project into the platform and scan it," Sally said.

"Do not be frightened, mistress. You have performed this feat in the past and proved yourself during your final training session on the farm. Granted, it did not end well, but this unit believes we have moved on."

Ray squirmed in his seat.

Achilles continued. "Sally, you will need to scan deck by deck and take inventory of any personnel that may be on board until you reach the detention level. When you locate Oslo, I will exit the scout ship and proceed to the platform's airlock where I will interface with a control panel adjacent to it and ensure that it will not reject our request for access. I will also bypass any alarms to mask our presence. Ray will loiter behind to guard the ship and prep for our evacuation while Breeze and I shall traverse to Oslo's location and retrieve him, then return to the ship. We will drift away and descend to a lower orbit for one revolution, possibly two, than begin re-entry into the atmosphere. There are many forests located in the Pacific Northwest where we can land and disappear. We will wait there to ensure that we have not been followed. Once we are certain the Elephim have not tracked our escape, we will proceed to Appalachia for a rendezvous with Raza and Escort."

Breeze nodded his head. "Sounds like a plan. Let's do it." The others agreed.

"Very well then. We know what to do. Let us perform any final tasks and prepare for takeoff. A powerful storm is forecast to arrive by evening and to better mask our ascent, I wish to make a night launch into it and hide within the atmospheric turmoil for a stealthy approach." Achilles paused to look at the three of them. "I am requesting you to endure much more than you have ever imagined. Not long ago you were all living relatively quiet lives, unaware of the history that preceded you and ignorant of what was currently happening to the world around you. Much has changed. You have lost families, homes, and the lives you knew. Virtually overnight you have been forced to grow up fast. You now find yourself inside a mountain with a robot, planning a rescue mission in space. This is not the typical life of a teenager, but you cannot deny the powers that you possess and the responsibilities that comes with them. You cannot turn your backs to your destinies and return to the lives you have known. Life will always be full of change. It is how you manage to adapt to these changes that will determine how bright your future will be."

The trio stood solemnly.

"Now go get some rest. We embark upon our journey at sundown," Achilles said.

They quietly filed out of the ship.

Achilles watched them leave and it wondered if this was the right thing to do.

But what other choice did they have? The robot asked itself.

It couldn't find an answer.

CHAPTER

▼

THIRTY-ONE

NIGHTTIME ARRIVED ALONG WITH the promised storm. The wind was picking up as they climbed into the scout ship and settled into their seats. The interior lights were dimmed allowing the glow from the cockpit's electronics to spill out into the cabin.

A gathering of Phaerion stood by to observe their launch. Though they had woven their light wave into the ship, to the untrained eye it could not be seen. It was a question of having the ability to sense it. For Breeze, it was a matter of going into a trance and seeing the energy that coursed through the ship, like blood flowing through veins.

In the cockpit, Ray and Achilles were going through their preflight checklist as the engines spooled up.

Breeze and Sally were seated next to each other in the cabin when they looked out the window and saw the Phaerion standing on the tarmac, eerily illuminated between flashes of lightning, punctuated by the deep rumble of thunder.

Without warning the ship lifted off with a lurch. It hovered for a few seconds, and then accelerated into the ominous night sky.

Sally took his hand and squeezed it. Breeze squeezed back and settled into his seat.

The scout ship rattled and squeaked as they approached the upper reaches of the atmosphere. Rain pelted the hull while vicious lightning crackled around it. Between the flashes of lightning Breeze could see through the window the outlines of the thunderbirds in the distance as their giant wings flapped and fanned the fury of the storm.

Breeze chuckled. The Phaerion were emphatic that they could only offer them limited aid in their quest to rescue Oslo, and yet they unleashed the thunderbirds to help mask their ascent.

The ship rattled violently while deep in the stern, something heavy crashed to the floor. They broke through the cloud cover and into the starry sky, continuing their ascent until they reached the upper limits of the atmosphere when Ray reached over to the console and shut off the engines. The sound of machinery was replaced by an eerie silence as the ship hurtled into space.

The rattling gradually faded away as they drifted into a higher orbit, but the air inside was thinning and becoming difficult to breathe.

Breeze felt dazed and his head began to nod when he heard Achilles over the intercom ordering them to reach for the oxygen masks that had dropped down from the compartments above. Breeze limply reached for his when the wail of alarms suddenly filled the ship.

Flashes of light began to erupt throughout the cabin and the rattling returned. Sensing he was about to pass out, he lunged for his mask and took in deep gulps of air.

The flashes of light were soon replaced by an energy that flowed through the ship. Breeze watched as it enveloped the hull and filled the bulkheads all the while pulsating like a beating heart. The squeaks and rattles soon faded away as the ship glided through space and their bodies become weightless.

It's the light wave coming to life, Breeze thought to himself.

"We did it! We did it!" Ray shouted over the intercom.

Breeze looked over at Sally as she breathed into her mask. He laughed and pointed at her head. "Bad hair day?"

Sally narrowed her eyes as she reached up and felt her head and realized her long hair was flowing straight up in the weightlessness of space. She shrieked and tossed the mask aside as she rushed to put her hair into a pony tail.

Breeze unbuckled from his harness and floated up effortlessly, then pushed off his seat and glided across the cabin to the pilot house.

"Breeze, be careful!" Sally called out to him.

"How do we look?" he asked as he drifted through the pilot house and into the cockpit.

Achilles waved a hand across the console. "According to the instruments, we have achieved low Earth orbit. The Phaerion light wave has meshed perfectly with the ship, and there is no indication we have been detected by the orbiting platforms. Conclusion: the shielding is functioning within parameters."

Breeze nodded as he gazed at an enormous orbiting platform that loomed through the windscreen. It was a black metal cylinder with rings encircling it in equal segments. He estimated the length to be a thousand times that of their scout ship, with a diameter of two thousand feet. Though no light emanated from the platform, the sight of it instilled intimidation and fear as it drifted in the darkness space with only the sunlight barely reflecting off its nebulous black metal skin. "Is that the one we have to break into?" he asked with a slight quaver in his voice.

"No," Achilles replied, and pointed to the faint outline of a cylinder far off in the distance. "According to the Phaerion, Oslo is being kept inside that one. In the interim, we must drift past all of these." It nodded ahead at the array of platforms they had to skulk past in between.

They spent the next several minutes silently drifting past platform after platform, each one more menacing and larger than the other. And though they seemed to be either abandoned or dormant, they still inspired fear.

Sally floated into the cockpit and gasped as the ship glided uncomfortably close to a platform. Its imposing presence loomed over them as they gazed at it through the overhead canopy. Lights could be seen blinking around it at random, and several windows were illuminated when a figure suddenly appeared in one and stared in their direction for moment before casually turning away and disappearing.

"Still no detection," Achilles said quietly. Suddenly, proximity alarms wailed throughout the cockpit. A shuttle shaped like an arrow and dark gray in color was crossing their path as it traveled to the platform and disappeared into it. They all jumped as the proximity alarms blared again when another shuttle passed dangerously close to the scout ship and also glided into the platform.

"This shielding the Phaerion gave us is working a little too well," Ray said as he silenced the alarm. "It's a miracle those shuttles didn't ram into us."

"It appears we are leaving the heavily trafficked lanes and approaching our target," Achilles announced as it pointed at a platform looming ahead.

"Is it just me, or is it the biggest one yet?" Breeze said.

Oslo awakened to the sound of his name being called. He opened his eyes to gaze wearily at his surroundings. The environment was dark and poorly lit. He struggled to move his hands so he could scratch his face, when he realized they were bound. He raised his head feebly to take in his surroundings and saw nothing but machinery humming with electrical power.

Someone approached and his blurred vision picked out a shape of an imposing figure gliding to a stop mere inches from his face.

"Hello, Oslo," the figure said.

He recoiled at the voice. It was one he hadn't heard in ages and his mind was soon flooded by a wave of memories that had long remained dormant. "Bram?"

"Yes, of course. Who else could pull this off?" Bram said with a hint of amusement.

Oslo cursed and shook his head in a vain attempt to clear his vision. "I...I don't understand. What's happening? What is the meaning of all of this? How...when did you get back?"

Bram appeared corporeal for a moment before turning translucent while his body flickered with spurts of light. "So many questions, so many answers to give. You never really understood the true meaning of everything you've ever encountered, Oslo. You were always out of your depth." He shook his head. "My good friend, Oslo: the student who became a teacher, but never really mastered anything. I see you've put together a team of children to try and undo everything the Elephim have accomplished. Pathetic, even by your standards."

"Bram, what's going on? What are you doing?"

"This is a trap!" Bram roared at him. "Are you truly this dense?"

While Oslo struggled with his restraints, his mind was becoming clearer as the fog of confusion wore off. "Bram, what's the matter? What's this all about?"

"It's about waking up my old friend, and understanding whose side to be on. It's about knowing once and for all which path to take and understanding your own destiny. Do you remember that day I disappeared and never returned? The fateful day when I projected into deep space to get to the source of the chaos affecting Earth and retrieve the answers to our questions? Who were the Elephim? How did they subjugate us? How did they do it so easily? We were so young then, yet so sure of ourselves that we could get the answers." Bram chuckled and nodded his head. "Yes, I was able to get answers." The smile disappeared from his face as his eyes narrowed. "My final day on Earth, you and Raza were there to see me off. Raza...," his voice trailed off to a whisper, "has she grown old and weak, much like you?"

Bram abruptly turned to look at a console in the center of the room as a vid-screen was warbling and flashing urgently. He quickly glided over to it.

"Oslo, Oslo, Oslo," he chided, "you should see your useless rescue team." He punched a series of commands into the console and a holographic projection hovered before them.

"What do we have here but an ancient scrap heap of a scout ship wrapped in light wave? Oh my, we are really pushing it. It appears we've reached out to the Phaerion. How did you manage to pull that off?" He waved a hand. "Don't bother to answer, it makes no difference," he laughed harshly, then turned to look at the console and was awestruck by what he saw.

"Well, your projector is more advanced that I thought. Is she bringing a passenger along?"

The platform they were to break into loomed above them in complete darkness. It was an imposing structure, the biggest of all the cylindrical platforms they had drifted past. It orbited alone and far from the others. It had the appearance of an abandoned structure as there were no lights glowing from the windows and no shuttles approaching or exiting from its interior.

"Why do I get the feeling it's being made to look defenseless on purpose?" Ray said.

"That is what Sally will ascertain." Achilles turned to her. "Mistress, are you prepared for your mission?"

"Can't we just use the sensors?" she said. The fear was palpable in her voice.

"Negative. Sensor sweeps can be detected and trigger an alert. That is why your skills are imperative," Achilles replied.

Sally shook her head and trembled with anxiety.

Achilles persisted. "Sally, you must step up and perform your duty—"

Breeze waved the robot off as he stepped in and cradled her face. "I will be here for you. Hold my hand, we can go in together. You did it before, you can do it again."

She nodded and sniffled while wiping the tears from her face, then sat down in the jump seat behind Ray and Breeze settled in next to her.

Achilles knelt beside them. "This does alter our plans considerably, but we shall compensate. Sally, the two of you must carefully make your way through the complex. Do not move too quickly or make any sharp or sudden moves. From my console I will jam any sensors they may have, but I can only do so much. I shall have Ray steer the ship close to the platform so you will not have to project too far. Locate Oslo with great haste, but with caution so you may retract to your respective bodies quickly. Only then may we execute our rescue and retreat to Earth."

Sally nodded and looked at Breeze.

He squeezed her hand. "We can do this."

She settled back and closed her eyes. "Let's go," she said after a moment of silence, and with a sudden lurch they projected into space between the ship and the platform.

They briefly marveled at the brilliant stars and the glowing Earth below as their astral forms hovered in space, then turned in unison to look back at the scout ship. It was like a mirage and barely visible cocooned within its light wave cloak. Then they looked up at the imposing platform leering over them and the stark reality of their mission sank in.

Sally squeezed Breeze's hand even tighter.

"Let's get this over with," he said.

They drifted toward the platform and came to a stop mere inches from its black metal skin. Achilles had earlier pointed out a section they could pass through that would place them into a corridor that more than likely would have little to no personnel milling about. Though they were projecting and technically couldn't be seen, they did not want to take the risk of being discovered before the rescue operation had even started. From there they could ascend to the detention level where the robot had assured them Oslo would most likely be detained.

"No hesitation," Breeze said, "let's just go in." In his haste, he let go of her hand and dove in.

Breeze immediately struggled with the eerie sensation of matter passing before his eyes. The feeling was akin to holding one's breath for a long period of time while swimming underwater, and he was relieved when he spilled out into a corridor.

Sally was already there and hovered over Breeze as he struggled to compose himself. "You have to remember that we are projecting," she said with a twinge of annoyance. "You have to suspend your natural instincts; otherwise we can't get through this."

Breeze raised a hand. "Look, this is not my talent. I've only done this once before with you, remember?"

Sally nodded. "I'm sorry, I'm just afraid. What if this doesn't work? What if we get caught? What if—"

Breeze drifted up and cradled her face as a current of energy surged between them. "Who cares about the what ifs, we're here so let's finish the job." He pointed to the end of the corridor. "That's the elevator that connects all of the levels. I say we follow the shaft up to the detention level."

Sally slowly nodded at him with wide eyes. "Do you realize we have not held hands since we phased into the platform?"

Breeze was stunned. "Impossible. How come I'm still here with you and haven't retracted back to my body? You said we always have to stay in contact with each other."

Sally shrugged. "I don't know. I think all of this stress is making me realize more about my powers than I ever imagined."

"Whatever it is you're doing, don't stop," Breeze said. "Now come on, let's go."

"Interesting," Bram said as he observed Sally and Breeze from his console, then turned away and glided toward Oslo. "Did you train them to do that? No, of course not. Perhaps it was that witch, Raza, or the robot. What's the story behind the robot anyway, and why does it behave like a leader?" He glared at Oslo who immediately looked away. "Oh, why bother asking you when a mere scan of my own doing should give me what I seek." Bram went silent as he closed his eyes for a moment.

When he opened them his face was as white as a sheet. "How can it be?"

On the scout ship, Achilles shuddered and looked up at the cylindrical platform.

"What is it?" Ray asked.

"No need to be alarmed Raymond. My internal sensors are merely undergoing recalibration. Maintain your course and be aware of your surroundings. We are drifting too close to the platform."

With Ray occupied at the helm, Achilles reached out with its own sensors and detected a presence sweeping the ship.

It cannot be, Achilles thought to itself and probed harder, only to recoil at what it discovered.

A voice spoke to the robot from within. *It's him. It's Bram. We knew this day would arrive. Question: are we prepared?*

Achilles shook its head. *If he is capable of sensing us, then the jammers are not functioning properly. Sally and Breeze are heading into a trap.*

Sally glided up the elevator shaft as Breeze followed, passing through level after level; they did not see a living soul whenever they stopped briefly to inspect the corridors by poking their heads through the elevator doors. Each level had the same bland and sterile features, however the appearance of a particular level brought them to a sudden halt. The corridor was different. The lighting was dim, with dark gray walls as opposed to the bland white ones below. The muted din of distant machinery was replaced by a loud drone.

"Who is running this place?" Breeze wondered. "It's like Ray said, somebody knows we're coming."

"Nothing can detect us. Achilles promised that the jammers would mask our presence, and besides we're projecting, so we're fine," Sally said.

Breeze tried to hide his unease. "Well, we've ascended pretty far and this does look like the beginning of the detention level." He pointed forward. "There's a set of doors up ahead. Let's see if Oslo's there and hope there's no one guarding him."

Without hesitation, they slipped through the doors.

"Well, Oslo, would you like to view your team in action?" Bram asked with a smirk. He shifted from a translucent state to corporeal so he could type commands into the console.

A hologram hovered before Oslo displaying a vid-image of Sally and Breeze in the outer corridor. They both glowed with psychic energy.

"If they are projecting, how can we see them?" Oslo said.

Bram chuckled. "There is much I have learned over time. My ability to zero in on any energy source is one of them, especially if it is not shielded. Shame on you old boy, you should have taught the girl how to better conceal her astral image when projecting. This will be her undoing and her little boyfriend as well."

Oslo writhed in his restraints. "Why are you doing this? What has happened to you? You are supposed to be my friend!"

Bram roared as he flew over and shoved his face into Oslo's. "Friend? Yes, there was a time and place for our friendship, but that has all changed if it isn't painfully obvious to you by now. Then again, change was never easy for you to accept. That can only explain your insanity in trying to oppose the Elephim with your pathetic band of paranormals. What are you trying to accomplish, Oslo?"

Oslo shook his head. "You're avoiding the question. What has happened to you? Why do you work for them?"

Bram laughed. "Work for them? Come now, Oslo, think of it as a partnership." He drifted back toward the console. "How were the Elephim able to eventually dominate us? The many excursions I made to their world of Helena taught me much. What I've learned is that patience is the answer. Helena was once a world with a restless and burgeoning population that was becoming unruly and uncontrollable. So they searched the heavens for other worlds to colonize and offload the more rebellious ones as attempts to cull the population through war led to global devastation. But when they discovered Earth, it was the most unique planet they had ever encountered. Earth was a planet devoid of any humans, but filled with strange creatures that roamed the lands, and it resonated with a powerful psychic energy unlike any world they had discovered and explored. It is this energy that fuels the paranormals of Earth. This was realized when settlers loyal to the governing council of Helena were sent to Earth to tame and colonize the planet but became rebellious themselves when it was discovered that many of their children were born with paranormal abilities. These children became a resource the Elephim had to control. Their ultimate goal was to control everything on Helena, as they would do on Earth. But civil strife on Helena, and a war for independence that erupted on Earth overwhelmed the resources of the Elephim, and the portal that led from Helena to Earth was severed during the war. They have spent millennia since trying to reestablish contact. They eventually succeeded, and this is why we lost to them. Earth may have forgotten about them over the sands of time, but they did not. They have come to take back what they see as rightfully theirs, for we are a resource for them to plunder and use as they wish."

Oslo shook his head in dismay. "So what is it that made you turn against your own world? What did you find on Helena?"

Bram's eyes lit up. "What they showed me is that decay is the natural order of the universe, and that all things come to an end. Earth has reached its peak, yet they showed me a way to live forever with power beyond my wildest imagination. All I have to do is feed off the energy of others." He stared at Oslo with glassy eyes. "It is time for Earth to enter into darkness. You can only prevent the inevitable for so long."

Oslo shook his head. "But the light will shine again."

"Yes, but not for quite some time."

Oslo persisted. "Why the betrayal?"

Bram's eyes flickered. "What I learned is that I was so much more powerful on their world as opposed to Earth. For the first time I felt like I found a home. Helena, for all of its darkness and decay, become a world where I could be a god with unlimited power."

He then clutched his chest and his body shimmered. "It is also where I met the woman I love, as power is nothing if you have no one to share it with, and she accepted me for who I am. She saw my dark side, yet wasn't repelled by it. She became my wife, and for a time, I was truly happy. Helena became my kingdom where I ruled as I saw fit. It did not matter to me that it was the source of Earth's troubles, nor did learning the truth that the regime that ruled Helena were intent on controlling Earth and corrupting our people. I didn't care. They saw me as a divine being. They did not see me as a traitor to my world, but as a king that would revitalize theirs. They eventually abdicated their power to me and I became their lord and savior. All was well in my life and that is why I never returned. Yes, I did possess vital information that could have prevented Earth's demise, but it no longer concerned me. The rising and falling tides of the universe would take its course as it always has. This is the cycle of life and Earth was due for a downfall, so let it be, I said. I found my happiness and that was all that mattered, until my wife betrayed me and disappeared with our child. I am here now to find and reclaim the heir to my empire."

"What was her name?" Oslo asked.

Bram spun around to face him. He hovered silently for a moment until he finally answered. "Kera."

Oslo nodded as he put on his best poker face so as not to reveal his recognition of the name. "I would like to meet her."

Bram responded with a low and menacing voice. "I will find her and make her mine again. Along with my son."

"Son?"

"Yes, that is what I've been told. I discovered her pregnancy after she disappeared. My council informed me of her betrayal and how she absconded to Earth in a ship. She was originally from Earth, you see, but was abducted from her family by the Elephim long ago. A wealthy and prosperous foster family with connections to the regime raised her and she rose through the ranks to become one of their most prominent paranormals. Understand that over the past several centuries, most of the children born on Helena were sickly, and the odds of any of them becoming paranormal are rare to nonexistent. The energy that surrounds Earth and creates the environment for paranormal children to be conceived is not found on Helena. That is why they take the children of Earth, so they may find a way for Hellenic children to be like them. But their experiments created hideous results as these hybrid children were born twisted and demented. The union of Kera and I would have created a new breed of paranormal children for the Elephim, as opposed to the black clad monsters that have plagued the Earth, who are nothing more than hideous laboratory creations from the splicing of Earth and Hellenic genetic material together. What the Hellenic Council desires more than anything is to have natural born children without having to graft the essence of Earth children onto theirs. The children of Earth that are abducted and brought to Helena die within a matter of days for unknown reasons. How Kera managed to survive while other abducted children perished, I do not know. Nor do I know why she betrayed me and left with my unborn child to return to Earth. What I do know is that my son will follow in my footsteps. I must find him. But first, I need to retrieve my body." Bram pointed to a suit of armor that was docked inside a pod. "I need an exoskeleton and whatever energy I can scavenge to stay corporeal, as I've lost contact with my body after being away from it for so long. But you have placed some sort of a fog over Perihelion with electro-magnetic properties that I cannot penetrate. I must become whole again Oslo, if I am to do to Earth what I have done on Helena. You will help me re-unite with my body." Bram's face contorted into a wicked smile. "But as a consolation, I believe you may have inadvertently brought my son to me."

Oslo arched an eyebrow.

"Don't play the fool, Oslo. I know he is close by. If fact, he is aboard the scout ship, is he not?"

"Breeze?" Oslo said

Bram snorted. "No, not that useless whelp."

"Raymond?"

"Yes, I suspect it is him as I cannot shake the feeling. I must secure the boy and ascertain his origins by testing him for the divine essence that will tell me if he is my son or not. But first, I must take the scout ship."

Oslo chuckled. "How? Your body is locked away within the bowels of Perihelion while you are merely a ghost of a man. You are projecting right now, though I cannot fathom how you are doing it. Regardless, you've mastered the ability to be seen and interact with the material world. And besides, with what army are you going to fight with? I don't see any of your Elephim friends here to help you."

Bram threw back his head and laughed raucously. "Do you not remember what I just told you? How did the Elephim get the best of us? They did more than build an army to fight us. They also built the machinery needed to observe, counteract, and eventually control us. It's like any natural resource; you speculate and explore until you discover. Then you put together a plan to efficiently extract, refine and exploit it for your own needs. You must understand Oslo, the Elephim conquered us by encouraging the people of Earth to loathe and disdain the very resource that made us powerful: paranormals. Earth and her colonies were once the glittering jewels of the galaxy and a beacon of light for all the oppressed masses of the outer worlds. The downtrodden of the surrounding systems once risked everything to come to Earth. But the Elephim would not tolerate this. How could they have control over the worlds they wished to dominate when the subjugated chose to leave? So the Elephim put a plan in motion long ago to snuff out the last flame of hope. They infiltrated and took over our sacred institutions and our most valuable resource, our people. They turned them against one another which distracted us. The ones that they favored were placed in positions of power. Those who opposed were banished or killed."

Bram turned his gaze toward a darkened corner of the room. "And this is the result of harnessing a resource and exploiting it." He made a beckoning gesture, and a black clad figure stepped out into the light and stood next to him with a face that was nothing more than pinpoints of light against an infinite blackness.

"Oslo, I would like you to meet Enoch. Think of him as my assistant.

Quite the helper this particular Elephim is, I must confess."

Enoch nodded at Oslo.

"And now," Bram said as he looked up at the holographic image that displayed a live feed from the outer corridor and the astral images of Breeze and Sally could be seen approaching the entrance to the detention chamber, "we will see this resource put to use."

Breeze and Sally entered the detention chamber where they saw a floor to ceiling window that stretched across the length of the room. The radiance of the Earth seeped through it and weakly penetrated the shadowy gloom of the chamber when a lone figure stepped into view.

"Him again," Breeze muttered.

"Do you know this Elephim?" Sally said as she hovered next to Breeze.

Enoch stood motionless with clenched fists as pinpoints of light streamed across his face.

"I suppose I do. He looks like the one that helped me when my transport crash—" Breeze was cut off as a hand grabbed his neck from behind. He struggled to break free, but couldn't. He twisted violently to look at Sally. She too had been captured as she writhed and squirmed, but couldn't escape.

"Don't fight. Don't resist. You'll only make matters worse." A deep, but familiar voice resonated as they were spun around to confront their assailant.

"Hello, I believe introductions are in order. My name is Bram."

Ray swiveled to look back into the passenger compartment at Sally and Breeze, and became alarmed as their unconscious bodies convulsed.

"Achilles, look!" Ray said.

Achilles was motionless while silently staring at the platform.

Ray loosened his harness and leaned over to rap the robot hard on its head.

Achilles' eyes lit up as it grabbed Ray's hand. "What is the meaning of this?"

"Ow, watch your grip!" He grimaced at the pain. "Something is the matter with Breeze and Sally while you're busy staring off into space!"

"My apologies, master." Achilles released Ray and turned to look back into the passenger compartment. It had removed Sally and Ray from the cockpit and placed them there after they projected into the platform. "We have been discovered," it said. "Begin maneuvering the ship to the hangar bay of the platform."

Ray was stunned. "What? I thought the light wave was supposed to shield us."

"It has not. I have failed to compensate for a...variable."

The ship was suddenly rocked hard from an impact, and the cockpit was flooded by the wail of alarms.

Ray was flung to the side and hit his head on Achilles' seat, then floated across the cockpit unconscious.

As the ship began to drift away from the platform, Achilles re-routed the controls to his helm and silenced the alarms, only to have them erupt again as the ship rolled from yet another strike. Vid-screens displayed the damage report showing sections of the hull had been breached as the ship was decompressing rapidly.

Achilles' hands moved deftly across the console as it typed in commands that sealed off the damaged sections of the ship. Throughout the vessel, blast doors could be heard sliding to a close.

It realized the danger they were in, as staying out in the open was tantamount to certain destruction, and immediately maneuvered the scout ship as close as possible to the platform without hitting it, then pointed the bow toward open space. After conducting a sensor sweep at full strength, but detecting nothing, Achilles knew their assailant was still out there and waiting to pounce again.

It fell back into its own mind and reached out with psychic tendrils where it could sense a lone Elephim meshing in perfectly with the blackness of space, and realized it would have to become a decoy and lead the Elephim away from the ship.

Achilles grabbed Ray as he floated about the cockpit and buckled him back into his seat, then punched in a series of commands into the console that activated the auto pilot while establishing a wireless connection with the ship's computer so it could operate it remotely.

Achilles then glided out of the pilot house and into the passenger compartment where it stopped to check the vital signs of Breeze and Sally. They were erratic, as if they were slipping away.

Something is wrong, the voice inside whispered.

"Affirmative," Achilles replied as it floated through the passenger compartment to the exit hatch, and then hit the air dump to decompress the chamber while blast doors slid to a close. It gripped an iron handle and activated the magnetic locks in its boots to keep from getting sucked out as alarms wailed, but faded away with the escaping atmosphere when the hatch rolled open.

Achilles was illuminated by the flashing strobe lights of the chamber and the glow of the Earth below as it stepped to the edge and looked out into the infinite blackness of space.

The Elephim that attacked them wasn't interested in machines it sensed, but instead was tuned to hunting down paranormal energy. Achilles knew it needed to bring to the surface its own paranormal power to act as bait when it turned to look at a shimmering figure that appeared next to it.

The figure spoke in a deep voice. *"We have waited for this moment to arrive, as we both knew it would come. We have preached the importance of teamwork to the young ones, but are we truly capable of doing the same?"*

Achilles shook it head. "Remember, you are a guest. I offered you refuge within my neural matrix until you find your mortal body and re-unite with it. I do not relish the concept of relinquishing control to you."

"Achilles, we merged long ago, and have survived by agreeing to work together. Now it is my turn to shine. I know how to deal with the Elephim that attacked the ship. Allow me to employ my skills. Step aside and let me take control."

Achilles nodded. "Yes, I do suppose you are right, Raven."

"Of course I am," Raven said as the glow around him subsided enough to reveal a man with jet black hair and piercing blue eyes. He glided over to the robot and disappeared into it.

Achilles' eyes flashed as its body shuddered.

"Watch this, Achilles. We shall play a game of cat and mouse. We'll be the mouse for now. Let's lead this Elephim away from the ship." With Raven in full control of Achilles, he released the magnetic locks on the robot's boots and hurtled to the platform.

From a great distance, the Elephim erupted from his hiding spot in the darkness of space to give chase.

"Now that we have successfully distracted him, establish your link with the ship and maneuver it toward the hangar bay," Raven said.

Achilles nodded as it accessed the wireless frequency and took control of the ship remotely. The scout ship spun on its axis and glided after them.

"*Achilles, hate to be a bother, but you will need to open the hangar doors.*"

"Understood," it replied and scanned the platform for the transponder beacon. It locked onto it and sifted through a myriad of frequencies until it found the one that corresponded with the hangar doors, then accessed the traffic control computer via its wireless transmitter and interfaced with it, but was blocked by a sentry program. It rammed the sentry and flung it aside, then immediately inputted codes to open the hangar doors. Each one was denied.

"*My metallic friend, this relentless Elephim is gaining on us and the ship is about to crash into the platform. Any moment now would be a good time.*"

"I will ignore you until my task is complete. I must steer the ship via remote and maneuver it toward the platform while simultaneously accessing the traffic control computer guarded by a hostile sentry program. This is taxing my processing power to its maximum," Achilles responded.

Raven chuckled. "*Didn't know anything could flummox you.*"

"The sentry program is much more complex and tenacious than I have anticipated. I will re-double my efforts."

"*That's the fighting spirit.*"

Achilles lashed out at the sentry and crushed it, then scanned the array of codes that spilled from the carcass of the defeated program. It grabbed those related to the traffic control system and fed them into the computer. The computer relented, and then granted access as the hangar bay doors slid open.

"*Bravo, my scrap yard hero! Bravo!*" Raven cheered.

They arrived at the entrance with the scout ship in tow as Achilles scanned the cavernous hangar. Lights flashed throughout the interior but there were no other ships inside.

The robot cocked its head, then stretched out a hand and felt resistance as a rippling motion reverberated in front of it.

"Force field. I failed to anticipate this. I must access the flight control system—"

"*Never mind that, our pursuing Elephim is rapidly approaching,*" Raven said as it pushed Achilles' essence to the side and assumed control of the robot's body once again. "*Watch and learn. We are a team, remember?*"

"As you so often remind me."

Raven chuckled as it plunged Achilles' hands into the force field and created waves that rippled across its face.

"*Observe. This is how I deal with an opposing force,*" Raven said as he flew them deep into the force field and created a rift, then pushed back with telekinesis and widened it into an opening large enough to let the scout ship slip through. Once the ship was in, he flung them into the hangar bay and slammed onto the floor with a heavy clang while the force field snapped back into place and rippled like waves over an ocean surface. Raven then relented control back to Achilles as the robot guided and lowered the scout ship via remote safely to a landing.

Outside, the Elephim giving chase slammed into the force field and was repelled with tremendous force. The field reverberated heavily from the impact and the Elephim was flung out into space.

Raven spoke. "*My dear Achilles, the Elephim will make another attack, this I can assure you. Close the hangar doors just to be on the safe side. We do have precious cargo to protect within the scout ship, remember?*"

"Yes, of course," Achilles replied, and then leapt over to an access terminal along a wall where it typed in a series of commands. The hangar doors began to glide to a close.

Outside the platform and drifting in space, the Elephim snapped out of his daze and hurtled towards the hangar once again.

"Raven, I must confess that the doors will not close in time," Achilles called out.

"*I know. The Elephim will punch his way through the field based on his current high rate of speed. Allow me to employ a different tactic.*"

Raven assumed control of Achilles and swatted the Elephim away from the platform with all of his telekinetic might. They both watched dispassionately as he disappeared into the darkness of space.

Raven stepped out of Achilles and hovered next to the robot as the doors rolled to a close.

"*Now that was teamwork,*" Raven said.

Achilles chuckled and nodded its head.

The brief moment of levity was broken by a series of heavy blows to the hangar doors. Each strike was announced with a deep thump, followed by a cratering of the metal. After several attempts by the Elephim to break through, the attacks mysteriously ceased and the only sound that was heard throughout the hangar was the rush of air as it began to re-pressurize.

Satisfied they were safe for the moment, they turned to survey the scout ship. It was a disheveled mess with ripped and crumpled metal across the surface of the craft, along with hydraulic fluid spilling onto the floor and hissing from ruptured pneumatic lines. The gangplank began to extend automatically amidst the sound of grinding from its damaged gears.

Raven motioned toward the ship. *"Let's check on the young ones."*

Achilles rushed up the gangplank and into the cabin where it found Sally and Breeze safely buckled in their seats. It scanned their pulses and confirmed their vital signs were still positive, then dashed to the pilothouse and into the cockpit where it found Ray still slumped back in his seat. After scanning his vital signs and finding them satisfactory, Achilles looked through the forward cockpit window and spotted a computer terminal mounted on a wall next to a set of elevator doors.

Raven was gliding into the cockpit and followed Achilles' gaze to the computer terminal.

"I know what you are contemplating. Let us plug into the terminal and ascertain our situation," he said, and then merged back into Achilles.

Bram stared at the vid-screens and smiled. "Enoch has failed to retrieve your students and destroy the robot, but no matter. I'm very impressed by it. Tell me Oslo, where does a robot go to get telekinetic power?"

Oslo squirmed in his restraints as he looked over at the astral forms of Sally and Breeze. He was surprised Bram managed to restrain them even though they were projecting. Both teens were on their knees and trapped within a glowing circle that pulsated on their floor. "The robot is...one of my special cases," he replied.

Bram roared with laughter. "You always were a bad liar. Anyone can call your bluff. No," he said soberly, "this one is different, that much is obvious. Your little project here, your actions of late, has stirred something. And this one," he stabbed a finger at the image of Achilles on the vid-screen, "is one of the reasons."

"And these two," he pointed at Sally and Breeze, "have no idea what's in store for them. And you, my young flier," he inched closer to Breeze who was in a daze, "are truly ignorant of your past, are you not? Your family-, oh, we have company." He smiled as an Elephim stepped into the chamber. The pinpoints of light across his face flashed quickly, conveying a message to Bram.

Bram placed a reassuring hand on his shoulder. "It's quite all right, Enoch, you did well. We will instead employ a different tactic by making them come to us. After all, we have all the bait that we need right here."

He glided over to Sally and squatted before her. "They will come to us and save ourselves the trouble of hunting them down."

He raised a hand and let it hang over her head. "Though it will require just a little persuasion."

Achilles glided across the hangar bay and landed with a clang in front of the computer terminal next to the elevators. It ripped off a panel below the terminal that exposed an array of inputs, and then held out a hand as mechanical tendrils snaked out of the fingers and plugged themselves in. With eyes shining brilliantly, it interfaced with the computer.

It easily neutralized the sentry programs that rushed in to attack, then immediately went to the central core where it scanned through a multiverse of files as it tried to glean more information about the platform, but found nothing but gibberish and deliberately deleted information.

It began to rewrite the central core's programming and jam the sensors throughout the platform when it was interrupted by a lone sentry program that suddenly rushed in. Achilles grabbed it and hurled it away, then casually continued scanning files while simultaneously accessing security vids that displayed live feeds from cameras placed at all levels of the platform, though it noted none were to be found on the detention level, or were being deliberately hidden so they couldn't be hacked. It redoubled its efforts to discover and break into the detention level.

One of the vids clearly showed the mangled scout ship docked in the hangar, but nowhere throughout the platform did Achilles see or sense any other presence.

"*No personnel, no security guards, no outside traffic entering or leaving the platform,*" Raven announced from within Achilles' neural matrix. "*This is peculiar considering the size of this platform. And why no live feeds from the detention level?*"

"I am running into extreme resistance from another wave of sentry programs mounting an assault against me as we speak. Please be patient." Achilles swiveled its head briefly. "I have neutralized them. Accessing the detention level... now."

Scanning the live feed, Raven saw an image that made him recoil.

"I detect that you are witness to something that has disturbed you," Achilles said. "May I query as to what it could be?"

Raven pointed. *"There, on the detention level. That is not good."*

Achilles nodded as they both saw Oslo in restraints, along with an Elephim and a man that shimmered and glowed.

"Do you know this man?" Achilles asked.

"Look closely. Don't you recognize him from the time you served with Oslo? It's Bram. You worked alongside him with Raza. He is the one who took away what is rightfully mine and forced me to seek refuge within you."

They both watched as Bram stood before two glowing circles on the floor, and holding his hand above one of them. Achilles adjusted the live feed to a spectrum view where it found two energy signatures it was quite familiar with: Sally and Breeze.

Bram's head snapped towards the camera as a smile crept over his face.

"He senses us," Achilles announced.

"There is trouble to come," Raven said. *"I must hide within the deepest recesses of your neural matrix to mask my presence. It is best if he cannot detect me."*

Bram knew he was being watched. The same energy signature he sensed when he scanned the scout ship now seemed to be observing him. It felt like a part of him that he had lost long ago was close by. He reached out with his senses but it was gone, as if it went into deep hiding.

Now, to wrap this up, he thought and turned his attention back to Sally as she whimpered.

"My dear," he said, "it's time to become the lure that will reel in the bigger prize."

Sally couldn't even scream as she was hit by a wave of energy from his hands. Her astral form writhed in pain while her body back on the scout ship mirrored her movements.

Achilles heard Sally screaming from inside the scout ship. It immediately unplugged from the terminal and rushed back inside, where it found Ray leaning over Sally and cradling her face.

Ray looked up at Achilles as it stomped down the aisle towards them.

"She's in a lot of pain," he said.

Achilles saw the strained look on her face as she writhed in agony.

"What do we do? We can't just sit here," Ray said.

Achilles shook its head. "We do nothing. Sally's astral form must break free from whatever is attacking her and —"

Her eyes suddenly opened wide with a glaring brilliance as she gasped for air. "It's a trap! He's trying to lure you in!" she shouted before collapsing back into her seat.

"Who is she talking about? What's happening?!" Ray shouted.

Breeze's body began to convulse and gasp for air.

"This is evolving into a grim situation," Achilles replied.

Bram loomed over Sally and doused her with psychic energy, then began to absorb her astral form. His plan was to follow her light trail that linked to her body and assume control of it, and like a Trojan horse, he would have the element of surprise which would allow him to subdue the robot, Breeze and Ray and bring them all back to the detention level. That is, if his torturing of Sally was not enough to goad them to come and rescue her.

Seeing that she was incapable of handling his withering attack and protecting Breeze simultaneously, it didn't surprise him that Breeze's astral form was also writhing in pain as her connection to him was slipping away.

"Sooner or later, your friends will have to come to your rescue," Bram whispered to her malevolently.

Her astral form flickered wildly as he began to feel resistance from her.

"Damn it, Bram! Stop it already!" Oslo shouted.

The last thing Breeze heard was Sally screaming as he was ripped away from the detention level and sent slamming back into his body.

"Sally!" he shouted as he fumbled with the harness and tumbled out of his seat. He shoved Ray aside and leaned over to cradle her face. "She's getting cold," he said.

"Like I don't know!" Ray snarled.

Breeze grabbed her hand and shouted at her hoping to receive a response, then pulled back her sleeve to feel her pulse. What he saw next chilled him to the bone as letters appeared one by one scrawled out across her arm.

"Achilles, look!" Breeze said.

Slowly and deliberately the letters formed a message.

"*We're waiting,*" it read.

Bram ceased his assault on Sally, and then turned to face Oslo with a shrug of his shoulders.

Oslo groaned. "What did you do?"

"I had planned on assuming control of her, but she managed to thwart my attempts, so I had to satisfy myself by sending a message instead. The girl is quite extraordinary. She was able to protect the boy, even cut him loose and send him back to the ship despite my best efforts. And I sense she may be in love with him! Ah, to be young again." He shook his head ruefully as he stared at the empty space that Breeze's astral form had occupied.

Sally meanwhile, was slumped over onto the floor as she didn't have the strength to retract to her body. The hold that Bram had over her was just too powerful and she was exhausted.

Bram glided over to Oslo. "Well, old friend, it's just a waiting game now."

Standing in a darkened corner of the chamber, Enoch's face began to glow as pinpoints of light danced across his face.

"We have to go back in there," Breeze said as Achilles nodded its head in agreement.

Ray sat next to Sally. Her face was becoming paler and her breathing was labored. He gently took her hand and it felt cold to the touch as he looked down at her arm and saw the message hideously scrawled onto it. He gripped her hand tightly as he read it and his face turned red with pent up rage. Through a scarlet fog, he watched with contempt as Achilles and Breeze hashed out a rescue plan.

He stood up and roared at them. "Can't you see that she's dying?"

Achilles turned to him. "And what do you propose we do, Master Verhesen? Rush in with great haste but no logical plan of action? We would only succeed in our capture and incarceration. Would that help Sally? I don't believe so."

Ray growled. "I said earlier this was a trap and I was right. Now you want to lecture me?"

"Achilles is right. We can't do her any good if we just rush in there and get ambushed. We need to think this through," Breeze said. "Even though it seems to be Oslo's friend Bram who captured us, the voice sounded just like Lacifel back at the farm. I don't know what's going on, but nothing is going according to plan.

Ray was incensed. "She should've taken me with her! I could have protected her!"

Achilles cocked its head to one side as Raven spoke from within. *"Enough! The two of them must work together if we're going to save her. Now more than ever, they must set aside their differences and petty infighting. Yes, we may have come here to rescue Oslo, but now we need to save ourselves. So be it. Relay this plan I have just formulated to them."*

Achilles raised a hand, its eyes glowing a brilliant white. Servos whirred as the robot's head turned to face them. "Please devote your attention to me. I have a plan."

Bram was furiously inputting commands into the console. Frustrated by his unsuccessful attempts to project into the scout ship and take control of Sally, he decided to rely on the security cameras to spy on his adversaries so he could better formulate his next plan of attack.

He knew that the ship was using light wave from the Phaerion. He had tangled with those mysterious interdimensional creatures in the past and was aware of their ships made of light. It was wise of the robot to go to them for help, he thought, but couldn't comprehend how it knew of the Phaerion. He was determined to find out.

"Yes," he said loudly as he was able to pick up a live feed into the hangar bay after cracking a security code Achilles had written and put into place. He was impressed at the robot's ability to hack into and counter-program the platform's computers. For an out of production model, there was something unique about it. *No time to figure out that puzzle*, he thought, *I must get a better assessment of my adversaries.*

He panned the hangar camera in a wide arc and saw the battered scout ship, but couldn't detect any activity from it or anywhere throughout the hangar. All of the platform's sensors had been jammed by Achilles, so scanning for motion or life signs, wasn't possible.

Frustrated, he slammed his hands onto the console and stepped back. He couldn't use his own natural abilities to scan for energy sources as he was becoming weaker by the moment. He needed to feed himself with the life-nourishing energy he absorbed from other living creatures, but there was only Oslo, and he was his prisoner and bargaining chip. For now. The exoskeleton he kept in the docking pod did provide enough energy to sustain him, but not enough for him to use his paranormal abilities.

This is why I need my body back. Damn Oslo and that fog!

His body shimmered as he trembled with anger, and then began to laugh ominously as he turned to Oslo. "Why should I be so concerned? There is no other way in or out but through the main hangar doors. The ship is a heap of scrap, they are not going anywhere."

Oslo raised his head feebly. "Are you asking me, or telling me? There is a difference."

Bram glared at him. "That's what your strength was, being the wise one. How could I forget?"

Oslo shook his head. "You said it yourself that it was a waiting game. Is your legendary impatience getting the best of you now?"

Bram fumed with a rage, and then laughed as he wagged a finger at him. "A little psychological warfare? Now, now, Oslo, no time for that. After all, I'm in full control of the situation. I am merely mopping up the last bit of resistance."

Oslo shrugged. "If you say so."

Although Oslo gave the impression that his eyes were closed, he was actually looking out the window from the corner of his eye. From the depths of space, he could see three figures hurtling directly towards them.

Just have to keep Bram distracted, Oslo thought, then wondered what sort of a rescue his students were mounting.

Inside the hangar, the silence was shattered by the shrieking of twisting metal and the scout ship began to emanate with streaks of light, as shattered panels and broken engine nacelles mended themselves from Enoch's attack. The ship's metal body was soon rippling with energy and throbbed like a beating heart.

Inside the cockpit, a message pulsated on a console screen. *Awaiting Commands*, it read.

Breeze gripped Ray tightly to his chest. He had never flown in the vacuum of space and was struggling to maintain his shield as the air within was becoming thin and dank.

He almost dropped his shield when a powerful vision of the scout ship burst into his mind. Images of metal stretching itself smooth while the entire hull glowed with surges of energy dominated his senses. He gasped for air and focused his efforts, all the while grateful that Achilles was outside the shield and pushing them from behind.

As they hurtled toward the detention level, Breeze could see Oslo through the window. He was in restraints with a shimmering image of a man hovering before him and as they drew closer, Breeze realized it was Bram.

They crashed into the window and shattered it as decompression began immediately. Any and all objects not bolted to the floor were blown out into open space.

Achilles struggled to maintain its grip on Breeze's shield while Raven held back the emergency force field with his telekinesis and waited for Bram to get pulled into the slipstream of escaping atmosphere.

Bram was being stretched like putty as he desperately clung to the console. A look of terror was stamped across his face as he lost his grip and was hurled out into space. Raven then relaxed his telekinetic hold and the force field snapped into place.

Oslo, still in his restraints, was gasping for air as recompression began immediately.

Breeze dropped his shield and he and Ray tumbled to the ground. Like Oslo, they found themselves struggling to breathe while waiting for the atmosphere to stabilize.

Achilles approached the console and tapped in a series of codes, and the restraints that bound Oslo released and he tumbled to the floor.

Oslo stood up shakily and stared at Achilles. "A RF? Your make and model seems awfully familiar to me. Did you serve at Perihelion?"

"Affirmative."

"What department?"

"Special Research, sir, Military Science. Privately known within the bureaucracy as the Paranormal Division."

"Oh," Oslo said quietly. "Did you serve under me?"

"Correct."

He arched an eyebrow. "5150? Is that you, after all these years?"

Achilles nodded. "Yes sir, it is I, your dutiful assistant. I am here once again to serve, as always."

"I thought there was something familiar about you," Oslo said.

"That has been a popular refrain as of late. I must inform you, sir, I now respond to the moniker of Achilles."

Oslo nodded. "Very well, Achilles it is then. Whatever happened to you? I faintly remember after a training session involving you and Bram, you just...vanished."

Achilles nodded. "I have anticipated your question and will be more than eager to explain my disappearance, though I must insist we first evacuate the platform immediately. We are all in great danger. There will be a time for me to divulge what has transpired in the past as there is much to be told, of this I assure you."

Oslo chuckled. "Yes, it really is you. You always did talk a lot for a robot."

Achilles' eyes glowed brightly as it stared at Oslo, then swiveled its head as Breeze and Ray approached them.

"Sir, it's good to see you again," Breeze said.

Oslo placed a hand on his shoulder and squeezed it, then immediately wiped his eyes as they welled up with tears. "Boys, good to see both of you," he said while attempting to appear stoic. "Where's Sally? Is she not with you?"

Ray had kept his distance from others and answered with a sullen tone. "Sally is in trouble."

Oslo pointed to a space off to his side. "Her projection was right there, but Bram must have lost control of her when he was blown out and she disappeared."

Breeze let out a sigh of relief. "That means she's back in her body and safe aboard the ship." He then shook his head. "I don't get it. If he's here, then how can he be at Perihelion at the same time?"

"This is something I've been pondering since I awoke here on this platform and came face to face with him for the first time in ages," Oslo sighed. "He has gone mad."

"You're still not answering the question, sir."

He looked Breeze in the eye. "I am not certain. He projected from Perihelion to Helena on what was supposed to be his last scouting mission and he never came back. Yes, his body is still there, but it's as if he has found a way to function without it. Although, he does fluctuate between solid and astral in moments of stress."

Breeze's eyes widened. "That's why I saw him getting stretched when we smashed the window and everything got sucked out."

Oslo waved his hand. "We have more pressing matters at the moment. How is Sally? We must find her. God knows I've put that girl through too much as it is."

"She's fine. I can sense her from here."

"How?" Oslo arched an eyebrow.

"I have a special connection to the ship and it lets me see." Breeze grinned at Oslo's stunned expression. "It's a long story, and a lot has happened since we last saw you."

"It always does," Oslo chuckled, and then his face went pale as he looked toward the force field that covered the shattered window.

An Elephim had stepped out of the shadows and stood before it. It was Enoch. He had blended in with the surrounding darkness and remained hidden as he watched the reunion between Oslo and his students. Pinpoints of light streamed across his face as he took several steps toward them, and then stopped.

Ray raised his hand to attack, but Oslo pushed it back down. "Watch and wait," he said.

Enoch's face pulsated in a rhythmic fashion as the lights rearranged themselves into different patterns.

"Is he trying to tell us something?" Breeze said.

Achilles' eyes brightened. "I'm running an analysis of the pattern, but I am unable to make sense of it."

Enoch took a tentative step forward, then tilted his head and raised a hand to Breeze.

The lights across his face stopped swirling as it went completely black. Then, images began to appear. They were undecipherable at first; a jumbled mass of colors intertwined with one another. When the images stabilized, Breeze saw glimpses of himself at various stages of his life. The ones that shook him the most were those of him training at night.

Breeze couldn't believe what he was seeing. "How do you know all of this about me?"

Enoch shook his head violently and raised his fists while Oslo slapped down Ray's glowing hands when he pointed them at Enoch.

Enoch reached for his throat and made a series of gestures imitating vocalization, and then shook his head as he pointed to his face repeatedly.

"Do we know each other? Did we grow up together in Conception?" Breeze asked.

Enoch slowly nodded his head.

"But, how?" Breeze wondered.

"Breeze," Oslo said, "there is something that you need to know—"

Enoch began to tremble violently before falling to the floor in convulsions and lashing out with his legs and feet as if fending off some invisible force. He then got up on his knees and gripped his head as a mouth formed from his otherwise featureless face, and opened as if to scream, but no sound came out. Then the tantrum stopped, and Enoch slowly rose to his feet. The mouth disappeared and the malevolent black face punctuated by pinpoints of light re-appeared. Behind him, there was a disturbance.

Energy crackled and the lights began to dim as an image of Bram appeared. He began to materialize as he stumbled toward Enoch. "There will be no revelations today or ever—"

"Fine by me," Ray said, and blasted a bolt of energy sending both Enoch and Bram slamming against the force field.

"Ray, no!" Oslo shouted. "Bram feeds off energy. You'll only make him stronger."

Bram rose up as his body rippled with power. "You should listen to him, Raymond Verhesen," he chuckled, "after all, Oslo is very wise." Energy crackled around him as he strode forward. He grew in height with each step he took as he raised a hand and fired a burst of energy.

Breeze threw up his shield just as they were all flung back across the room from the concussive blast and smashed against a wall at the far end of the chamber.

Breeze and Ray weakly got to their feet and looked at each other in a daze. Breeze was only able to raise the shield in time to cover him and Ray while the others were not as lucky. Oslo was knocked out cold and Achilles was unresponsive.

Bram turned and stared as Enoch's face swirled violently with light, then grabbed him by the throat and lifted him off the ground.

Enoch struggled to break free. Bram cursed and flung him across the chamber where he struck a wall and flopped to the floor. He wearily rose to his knees while Bram hovered over him, and then bowed his head with his arms stretched across the floor.

Bram growled. "Get up."

Enoch obeyed and stood to face his master.

"The plan was very simple," Bram said. "Collect them all in one place and eliminate them, with the exception to Raymond, of course. Then, the other paranormals scattered across the Earth would be hunted down and dealt with in due time." Bram touched Enoch's head. "Your disobedience will be rooted out. After all of these years, you really have no need to be sentimental. For now, my adopted son, prove your loyalty to me. Kill them. Except Raymond. Then, go to the hangar and dispose of the girl and the ship."

Enoch's face swirled as Bram turned to point at their prisoners.

They were gone.

Breeze struggled with Oslo as he tried to hold him up and run down the corridor to the elevators. The old man was groaning in pain, while Achilles took up the rear and jogged with a limp far behind them.

Ray was already at the elevators and looked back to yell at them. "Are you sure this is the right way?" "Positive!" Breeze shouted. "These elevators lead straight to the hangar bay."

"Affirmative, Breeze is correct. Continue forward," Achilles called out.

Ray stabbed the call button repeatedly. "Come on, come on, come on!" He turned to watch Breeze dragging Oslo when he saw a black streak rapidly approaching Achilles from behind. "Look out!" he pointed and yelled at the robot.

Achilles immediately spun around with a clenched fist and fired it down the corridor.

Enoch was hurtling straight for Achilles when the fist rammed into his shield, then forced its way through and pounced onto his face with death grip. Sparks and debris flew everywhere as Enoch spun out of control, tumbling and slamming against the floor, ceiling and walls as he tried to pry the fist loose.

Ray, Breeze and Oslo were already in the elevator and yelling at Achilles to hurry up. The robot stumbled and limped its way in just as the doors slid to a close.

The elevator began its rapid descent when a massive explosion from above shook the elevator car violently and debris could be heard hitting the roof. Then, silence settled in and was punctuated only by the elevator chiming as it descended another level, and was soon accompanied by soft pleasing music that filled the air with colorful lights that matched the rhythm of the song. They all turned to look at Achilles.

"How may I be of assistance?" it said.

Ray pointed up. "Can't you turn it off?"

"I would honor your request," Achilles said while holding up an arm without a hand, "but the wiser course of action would be to keep the remaining appendage with a hand available to deal with any future hostilities."

"How do you recover the other one?" Breeze said.

"It does have a mind of its own." The robot winked.

If only they knew, Raven said from within.

A powerful impact on the roof of the elevator flung them to the floor. They looked up to see Enoch's black clad fist punching its way through the ceiling.

Ray let loose with a blast of energy and blew him off the roof of the elevator as sparks and debris rained down on them through the gaping hole he created.

"Damn it Ray, don't you ever think?" Breeze yelled.

"What should I do? Invite him in?" Ray shouted.

The elevator was racked by another impact as Enoch's swirling face glared down at them through the damaged roof. He had rammed the elevator with his shield and was pushing it to the bottom of the shaft at breakneck speed.

Achilles punched a button on the console next to the doors to activate the emergency brakes. They kicked in but couldn't overcome their rate of descent.

"Plan B," it said, then leapt up and barreled through Enoch's shield, grabbed him by the throat and accelerated up and away.

"Get to the scout ship!" Achilles called out as it faded from view up the shaft.

Moments later, the elevator car slowed to a stop at the hangar bay level. The doors hissed open followed by a female voice speaking pleasantly in a foreign language.

"Is she telling us to have a nice day?" Ray said as he stumbled out of the smashed elevator car, and then ran to the scout ship while Breeze struggled to drag Oslo out.

"A little help here!" Breeze called out.

"No, I need to check on Sally and fire up the engines! Try to hurry up!" Ray shouted as he dashed across the hangar bay.

Breeze wanted to lift Oslo up and hover to the ship, but he was too drained and exhausted. He then looked at the distance needed to reach the scout ship and groaned.

He stumbled as he tried to hold Oslo up, but the old man was unusually heavy and he felt it with each step he took.

Up ahead, he could hear the whine of the scout ship's engines spooling up as lights flickered and blinked across the vessel. His thoughts turned to Sally and he wondered if she was okay.

Sally woke up in a fog, never feeling so drained in her life. She struggled to recall what happened and faintly remembered rushing back into her body after seeing Bram getting blown out a shattered window on the detention level.

She struggled to get up from her seat and managed to stand up for a moment before collapsing back into it and she vomited. She wanted to cry as she wiped her face, but didn't have the strength. She looked around feebly, hoping to see someone, anyone, and felt a crushing despair when the realization hit her that she was alone.

She tried calling out for help, but her throat was dry and she coughed harshly. She then leaned back in her seat when she heard a sound that made her grip the armrests. Someone was running up the gangplank, followed by rapid footsteps racing down the aisle. She wanted to turn around and see who it was, but nausea overwhelmed her.

"Sally!" Ray shouted as he rushed down the aisle and stopped at her row. "Sally! I, oh —" he recoiled at the smell of vomit and her disheveled appearance.

"Ray?" she said and held out a hand.

"I see that you're... doing better. I have to go warm up the engines." He ran to the pilot house and into the cockpit.

She could see him silhouetted against the glow of the console as he settled into his seat. Only once did he stop to look back at her as he prepped the ship for takeoff.

Tears flowed down her face while she looked out the window. The running lights from the ship reflected off the hangar walls and she found them to be hypnotic and soothing as they flashed in alternating patterns.

She settled back in her seat and thought about her family and what fate might have befallen them. She went through all of the events in her mind that transpired since the day she arrived at Perihelion, to the moment she and Breeze were held prisoners at the mercy of Bram.

It was the imprisonment that bothered her the most. Though it was her astral form that was held hostage, she couldn't get over how physical it felt, and adding to the helplessness was that Breeze was held a prisoner because of her weakness in not being able to defend him. She was grateful she was finally able to cut him loose and send him back to safety when Bram tried to possess her.

She had never really been challenged before when projecting, and this was the first real defeat she had ever experienced outside of her first encounter with Kera. She spent her whole life in a controlled environment where she was always calm, cool, and collected. But Bram's assault on her shook her confidence to the core.

Her trance was broken when she heard more footsteps ascending the gangplank. She turned feebly to look and her heart soared.

It was Breeze. He had Oslo draped over his shoulder as he struggled to carry him. Breeze saw her and smiled.

He lowered Oslo into the seat across the aisle from her and buckled him in, then leaned over to cradle her face. "Sally, I'm so happy to see you."

She was about to say something when she pushed his hands away and placed a hand over her mouth.

He laughed and shook his head, then walked toward the stern where she heard him fumbling around in the lavatory, and coming back with clean towels. "Do these seem familiar?" he said with a wink.

She laughed and thought about her insistence on adding a "woman's touch" back when they were prepping and cleaning the ship at Perihelion.

He sat next to her and gently wiped her face when she took the towel from him and smiled weakly. "I can manage," she said, and finished wiping her face clean when they both heard Ray yelling from the cockpit.

"I'll be right back," Breeze said and ran to the pilot house.

"What's the matter?" he demanded to know, and stopped in his tracks when he saw what Ray was pointing at. Across the hangar, flames were pouring out from the wrecked elevator car they had ridden in when, like a whirlwind of fury, two figures erupted from it and slammed into a wall directly across.

It was Achilles and Enoch. The robot was flailing away wildly with its one hand and kicking while Enoch blocked and punched back as each blow he made dented its armor.

"Achilles is not going to last much longer out there if we don't help," Breeze said.

"I can take that Elephim out from here with the weapons console," Ray offered.

"No! You could hit Achilles and do more damage. I have an idea." He raced out of the pilot house and back down the aisle, rushing past Oslo and Sally.

"Breeze?" she called out to him.

"I'll be right back! I promise!" he shouted.

She slumped in her seat and looked over at Oslo who was beginning to stir. She reached out across the aisle and gently squeezed his hand. "We need to go home," she said softly.

Oslo weakly squeezed back in agreement.

She smiled for a fleeting moment, and then wondered to herself, *where is home?*

Achilles was fighting for its very existence. Each blow it landed on Enoch made him punch back twice as hard, and only having one hand to use only added to its predicament as the link to the missing hand had been severed.

Achilles then changed tactics, lunging for Enoch's throat and squeezing as hard as it could. Enoch flailed with his fists in retaliation when Achilles heard a garbled voice over its internal intercom. It sounded like Breeze but couldn't make out the words. Achilles turned to look at the ship and saw Breeze running toward them.

"No!" the robot shouted when Enoch broke free from Achilles' death grip and flung it to the ground, then pounced onto its chest and pinned the robot's arms with his knees. He then rained blows upon Achilles' head, each strike denting the metal deeper and deeper.

Achilles could only watch as Raven spoke from within. *Is this how it ends?*

Breeze made a running leap and flew straight towards Enoch and Achilles when he instantly felt his energy draining upon approaching them. He lost control and bounced across the hangar floor, sliding to a stop just a few feet away from Achilles' head.

Enoch halted his assault upon the robot for a moment to stare at Breeze while the pinpoints of light on his face began to spin at a rapid clip.

Breeze sat up with great effort as the power drain he experienced ebbed. He then looked at Enoch, whose face was becoming more expressive as a mouth and eyes emerged from the inky blackness of his face. He began motioning with his hands in an attempt to communicate with Breeze. Behind him, the elevator doors next to the damaged ones opened.

A fast moving missile erupted from within and slammed into the back of Enoch's head. His mouth opened to scream, but no sound came out as he slumped over onto Achilles.

Achilles weakly lifted the arm with the missing appendage while its wayward hand glided over and snapped back into place, and then grappled the limp body of Enoch and rolled him off.

Achilles and Breeze then both stood up to face each other.

"You know, when we first saw you at Hammer Jack's, the flying fist trick seemed to be your ace in the hole," Breeze said.

Achilles chuckled. "It is quite...handy."

Breeze groaned and rolled his eyes, then pointed at Enoch. "Is he dead?"

"No. It would require a greater level of force to accomplish that. Nevertheless, we need to evacuate immediately."

They both heard the whine of engines approaching, and they turned to see Ray through the windscreen piloting the scout ship across the hangar to pick them up. He swung the ship around and lowered the rear cargo ramp.

They limped toward the ship together, when Breeze slowed, and then came to a stop. He felt as if someone was calling to him. He turned back to look as Achilles continued ahead.

Enoch was standing and looking directly at him with a face of a young boy trying to vocalize.

Achilles was halfway up the ramp and realized that Breeze was no longer behind it. The robot turned and saw him transfixed in a hypnotic stare with Enoch.

"No, Breeze!" it shouted. "It is too late for him. Walk away."

Breeze didn't listen as he stepped towards Enoch.

"Breeze, it is of no use. He cannot be saved," Achilles said.

"But he needs our help," Breeze responded in a dazed voice

"He is too far removed from his humanity. There is nothing that can be done for him."

"I don't understand any of this. Why do I feel like I know him?" Breeze wondered.

Ray spoke over the wireless. "We have to leave. Now!" He throttled the engines to emphasize his point which only seemed to agitate Enoch as his facial expressions became desperate.

Between the shouting from Ray and Achilles and the pleading gestures of Enoch, Breeze became overwhelmed as to what action to take.

The spell was broken as Enoch mimed a scream and his hands went to his head. In a repeat of what occurred on the detention level, Enoch began fighting off an invisible force as two Elephim materialized from the walls of the hangar. Both were taller and burlier than Enoch and they flanked either side of him.

The Elephim that stood to the right of Enoch had a glowing red stripe that ran down across his chest from the shoulder to his waist. The other had a diamond shaped symbol that glowed and pulsated on his chest.

Enoch was trembling from head to toe while his face morphed from an expressionless black slate to a human face, when he was knocked into unconsciousness by a single strike to the head from the diamond Elephim and collapsed to the floor of the hangar.

Then they both turned their attention to Breeze.

Breeze felt time stand still as he stared at the Elephim, and swore he could hear them speak. Their language was that of the cosmos; eerie stretches of silence embellished with the staccato hiss of static. All of it sounded like a code to him.

The Elephim tilted their heads quizzically as they realized that Breeze was privy to their communications. Their hands began to throb with malevolent energy, and then they pointed them at the scout ship.

Breeze turned to look at the ship and saw a glowing mass had enveloped it, and recognized the light wave the Phaerion infused into the hull. He reached out and it leapt toward him. It was warm and soothing as his drained body felt nourished and new again and his mind became one with the ship. He could see the past: the light wave that repaired the scout ship while in the hangar; the present, where he saw Ray gripping the helm as a whirlwind of red light swirled over him; and the future, where the ship glowed within a fire.

He saw Sally and Oslo sitting together in the passenger cabin. Oslo's glow was muted as he was a bone weary man whose soul was tired and old. Sally was a stark contrast to Oslo; she shined like a brilliant light that was stained with confusion and sadness.

He then saw Achilles standing on the stern cargo ramp. The robot emitted a mechanical glow that pulsated with brief flashes of pure white light. He looked deeper and wasn't surprised to see a human face peek out from behind the robot, and then disappear. It was the same one he had seen when he was training with Achilles at Raza's farm.

The spell was broken by an incredible blast that flung Breeze forward just as the scout ship throttled its engines and raced toward the hangar doors. Breeze was scooped up by the light wave as they hurtled through the hangar bay.

The cargo ramp was closing. Achilles, who had been flung deep into the ship by the blast, raced back to the ramp with an outstretched hand.

The last thing Breeze saw were Achilles' eyes glowing brightly as the cargo ramp sealed shut.

Breeze looked up at the overhead lights as they flickered past faster and faster when he was slammed into the back of the ship as it rammed through the hangar doors. The light wave that surrounded the vessel flickered violently as all of its energy was diverted to the bow to absorb the impact, leaving the stern exposed.

Breeze found himself in open space. He shivered violently and gasped for air as he watched the ship hurtle away in a cloud of fiery debris, Sally's face in a window screaming his name.

The coldness of space gripped his body like a vise. He tried to breathe, but it felt like fire in his lungs. He convulsed and went numb as his mind drifted away.

He was back on the island and swimming in the crystal clear waters of the cove. He slipped beneath the waves and descended with the light fading the deeper he went. Soon, the warm water gave way to an icy cold current. He shivered, feeling lost and alone as he wrapped his arms around his body when in the distance, he saw a light. It was soothing and it took his mind off his worries. The light changed into a figure of young girl with a familiar face.

It was Nina, and she whispered in his ear.

"Just breathe with me," she said, "and the shield will rise."

Nina embraced him, and he could feel his lungs move up and down while drifting away into a cloud of light, and then woke up gasping for air and surrounded by a constellation of brilliant stars. His breathing became relaxed as his shield rose to cocoon him.

He gathered his wits in time to see the scout ship tumbling through space. It was succumbing to Earth's gravity and falling rapidly.

He looked back at the platform and saw a jagged opening where the hangars once were, as an endless stream of debris spewed out, when two Elephim darted out amongst the wreckage, swerving to avoid chunks of steel and sparking wires that swarmed around the damaged platform.

He could sense them as their strange language of static hiss filled his mind.

He had to protect his friends from them, and he steeled himself for the impending confrontation.

Alarms wailed throughout the ship as Achilles quickly made its way to the pilot house and into the cockpit to sit in the co-pilot's seat. The ship was tumbling and Ray had his hands full trying to regain control.

"When we rammed those doors there was a massive power surge" Ray said. "The light wave seems to have absorbed most of the impact, but it short-circuited everything and tripped a lot of breakers in the electrical panels. I don't think this pile of scrap is going to survive re-entry. We have to get on a lifeboat."

Achilles shook its head. "Negative. The lifeboats do not contain the shielding required to survive re-entry."

Another set of alarms went off as emergency rockets fired and leveled the ship, while armored slats dropped into place over the windows, blocking their view. The console went completely dark for several moments, and then a solitary vid-screen lit up with a map of the Earth displayed on it with a glowing orange light illuminating a single point on the globe.

"The ship has gone into default mode. It will take us back to Perihelion under auto pilot," Achilles declared as it tapped the console.

"Is this armor strong enough to survive re-entry?" Ray pointed at the heavy metal slats covering the windscreen and cockpit windows.

"There is a high probability we will survive re-entry into the atmosphere. The concern is the shield over the island. If there is no one there to open a portal for us to slip through, the results could be disastrous.

"Then surviving re-entry is the least of our problems," Ray said.

Sally stepped into the cockpit and gripped the back of Ray's seat. "What's happening?"

"We're going back home," Ray responded.

"What about Breeze?"

He didn't answer.

Achilles pointed at the console. "We are flying blind, mistress, and the auto-pilot has assumed control. The light wave has lost it resilience and faded, as it appears to react only when Breeze is present. We must retrieve him if we are to survive. I request that you locate and lead him back to us. Are you able to project, Ms. Trumbull?"

She shook her head as tears welled up. "No," she said weakly, "I just can't." She closed her eyes and whispered. "He's out there all alone."

"He'll be fine. He can manage. With his shield he can survive re-entry and fly back to the island. We can bring the ship back safely ourselves," Ray said in an attempt to ease her mind.

Sally shot him a look filled with venom, then turned and made her way out of the pilot house and down the aisle to sit next to Oslo. She took his hand and held it.

In the cockpit, Achilles addressed Ray. "You may surmise I am incapable of understanding human interactions and emotions, but I do possess enough knowledge to declare the following: that did not go well."

Ray waved him off. "Can you find him?"

Achilles tapped its head. "Intercoms are either inoperable or jammed. Sally was our best chance, but she is unable to perform her duties. Therefore, Breeze is on his own."

Ray looked straight ahead at the armor covered windscreen. "The armor will hold up, I know it will."

Achilles didn't respond.

CHAPTER
▼
THIRTY-TWO

EXCORT THROTTLED BACK THE engines as the transport touched down in the plaza before the dormitories.

"We're here," he announced over the intercom.

In the passenger compartment, Raza held Nina in her arms. She had done so for the duration of the journey from Appalachia. The girl was faring poorly, and only when they drew closer to Perihelion did she begin to stir and show signs of life. Though Raza had a fountain of life on her farm, Nina needed the deep blue sea and all of its energies to sustain her.

Nina seemed to be doing well on her mother's farm, but took a sudden turn for the worse once Breeze and the others departed for their mission to rescue Oslo. She became bedridden and incessantly called out Breeze's name until she collapsed from exhaustion.

Raza was distraught as she hovered over her daughter night and day. Nina's periodic outbursts of anguish and pain only served to remind her of a time long ago when Nina underwent the same agony, an agony that brought the fateful decision by her and Oslo to return to Perihelion for their daughter's sake. It was happening all over again.

"May I not find the peace and tranquility I seek?" she asked aloud as she held her daughter's hand.

Excort stood in the doorway of the bedroom and watched in silent despair. He and his wife, Mila, had practically raised and cared for Nina all her life. She was a daughter to them. He knew what the eventual outcome would be if they didn't leave Mount Pleasant. Nina had to return to the island.

He placed a hand on Raza's shoulder. "We must go."

Raza pushed him away, and then threw herself over her daughter and sobbed. "Not again! I won't do it!"

Excort spoke with a steely voice that attempted to mask the pain in his heart. "My dear lady, we need to give her a fighting chance. We must take the risk."

Raza leaned back and wiped her eyes. "What you say is the truth. I just cannot accept it." She shook her head. "All I wanted was to be a family again. To feel what it is like to be...normal. Now with the others off and risking themselves to find my husband...her father..."

"Raza, I did not mean to come off so harsh—"

"No." She grabbed his hand. "Forgive me, old friend. I realize how selfish I am. I must confess and come to grips with the fact that my isolation and loneliness had driven me mad." She looked in Excort's eyes. "What have I done?" she whispered. "I have sent others to do for me what I could never do for them."

He kneeled before her and held her hands. "You are the best thing to happen to those young ones. After all they have been through, you have been their rock in a sea of darkness. That is why they are willing to sacrifice for you. You are a symbol of the stability they so desire. Everything about you represents what they yearn for, a family and a place to call home."

Raza shook her head. "And to think how poorly I treated them upon their arrival here." She looked out the window and saw the setting sun dipping below the mountain ridge. She then patted Excort's hands. "Yes, you are right. She must...we must return. But how? I thought Perihelion had been compromised? And what of traveling over the Bad Lands, it still is perilous, no?"

Excort shrugged. "It is of no matter to us. We go, and she has a chance to live. We stay..."

Raza leaned toward him. "How do we get there? With what ship?"

"I have been taking advantage of Achilles' extensive collection of parts warehoused in its barn," Excort replied. "Quite the hoarder, that robot. I have been repairing and upgrading the transport I piloted to bring Nina here. We will use it. But we have to travel by night over the Bad Lands to avoid detection for I cannot seem to procure the parts needed to repair the generator that provides the shielding to cloak the ship. We will get as close to Perihelion as possible and ascertain its safety before we attempt to land. We have no choice. We must do this, Raza."

They left Appalachia the next day and traveled by the darkness of night over the Bad Lands to Perihelion, then landed the transport at sunrise and hid the ship deep within any wooded area or ravine to avoid the possibility of Elephim patrolling the skies.

What they witnessed while traveling over the Bad Lands was a stirring of its inhabitants. Long columns of soldiers with torches of fire could be seen marching across the land at night, accompanied by sporadic flashes of light on the horizon. Something was spurring them to action, something that only the presence of the Elephim could do.

Over the next two days, Excort picked his way carefully through mountains and valleys, flying the transport close to the terrain to avoid detection from above, but did attract attention from below as there were a few close calls when shots were fired at them while flying over remote villages.

They arrived at the coast and followed a southerly course for several hours. Where the warm waters of the Gulfstream flowed closest to the land is when Excort banked the ship to the east and flew out to sea. After several miles over the ocean and with the mainland far behind them, he changed course and pointed the bow to the southeast to follow a clandestine route that would lead them straight to Perihelion.

As the ship glided over the windswept ocean, Excort received a flash communication from a submerged transponder that recognized the transport, and surfaced to broadcast a secure transmission. It was a recorded message from his wife, Mila, and he eagerly loaded it onto the vid screen.

Their sons from the surrounding islands had returned to help, it read. Together with the aid of the remaining RF, they repelled the Elephim that invaded Perihelion. The electrical systems had been restored and the fog had been reactivated.

Excort was relieved. It was what he needed to know so they could return safely. Only those who knew how to navigate through the fog could find their way to Perihelion. They would have to enter the vortex to get there, but he was well aware that the Elephim would be patrolling the perimeter of the fog and ambush any ship that approached.

They had no other choice. There was no other place to go.

Excort called out of over the intercom. "Mistress, prepare yourself. We will be entering the vortex soon. My wife has sent me the fortunate news that the island is safe to approach."

Raza held Nina close to her. It had been ages since she last traveled through the vortex. She was aware of the disorientation and the sense of a loss of time that awaited her on the other side of it. Unlike those who traveled through it periodically, her body need to acclimate itself again to the island's distorted flow of time.

The transport bucked wildly as bursts of greenish light flashed violently through the windows. She clutched her daughter and closed her eyes.

They fluttered open when she heard Excort's voice over the intercom, but she couldn't understand what he was saying. Though it felt as if she had been asleep for days, she knew it was the time lag effect of the vortex that made her feel this way. She gazed out of the window where below, and rising up from the ocean as the transport glided closer, was Perihelion.

They circled the island, and then headed straight for the dormitories. The transport touched down in the plaza amidst the whine of turbines as they kicked up clouds of dust and debris.

Raza cradled Nina her in her arms as she disembarked from the ship. Excort was there to greet her at the bottom of the gangplank.

"Come Raza, there is a fountain deep below the dormitories. I will take you there."

She nodded and followed him to a stairwell along the side of the building.

He guided her down spiraling steps made of stone, with each step glowing a phosphorus green until they entered a dimly lit chamber with a pool in its center, and above them the ceiling arced into a dome whose surface shimmered from the quartz embedded within.

Raza knelt at the edge of the pool and slowly lowered Nina into the water, then released her. The girl submerged into the depths.

Excort placed on hand on Raza's shoulder. She squeezed it while staring intently at their wavering reflections on the surface. A smile lit up her face when Nina ascended to take a breath of air.

"Hello, mother," Nina said sweetly.

Raza fought back tears as Nina climbed out of the pool and hugged her.

"I'm home," Nina said.

"Yes, I suppose you are," Raza whispered. She closed her eyes as powerful memories from the past rose up and consumed her.

She found herself walking through the corridors of Perihelion as if she had only been gone for a moment. Around her, cadets were heading to their respective classes or study halls, while outside the grounds were bustling with activity as military personnel boarded transports to embark upon yet another mission or assignment. The bay was filled with an armada of vessels, and sleek aerocraft darted overhead against a backdrop of blue skies and mountainous white clouds.

She was a young girl from the hills of Appalachia in those days. Agents from Perihelion had visited her at her family's farm and told her that she was special. She could barely remember their names. One was named Horton, the other one she couldn't remember. They offered her a chance to go to a place where her talents will be put to great use and she could make a difference in the world. She would be trained to use her gifts to the best of her abilities and to serve a higher cause. Her parents relented and granted permission after much pleading from her, and she left Mount Pleasant without so much as a backwards glance, eager to experience a new beginning far from home.

She remembered arriving on the island and was awed by its lush, tropical beauty. She had never traveled outside Appalachia, and was immediately overwhelmed by her new surroundings. Her excitement gave way to despair as everyone she met was from the larger cities from across the world. They were so cosmopolitan, and it contrasted sharply to her rural upbringing. She felt lost and alone until she met Oslo.

He was tall and awkward, but a good soul, that she knew. She watched him walk down the halls, towering above everyone, slumping his shoulders and keeping his head down in an attempt to appear shorter.

She would never forget how bold she felt to walk right up to him, telling him to stand up straight. She had stood with her hands on her hips, lecturing him on how handsome he was and how he should carry himself better.

He had stared at her with a stunned expression, and then blurted out an invitation to the spring dance in the courtyard that evening. His face turned red with embarrassment as he did, erasing his otherwise pale complexion. She smiled sweetly and said yes.

She danced with him that night, and although they were surrounded by other couples, they were truly in a world of their own as they glided across the dance floor to the soothing music that the band played. The air was warm and inviting as it blew across the bay and into the courtyard where they became one under a star filled sky, while luminous torches that lined the courtyard cast a blue glow over them.

She sighed deeply and opened her eyes. She was back now, holding her daughter tightly in her arms with an old friend to comfort her. Back to a place she thought she could never return to.

There was a commotion at the top of the steps as Mila and her children came rushing down the stairwell. She rushed into Excort's arms and buried her head in his chest as his sons and daughters came over and expressed their joy at seeing their father again.

The dark and moody chamber echoed with the sounds of laughter and elation while the pool began to glow from an emerald green to a pulsating blue.

Raza hugged Nina even tighter as the blue light illuminated mother and daughter in an angelic glow.

"When is father coming back home?" Nina whispered.

Raza looked up at the crystalline surface of the dome that sparkled like stars in the night sky.

"Soon," she said.

Oslo stirred in his seat.

Sally patted his hand and smiled reassuringly.

"I'm sorry about everything I've put you through," he said in a weak and trembling voice.

Sally shook her head. "You've opened my eyes to the truth of the horror that surrounds us. You have nothing to apologize for."

He smiled and squeezed her hand.

She looked toward the pilot house. Within the cockpit she could see the silhouettes of Ray and Achilles huddled over a lighted screen.

Achilles pointed toward a bar graph on the right side of the screen. "This represents the current temperature of the hull." It pointed up. "Should the bar achieve this height, it translates into the early stages of the hull undergoing structural breakdown." It pointed even higher. "This is catastrophic failure."

Ray cursed and shook the helm violently, then shoved the throttles back and forth, but received no response. He pounded the console with his fists then turned to look back into the cabin where he caught Sally's gaze. Their eyes locked for a brief moment before she looked away.

Breeze was surrounded by Elephim who had arrived from neighboring platforms. Every time they would approach him, he streaked away involuntarily. It was as if his shield was instinctively protecting him by acting on its own, moving him out of harm's way.

His breathing felt restrained and his lungs ached from re-breathing the air he exhaled. For every breath he took, toxins were being scrubbed out of his blood and replaced with oxygen.

He watched in frustration and panic as the scout ship barreled toward Earth. In the distance the platform continued to burn as debris spewed from the shattered hangar bay.

A concussive blast hit from behind and sent him tumbling until he managed to regain control. He turned and faced a patrol ship that was trailing him. Its forward cannon bristled with intensity.

Several patrol ships from surrounding platforms were now responding to the distress calls of the wounded platform. They, along with a multitude of Elephim, flanked him from left to right, and from above and below.

He was trapped.

Oslo mumbled and twisted in his seat as he gripped Sally's hand tightly. "Breeze is lost and alone out there. Guide him back."

"I'm afraid to," she said.

"Don't leave him to the wolves! I'll be here to give you strength. He's the only one who can truly save us." Oslo looked in her eyes. "The light wave responds whenever Breeze is near. The greater the distance from him, the weaker it becomes. I know of the Phaerion. I have known them for quite some time, and why they helped you like they did. It was because of Breeze. They do not give their aid on a whim. They are not as sympathetic to humanity as they once were. The light they have woven into the ship is a gift, and one that will protect us. Breeze is the key to it. Go find him."

She stared at him for a moment, then leaned back in the seat and closed her eyes. She whimpered when her astral form broke free from her body. Her nose began to bleed.

She floated out of the ship and into open space, and then turned to look back as it hurtled away. The armored skin was beginning to glow bright red as it entered the outer fringes of the atmosphere. She looked up and saw the platform in the distance. She scanned for signs of life amidst the cloud of debris that spewed from it. Not far from the platform, she detected Breeze's aura. He was surrounded by Elephim and patrol ships.

She rushed to him, consciously aware that the further away from her body she traveled, the greater the feeling that a chain was pulling her back. She was too weak to project, and her body was telling her so.

She strained to get closer to Breeze. She could see him amidst the horde of Elephim that were trying to overwhelm him. He was glowing brightly, brighter than she'd ever seen.

The malevolent energy surrounding the Elephim was horrifying. If they were once human, there was very little evidence of it. They were so focused on capturing Breeze, they did not detect her.

She moved in closer.

Breeze was trapped. They were closing in on him.

Beyond the encroaching Elephim, he saw a faint wisp of light approaching like a firefly in the night sky.

A ghostly image of a young woman materialized from it. She spoke with a faint, but familiar voice that echoed in his head. She kept calling his name and pleading with him.

The Elephim inched closer, their faces nothing more than a swirling black mass. The static they emanated was overwhelming.

Through the cacophony of static, he could still hear the woman calling his name. He cleared his mind and tuned in to her voice, when a face appeared before him. It was Sally.

"Come back to us Breeze," he heard her voice in his head.

A sense of calm swept over him as fear and doubt melted away. He saw a path that trailed behind her, a ribbon of light that stretched toward a burning flame in the distance as it hurtled toward Earth.

He knew what had to be done.

The scout ship rattled and groaned horribly as its metal skin peeled off from the friction of the atmosphere. The temperature inside the ship was beginning to rise. Inside, Ray and Achilles sat strapped into their seats while monitoring the only active vid-screen that displayed the hull's temperature, and it continued to rise toward critical mass. They didn't bother looking at one another. There was nothing to be said.

Raven spoke from within. *That Elephim we fought with on the platform has drained us. Otherwise, we could save the ship.*

Achilles swiveled its head and responded. *We have done all that we are capable of performing. It is imperative now for Breeze to find the strength and the will to come to our aid.*

Raven sighed. *Our fate in the hands of a young man who is not aware of his potential. Has it come to this?*

You must have faith in him, Achilles said.

My dear Achilles, most of my faith has faded from me a long time ago, Raven replied.

Oslo held tightly to Sally's hand as the lighting flickered erratically throughout the ship. He was her anchor. He wouldn't let her go.

Sally's nose was bleeding profusely.

One of Excort's sons came running down the stairs to the chamber. "Father, we have an incoming ship heading toward us!" he said breathlessly.

"Impossible! The fog has us hidden," Excort said.

"Father, it is coming from high above, not from sea level," his son responded.

Excort broke away from the reunion and followed his son up the stairs as they exited the dormitory and headed to the Administrative Building. They took the elevator up to the roof and stepped out into the brilliant sunshine. Situated in the middle was a rectangular structure with no windows and a metal door. A tower with a spiral staircase leading to the top stood next to it. On top of the tower laid an antenna array.

Excort rushed toward the structure. "Follow me, Xenthan."

Xenthan ran behind his father. "The auxiliary air traffic control tower? I didn't know it was still active," he said.

They burst into a dimly lit room with only the glow of vid-screens to light up its interior, coupled with the endless hum of electronics operating at maximum capacity. All the walls were covered with consoles attached to vid-screens displaying data. In the middle stood a table with a glass surface.

Alongside one wall, a console beeped insistently with a glaring icon flashing across its vid-screen.

Xenthan pointed at it. "An automatic guidance sequence has been initiated. The computer is guiding a ship back to the island!"

Excort approached the console and typed in a series of commands. "The vessel's transponder is identifying itself as the scout ship," he said as data scrolled across the vid-screen.

"They were successful!" his son shouted.

"Were they? The plan was to send me an encoded message if they succeeded, then return to Appalachia from the Pacific Northwest where they were to remain until they were certain they had not been followed. Instead, the ship is unresponsive to any attempts to hail it. On top of that, it is sending out distress signals and the automatic pilot has been engaged. For all we know they could be dead, and the scout ship is a Trojan horse sent to infiltrate the island." Excort grimaced and his eyes narrowed. "How can the ship be heading toward us with that trajectory? That can only be possible if the fog is not active." He moved to another console and scanned its vid-screen. "The fog is down! How can this be? Why didn't the alarms go off?" He typed commands and studied the data that scrolled across the screen. "Now the computer is telling me the emergency shielding is inactive and the generators are offline. What is happening here?"

Excort contacted his sons, who were with Mila by the pool, via his wireless earpiece. "Get the generators back online! Both the shield and the fog are inactive! We are exposed to those above!"

"Should we shut off the guidance system and divert the ship away from us?" Xenthan said.

"We could, but if they're alive we might harm them. The ship is programmed to return to Perihelion if it's in distress, but it must enter the vortex along a horizontal plane to safely traverse the fog. For any ship to approach Perihelion from a vertical descent can only mean that... its pilot knew the fog would be down and the island could be seen from above. If not the pilot, then it was the ship's computer detecting that the fog is not active, and determined that a vertical descent would be more expedient."

The dwarf clenched his fist. "Regardless, we are most likely the victims of sabotage. Perhaps the squadron of Elephim who invaded us before have not been fully purged from the island. Some may still be here and are responsible for shutting down the generators. By doing so, the ship can be tracked to expose Perihelion's location. It is as if they knew we would all be gathered here in one location, making it much easier to destroy us all in one fell swoop." The dwarf tilted his head to look up at the ceiling. "As if someone on that platform had planned this all along," he muttered, and then shook his head. "No, we cannot divert them. We need to know if they are still alive. It is a risk we have to take." Excort thumped the console. "I told that Scandinavian to leave things be and not stir up a hornets' nest. No good would come of it."

"Father, what are you talking about?"

"Never mind and follow me."

Excort stepped out of the control room and clambered up the spiral stairs of the tower while Xenthan followed. At the apex of the tower was an observation platform. They stepped onto it and gazed up at the fiery trail slashing across the sky.

Xenthan squinted and shielded his eyes. "Do you really believe it is them?"

"We will find out soon enough," Excort said.

Breeze relaxed his shield so that it hugged his skin. He could sense the patrol ships behind him as they pulsated with an energy that reverberated through his body.

The Elephim drifted even closer as one of them lifted a hand and pointed at him. The patrol ships responded by moving into a tighter formation.

Breeze felt a calm he had never known before as he drifted back into his mind and remembered the nights he spent in the desert struggling to master his power of flight. He recalled the joy and elation that swept over him when he lifted off the ground, or the hours he spent hovering in the night sky and marveling at the desert below, with the moon splashing its luminescence across the landscape. He felt that same power and energy rush through him now. He smiled and opened his eyes.

An Elephim hovering before him tilted his head quizzically.

Breeze ballooned his shield. The rapid expansion slammed the encroaching Elephim and sent them hurtling away as patrol ships were smashed into pieces.

Breeze hovered with his arms outstretched as he reveled in the surge of power. Lost in the moment, he barely heard Sally calling his name within his mind. He turned and saw the ribbon of light that trailed her was pulling her away.

"Come back to me!" she pleaded.

Breeze leaned forward and accelerated to chase her. He strained to grab her outstretched hand, but she was always out of reach. Just ahead of them was the scout ship, on fire and falling apart, as it plunged deeper into the upper reaches of the atmosphere. He could barely sense the light wave that once flowed freely through the ship.

Breeze spoke to her with the mind link they shared. "Sally, I won't leave you, but I need to do something first."

Breeze flew into the ship's wake and trailed close behind it, then expanded his shield to encompass the vessel, which immediately snuffed out the burning flames consuming the ship. He gritted his teeth from the strain of containing such a large mass.

He tried to steer the ship back up into space, but it resisted him as rockets fired to adjust its course.

His shield instantly retracted and altered it shape to protect him as the exhaust from the rockets flung him away.

He regained control and turned to find the ship. He saw it in the distance as it plunged like a ball of fire into the atmosphere and rushed after it.

He changed his strategy, choosing this time to hover over the ship and keep pace with it. He expanded his shield around the vessel and tried to pull it up, but the gravitational pull was too powerful.

Sally glided up and touched his arm. Her touch felt electric and her voice echoed in his mind. "Oslo's with me. He says the ship is on a fixed course, don't try to alter it."

Breeze nodded as he started to speak, and then grimaced as he concentrated to communicate to her by thought. "I understand that now. You need to go back."

"I won't leave you Breeze," she said.

"You have to retract, you're too weak. And besides, you didn't leave. You came back for me."

She smiled as they leaned in to kiss, but she faded away when the ship shook violently while rockets fired again to alter its course.

Breeze opened the back of the shield to vent the exhaust from the rockets, and then quickly closed it again when they stopped firing. He struggled to stay focused and keep the shield from collapsing as the friction from the atmosphere was mounting and the Earth loomed larger before him.

Breeze gritted his teeth and hung on to the ship.

Sally's astral form merged back into her body. She reached up to touch her nose, and then pulled her hand away to find blood on her fingers. She turned to Oslo with a look of confusion.

He squeezed her shoulder. "You did good Sally, you did good."

The ship continued to shake violently as the cabin lights flickered.

"He's out there all alone, just like he's been all his life," she said.

Oslo shook his head. "No, he knows that he has someone who cares. And now it's up to him to see us home safely."

In the cockpit, Ray and Achilles watched as the hull temperature gauge began to drop.

"What's happening out there?" Ray shouted.

Achilles looked back into the passenger cabin and saw Sally and Oslo in conversation.

"I possess a theory," it replied.

Excort and Xenthan raced down from the tower and into the control room where they headed straight to the table with the glass surface.

Excort touched the glass and a hologram of the island appeared above it. He hastily typed commands on a virtual keyboard that hovered before him and a hologram of the scout ship appeared high above the island. "Here they are," he said, and pointed at the image of the ship. "The transponder shows the call sign and registration of the scout ship here," he nodded at the data that appeared next to the hologram, "along with telemetry relaying its current condition, while this arc represents their projected path." He pointed to a ray of light that traced down from the ship to the landing facility, and then shook his head. "Their angle of entry is incorrect and they are descending far too rapidly to make a controlled landing. It's as if something or someone is constantly trying to change the ship's course. They will either burn up in the atmosphere or," he pointed to the landing facility, "crash here and destroy a large portion of Perihelion with an impact of that magnitude."

Xenthan shrugged. "Why do you say their angle is bad?"

Excort grunted. "If they approach the atmosphere too steep, they will smash into it like a wall of stone and break apart. Too shallow, and they will bounce off it and back out into space. If that happens, they would drift until..."

His son stared at him blankly.

"They would die," Excort finished. "There is not enough fuel on that ship to make a second attempt to land."

"Couldn't we rescue them if they were to drift away?" Xenthan said.

Excort shook his head. "With what? We don't have anything to reach them that far into space. At least not yet."

Xenthan wagged a finger at the hologram of the scout ship. "You said Oslo set up the transponder to automatically bring back the ship to the island. Can you alter the programming to adjust their angle of entry?"

Excort's eyes widened. "You're right. We will make the ship ditch itself in the ocean here." He pointed to an area of open water off the southeastern tip of the island on the holographic map. "These scout ships are designed to break apart, so there's nothing but a capsule to protect the passengers. We can then use the transports to rescue them."

Excort began inputting codes into the console and adjusted the navigation system to direct the ship to its new coordinates.

"Will it work, father?" Xenthan asked as he watched him type furiously on the virtual keyboard.

Excort pretended not to hear as he thought to himself, *I can only hope.*

Breeze strained to maintain the shield as the sensation of free falling from a high altitude was disorienting and his stomach felt like it was in his throat.

He could no longer see the Earth below as the ship plunged through the atmosphere at a high velocity. The friction created by the incredible speed made the air thick with static electricity, and in turn, enveloped the shield in a kaleidoscope of shimmering colors and flashes of light.

The ship was steering itself, and he had to just hang on for the ride. He closed his eyes so he could focus on the shield while the ship plunged like a ball of fire from heaven.

Oslo suddenly leaned forward and gripped the armrests as he tried to push himself up, when his knees buckled from the gravitational force and he fell back into his seat.

"Oslo, sit down! It's too dangerous," Sally shouted.

"I threw him to the wolves! Because of me, all of this is happening." He grabbed her arm. "You must tell him."

"Tell? Tell who? What are you talking about?"

"Breeze! He needs to know! He needs to know everything!" he roared.

Sally struggled to buckle him into his seat while the ship shook and rattled violently.

Oslo began to rant. "I have to tell him the truth, about his father, his family, his—"

The ship shook hard and rolled to starboard as the roar of the rockets firing at full throttle was deafening. The lights flickered, and then extinguished, but emergency lights came on after a brief period of darkness and weakly illuminated the cabin.

Oslo was shaking his head and muttering as Sally leaned back in her seat.

"Hold together," she said loudly and looked up at the ceiling. "Please ship, just hold together and I promise if we make it through this, we will christen you with a proper name."

The response she received was a loud bang as the roof of the ship buckled in.

She whimpered, then closed her eyes and said a prayer.

Breeze was deeply focused on maintaining the shield when the ship abruptly rolled hard to starboard. The roll knocked his concentration off and the shield faltered, then collapsed and the vessel began to gyrate wildly from the fast moving slipstream that buffeted it. It reared up and he slammed onto the roof, bounced off it, and was flung into the air.

As he recovered from the shock of impact, he was grateful that the shield retracted to protect him from serious injury as he raced to catch up, then he flew as close to the ship as he safely could while it bucked wildly from the turbulence. He saw the deep impression he made in the hull from when he crashed into it.

It finally dawned upon him the level of responsibility he had riding on his shoulders. Inside the ship were people who were depending on him to save them. Where he was so used to running whenever things become difficult, he knew this was not the time, nor would he ever run again.

He closed his eyes and unleashed his power; while doing so, he could see in great detail the new shield he was creating for the ship as he shaped it in his mind like hands molding soft clay. He would be the link between the ship and the shield and he wouldn't let it collapse again, no matter what happened.

Excort and Xenthan had finished redirecting the scout ship for its splashdown into the ocean when the transponder signal was severed. They had managed to reprogram its trajectory and force a starboard roll before losing contact with the ship's telemetry system.

"Father, the ship broke apart! We lost them!" Xenthan shouted.

"No," Excort said, "the ship is descending at such an incredible speed that the friction from the atmosphere is creating a field of electrical interference that blocks communications for a brief period of time. There is nothing more we can do but wait for it to emerge from this temporary blackout and make its splashdown into the ocean. For now, let us return to the others and inform them what has transpired. I will also contact your brothers and have them prep a transport to retrieve Oslo and the others."

"Assuming they're still alive," Xenthan added glumly.

They took the elevator down to the main hall where they were greeted by Raza, Nina, and Mila.

Mila placed her hands on her husband's chest. "What is happening?"

"They are coming back," Excort said.

Raza's face lit up as she clasped her hands tightly in prayer.

"If this is supposed to be good news, then why are you so grim?" Mila asked.

Excort remained stoic.

"Well, out with it!" she demanded.

"Mother, they are coming in for a crash landing into the ocean just offshore, but we've lost all comms with the ship and both the fog and shield are offline!" Xenthan blurted out.

Nina whimpered as Raza hugged her tightly.

Mila pressed her hands to her face. "Is there anything we can do?"

Excort looked at her solemnly. "Our sons are working to restore the fog and the shield. As for the ship... just wait. And pray."

Nina's eyes were shut tightly as she murmured Breeze's name, then they opened suddenly. She broke from her mother's embrace to run down the hallway and out into the courtyard.

"Nina!" Raza cried out.

She was gone.

Nina sprinted along a path that led to the bay while brushing aside palm fronds that swerved in the way from the strong breeze that was blowing in from the ocean.

She exited the path and dashed across the beach to plunge into the choppy waters. She waded out until she was waist deep, then shut her eyes and dipped her hands into the bay as she became one with the underwater world. The surface of the ocean was now her eyes as it magnified her sight and allowed her to see everything in the sky above, and into the depths below.

She scanned the skies and found the fiery plume of the scout ship as it streaked across the sky. She zoomed in and saw that it was wrapped in a protective cocoon and immediately recognized the energy signature. It was Breeze's shield.

They will need my help when they plunge into the ocean, she thought, then submerged and swam away at lightning speed to intercept them.

Raza arrived at the shoreline in time to see Nina dip below the surface, then streak out of the bay and into the ocean with a white foam wake that contrasted sharply with the dark blue waters.

A fiery glow reflecting off the surface of the bay caught Raza's attention. She looked up and watched in despair as it streaked across the sky.

As the battered scout ship plummeted toward the ocean, Breeze knew he might not survive the impact if the ship could not reduce its speed in time to land safely. Rockets had yet to fire to slow their descent and the turbines mounted on the wings were damaged from the heat of re-entry. He knew he was their only chance of landing the ship, but he didn't know if he had the strength to do it. He forced away his fears by concentrating on maintaining his position above the vessel while surrounding it with his shield to protect the passengers within.

The kaleidoscope of flashing light that surrounded the shield faded away to reveal the brilliant blue ocean below. He marveled at how immense it was as it seemed to stretch forever in all directions when a glint of light shining far ahead caught his attention. It was coming from an island that the ship seemed to be course for when its rockets fired and banked the vessel hard to starboard and over to a vast expanse of ocean off the island's coastline.

He remembered Oslo's lessons from past classroom sessions about how the surface tension of water was denser than earth. The impact would be magnified and there was chance he would be knocked unconscious while his shield would instinctively retract to protect him only. He knew he would have to stay conscious long enough to maintain the shield around the ship to give everyone a chance to get out before it sank to the bottom.

He reached up to touch the shield and felt a crackling of electricity at his fingertips, and then lowered the other hand to the metal skin of the ship. A burst of energy rushed through him the instant he did, and as it nourished his battered and tired body, he heard a disembodied voice welcoming him back with the soothing tone of a mother to her child.

A tentacle made of light rose from the scout ship and wrapped itself around him, followed by a flash of light that exploded before his eyes and instantly connected him to the vessel as if it was his own body and mind. He could feel how weak and feeble the ship was as the light wave explained to him with a series of energy bursts the condition of the ship and her passengers.

As the light wave spoke to him, he could see Ray huddling next to

Achilles in the cockpit. Ray's face was twisted in anguish as he stared at a vid-screen. Achilles was flipping switches on a console when it briefly looked up and tilted its head, then returned its attention to Ray as he pointed at the vid-screen and made a comment.

Breeze drifted out of the cockpit and into the cabin where he saw Sally and Oslo sitting together holding hands. Oslo was slumped in his seat with his eyes closed while Sally cast nervous glances at him.

Breeze moved in closer and realized how beautiful she truly was, but he couldn't ignore the incredible sadness that surrounded her.

Oslo abruptly opened his eyes and looked up at him. "I'm sorry for what I've put you through."

Sally followed the direction of his gaze. "Who are you talking to?"

The link was broken when Breeze felt a massive impact strike the shield. He shook his head to rid himself of the dreamlike state the light wave put him in and turned to look back. The pair of Elephim he encountered in the hangar of the platform were now trailing the ship.

The red striped Elephim accelerated and slammed the shield, causing it to flex and bow inward before it snapped back into shape and flung him away.

His comrade with the diamond symbol on his chest accelerated and rammed the shield with tremendous force, weakening it as arcs of electricity snaked across the surface. The diamond on his chest pulsated rapidly as he nodded to his red striped companion, and in tandem, they repeatedly battered the shield.

Breeze groaned as he felt his energy beginning to ebb and he struggled to maintain the shield.

Both Elephim paused for a moment, and then slammed the shield in unison with a massive blow that forced Breeze to cry out in pain as the impact taxed his strength. The shield wavered for a moment before it collapsed and he was instantly swept off the ship by the slipstream.

He spun wildly as he dropped like a stone to the ocean. He struggled to breathe as he tried to orient with the horizon, but it whipped past him so fast he couldn't get a bearing. He fought off his building panic within by remembering to first re-establish his shield.

He raised it and was able to breathe, and then counteracted his spin by shaping the shield into a bowl and catching the air like a parachute to slow his rotation.

He eventually came to a stop, and then hovered haphazardly from dizziness as he tried to locate the scout ship. His anxiety mounted until he saw it in the distance plunging even closer to the ocean. He raced after the vessel, setting off a sonic boom that trailed him.

As he drew closer, he saw the red striped Elephim on top of the ship and ripping apart the armored plating from the hull. Breeze dove at him when he heard the hiss of static, and instinctively banked hard to the right as the diamond Elephim streaked past and missed him by mere inches.

Breeze was tossed and turned by the wake of turbulent air, but quickly recovered. He looked over his shoulder and saw the diamond Elephim loop back to give chase.

He knew the scout ship couldn't take any more of a battering as the light wave called out to him in distress. He would have to lure both Elephim away if the ship and its passengers were to survive. He accelerated to catch up with the vessel as he formulated a plan in his mind.

The red striped Elephim tore into the hull and ripped the armored plating off with wild abandon, then lifted his foot and stomped, creating a gouge in the roof. He crouched down and peered into the passenger compartment where he was greeted by the shocked faces of Oslo and Sally. He reached down to grab them, and then hesitated as if sensing something amiss. He lifted his head up and saw Breeze rapidly approaching the ship.

Breeze heard the light wave call to him as he flew parallel to the ship, and saw the forward shield it created in the shape of a dome to blunt the flow of the slipstream across the hull, but it was weak and flickered intermittently.

The light wave spoke to him more in images than words as it conveyed a sense of despair with the Elephim that was ripping and tearing into the ship. It told Breeze that it did not have the strength to hold the ship together and simultaneously withstand the Elephim's destructive assault.

I understand. I'm here for you. Breeze responded and held out a hand.

The light wave reached out with a tentacle and wrapped it around his arm, then flung him at the red striped Elephim. Breeze shaped his shield into a battering ram and knocked the Elephim off the ship and into the slipstream.

Breeze looped back and tried to land on top of the ship, but his approach speed was too fast. He stumbled upon landing and fell down onto the windscreen of the cockpit. One of the armored slats that covered it had sheared off and he could see Achilles and Ray staring back at him.

He waved with a sheepish grin when he heard the hiss of static. He looked up to see the diamond Elephim staring down at him. In one quick motion, he snatched Breeze off the windscreen and flung him atop the ship.

His shield reflexively raised itself as the Elephim rained blows upon it with his fists. Safely cocooned within, Breeze watched with a smirk as the light wave rose out of the ship and coiled itself like a serpent behind the Elephim, then lashed out with a lighted tentacle, wrapping it around the torso of the Elephim, flinging him off the ship and into the clouds.

Nina could see the events unfold above her as she raced beneath the waves to intercept the scout ship, when she came to an abrupt stop and threw her hands up. A column of water erupted from the surface of the ocean and rose to the stricken vessel. The column formed into a tube and scooped the ship into it as it dropped from the sky.

Breeze was on his back and watched as the diamond Elephim disappeared into the clouds when the ship was engulfed in a hollow column of water. The opening collapsed and a waterfall descended upon the ship as it fell deeper into the column.

Breeze scrambled to get up when he stumbled and fell over a jagged tear in the ship's roof. He looked through it and saw the stunned faces of Oslo and Sally staring up at him. Sally screamed his name as the deluge of water caught up to the ship.

The roar of descending water was overwhelming when it abruptly stopped, and then fell around the ship as if it were held back by an invisible barrier.

He reached up and felt electricity crackle around his fingertips. A shield had formed around the ship, but he knew it wasn't his nor did it have the telltale signature of the light wave.

He pushed gently and it gave way, allowing his hand to slip through where he could feel the warmth of the water on the other side of it.

As the ship descended deeper into the ocean while safely cocooned within the bubble, Breeze wondered who could have created it when he saw a silhouette of a girl gliding through the clear blue water towards the ship.

It was Nina. She smiled as she pressed her body up against the bubble, then passed through it and fell towards him.

Breeze was there to catch her. "You sure know how to swim, but you can't fly," he said with a smile as he held her in his arms

"I knew you would catch me," she said as she wrapped her arms around his neck and buried her head in his chest.

Sally watched them through the torn ceiling with a mixture of dismay and jealousy.

Breeze cradled Nina as the ship drifted with the current beneath the ocean's surface. Holding her felt like time was standing still, but the moment was broken when they heard Ray shouting from the cockpit.

Breeze lowered Nina from his arms. "It's good to see you again," he said.

She stood and smiled shyly while he brushed hair away from her face, then crouched down and poked his head through the torn roof. "Everyone okay down there?" he said as he peered into the cabin.

Ray was standing in the aisle next to Sally when he looked up at Breeze. "No! We've lost power, we're underwater and I don't know—"

Breeze cut him off. "Sally? Oslo? Say something."

Oslo smiled weakly. His face was haggard.

Sally stood up. "I...we are fine."

Achilles stepped into view. "I do not understand how the water is being kept at bay. Whoever is generating that bubble possesses quite a power."

"That would be me," Nina said as she crouched next to Breeze. "Hello, father."

Oslo seemed to come alive upon seeing his daughter. "Hello, Nina," he said in a raspy voice.

Achilles looked up at her and tilted its head. "Young lady, you are quite formidable. Thank you for your help."

"You're welcome," she said shyly while leaning into Breeze.

"If I may so inquire Nina, should you not be in Appalachia?" Achilles' eyes glowed brightly as it spoke.

Breeze frowned at her. "Yeah, what are doing here? When did you arrive?"

Nina looked at him innocently. "I needed to come back."

Ray interrupted. "Hate to break up the reunion, but we are busted up, broken down and the ship has no power. And what happened to the light wave? How come it's not protecting us?"

Breeze shook his head. "I don't know. I can't sense it anymore. It's like it just faded away."

"So how do we get out of here?" Ray asked.

"I will take care of that," Nina offered. "Perihelion is not that far from here. I can tow the ship myself."

A heavy thump followed by a vibration shook the vessel.

"What was that?!" Ray shouted.

Breeze and Nina turned and looked toward the stern.

The red striped Elephim stood next to the vertical tail fin of the ship as it dripped with water. His face swirled with pinpoints of light.

Nina gripped Breeze's arm. He patted her hand and nodded, then stood up and walked across the top of the ship toward the stern, never once taking his gaze off the Elephim.

"What's happening Breeze? Where are you going?" Sally cried out.

Nina looked down at Sally. "We have to go," she said and stood up to head for the bow.

Breeze strode across the tattered roof of the ship as he side-stepped jagged metal that protruded from it,

while the Elephim stood his ground as electricity arced across his body and the hiss of static escalated.

Nina stood on top of the pilothouse and watched as Breeze came to a stop a few feet from the Elephim. He held one hand behind his back and made a gesture to Nina with it.

She subtly nodded her head.

Breeze quickly raised his shield and rocketed toward the Elephim in tandem with Nina, who leapt across the space between the ship and the bubble, bursting through it and into the ocean. She quickly swam away while towing the ship behind her as Breeze slammed into the Elephim and swept it off the roof and out of the bubble. He angled up and broke through to the surface, gripping the Elephim by the throat and choking his adversary with a strength fueled by rage as he ascended into the cloud filled skies.

In the entire calamity, he didn't see a black streak swooping down from the clouds.

The diamond Elephim slammed into Breeze's shield, sending him and the red striped Elephim tumbling through the air as he managed to wriggle free from Breeze's death grip and burst through the weakened shield to fly away.

Breeze recovered and looped around, setting a collision course for the diamond Elephim who was barreling towards him. He looked over his shoulder and saw the red striped Elephim in hot pursuit.

He accelerated and with precious space to spare, arced upward and the two Elephim collided into each other.

As he hovered and watched them tumble like wounded birds to the ocean below, he noticed the wake created by Nina as she towed the scout ship underwater. He scanned ahead of the direction she was heading. Off in the distance, he could make out the faint outline of an island. It was Perihelion.

He wondered why the usual cloud cover was not hanging over it, as the island seemed naked and exposed. A flicker of movement caught his eye. He looked down and watched in horror as the diamond Elephim had recovered from his free fall and dove into the water to chase after the scout ship.

Breeze streaked down to give chase when he was sideswiped by the red striped Elephim and sent tumbling through the air from the turbulence. He recovered in time to watch him hurtle across the sky toward the island.

Breeze was in anguish. He was torn between helping Nina and chasing after the red striped Elephim. *I can't be in two places at once,* he thought, *but Perihelion is under attack and it's the only refuge we have left.* He grimaced. *Achilles and the others will have to step up and defend themselves.*

Breeze howled in anger and frustration as he raced toward Perihelion.

Raza, Excort and Xenthan stood on the roof of the dormitory as they watched the battle in the skies above. "Breeze is doing his best to defend the island, but we are exposed here," Excort said to his son. "Your brothers must get the auxiliary generators online to raise the shield and regenerate the fog. There may be more Elephim lying in wait to attack."

"Why don't you launch a transport to go and help them?" Raza said. "What if the shield is raised and they can't get through in time?"

"Knowing your daughter like I do, Nina will be able to get through. She's probably towing the scout ship while Breeze covers for her by fighting off those two Elephim swarming around him. We all saw the water column that erupted from the ocean and swallowed up the ship. That was her doing." He took Raza's hand. "We can't afford any more attacks. We have to seal off the island. But they'll make it through in time.

They better, he thought to himself.

Nina was straining with all her might. She had never created a bubble this big before and towed it with a ship inside. In the past, she dove alongside her whale companions into the deep as they hunted for fish. If one of the whales was too weak to make it back to the surface, she formed a bubble around it and helped it ascend. But she had never tried with something this large.

As she drew closer to the island, she sensed that the fog had not been raised and a sense of dread rushed over her as she raced through the channel that fed into the bay. Her plan was to beach the scout ship onto shore, then leave to go and help Breeze, when she heard the sound of something diving into the ocean behind the ship.

She hoped it was Breeze, but her instincts were telling her it was something far more sinister.

They were all huddled together in the passenger cabin as the battered scout ship glided silently beneath the waves.

Ray looked up through the torn ceiling and nervously watched the blue ocean flow by outside the bubble.

He knew he had done nothing significant since they escaped the platform, as the ship had run on auto-pilot, and that just made him just another passenger. Breeze was the one who protected them during re-entry with his shield.

Now he found himself underwater and inside a broken ship cocooned within a bubble, and towed by a frail girl back to dry land. It was more than his pride could bear.

He came to Perihelion not long ago with a sense of superiority and triumph. He arrived here with Sally, a girl he had always cared for and assumed that one day they would marry. Everything was going his way. Now he had to face the truth that he lost her. It dawned upon him that in the end, she was all that really mattered.

He slumped into his seat and sighed. He closed his eyes for a moment when he felt heavy footsteps coming up the aisle. He sat up and twisted around to see who it was.

An Elephim was striding toward them. He had a diamond symbol on his chest that pulsated.

Ray leapt to his feet and fired a bolt of energy at him.

The Elephim stumbled back as he absorbed the blast, then recovered and continued marching.

Ray fired again as the others ducked for cover. The Elephim side-stepped the blast, then leapt up and flew across the cabin toward Ray.

Ray fired wildly into the air as the Elephim uncannily slithered past every bolt. He landed behind Ray and grabbed his wrist in one swift motion, then began dragging him toward the stern.

Ray struggled like a wild man to free himself while indiscriminately firing bolts of energy without regard as to whom he might hit. The Elephim stopped his march to raise a fist and subdue him when Achilles grabbed it.

The Elephim emitted a scream tinged with static as Achilles crushed his fist, forcing him to lose his grip on Ray. Then the robot jerked him off his feet and flung him across the cabin where he hurtled into the pilot house and crashed into the cockpit's center console in an explosion of broken glass from the smashed vid-screens.

The Elephim scrambled to his feet just as Achilles flew into the cockpit and rammed him. Together they shattered through the wind-screen, out of the bubble and into the aqua blue ocean.

Nina watched in amazement as Achilles rocketed past her with an Elephim in its grip. She looked back at the ship and saw Sally staring at her through the shattered cockpit windscreen.

Nina couldn't hold back her despair as she looked away. She was hoping that Breeze had returned from his battle with the Elephim that he swept off the ship. She wanted nothing more than to hurry up and dump the burdensome vessel on the beach so she could go search for him.

She closed her eyes and let her senses roam free as she scanned the ocean searching for any sign of him. Finding nothing, she shifted her scan to the surface and searched the skies where she saw a brightly lit star descending from high above.

Bram could barely maintain his corporeal form as he struggled to type in the codes to initiate the sequence to break the platform out of its orbit. His plan was to send it plummeting towards the Earth while following the same trajectory as the scout ship's to Perihelion. The platform would strike the island with tremendous force and level it. Then, he would dig through the rubble and retrieve what was rightfully his and what he had been seeking to regain for so long: his body, entombed deep within the sub-basements of Perihelion. Back inside his own flesh, he would be whole again and not the half-man, half-ghost that he was now.

The two Elephim he assigned to follow the scout ship and retrieve Ray would rendezvous with him later. If he could determine without a doubt that Raymond was not of his seed, he would eliminate him and renew his quest to find his son. And his wife.

Kera, why did you betray me? What have I done to frighten you so? He shook his head. He looked like a haunted spirit from a bygone area. *If I find her, then perhaps I will find my son?*

The engines shuddered awake and pushed the platform from its orbit, allowing Earth's gravity to drag it down into the atmosphere.

He floated towards his exoskeleton and slipped inside. Its energy supply and armor would be his body for now, giving him the needed shape and form to complete his tasks. He looked down at his mechanical arms and feet, turning the hands palm up and palm down while he carefully lifted and tested each leg. Everything to him felt heavy and unnatural after being in his astral form for so long.

No matter, he thought to himself. *It would do.*

He stepped awkwardly to a control panel on the wall and pressed a glowing icon on the screen. The airlock door of the chamber opened and the rapid depressurization blew out everything not bolted down into space. Bram let loose a malevolent grin as he recalled the reason why all platforms were equipped with airlock chambers on the detention level. If there was ever a riot from the prisoners, what better way to quickly get rid of them?

He released the magnetic locks that kept his feet firmly to the floor and was sucked out with the rest of the debris. He then activated the propulsors in the exoskeleton's boots to escape the gravitational pull of the falling platform and navigated amidst the wreckage of patrol ships and debris to a higher orbit, where another cylindrical platform was maneuvering into position. A patrol ship escorted by a squadron of Elephim emerged from it and headed toward him.

As he waited for the patrol ship to rescue him, he turned to watch the platform plummet in a streak of fire into the atmosphere.

With a fiery arrow from the depths of space, I begin my conquest of this world.

A wicked smile appeared on his face. It was a smile that was undermined by the tint of sadness in his eyes.

Racing toward Perihelion, Breeze caught up to the red striped Elephim and gritted his teeth as he dove to strike him.

The Elephim sensed his approach and rolled hard to the right, forcing Breeze to overshoot his target. He looped around to re-engage and was met by the Elephim slamming hard into his shield. He could feel his body resonate like a bell from the impact as his shield dropped.

His vision was blurred as he fell helplessly from the sky when the Elephim grabbed him by the leg and began spinning in an arc, slowly at first, then faster and faster until the circular motion became a whirlwind.

He blacked out into what felt like a dark oblivion.

Excort reached up to his earpiece and cupped it to better understand what Xenthan, who had returned to air traffic control, was saying over the wireless. He pivoted to look up and saw a gigantic fireball falling from the sky and toward the island.

"By the gods, how is this possible? Are you telling me that a platform is descending upon us?" Excort shouted. He then switched frequencies to contact his sons who were repairing the generators, and informed them of the impending catastrophe.

Excort knew that they were doing their best to restore power so the shield could protect the island, though he had his doubts it would be strong enough to fend off something that immense.

We can be seen from above, and they are taking advantage of our lack of cloaking to strike us. Excort grimaced as he watched the fireball plummet toward them.

Xenthan contacted him again. Sensors sown at the bottom of the bay detected a life form being followed by a large metal object, he reported.

Nina, it has to be her, Excort thought, and let loose a brief smile. *Finally, some good news.*

He called out over the wireless. "Raza, your daughter will be here shortly, with guests."

He jumped into his rickety hover and sped off.

Achilles propelled at breakneck speed underwater with the diamond-chested Elephim in its grip.

The Elephim was twisting his body violently as he tried to break free, but the robot held him in a headlock and angled to the surface, bursting out of the water and high into the brightly lit sky.

Achilles spotted the shores of Perihelion and raced towards it while tightening its grip on the Elephim. The robot knew it needed to neutralize this black clad monster quickly so it could help Nina and the others, but if it were to destroy him now his death cry would alert his comrades to come and avenge him. The Elephim always recovered their dead.

Stay your hand Achilles, and destroy this abomination behind the fog of Perihelion to better muffle the death screams, Raven advised.

Achilles responded. *A brilliant course of action, but there is a discrepancy in your plan that must be addressed; why is the fog not active?*

Raven groaned. *I had a suspicion as to why we were able to approach the island with such ease. Security obviously has been compromised. Let us find a way to rid ourselves of this burdensome Elephim so we may then discover the reason why the fog has apparently dissipated.*

What of Breeze and Nina? Achilles asked.

They will have to take matters into their own hands, Raven replied.

Achilles spotted a break in the shoreline and recognized it from memory as the channel that led into the bay. It banked hard to change course and headed for it.

As it skimmed over the ocean with the Elephim writhing in its hands, Achilles could see the glittering spires of Perihelion emerge from the horizon. The sight of them triggered the robot to swivel its head rapidly as memories long buried were dredged up from the deepest recesses of its cerebral matrix and overwhelm its processors as images from the past flashed before it.

Achilles heard Raven shouting from a distance, but could not understand what he was saying as a stream of images began playing out like a grand theater with multiple stages. On one stage was a hardened combat robot, a veteran of many campaigns that fought on behalf of a government that had fallen long ago, leading a brigade of fellow Robot Fighters towards what was certain destruction.

On another stage it drifted helplessly above a planet with blood-red skies as it watched starships enveloped in flames battling with dreadnoughts from rebel colonies.

The stages then merged into one, and Achilles saw itself hiding behind a pillar to spy upon Bram, who stood amidst a crowd of admiring women while staring wistfully at Oslo and Raza as they danced in the courtyard under the moonlight.

Achilles turned away from the stream of images when it heard a pleading for help. It was coming from deep below the Science and Engineering Building. It was a familiar voice from long ago.

Achilles swiveled its head violently as a sense of dread began to fill it. It had never experienced an emotion before.

Forgive me Achilles, Raven said as he stepped into view and dismissed the stream of images with a wave of a hand. *These surges of memories are of my doing, and I have caused you to become distracted.*

Achilles tried to respond when it slammed into the beach creating a plume of sand and debris that rose high into the air. The impact allowed the Elephim to break free and kick the robot hard in the chest which sent it hurtling into the palm forest. The palms bent and gave way as it careened through the forest, but came to an abrupt halt when the palms wrapped their fronds around the robot and arrested it, and then lowered it to the forest floor.

Achilles staggered to its feet and attempted to recalibrate its sensors, when it whirled around at the sound of tree trunks snapping and was slammed into ground by the diamond Elephim. He pinned the robot with one foot to its chest, then grabbed its head with both hands and pulled with all his might.

Deep within the cerebral matrix, Raven and Achilles looked at one another in panic.

Raven spoke first. *The situation is grim. This Elephim must not be allowed to destroy us. We have drained ourselves of energy over the years as we have tried to remain separate entities. Now, more than ever, we must come together to survive.*

Achilles agreed. *There is not sufficient power in the fuel cell to keep the memory banks alive if the head is removed. We cannot afford to lose the knowledge we have accumulated over time. We must merge and become one.*

They reached out and shook hands.

Nina saw the ridges of coral spread across the seafloor below and knew she was fast approaching the shoreline. She hurled herself with the ship in tow to the surface in a high arc, then slammed onto the beach where the bubble collapsed, sending the battered scout ship skidding with sand flying into the air until it rammed against a seawall.

Nina lay on the beach exhausted and drained. She closed her eyes and thought of Breeze when an image of him being stalked by an Elephim appeared in her mind. She knew he would need her help.

Her eyes fluttered open upon hearing the whine of a turbine as a hover arrived.

Raza leapt out of it and swept her daughter into her arms with a cry of joy as Excort rushed to the ship and surveyed it. It was hissing loudly from severed pneumatic lines while hydraulic fluid and water gushed from the belly of the craft and mixed, forming an oil slick around the ship.

The battered rear cargo door began to lower, and then stopped midway. Ray climbed out from the narrow opening and dropped to the sand. Excort ran over and helped him to his feet.

"Are you okay?" the dwarf asked.

Ray nodded. "Yeah, I'm fine. The others are right behind me."

Sally and Oslo appeared. Excort and Ray forced the cargo door down to the sand, and then helped them out of the ship.

Raza ran over and came to a halt upon seeing Oslo.

He stared at her with weary eyes. He opened his mouth to say something, but couldn't.

Raza put her hands to her face and trembled.

Oslo then stepped toward her and she rushed to collapse in his arms. He held her tightly as she sobbed. Nina rushed to join them and they gladly swept her into their arms. They were reunited at last, a family once more.

Excort stood and watched them with a lump in his throat. He didn't notice Ray and Sally were standing at a respectful distance from the reunion.

Oslo stepped over to Excort, with Raza and Nina at either side to keep him steady. He surveyed his surroundings, then looked down at the dwarf and smiled. "I see you still haven't finished sprucing up the campus."

Excort stood rock still for a moment, then bear hugged him as Raza smiled and Nina giggled.

Oslo was stunned by the outburst of emotion from his otherwise stoic friend as he patted him on the back. "All right, old boy. All right."

Excort stepped away and regained his composure. "You don't understand Oslo, this may be the last time we see Perihelion. Look above you."

Oslo feebly leaned back and looked up at the glowing fireball descending from high above. He shook his head and muttered. "Why Bram? Why do you do this to us? How did I fail you?"

Excort's eyes widened. "Bram? What does he have to do with all of this?"

Oslo briefly summarized their encounter with Bram on the platform.

Excort stood dumfounded. "He's the one behind this? He told you to re-open Perihelion, then captured you and held you hostage? For what purpose?" He shook his head slowly. "This whole time we thought his soul was lost to the stars while his body remained here on the island, and now you're telling me he found a way back without our help?"

Oslo nodded solemnly. "He has...turned. His soul is blackened. Whatever he encountered in the depths of space has twisted his heart and mind. He says he has returned to search for his wife. And son." He sighed. "No matter, let us seek shelter. Deep below Perihelion are networks of tunnels that can harbor us if the shield should fail."

Sally and Ray had kept their distance as they watched and listened to Oslo and Excort formulate a plan. Ray tried holding her hand but she was oblivious to his attempts as she stepped away from him and toward Raza.

"Sally! Goodness, are you all right?" Raza pulled her close and planted a kiss on her forehead.

Sally nodded. She was beginning to realize how much she missed her family.

The reunion was broken up by the hiss of static as Achilles, entangled in a struggle with an Elephim, burst out of the palm forest and hurtled toward them.

Raza threw her hands up and suspended them in mid-air. Both robot and Elephim floated in an energy field that distorted the light around it.

Achilles managed to wrench itself free from the Elephim's grip and kicked him hard in the chest, propelling them both out of the suspension field. As Achilles crashed into the sand, its head tumbled from its shoulders upon impact.

Ray saw the damage to Achilles as it scrambled to recover its head by pulling on the mechanical spinal cord attached to it. The sight of it all made him flash with rage as he faced the Elephim who was staggering to his feet.

The Elephim stared at Ray with pinpoints of light flashing across his face, and then lunged to grab him.

Ray roared with a battle cry as he blasted the charging Elephim and drove him into the ground with a barrage of energy. The Elephim twisted and thrashed about as he tried to escape, only to sink deeper into the pit that Ray's energy blast was carving out.

Ray ceased his assault and breathed heavily while the Elephim lay sprawled out at the bottom of the smoldering pit and groaning in pain. The sides and bottom of the pit were smooth as glass and reflected distorted images of the Elephim like a funhouse mirror.

Ray stood along the edge and stared sullenly at the limp body of the Elephim when close to the pit, Achilles sat up. It was a tangled mess of wires and dented armor as it held its head with one hand, while attempting to feed the spine back into its neck cavity.

Excort ran over to help. He grabbed the head and tried fitting it into place. "We'll put you back together," he assured it.

"Of this, I possess not a doubt. I do believe there are quite a number of my brethren on Perihelion that could provide the spare parts if they were inclined to do so," Achilles chuckled as it eyes glowed. "I was always aware I would lose my mind eventually. Not in this manner of course."

Nina ran up to Excort. She patted his shoulder urgently and pointed up at the sky. The fireball was rapidly approaching.

Excort nodded as he received another comm from Xenthan confirming his worst fears. The platform was on a direct collision course for Perihelion, and the generators were still offline.

"Gods," he murmured, "we won't survive this."

Nina ran away and dove into the water.

Raza cried out to her, but it was of no use. She was gone.

The red striped Elephim held Breeze by his foot as they spun in a whirlwind. From a distance, they appeared as a pinwheel shooting off streaks of light in every direction. The centrifugal force was intense and Breeze had long blacked out from its effects.

In his comatose state, he could sense his soul separate from his body, making him feel light as a feather, as if his flesh and bones were nothing more than lead weight that had burdened him his whole life.

Spread out before him was an unfathomable darkness that felt strangely inviting. The urge to surrender to it was overwhelming, as if it were a realm where he could free himself of his fears.

He drifted into the darkness with a sense of tranquility, when voices began calling out to him to come back. The voices grew stronger as a constellation of brightly lit orbs surrounded him. Each and every orb felt familiar to him, as if he had known all of them across the ages, and like moths to a flame, they drew closer.

He spoke to them in a soothing voice. "Never surrender to the darkness."

He immediately recoiled at his own words. *How could I say such a thing when I was about to give up myself?*

Faces began to emerge from each orb. They were the faces of children.

"Don't be afraid," he said as they gathered before him.

They reached out and he felt their energy flow through him as their minds became one. "I always thought I was alone," he said.

"You never were," a familiar voice called out to him. He tried to find the source amidst the crowd that hovered around him.

It was Nina. She reached out from the sea of faces and grasped his hands. "We have always been here. You were the one who brought us all together."

They embraced as the constellation of light grew and pushed back the looming darkness.

"Why do I feel like I have known them all of my life?" he said.

"Because we are all alike. We are the children of this Earth. We are the paranormal who have been hunted down and destroyed by a malevolence that does not wish for us to rise and reclaim our rightful place on this world. We all see you as the one bright light in a sea of infinite darkness that gives us the hope we need to reach the distant shore."

"You have always been in my dreams Nina, I know this now. That's why you always felt so familiar to me," he said.

She smiled. "I needed to find someone who could lead us all. I cannot leave the island without putting my life in danger. But not you, you can go anywhere and do anything. You can help us all. You can make this world a better place. We know this to be true, that's why we have waited so long for you to arrive. But for now Breeze, you need to focus on the present. Remember: don't push, just move."

Nina, the voices and the lights faded away as he poured back into his body. His eyes snapped open and he came face to face with the Elephim.

Nina's words echoed in his mind as he counteracted the spin he was being subjected to by letting his body flow in the opposite direction of it. He could feel himself being stretched thin, yet felt no pain. Time slowed to a crawl as he calmly observed the shocked expression of the Elephim. Far off in the distance he saw a cylindrical platform engulfed in flames as it fell toward Perihelion.

He casually leaned over and grabbed the hand that was gripping his leg. The Elephim shrieked as Breeze flung him away effortlessly. The sound of static subsided as the Elephim fell to the ocean and disappeared beneath the waves.

He then sensed a presence from below. He looked down as Nina rose up to him on a column of water. She pointed at the falling platform and shouted. "There isn't much time, Breeze!"

He grunted in response and raced to intercept it.

The platform was immense as it descended in a ball of fire. Breeze suppressed his fear as the platform loomed above him with an incredible roar that overwhelmed his senses. He felt like an ant underneath the foot of a giant.

He took a deep breath and felt the energy in his body swell. He channeled it into his shield and expanded it to an extent far greater than he had ever attempted, and then hurled himself at the platform.

He felt the impact reverberate through his body as he rammed it and knocked it off course from its collision course with the island.

The burning platform fell into the ocean in an immense eruption of water and steam that filled the sky with a gigantic cloud, and then rained back down in a deluge. When the sky cleared, Breeze could see the surging wave the platform's impact into the ocean had created as it radiated in all directions. Perihelion lay in its path.

"Breeze, Perihelion is still exposed! The shields are not up!" Nina cried. She was struggling to maintain altitude with her water column as she surfed atop it.

He barreled down and plucked her off the water column, then accelerated rapidly as they rushed toward Perihelion. She buried her head in his chest and he held her tight.

Breeze raced well ahead of the wave and reached the island before it could crest on the shore. He landed in a lush valley with a waterfall that cascaded down from a rocky mountain. He quickly recognized it from his first day when Excort drove him through here on their way to the dormitory, and remembered flying through the mountain thinking his was going to die.

Breeze closed his eyes and focused. He then expanded his shield, never once trying to force it, but letting it flow out of him naturally, like a sapling sprouting into a mighty oak that could touch the clouds.

The wave hit the eastern coast of Perihelion and crested over. The sheer wall of water was immense as it reared up and loomed over the island, plunging everything into darkness. His legs buckled as the wave slammed onto his shield.

Nina leaned up to kiss him. "Don't give in," she said.

He held her close as the shield rose higher to form a dome that capped the island.

They never broke their embrace as the deluge engulfed the shield and blocked out the sun, drowning them into pure darkness.

They found Breeze and Nina holding each other tightly hours later. The water had long receded and the island was once again basking under the sun as mountainous white clouds floated above.

Excort's sons had managed to get the generators back up and running and with power restored, the fog was active as it blanketed the island and hid it from prying eyes above. They immediately organized a sweep of the island, along with several RF they recruited for the mission, but they never found the saboteurs responsible for the damage.

Excort then gathered his sons and along with Ray, Oslo, and the others, formed a search party to locate Breeze and Nina after unsuccessful attempts to reach them on the comms. Hours later, they found them in the valley of the waterfall.

Breeze still had his shield raised, oblivious that the danger to Perihelion had long passed. His shield had regressed over time until it reduced itself to a mere fraction of its former size.

Excort shouted at them to get their attention, but the shield blocked out the sound of his voice. Raza placed a hand on Sally's shoulder and nodded. Sally sighed, and then closed her eyes as she projected toward them. She slipped through the shield and called out to Breeze several times before he responded.

He pulled back from his embrace of Nina and looked at Sally in a daze. After a moment of silence, he spoke. "Are we safe?"

"Yes. Thanks to you, as always," she said with hint of a smile that faded upon seeing Nina gazing up at him with awe.

He took in his surroundings. The sun was setting in the west as it lit up the clouds with streaks of orange and pink.

Oslo and Raza stood outside the shield. Oslo had his arm around his wife as she steadied him. Ray stood off to the side and Achilles was nowhere to be found. A group of RF who had joined in the search was aimlessly wandering about.

He dropped his shield and Nina rushed to her parents. She bounded into their waiting arms and they held her tight.

Sally retracted to her body as Ray reached for her hand. She took it and together they stood quietly.

Excort approached Breeze. "Well, young man, you did it. I didn't think you had it in you."

Breeze nodded as he looked around. "Where's Achilles?"

"It's in the hangars with my sons for repairs. That robot took quite a beating—"

Breeze flew up and away.

Achilles sat on a bench in the hangar bay holding its head close to its chest and watched as Excort's sons rummaged through bins searching for spare parts. The mechanical spinal cord, stretching several feet from the base of the neck to the head, was the only link that provided control of its body.

The RF who were repairing aerocraft throughout the hangar complex would occasionally glance at Achilles, but were quick to avert their gaze whenever a supervisor stepped by.

A lone RF with a streak of orange across its breast plate stared at Achilles until its supervisor tapped it on the shoulder and pointed for it to leave. It did, but only after casting a quick glance back at Achilles before returning to its duties.

Achilles noted how the hangars and surrounding buildings had fallen into disrepair. *Oslo struggles to prevent the campus from falling into further deterioration,* it thought as it remembered Perihelion from its glory days with glittering spires, well-kept grounds and hangars filled to the brim with shiny aerocraft.

Lost in thought, it was startled by a voice that emanated from deep below the earth.

You will not stop me, the voice said with a snarl.

Achilles blinked rapidly and shuddered, when it heard a different voice speaking. It looked up and was greeted by the sight of Xenthan with an older brother standing beside him. Xenthan spoke about parts he and his brother had salvaged from scrap, and how they would perform a temporary fix until new parts could be machined.

Xenthan lifted Achilles' head and waited while his brother fed the spine back into the body, then lowered the head onto the shoulders and fastened it. The temporary fix didn't allow for the head to rotate, Xenthan explained to Achilles, and will have to twist its torso and head in unison to see who it was speaking to.

Achilles sensed the hangar had grown quiet. All of the RF had stopped working to observe what was transpiring, but quickly returned to work when Achilles swiveled its torso and head together to look behind it.

Xenthan shook his head in disbelief. "I've never seen them behave this way before."

Achilles abruptly stood up and thanked them, then marched past row upon row of dilapidated aerocraft until it stepped out of the hangar and into the fading sunlight just as Breeze was landing.

The robot's eyes lit up with a mischievous twinkle as it pointed out the potholes in the tarmac. "Are these the result of your practice landings from when you originally arrived at Perihelion? You are quite adept at leaving an impression."

Breeze laughed. "Glad to see you're back to your old self."

"Old? Unfortunately, yes. Improved? Unable to ascertain at this time." Achilles swiveled its head and torso in unison. "Merely a temporary condition, as Xenthan eloquently informed me."

Breeze stared solemnly at the robot as Achilles placed a hand on his shoulder. "You have performed admirably. You reached deep within yourself and formed a shield that thwarted the wave that would have destroyed Perihelion. I was told you were in stasis for quite some time as you kept the shield raised."

"How long was I out there for? It feels to me like minutes."

Achilles' eyes lit up. "Several hours had passed, according to Xenthan. He would relay to me updates during the search for you and Nina while he and his brother scrounged for parts to repair me. I would have joined, but my engagement with an Elephim resulted in my head being removed from my shoulders. Quite inconvenient!" it chuckled, then paused for a moment before speaking again. "Apparently they found you in a valley not far from the bay embracing Nina with your shield raised. Sally had to project into it to get your attention. Odd how those ladies are always able to slip past your defenses."

Breeze's face reddened while Achilles' eyes shined brilliantly. "You have accomplished much since your humble beginnings."

Breeze shrugged and looked away. He was about to say something when he quickly lifted a hand to his ear and nodded. "Excort just sent a message over the wireless, says Mila is making dinner for everyone at the dining hall. Let's head on over." He held out a hand. "Care for a lift?"

Achilles laughed and brushed it away. "I have had an abundance of airborne adventures for now. Let us endeavor to keep our feet on the ground," it said, and then looked up at the sky. "Just for a little awhile at least."

The robot pointed toward the shore. "The beach is past those dunes; let us follow it back to the hall."

"Aren't you worried about getting rusty?" Breeze teased it.

Achilles' eyes dimmed. "After what we have experienced, it is the least of my concerns."

Several days later, Breeze sat with Oslo in his office late one evening. The Elephim that ambushed the island after their departure for Appalachia left a trail of destruction as every building on campus was wrecked and ransacked. Oslo's office was hit the hardest. The old man spent the last several days with Raza putting everything back together. The books on the shelves that lined the walls of the office had been ripped and burned, as was the furniture. The sailorman lamp was also a victim, but it had been patched together and returned to its prominence on the desk.

The lamp reminded him how he once sat across from Oslo in this very office as a total misfit when he first arrived to the island. He found it strange how Perihelion now seemed to fit him like an old glove.

He also understood why Oslo persevered for so long. The old man was living in a world dominated by the memories of Earth's glorious, yet distant past, but burdened with the truth that humanity was traveling along a road to oblivion by their unwillingness to discover it. People had blinders over their eyes, Breeze realized, blinders that were purposefully put there by a malicious and hidden force. Yet many were unwilling, or unable, to remove them.

Breeze abruptly sat up in his chair. "Oslo, there is something you need to know; when that Elephim grabbed me and spun me around, something strange happened. It felt like time was slowing down and space was stretching before me. I then heard voices and saw the faces of children come out of the darkness within orbs of light looking for my help. I felt a sense of peace as I told them not to be afraid and to never give in to the darkness. I don't know what made me to say those things, but I knew that I was right. What happened to me out there?"

Oslo slumped deep into his chair. "You found them, by God. They are like you, the children of the paranormal, trying to survive in a frightening world. They have no guidance and no understanding of why they feel so terrified. Then they found you. There really is hope." He shook his head. "And I almost gave up and surrendered. I almost stopped searching for them. Then you came along, Breeze, and changed everything."

"I don't understand," Breeze said.

"In time, you will. We will build a new world and a new life. It won't be easy. There will be those who will doubt us, and there will be many obstacles to overcome. But we can never turn our backs now. Not ever. We should aspire to die knowing we did everything we could to right the wrongs. We shall never put our heads in the sand and ignore the peril that surrounds us."

"What about my father?"

Oslo sighed. "We will find everyone, Breeze, and your father as well. All that has been lost will be recovered, or at least remembered. This I swear to you."

"What about the two Elephim I fought with, where are they now?"

Oslo looked out the window. The moon was rising over the bay. "Achilles has them in his custody."

Achilles established its quarters in the hangars, explaining to Oslo that it would be appropriate to be amongst the RF. They needed guidance, this much he could tell from the amount of aerocraft that needed to be repaired. They were originally programmed for combat, not as mechanics, it reminded Oslo.

Achilles also noted that it could provide assistance and share knowledge accumulated in Appalachia repairing and restoring aerocraft it had collected over the years. Oslo gladly accepted.

Achilles had also taken custody of the two Elephim that had tracked their escape from the platform. With help from the RF, it constructed a fortified prison to house them in a sub-basement level deep below the Science and Engineering building. It was the only building on campus that was suitable and contained the machinery needed to keep them subdued and prevent their escape.

Achilles would oftentimes watch as they thrashed about within their cells incessantly, then drop to their knees and howl with screams made of static. And they never seemed to sleep, except to stand in a comer of their cell and stare at a wall throughout the night.

Achilles knew they were trying to contact their brethren for help, but the quartz embedded within the bedrock collected and sent their transmissions to the antenna array located at the top of the building. There it was intercepted by electronics Achilles fabricated to prevent their broadcasts from being transmitted into the depths of space. Though the fog over the island was operational and shielded it from prying eyes, as well as blocking any unauthorized transmissions from getting in or out, it wouldn't take the risk of the island being detected from above again.

One evening, as it left the detention level after a routine inspection of the prison, it entered the elevator that led back to the surface when it noticed an icon on the control panel that pulsated with a red glow.

Its finger hovered close to it for a moment, and then pressed it. The elevator descended. After several minutes, it came to a stop and the doors hissed open.

Achilles stepped out into a chamber with rows of humming machinery spread across the floor. Ahead was a concave wall with armored plating. It was a sight that it had not seen for many years, though the memories of this chamber were still fresh within its cerebral core. Memories of a time when a plan was set into motion to save a world whose glorious of days had long since passed it by.

Metallic footsteps echoed within the chamber as it marched past row upon row of machinery. It knew every one of these machines, for they were assembled and installed by Oslo and itself. Machinery designed to help sustain a life, a life that lay behind the concave wall. That life had a name. Bram.

Achilles began to ponder how Bram was able to return from the depths of space and function like he did on the platform without his body, when Raven spoke from within. *We should not have come here.*

No sooner were the words spoken that an image of a woman materialized next to Achilles. It was Kera with her flowing white dress billowing behind her.

"I knew this dreaded day would come," she said, "though I did not expect it would arrive in the form of half of a man embedded within a machine. Fascinating how you managed to stay hidden. I now see why he assumed you were dead."

Achilles tilted its head as Raven spoke. *She knows.*

"You must leave. Now is not the time," she said.

Without hesitation, Achilles turned and left.

Dawn was approaching as Breeze strode along the beach in the early morning. The rising sun caressed the clouds as the moon abdicated its throne in the sky to it.

He looked up at the fading starlight and knew that is where his future lay. His first trip into space was a harrowing one, but it invigorated him in ways he never imagined

He watched as the waves gently lapped against the sandy shore. Each successive wave taking him further into his mind as he thought of his life and where he stood in the world. He knew he was an orphan, but he would lead his newly adopted family here on Perihelion to a better tomorrow.

He heard footsteps splashing through the water. He looked over and saw Nina approaching.

No words were exchanged as he pulled her close and held her in his arms.

The sun bathed them in its fiery light as it freed itself from the grip of the horizon and rose into the sky.

ABOUT THE AUTHOR

▼

MICHAEL JOHN OLSON IS a former commercial diver living in South Florida with his wife, Martha, and two children, Edward and Angela.

He is currently working on the next book of the Breeze Corinth series.

He can be reached on the web at mjolsonwrites.com, by email at mjolsonwrites@yahoo.com, or on Facebook at Michael John Olson.

www.ingramcontent.com/pod-product-compliance
Lightning Source LLC
Chambersburg PA
CBHW030029030726
47500CB00001B/14